PRAISE FOR
KALYNA THE SOOTHSAYER

"[D]elightful debut fantasy adventure . . . **Put your trust in Kalyna's hands and let her build a story** around the two of you. Parts of it will speak to your own specific fears and desires; other aspects will be entertaining fictions, until you discover the devastating shard of truth within."

—NPR

"A gorgeous, layered debut, both **intricate and propulsive**, with a singularly brilliant heroine at its center. Kalyna is a twisty, entrancing, and totally unique entry into epic fantasy."

—**Ava Reid**, bestselling author of *The Wolf and the Woodsman*

"An engaging read with **unique prose and a strong-willed, witty protagonist** to adore."

—Tor.com

"Full of hilarious wit, intrigue, spycraft, and charlatans, *Kalyna the Soothsayer* is **a classic adventure with a sardonic twist**. At the turn of the last page, I was sad to leave these lovable rogues. I've been waiting a long time to read an intelligent swashbuckling story like this . . . it's the perfect fantastical escape."

—**Marissa Levien**, author of *The World Gives Way*

"Kalyna is a character after my own heart: a conniving liar whose love for her family threatens to be her downfall. **Hilarious and heartbreaking** by turns, *Kalyna the Soothsayer* is a reminder that if you can't see the future you want, sometimes you have to make it."

—**C. L. Clark**, author of *The Unbroken*

"**A glorious confection of a novel**, with characters you will adore. Politics, prophecy, scams, adventure, and a world that you'll want to come back to again and again. I'm no soothsayer, but I see you falling in love with this wonderful book."

—**Trent Jamieson**, Aurealis Award–winning author of *Day Boy*

"The intricate worldbuilding includes intriguing court politics and nefarious plotting galore. [Kalyna] is both a witty and a determined heroine. . . . **A fabulous puzzle box** of a fantasy novel."

—**Foreword Reviews**

"**A brilliantly constructed character, endlessly multilayered and relatably conflicted**, with a scarred interior that nonetheless perseveres by sheer survival instinct. Kalyna's inner monologue is a delicious parade of sharp political commentary, pragmatic callousness, reluctant hope, internalized self-loathing, wounded desire, the driest sense of gallows humor, and a drive to independence made of the hardest bedrock. . . . Engrossing."

—**Nerds of a Feather**

ELIJAH KINCH SPECTOR

KALYNA
THE
SOOTHSAYER

EREWHON

an imprint of Kensington Publishing Corp.
www.erewhonbooks.com

EREWHON BOOKS are published by:

Kensington Publishing Corp.
119 West 40th Street
New York, NY 10018
www.erewhonbooks.com

All Kensington titles, imprints, and distributed lines are available at special quantity discounts for bulk purchases for sales promotions, premiums, fundraising, educational, or institutional use.

Special book excerpts or customized printings can also be created to fit specific needs. For details, write or phone the office of the Kensington sales manager: Kensington Publishing Corp., 119 West 40th Street, New York, NY 10018, attn: Sales Department; phone 1-800-221-2647.

Erewhon and the Erewhon logo Reg. US Pat. & TM Off.

ISBN 978-1-64566-072-9 (trade paperback)

First Erewhon trade paperback printing: April 2024

10 9 8 7 6 5 4 3 2 1

Printed in the United States of America

Library of Congress Control Number: 2022932280

Electronic edition: ISBN 978-1-64566-039-2

Edited by Sarah T. Guan
Cover design by Sasha Vinograd
Interior design by Cassandra Farrin and Leah Marsh
Author photograph by Sylvie Rosokoff

For Brittany Marie, who told me to
stop working on an irretrievably broken
novel and start on this one instead.

But everything must finally fall in war, or wear away into the ultimate and universal ash. The triumphs and the frauds, the treasures and the fakes.

—Orson Welles, *F for Fake*

Some of the People Who Made My Life Harder

My Family

ALJOSA VÜSALAVICH: My father, the greatest soothsayer I have ever known. (His second name means "son of Vüsala" in Masovskani, because he was born in Masovska.)

VÜSALA MILDOQIZ: My grandmother, the worst person I have ever known. (Her second name means "daughter of Mildo" in Cöllüknit, because she was born in Quruscan.)

Those Who Have Their Own Armies

KING GERHOLD VIII: King of Rotfelsen. Quite blank in face and mind. His army: the Reds.

QUEEN BIRUTÉ: Wife of King Gerhold. Originally from Skydašiai. Her army: those amongst the Reds who obey only her.

PRINCE FRIEDHELM: Younger brother to King Gerhold. Seems to be a thoughtless, sybaritic prince; is both more than that and exactly that. His army: the Yellows.

HIGH GENERAL FRANZ DREHER: The somewhat avuncular defender of Rotfelsen. His army: the Greens, who actually fight wars and guard the borders.

COURT PHILOSOPHER OTTO VOROSKNECHT: A dangerous fool who talks a lot. His army: the Purples.

Those I Met in Masovska

EIGHT-TOED GUSTAW FROM DOWN VALLEY WAY: The name tells all you need to know.

RAMUNAS: A flamboyant legal advocate and informant, who likes to send messages by terrifying bird.

KLEMENS GUSTAVUS: A very important little rich boy. Heir to a number of changing banks.

BOZENA GUSTAVUS: His slightly smarter sister, whom I heard of in Masovska.

LENZ FELSKNECHT: Best forgotten.

THOSE I MET IN ROTFELSEN

TURAL: The Master of Fruit, and my neighbor. Eccentric, but nice.

JÖRDIS JAGLOBEN: Chief Ethicist, and my neighbor. Perhaps also nice?

VONDEL: Tenth Butler to High General Dreher. A real stickler for etiquette and tradition, but not in an overbearing way.

GUNTHER: The tall barkeep at the Inn of Ottilie's Rock. Beautiful smile; supplier of starka.

AUE: A talented doctor who looks after royalty and nobility.

GABOR: Very chipper for a man who lives in a cave.

MARTIN-FREDERICK REINHOLD-BOSCH: A young swordsman employed by the High General. Within spitting distance of the throne. Arrogant, but pretty.

"DUGMUSH": A tall and frightening soldier in the service of Prince Friedhelm. I had trouble remembering her name.

BEHRENS: A sharpshooter in the service of Prince Friedhelm. Quite friendly, when he isn't looking down the barrel of his harquebus.

ALBAN: A brute in the service of Court Philosopher Vorosknecht.

SELVOSCH: The Lord High Quarrymaster. Unpleasant.

EDELTRAUD VON EDELTRAUD: Mistress of the Rotfelsen Coin. A powerful and nervous noblewoman.

ANDELKA: An emissary from Rituo, one of the countries that make up the Bandit States. Acts as though she is very important.

OLAF: A lucky drifter.

CHASIKU: A threat.

KALYNA
THE
SOOTHSAYER

PART ONE

MY MOTHER

"You killed your mother twice over, you know," said Grandmother.

She pinched my cheek ironically and chewed on her gnarled, old pipe stem. Grandmother seemed to get more from rolling it around between her white teeth than from the scant smoke that leaked out.

I sat still in the dirt at her feet and rubbed my cheek where her thumbnail had left a deliberate indent.

"You killed her first, of course, with your birth: when you selfishly tore your way out, making your poor mother bleed so, so much." Grandmother removed the long wooden pipe and curled her papery lips to luxuriously exhale a small amount of smoke.

I nodded slowly. I meant to show I was listening, but it looked like I agreed.

"And you killed her *again* two days later, when she, weakened and bloodless as she was, learned from your father's visions that you would never possess the Gift."

I nodded again from where I sat, looking up at Grandmother as she noisily replaced the pipe between her teeth. Her hard face, the small tattoo above her left eyebrow, peeking out from her scarf, and her thin old nostrils, full of char.

"Maybe," I hazarded, in a squeak, "maybe she only died from the bleeding? Maybe . . . maybe I only killed Mama once?"

Grandmother looked down at me, then closed her eyes as though she need see nothing else ever again.

"Finally," Grandmother sighed, "she admits it."

As she sat back in her red velvet chair, unmoving, I wondered if Grandmother had died. If she had savored a last bitter happiness after I admitted the evil I'd done in this world and then, pleased with herself, expired.

If only.

Had I the Gift, I might have known better. I might have known that as I passed through the years, I would do so with Grandmother always at my back—remaining stubbornly, infuriatingly, alive and lucid.

Two of those decades later, I was twenty-seven and still sitting in the dirt at the foot of her chair, from which the velvet was all gone. Grandmother was unchanged since the day she told me I twice murdered my mother, except that her pipe was empty and unlit: she couldn't smoke anymore, said it made her cough too much, so she spent her days chewing the cold pipe stem and spitting.

Grandmother was my father's mother, and she cared for him above all else. Nothing ever seemed good enough for her son, and so we couldn't understand how she had come to genuinely love and miss her daughter-in-law. But she did, fiercely.

It was to Papa that Grandmother had passed the Gift, and through him that it was meant to go to me. The Gift had been in our family for generation upon generation, through thousands of years; farther back than even Loashti nobles traced their lineages, let alone poor nomads like us. The Gift cared not for gender, legitimacy, national boundaries, nor family name, and was all that delineated our family down through the ages.

Until me.

AUTUMN FURS

At the end of autumn in that, my twenty-seventh year, our horse died. The following day, I untied the furs that had been stored neatly at the peaks of our tents. The soft remains of long-dead polecats, wolves, and marmots tumbled down, thick and stale, smelling like the previous winter in the kingdom of Quruscan: all cold mutton and maple and mildew. We had spent this autumn, which was now ending, on a grassy hill in the Great Field, north of the town of Gniezto, in the kingdom of Masovska.

Our goal was to keep from starving to death during the onrushing winter, just like it was every autumn. But now we were stranded with no horse, serving our few customers and building up meager winter supplies, which would mean nothing if we froze in our tents. I tried not to think of all the ways we could die before spring, nor of how we would ever afford a new horse. For now, I could only roll down the furs to keep out the cold winds.

These winds had cut through the Great Field all autumn, and would only worsen in winter, as I remembered from previous years we had spent here. At least when the snows came, we could winter among the tents crowding the Ruinous Temple. Perhaps it would have been better to go broke buying Papa a room in an inn, with four walls and a roof, but our family's way has always been to move. Walls are traps.

In my time, we moved from place to place at a greater speed than even my ancestors had. We did so to escape reprisals, you see: sometimes long before my ruses were discovered, and sometimes fleeing angry mobs. I was, after all, lacking the Gift, and therefore an inveterate liar.

THE GIFT

The Gift is that of prophecy and soothsaying. Anyone possessing it can see the future, with limitations: the most important being that the better known a subject is to the bearer of the Gift, the less can be seen. Such a future is, to put it simply, blocked by the clarity of the present. This is why Papa and Grandmother couldn't see my future, nor their own, nor each other's, and why no one saw my mother's death coming. This is also why a fortuneteller must make her living telling the futures of strangers, rather than making herself very rich by knowing whom to befriend, whom to kill, or where to open a changing bank. The moment any threads threaten to involve the soothsayer, she is less likely to see their ends.

This limitation can be stretched and twisted when the bearer of the Gift is near death. Papa almost died of sickness and starvation when he was looking after my mother in her final days, and it was in a fit of near-death, when his spirit was not so close to us, that he gained the distance to see that the Gift would never be mine. Knowing this, of course, killed my mother. Finally. Again.

These capricious workings of the Gift are another reason I prayed for Grandmother to finally die, as was her due. Perhaps on her deathbed she could tell us if there was any chance of the Gift skipping a generation, of my child not being hollow like its mother. However, by the time I hit my mid-twenties, she seemed to have decided the line ended with my father. Perhaps, in her old age, she once came closer to death than she ever let on, foresaw my failure, and then clawed her way back to life to continue tormenting me?

I often wonder whether the Gift is in me somewhere, and instead of being broken, I am simply too stupid to access it.

THE GREAT FIELD

Masovska's Great Field was not very great. It was less than a mile wide, and only a few miles long. In Quruscan's minor steppes, for comparison, the grass could stretch in every direction until you got lost and spun in circles and felt as though you were drowning on a dry sunny day. I have heard that the major steppes drove travelers insane, and had oak-high grasses riddled with the corpses of birds in sizes never seen by polite civilization. The birds had, supposedly, lost their minds and their way as surely as any human traveler.

The so-called Great Field, however, was just a patch of shrubs and hills, with a sad old ruin in the middle. This Ruinous Temple had been constructed long before recorded history, from that supposedly unbreakable stone of the Ancients, before it was, somehow, torn apart. The prevailing theory was that the Ancients built the place to enact the hubristic, and *ruinous*, act of speaking the gods' names out loud, thus dooming themselves. (No one ever seemed to ask how many names they got through before disaster struck.) Whatever its origin, from the Ruinous Temple you could see, and hear, the forests at the Field's borders. I suppose the Field was considered "Great" because most of Masovska was forest: the kind where trees grow so tightly into one another that there's no room for air or light, yet somehow giant boar and packs of wolves can slip between. The Great Field may well have been Masovska's only field that was not human-made.

But, I suppose, to those who had seen no better, the Field could be "Great," and in those days, it bustled with commerce right up to the edge of winter. Due to a local ordinance about A Certain Sort of Business, one could always find merchants, hucksters, prostitutes, mystics, messiahs, revolutionaries, and others who didn't fit Masovska's mores camping out in those shrubs and hills outside of Gniezto. The most lucrative ones formed a marketplace in the Ruinous Temple, which led to fistfights and sales wars, until winter chased away those who could afford to run.

We untrustworthy parties banished to the Great Field maintained cold cordiality with one another: businesslike, but never trusting. I have heard of fanciful thieves' guilds—secret criminal societies buttressed by codes and mutual respect—that may or may not have existed outside of stories, but the trick of the Great Field was that everyone there felt themselves to be more legitimate than the rest. Surely one was dishonest, but he was not *sacrilegious*; while another was sacrilegious, but not *foreign*; and the foreigner could at least be sure that she was not *unladylike*; and the unladylike knew that she was not some disloyal *dissident*; and so forth. This way of looking at one's neighbors was not conducive to respect or professional courtesy.

When winter arrived, most residents fled to more sturdy surroundings in towns and villages, where they continued to bicker, but those like us who could not afford traditional lodgings would crowd uneasily beneath huge canvases, heavy with snow, in the Ruinous Temple. I had pleasant memories of this arrangement from childhood, back when new smells, new voices, and excessive cold made things exciting. Papa told stories back then, and made it an adventure, but later I saw how close we came to having our food, clothes, and furs stolen. Not that a stable community has ever been quick to shelter my family either: few care for the survival prospects of an invalid huckster, his diminished shadow of a daughter, and his rancorous mother.

It lay upon me to keep Papa (and, I suppose, Grandmother) from starving in winter, and this year I was doing a terrible job. We did not have enough salted meat or kasha for half the season, and we could not even eat our horse. Yellow blight had sent the poor beast off to canter unsteadily across the sky with his twenty-legged horse god, and his meat was quite poisonous (although his hide would serve to patch up our tents). So, on the morning that I set the tent-furs, I saw a horrid bird landing on our hill, and hoped that it carried good news.

A Lammergeier

The bird was a huge, red-eyed lammergeier, with black and white streaked wings longer than I was tall, and a body the bronze of sunset. It carried a message from Ramunas, for whom a gray messenger pigeon would have been passé.

The curled parchment tied to the beast read: "GNIEZTO SQUARE, TOMORROW MORNING. FOR EIGHT-TOES. —RAMUNAS." As though such a message could have come from anyone else. For tasks like this he had bought this terrifying bird, had it trained, barely, by handler-mages, and forced me to disengage the parchment from its gnarled, angry claws. I think the thing sneered at me as it flew away.

Ramunas was an ostentatious informant who often helped me form my false prophecies: he seemed to know everything that went on in the town of Gniezto, and the greater Gniezto Oblast that surrounded it. I had met him early during this stay in the Great Field, and his information had more than once paid for itself. Whether or not I liked him, he was effective and cheap, and always seemed to know a little more than anyone else I could afford. How such a flamboyant and theatrical man learned so many secrets was still beyond me. I had told him that even a prophet needed a bit of help and context for her visions, at times—which, in my father's day, had been true—and Ramunas either believed me or did not care about my legitimacy.

What Ramunas had to tell me about a customer I knew as Eight-Toed Gustaw from Down Valley Way, or why it needed to be said in Gniezto proper, I did not know. But a promise of decent information, even for a price, was welcome. All good news was holy, just then.

Once I was sure the flying beast was gone, I checked in on Papa and assured him that, yes, there actually *had* been a great bronze bird. I held his shaking, sweaty hand and kissed his red-brown brow until he went back to sleep.

EIGHT-TOED GUSTAW FROM DOWN VALLEY WAY

When he had been able, Papa had taught me how to get by as a sooth-sayer on observation and generalities, which even those with the Gift must employ. I can often tell a man he will throw out his back if I see how he carries his goods, or tell a pretty young woman she has an admirer because of course she does. One with no skill, like myself, can do decent business with finesse: telling customers what is apparent, what they want to hear, and what is deeply vague. The rest is made up through theatricality, distraction, and research, such as that which comes by lammergeier.

Which brings us to Eight-Toed Gustaw from Down Valley Way. Gustaw was the best sort of customer: a returning one. Fourteen years previous, our travels had brought us to the Great Field. Back then, Papa had still been the soothsayer, even as his health failed and his mind hiccoughed, and Eight-Toed Gustaw from Down Valley Way had possessed a shorter name.

On a summer day in that year, Gustaw and his stupid friends drank at the Ruinous Temple market and stumbled about the Great Field, laughing and fighting and sweating as men in their early twenties do when they're drunker on blazing sunlight than ale. Sallow Gniezto residents lose their minds when they are not shaded by trees. At our tents, Gustaw's stupid friends dared him into a session with the spooky, exotic, legless soothsayer. I curtsied carefully and pivoted to usher Gustaw inside to see my father. His stupid friends leered at me and retched shredded goat meat onto the green grass.

Papa could barely do his job by the time I was thirteen. He was no longer the unflappable, endlessly confident prophet of my early years, who could recite perfect mixtures of truth and lie while running about on his hands faster than most men did on their legs. No, that day, seated on his great pillow, his hands shook, knocking over candles and ruining the mystique, and he often forgot the very real futures the Gift showed him. He did manage to blurt out that if Gustaw wasn't careful, his left foot would be injured. Gustaw laughed his way outside, where his stupid friends burned their pale skins in the sun and suggested that the legless man only wanted to put a scare in him.

Based on the name Eight-Toed Gustaw from Down Valley Way, I'm sure you can guess what followed. Gustaw and his stupid friends got into a drunken altercation that night with a man who was not drunk, and who was armed. A cross-guarded sabre took off Gustaw's big toe and the one next, along with a triangular section of his foot.

Eight-Toed Gustaw from Down Valley Way visited us again eight years later, when I had taken over from my father and we once more spent a season in the Great Field. That year, I (somehow) foretold Gustaw's yet-unborn third daughter in enough detail to be convincing.

Now, in this waning autumn when I was twenty-seven, Eight-Toed Gustaw from Down Valley Way had come to us once more. He had come to respect and fear the Gift, and was well-liked enough in his community that some others did too. What's more, Gustaw possessed some sort of affection for us: perhaps as a nostalgic vision of the end of mindless youth, and the beginning of slightly less mindless adulthood. I believe he still had the same friends, but they may have become less stupid.

He paid me in copper coins for a pleasant chat laced with vagaries and wish fulfillment. It was all so simple that I got none of the thrill of a well-executed deception, until he asked if there was any money coming his way. Here I found the seeds of a greater piece of fraud, and asked him to return soon if he wanted to learn more. I did not ask *him* why he expected to become richer.

Instead, I asked Ramunas. And a week later, I received his lammergeier.

FATHER AND THE GIFT

It was not long after Gustaw's severing, when I was thirteen, that Papa became too sick and distraught to work. I became his broken replacement. Sometimes luck would bring him a prophecy I could use, but I never counted on that.

You may wonder why my father could not do the soothsaying himself, as he was still possessed of the Gift. Why, instead, a broken failure like me? The short answer is tradition. In the extended history of our family, the next one with the Gift has always taken over upon turning twenty, no matter gender, station, or parentage. (We are like royalty and nobility, in that we actually track our ages very carefully.) At this time, the parent was meant to sit back and enjoy the fruits of their labors, advising future generations while no longer being expected to laboriously pick through their own fevered visions.

The long answer is that Papa's mind was troubled. When my mother was dying, he took terrible care of himself and became afflicted with both freezerot and redspit: these and grief addled him. His Gift was there, stronger than ever, but he lost tact, showmanship, restraint. If one asked my father about their future, they would hear *everything he could see*, with no preamble, no teasing, no vagaries, no withholding.

Imagine asking a soothsayer if this year's harvest will be good and being told that it will be passable, and also your wife will be taken from you by a noble in a year, your son will die of consumption in two and a half, and you will follow only four months later when you hang yourself, unsuccessfully at first try, from that rotted beam in your home, which you chose because deep down you did not have the courage to end it all.

Now imagine that the string of deaths told to you includes your neighbor, a stranger, and a woman not yet born. His visions were scattered: he might see one innocuous moment from ten years in a customer's future, or get snatches of tomorrow for everyone within three miles. Papa was done with the business long before I turned twenty.

Grandmother also had the Gift, but refused to help. Even if it meant we starved. She would watch me, angry at how bad a job I did, but offer nothing beyond her "encouragement."

"You're the soothsayer now, aren't you?" she said when I was fifteen. "Aren't you supposed to be getting us fed? Do whatever it takes: you could hardly debase our line further than you already have." She spat. "And when you *fail* and my sweet Aljosa *dies*, he will be better off, while you will deserve whatever comes to you."

ON FOOD

After receiving the lammergeier, I worked until the evening. I had a few customers, who only required a little knowledge of human nature and a lot of leading questions, while I distracted them with smoke and trinkets. I smiled at each one as though they were the only person in the world, and when they believed me, I drank it in.

Besides that, I cleaned, packed, counted, and worried. A few townsfolk wandered past our hill in search of whatever sort of business they were looking for, but it was a quiet day in a quiet time of year. When the sky was red and the sun had disappeared behind the forest, I circled behind the large tent toward the fire pit, to make a weak stew over a weak flame.

My family of three traveled with two tents: one for plying the trade and one for Papa and me to sleep in. Grandmother stayed in the cart, where she could benefit from wooden barriers on all sides but the roof. A canvas on a stick was set up in the cart to keep me from seeing her angry gaze, and it was becoming too cold for her to place her skeleton of a chair outside. I wondered what would happen if the cart were to just roll down the hill and crash at its base while Grandmother lay inside.

She would survive on spite, I'm sure, and we would no longer have a horse *or* a cart.

The fire pit sat between the tents and the carriage, exactly where I had cracked half my fingernails and purpled my toe digging it months earlier. It was sheltered there, but with the cold winds picking up, I would have had to put my feet directly in the burning coals to keep warm. At least the fire lit, this time.

In my life at this point, food held no joy for me. I had wisps of memories from early childhood in which Papa, walking over to the fire on his hands and putting on the brave face of an adult, had cooked for Grandmother and me with something approaching relish. I remembered looking forward to the sounds of frying, and of onions and turnips shifting noisily about a pan. I even remembered that I liked their smells and tastes, but had no recollection of *how* they had actually smelled and tasted. Just that I had liked them.

Barring those phantom happinesses, meals had only ever been sustenance to me. I bought the cheapest and most filling foods—beans, potatoes, sometimes the intestines of a scrawny pig or goat that had been sold cheap—chopped them and boiled them into a sad stew every night. Grandmother always said that spices were decadent.

I would then bring a piping hot bowl of mushy stew to Grandmother. That evening, she was bundled in the back of the cart, leaning against her old, stripped frame of a chair, which lay on its side. Two eyes and a dead pipe stuck out from between blankets. She spat on the floor of the cart and cursed me for a failure, and my food as well. Had I brought her a perfectly poached egg of cassowary, imported from Loashti reaches, she would have done the same. And called me "soft" besides. So I knelt in the cart, let her think it was in obeisance, handed her the bowl, and hoped she burned her tongue.

"What, freak?" she snapped.

I had said nothing, but she saw through me. I shook my head and muttered, backing out of the cart and leaving her to her useless rage.

A few moments later, I heard her yelp at burning her tongue. I smiled broadly at my tawdry, pathetic revenge and sat back by the fire. In a few hours, Papa would wake in the middle of the night, and I would have his soft and lumpy stew ready for him.

I stared at the empty, cold kettle leaning against a rock on the far side of the fire pit. My throat parched in that moment, as though it had waited for me to notice it. We were almost out of tea, and could use more root vegetables besides. I had in total thirty-six Masovskan copper coins, officially called "little grivnas," and ten of those would go to Ramunas in two days. Gustaw would have to pay me more if we were to survive the winter. A lot more.

MY FATHER

I was in the large tent sweeping the rug when I heard Papa snort and moan through the canvas; he had woken up. The broom clattered against the dais behind me as I ducked outside.

I did not throw on a shawl, and just the twenty steps from the large tent around and back to the smaller one chilled me. I was shivering when I rolled down the leather door-flap behind me and saw my father.

Right by the door was the tall pile of furs, blankets, and pillows that made Papa's bed, which lifted his prone body up high enough that when I sat on my own bedroll, I could look him straight in the eye. Having no legs, Papa and his bed didn't take up much ground, and so I slept on a small cushion flush against the ratty, old bearskin rug. I wonder what great warrior far off in our lineage must have killed that striped Quru bear—my family tend not to be that type.

"Welcome, stranger," Papa coughed out as I approached him, smoothing his gray beard, "to the tent of Aljosa the Prophet! In this humble place I will untangle the strands of fate that— Oh! It's you, Kalynishka!"

He laughed at his little joke, the same little joke he made every night.

I sat on my bedroll and took his hand. It felt like a clammy little sun, radiating heat even as his teeth chattered. Papa's drawn face rolled toward me, and just as quickly as he had smiled at his joke, the corners of his mouth fell.

"Oh, Kalynishka, I'm not well."

"I know, Papa. I know."

From the cart next door, Grandmother coughed herself awake. Her throat was a desiccated wasteland, but the cough was still exaggerated. She didn't like me, but she didn't like being left out either. Good. I ignored her.

I cared for my father as I did every night. Did he want some tea? He did not, but I brought him what I had brewed for myself and made him drink it. Would he eat? Just a bite, Kalynishka, just a bite, but he emptied the bowl. Once he was as sated as he was going to be, Papa settled back into his bedding and passed gas. I drew the furs covering his torso up to his neck, tightened his fur hat, and braced myself for what was always next: the Gift would come for him.

When Papa was comfortable and relatively awake, he began ranting about sundry futures, most of people he would never meet. It always pained him, and was almost never helpful. Often he would only see red and brown and green, maybe a tree, a button, or a stepping boot heel. Now and then he would see actual events, like an old woman dying or a boy touching himself. He was never sure what he was seeing; each vision was a question, a melting mist. He had no control over the Gift, and any attempt to concentrate on what he saw, or to see anything specific, ended in frustration.

That night, I held his hand particularly tightly and hoped beyond hope he would see something relating to Eight-Toed Gustaw from Down Valley Way's inheritance. I did not ask anything of him: Papa liked very much to feel useful, but not half so much as he hated to feel useless.

For a good half hour, Papa twisted and held my hand and muttered vagaries.

"A clove of garlic, Kalynishka, rotted. There is a bird. A string? Thousands of them, in all colors! Fluttering in the wind—and that wind is so strong, Kalynishka, so strong. Stone walls and lanterns, and blood and corn. Blood *on* corn. A great eye and a limping mustache. Sand? Where in the world could there be so much sand, Dilara?"

Dilara was a Quru name, my mother's.

I daubed his brow and leaned in to listen closer. I did this every night, even though he always looked past me and never noticed. Papa was plagued by things only he could see, and since he was beneath the notice of most people, it seemed only right that someone be there to hear him. Even so, his colors and objects became chatter to me, and I listened only for knowledge of Gustaw's future. Or my own.

". . . Kalyna."

Papa was looking at me unwaveringly. I met his gaze, and he stared directly into my eyes.

"I . . . Yes, Papa?"

"Kalyna," he repeated. "Listen." His voice was firm. The set of his jaw showed a conviction I hardly remembered in him.

I nodded. His face didn't move, but his gaze was far away again. A tear formed in his right eye.

"This country," he began, "this country will collapse in chaos and war, Kalyna."

I exhaled. It was nothing about Gustaw or myself. I daubed his brow again and then leaned in to hug him. "Of course it will, Papa," I said into his ear. "They all do. Countries and borders are fluid, and they are moved by war. Now try to relax."

"No!" He tore himself backward out of my grip, which he had never done before. His whole face full of . . . not terror, but deep sadness.

"No," Papa repeated quietly, understanding that he had been too loud. "No, no, Kalynishka, some endings are worse than others." He shook his head. "This one will be very bad," he said as though he were appraising a rotted apple.

I wondered if perhaps we could use this information. Prophetic books of future history sell wonderfully, if convincing.

"No weak skirmishes and redrawing of borders," he continued. "War will pour in like a deluge, change will come to mountains, valleys, and steppes with fire and sword. Not just Masovska, but the whole Tetrarchia. Survivors will not live the same lives beneath different flags, they will be ruined and enslaved, or strung out beneath the sun with their entrails stretched across the landscape, and their children thrown among Rotfelsen's shattered remains. Do you see? When our country ends, it will end terribly."

I sat back to look at him better. It was entirely dark outside, and I kept only the smallest lamp in the tent with him. Grandmother coughed quietly from the cart; she was probably back to sleep.

"But when will this all happen, Papa? This terror and entrailstretching?" I asked. "Fifty years from now? Five hundred? In a time so different that you can barely recognize—"

"Three months." He blinked.

"Oh," I said.

ŞEBEK IN A CLOUD

"Let me tell you a story, little monster," said Grandmother.

I chopped wood harder and louder.

It was the morning after my father's prophecy. Our corner of the Field was quiet, and it was the kind of sunny, calm, cold day that I suppose one is meant to languidly enjoy by an outdoor fire. Perhaps with friends. I was by the cold fire pit, trying very hard to *not* see the Great Field as the part of Masovska best suited to mass graves for the nameless. To not imagine farmers penned into the Ruinous Temple and slaughtered. But slaughtered by whom? Where would this destruction come from? How literal were words like "deluge," "fire," and "shattered" in Papa's mouth? How could this be our *future*, when for years, Papa had seen the lives of others stretch into the oncoming decades? I tried to distract myself with anger at Grandmother and succeeded marvelously.

She sat on the lip of the cart and began to tell me about when she and my father had stayed in a village called Şebek, long before I was born. This was the story she *always* told when she wanted to yell at me about duty.

"Şebek," she explained every time, "is a series of baskets that hangs between two mountainous outcroppings, themselves atop a higher mountain. You could say the town is at the crotch of the peaks. Şebek floats in the clouds, all baskets and nets and wooden platforms. It was well hidden, and we were on the run. You scowl at one idiot child and suddenly you are to blame for it dropping dead? Honestly. Not my fault the parents didn't pay me to see whether their brat would get a bog-plague."

From here she went on, as always, about how she had coddled Papa in his youth. "*If* ever I had a flaw," she said, "it is that I love too much." As such, she had not yet let him take over the business when they were in Şebek, despite Papa being "twenty-two, full of the Gift, and flush with showmanship."

I mouthed the words along with her under my breath when my back was turned, making angry faces she would never see.

The long and the short of this oft-told story was that while they were there, Şebek was attacked—whether by the town's enemies or my family's, she never knew. Either way, nequş birds were released into the village: little flightless, scuttling creatures that eat nothing but oily plants, giving their feathers a gloss that can be easily lit on fire. They ran about, leaking flame and causing havoc. Papa found his mother and led her down the mountain, running on his hands and quietly scouting ahead to see whether the way was clear. During that perilous escape, he repeatedly avoided mobs that were drawn, I'm sure, by Grandmother's refusal to keep her voice down.

Once they were both safe, Grandmother realized Papa was truly an adult, saw the error of her ways, and the family business passed to him.

"And *he*," she finished, as always, "went on to do his duty as a soothsayer! Unlike the twisted doll that he spawned."

I kept chopping.

"Perhaps you should give up soothsaying entirely," she said. "The Gift is dead. You killed it with your sloth, just as you killed your mother. Why pretend to be what you are not? Let my son and I die in peace—by which I mean on the road—knowing that we did everything we could to continue our illustrious line. Until you destroyed it."

I laughed to myself at the very idea. Nothing would make her more angry than if I stopped being a "soothsayer."

"Did you say something, freak?"

"A splinter was in my mouth."

"Just so."

In the light of day, the previous night's prophecy seemed a dream. But it had looked real enough to my father, realer indeed than my presence, his existence, or anything of the last two decades. I would have been stupid to ignore him. When things fall apart, women, foreigners, cheats, and mystics are always dragged out, humiliated, ruined, and slaughtered first. I was all four of these. We had to escape the Tetrarchia's doom.

Once I was done chopping wood, it was time to go to meet Ramunas in Gniezto. I wore an orange dress of tightly wound, thornproof wool, and wrapped two shawls about my holed sheepskin coat, packed a satchel with copper coins and incense, and slipped my sickle into my belt.

SICKLE

A sickle as a weapon is an awkward thing, but I like it. With its short handle, it's small enough to be hidden in skirts, with a wickedly curved blade that can discourage troublemakers without the pinpoint accuracy of a stiletto. And if one poses as a farmer's daughter, it needn't even be hidden.

Those of my lineage are no hussars, but I have learned to defend myself. When one travels up and down these beautiful kingdoms of bandits, pimps, and con artists (like myself) accompanied only by an ancient grandmother and a delirious father; when one is a relatively young, unmarried woman who is not forever wreathed by threatening relatives; when one looks "foreign," and practices a trade that regularly incites anger, one must absolutely be able to open a forehead or hack off a hand here and there.

There are, in fact, stained and cracking combat treatises for the sickle, illustrated with paper-flat men in the rounded and buttressed clothing of centuries ago, holding stances and demonstrating cuts. Such documents for sword, spear, harquebus, and other actual weapons were only legally owned by nobles, but those for sickle, pitchfork, or pliers (terrifying) were intended for peasants. I believe they hearkened back to the constant border wars in the time before the Tetrarchia's formation, when peasants were conscripted into battle and never outfitted; when it was useful to roil up the peasants against the "foreign" nobility.

By my own time, centuries later, our nobility had learned they had more in common with each other than with their local peasantry. I bought my sickle treatise in a Hidden Market on the Masovska-Skydašiai border when I was a teenager, plucked from amongst a stack of nationalist, separatist, and otherwise dissident literature. It was, by then, quite as illegal as a real weapon treatise: nobody wants farmers to know how to murder—or, even worse, *parry*—with their implements.

Unfortunately, knowing the enormity of what was coming for the Tetrarchia made my small piece of sharp, curved metal much less comforting. Perhaps our nation's destruction would come from the commoners rising up and turning their pliers upon the nobles? A nice thought, but I doubted it would make me any less likely to die in such a war.

RAMUNAS

It felt incredibly dangerous to go into Gniezto's very seat of power, but I had little choice. Besides, wouldn't we all die in three months? Or perhaps I could make enough from Gustaw to escape, and only *everyone around me* would die. Lovely.

I met Ramunas, my informant, in Gniezto proper: at the government square, between the squat green municipal building and the squat tan guardhouse. He was wearing the brown robe and ceremonial gorget of an advocate, but the robe was held together by glistening horn clasps and splashed at the arms and collar with stitched blue flowers in groups of three. When he moved, his robe shifted to show off its lining, and spiderwebs of gold lacing appeared in small bursts about his legs. Ramunas was from Skydašiai, Masovska's warmer neighbor to the north, but he always wore some version of local garb, in colors of an intensity one would never find on an actual Masovskan. Skydašian clothing tended toward brighter dyes than Masovskan, but Ramunas would have been excessive in his homeland as well—he was just that type.

He offered me his arm, which made me uncomfortable because I had seldom before walked arm-in-arm, publicly, with anyone who wasn't Grandmother. But he gave me a nudge, and I hooked my arm into his, finding that the sensation was not unpleasant.

"Not ashamed to be seen in town with a Ruinous Temple prophet?" I asked.

"There is a mania for the theatre of law in Gniezto, you know," he replied. "It is why I came here. And, as a respected advocate, if I meet with any shady characters on the side"—he nodded at me—"why, they must simply be part of a case."

"Why sell me information at all?" I asked. "Surely, my ten little grivnas aren't much to a *respected advocate*." I had long since stopped attempting to charm Ramunas; he reacted better to bluntness.

He made a face at my tone, but answered my question. "While I don't mind a little more spending money, it's mostly because the information I feed you helps the Gniezto locals you relay it to. A way for me to assist my neighbors when going to court isn't viable." He shrugged. "And today, Kalyna Aljosanovna"—he flourished a hand out of its sleeve and pressed it to his chest—"is on the house."

I shook my head at him, but was also relieved to hold onto my ten copper coins. Arm-in-arm, we began to take a sort of stroll around the square.

Ramunas often confused me, but he had been right about Rotfelsenisch nobles buying up beet-growing lands two months ago, and about Olga Child-Skinner after that. With his help, I *had* in fact been able to help a few people, even save a life, and get paid a bit besides. As informants went, Ramunas had done right by me. So far. I suppose it saddened me to imagine him slaughtered.

"So, what's this about my customer?" I asked in his native language of Skydašiavos.

"Well, Kalyna Aljosanovna, your Eight-Toed Gustaw from Down Valley Way has an uncle," he replied in the same. "A good uncle to have."

"Good how?"

"He is rich, and he is dead."

I leaned closer. "And will his money fall to Gustaw?"

"Shouldn't a prophet already know this?"

I glared at him.

"Yes! Yes, it will!" He threw up his free hand and laughed. "Maybe."

We turned a corner and began another circuit of the square, passing a statue of a male figure with one leg bent and the arm up, hips jutting. It was a figure in the unbreakable Ancients' stone: a beatific god swiped from the Ruinous Temple. At least, it was assumed he was a god—assumed that each of the Ancients' statues of impossibly supple humans corresponded to deities in our own "pantheon," which was but a lumpy and incomplete rabble. The gods of the Tetrarchia existed in shapes we sometimes could not depict, going by names only the priests of their orders could say; they were cobbled together from hundreds of long-subsumed peoples, all of whom came to these lands long after the Ancients spoke themselves into oblivion.

I, like everyone, had my favorite gods, whom I hoped would look after me, and whom I will absolutely not vex by writing their names here. The goddess of travelers is, naturally, near to my heart; I have always prayed to the trickster god, but that is not devotion so much as compulsion; and for some reason I have always had a deep love for R——, the local goddess of Keçepel Mountain.

As for the "god" whose statue had been taken from the Ruinous Temple, a dove was perched on his phallus, and his blue-veined buttocks looked to me like they were cold. Behind him was another statue in the same pose: a great local judge, whose jowls were perfectly carved into a workmanlike granite. Unlike the old god before him, the judge's stone would break beneath cannonballs. Also, he was clothed.

"Gustaw's uncle," Ramunas continued, "is also a Gustaw. Gustaw Close-Hand, he's called."

"'Close-Hand.' Not a good sign for his inheritance."

"It is for your farmer friend. You see, Kalyna Aljosanovna, there's a great distance of land between these two Gustaws: they may have met once, or never at all. The family on *this* side of the western forest"—he jabbed down toward the muddy ground—"are meager farmers, and on *that side*"—he pointed in the general direction of the western sky—"are very rich."

"So has . . . that family"—I pointed at the sky—"decided to favor this one?"

"Not exactly. Gustaw Close-Hand is why that arm of the family is rich. He made his fortune in the fish market—beginning as a simple fisherman at a nearby lake, and ending up as the mogul of the Tetrarchia's largest changing bank. Your Gustaw," he said, "is probably hoping for the funeral gift."

"The what?"

"You aren't from Masovska, are you?"

"I was born here," I said. It was the truth.

"Really?"

It was easy to see why he doubted me. Coming from about the center, north-to-south-wise, of Skydašiai, Ramunas was light brown, with curly hair, neither of which were considered to be Masovskan. I shared some of his features, and others besides. My family, over the centuries, had come from everywhere, and so I looked foreign everywhere.

"Yes, really," I said. "But do go on."

"Well, the funeral gift is important here in my adopted home. You see, if the deceased is the last of his or her generation in the family, ten percent of their belongings are split between all extended family who are not properly in the will. That is the funeral gift. It isn't law, but tradition."

"Ah. Not the sort of tradition I would expect a man called 'Close-Hand' to go in for."

"True enough, Kalyna Aljosanovna. He did something worse."

He paused for effect. I groaned at him.

"Gustaw Close-Hand," Ramunas continued, "had three children: Bernard, Bozena, and Klemens, whose family name became Gustavus, as a way to separate themselves from the rest, who are identified by 'Eight-Toed' or 'Fish-Eye,' or, well, 'Close-Hand.'"

I nodded.

"Old Close-Hand raised his children as rich and spoiled as could be, but it seems near the end of his life, the old mendicant had a crisis of conscience: most likely, this was after Klemens killed a vagrant for fun and was never charged. Allegedly. The patriarch decided that his children needed to earn their fortunes, just as he had; that this was the true path to redemption."

"Isn't redemption for murder meant to be found in prison?"

Ramunas smiled. "The rich are not like us. So, in order to keep his spawn from staying spoiled, Close-Hand chopped up the inheritance—the whole thing, no measly ten percent—between all relatives of the next generation. His children, his nephews and so on: they all get the same amount. Just enough to coax future ventures into being." He clicked his tongue. "Of course, his children still get his banks and other businesses, so they won't exactly be destitute."

"Then Gustaw, *my* Gustaw, doesn't have much coming to him."

"Ah-ha!" laughed Ramunas. "But you see, a pittance to the Gustavus children is a great deal to our eight-toed friend."

"How m—"

"Fifty grivnas."

In Masovska, a grivna was a gold coin. Hence, silver coins were "lesser grivnas," and the coppers that I had on me were "little grivnas." I had only ever owned one solitary gold coin of any sort at a time. And not often. I breathed a huge sigh of relief and actually did allow myself to smile. Perhaps grin. I was saved.

"Well," I said, "that sounds grand. Why did I need to be here for you tell me all that?"

Ramunas bowed and flourished toward the courthouse. "Come on in and I'll show you."

ADVOCATES

We walked quietly, still arm-in-arm, into the courthouse from the government square. A bored guard in a mud-spattered tunic and helmet, whose cross-shaped sword hilt did not look like it was attached to anything, watched us enter the squat courthouse without bothering to crane his neck. The vestibule was a wide, low room in chestnut with a straw floor, and there was a small crowd milling about there, waiting to be allowed into the gallery.

In the crowd, I counted seventeen elderly locals who chatted while waiting for a warm place to sit, away from their homes and demanding families. They leaned against long-grubby paintings of kings, officials, local martyrs, and forest landscapes. There were nine or ten children, of ages ranging perhaps from three to fifteen, spitting and running about the room on their own or in packs, but never with adults. There were also two drunks. The vestibule was filled with those who had no work to do in the morning.

Ramunas assured me this was a normal crowd for a day on which no major decisions would be brought to the courthouse. I marveled at how boring Gniezto must be if an exciting day at municipal court was all that was available for those who were not in the Great Field.

However, somewhere on our way to the other end of the vestibule, where a harried official awaited us, I noticed that these elders and children and drunks looked genuinely interested in being there. Excited, even, to spend their day listening to advocates outline arguments and quote minutiae. A lone little child, blowing snot bubbles and wandering between the old-timers' legs, asked another child, excitedly, if Przemysław, the famous advocate, would be arguing today.

Ramunas had not lied about Gniezto's fascination with the "theatre of law." What a terrifying people.

The official at the entrance to the gallery wore a long gray robe with thick black clasps across the chest and gray fur at the shoulders. He was shivering anyway, probably because the vestibule floor was mud and straw, and his leather boots were coming apart at every seam. He sighed unheard imprecations at a group of teenaged boys fist-fighting in that way that's never clearly a practice game or a real grievance, until he saw us.

The official's gray little face lit up when he saw Ramunas. He grabbed my informer's bejeweled hand, which was a most affectionate greeting in Masovska, and gushed about how happy he was to see him in today. I may as well have not existed to this official, which was fine with me.

The muddy ground, the gray official, the sad drunks excited for a chance to see advocates bicker over property rights: it occurred to me that a fop like Ramunas probably brightened these people's days with his over-practiced grace and garish colors. He illuminated this cold land of wolves and treatises.

We were gestured into the court itself, which thankfully had a real floor of creaking pine. It was a wide, low room filled with pews that may have been torn from a small temple. By the entrance, there was a row of wolves carved from wood painted brown and gray, each baring its fangs and raising its bristles in anger. Those bristles were horsehair and the wolves were boot scrapers, of which I made use.

Far from us, in the front of the room, was a small barrier separating the pews from a raised dais. The dais was marble that must have been shipped westward from Rotfelsen, and was the only part of the room not made of wood. It may well have been the only thing in Gniezto proper made of stone that wasn't a statue. Atop the dais was a small pot of red clay.

Advocates and whoever else were involved in the day's cases were bustling about, rustling papers and muttering to each other, or actively *not* muttering to each other. The pews were mostly empty, waiting for the elderly derelicts and violent youths gathered outside.

We sat toward the front of the courtroom, alone, on an uncomfortable pew. Everyone near the dais greeted Ramunas with smiles or conversation. One or two of them greeted me as well; I coughed and nodded, then sat in silence as Ramunas chattered until the doors were finally opened for the Masovskan rabble.

Once the coughing, laughing, and running had subsided, the pews were a good two-thirds full. A boy who had been half-trampled by older girls was trying very hard to stop crying. The judge entered in front of us, carrying a ceremonial hammer, and walked slowly toward the dais. A grouse drummed at the window frame—which was large, with no bars or glass.

Ramunas assured me that on the occasion of a very important or sensational case, the aisles would be full of spectators stepping on each other, cursing, and fighting up until the moment the proceedings commenced, while yet more people nearly fell in through the windows. He kindly elaborated the sorts of cases to draw crowds: a ghastly murder, a great swindle, a charlatan unmasked. This last one made me quiet.

The commencement was signaled when the judge smashed the red ceramic pot atop the dais with his hammer. It was to represent, Ramunas whispered to me, that any decisions following its destruction would be just as irreversible. The pot had looked utilitarian and rustic in life, but its shards showed a vessel too thin, delicate, and easily broken to have ever been used for carrying anything. The clattering of ceramic shards with the judge's ornate silver hammer shut up every mouth in the room.

The judge himself was a round man in a pink powdered wig. I don't know if it was meant to be pink, or if its red had faded. The wig's ends stood straight up, looking as though his brain was frozen in the process of blowing out the top of his head. I would have laughed if I hadn't noticed that the teenager next to me with the at-least-twice-broken nose, who had shoved an old man down in order to sit in the front, was silent with admiration.

The judge presided over five disputes before Ramunas jabbed my ribs to make sure I was paying attention. Those first five were divorces, land rights, and some things I didn't understand. Investments? The room was riveted. Sometimes they cheered, but never for the accused or accusing, always for the advocates. I tried to pay attention, but the encroaching possibility of freezing to death before I could starve, or starving before my entrails could be spread throughout Masovska, or even successfully escaping while the victors in these cases stayed to die, didn't make it easy for me to care about such things.

With my ribs aching from Ramunas' elbow, I trained my eyes on a man the judge was now addressing for this sixth case, which Ramunas so wanted me to see.

"Name," demanded the judge. If he could have sneaked a rolled R into the word "name," he would have.

"Klemens Gustavus," sighed the man on the stand.

I didn't need Ramunas to jab me anymore: this was the youngest son of Gustaw Close-Hand. Klemens sat straight, with his hands on his knees—proper—and looked the judge directly in the eyes. There was nothing to criticize about his manner, his words, nor even his tone, and yet there was *something* wholly disrespectful and indignant in him that I couldn't define. It was as if showing respect, not for a judge, but just for the time and existence of other humans, was an act that he was putting on, and he wanted us to commend his performance.

It didn't surprise me that this was the Gustavus child who had once, supposedly, committed murder and gotten away with it.

THE GREATER EASTERN TETRARCHIA

The judge swore Klemens Gustavus in the same way he swore in everyone that day: four times, once in each major language of the Tetrarchia.

The Tetrarchia—if you, whoever you are, are reading this hundreds of years removed from me and have no history—was a tetrarchy, a country made up of four separately ruled parts, as its name implies. So, all of its most important administrative and legal duties were executed in four languages. Before our Tetrarchia was born, the very idea of a tetrarchy, or any differently numbered combination, was only a theoretical exercise: argued for or against in rhetorical treatises, but never put into practice.

Soon enough, I would come to learn *far more* about the politics of my country than I had ever wanted. Nonetheless, let me explain what I, as a laywoman, already knew by the time Ramunas took me into that little Masovskan courthouse. By then, I had been all over, and beyond, the Tetrarchia, which I was now planning to escape.

As I told my father, kingdoms and borders are always fluid, no matter what a king and his advisors would have you believe. As I understood it, our great country was once a mass of city-states that warred with, absorbed, and wiped out one another. Each had its own language and culture and ways and exports, and even within a city or town, there were varied traditions and peoples. Over time, these coalesced painfully into seven to ten kingdoms, which eventually boiled down and reduced to four, wedged tremblingly between mighty Loasht to the north and the whirlwind Bandit States to the south.

These four kingdoms—cold and superstitious Masovska; jagged and paranoid Rotfelsen; precarious and discrete Quruscan; fertile and motley Skydašiai—leaned against each other for a few hundred years, skirmishing, trading, and taking each other's measure, until a surprising decision was reached.

The official version was that the four kings recognized the spark of divine rule in each other and, instead of risking further war, banded together. This began the Tetrarchic Experiment, in which one gigantic country was ruled by a council of four monarchs.

The version I heard in taverns across the breadth of the Tetrarchia was that the merchant guilds got sick of having their goods raided in every half-war between kingdoms. So, they banded with a group of young knights who were desperate to prove themselves in greater battles, and forced the kings into a corner: genuine compromise or all-out, four-way war. This began the Tetrarchic Experiment, in which one gigantic country was ruled by a council of four monarchs.

Certainly, unification in the face of the Bandit States' constant war, and Loasht's looming, antique power, didn't hurt.

The Tetrarchia was always a country too large for itself. It had no natural or cultural reason to be one nation, besides a strange quirk of mercantile history. The Tetrarchia's four monarchs, complacent in their safety, only met once a year (at the Council of Barbarians), and could hardly stand one another. Masovska felt that its bitter cold kept its people strong, and that everyone else would collapse without wood imported from its vast forests. Rotfelsen believed similarly about its exported stone, and viewed the rest of the nation with stewing, insular disdain. Quruscan deemed itself unconcerned with anyone unable to survive its mountains and steppes, and it was felt that they alone protected the Tetrarchia from Loasht. Skydašiai was *also* the Tetrarchia's "only" protector from Loasht, and provided most of the nation's produce besides.

Outside of the most sweeping laws, nothing was consistent from one kingdom to the next: not culture, legality, manners, or how regions within each kingdom were defined. The very idea of unity within the Tetrarchia was laughable: we were held together by momentum and fear. Fear of the Bandit States, fear of Loasht, and fear of our own internecine squabbles bubbling up once more.

Each kingdom had its own official administrative language, which was used, unsuccessfully, to grind out the dozens of other languages that still existed within its borders. Swearing in and sentencing were given in all four official languages: Masovskani, Cölluknit, Skydašiavos, and Rotfelsenisch, as were royal decrees, customs forms, money-changing, and pronouncements made before executions. All of the *other* languages became half-remembered dialects, mournful prayers, separatist rallying points, and the like.

The country's full name was The Immovable Confluence of Four also Being the Greater Eastern Tetrarchia of Dirt, Rain, Stone, and Wood Watched Over by the Divine Four Kings of All Known Time, but I had only heard this said out loud once or twice in my life. I had been to its every corner, and spoke all four of its official languages (among others), but, like most citizens, I knew our kingdom as the Greater Eastern Tetrarchia, or simply the Tetrarchia.

KLEMENS

Once Klemens Gustavus had repeated "on my soul" in four different languages, some of which he may not have understood, he leaned back ever so slightly. An inch, maybe. It gave the same impression as if he had thrown his leg up over the barrier, loosened his shirt front to scratch his chest hair, and burped. It amazed me how much contempt he could convey while giving no real offense.

Klemens was a medium-sized man with hair that may not have been black, but looked that way when it was greased down to both sides of his head. I could smell the fishgrease he used from where I was sitting, as well as the lavender with which he tried to stifle it. He had the thick mustache of a grown man grafted over a youth's beard: all spots and neck patches and tufts beneath the eyes. He wore a long coat accented with fur that had been dyed a bright, unnatural blue. The coat itself had heavy clasps, a large collar, and a lined hood, as if to suggest he had trudged all the way through the forest to Gniezto on foot, and was ready to leave the same way at any time.

I had by now learned that it was normal for anyone on the stand to have their advocate hovering just behind them, ready to pounce on any untoward recriminations. Klemens' advocate, a reedy little man who gulped constantly, looked like he had never pounced in his life. He blinked and drummed his fingers on the back of his client's chair and gulped some more. He was there to dutifully find cause for whatever Klemens wanted—even I could tell that. And if it was obvious to me, this litigation-happy Gniezto rabble must have been picking up on all sorts of signs and symbols about the power the magnate's son wielded.

I glared at Klemens hard, squinted, and prayed that if the gods had seen fit to delay my Gift, they would give it to me in this moment. I wanted to see what would come to the rich brat, just to feel a bit of power. But then, I knew what was coming to everyone here, didn't I?

"Klemens Gustavus," boomed the judge, "do you know why you sit before me today?"

"No," Klemens lied.

The judge sighed and looked at the reedy advocate. "Counsel, your client . . . ?"

"My . . . my client," sputtered the advocate, "would very much like to be fully apprised of whatever it is that—"

"Fine. Fine," sighed the judge. He pushed up the pink wig to scratch his hair, which was gray-brown. "Klemens Gustavus, you are here today as a representative of your family in the matter of your father, Gustaw Close-Hand's—"

"Gustaw Gustavus," corrected Klemens. He interrupted as though this had been a natural break in the judge's speech.

The judge chewed so far down on his lower lip that I heard his teeth scrape at beard stubble.

"Gustaw *Close-Hand*," the judge continued, "never took that name."

At this point, I gathered that Klemens was not accused of anything, as there was no other advocate involved, and so the judge had to bear the brunt of him. I spared a quick look behind me to see that the crowd had grown bored at the lack of sparring advocates. One child began punching her neighbor.

"You are here," the judge tried again, "as a representative of your direct family, the progeny of Gustaw *Close-Hand*."

The judge glared at Klemens, who kept silent but put his nose in the air.

"This is in regard," the judge continued, "to your late father's bequest."

Klemens nodded. Slightly.

"It seems that your father's will, which was read at an inquest in your home of Rybochyksta, named certain beneficiaries in the greater Gniezto Oblast, is that correct?"

"Must I answer a judge's questions as though he is an advocate?" Klemens bent his neck back to pose this question to his own advocate, but his eyes never left the judge.

The reedy man behind him gulped loudly, and a ceremonial silver gorget with an engraved skull upon it bounced up and down along his neck. "Well, sir, yes, sir. That is, if you do not, he will call up an advocate to ask the same questions for him. Then you will have to answer."

Klemens pondered this. He seemed to be working over in his mind how much theatricality made him look in control, and how much would be too much. Ramunas put his hands on the pew and strained, almost standing up. His eyes were wide. He was waiting for the judge to call for a volunteer. I found myself admiring something in him.

Klemens looked around slowly to gauge the reaction of the crowd. He seemed to notice Ramunas' eagerness, and frowned.

Klemens sighed. "Yes, there are beneficiaries of the will in this general area."

Ramunas also sighed. The bench creaked and settled.

"Well, this hearing has been called," said the judge, "because your family never informed local beneficiaries, nor the local government"—at this, the judge indicated himself with a flourish—"that this was the case. It was only by luck that we learned of it here in Gniezto."

Klemens smiled a little too wide for my taste and leaned toward the judge. "Luck indeed. I wonder who tattled, eh?" he asked in a stage whisper.

The judge cleared his throat pointedly. I glanced at Ramunas, and wondered if he had been the "tattler." He betrayed nothing.

Well, likely enough, Masovska would collapse in fire and pain before Ramunas' nosiness got him killed. One could only hope.

"Why were no beneficiaries informed?" asked the judge.

"We rather felt it was a beneficiary's responsibility to dig out his own gold."

"Any beneficiaries are your own family!"

Klemens shrugged.

The judge sighed and rubbed his forehead. He did not seem to notice his wig shifting back. "Klemens Gustavus, this court will send couriers to all local beneficiaries. Your family is hereby required to reimburse the payment of these couriers, is that understood?"

Klemens narrowed his eyes. "Is that enforceable?" His advocate cleared his throat and began some half words.

"It is not," replied the judge, "but it will be cheaper than the lawsuit that will ensue if you refuse."

A child just behind me cheered prematurely, and then let the cheer die out halfway as he realized he was too young to know which parts he was meant to care about.

"I accept." Klemens smiled in a way that suggested he was not acquiescing at all. "Besides, I'm going for a little jaunt tomorrow, and haven't the time for a lot of legal nonsense."

The judge grumbled.

Klemens Gustavus stood and gathered up his coat in preparation to leave. After taking a step away, he stopped and turned around as though he had just thought of something. I rolled my eyes.

"A small question, Honored One."

"Yes?" said the judge through his teeth.

"Seeing as my family is *paying* for these couriers, it seems only right my sister Bozena be allowed to review and approve their schedules, routes, and expenses. To confirm that they do not travel all roundabout to the nicest taverns, you know."

The judge waved him away telling him that yes, that would be fine. Ramunas nudged me hard in the gut to make sure I didn't miss the significance.

I had not. Klemens Gustavus certainly planned to have those couriers murdered before they reached his extended family. I put my head in my hands and groaned at what I would have to do next. It seemed that before I could freeze to death, before I could be murdered in a great war, I would die along the road Down Valley Way.

TWO NIGHTS FROM NOW

A few days later, Eight-Toed Gustaw from Down Valley Way came trudging up our hill. I had been practicing a stance from my sickle treatise, with the blade by the left side of my face, ready to strike down or across, as needed, while Grandmother screamed that I was handling Papa's freezerot all wrong. She preferred to believe that old illnesses still lingered on inside him, rather than accepting that his mind was troubled.

When Gustaw got to the top of our hill, Grandmother swallowed her next insult and was quiet. Gustaw rubbed his bald head, and then shook my hand enthusiastically with his great, calloused mitt.

"Kalyna Aljosanovna"—he smiled down at me—"you have gotten big. Did I tell you this last time I stopped by?"

"So have you. And you did not."

Gustaw laughed. His breath smelled of beer: a faint whiff of dark stout to get him through a cold day, not the reek of watery summer ale from his youth. I ushered him into the large tent in front, with its pointed top that dripped lace and fringe, holding up the curtain of shimmering glass beads for him.

"Thank you," he grunted.

"Of course. You are now in the presence of a prophet," I said as though we were joking together: Gustaw had heard such greetings many times.

The large tent was not for sleeping: it was too nice. At its center was our small dais, made of various and variously shaped cheap woods that had been stuck together, and painted to look, in dim light, like mahogany. A heavy Quru rug crushed the grass, and atop it were large pillows: the most comfortable things we owned. I sat on one pillow and Gustaw fell into the other, across the dais from me.

Inside the dais were cards, crystals, chicken feathers, and everything else I used to stall and distract. But today I only used my bright purple dress—advertisement and distraction in one—and lit the swan-shaped incense holder. I breathed in the smoke and felt a rare moment of ease. Gustaw needed a real prophecy from me, and I suppose I had one. If it didn't come true, I would not live to see his disappointment.

Ramunas had gotten his hands on the couriers' schedules, which I *would* have to pay him back for, and so I had formed a plan. The plan was not good, or smart, or likely, but it was all I had. With great, impossible, godly luck, and money, we would escape the Tetrarchia right away, before the snows stopped us, before its collapse, spending everything and ruining ourselves in the process, while poor Gustaw would barely get a chance to spend his new fortune. There was something to look forward to.

"I have been thinking, madam," began Eight-Toed Gustaw from Down Valley Way, "about when you said I would ride in a carriage someday?"

"And you will," I said, leaning forward, chin on my hands and elbows on the dais. I prayed for the pasted wood to hold.

"When?"

"Gustaw," I smiled, "if I knew everything, I would tell you everything, but that is not how it works." I tapped my temple. "You know how it is: the demigods rule the future, and nothing else, so they are jealous of it. If I take too much of it . . ." I reached out in a grabbing motion and trailed off, letting him take this only as literally as he wished to.

"You only rent, eh?" he asked, smiling.

I nodded. "Just so."

He nodded back and grinned. He believed me, but also wanted to feel savvy to the game we were playing.

"We have known each other forever, so I will not spout a lot of nonsense," I lied. "A great change is coming in your life."

"Good change, I hope."

I straightened, went from chummy to mysterious. He had leaned in to meet my low gaze, and so I was now looking down at him.

"Yes, very," I said.

"Are . . . are you sure?"

"Has my family ever steered you wrong?" Imperious, now.

"No."

I smiled and nodded.

"Two nights from now," I moaned from somewhere deep in my abdomen, eyes closed, lips trembling, "when your animals show great unrest in the darkest time, if you begin to make ten circuits 'round your home, your fortune will come on horseback."

"My fortune?" Gustaw replied.

"Yes."

"A *monetary* fortune?"

"Yes."

"How much?"

"Enough that I hope you will not forget a lowly beggar prophet."

"Oh! Of course not!"

Then there was a long pause as Eight-Toed Gustaw from Down Valley Way considered my prophecy. Eventually, I shifted forward on my pillow and opened one eye to see what he was doing.

Gustaw's massive hand stroked his massive chin, and he looked at me intently with large brown eyes. He reached down and scratched his left ankle, probably because he couldn't reach through the boot to his truncated foot.

"'Ten circuits 'round my home,' you say?"

I nodded slowly.

"Now what exactly is a home, according to the knowledge of the Ancients and demigods? Am I to go ten times 'round my shack, madam? Or the gates of my farm? Or the farthest borders of my lands?"

I opened my eyes the rest of the way and lit a new pyre of incense, more for the smoke than the smell. Better he not see me clearly. Even through my worries, I felt a tingle of the thrill that comes with successful trickery.

"Your farm, Gustaw. Circle your farm."

Circuits around the farm would, I hoped, take him long enough for me to enact my prophecy. The unrest of the animals was a way to make him wait a good while. At some point in the night, either the courier or the fighting would rouse them, or he would simply convince himself he heard his animals squealing.

Gustaw sighed and nodded and checked again, just to be sure, that if he followed these instructions his fortune would be made. I reminded him that the fates are fickle, but it would not be the first time my family accurately beheld his future. I then felt a jabbing pang of guilt because, from Papa's prophecy, I almost certainly knew what Gustaw's short future held.

If I succeeded and he got his money, I thought to myself, then perhaps I could tell him about what was coming, and we could escape together. Being piled into a carriage with Gustaw and his family did not seem like the worst way to leave the Tetrarchia. At least we would have company, and money, in our desolation.

Gustaw sucked his lip and nodded, glanced at his foot, grunted up off the ground, assured me he would go 'round ten times, and limped off. I slumped against the side of the tent, exhaling loudly at the effort of being charming and aloof, conspiratorial and unknowable, all at once. The tent shook slightly.

I felt bad asking him to do so much walking: he did, after all, have only eight toes. But even where fate is concerned, a human must feel they are doing something.

FREE WILL

Now, you might think that Eight-Toed Gustaw from Down Valley Way would wonder why it was he had to do *anything* in order to make the future arrive. After all, is the future not inevitable? Well, you would be very wrong.

After all, if a drunken man had listened to my father fourteen years earlier, he would be called Stupid Drunk Gustaw from Down Valley Way. A prophecy that comes through the Gift is not immutable, but it is the most likely outcome, although the how and the why are not always clear.

For example, imagine a man coming to my father back when he was at the peak of his powers, in the prime of his life, with a brown beard and a booming voice, our large tent perfectly outfitted. Imagine, as I say, that a man comes to him with general inquiries: no particular aim or hope, just curious about the future. My father smiles, closes his eyes, and sees that on the following day, this man will fall and crack open his skull, dying. He tells the man this, but does not see where, when, or exactly how.

This unlucky man may spend the next day walking carefully, eyes on the ground, searching every pothole and pebble, and in doing so, not see the cart that barrels into him, knocking him over and killing him exactly as foretold. How *ironic*, you may think. On the other hand, it's entirely possible he'll spend the next day walking carefully, always watching where he is going, and in so doing avoid what my father saw, going on to live for thirty more years of fulfillment and happiness.

And yet, my father had often seen thirty or forty years into happy futures spent in the Tetrarchia: spent right where we now know there would be war, slaughter, and possibly natural disasters, depending on how literal my father had been. Deluge or no, something in our country had changed recently, some new wrinkle to old problems, most like, that made disaster the most likely future by an impossibly high margin.

If everything my forebears saw in their visions was ironclad, they would never have made enough to live on. Giving someone *exactly* what they wanted was the domain of those sorcerers who enacted spells through complex ritual and elaborate set design, while still managing to fail most of the time. Our customers simply wanted to know how to find fortune and avoid catastrophe, or they wanted to be reassured that the future was exactly what they wanted.

Knowing a possible future gave one, at least, the chance to act. This was why it was good to give Eight-Toed Gustaw from Down Valley Way some extra work.

This was also why we had to escape. There was no way I knew of to make the entire Tetrarchia avoid its end in three months. I could mourn it later, with the other refugees.

SAVING GUSTAW'S MONEY

A small dirt road, barely wide enough for two horses abreast, wound down through the impossibly thick Masovskan forest into a little valley, toward the farm of Eight-Toed Gustaw from Down Valley Way. I was not walking on it.

Instead, I was stumbling through the underbrush on the right side of the road, leaving at least one layer of trees between myself and anyone who came down in the open air. It was late at night, and I hadn't seen a single worthless soul since leaving the Great Field, but I was best hidden nonetheless. The moon was just bright enough to illuminate the road, while only penetrating the forest enough to show what was directly in front of me.

I drummed the handle of my sickle idly. Stuck in my belt, the point rasped quietly against my plain, rough leather trousers. I became bored, and so began to reflect on whether moving and fighting was actually easier to do in so-called men's clothes, like trousers, or whether growing up in the Tetrarchia had simply convinced me that it was so. Though the rules changed (maddeningly) from kingdom to kingdom and town to town, violence in my home country was generally considered to be masculine, and so if a woman involved herself in it, she was expected to look the part. It was all rather silly when I thought about it too much, especially considering how differently the *supposed* divide between men and women was often viewed outside of the Tetrarchia's kingdoms.

It was about then that a twig snapped under my boot, and I cursed myself for a fool because I had not been paying attention. I hoped it hadn't mattered this time, as there were owls, crickets, and creatures I preferred not to think about making noise all about me. I had heard nothing of a human being, but even so I went slower and quieter downhill through the rocks and bushes.

A courier was on the way to Eight-Toed Gustaw from Down Valley Way tonight, and I was sure that Klemens Gustavus had planned an ambush. One could pay the court's required fees and afford mercenaries to lie in wait while hardly denting fifty grivnas.

I assumed that Klemens and his siblings had similar ambushes ready wherever their distant relatives stood to gain fifty grivnas. No matter how convenient it might be for *every single courier* to have their throat slit on the road, there would be, Ramunas told me, no real evidence that could be brought against rich, important defendants who ran a major bank. It was a shame I couldn't help these other unfortunate cousins, but I had to harden myself to that sort of feeling. War, disaster, or whatever was coming would swallow them all up soon enough.

I crested a small ridge, and through the trees saw the bottom of the little valley far below. It was all a dark mass, with no individual tree and no piece of road making itself known, all surrounding one little lit-up spot in the center. Gustaw's farmhouse was no larger than my thumb from this distance, but there were lanterns lit outside, showing me its round-topped, squat little shape.

Seeing a warm, safe home nestled in the middle of that forested valley made me realize how cold I was, and I pulled my shawl tighter around my shoulders. I wondered if a tiny Gustaw was trudging around his farm in circles yet.

I heard a lone horse clopping somewhere far away uphill, behind me. I arced toward the road to avoid a particularly thick clump of trees and allowed myself a deep sigh. If it was only one horse, then it was probably the courier bringing Gustaw news of his payday. Perhaps, I thought, the Gustavus brat was going to leave the poor wretch alone after all. Then I nearly tripped over the first mercenary.

He had been crouched by the road, looking intently up it toward the far-off sound, and had never thought to glance into the trees. He was in a bush, bracing himself against the ground with one hand, and I honestly didn't see him until I had crushed the fingers of that hand beneath my heel. He did not cry out.

I, idiot that I am, mumbled, "Pardon!" before I could stop myself.

Instead of a pardon, I received a dagger in my left arm.

I reeled back and fought very hard to use my right hand for drawing my sickle, rather than for pressing the wound on my left arm. I lifted the sickle to the left side of my head. I knew the mercenary didn't need to yell for his cronies to hear us, and sure enough, I heard shuffling through the underbrush come toward us.

The mercenary was still crouching, dagger out, with the moon behind him. I saw the outline of a carefully curled mustache. He was certainly not some starving forest-dweller. Others were crashing closer through the bushes, and I saw one more run across the road from the other side. They said nothing, but did not hide their footsteps. I had to finish with the man in front of me quickly, and I hoped he was distracted enough by his pain to fall for something simple.

I feinted and pivoted back when he stabbed up at me. Then I cut his knife hand clean off. It flew away into the forest, blade glistening with it. He made a gulping noise and bent over forward. I kicked him in the face to keep him out of my way.

At least two were almost upon me from behind, and there was another who had crossed the road somewhere in front of me. I dashed deeper into the forest, away from the road, slipping behind two huge trees grown together. I dropped to the ground and bit my lip. One mercenary tromped toward me, but I couldn't see him in that thick forest until his boot landed a hand-span from my face. I whipped the sickle blade around and sliced open his boot, as well as his tendon.

I never saw this one's face, but he was not as stoic as his comrade. He fell close enough to lie screaming in my ear. The horse was coming closer now, and it seemed to have sped up.

Now that no one was surprised, and the others knew where I was, I needed to get out of the forest and onto the road. I didn't want the courier to see me, but I very much *did* want to see whoever was coming for me next.

You don't realize how instrumental your arms are in keeping balance until you have to leap to your feet with a weapon in one hand and a wound bleeding down into the other. I flopped up awkwardly, inadvertently kicking the screaming man in the process, and sprinted out toward the road.

I dashed through the trees as well as I could. Somewhere in that dark forest, I actually bumped right into another man, the same way one would in a crowded marketplace. He grunted and reeled, and I heard a blade cut air behind me. If my hair had not been tied up tight, I would have lost some.

I burst out of the bushes into the road, which the moon was turning a brilliant silver just below the ridge. The horse could not have been far now; its hooves drummed down toward us.

Two men came out of the forest after me. They were absolutely not desperate highwaymen: freshly shaved, with pristine fur caps and gold chains that clanked against their cloaks. They also both had sabres out. I felt myself hyperventilate. I put the sickle up by my head, and lifted my aching left arm to grab hold of my shawl.

One was a half-step in front of the other. I dashed right of him, putting him between myself and his comrade, and threw my shawl into his face. I stepped in and cut him down, across the head and neck. I felt him yield, and the cream-colored shawl stippled with red as he fell.

The remaining mercenary leaped over the fallen body toward me, and I backed away. He was all that was left of the Gustavus' thugs, and I began to feel truly confident. I thought I could really do this; perhaps there were things in this world I was good at.

He disappeared as I fell over backward. I yelled, "Cock!" as my head hit the packed earth. The mercenaries had stretched a tripwire across the road for the courier's horse, and I stumbled right over it.

My ears were ringing as this remaining mercenary appeared above me. I don't know if he was a large man or just looked that way when I was on my back. He raised his sword, and suddenly disappeared.

I blinked and shook the noise out of my head as I sat up. The mercenary was sprawled on the ground in a puddle of blood, unmoving. As my ears began to work again, I made out the last echoes of a gunshot I hadn't initially heard.

I looked around for the source of the shot before realizing the courier's horse was nearly upon me, galloping down. I fumbled with the tripwire, hacking at it with my sickle.

I saw the heads of horse and rider bob up above the ridge. Even in the middle of the night I could see the horse was wide-eyed and frothing. My bloody left hand joined my right on the sickle's handle. My left arm felt like it would wither and fall off.

The horse's full body appeared. The tripwire severed and snapped away from me. I fell over backward and rolled clumsily into the bushes as the horse tore past and headed down the road towards Gustaw's farm. I lay there and watched it, deciding that, when Gustaw came to pay me, I would tell him everything Papa had seen. That we *would* escape this doomed country together, northward into Loasht itself.

I never saw if the courier was tall or short, scared or composed. They never knew I had been the guardian of that night's journey. The horse turned that last mercenary's skull to jelly.

KILLERS

There were two dead mercenaries in the road, one of whom I had killed. At that point in my life, when I defended myself, I gave out flesh wounds or cut pieces off of people. I had only ended a human life once before, when I was still mostly a child. That first time, I had felt nothing but relief at my safety.

This time, I lay in the forest and waited for the knowledge that this had been a human being, born of human parents, to draw a reaction from me. Nothing came. It felt no different than wounding someone. I decided I did not have the room in my life to agonize over men who had been trying to kill me.

But who had killed the second mercenary?

There were still two injured, but alive, mercenaries somewhere in the forest. How injured were they? I could not remember. Were they near me now? Would they come for me soon?

For one unreasoning moment, I intended to get up, traipse into the road, and take my shawl back from the man I'd killed, looting his pockets in the process. I shook that thought out of my head: whatever hidden harquebus had killed the other one could surely have been reloaded by now. There was no reason to think this shooter wanted to be my savior. The Gustavuses must have had many enemies.

I heard shifting and cracking move through the forest, louder and more deliberate than the mercenaries had been earlier. I sat up quietly as I could, wincing in pain when I pushed myself up with my hurt arm—I had entirely forgotten about it. At least two pairs of boots crunched uncaringly through the underbrush. I sat awkwardly and gripped my sickle. Could it have been the first two mercenaries coming for revenge? I hoped they would be too badly injured to bother. But then, I was injured too.

"Wait—!" croaked a voice in Masovskani. Then there was another shot, so close it deafened me. I turned toward it and saw, between the trees, a dark yellow smudge.

I caught another such smudge in my peripheral vision, moving in time with the sound of boots in the forest. I turned to look and heard another sound, like an animal scrambling through the dirt. The yellow smudge lifted an arm and a lantern shined out ahead of it, illuminating a man who was desperately trying to crawl away on his elbows. One hand was broken, the other a stump.

A final shot, and this time I saw the report light up its section of the forest even brighter, for just a moment. I almost fell over backward.

I sat perfectly still. Scrambling on injured limbs clearly did not arouse the sympathy of these mysterious yellow smudges. I heard them speak to each other in guttural, halting Rotfelsenisch, too quiet for me to make it out. My heart seized up so wildly in that moment that I still wonder if I died then, and the rest of the story I will tell you has simply been a terrible afterlife.

The lantern went out and I was in pitch blackness. I heard more boots, more crunching branches, more Rotfelsenisch, and I prayed that it was as dark where I was as it looked to me.

Something nudged my back. I turned, and it was a man in a yellow soldier's uniform, holding a long-barreled harquebus. Another was walking up behind him.

"Kalyna Aljosanovna?" said the first one.

I nodded numbly.

"Come with us, please and thank you," he said, in Rotfelsenisch.

CONSCRIPTION

I was relatively sure I had seen a soldier in yellow before, the last time I was in the suspicious little kingdom of Rotfelsen, but what that meant escaped me. That kingdom of our Tetrarchia was a confusing mess of parti-colored armies, as though someone had covered it in confetti, and then given that confetti swords. The last time I had been there, I remembered seeing Rotfelsenisch soldiers in green, mostly, and some in yellow. There had been other colored uniforms, but I could not place them in that moment.

These three yellow soldiers, all men and all harquebusiers, led me back up the road for a good mile. They surrounded me but, surprisingly enough, did not jab me with weapons or tell me I was scum. This did not convince me I wasn't on my way to death. They were almost chatty, but told me little useful. The moonlit road was a very different experience on the way back.

"We had to come awfully far out here to find you," chirped one. "Were you trying to escape those brigands?"

I grunted.

At about a mile, we came across a great road that sprouted off from ours, and it was indicated, politely, that I should sit on a large stone at its entrance.

"You must be tired," said the lead, who had done most of the talking.

I almost pointed out that of course I was, I only did all the fighting, while they came in afterward to execute the survivors. But thought better of it and sat.

One of them ran off down this other road, which, despite its large width, twisted off into the forest, and another knelt next to me, to poultice and bandage my bleeding arm. He told me that I could see a flesh-alchemist tomorrow, and then it would be just fine. I did not thank him. In some "civilized" places, the condemned must be healthy before execution, for some reason I do not fathom.

I wondered idly if I should have let the arm gangrene and fall off. Then I would have a soothsayer gimmick. If only I didn't also need it to cook, clean, chop wood, guide our cart, tuck in Papa, defend myself, unpack tents, pack tents, and someday get up the nerve to slap the bile out of Grandmother. If I survived the winter. If I survived this night.

I sighed. I had been terrified for hours, and was simply too exhausted to work up any more terror. If they killed me, they killed me.

I wondered if the courier had made it to Gustaw yet. Was he cavorting through his home, hugging his wife, crying? I hoped so. He deserved that, at least, even if he wouldn't have time to spend it. Even if there were ants in this forest that would probably outlive the very society that made his money viable.

I was tired and, I admit, a little loopy, so when I heard a rumbling, I assumed, first, that it was in my head. Then I wondered if Papa had been off by three months, and the armies were coming now.

"Fine," I said, "let them come."

The soldier finished his bandaging and gave me a perplexed look. I shrugged it off. He could think what he wanted, but the rumbling was getting louder.

I looked down the road, over the soldier's head. The rumbling got even harder to ignore, and a bright light shone out from between the trees. Then I saw, rolling around a bend in the road, the largest carriage I had ever seen.

It was the size of a small hut, had eight wheels in total, and was dragged by ten horses, each much larger than our dearly departed, rock-kneed old horse. Its body was wood, like any other carriage, but its sides were reinforced with iron layered in sheets like an old suit of armor, complete with overly intricate swirls and spikes. The top formed into a silver and red turret that I soon realized was not an ornament. The carriage actually had a small, pointed second story. I could see all of this thanks to great lanterns that hung from its corners: it seemed to travel in a halo. I wondered if it was here to take me to join my ancestors.

Two soldiers, also in yellow, sat in front, one guiding the horses while the other hoisted a harquebus on his shoulder. I would soon learn that the three who walked me here had their own perches, at a small railing on the carriage's roof, and atop an outcropping at the back, respectively.

The carriage ground to a halt just in front of me. I stood up, bewildered, as a door on its side creaked open, revealing an interior of dark green velvet with deep purple trimmings.

A man who was not wearing a uniform stepped out with a slight limp.

"Kalyna Aljosanovna the soothsayer," he said, "for the good of the Greater Eastern Tetrarchia, and its Divine Four Kings, in the name of His Most Serene Majesty One-of-Four Gerhold VIII"—he winked, as though it were a joke between us that he was using such formal language—"I hereby requisition the use of your Gift."

This man's clothing, pinkish skin, and the stop-and-start rhythm of his language made it clear enough to anyone that he was from Rotfelsen, the kingdom in the southeastern corner of our Tetrarchia. At his side he wore a long, thin rapier with an ornate, enclosed hilt, unlike the Masovskan cross-guarded sabre. He also wore a yellow silk doublet with leather riding trousers and only a blue half-cape on top, with no robe to keep warm. He knew he would not have to stand outside in the chilling local winds for long.

My pain and exhaustion disappeared in the face of pure, numb confusion.

"I . . . I'm sorry?" I managed to say.

He walked up to me, favoring his left leg, and stopped at the perfect distance to be in control of the space I occupied without being invasive. The lantern light flickered on the right side of his face. His jaw was set, but not too hard, his face angular and serious without being stern, neither enjoying nor abhorring his duty. His dark brown hair was gray-streaked and worn long, but messy and nearly vertical, as though he had just woken up from his carriage bench, and his mustache was heavy without support from a goatee, which went against Rotfelsen noble style. He was dressed well, I gathered, because he was some sort of officer or official, but it was also clear that he came from peasant origins.

He pulled a parchment from his belt, its rustling louder to me than the harquebus shots.

"My name is Lenz Felsknecht, and I have here an order signed by the hand of His Most Serene Majesty's younger brother, Dutiful Prince Friedhelm, Landgrave of the Two Great Caves and the Spire, that calls for the requisition of—"

"You can't 'requisition' my Gift," I said. I felt I had taken a bit of his measure, and the melting of pain and exhaustion had allowed me to return to myself. "It's part of me, do you understand? Attached. In here." I pointed to my temple, perhaps condescendingly.

"Just so. But as I doubt bringing only your *head* will do, you must come with me."

He opened the parchment and showed it to me. I had seen a royal seal once or twice before, although never on orders concerning me. It certainly looked legitimate. So did the harquebusiers. He laid his other hand, in a thick glove, on my shoulder.

"Step into the carriage, Kalyna Aljosanovna," he said. "We've kept a close eye on you, and we know the great prophetic strength of your Gift, of which . . ."

Was this sarcasm? Did he know?

". . . the Prince has need. Think of him as a customer. One who will pay well, but whom you cannot turn down."

In that moment, I think I could have gutted him with my sickle and run off through the dark woods before the harquebusiers took decent aim. It occurred to me, but did not seem worth the immediate effort. Had I a better idea of what was coming, I would have tried.

PART TWO

FORCED LUXURY

I would have enjoyed traveling in that carriage, with its plush seats and its safety, if not for the company, the destination, and having been kidnapped.

The monstrous vehicle's interior, not including the unnecessary turret on top, was larger than my family's two tents put together. Lenz and I began by sitting diagonally at opposite ends, on separate seats against the front and back walls, respectively, and there were two more rows of seats that ran through the center, separating us. It was almost too much space for me. It made me feel uncomfortable; adrift. This monstrosity could have sat twelve spoiled nobles in relative comfort. Soldiers sitting on the floor could likely have numbered twenty, provided most of the filigrees and luxuries were removed to make room for them.

Yet none of the harquebusiers were inside with us. They sat on little platforms with guardrails, and took shifts sleeping in an enclosed area about the size of my bedroll, which bulged out from the back of the carriage. There was no door between their sleeping chamber and where we sat—this carriage was also built to be a prison, if necessary.

So, Lenz and I had the inside of this rolling cathedral to ourselves, and I sat as far from him as possible. The benches were backed with silk cushions, and the carriage interior was all rich woods and velvets, with gold-plate in the shape of grape leaves everywhere—as though anyone in Rotfelsen's dank caves had even seen a grape that wasn't first stomped and turned into wine beneath a Skydašian sky. Overall, this carriage was more expensively designed than any building I'd ever been inside; and perhaps more sturdily built (excluding dungeons).

As the soldier patching me up had promised, we did indeed stop to find a good flesh-alchemist, who cheerily got on board and spent a good hour mending my arm as we rolled along. I had been injured many times in my life, but only rarely been willing (or able) to pay for flesh-alchemy. It was still quite impressive, to me, to see how his gritty little salve, still warm to the touch, closed up my wound before my very eyes, although Lenz seemed quite disinterested.

Of this relatively new art, Grandmother had always said, "Bandages and bed rest were good enough for our ancestors, and they're good enough for you!" Never thinking, of course, of all the necessities and luxuries she enjoyed that many of her ancestors had not: tobacco from the Bandit States, Loashti gunpowder for a soothsayer to make a stunning entrance, the velvet she'd torn out of her chair. Flesh-alchemy had simply been unlucky enough to come about during Grandmother's adulthood, and was therefore a decadent luxury. (Unlike *tobacco*.)

She also did not bother to think of how her own grandfather, Huso, had escaped a mob only to bleed to death of a wound that could have been easily fixed by flesh-alchemy. But, of course, this new medicine was no help for internal bleeding, and so would have done nothing for my mother when I killed her.

The flesh-alchemist was a pleasant little man in a fur coat whose normal rate was a *ludicrous* (to me) ten gold grivnas. He was given another ten for his silence, and five more besides to pay his way back home from the nearest inn—a trip that would cost, at most, a few silver grivnas. Lenz had just handed out half of Eight-Toed Gustaw from Down Valley Way's fortune on fixing my arm. I stared up at my kidnapper, who was standing by the door, as the carriage lurched back to life.

"Why," I asked, "could the Dutiful Prince Friedhelm, Landgrave of the Two Great Caves and the Spire, not come to my tent like a decent person?" I looked down at my arm, flexing it lightly and feeling the newly knitted flesh tingle.

"Gniezto is farther than our good Prince can travel just now," said Lenz. "It's a well-kept secret that Prince Friedhelm is one of the hardest working people in Rotfelsen."

"Is he in Masovska at all?"

"No."

"You . . ." Lenz may have heard me grind my teeth. "You are taking me all the way to Rotfelsen, aren't you?"

"Did you think the Landgrave of the Two Great Caves and the Spire was just over the next Masovskan hill?"

"I dared to hope."

At least Lenz did not laugh at me. He braced his hand against the wall of the carriage, but did not move to sit down.

"Surely you know," he said, "that most Rots don't like to leave their land."

"'Land' is generous," I sneered. "Their rock, you mean. But of course, who would ever want to leave such a *charming* place?"

"Personally, I quite enjoy travel."

I was feeling very Masovskan just then, and almost told him just where in his Prince he could travel. But I held it in.

"*Sir*," I said instead, "I have customers, one of whom owes me a payment, and an invalid father besides. I cannot simply disappear from Gniezto without a trace."

I did not tell him I also had an informant to pay off and a societal (or natural?) collapse to avoid.

"It seems *someone* in Gniezto didn't want you around anymore," he said. "Some well-off type dislike his fortune, perhaps? We took care of his goons for you, and the Prince will pay you more than any other customers could."

I groaned theatrically. Even if this Lenz were to give me five hundred Masovskan grivnas, I had done *so much* for a fragment of Gustaw's fifty.

"And," he continued, "your father and grandmother will be spirited to your side. I have a suite, complete with servants and four sturdy walls, prepared for them."

I admit that the thought of Papa being comfortable and safe for the winter would have been tempting, if we didn't need to escape the Tetrarchia entirely. If I ignored the imminent collapse of our country, then my jailer was promising to do more for Papa than his own daughter ever had. Provided Lenz was telling the truth.

"Just a little way from here," he said, "is another carriage of ours, which I will send back for your family, and your things, and bring them after us. At a less strenuous pace than you and I are traveling. The soldiers within will collect your father and grandmother, as well as your possessions."

"No soldiers!" I hadn't meant to yell, but I did. A harquebusier on the roof knocked against the hard metal door to make sure Lenz was alright.

"All's well!" Lenz yelled upward. He walked back to his side of the carriage and sat.

"No soldiers," I repeated, quieter. I stood up and paced the carriage to do something with my energy. My hands were shaking, and I stopped myself just before pulling at my own hair many times. "Everywhere we go, we are hunted, arrested, blamed, burned. If a woman has a miscarriage, I must have looked at her; if vengeful spirits have been causing trouble, my father drew them with his madness. More often than it's an unruly mob coming for us, it is *soldiers*."

I threw my arms up and turned away from him. The carriage bounced and I stumbled, which didn't look very threatening. I turned back to face him, glaring.

"If Grandmother sees soldiers coming for her," I said, "she'll do whatever she can to get my father and herself killed, rather than captured. She will be surprisingly good at it."

"And so I should . . . what?" Lenz was listening, but seemed unbothered.

"Put some of your soldiers in servant's livery, and have them say I'm . . . I'm working for the Prince of my own free will, which is but half a lie."

"Hmm." Lenz scratched his head. "That's a lot of trouble."

"I can also be a lot of trouble."

"I'm sure you can. I'll see what I can do."

Would he? Or was he was only humoring me while he left them to starve? Or freeze? I had only his word to go on.

I walked back and fell into my seat. "Well . . ." I laughed to myself. "Maybe it would be all right if Grandmother was . . . misplaced along the way."

"Don't say that unless you mean it."

I looked back at Lenz, and he seemed serious—more so than when conveying the Prince's orders. Who *was* this man?

"If you mean it," he continued, "it's done."

I may have considered his offer.

But finally, I said, "Forget it."

"Forgotten."

The carriage rumbled through the Masovskan forest, and I glanced at the sun beginning to rise above the trees. Lenz stood up and opened a compartment. In it was a large and ornate gleaming silver samovar, which rattled softly with the carriage's movement.

"You don't smell good enough to be a spoiled noble," I said.

"Just a soldier, Kalyna Aljosanovna." He pointed with his thumb to his yellow doublet. "The luxury is for you." Then he poured two cups of tea.

"When a powerful man abducts a woman, the luxury is never for her. You are showing me your power."

"I am showing you the Prince's power."

"Hmm. I wonder what he really wants from me."

"What do you think?" he asked as he watered down the tea.

"Perhaps the Prince has a *social disease* and rubbing the ashes of a prophet on his balls will cure it."

"That's ridiculous," he said, walking over to me. Then he smiled. "The Prince is nowhere near as lecherous as his reputation. Hardly anyone could be."

I shrugged and grimaced. "I've never heard of your blasted Prince, or his *reputation*. I'm just assuming."

"I promise you, Kalyna," he said as he handed me a teacup, "his only interest is in your Gift."

"What does he want from my Gift? To supplant his brother, I suppose?" I sniffed at the tea.

Lenz then proceeded to tell me what it was the Prince wanted. He did so in every human being's favorite way to communicate: through a story about oneself.

LENZ'S STORY

When I first came to the Dutiful Prince Friedhelm's apartments in the Sunset Palace, Kalyna, I was dressed to be murdered.

My full formal uniform—green, at the time—was stiff with disuse and completed by a great empty space on the chest for the medals I did not have. My hair and mustaches I had combed, curled, twisted, and slicked so heavily that I could not tell my own sweat from running pig fat. With all that and my limp, I was a sight to behold.

The Prince's guards—yellow, they wear, as I do now—took my sword but allowed me to wander his apartments unaccompanied. I assumed this was permitted because I would not leave those apartments alive, and I decided that if I was to become a corpse, I would see absolutely every room first. Have some new sights to mull over while I waited in the void for the spirits of my ancestors to come find me.

Prince Friedhelm's apartments, with which you will soon be familiar, are a dizzying array of sitting rooms, library-studies, bedrooms of sundry themes, and a complex of baths. You can tell one sort of room from another by the variety of couch that it has. (They *all* have couches.) Some are sectional and curved for lounging groups, some are straight and comfortable with an end table on which to set paperwork when the eyes get tired. One couch is velvet, and its armrests are gold-plated nudes bent at ninety degrees.

Thus I lingered before entering the audience chamber. I saw every book, wall, and device in those apartments, in order to delay my death a little longer. I see you are disappointed I did not meet it. A guard in yellow eventually indicated that I should really get going, and he did so unkindly, as the Yellows and the Greens have never been close. Rotfelsen has four separate armies, you see, each of which supposedly serve the kingdom, and through it our greater Tetrarchia, in their own way. None of them like one another.

Now, this was only last spring. At the time, I was a minor officer, unnoticeable by my own design, in High General Dreher's army. In other words, I was a Green. The way I looked at it, I'd made a deal with my superiors: I took a bullet in my left leg for Rotfelsen during a skirmish in my youth, and now I would fill out acquisitions forms for grain and saltfish and carry no ambitions, so long as they sent me limping into no more battles. Raids from the Bandit States would be curbed well enough without my sword: I was happily beneath anyone's interest.

Oh yes, I was also stealing privileged information. Constantly. Not for any purpose, mind you, but it's amazing how many matters of grave importance will be written right into the blandest paperwork with no thought as to whose eyes may run over them. I had in my home books upon books I'd written with my own hand, filled with secrets about the army, the nobility, the royal family, our neighbors, and anything else. I had no use for any of this, but it seemed such a waste not to collect what was right in front of me every day. I was driven chiefly by curiosity, incredulity at so much being available to me, and deep boredom. Of course, I knew it was dangerous, and perhaps a part of me wanted the excitement.

So I thought I knew why the Prince had called me from my windowless office, up to his towering and very windowed one. I was to disappear, or go out those windows and bounce on the red stone, after he figured out what my shadowy, and entirely fictional, masters wanted with my secret history, and how much I had told them. I fancied I had been taken for a Loashti spy.

I paced the Prince's audience chamber and pretended not to notice the secret door in his bookshelf. A room has never had a secret passage that did not also have a secret peephole, so I behaved myself. There was a very sharp letter opener on his desk, and I wondered if he expected me to pick it up and hide it.

Soon enough, the Prince came out of his bookshelf and looked me over. He's a short man who bears the features of the inbred, a strange jaw and nose, but is also the rare royal who would attract admirers even as a tailor or blacksmith. But you'll meet him soon enough.

He greeted me warmly and asked if I'd drifted back toward his desk because I recognized what he was reading. I lied and said that I had. The open book on his desk was in my handwriting: a volume on his older brother, King Gerhold VIII, open to a page on our monarch's childlessness.

"'Many in the court'"—the Prince quoted a passage of mine from memory—"'whisper that the King has specific predilections that keep him from fathering children. Such as an interest in men, or . . .' Well, you know. 'And,'" the Prince continued, in my voice, "'that such desires could also explain his periodic disappearances to his hunting lodge down in the southern caves. But this seems unlikely, as to marry and create royal offspring is a duty beyond something so simple as personal tastes. More likely, the King or the Queen simply cannot have children.'"

The Prince then asked me from whom these speculations had come, and I told him they were my own.

The Prince told me it was treason to even suggest that the King's issue was anything but potent. It was also treason to suggest the King may have preferred men, as such things are frowned upon in Rotfelsen, past a certain age. Although the Prince was quick to point out that this would not have been a great hindrance.

"I assure you," I remember he said, "to ensure his legacy, a King can grit his teeth and bear anything."

I told him that was exactly what I had been trying to say in my book.

"Lenz Felsknecht, Acquisitions Officer in the High General's army," he said to me, "why do you suspect you're here? Assuming it's not to have you thrown from my window, which it may well be."

I told him I was sure I didn't know.

Now, I'll always remember this next thing he said perfectly: "These books of yours are better curated and organized than any records I have seen."

I thanked him for the compliment, of course, and then told our Dutiful Prince Friedhelm, "You want my help in intriguing against your brother."

The Prince laughed and asked me why in the world he would ever want that.

"If," the Prince told me, "my brother dies, or is exiled, while childless, I am King. If my brother survives every plot against his life, and manages to somehow produce an heir, what do I receive?"

"Nothing?"

"Nothing. Except a lifetime of riches and parties and pleasures with no consequences. I love my brother no more than an evil prince from an old story does his, but the last thing I want is his death before I have a niece or nephew."

In all my prying, I had not suspected our Prince was so motivated.

"But the plots in our wretched kingdom grow faster than the divided King's Guard can prune them. No matter how hard I have tried, I am not so blind to politics as to miss how suspicious centuries living in *this place* have made us. I feel that in every little hollow there is sedition breeding—that our people get strange ideas when they live away from the sun for so long. So, your job will be to serve me, as one of my Yellows, in keeping my brother safe from the shadows to ensure my indolence. I can't use anyone known to the court."

I bowed and accepted this new position immediately, to preserve my life.

"Keep my brother alive, Lenz, at least until he can have children *somehow*. Keep this festering boil of a kingdom from bursting until I've died happy in my wine and my lovers."

Don't Bring Me Near the King

I sat quietly through his story, holding a cup of untouched tea in a sad attempt at repose. We were still somewhere in Masovska's thick forest, and it was only midmorning. The tea smelled strangely intense, almost like smoked meat.

"Well," I said, "now I know what the Prince wants, but nothing about *my* involvement."

"Oh, that." Lenz laughed. "The Prince thought a prophet might be useful. For anticipating plots."

"You could have just said, 'We're spies!' and skipped the story."

"I wanted you to understand my position in all this."

"I do not care to."

Lenz shrugged and sat back, scratching his messy hair. The carriage crashed over a bump in the road.

"So," I said, putting down my untouched tea, "the Prince wants me to read the King's future and point out a couple of dignitaries who are eyeing the throne for their masters, for a hefty fee."

"Essentially. We will be there just in time for the Winter Ball."

"What's that?" I asked.

"The Splendid Royal Ball of the Entering into the Winter Months, Wreathed by Snow and Ice, although likely none will have formed yet. It's a party with hundreds of guests, some of whom may have harmful plans."

"Perfect, I can see all the dignitaries and third-tier royal bastards in one place." I clapped my free hand against my thigh, with finality. "A good night's work!"

It would be a crowning achievement of lying for me, the monumental fraud, to successfully prophesize for a king, a prince, and a spy. So satisfying would be the success, and so easily could I afford to get Papa out of the Tetrarchia on a Prince's money. I would escape the Tetrarchia in time *and* be proud of my greatest deception. Perhaps that would comfort me through the long hours of contemplating my homeland's death from afar.

But Lenz looked very sorry about what he was about to say. "No. You are conscripted to join me as a spy for . . . quite some time. The ball's a good start, but we will need regular reads on the court."

"How long?"

"Well, your father and grandmother will have a nice warm place to stay for the winter. For the next few winters."

"The next—!" I gulped back the rest.

"Kalyna Aljosanovna, you will know too much for us to just let you go."

"Then don't tell me your secrets! I don't care to know them. And I could not begin to care about royalty."

"You're a soothsayer."

"Then *don't bring me near the King*!" I cried. "That way I will know nothing!"

"You may well never see the King," said Lenz, "but you'll tell us about many important people."

My head spun. How long could an imposter possibly survive at any court, much less the insular and cagey Rotfelsenisch court? What's more, were I whispering false prophecies into a Prince's ear, couldn't my incompetence then be *directly* responsible for the Tetrarchia's collapse?

This last was actually a strangely comforting thought.

But what was not comforting was the image of Papa waking up alone and confused in his tent. What was certainly not comforting was the fact that this job for a sybaritic prince was not going to be the greatest con of my career, but a death sentence. Even without the looming end of the Tetrarchia, there was no freedom on the horizon.

Every failed prophecy would be a chance to be discovered and executed, and every successful one would keep me there for when Rotfelsen crumbled to red dust beneath Papa's prophesized destruction. I would have to reform my escape plans, as leaving the Tetrarchia from Rotfelsen was entirely different than from Masovska. Rotfelsen's very structure was that of a fortress—it was the hardest kingdom to escape, as I knew from past experience. Could we make it south into the Bandit States while they picked at the edges of the Tetrarchia's despair? I was doomed.

I watched the Masovskan trees speed by through the window's bars and thought about them being leveled for siege engines. Even then, as winter encroached, most were still green and vibrant. As I stared out, Lenz spoke about paying off my Gniezto debts, about making sure to collect my fee from Eight-Toed Gustaw from Down Valley Way, and all other manner of things to show how much he knew about me. At least he did not seem to understand my relationship to Ramunas.

"How long did it take you to get to Gniezto?" I finally asked.

"A week, at full speed."

"A week? I'll be trapped in here with you for a week?"

Gods, a *whole week*. I would arrive in Rotfelsen's capital, Turmenbach, with maybe two and a half months until the Tetrarchia was supposed to collapse around me.

"Yes," said Lenz, "we will be stuck with each other for a week, before we are stuck with each other for years."

I sat still, staring at him for a good minute or two, and then realized that I was very tired. I said as much.

"You can sleep in the turret," he said.

"'Can,' so I have privacy? Or 'will,' so I am farther from the doors?"

"Yes to both. Although the doors are steel, and locked, with harquebusiers watching the road fly by at impossible speeds."

I sighed. I was beginning to have trouble keeping my eyes open.

"Will my father catch up with us along the way?" I asked.

"Oh my, no. We will change horses, but otherwise it's straight on through half of Masovska and into Rotfelsen. No stops. Your elderly family will be stopping for rest, so that they are not constantly jostled."

I had not gotten to say goodbye. Papa would be so scared and confused when Lenz's people came for him, however they were dressed. If Lenz wasn't lying and they did so at all. Papa might simply sit in the tent waiting for me until he froze or starved. Or perhaps Lenz's soldiers had slit his throat and been done with it. I had no reason to think I would see Papa ever again.

I was now tired enough to realize that the carriage could have been crashing off Rotfelsen's red cliffs and I would have fallen asleep in the middle of it. I did not even have the energy to continue worrying about Papa.

Tomorrow. Tomorrow there would be much worrying.

I stood up and stumbled to the little ladder. I remember from later in the trip that where each of the ladder's rails punched through the sides to anchor itself, there was a bronze face staring out the other end, as if to guard anyone ascending it. All human faces, and each one different.

I certainly didn't notice this on that first evening, however. I have a vague memory of being halfway up the ladder, and the next thing I remember is waking up in the turret the following day. I was wrapped in five blankets as I pulled open the curtains to see the harquebusier on the roof. He smiled and waved at me.

BOHDAN'S BOTANICALS

That next morning, I was presented with a few sets of clean clothes and a bright sky above the Masovskan woods that did not look like they could ever become a battlefield, or be even the least bit affected by human concerns. I changed, awkwardly, from trousers back into a dress inside the little turret, kicking its sides a lot in the process and feeling the new alchemy-crafted skin on my arm stretch strangely. Thus, I stopped looking like some midnight cutthroat, and was once again a soothsayer. The dress was a deep ochre with blue-green embroidered accents—the sort of colorful clothing I preferred, but better made than anything I owned. Pity it was tight in the shoulders.

I climbed down the ladder and was provided a warm meal of roasted beets and turnips scrambled with egg and thin slices of ham, alongside a mug of warm cider. The food and drink had waited for me on a little table rooted to the floor, the surface of which was on some sort of hinge that kept it always upright and still, no matter how the carriage bumped and rolled beneath us. I cannot pretend I understand how that worked.

Part of my family's excuse for meager meals had always been that we were constantly traveling, and yet here was travel desperate to seem like decadent, stationary life. I have known nomadic peoples who traveled with a collection of huge tents, each with thick rugs and wooden furniture, serving a feast of pickles and preserves, but they never acted as though they were *not* traveling. This thing was pretending to be a house as it bumped along the road. But I supposed the Rotfelsenisch mind always craved *enclosure*.

"Is a cook sweating into a fire in that closet?" I asked with my mouth full, spitting bits of ham. I pointed with my spoon to a small closet at the rear of the carriage, which could not have fit more than three jackets and some boots.

"We changed horses at an inn ten minutes before you woke; this was cooked there." Lenz was picking at a plate of the same, and still did me the courtesy of sitting at the far side of the carriage. He seemed annoyed at having to speak up.

"Ah."

"We have alchemically warmed pots stored below us"—he stomped on the floor—"filled with that cider, soups, stews, and we have the samovar as well, but I assure you that's the limit."

"Oh yes, quite limited," I grunted as I crammed the rest of the ham and the last round of turnip into my mouth. The food and cider were both delicately spiced with flavors I did not yet recognize, but the child at the bottom of my consciousness stirred with memories of Papa crushing small leaves in his palm and sprinkling them over a pan.

I thought about allowing Lenz to sit closer, so that we could chat and I could try to wheedle useful things out of him, until I remembered I was being kidnapped in a carriage dripping with soldiers. Suddenly I did not have the energy for such subterfuge. Later. We had a *week*, after all.

"There's a library in here, you know," said Lenz.

"Naturally!" I said.

He indicated a handle on the floor. I knelt, grabbed it, and yanked up as hard as I could, only for the bookshelf to slide up so easily that I fell on my rear. Lenz was good enough to pretend he had seen nothing. The bookshelf came right up out of the floor to my waist: a square column with books on all four sides.

"About half of them are my own volumes," said Lenz. "Just a few slices of my history that are pertinent to those we'll see at the Winter Ball."

I looked up at him: smiling and relaxed, the way someone with power over one's life can afford to be. I wanted to jump up and throttle him. I was sure I could at least kill Lenz before the soldiers got to me.

Sitting on the floor, I gritted my teeth, grabbed a book, and began reading Lenz's extensive secret history of Rotfelsenisch politics—the work that had gotten him in trouble, and also hired. This would, I hoped, give me somewhere to begin when I was trapped in Rotfelsen, producing futures for the Prince. Lenz didn't wonder why I needed to read them because he understood how the Gift worked, and so knew the importance of context.

Context, however, I did not achieve, at least not yet. I began eagerly, for here was a chance to better formulate my "prophecies." But with no points of reference for the major figures, scandals, and battles, it read as a jumble of guttural monikers and meaningless observations.

Reading about the royal family and all attendant nobles was useless—I had no faces to put to names. How was I to know Frederick from Johann-Frederick from Frederick-Johann in a pinch, when all were names on paper, and all heirs to the Dukedom of the Blue Fields, of which I had never heard? The current, ailing Duke was Hans-Robler XII, not to be confused with Robler-Hans IV, Viscount of the Web Tunnels, who had been mentioned twenty pages earlier as a minor leader of the South Cave Separatists, who had attempted to split off from Rotfelsen entirely.

Every person, place, political idea, or event I did not know had to be further researched, and within its definition—if one was even provided—I would find more I did not know. The words all made sense on their own, but together it was a jumble of strangers doing things to each other that I did not understand.

I gave up and slammed one of Lenz's volumes shut in frustration. These idiots would all be dead soon anyway. He sighed and told me that if I wanted something else to pass the time, there were other works, which he had not written.

I had initially learned to read all my languages through unfulfilled contracts, vicious edicts, and wanted posters. (In my teen years, one such poster, covered in the globes and loops of Skydašiavos, claimed that my presence had "soured almond milk and twisted the beanstalks of unmarried young men like sourdough pretzels.") But the only time before my trip with Lenz that I had *enjoyed* reading had been in my fifteenth year, when Papa caught a pneumonia so bad that we spent a week with a doctor. I hemorrhaged silver that week but refused to leave his side, and so spent his sleeping hours reading medical texts. It helped me learn where to cut people.

So, now that I had nothing to do, I would try to learn more. I looked at what else Lenz had in his little library: *The Fundamentals of Historical Ethics as Told Through the Failures of the Pre-Tetrarchic Eras*, *The Cleaving Battle of Selju Cliffs*, *Half-Fabulous Creatures of Misted Places*, *Loashti Diplomacy*, *Goëmann's Honey Conspiracy*, *The Skydašian Tower of Nine-Toed Feet*, and on and on and on. There were some whose titles were in archaic forms of Rotfelsenisch beyond my understanding.

I chose *Bohdan's Botanicals*, second edition, because I hoped to learn how to poison my captor. The title *Bohdan's Botanicals* was alliterative in Rotfelsenisch, but not in the original Masovskani from which it had been translated. The words of each page's descriptions wrapped themselves about a desiccated flower, leaf, or stem pressed onto the page. It must have been a terribly expensive book to produce. Many times, the guide's informative prose broke down amidst invective against "the Skydašian bandit-naturalist Adomas."

I searched and searched that book for a harmful flower to crumble into Lenz's tea. Unfortunately, every hallucinatory candleflower, itchy dogwhisker, and purple poison rotprick was divested of its poisonous innards before pressing. The prose excitedly promised this on every page. I wonder if the first edition had caused poor Bohdan a lawsuit. I hope he stayed out of Gniezto.

THE COUNCIL OF BARBARIANS

By the third day of our trip, Lenz had formed strong opinions about how little preparatory reading I'd done. So he told me why the Winter Ball was so very important, hoping that this would convince me to pick up his histories again. I had not only avoided them because they were mystifying: reading those books began to feel like a capitulation to the desires of my jailer. I knew that if I was to survive this Winter Ball, I would need to learn something ahead of time, but I continued to tell myself I would get to it *later* in our trip.

The Winter Ball this year was when the King would begin to entertain delegations from the other three kingdoms of the Tetrarchia, as well as his own, in early preparation for the Council of Barbarians. The Council's existence was a fact of life in the Tetrarchia, but I must remember that someone reading this may well be from anywhere else, so I will explain.

Every year at the dawn of spring, provided there were no succession crises in process, the monarchs of the four Tetrarchic states—Rotfelsen, Masovska, Quruscan, Skydašiai—would meet in one of their capitals to discuss the running of our lumbering, unwieldy monster of a country. This was officially known as The Divine Monarchic Council of Pure Blessed Blood for the Furtherance of the Greater Eastern Tetrarchia as a Bulwark to its Devious Neighbors and a Net Spread to Catch the Dropped Blessings of Its Gods.

"Council of Barbarians" started as a tongue-in-cheek title, used behind closed doors by drunken clerks and ministers. It came out of the fact that, at the Tetrarchia's advent, each of its states officially saw its neighbors as, well, barbarians. So when all those retainers and delegates and clerks and ministers drank together, they were tickled to find that they all used different words for the same thing. Well, tickled when they were not fighting. Naturally, each Tetrarchic state *still* sees its neighbors as barbarians, but not as a matter of policy, and the names are subtler.

In those shaky days of the first councils, the kings and ministers who took part were so quick to threaten abdication or war, so eager to stab one another in the back (literally, I mean), that they were, by any metric, barbarous. But the name "Council of Barbarians," which had originally been whispered (and drunkenly shouted) in secret, began to wriggle its way toward acceptance. By a hundred years into the Tetrarchic Experiment, it was being inscribed on everything but the most official papers, and being said everywhere but the Opening Invocation. By this time, the proceedings had become less violent than pettily bureaucratic, and even the monarchs enjoyed the short and playful name.

So, once a year, as winter faded and spring crept in, the Council of Barbarians would meet in a capital—Skydašiai, Masovska, Quruscan, Rotfelsen, Skydašiai, and so forth, in that order—to discuss matters of state. About infighting and drunken clerks, I have a working knowledge, but if you wish to learn statecraft, you will have to look elsewhere.

I doubt it will surprise you to know that the Council of Barbarians was scheduled to meet in Rotfelsen just *three months* from the day my father had his vision. Specifically, his *very* clear vision of the Tetrarchia's end, which he had then said would happen in "three months."

FÁNTUTAZH LAKE

Soon enough, the forest we were passing through was thicker even than the one Down Valley Way. The rumbling of our metal terror scared the wolves, tree cats, and hoopoes away, so all I saw through the bars of my window was a wall of trees and occasional beams of sunlight.

When a sad, desperate group of bandits, or separatists, or loyalists, or whatever they were emerged from the trees to waylay our carriage, the harquebusiers handled them so swiftly that Lenz did not even look up. I watched their starved bodies disappear behind us, and wondered what fickle gods had put me in this monstrous, armored luxury carriage, rather than out there with them.

But then, perhaps they were lucky. I still did not know what exactly was coming, but perhaps being shot quickly in a forest was better than whatever I would have to deal with. Better than the terror of collapse, the uncertainty of invasion, the bleak drudgery of prison camps, the pain of forced marches. After all, *they* had died knowing the Tetrarchia was a thing that existed, and would continue to exist—for all the comfort this thought may have brought them.

"Isn't it nice to have soldiers to do the fighting?" asked Lenz, a bit after the encounter. "This is how it will be, from now on, Kalyna: I'll read the past, and you the future, while we sit comfortably far from the dangers we see."

Remembering, just now, that Lenz said this has caused me to suffer a fit of laughter.

There were, of course, breaks in that Masovskan forest, and near the halfway point of our journey, we passed Fántutazh Lake. At the inn by its shore, I received a cask of piping hot fish stew, the taste of which I wish I remembered better. Trees don't grow a mile from the lake in all directions, although no one knows quite why. There is a theory that the Ancients over-planted and mined the land until it was near barren. I read this as a quick background note in Lenz's exhaustive history, which I was now attempting to tackle by starting on the strangest tangents I could find.

Fántutazh Lake itself is immense, and shaped like a horseshoe. I knew, from a previous visit, that the city hall sat in its interior bend, where water protected it on three sides. That is the one place in Fántutazh where trees grow on land. There are also the sinuous, flexible trees that grow right up from the water and dot the lake.

When I was younger, a boy showed me how young lakefolk swam out to those lake trees, perched in them, and caught, with darts and nets, those fish that eat only the moss that grows at the base of such trees. The boy told me that when one became too heavy to sit in a lake tree without it bending down to the water, leaves skimming the surface, then one was considered a full adult, ready to hunt other sorts of fish. Larger and more robust fish, but less tender. Such adulthood comes late there, but when it does, they grow quite stout indeed. He was not yet stout, and had the most lithe legs I had ever seen, like a statue from the Ruinous Temple. I would have stayed up in the tree with him more often, had my father's wails not carried easily across the surface of the lake. I was so embarrassed by his pain, back then.

As I passed the lake in my carriage-prison, an adult with no time for lithe legs and treetop whispers, I wondered if the boy was still somewhere on Fántutazh Lake, too heavy for the trees now, floating in a boat past fluffy, paddling grebes with minnows in their beaks. Or perhaps he was in one of those huts, each one wafting lazy notes from stringed instruments, with a similarly stout wife, raising children who scrambled out into the trees.

BORDER LANGUAGES

Crossing any border that isn't an ocean is incremental, even when entering a place as singular and fortressed as Rotfelsen. Populations always change like the layers in a Quru cake, where each is a different flavor, but the syrups seep into one another: the orange syrup inflects both the berry and the lychee layers, while the orange layer itself tastes faintly of tangy berries and sweet lychee. (This comparison did not occur to me at the time, as I had yet only eaten Quru cake of the stale, week-old variety.)

Populations especially melted into one another in a place like the Tetrarchia, where we were all, technically, one happy family and country. The borders between our four kingdoms were wide open even to the most wretched and despised citizen, although it seemed an almost yearly occurrence for some monarch or dignitary—usually a Rotfelsenisch one—to suggest reversing this.

Closing the borders had never yet been managed: the desire of one kingdom or ethnic group to seal themselves off from the outside world, to bask in their sameness, seemed unable to survive the needs of capital. Merchants liked being able to travel from kingdom to kingdom, and they would not allow too much paperwork or nationalism to get in their way. It seemed that the Tetrarchic Experiment was simply too big to be pushed backward into the realm of ideas, at least by anything less than war and destruction. Utter destruction. Which I expected very soon, at the exact time of the Council of Barbarians.

The last Masovskan inn where Lenz and I changed horses and got fresh food was little different than the first one in Rotfelsen would be. Both Masovskani and Rotfelsenisch could be heard lilting and tumbling, respectively, in through the carriage's barred windows, in a variety of border dialects. When the matron of the inn counted out Lenz's change in little grivnas, her numbering was in another language entirely. It is always in numbers, at outposts, that the last breaths of a language hang in the air.

We did not see Rotfelsen's characteristic red cliffs looming up above us, as I had in past trips to that kingdom, because the forest was simply too thick. Soon our carriage entered a wide tunnel, the mouth of which was hidden by trees, bushes, and guards. Inside the tunnel it was too dark to see the color of the stone, except for a halo around the odd wall-socketed lantern, and we began moving upward. Only one place in the world that I knew of had roads through solid rock.

An hour after entering a tunnel in the thick forests of Masovska, we emerged high on the elevated cliff roads of Rotfelsen, beneath the wide sky, without a tree in sight. Lenz sipped tea and watched huge plateaus of red stone appear out his window, sighing with the wistfulness that comes from returning home. A sensation I have never felt.

I looked up from a volume of Lenz's secret history and decided to say *something*, in order to break his reverie and steal at least a little happiness from him.

"And what does King Lubomir XIII of Masovska think about a guarded Rotfelsenisch tunnel road in his forest?" I asked.

"I expect," he answered, "he thinks about it as intently as you think about the blood moving through your veins."

"Well"—I stretched my arm—"I've been thinking about *that* much more lately, as this injury closes up. The new skin still feels slightly off."

"It will feel normal soon enough. And you're welcome."

"I'm sure it would have healed eventually without flesh-alchemy."

"I meant," he said, finally looking at me, "for saving you from getting killed in Masovska."

I supposed he had. But we were all doomed anyway, so I didn't let it endear him to me.

"Masovskans," he continued, "aren't fond of outsiders."

I laughed unhappily. "That is audacious, coming from a Rot. I have not yet found a people that *is* fond of outsiders, although your kingdom may be the worst." I sipped my own tea, and made my own show of looking out the window. "Anyway, I am Masovskan."

"How do you mean?" He did not ask it like a cagey spy, more like a student fascinated by his subject.

I smiled because here was proof he did not know everything about me. "Well, I was born in Masovska and my name is Masovskan. What more do you need?"

"You don't look it."

"Of course not."

"You look . . ."

"Foreign?" I looked back at him. Training my gaze directly on his. "That is as much my birthright as the Gift. My family are wanderers by necessity, and we have been everywhere. In my family, each child's name is appropriate to the land of its birth. How else to name ourselves? It has always been so, since even the families who rule the Tetrarchia were nobodies squabbling over long-forgotten city-states. Long before that, even. By purest coincidence, my father was also Masovska-born, hence Aljosa."

"Your grandmother must have been born somewhere in Quruscan. Vüsala, yes?"

So much for reveling in Lenz's ignorance. Grandmother liked strangers even less than she liked me; how had he learned her name? But then, I was no stranger to paying informants. Lenz may have even learned about me from Ramunas, although I preferred to think better of the Skydašian advocate than that.

"So then you aren't really . . ."

"I am as Masovskan as I am anything. And I am *everything*."

"Is that so?"

"My nose is too hooked for Rotfelsen, my eyes too narrow for Masovska, my hair too curly for Quruscan, with a bronzy redness only seen in our Loashti neighbors, and my skin too dark for roughly half of Skydašiai. I have got something from everywhere and I am exotic to all. It is useful for business, and also for being dragged out by a mob to be throttled. Throttled first, if I'm lucky."

"Well, that won't happen here."

"I have heaved my father onto my back and fled your fine land before."

"Isn't it your land, too?"

"Of course. The whole Tetrarchia is my people, and I am also a foreigner here."

"Sounds inconvenient."

"Yes. Especially when it gets me kidnapped and forced to read dry histories."

"'Dry'?" he cried, with mock insult, which I suspect was covering up real insult.

"Is there anyone," I said, holding up the book, "in this volume that you, or the Prince, think I should particularly keep an eye out for?"

"I don't want to prejudice you. Have your context, and we'll see what you . . . *see* when you're in the palace."

I decided to smile at him in answer. Not a big smile, just enough to let him think I was being a good student. Then I went back to reading about the many suitors of someone named Edeltraud von Edeltraud.

Soon after, we rolled up to that first Rotfelsenisch inn, which *was* just like the last Masovskan one, except that it sat atop a high cliff of red rock. Next to it was a little outpost changing bank (owned, I learned later, by the Gustavus siblings) where we traded in Masovskan grivnas for Rotfelsenisch gold marks stamped with the smooth, expressionless face of Rotfelsen's King Gerhold VIII. I was well and truly trapped now.

ROTFELSENISCH GEOGRAPHY

In the last days of our trip, the carriage dipped in and out of tunnels in the rock many times, sometimes for intervals of only a few minutes.

The kingdom of Rotfelsen was contained almost entirely within and upon its great red cliffs. It was, mostly, one huge piece of red rock, as though the gods had made an island for the guttural, pink people but mistakenly dropped it onto a continent instead of in the sea. There was no sign of impact in the surrounding dirt, but jutting up out of the ground was a bulging, many-sided, multispired rock of tiered cliffs the size of a small kingdom. A rock that *was* a small kingdom, with a verticality that made it larger and more populous than its length from end to end would suggest. Some towns were entirely enclosed, while others were entirely on the surface. Most, and major cities particularly, were both. There were a few small tracts of dirt (primarily farmland) beyond the rock that were claimed by the kingdom's borders, and most Rots acted as though the people living *there* were the strange ones.

No one in Rotfelsen seemed to find their way of living odd: the feeling in the rest of the Tetrarchia was that the Rots must spend all their time, every day, telling each other it was all perfectly normal. (At least I have the humility to know that my upbringing was abnormal.) Rotfelsen was still very much part of the Tetrarchia, taking part in trade, and even immigration, throughout the larger country, but it also felt the most apart from the rest of us. And, for the Tetrarchia, that was saying something.

Of course, the Rots also lived in a giant fortress, which may have helped create and sustain the kingdom's insular nature. Conquering a mass of rock webbed with towns and tunnels is hard work, even if those towns and tunnels could also become furnaces. In fact, a number of entirely enclosed Rotfelsenisch towns had cave walls still blackened by fires from Skydašiai's most earnest attempt at conquest in the days before the Tetrarchia. Such scorch marks were often preserved intentionally as proof that invasions had failed, and as reminders to distrust Skydašians.

However, these days such threats supposedly came from the Bandit States to the south: always a popular topic of conversation because they were scary, but not *as* scary as Loasht. This insulting name represented a group of small nations that shared some linguistic and cultural forebears, but were otherwise unrelated. Some people from some of these states had histories of raiding Rotfelsen and Masovska, and of attacking trade convoys, and so the name Bandit States was born. Where their governments ended and local criminals began was often blurred from the Tetrarchic point of view, as was the role of our own history of attacks upon them.

Conventional wisdom told us that Bandit States' raids never got into Rotfelsen's actual rock anymore, thanks to the kingdom's courageous and powerful High General. Certainly, sometimes they would maraud at the southern border, pillaging those Rotfelsenisch farms and villages unfortunate to exist on normal land outside the rock. In those cases, the High General's army would sweep out and burn some of *their* villages as a matter of course, but they never stayed to protect their people on those dirt outposts. (And whether they would even burn the villages of the "correct" Bandit State is up for debate.)

The singular variety of stone making up the kingdom, which was red but not porous or volcanic, had been named, simply enough, rotrock. Would this great stone shatter in the spring, or had Papa's talk of "shattered remains" been metaphor? Since it was to happen at the same time as the Council, I leaned toward the cause being war or political unrest, but in that case, how would the entire kingdom of Rotfelsen simply . . . break?

The villages within the rock had gardens of cave plants that I could not see very well, often surrounding whole lively town squares that seemed to exist only within the light of torches. I would catch flickers of people living their lives, arguing, laughing, buying groceries, completely within some great cave strewn with stalactites. Then, every time we rolled out onto the surface, in the open, I saw green patches, some nearby and some on sections of rotrock thousands of feet below us. There were, of course, no great farms nor fields on the rock, but Rotfelsen was full of imported fruits and vegetables that could be grown in pots of imported dirt. There were also great numbers of ornamental gardens, full of flowers and ginkgoes and other plants that could only exist there through trade with the outside world.

The strange feeling of traveling through Rotfelsen is that of being within subterranean caverns while knowing yourself to be far above the *actual* ground. The tunnels through which we passed varied as much as any roads do. Some were wide, some barely big enough for the monstrous carriage (at one time, a poor merchant had to back up for a good hour to the far end of the tunnel so we could pass: the harquebusiers were apologetic, but firm), some were public and some private. Most were natural tunnels, caves, and cracks, expanded to a width appropriate for carriages, while others had been carved out entirely by exhausted human beings. In every tunnel, lamps were hung and still burned, making iron and copper deposits, which were sometimes in the process of being mined, glimmer on the walls like lines of saliva. Rotfelsen's wealth was in its stones and metals.

From past trips, when I was not escorted along the King's own routes, I remembered many dark, disrepaired tunnels that threatened to fall in at every moment. My family sometimes lived in them for weeks, in total darkness, to avoid being murdered. We did not work in Rotfelsen often once I took over the business—how do you con a person whose thinking you cannot understand?

A Million Little Feet

On our last day of travel, the Great Field felt very far away indeed. We passed through our final tunnel, which had so many torches as to feel like a Skydašian midday, and which would deposit us at Rotfelsen's palace grounds, above the capital city of Turmenbach. I had never been to that city before, and wondered whether its people resented the royals above them—whether the secret tunnels we traveled existed in order to avoid seeing the lower classes at all.

Then I wondered how I would ever escape this place. Perhaps by jumping off the edge of the kingdom.

"I understand Turmenbach is quite big," I said. "There must be fortunetellers and mystics here. Why didn't you kidnap any of *them*?"

"We looked into it. They were all frauds."

"How did you know?"

"They didn't recognize the Prince after a little spirit gum, and had . . . unfitting futures for him."

I cocked my head to the side and looked at him. I forced a hint of smile, both to disarm, and to hide a dull fear in my gut of such tricks being played on me.

"But I was spared this indignity?" I asked. "Or are *you* actually the Prince? I have never seen the Prince of Rotfelsen before, so I don't know how I'd be expected to—"

He laughed. "No, Kalyna, I am not the Prince. Unlike our local frauds, you already had a reputation."

I thought of Eight-Toed Gustaw from Down Valley Way telling his friends about my family. I hoped he was living it up, maybe in a quick, sporty little carriage, wearing a ring on every finger.

"And," Lenz continued, "unlike them, you don't promise *everything*. Futures, pasts, demons from the hells, control over unborn grandchildren, communion with gods, conversation with ancestors, and so forth."

I laughed. "Your Rotfelsenisch frauds sound very presumptuous. And your people sound deeply gullible."

I went back to trying to read one of Lenz's books, while wondering what tricks he or his Prince might have in store for me. Outside, travelers were yelling as they passed one another. In that echoing tunnel, I couldn't tell which yells were friendly and which were threatening. I tried to imagine life when *every* yell, every raised voice, is echoed and echoed and echoed. It sounded like a nightmare.

After a bit, Lenz stood up and hunched over near my window.

"Kalyna," he said, "I want to show you something that isn't in any of the books here."

"Is it more rock?"

"Well, yes. The walls of this tunnel are very smooth, aren't they?"

I peered out the window. The tunnel walls were indeed unbelievably smooth, like polished marble or the unbreakable stone pillars of the Ancients. The tunnel was so well-lit that I saw mineral deposits snake through the smooth surface.

"Very impressive. Thanks to the fussiness of a past king? So intent on perfection that he also forbade mining the ore?"

Lenz shook his head. "This is not man-made. There *is* a law against mining here, that much is true, but it is to preserve the evidence."

"Of?"

"Creatures."

"That is very scary and unclear."

"Go up into the turret and take a look at the tunnel's ceiling. It's just as smooth, despite how difficult that would be for humans to carve effectively. It's a very high ceiling."

"In Masovska, they have these things called ladders that—"

"If you can see the ceiling's center, you will notice a further indent running the full length. That's from the ridge of the thing's spine."

I must have looked skeptical.

"This tunnel was fully formed deep in the rotrock when humans discovered it long ago, burrowed by some sort of creature. There are more throughout Rotfelsen: all the same size, with the same spinal indent at the top. Old texts say that, before these tunnels got carved up by a thousand carriage wheels, the floors carried the indents of a million little feet, each no larger than your index finger."

"You just like for me to know how smart you are, don't you? How many facts you amassed while others did their jobs and had lovers."

"I think it's interesting," he said with a shrug.

"Fine." I set down my book and moved toward the ladder. "Is this part of some lesson? A way to teach me how little I know, or what danger I'm in?"

"I just think it's interesting."

I climbed into the turret, and I saw exactly what he had described. The indent from some great thing's spinal ridge stretching off down the tunnel in both directions. I thought again about the possibility of Rotfelsen literally shattering. From within, this time.

THE SUNSET PALACE

Somewhere in that tunnel I fell asleep, and dreamed of my father. It may surprise you to know that in those days, I did not dream of him often. The details don't matter, but he told me I had the Gift, and then I saw the Tetrarchia destroyed.

I was awakened by a harquebusier wrenching open the wrought iron door to the armored carriage. I blinked and remembered the carnage of my dream, knowing it to be the first bleeding of prophecy through the cracks in whatever dam had kept me useless and untalented. I felt Papa's words—that I had the Gift—deep in my chest. I did not feel sad about the violence that would come, only happy that the Gift was in me after all.

Once I sat up and the dream began to fade, I knew this was not so. It was not *prophecy* to envision what my father had already told me. Reality returned and I fought off the lingering joy.

I woke fully, and saw Lenz standing patiently outside the carriage door, sunlight shooting through the spires of his mussed hair. Somewhere, a bird chirped.

I stepped out onto a windy plateau, surrounded by armed soldiers who watched me closely. The very tired and dirty harquebusiers who had traveled with us were relieved by a small group of fresh soldiers in yellow: these carried swords, not harquebuses, and included a few women in their rank, unlike the harquebusiers.

We were up on the surface of Rotfelsen, with great gardens and manors behind us, and a clear blue sky stretching above us in all directions. Many of the buildings up here were built out of exported wood or non-rotrock stone. Those that were cut directly from the rotrock were constructed to mimic the look of regular buildings that had actually been, well, *built*, with grooves in their façades pretending at arches and bricks. I supposed Rotfelsen's government liked to pretend it ruled a kingdom like any other, rather than a maze of tunnels and caves beneath its feet. In front of us, blotting out part of the sky, was a tower hewn from solid rotrock, studded with marble and jade, that cast a long, jagged shadow.

Lenz smiled broadly and pointed up at the tower. "That is the Sunset Palace of the Rotfelsen Kings."

"Naturally."

The Sunset Palace was too old to pretend at being any other kind of castle. In fact, it was likely the oldest home in the entire Tetrarchia that had been continuously in use. Long ago, someone got to the top of Rotfelsen, found a jagged outcropping, and carved it into a fortress. Over the years, its wings were further shaped into one style or another, depending on the fashion of the time, and huge sections of iron, gold, jade, and even marble were pressed into the outer walls here or there. Outcroppings and buildings around its base, too, became smaller satellites in clashing styles.

The result was a formless, jutting, sloppy, gaudy mess. I was struck by just how much it looked as if a giant child had slapped the thing together. It seemed ready to topple under its own weight right off the kingdom it ruled. Which, I supposed, it very likely would. And soon, too. Maybe it would fall so hard that Rotfelsen itself would crack in half? Unlikely, but once I thought about it, the imagery wouldn't leave my head.

We went into that silly thing through a humble servants' entrance, which still had double doors, and hobbled our way up a narrow staircase through deep red walls. As we passed each floor, I would see a mass of windows in haphazard arrangements, many of them cracked. I felt ignored and constantly watched at the same time.

My legs and back ached from a week of sitting, relieved only by storming up and down the length of the carriage, so I didn't mind the exercise. At least, not for the first few flights of stairs. Lenz's soldiers, as always, were thankfully too well-behaved to prod me with their weapons. This did not diminish their threat.

As we trudged up the stairs, a cook's assistant knocked into me as he dashed down, leaping three steps at a time to avoid his superior. The cook herself—identifiable by a tall hat and gold trim on her apron—was red in the face as she screamed and gave chase, throwing bits of cold chicken at him.

"They're in a tizzy," I said, mostly to myself.

"The Winter Ball *is* tonight," Lenz replied.

Tonight. And despite all my reading, I knew so little of its guests. My heart began to speed up and my hands began to shake. Then I turned a corner and saw a Rotfelsenisch soldier in a uniform of rich purple leaning against a balustrade. I heard Lenz inhale sharply through his nose.

The soldier was completely still, a purple smudge against the rotrock wall. His left hand sat on his sword hilt as he watched us closely. One of our soldiers in yellow glared at him, jawbone clenching. The purple one smiled. Our soldiers regarded the one in purple, and the shuttered windows which may have hidden an ambush, until we were a floor above him.

I didn't know what a purple uniform meant: Lenz's books mentioned "the Purples" quite often, but with the assumption that a reader would already know who they were. Then I remembered Lenz's story about the Prince going incognito to *test* local soothsayers. Perhaps I'd get lucky, and he'd reveal my fraud and kill me before I had to deal with the ball and the soldiers and all of that.

I was not comforted. My hands shook, and I got much hotter and sweatier than even climbing that many stairs warranted.

PRINCE FRIEDHELM

So, after too many stairs, I ended up in Prince Friedhelm's office. By the time we got there, I was a swampy mess, which did not stop my teeth from chattering. I eyed the desk and did not see the letter opener from Lenz's story—either because Lenz had advised caution or because the Prince had opened no letters today. Or, perhaps its earlier appearance truly had been a test. What tricks would the Prince pull to test me? Would I meet an impostor Prince and be expected to know it? But I would look ridiculous if I met the real Prince and called him a fake.

Prince Friedhelm's office was as Lenz had described it, but its opulence still astounded me. There were, of course, art and books and exquisite furniture—but even his pens and paper, his collection of pipes, his water glasses, looked terribly expensive. I couldn't always pin down *why* they seemed so, but they did. It was something about their, well . . . comportment.

The far wall, toward which the desk faced, was the largest glass window I had ever seen in my life. It was the entire top two-thirds of the wall—the bottom being the only place in the room where the rotrock of the Sunset Palace was visible. A window that size gave the impression of the outdoors intruding in on the room: the expansive sky and the vistas of jagged and rolling rotrock may as well have been standing next to us. Far beyond those blooming red cliffs, I could see verdant green forests that may have been in Masovska or one of the Bandit States, I was too disoriented to know. I felt that I was flying, or drowning. I felt that the plumes and canyons of rotrock would come devour me. I felt that because I could see them, I *owned* them.

I caught my breath and turned to the wall across from the window, which had a bookshelf that was clearly a secret door, and, unlike Lenz, I found the secret peephole as well. It was behind a bunch of pink flowers in a porcelain vase that had bulls painted on its sides. Virile bulls.

I wondered how many other peepholes there were—for reasons of security more than lechery. A man entered the room with a loud slamming of the door, and walked toward us in such a way as to always leave a line of sight between myself and certain corners or pieces of furniture. I was sure there were sharpshooters hidden everywhere, ready to end me the moment I made a mistake.

This man who had entered the room certainly seemed like the Prince Lenz had described: strangely attractive despite (or because of?) his weak jaw and upturned nose. His attraction was not so simple as the pull of his power—that attracts many people, but has never drawn me. In many situations throughout my life to this point, I had possessed less power than whomever I dealt with.

Or was this *not* the Prince, and therefore powerless? He could have just been a strange man Lenz had described to me as part of a test. Whoever he was, he all but stormed into the room.

"Your Highness," Lenz began, "allow me to introduce Kalyna Aljosanovna the soothsayer."

"Yes, hello," the man said, before pivoting to face Lenz and, without taking a breath: "We have a problem."

"What sort of problem, Your Highness?" Lenz's manner toward the man certainly seemed like that of trusted underling to royalty. But of course, he was a spymaster and, I would hope, a decent actor.

"Another conspiracy against my brother, of course," grunted the man, waving a hand. "But we aren't fumbling about in the dark for petty plots this time, Lenz. They approached me a few days ago, while you were away."

"Who did?"

Lenz had gone from concerned bemusement to intense attention in a moment. This, and the way the man said "my brother" as though it was sour in his mouth, began to convince me that this truly was Prince Friedhelm, and that this crisis was real. Perhaps, if I was very lucky, this new plot against the King had broken their plans to test me.

Yes, lucky, that's what I would call myself.

"Selvosch," the Prince replied. "The oaf. He spends too much time down in the caves and mines, if you ask me. He, or whomever he is working for, seem to think they can put me on the throne." He laughed exactly one time, sharply. "Why, it's *almost* as though the court finds me untrustworthy."

I wondered the obvious question: Why not accept their offer? If he was going to be a figurehead, didn't that neatly let the Prince have the indolence he so craved? His aim, after all, seemed to be remaining free of the duties of running a kingdom. I did not wonder this out loud, and neither did Lenz.

"Selvosch," murmured Lenz. I vaguely remembered the name from my reading. "Did he say anything about whom he was working with?"

"No, no, of course not. He intimated that there were powerful people, and I intimated that I was interested, if they were indeed so powerful. I said he could not have my full support until I knew who his comrades were, and he that I could not know who his comrades are until he had my full support." The Prince wound his hands about as he spoke. "There must be someone very big involved, if they were powerful enough to make our Quarrymaster the one to out himself as a potential traitor to a royal." He grinned mirthlessly and placed a hand on his own chest. "Even if that royal is known for being 'listless,' 'licentious,' and 'irresponsible.' Which is all about half true. I'm sure the Queen is involved."

"I'm sorry, what?" said Lenz.

"The Queen. More than half of my brother's soldiers are loyal to her anyway, for some reason, and—"

"Not that part." Lenz did not seem to realize he had interrupted a Prince. "You *agreed* to take the King's place?"

For the first time since he had entered the room, Prince Friedhelm seemed to be at a loss for words. He even shrugged. "I . . . well, no. But I let him think I was interested."

"You . . ." Lenz drooped his head for a moment, and lifted his hand, as though to clasp it to his forehead. Then he thought better of it and stood straight. "You . . . may have committed treason, Your Highness."

"Well, I didn't say, 'Yes, kill my brother!'" replied the Prince. "I wanted to learn more, and I may have panicked a little. It seemed the best way to get Selvosch to keep talking to me."

"And did he keep talking to you?"

"A bit," said the Prince. "'By the end of the ball,' he told me, 'you had better have chosen a side.' I told him I would be happy to, once I knew who was on which side. Then he just waggled his finger side to side and repeated, 'By the end of the ball,' like the daft thing he is."

"Which is tonight," I heard myself saying.

"Just so," replied the Prince.

Lenz bit his lower lip. "Perhaps," he said, "you should warn your brother."

"He would not listen to me if I did," said the Prince, with great finality. "His *Skydašian* wife is competent, of course. Competent enough to command more than half of his soldiers. I would tell her, if I trusted her."

I cocked my head to the side at that. If the King could get by with so little action, so little competence, why did the Prince want so badly to avoid taking his place?

"The rest of the court," the Prince went on, "all think that I am like my brother: inactive, indolent, a living slab of rotrock. But where he is governed by no impulses at all, they think that I only act toward my own pleasures. Which, in a sense, I do, but at least I can think ahead." He clapped his hands together. "So then, how to keep him alive? Perhaps he can be convinced to spend another week or two at his hunting lodge, down in the depths, and we can break out the Twelfth Recourse?"

"Your Highness," said Lenz, clearly trying to be patient, "why don't you meet the Eleventh Recourse, first? Maybe she can help." He gestured toward me.

Well, that was no pressure at all. I smiled.

"Yes, yes, we've met," grunted the Prince.

Then he turned to face me and, to my surprise, smiled back. I saw then a bit more of how magnetic he could be, when he wanted to. He had gone, with a look, right from acting as though I wasn't there to acting as though I was the center of his world. He almost convinced me of it, except that I was quite used to making others feel the same way. It was as much in the body language as in the smile: open yet conspiratorial, as if shutting out everyone else.

"Kalyna Aljosanovna," he continued, "what will happen at tonight's ball?"

I stalled. "Well, it's hard to say . . ."

"Your foreign Gift works by proximity, yes?"

I nodded.

"Now you've been in the palace. What have you seen of tonight in these walls?"

"My Gift works in proximity to *people*," I corrected, as obsequiously as I could. "Have the guests arrived?"

"Not most, no. But you must see something!"

I tried to smile again, to find some remaining reserve of my duplicitous self, of the part of me that enjoyed the game. This wasn't a test with disguises and great ruses, but if he did not find the answer convincing, I suspected I would be killed, and Papa left in a ditch somewhere. If Papa had not already been left in a ditch somewhere.

I shook thoughts of whether Lenz had told the truth about Papa out of my head, along with anything about the violent end of the Tetrarchia itself. I tried to remember how I had spoken to Eight-Toed Gustaw from Down Valley Way.

"Well, Your Highness," I began, "I've only just arrived in your fine palace. There will be pressing crowds, of course, drunken arguments, duels, that sort of thing."

He raised a skeptical eyebrow.

I curtsied graciously and grasped for something. Anything. I would deal with the consequences tomorrow. I thought of the Prince's clear dislike of the Queen, and how readily he would eat up anything I said against her, but decided those waters were too deep to wade into—until I needed to. Then I thought of the soldier in purple on the staircase. I still did not know who commanded the Purples, but based on Lenz's histories and his reaction at the time, it seemed likely it was someone who did not much get along with the Prince and his Yellows.

"And, well, the Purples are planning *something*, Your Highness. They will be out in force, possibly more than you expect. As I'm new to your land, I admit I don't know what would be 'normal,' but I am seeing quite large numbers of them. And ulterior motives. So, I would suggest keeping your eyes on them."

I hoped that whoever commanded the Purples was not actually a good friend of the Prince's. Friedhelm looked thoughtful. He opened his mouth to speak; I held my breath, and my curtsy.

"Nice to meet you, Kalyna Aljosanovna," he said. "Glad to have you on our side."

I thanked him quietly, and the Prince dismissed us with, "Now, go save my brother!"

It took great restraint to not run out of there. Somewhere behind me, I heard the Prince clicking his tongue and muttering, "Now what will I do with all this spirit gum?"

THE ELEVENTH RECOURSE

We made our way quickly out of the palace, and into a spry little carriage with none of the amenities of the last one. The front was open and the railings that kept us from falling out were carved to look like racing horses. My head swirled with questions: Who ran the Purples? What was our next move? Where could I get something to eat? Where would I sleep if I survived the night? Where were we going right now? Was that how Lenz and the Prince normally interacted? Why didn't the Prince want to be King? Was Papa really on the way to join me and, if so, would I be alive when he got here?

Would I meet someone at this ball tonight who would be directly responsible for the disastrous end of the Tetrarchia? Would *I* destroy the Tetrarchia?

There was only the driver, Lenz, two other Yellows, and myself in the carriage. Now, with relative privacy, and in Masovskani, I could ask the question that was burning inside of me the most.

"Eleventh Recourse?" I asked Lenz.

He laughed. "Really, that's what you want to know? Not who Selvosch is or—"

"We'll get to all that. What is this nonsense? I assume you create new 'Recourses' to stay useful, so he doesn't kill you."

"No, no. They are all his genius ideas." Lenz pressed his right hand to his chest, and said with mock-seriousness, "I was the Sixth Recourse."

"So they're all people, then? Strange talents he draws from wherever his fancy leads him?"

"Exactly."

"Who are one through five?"

"A few aren't dead."

"That's not an answer."

He sighed and turned to face me in the cramped carriage. "Our Prince can be a fanciful man, who sees plots against his brother everywhere. But he also is not *wrong*, half of the time. So Friedhelm wants as many solutions hidden away for a rainy day as possible. A researcher was Sixth Recourse, prophecy was Eleventh."

"What's the Twelfth?"

"That's a secret. But please do let me know if you have a vision of it, and how it works out."

I rolled my eyes.

"And," Lenz continued, "lest you think the Prince is unreasonably suspicious, this is far from the first such plot we've uncovered. It's simply the way Rotfelsen has always been! I think our way of living, squirreled away as we are, has led to a lot of interesting thought and contemplation over the years. But it has also led to a lot of strange people sitting in the dark and convincing themselves of the most outlandish things."

"No wonder you kidnapped me. No one would move here by choice."

He ignored me and rubbed his chin thoughtfully. "*This* plot is by far the most daunting yet, if someone as powerful as Selvosch isn't even its most important participant. He's the Lord High Quarrymaster, you see."

"Which means?"

"He masters the quarries."

I did not respond to that. Instead, I leaned forward, hands on my knees, and asked, "Why don't you think your Prince wants the job? Of King, I mean."

"He hasn't told me, outside of what I've already told you. He may think, as I do, that these conspirators would eliminate or lock up their figurehead as soon as possible."

"So that's *these* conspirators. But what about generally? It doesn't sound as though the King is saddled with too many weighty decisions or great responsibilities."

"Prince Friedhelm does not deign to share his reasons."

"Well, if he told you he *did* want to supplant his brother after all, would you help him to do so?"

Lenz was quiet. I stared at him for a moment, but he just looked out the window. I continued to stare at him, hoping to make him uncomfortable.

The two Yellows sitting with us, a man and a woman, did a very good job of not looking surprised, curious, concerned, or anything of the kind. They were both tall, broad-shouldered, and blonde: a very Rotfelsenisch look. The man was leaning forward to watch the road ahead, and the woman was absentmindedly cleaning or sharpening her dagger—absolutely unafraid of a possible bump in the road causing her to lose a finger.

"Kalyna," Lenz finally sighed, "I take no pleasure in imprisoning you, but look around: autumn is so mild up here and our winter will be nothing like Masovska's. You have food, lodgings, and luxuries that your family will share, all while you are paid in gold marks directly from the royal coffers."

"I had no choice in it."

"Did you ever make a choice to be what you were? A roving prophet living a life of mistrust better suited to a charlatan?"

Charlatan.

"My family," I said, "were never meant to be court seers for two simple reasons." I stared fixedly at gardens going by out the window and continued quietly, from memory. "First, it is our duty and burden to give our services to all classes of people; this is how we have thrived since millennia before any kingdoms of the Tetrarchia were founded." It seemed I spoke in my father's voice, from when I was a child perhaps, or from before my birth. I heard his deep, confident resonance shake my inner ears and my jaw. I felt his pride in a job well done, and my own at a job well faked, as though the ghost of the man he had been stood before me.

"Second," I continued, "just as we are the first murdered when things go wrong in a community, the seer is the first executed when things go wrong at court. But escape is easier from one than the other. Slipping out of a town in the night is difficult; escaping a *palace*"—I put up my hands to indicate all around me—"is impossible." I almost said "nearly impossible," but decided to sound more resigned than I was. "This is how we have *survived* since millennia before any of the—"

"Yes, yes, I think I know that part," said Lenz.

I folded my hands in my lap and looked at him.

"Well," he said, "you at least deserve better food and lodgings, and you will have them. Comes with the job."

A more comfortable life, until the Prince got me killed. Or *had* me killed.

"Do not pretend this is for my benefit," I said.

"Never. Your benefit is a symptom." He smiled and leaned forward, lifting his stiff left leg with his hand and grunting as he uncrossed it from his right.

We were done talking, for the moment. The Sunset Palace had gotten at least slightly smaller behind us, and before us were rows of wooden buildings, separated by hedges and gardens. We were taken to one of these, a four-story wooden servant house, surrounded by pleasant gardens and tall walls, blocking all the rest of Rotfelsen's surface except the top of the palace, which still towered above us to the west. It was all very cozy, if wreathed by yellow soldiers. One could have never guessed we were on top of a giant rock full of people.

Lenz ushered me into the servant house, and up the stairs to a chamber on the top floor. No soldiers followed us, for once, but a quick glance out a window showed that they surrounded the building. The room, which I was told was mine, had something of the quaint country home to it, if polluted by ornate luxury; as though this house was where the palace stored its leftover furniture.

A small woman was standing in the corner. She held a handful of string and looked very anxious, tapping her foot pointedly as I walked into the room. When I stopped, she snapped her fingers at me four or five times.

I ignored her and leaned against the wall, crossing my arms like an angry child. Lenz sighed. He did not lean against anything, and I could tell that this was a painful weight on his bad leg. Good. He nodded to the anxious woman, and she scurried over to me. A bird chirped on the windowsill, a pleasant little puffball preparing for winter. Why had birds bothered to fly all the way up here, I wondered. Or had they been imported too? To give the borrowed trees and grass the right ambiance?

"Very nice," I said, to Lenz, who was standing in the doorway. We were still speaking Masovskani. "And when will my father arrive?"

"Maybe another week," he replied. "With your grandmother, too, of course. I did not want them, with their frailties, to be forced to hurry."

"Do you know—" I began, before the woman jammed her hand into my armpit. I glared at her before I could stop myself, but she ignored me anyway. I looked back at Lenz and tried again: "Do you know how cruel it is to make my father go through his nightly fits while I'm not there to help him?"

"Your grandmother—"

I laughed loudly and sharply. The anxious woman, who had been counting under her breath and pressing a long string against my leg, flinched and lost her place. I leaned down and smiled at her, putting a hand lightly on her shoulder. She flinched again.

"I didn't mean to scare you," I said in Rotfelsenisch.

She coughed and went back to measuring and quietly counting.

I tried again: "I notice you're counting in Sugavi." Sugavi had once been the language of the lower eastern sixth or so of Rotfelsen.

She glared up, seemingly mortified, then looked back down to continue counting.

I sighed. "Well, I see you have not put me in a cell," I said to Lenz, back in Masovskani.

"You have free rein of this agreeable little servant house, with its unbarred windows and innocent denizens. The guards will stay outside, mostly."

"And my family?"

"Will be kept rather far away from you, most of the time."

In order to glare at Lenz, I had to look around the anxious woman's head. She was measuring my collarbone, it seemed. If she understood Masovskani, she hid it well. Lenz scratched his unruly hair.

"Will they—" I stopped when the woman wrapped a string around my thigh and nearly yanked me off balance. I almost yelled at her, composed myself, and looked down again, smiling at her and trying Rotfelsenisch again.

"Hello. My name is Kalyna Aljosanovna. What are you doing?"

"She is measuring you, Kalyna," said Lenz, still in Masovskani. "The ball is tonight, remember?"

"Why can't she tell me herself?" I asked, still in Rotfelsenisch.

The tailor coughed loudly.

"Because her job is to measure," Lenz sighed. He had now switched to Skydašiavos—just for fun, I supposed. "Not to chat or listen in. To be discreet, especially when making clothing in a great rush for a mysterious stranger."

"She'll be making a ball gown in a day?" I joined him in Skydašiavos, although I don't know what I was proving.

"A guard's uniform." He smiled. "You will still *be* guarded, and you will not be armed."

"Fine."

"And you will be trained on how to comport yourself."

"Before tonight?"

"Don't slouch, don't hide, don't hurt a noble. Try not to get killed by the other soldiers. There, you've been trained."

"Why will soldiers try to kill me?"

"Did you *actually* read my books?"

"There's a lot in there, Lenz. You should be very proud. Will my family know they are prisoners?"

"I hope not. But they *are* prophets."

"Not professionally," I said. The tailor pulled roughly at my waist.

"Besides"—Lenz loosened, trying to put me at ease, as though he would walk in and clap me on the shoulder any moment now—"they will share a building with our best doctor. You will be glad I came along, eventually. Your father might even improve." He did not actually walk into my room, however, which I appreciated. A little.

I considered what he had said about the "best doctor," but continued to scowl. Sunshine streamed into the room, which was larger than any of our tents. Comparable in size to the carriage Lenz and I had shared, in fact. And this whole room would be mine?

The tailor, who had never said a word beyond whispered Sugavi numbers, stood up straight and nodded curtly.

I still only had Lenz's word that my family were on their way at all. Perhaps they'd been left to freeze, or had their throats slit. A jailer does love to dangle false hopes and then snatch them away—just ask the Quru warden who insisted the accusation of conjuration against me was "being reviewed," every day for a month, when I was twenty-two. (I got a sort of revenge on him eventually.) But now, as much as I loved and worried for my father, I also desperately wanted to wring him for new prophecies.

"Anyway"—Lenz turned slowly away from me on his good leg—"I do have preparations outside of you. Do nothing stupid, Kalyna Aljo-sanovna. It is beneath you. And besides, there is very nice liquor in the cabinet. Courage juice."

"I thought you wanted me *not* to do anything stupid."

He shrugged and turned to leave. "Tonight, Kalyna," he said in Rot-felsenisch. "I hope you'll be ready."

"You must be as sick of me as I am of you," I said.

Lenz nodded emphatically before limping down the stairs with un-even thuds, followed by the tailor, who looked miserable.

Here is what I thought at that point in my life: people only give each other liquor to make them do things they will regret. I did not open the cabinet.

TURAL

My room in the servant house was the largest I had ever inhabited, and from its windows I could see over the walls to other, similar servant houses. The looming tower of the Sunset Palace, glittering in the sun and always in view, made everything feel very small. I could also see the sprawling manor houses of the nobility, which made a line in front of the palace, defending it like cannon fodder. The palace grounds were essentially their own city, complete with transplanted trees and bushes to line walkways, larger roads for carriages, and soldiers' barracks at the edges, color-coded for each of the four armies of Rotfelsen. But there was a real city, Turmenbach, below it, full of poor people, normal people, the types I'd worked for (and run from) over my life. They lived largely within the rock, not up here in a false garden. How did they view us?

My room had two chairs, a bed, a desk, and a bookshelf. The books were all general sciences, histories, religion, and the like, alongside copied volumes of Lenz's secret history. These last volumes, he assured me, had been cleansed of "the juicy bits," lest a maid get too curious.

I knew well enough that I needed to continue studying royals and nobles and soldiers, and all the other powerful types who would be at the ball: all those people who might want to topple the King. But after a week shut up in that carriage, with Lenz looking so damned *proud* of himself, continuing to study was the last thing I wanted to do. I decided that I would figure it out as I went—I'd always managed before—and chose to explore my new domain and prison. I was sure there would be no secret escape hatches, hidden doors, or unguarded tunnels through the rotrock, but it seemed like a fine idea to check. I could not escape until my father had arrived, but best to have a plan.

I listened at my door to make sure no one was in the hallway. The entire fourth floor of the sunny house seemed quiet. I stepped out and walked slowly, hearing the squeak of my boots, which still carried Masovskan dirt in their crevices. I felt as though I was sneaking through a hostile land, invading a fortress, even though there was nothing *wrong* with simply exploring one's new home. They didn't have to know I wanted to escape their country before everyone died horribly.

Six steps from my door, something appeared in the corner of my eye. I turned to see a man sitting perfectly still in the room next to mine, watching me.

He wore a white smock stained with green and orange, and a black cravat tied lazily at his neck. He had one leg crossed over the other on a high stool, and was sipping from a glass of water. When he saw that I had seen him, he leaned forward, raised a thin black eyebrow, and wound his free hand as if, I thought, to say, "Go on . . ."

I turned to face him, arms flat at my sides, and raised one at the elbow in an awkward wave.

"Hello," I began, "My name—"

"Oh!" he cried. "Ohhhh!" He looked at the ceiling, as if to ask why it had forsaken him, and his shoulders fell.

"—is Kalyna Aljosanovna. Are you hurt?"

"You are new," he said. "You are new. Come in, please. Please. I'm sorry." He waved me into his room.

It was nearly identical to mine, but lived-in. Every surface or cloth was stained with different colors, and on the walls were still life paintings of glistening fruit.

"I am sorry. Sorry," he repeated. "Everyone on this floor keeps quiet when I conjure. I got angry. But you are new, and it's unfair of me besides."

"Conjure? Are you a—"

"A chef. Yes, a chef."

Chef would have been my last guess in the world.

"Of course," I said.

We introduced ourselves to each other. Tural, for that was his name, was a wiry sort, with an intense stare, shining black hair, and a thin mustache. Upon closer inspection, he was younger than he acted, somewhere around thirty-five. He was Quru, as you may have guessed from his name. But if you don't know, Quruscan was the mountainous kingdom in the northeast of our Tetrarchia, which had been historically (somewhat) safe from Loasht due to a lot of very treacherous mountain roads, which the Quru were in no hurry to maintain.

"You live next door?" He pointed to the wall we shared.

"For the moment, yes."

"You work in the palace?"

"Sometimes."

"Ah!" He set down his water and stood, looking knowingly at me. He was almost exactly my height.

"Are you . . ." I asked slowly, "the *Head* Chef of the palace?"

"Head Chef?" Tural laughed. "Who wants to be Head Chef?"

"I don't follow."

"Head Chef," said Tural, "is a tanner who is also a cooper and a chandler and a tailor and a blacksmith. Does many things; good at none. *None of them.* Head Chef means living up in the palace, not out here, only being good at sucking up to the royal family." He smiled. "I can be good at that, when I must, but not my job."

"I . . ."

"I am a specialist! The Master of Fruit! Specifically and exclusively." The volume of his voice rose and fell in that Quru way, even as his Rot-felsenisch pronunciation was perfect, if oddly phrased.

The very idea of a cook who worked only with fruit seemed so excessive as to be fundamentally inhuman. I must have looked mystified.

"Do you think this is strange?" asked Tural.

"Well, yes."

He smiled. "Not wrong. But do you know, Kalyna, how many *tons* of food the palace's kitchens produce?"

"I don't."

"Yes. Yes. You are new." There was no judgment in his voice. I felt relieved.

"The Head Chef," he went on, rolling his eyes at his superior's title, "gives guidelines, and it is we beneath him who form these into meals for the lower chefs to create. There is a Master of Breads, a Master of Cakes, a Mistress of Fowl, a Master of Rice, two acrimonious Sub-Masters of Noodles, and so forth."

I almost asked how many of these could be necessary, but then suspected I would be trapped in conversation for hours.

"I," he continued, "know every fruit that grows in the Greater Eastern Tetrarchia, and many from beyond. But it is a lot, so I must conjure."

"Are these food masters normally . . . sorcerers?"

He laughed a strained sort of laugh. "No," he said. "No, no, no. A sorcerer cannot simply 'conjure' fruits from the air. If they could, I would be homeless. No, I . . . Well, you see . . ."

He put a finger on his chin and thought for a moment. Someone stirred in the hall; hearing Tural's voice must have let them know that he was no longer "conjuring."

"Look," he said. "Krantz is the Master of Pork, you see?"

"Yes, I think. Does he also live in this building?"

"What?" Tural was shocked. "No! You cannot make food masters live with one another—they would murder. One feast day, *I* would be the King's pork, you see?"

"Yes."

"No, no, no. Ha. Me to live with . . . ha. No."

"Of course."

"Krantz is the Master of Pork." He held up a thin finger, gesturing at nothing. "If Krantz wishes to see whether a certain pork cooked in a stupid pork way will go nicely with the chard of the Mistress of Leaves, or with the Master of Breads' tangy Skydašian bread, all he—Krantz—must do is kill one of the palace pigs. There are always pigs."

I nodded intently.

"Now. Say the palace is planning, during the winter, for a feast in spring. 'Tural,' they say, 'we want fresh berries with this tart!' Where am I to find the berries that will be fresh in spring when it is winter?"

"You can't."

"Precisely! Even with our alchemy and our hothouses, we cannot grow things so out of season. How am I to know if a tungenberry compote would go with, say, the Master of Cakes' sweet-mushroom cake, or the Mistress of Tarts' spring mint tart? How am I to know that a different berry would not be better?"

"I do not know." At the time, I did not even know the difference between a cake and a tart. Grandmother would have said I was better off that way.

"I must have silence and conjure them," explained Tural. "I must sit very still, cleanse my palate"—he pointed to the water glass by his velvet-slippered foot—"and imagine, unaided by taste, the flavors of the berries, or any other of a hundred, hundred fruits. I simply imagine them, you see—remember. *Conjure* their memory, like you do the smell of an old lover's hair, or the sound of your long-gone grandmother's voice."

If only.

"After all," he continued, "we do not have *berries* living in the stables year-round, grunting and eating slop. I am not some . . . *pork* master."

"But the Winter Ball is tonight. Don't you have your fruit?"

He laughed. "If only those unpacking the Masovska peaches cared as much as you do! But yes, tonight is all sorted, and my underlings are working at it. I have nothing left to do, for tonight. I am planning ahead, for a King's Dinner next week."

"That is very . . . industrious." I reflected upon the fact that I felt entirely unprepared for tonight. "Well, I'm sorry I disturbed you."

He smiled. "You are new. You are new. What are you? I am the Master of Fruit. Also on our floor is the Master of Pillowcases, the Chief Ethicist, the Lavatory Captain, and such. Each high-ranking, but none of us report to royalty, and the menials here serve us. You are similar?"

I tried to hide my shock at the fact that there were people here who would serve *me*. I chose, instead, to look more confident in my new position.

"Well," I said, "I *did* meet the Prince today. But he barely spoke to me."

"Ah! Well, you are no chef, philosopher, or janitor because they know better than to board disciplines together. What are you?"

"An intelligence officer." I had spent a moment imagining how the house and its inhabitants would react to a soothsayer, how many fortunes would be requested, how many chances for exposure there would be. The lie came naturally.

"Ah! Those soldiers—the Yellows—they are to protect you?"

"The ones out front? Yes."

"Protect you from those *within* the palace?"

"Perhaps."

"Ah." He touched the side of his nose, as if indicating secrecy, but then immediately continued: "These palace Rots, they love their intrigues and their paperwork."

"Is that so? I've never been this close to the Sunset Palace before, so I suppose I wouldn't know."

He nodded emphatically. "Oh yes. Intriguing and backstabbing, but everything must be backed up by three manifests signed in triplicate and so-and-so's seal pressed into such-and-such assassination order and so on."

I couldn't tell how much of this was a joke and how much was true. Tural clearly liked talking, and I began to wonder what I could draw out of him. Despite how tired and worried I was, I slipped into a playful bit of attempted charm and leaned in closer. "Assassinations?" I asked. "For the Master of Fruit?"

"What? No! Only Krantz would want me assassinated, and not *really*. I am exaggerating. It's just that, back in Quruscan, people keep to themselves, and trust one another. Rots are too much in each other's business. And fancy themselves too far *out* of the rest of the Tetrarchia's business."

"Do you have trouble here?" I asked him. "You know, being Quru around all these Rots?"

"No, no. Not up here. The court likes to appear cosmopolitan, you see. Although, I admit, I rarely go down into Turmenbach or any other caves. Perhaps that makes me a bad guest, but they scare me. Up here feels better: more like being in the mountains."

"So, you like it here? Even though it isn't Quruscan?"

He grinned. "Well, sometimes Quru keep *too much* out of each other's business, for my taste."

There was the lightest tapping on the doorway behind me. An apologetic maid, standing in stocking feet with her shoes in her hand, stood there.

"Ah, Master Tural, may we . . . ?" She trailed off and motioned her head vaguely toward the rest of the floor.

"Yes! Yes, yes. So sorry," he said. "I'm done for now."

She nodded, smiled, and slipped her shoes back on before clacking away. I supposed the tapping of her shoes as she walked would have disturbed Tural's "conjuring."

"I scare them. I don't mean to," he sighed, looking past me. "They live on the bottom floor and work to serve this house only. We are their masters as the King is ours, and theirs. They never see the inside of the Sunset Palace, and do not realize how unimportant we are."

I coughed and wiggled my eyebrows, nodding in the vague direction of the palace.

"Well, I am. *You* saw the Prince on your first day at the palace." He gave me a pleasantly conspiratorial look, which I returned.

"So, Tural," I began in, I must say, perfect Cöllüknit, "what do you know about who will be at tonight's ball?"

He looked a bit dazedly surprised at my switch to his native tongue, and then became thoughtful. He snapped his fingers. "Kalyna, I can give you an exhaustive list," he began, in Cöllüknit, "of which Rotfelsenisch nobles are allergic to stone fruits. I can tell you which royals, from *all four* kingdoms, mind you, have a sweet tooth, or have an aversion to the smell of citrus, or just don't *like* berries because of how they burst in one's mouth, and so forth. But beyond that . . ." He shrugged.

"Well, I may want a list of who's allergic to what. Later." I winked.

"Oh! I . . . Well, I don't know that I would actually be allowed to . . ." He trailed off.

I laughed and waved my hand at him. "Of course not, Tural! Of course not. Joking."

He seemed relieved and smiled. There was a ball to prepare for, an escape to plan, and who knew what else. I needed to go.

"Thank you," I continued in his language, "for sharing with me your mysteries."

That is what I literally said, but in that language of Quruscan, "mysteries" have a particular meaning. A mystery can be one's trade, one's personal feelings, one's deep religious observances, or any number of other personal things. It acknowledges that a great confidence has been given. Of course, it is generally diluted by casual use, and I meant nothing by it, really, beyond proof that I spoke his language and knew its intricacies.

I could not remember the last time that someone looked so happy to see me. Not my Gift, not a daughter to give comfort nor a young woman to give pleasure, but *me*. Tural smiled widely and waved me good day with a brown hand stained with purple. I did not know what to do with the warmth in my belly. I smiled back with a truly genuine smile, and then left quickly.

I walked to the ground floor of the servant house very slowly, and found no hidden passages or unguarded windows.

JÖRDIS

All my other neighbors, it seemed, were busy preparing their own small domains for the Winter Ball, so I went back to my room. Loath to read yet more of Lenz's serpentine histories, I paced back and forth for an hour. I should have been pondering how to manage the ball itself, because I would have to survive into next week to escape with my father. If he was truly on the way here. Instead, I formulated, and discarded, a hundred different ways to take Lenz hostage, or kill him, during the ball. None were feasible, but all were satisfying to imagine. I was particularly fond of the one that included a long dive down the stairs.

Finally, I got the sinking feeling that I should actually sit down and try to learn more of what was going on in this ridiculous kingdom. A few decent prophecies would, I hoped, please Lenz and keep me alive long enough for my family to arrive (if they were indeed on their way). Begrudgingly, I took one of Lenz's histories off the shelf, and spent some time staring at it, deciding whether to read it, put it back, or tear it apart. I opened it.

Rituo, it read, *is the largest of the Bandit States that directly abut Rotfelsen itself, and as such, it is the one with which we have the most history, good and bad. When things are good between us, Rotfelsenisch officials pretend they don't see all of the Bandit States as one great mass with no differentiations. When things are bad between us and Rituo, we conduct massacres, and not* only *in Rituo. The Tetrarchic mind is too caught up in itself and Loasht to ever be capable of imagining interrelated, yet independent, small countries.*

I knew that I should move to something more apt for tonight, but those cascades of Rotfelsenisch names were so impenetrable. I yawned and flipped a few pages to read more about the loose conglomeration of city-states to the south.

Skoagen is probably the largest of all the Bandit States. It has been the largest, as far as we can tell, for the past ten years, as they consistently bend, break, twist, split, and absorb. We know very little of the place—the last time High General Dreher and his army penetrated that far, on a punitive mission, Skoagen's people seemed to melt away from us into hills and caves.

There are some officers in our army who, when no one of import is listening, suggest that the recent spate of attacks by smaller Bandit States are somehow orchestrated by Skoagen's leaders. This, though the Bandit States have *never* managed to work together before, is—

I was interrupted by a knock, and opened the door to see a maid. The sun was beginning to set outside, and my room had turned bright red. The light hit the expanses of rotrock and bent around the Sunset Palace, which was named that for a reason, before it got to us. When did balls normally begin? Were people already on their way in? Was I late?

"Master Felsknecht," the maid began, "has requested that you take your tea in your room."

Requested indeed. He wanted me to continue all that studying of his brilliant life's work. So I sat at my desk as I was served, and picked at food I didn't notice, while drinking tea and pointedly reading nothing. The maid left the door open.

It began to occur to me that, in the eyes of Selvosch, the Quarry-master who had approached Prince Friedhelm, and his plotters, I was on Lenz's side, no matter how many fantasies of his death I entertained. Was I being watched by Lenz's soldiers? Was I being watched by his adversaries? Could I trust even the butlers and maids in our servant house? I was not used to having so many people around me at all times, even while I had so much space to myself.

I spat out the bite of food I had just taken, as though it would save me from poison.

"That bad?" asked a Rotfelsenisch voice from my doorway. I jumped in my chair, and snorted loudly.

I saw a short, round woman with a pile of blonde braids atop her head, in impeccable imitation of a local peasant girl style. Maybe it was just the early sunset, but she was positively rosy cheeked.

"No, I choked," I said as I stood. "Kalyna Aljosanovna." I wondered if I should extend a hand, or curtsy, or cross my arms over my chest, or . . .

She scuttled up to me and bowed at the most precise angle I'd ever seen.

"A pleasure," she said. "Jördis Jagloben, Chief Ethicist serving beneath His Brightness Otto Vorosknecht, Court Philosopher of Rotfelsen. Pleased to meet you, Kalyna Aljosanovna. I'm your neighbor!" She pointed to my wall.

It occurred to me that the Master of Fruit was wiry and severe, and the Chief Ethicist playful with a libertine's figure. Palatial Rotfelsen was strange indeed.

"You have a beautiful name," she continued, "although you don't look Masovskan."

"I . . . Thank you?"

She smiled broadly. "I'm sorry, Kalyna Aljosanovna, was that rude? I think it was." Jördis dropped her courteous demeanor and put a hand on her hip. "That's why I do ethics, not etiquette."

"Ah."

Even in her casual stance, she turned, perfect as gearwork, to look around my room. "And speaking of etiquette, the rest of the house was having tea together. A last sendoff to get good and full of tea mania before the Winter Ball begins."

"Yes, sorry. Work." I waved at the half-eaten food and closed book on my desk.

"Indeed. You work for the tall one who was here earlier, with the mustache and the limp, yes?"

"I do, yes. Lenz." I immediately wondered if I should not have given his name. Well, if he was trying to be secretive, he should have told me so.

"You're a Yellow, then! I suppose that makes me a Purple." She pointed her finger at me and wound her wrist in a circle in imitation of a rapier maneuver, before jabbing forward toward my stomach. "Better watch out or I'll *get you*." She laughed heartily.

"Yes," I said.

I was still not sure who the Purples even were, but I had already implicated them to Lenz and the Prince. Were they soldiers of *ethics*? That couldn't be right. Had I branded this perfectly nice woman a traitor without thinking?

"So, what *are* you two?" she asked.

"Intelligence officers."

"Is that the same as a spy?" She was acting very excited about the whole thing. Too excited, in my opinion at the time. But then, I didn't much take to excitement.

"Much duller," I replied. I returned her smile, although with perhaps a quarter of the intensity. I got the impression that Jördis was working very *hard* to be so smiley and friendly, and felt that she might react well to a calmer conversation partner. I pretended that I was at ease.

"A pity," she replied.

"You seem disappointed that nothing untoward or dangerous is happening here."

"A touch, perhaps. It seems this house is full of dull subjects."

"Well," I began, pointing to the other wall, "Tural is—"

"Oh, Tural isn't dull, but his *subject* is. He just manages to be decent despite it. But devoting your whole life to fruit is almost as boring as doing so to ethics."

I truly wasn't sure how to respond to that, so I chose to change the subject slightly. "Jördis," I began, putting on a look of worry, which I didn't particularly have to fake, "you said before that you're a Purple, yes?"

She rolled her eyes and made a big show of deflating. "Yes, I suppose I am. I can leave now, if you'd like."

"No, no!" I laughed. "What I'm trying to arrive at is, well, that I'm new here, and I am not entirely sure what that *means*."

Jördis was quiet for a moment, her brows furrowed, and then smiled again. "You really *aren't* a spy, are you? If you don't even know that?"

I nodded and hoped I did not look entirely too stupid.

"Well, the Purples are the soldiers of my . . ."—the next word seemed to sicken in her mouth—"*boss*, the Court Philosopher."

I suppose I should have looked more knowledgeable, appeared more aware of what was going on in this kingdom where I was now practicing intrigue. But I couldn't help being surprised to hear that the Court Philosopher had an *army*. This must have shown in my face.

"Rotfelsen's philosophies need their defenders as much as the King, the Prince, and our borders do, I suppose," Jördis explained. "Or so it's said. Many Purples are simply soldiers for the gold marks, but quite a few really believe."

"Believe what?" I asked.

She opened her mouth and made a strange noise for awhile, which eventually crescendoed into, "Look, we'll be here all night if I get into that. Kalyna, it was a wonder to meet you. And so nice to see this room in use again after the *incident* with the Butler of Anointing Oils for Lesser Nobles."

I never did learn what this "incident" was. Some spy I was.

I continued not studying. My position at the moment was as mortifying as *everything else* that had beset me recently. The death of our horse, the mercenaries of the Gustavus brats (was my Gustaw still alive?), the benign tyranny of Lenz and his master, a philosopher's army, and now . . . Planning for tonight while upholding a half-formed false identity (non-soothsayer) that was itself covering a false identity (soothsayer). Not to mention the fall of the entire Tetrarchia.

I had none of the giddy enjoyment of a confident, well-prepared lie fluttering through my innards. I couldn't even enjoy my spacious new home.

ONE OF THE YELLOWS

It was almost entirely dark when Lenz returned, with the tailor and my hastily altered guard's uniform. As I have mentioned, the expectations placed upon women changed considerably throughout the Tetrarchia, while remaining frustratingly similar in certain ways. In

Skydašiai, for example, about half of all violent and physical jobs—soldiers, handler-mages, blacksmiths, so forth—were held by women, but this was not the case anywhere else in the Tetrarchia. In Rotfelsen, women could have a number of professional roles, such as a tailor or a doctor—so long as they were decently deferential to their male peers—and there were a good number of women soldiers, which meant I would not look implausible at the Winter Ball, outside of my supposed foreignness. But in all of the Tetrarchia, to whatever extent women were allowed to work at "manly" occupations, it had to be accompanied by a masculine bearing, or wardrobe. Being a man was seen as something to *aspire* to.

Even I, growing up in my strange, nomadic family—a family that put stock in no mores that did not directly serve us—found myself thinking this way at times. And so, my Yellow uniform made me feel powerful. It had brown leather trousers and sleeves, with a red sash across the chest, while the doublet, hat, gloves, and cape were the yellow of a daffodil. This marked me as one of the Prince's Guard, though there was no loop for a sword on my belt, hindering my ability to *guard*. The doublet was wool, cut exactly to my figure like nothing I had ever before owned. Having something fit me so perfectly was a bit intoxicating.

I felt a thrill go through me when I learned that the tailor would also be dropping off more clothing cut perfectly to me in the next week or so.

I went downstairs alone, adjusting my gloves and feeling very dashing. I daresay the color of the uniform was more flattering on me than on those pink Rots. Then I saw another Yellow and my confidence evaporated. Lenz had told me they would stay *outside* of my new home, but this one was sitting on a stool in the servant house's kitchen.

When my footsteps stopped, the Yellow slowly turned her head to look at me. The look on her face was thoughtful, intense. I had seen this soldier before, when Lenz and I took a small carriage from the Sunset Palace to my new home, only a few hours before—she had been playing with her dagger. She was darkly blonde, tall, and lean, tapering down from broad shoulders. Sitting as she was now, she seemed entirely at ease in her uniform with a weapon at her side, in a way that suggested she could move from leisure to violence in a heartbeat. Her mouth was shut tightly, and she looked at me in a way I took to be cold, appraising.

She was quite terrifying and compelling. In front of her, on the kitchen counter, was a plate with a torn apart loaf of crusty brown bread and a pat of butter.

"Are you—" My voice went too high, and I cleared my throat. I tried again. "Are you here to take me to the ball?"

She nodded.

"Great. Well. Let's go. What's your name?"

She garbled out something that sounded like "Dugmush" through a mouthful of bread and butter.

She had not been, just now, particularly thoughtful, or appraising: she had simply been trying to chew. I was sure her name was not actually "Dugmush," but I was now too embarrassed to ask again.

She swallowed her bread and winked at me. "Don't you look sharp?"

I felt myself flush slightly. She was my guard, ready to commit violence to keep me from escaping, and yet I preened at the compliment. A base fear of her mingled with a desire to have her self-assurance, particularly while we wore the same uniform.

"Off we go!" she said.

I was then whisked off to the Sunset Palace under the close watch of real soldiers. It was time for the Winter Ball.

PARTIES

I found the Winter Ball to be disgusting.

Everything was draped in jewels, carved with the faces of past royalty, circled by ice sculptures to suggest a "winter" that had barely hit Rotfelsen. Men and women sweating into silks and furs discussed skirmishes and marriages and taxes and land-grabs, while scarfing the most carefully prepared food and getting very drunk. But none of this excess, these things I could never possess, were what disgusted me; at least, not directly. What disgusted me was that everyone there had friends, acquaintances, spouses, lovers, the freedom to gossip without being murdered, to rut without much worrying how a child would tie them down. They could have a drink or two because guards and civilization meant they were not always in danger, and they could eat because they knew the food would not run out by tomorrow morning.

Of course, this safety was an illusion, even without the destruction that was coming for the Tetrarchia. Perhaps the Turmenbach masses would rise up and crush them: this was an end to the Tetrarchia I found more palatable. Yet, imagining these thoughtless nobles as starving refugees in the coming months, preyed upon in the Bandit States, did not make me feel much better.

The first time I ever drank alcohol had also been the last time (until later that night). I had been fifteen, and a pretty girl in a Skydašian village offered me a sip of her father's liquor. I laughed, stumbled, fell.

I woke up in pig shit, at the back of a barn on a side of town I did not know. When I found my way back to my family's camp, Papa was babbling. Grandmother cursed me and beat me with a belt, and then a stick, for leaving my father to be tormented by the girl and her friends. They had thrown rocks at him from afar, and with each impact he had apologized. When I, covered in offal and bleeding, held him, he cried for my mother, Dilara.

When I saw those nobles guzzling spirits, laughing, plopping red-faced onto fainting couches, I envied them their leisure, and the freedom of their stupidity.

THE WINTER BALL

Oh yes, the ball.

I, idiot that I was (and mostly still am), had assumed a great, royal ball would take place on the ground floor of the palace. It would be easy for guests to find the party and, as the buttressed entry hall was the largest room I had yet seen in my life, I assumed it was the most impressive one the palace had to offer. Surely, it could fit everyone.

It absolutely would not have fit everyone. No, the entry hall was indeed only for *entry*. The rich and indolent passed through it, marveling loudly and insincerely, before leaving their attendants to mill about by the staircase, or outside, while they ascended to the royal clouds. How many of them, I wondered, had emerged blinking and disoriented from their caves deep in Rotfelsen—had traveled farther vertically than horizontally to get here? Perhaps emerging onto the surface and seeing so many stars was the first bit of glittering royal excess they beheld.

The main stairway was wide enough for a carriage, with railings of pure emerald gemstone, imported (I had to assume) from northern Skydašiai or Loasht. I think that if anyone tripped, they would not have grabbed that railing, for fear they might scratch it. One noble was carried up those stairs on a palanquin, although he did not seem partic-ularly weak. A squat woman, who was clearly not Rotfelsenisch, made a big show of being annoyed by him and trying to get by.

This great palace, those huge and gaudy stairs, it all seemed so friv-olous and yet so inviolate. As though this noble fancy was too big, too *stupid*, to ever be broken down and removed from the land on which it sat. But I supposed I knew better: it was all going to crumble, physi-cally or metaphorically. This staircase would tumble onto itself, perhaps, crushing these royals just as well as it crushed their servants and hangers-on.

At the top of those stairs—and only half as far as Lenz and I had climbed up the cramped servants' stairs earlier that day—were King Gerhold VIII's Royal Party Apartments. This was their official name. I never did learn how many rooms were in this suite: there always seemed to be another and, as far as I could tell, the in-demand monarch was always one room away. It seemed everyone wanted to see him, and no one ever did.

Wreathed through the guests, and crowded at every door, were groups of guards: most in red, many in green and purple, a few in yel-low. They were more interested in circling each other than watching the guests, and the Yellow who had brought me wanted to join them, so I was left to my own devices.

So, I tried to figure out which guests were plotting against the King. Or, failing that, to make up my own plot, accuse someone of it, and convince Lenz it was the truth. I simply had to survive until my father got here, then we could run away and leave Rotfelsen to crumble into dust.

Telling fortunes without the Gift, to those that want to hear them, is relatively easy. When a customer wants to believe, one can be vague. "I see you covered in a sheet" can be a death shroud or a comfortable bed, "I see your mother having a revelation" can be about your greatness or your terrible secrets, and so on. The customer shapes the vagaries to fit what they expect, if they even slightly believe you to be the real thing. And I must give myself credit for being good at acting like the real thing. So good that a master of secrets had not yet caught onto mine.

But *extracting* futures from assembled nobles and merchants was an entirely different set of skills. They did not *want* to believe I was prophetic, and in fact, it was better they not suspect. At best, I would be playing my game of setting up open statements to catch Lenz's assumptions, but even that meant actually *watching* these drunk idiots. An hour in, all I had prophesied was gout and burning crotch.

"Why don't you have a sword, soldier?"

I had not seen the speaker walk up beside me, as I had been standing in a corner, focused on a pale man with a thin beard and mustache. He had been speaking to a little curve of people, and I had gotten the idea he was important.

I turned slowly toward the speaker, a blonde and beardless Rotfelsenisch lord of no more than twenty-two years. The rapier at his side had a jeweled handle that almost tricked me into thinking it was never used. But the jewels on the pommel had been scratched many times, as had the guard, and he wore only one ring, so as to make gripping his weapon easier.

"I am not that sort of soldier," I said to him.

"Oh? What sort are you?" He smiled, and it occurred to me he might have been *flirting* with me. I was as used to unwelcome advances as most women, normally of the less genial kind, but, armed or no, I was in the yellow of a Prince's guard, sternly watching those around me. I could not see how he thought this was a good idea, unless he wanted to get into the Prince's business through me. I almost laughed at the thought.

My uniform *was* form-fitting, in a sense, but in service of emphasizing power: a triangle wide at the shoulders. The shadow I saw against the wall *was* mine, but it was a me who looked stern and implacable, which did not tend to be what men who leered at me wanted. Usually, *that* was wild, sensual exoticism—"feminine like a she-lion!" a man told me once. Had I possessed such a wildness to offer him, I still would not have. How ridiculous.

I will say that this youth did not leer, at least.

"The sort who does not need a sword," I told him. I looked back at the man holding court.

"Now you are being circular."

"Not my job to be friendly. There are attendants for that." I probably should have been less rude—after all, he could have been someone powerful (or the son of someone powerful), but I got the feeling this fancy boy would respond well to being neglected, just a touch. And if I were wrong, what would he do, imprison me?

"Is your job to stare at the Lord High Quarrymaster?"

In that moment, my skill at deception did come in handy. Because, upon learning that the man I had been looking at was, in fact, the same Selvosch who had approached the prince about supplanting the King, my heart jumped, but I did not so much as bat an eye.

"Maybe," I said. "That's certainly *their* job." I inclined my head toward the half-circle of eager listeners around Selvosch.

"Just a hobby, I assure you," said the blonde. He looked out at Selvosch and his admirers.

"Is he so entrancing to listen to?" I asked. "He does not seem so from here." It was a chance to betray so much ignorance, and be flippant to boot, but I had let the blonde set our tone. If I could learn anything useful about Selvosch, the only confirmed member of the plot against the King, I could maybe coast on that until I got a chance to escape.

"Entrancing?" the blonde laughed. "Oh my, no. But he is powerful, and rich, with a . . . captivating unpleasantness. But you could say that of most anyone here"—he trained his gaze on me—"except the soldiers. So! Perhaps you're a new type of sharpshooter? Or some sort of *magic* soldier, perhaps? I know the sorts old Friedhelm likes to recruit. A foreign mercenary? From Quruscan, perhaps? Or . . . farther?" He would not even mention Loasht by name. "You clearly aren't—"

"Rotfelsenisch? I am, but not entirely."

The blonde was fully facing me now, and certainly flirting. He was not badly formed. He had a dueler's body, lithe and narrower in the shoulders than myself. High cheekbones and piercing eyes. I was not, however, interested in flirting just then. I was also unsure whether *I* was what he wanted, or a means to some end. How many networks of spies were there? How many alternate spymasters were darting around, looking to confound Lenz?

"Meaning," he said, "that you are watching everyone, but you are a foreigner unaware of who everyone is?"

"If you like. And who are you?" I continued to stand straight, hands clasped behind me, like a soldier. Even as I spoke to him, I kept an eye on Selvosch, to be sure I did not lose him.

"Martin-Frederick Reinhold-Bosch."

"That's a lot of names. Couldn't your parents make up their minds?"

"Not really, no. That length conveys that my line is old and royal."

"Is it?"

"Well, yes, but the royal part is not so old. My grandfather was allowed to marry into unimportant royalty, you see, after distinguishing himself somehow." An exaggerated shrug. "But he was able to set up a better match for my father, and now here I am!" The false modesty was stifling.

"Here you are where, exactly?"

"Why, living up in the light rather than down in our ancestral caves. Knocking about the palace, watching for lecherous Uncle Friedhelm's treachery against Uncle Gerhold."

"You do see that I'm wearing yellow, don't you?"

"Well, one can hardly blame you for that. I know a man in my position *should* be looking to meet wilting, noble flowers—but I'm always drawn to a woman in uniform. The martial type."

I rolled my eyes, and let him see that I was doing so. I had a feeling that would only make him try harder.

"Well, I hate to disappoint you, ah . . ." I trailed off, making a show of forgetting his name. "But I'm not terribly martial. No sword, remember?" I grabbed at the empty space on my belt where a sword would have been.

He grinned and lowered his voice again. "But what *can* you do? It must be something."

I smirked. "Who are you asking for?"

"Myself."

"Well, I hardly know you. Who else?" I let my stance falter slightly, in order to gesture to his clothing in an . . . aggressive fashion. "You aren't wearing a color I recognize." His doublet was an inoffensive midnight blue, which flattered his complexion.

He laughed at that. "What if I said High General Dreher?"

"What if you did?"

"Would you tell me what sort of soldier you are, if it was for him?"

"Perhaps, but I'm not speaking to him, am I?"

"Not yet."

I began to suspect that this Martin-Frederick Reinhold-Bosch (I had in fact remembered his name quite well) had nothing more to offer me tonight. But I would keep him in mind: a royal with a way to the High General could come in very handy.

"I," I said, "am going to go over there now, and stare at people from a different angle. Thank you for the information."

The little blonde laughed and told me his name once more. He seemed quite sure he would run across me again, and he was right. Sometimes it seems everyone is better at seeing the future than me.

I walked past Selvosch as he was loudly demanding everyone agree with him that someone was a filthy, three-legged swine. They all agreed.

The Lord High Quarrymaster

I had passed Selvosch, the Lord High Quarrymaster, in order to better hear him for a moment, and to move away from the young blonde. Soon after that, I stood in another corner, still watching who spoke to Selvosch, and trying to see if any of them seemed conspiratorial about it. Of course, everyone was so coquettish and playful that it was quite hard to tell. Selvosch took his leave of the group, and I followed him into a small side room. My hope was to learn enough about him to craft a believable vision that could keep me alive until my father arrived.

If Papa was indeed being brought here at all. If he wasn't, if he had been killed or left behind to starve, what would I do? Still try to escape before everything came crumbling down so soon? Perhaps I would purposefully speed and aid that destruction, as some sort of terrible vengeance—it did not feel beyond me, just then.

But, for now, I watched laughing revelers in their silk doublets, too-tight hose, and enormous dresses cram themselves against each other on plush chairs and couches. It was early in the night, yet already these dresses and hose were crinkling into one another. The walls were adorned with bas-reliefs of various styles. I am no historian—and was even less one then than I am now—but even I knew these were each from different places and times. Some were of marble or onyx, some of rotrock that was separate from the room's own red walls, and a few were of that unbreakable stone of the Ancients, somehow. Any story these bas-reliefs told was unintelligible to me.

The nobles didn't care about me, and no other soldiers were visible. I slunk into a dark corner and felt relief.

"Hello, Kalyna Aljosanovna," said Lenz.

I don't know where he came from, but I managed to hide my shaking hands and turn calmly.

"Were you watching me, or Selvosch?" I asked.

"Neither. But the Party Apartments fold in on themselves. A ball can have thousands of guests, and yet one will keep seeing the same dozen people again and again. A marvel, really."

"Yes, marvelous," I said. "I suppose they wanted to imitate the confusing, twisting tunnels below."

"Wanted to, or could not help doing so," he replied. Then he dropped into Masovskani: "I am wondering why you're following the Quarrymaster so closely."

"Isn't he part of the plot against the King?"

"Yes, and he also knows that the Prince knows that he's part of that plot. I would prefer he not be followed by anyone in a yellow uniform." He sighed. "Trust that I have people with eyes on him, while you see to reading the futures of *other* powerful people, to learn who else is involved."

I sighed in false exasperation.

"Lenz," I said, "If I catch a few moments of every possible future in this palace, it will simply be a jumble. I must know whom to focus on."

"Well, if you had paid more attention to my histories . . ."

"By the gods, Lenz, there are things in your daft books about what the Ancients were and which areas they may have over-planted! Forgive me for not immediately finding the most important morsels while I was being *kidnapped*."

He shrugged, which I decided was the most I would get out of him on this.

"Tell me," I continued, "what the Lord High Quarrymaster actually *does*. Officially. This may give me an idea of who would be connected to him."

Lenz grunted in consternation and looked away for a moment. We watched the room idly, and I focused on a group nowhere near Selvosch, which seemed to be made up of important people. They were all laughing together on a couch shaped like the horseshoe of Fántutazh Lake, where trees float. Others streamed in and out of the room constantly—on their way somewhere, or looking for a place to sit. I could hardly believe how many people; it never stopped.

"Can you imagine . . . *I say*, can you *imagine*," one man was yelling to a group, "what would happen if we ever *did* go to war with Loasht?" He was trying to sound witty, and enjoyed the jolts of shock from his audience at the mention of that terrifying power to the north. "I say, can you imagine?

All those soldiers, from all four kingdoms, lined up in a row: Masovska hussars next to Quru mountaineer irregulars next to Skydašiai's puffed up Yams and so forth, all yelling in their own doggerel, with their own sets of maneuvers! Even our High General Dreher couldn't wrangle them: he'd have his hands full just telling our Purples what to do!"

A woman chimed in. "They would all fight each other before"— whispered, now—"the Grand Suzerain's forces even got to them!"

They all laughed at the *hilarious* image, convincing themselves it wasn't real. They suddenly quieted as a man went by in a tall flash of purple, followed by a stream of Purples.

"That's the Court Philosopher," said Lenz. "You said his Purples were up to something. Why don't you follow him?"

I got a quick look at the Court Philosopher's angular face and very tall hat, which jutted straight up. His soldiers glared at us as they passed. Once he had left the room, it began to buzz again. Selvosch did not seem to react one way or another.

"I rather think his men would notice," I said. "Is the High General here, too? I've heard he's rather important."

Lenz shook his head. "He doesn't do parties."

"I see. As to the Quarrymaster," I said, "I am sure he does not over-see production. Too low for someone like him."

"So you didn't *see* him with your Gift, then?"

"Not yet. Give me context."

"You are astonishingly unhelpful."

"I never said I'd be helpful. You assumed it when you *kidnapped* me."

He sighed, but did not turn to me. "The Quarrymaster," Lenz began, staring forward, "does not so much run Rotfelsen's many, many, *many* quarries as he rules them."

"How do you mean?"

"All the laws about what can be extracted: rotrock is a quite useful building material for the other kingdoms, although they usually like to paint it other colors so they don't 'look like Rotfelsen.'" He smirked. "And exporting the stuff also gives us more space for new homes and tunnels. We mine and sell a great deal of metals and gems as well from our beloved home. The Quarrymaster controls all of that, dictates where one can't dig, how much to take, which equipment is lawful, even worker safety." He laughed at this last one, at the very idea. "All go through Selvosch."

"No wonder everyone surrounds him."

"Most Rotfelsenisch landowners have quarries, because it's all that can be done with their property. Some also sell potatoes and other cave plants."

I smiled to myself at the thought of how little Selvosch would rule, if my father had been literal about those shattered remains. But I could not hold onto that smugness for long, as thoughts of the Tetrarchia's impending doom ran wild through my head once more. Would another Tetrarchic kingdom become fed up with living next to a big rock full of jewels that were slowly portioned out? Perhaps Skydašiai would finish their work of centuries ago, and simply crack the thing open to take what they wanted. Then there were the tens of thousands of miners who toiled deep in the dark to keep this place running: I would not blame them for rising up and crushing their masters. Or perhaps they would simply be unthinkingly directed to overmine the rock's foundations during the Council of Barbarians, and it would fall in on itself.

All the revelers became not just disgusting, but deeply stupid. How could they dance and drink when the country they ran was collapsing? When their way of life was going to end when winter did? *I* didn't know what would cause it, but shouldn't those in power see the end coming?

Or was it Rotfelsen's own aggression, or conquest, or infighting that would cause all of this?

Either way, no matter how stupid I told myself they were, I imagined their deaths in an avalanche of rotrock and wanted to cry.

"Well," said Lenz, "please don't allow me to distract you, my prophet. See what else you can see."

I bowed insultingly.

He repaid it with a similarly sarcastic bow and turned to leave, before stopping and turning back. "Oh, and Kalyna, do be careful."

My breath caught in my throat. "Of . . . ?"

"Earlier, some inflated Purple bumped into me, blamed me for it, and spent a *great* deal of time trying to goad me into a duel." He smiled. "It was all very transparent, and I'm sure that if I cared for that sort of honor, he'd have killed me."

"Pity."

From my first moment at the ball, it had been clear that the night would include duels between military doublets of different colors: they seemed positively twitching to do so. Already I had seen them jostle, side-eye, and spit on the floor when those of another color passed, much to the delight of the nobles.

"You'll be largely on your own if they make trouble for you," said Lenz. "Most Yellows are in the Prince's apartments, guarding him during his private, ah . . . let's say *adjunct* party."

"Keeping track of the Prince's conquests?"

"He's quite capable of that himself—the numbers aren't as high as he likes to pretend."

"Inspiring. So," I began to count on my fingers, "the Yellows are us, of course. The Purples are the Court Philosopher's army of idealists, yes?"

Lenz looked pleased with how much studying I'd supposedly done. "Yes, although I don't think they're all idealists. I certainly hope not."

"Fine. And the Greens are whom you used to be a part of: you know, the *actual* army."

"Yes." He looked irritated at that, which I liked. "They're the largest of the four, but are stationed throughout the country, not just up here."

"And lastly," I continued, "who are the Reds?"

"The Reds, Kalyna, are supposedly King Gerhold's own guards, his personal army, dressed in the color of Rotfelsen itself."

"'Supposedly'?"

"Despite being Skydašian, Queen Biruté has become quite popular. Probably because she has a personality." He shook his head. "The Reds are, I'm afraid, quite split between those loyal to the King and those loyal to the Queen. Unofficially, of course, but it's quite clear."

"And so, if a Red or a Purple or whoever comes for me, I can simply ignore them?"

"That worked for me, Kalyna, because I have a little power and am a man. It may not work for you."

"Then what will? I have far *less* power than you. What's the code of conduct here?"

"You *did* read my books, didn't you?" asked Lenz.

Then he left.

Phlegm caught in my throat, and I almost spat it onto the rug, which was made from the furs of hundreds of animals.

SKYDAŠIAN DUELS

Simply ignoring the Purples would not work for me, I learned, because no one would try to dispatch me through a duel in the first place. Although I could be a soldier in Rotfelsen, I could not fight a duel. The very idea of women dueling—with each other, or with a man—was seen as laughable in Rotfelsen, and in Quruscan as well.

In Masovska, I have heard, it had long been legal for a challenge to be issued between man and woman (still not between women), but the man had to fight up to his waist in a hole in the ground, in order to "balance out her infirmities." I never saw such a duel, and a man could demur without disgrace. It never occurred to lawmakers that a woman might have a sense of honor to affront, but then I've never really understood why honor was a thing that mattered to *anyone*.

But in Skydašiai, a man or a woman could challenge the other to supposedly equal and open combat at any time. A nice idea, insofar as any legal brawling is, but it seldom worked in practice because Skydašian women were consistently discouraged from learning the use of arms outside of those military branches that would have them. Most sword masters would not teach a woman, and most women would be shamed for the learning—unless, again, she was a soldier, in which case dueling was forbidden to her. All of this may serve to explain why I was in the habit of carrying a discreet sickle.

So, while the law of Skydašiai suggested that a woman could redress her grievance against a man (or, indeed, a woman) through lawful and godly combat, the reality was that such duels took the form of victimization. A man felt a woman had laughed at him, rejected him, slighted him by her presence, or otherwise shrunken his phallus, and in retribution, he challenged her—she who had never held a sword in her life, on pain of ridicule—to sabres at noon. She was then almost invariably killed or maimed to his satisfaction. It was to escape just such a duel that my family once fled Skydašiai, and I count myself not untalented at cutting men. Telling a spoiled, young fencing prodigy that you are not interested could be deadly there, in a way that was fully legal and public.

There is a sort of folk hero of Skydašiai, Aušra the Cleaver, who received army fencing training and then dropped out in disgrace before her first day as a soldier, due to being unmarried with child. Fifty years before my birth, reputedly, she roamed Skydašiai, waiting for just these sorts of brutes to challenge her: she never had to wait long, never had to incite or delude them to it. She would traipse out onto the battle-ground, in a dress, wobbly and unsure, nearly tipping over when she drew her sword. She would then give her opponents a deeply unpleas-ant surprise by moving into a perfect fencing stance, and proceed to kill or maim them. The maimings were *very* specific.

I could kill and maim, but had never dueled nor learned the sword. I am no Aušra the Cleaver.

MULTICOLORED, DUEL-HAPPY YOUTHS

Unsure of what to do next, I passed back into the room where I had met young Martin-Frederick. The groups of revelers had spread out a bit, as there was no Selvosch figure to flock toward. Music was playing from somewhere that I couldn't see, and laughter was becoming very shrill. A Red and a Purple were shoving each other, while a group of refined gentlemen seemed to be placing bets.

A hand was clapped onto my shoulder hard enough to hurt. I turned to see another group of Reds, grinning at me. Their leader leaned down until his face was even with mine. His cheeks still had baby fat, and he seemed entirely sober.

"I hear," he said, "that the Prince can't sleep at night without first sucking the High General to completion."

"The Prince sounds like a considerate lover," I replied.

Not having a response, he shoved me hard, sending me reeling back-ward. I'm sure I looked very powerful and martial flailing my arms and spinning around. I crashed fully into another reveler, who yelped and spun down with me. For a few moments, all I could see was the lace of her dress as it wrapped around my head.

The Red kept speaking, more to his comrades and the onlookers than to me, so I couldn't hear the specifics. I was too busy struggling to get out of those skirts, and babbling, "Pardon me," over and over again to the woman I'd barreled into. When I finally got free, the noble-woman was red in the face with laughter as a gentleman helped her up.

"What do you say, miss?" the leader of the Reds was asking her, over my shoulder. "Surely, this Yellow filth gave you a grave offense." He leaned toward me, hand on his sword pommel.

"Oh yes, certainly!" she laughed in reply. It was only a game to her, and to the other spectators.

The Reds stepped toward me, four in all. Armed, of course. I fought the urge to look around for people to run behind, for possible help, for an escape. Instead, I looked directly in the leader's eyes, and told my body to relax, to seem calm, above it all. I remembered something the young blonde had said earlier in the night, and my own thoughts when I was in the Prince's apartments that morning. I summoned all the trickster's confidence and tried to steady my voice.

"Be a shame to ruin our guests' fine outfits," I said. There was still definitely a tremble in the last few words.

The leader looked confused. This was good, because if he didn't get confused enough to ask, he could just kill me, easily. The Reds hung there for a moment, silent. My heart felt ready to burst.

"What do you mean?" he asked.

I smiled widely. I had him, at least for a moment, and knowledge of that flowed into me, let me feel I controlled the situation—whether or not I did.

"Don't you wonder why I'm not armed?" I asked.

"No," said the leader.

"Why?" asked one of the Reds behind him.

I thanked a few of my favorite gods, thinking the names that I could not say aloud, and cannot write here.

"Because I'm a sharpshooter, naturally. A harquebusier. Do sharpshooters duel?"

The lead Red looked directly at me, but his comrades, back where he couldn't see them, couldn't help looking around. Especially up above.

"It's bad form to walk amongst our guests with a harquebus," I continued. "But if you think the others don't have eyes on me, and you, at this very moment . . ." I trailed off on purpose.

"But," the leader began, "women can't be sharpshooters."

I did not know this. But now that I thought about it, there had been no female Yellows among the harquebusiers who had traveled with me from Masovska. I felt my heart seize in my chest.

"Let's go," said one of the Reds in the back.

"Women can't be sharpshooters!" the leader repeated, to his compatriot.

"Are you sure?" I asked.

"Maybe the Prince allows it," said one of the Reds. "Being a deviant and all."

"Not a chance," said the leader.

"She's not Rotfelsenisch, so who knows how it works where she comes from?" added another.

"Are you even sure I'm a woman?" I asked. At this point, I was simply trying to confuse them.

"Let's not risk it," said a Red who was looking very insistently in one direction.

I glanced that way, too. There was just a large painting—perhaps he had reason to think sharpshooters often hid behind it?

I winked at the painting.

"You don't really think—" the leader began.

"Why else wouldn't she have a sword?" yelled another of his men. "Come on, there's no shame in it."

They almost pulled their leader behind them, but they left. There was a general air of disappointment from the crowd, and one man even *booed*, first at the disappearing Reds, and then at me. I shrugged and walked up to him, grinning.

"You're next," I said, only because I was angry and relieved, and just maybe enjoying being the villain.

Who was in charge of all this? Rotfelsen hadn't had a real war in years, yet these soldiers were all young and angry, and no one seemed to mind their killing one another. Did they all go mad when they came to stay up in the palace's barracks, away from their tunnels?

The man in the last room, suggesting that the Tetrarchia's armies were too divided to fight Loasht, hadn't seemed to realize that even Rotfelsen's was too divided to get much done. Or perhaps, in their ignorance and violence, these multicolored, duel-happy youths would even be the doom of the Tetrarchia.

Had these men (or boys) been the Queen's Reds taking part in a plot against their King? Even worse, were these the King's Reds after me because they *thought* the Prince was indeed trying to overthrow his brother? Perhaps we would be mistakenly murdered by the King's protectors, while whoever wanted him dead skipped toward victory. Wouldn't that be a tragic and contrived ending to it all?

But what did I mean by "we"? Let the fools kill each other, I was getting out. I just needed to survive until my father got here. If vicious infighting would end the Tetrarchia, then there were no invaders to be feared. I could escape right into the disorderly, warring cities of the Bandit States while they picked at the Tetrarchia's carcass from the south.

I was brought back to the present when the party guest who had been booing me suddenly stopped. Then he laughed.

I wondered why he was laughing, right until something beige fluttered over my eyes. Then I was struck in the stomach and dragged away.

VOROSKNECHT

"Is this the one?" grunted a voice.

"It had better be," said another.

I knew those Reds had come back with reinforcements to kill me. That they were taking me somewhere unmenaced by the Prince's sharpshooters. I actually laughed bitterly at them going to all this trouble for me, the poverty-stricken, broken, mystic outcast, who knew that the end was coming soon. I do hope my laughing unnerved them.

When the bag was torn off my head, my eyes were assailed with brightness. The soldiers above me were nothing but menacing sunspots. As my eyes returned to normal, I saw one color overwhelmingly, and it was not red.

Everything, from the walls to the furniture to the uniforms, was a near-blinding purple. This must have been the Court Philosopher's suite. Had he already learned, somehow, that I had implicated him to the Prince when I was desperate for a prophecy about tonight?

The Purples grabbed me by my shoulders and dragged me through a hallway, past more purple rooms. The Court Philosopher's suite was just *slightly* smaller, and just *slightly* less opulent, than Prince Friedhelm's in every aspect.

"I am beneath you, O Prince," the suite proclaimed, "because I choose to be."

The Purples stopped before a large, purple door.

"Why does he need an army anyway?" I asked, bolstered by assuming I was already dead. "Whom do you people fight?"

If I hadn't put up my arms in time, they would've opened the great doors with my head. I was thrown into a study, and in its center, watching me, was the Court Philosopher. My neighbor, Chief Ethicist

Jördis, was with him. She looked unhappy. The doors slammed shut behind me.

The Court Philosopher of Rotfelsen was a tall, thin man in a tall, thin hat, as though a temple column was growing up from his skull. This, along with flowing purple robes, made him the perfect picture of a great king of the Ancients, as they have been depicted in paintings. Tetrarchic artists had no idea how the Ancients looked, and so fabricated a long extinct refinement based on nothing.

A book I once read, instead of one of Lenz's, quoted a woman who spent decades exploring ruins: she swore by all known gods, demons, and planets that the Ancients had not even been human.

But this is beside the point. The Court Philosopher looked like a fashionable painting. In his angular face and carefully groomed gray-brown beard could be seen all the self-assurance and serenity of those painted Ancients, who knew they were the pinnacle of humankind.

He stood behind his desk, caressing the skull of a skeleton that was posed on a stand. It looked like some sort of dog or large rodent, with extremely long and sharp fangs. The bones were dyed purple.

I started to curtsy, but realizing I did not have a dress, turned it into an awkward bow. My stomach and arms hurt. I imagined he was planning my beating, humiliation, or death. I didn't really understand how court intrigue worked (I still don't), so I decided to try obsequiousness. I did not know his name but, thankfully, there was a large bust of him next to his desk, and its base said "OTTO VOROSKNECHT" in large letters. The statue was purple.

"His name was Meregfog," said Vorosknecht, looking at the skeleton with great affection. "A wonderful pet."

I waited.

"His glands, they secreted something when he was unhappy. Something very painful."

I waited, and made sure to widen my eyes in interest.

"So!" said Vorosknecht, turning from Meregfog's poor skeleton. A dutiful Purple dashed up and wiped Vorosknecht's hands vigorously clean with a wet rag that smelled relentlessly tangy. "Kalyna Aljosanovna," the Court Philosopher said.

I stood still. Expectant.

"Kalynaaaaa Aljosaaaaanovnaaaaaa," he repeated. "You don't look Masovskan."

So I've heard, I managed to not say. I dipped my head respectfully.

"Meregfog was a good pet," he said, "because he could—theoretically, you understand—cuddle or poison someone for me. I couldn't well be held accountable for the actions of an *animal*."

I nodded.

"Ethicist Jagloben," Vorosknecht said to Jördis.

"Yes, Brightness," she replied from behind him.

Jördis seemed to be half of Vorosknecht's height, even though this was not possible (it must have been the hat). Gone was my gleeful neighbor, and in her place was a worried woman with a creased brow and a large purple sash, hands clasped tightly behind her back. I wondered if this was how I had looked around Prince Friedhelm.

"You know this Kalyna Aljosanovna?" asked Vorosknecht.

"Yes, Brightness. We just met today."

"Where does she come from? What is she? The viper disguised as a tree branch? Or the insect disguised as a peony?"

Jördis took a long breath. Since her master did not face her, she rolled her eyes. I wanted to smile at her, raise my eyebrows, or otherwise share the moment of annoyance with her, but I dared not. I didn't know her so well to rule out whether this was a trap. Perhaps making such a face was exactly what he was waiting for, as an excuse for his soldiers to gut me.

"I do not know, Brightness," she said.

"Well now, she must be some sort of dishonest, chameleonic creature."

I heard the Purples shifting behind me, weapons clanking.

"I . . ." Jördis faltered. "Must she, Brightness?"

"Why, Ethicist, did you know that your foreign neighbor here is a Yellow?"

"Brightness," I finally said, indicating my uniform, "I've hardly kept it a—"

"Ethicist Jagloben," Vorosknecht interrupted as though I'd said nothing at all, "did you know Kalyna Aljosanovna is a psychic?"

Jördis coughed and looked at me. "No, Brightness, I did not."

Vorosknecht smiled very widely and stepped out from behind his desk. He passed the bust of himself and approached a large glass cabinet full of small liquor bottles. The glass was stained purple. He poured himself a drink into a delicate, purple glass. I watched him do it, feeling intense relief that on his fingers were gold rings holding jewels of some other colors, just as a break from the monotony.

It really was a shame, because I *liked* purple. If I escaped this bad dream of a kingdom, I would wear it again.

"Our good Prince Friedhelm," said Vorosknecht, "has hired himself a psychic, Ethicist Jagloben, right under your nose. I wonder why." He downed the drink and replaced the glass, which a Purple then began to quietly wipe clean behind him.

"Why don't you ask the 'psychic'?" I asked, adding, "Brightness," and another bow.

Vorosknecht raised an eyebrow at me and said, "Huh."

I waited in mid-bow, trying not to shake.

"Ethicist Jagloben," he continued, "why do you think?"

"Well, Brightness . . ." Jördis struggled. She seemed to feel caught, the way it was for me when asked about a future I couldn't guess. It was clear Vorosknecht had a very specific answer he wanted to hear. "Well, Brightness," she said again, "I . . ."

"To *tell fortunes*," I said, standing up straight. "For the Prince. I kept it secret so as not to be pestered for the future of every neighbor in my house. That's the answer."

"Hm," said Vorosknecht.

"Would you like to know yours, Brightness?" Another dip of my head.

"Why not?" he replied.

He clearly thought little of my Gift (and who could blame him?), so I decided there was little point in trying to convince him of anything. Better to learn something, if I could.

"You and High General Dreher will soon be at each other's throats," I said. "Quite viciously."

Vorosknecht laughed derisively out of the left side of his mouth. "Oh, very good. Why, it's almost as if we have *never gotten along*."

Well, it wasn't a great revelation, but at least now I had an idea of where Rotfelsen's two armies *not* commanded by royals stood.

"Meregfog," said Vorosknecht, pointing to the purple skeleton, "was a tool. Prince Friedhelm also collects such tools."

I smiled nicely, but blinked too many times.

"You had some distinguished predecessors, psychic," said Vorosknecht. "There was the cooper who made hidden weapons, the chandler with the poisonous vapor candles, the, ah, 'dancer,' the librarian, the clown, and now this squirrely Lenz character, who is *also* a clown." He laughed. "I may have the order wrong. All tools. All more expendable to the Prince than this dumb animal," he said it with affection, "was to me."

At least he was speaking to me directly.

"But a psychic," he continued. "Ethicist, what are the *ethics* of using a psychic?"

"That would depend on how they are used, Brightness," said Jördis.

"Wrong!" He spun to face her, as though catching a child stealing sweets. Jördis jumped only slightly. "Ethics," Vorosknecht said, "as they stand, alone from all else, only dictate the uses of power, yes. But ethics alone cannot fully dictate whether something is right or wrong, is that not so?"

Jördis looked deeply unhappy. She was meant to agree with her master, but could not bring herself to. Her face turned red; she may have even shaken. She opened her mouth, closed it, looked away, looked back, and then Vorosknecht mercifully spun away to face my general direction.

"Of course it is!" he said. "Because the Ethicist and, say, the God-counter are separate viscounts of their own provincial, philosophical lands, aren't they? They live in the proverbial caves of thought—important, but siloed. You, Ethicist"—he waved a hand behind him at Jördis, who was standing very still—"can concern yourself with the use of power, but not the morality of that power's origins."

Jördis made a noise that was perhaps intended to sound like agreement; or she was releasing steam.

"The Godcounter," Vorosknecht continued, "keeps track of the gods—knows their caprices and hatreds—but does not understand how those divine preferences can be misinterpreted. I"—he placed a hand on his own chest—"of course, live beneath the bright sky of full understanding. I comprehend the intricacies, details, and intersections of *all* our disciplines. And, with such a perspective, I counsel the court and enact laws that protect our people's morality. But also"—he turned to me—"*from* this perspective, Kalyna Aljosanovna, I see that any use of your power is deeply, philosophically troubling."

"How do you mean, Brightness?" I asked.

Was he using my supposed Gift as an excuse to have me killed?

"Your powers are a curse, a moral travesty, setting you apart from other human beings, placing you—in the eyes of *some*—above even philosophers, kings, and other thinkers."

"I don't place myself—"

"You peer into what should not be the realm of man," he seethed. He began to pace, purple robe fluttering about him. "Only the demigods should see what is to come; it is for mankind's greatest thinkers"—he did not actually point to himself—"to extrapolate and interpret!"

"And yet, Brightness," I asked with my best innocence, "didn't the gods give me this Gift?"

"What?" He seemed disappointed that I could think such a thing. "Either gods cursed you or demons blessed you, which round out to the same thing."

I took a deep breath. "Why, Brightness," I said slowly, "can't this be a gift from the gods?"

Vorosknecht smiled serenely. "Because if humans were meant to see the future, why would the holder of that power be a mongrel nomad? Such a gift would be given to those who could put it to the best use, or it would be given to everyone like smell and taste. The gods don't hand out extra senses on a whim."

"What about all the old stories of a god's chosen champion or martyr who—?"

"A sky-chariot? The strength to move mountains? Or the power to die over and over again? Honestly."

He began to pace again. I shifted my weight to one side. I was tired of standing at attention.

"That," Vorosknecht continued, "was back when the gods were at war with each other; now we live in the glorious days when they are at nominal peace. This is why the past is full of stories of such heroes, and the present is not."

I always felt this was because gifted heroes born into our era would have been run out of towns or burned. In fact, I had quite a few well-supported arguments along these lines that I had thought up during long trips, but I felt that sharing them wouldn't help me just then.

"Well," I said instead, "I also see the present, Brightness, and yet I have known men and women who could see nothing. You can walk, but my father can't. How is this different?"

Rather than being angry, Vorosknecht only seemed put upon, which was so much worse. "You fail to grasp." He demonstrated this by grasping at the air with long fingers. Then he closed his eyes, pressing the bridge of his nose until those fingers turned white. "The blind are made that way because the god who dwells in darkness cursed them; those who cannot walk were cursed for hubris by the god of the hunt; do you see? This is all simply laid out if you can only understand the world around you."

I nodded. Waiting for the knife in my back that was surely coming.

"Similarly," he continued, "you have been cursed by something that taunts you, that makes you think you're special."

I blinked back a tear. I would not let him know that he had mistakenly pricked something within me. I began to wonder if I could somehow hold him hostage, drag him out of the Purples' sphere of influence, and then *murder* him.

I couldn't, but at least he would die in two months with everyone else. This whole, gaudy room would be a great purple stain in a mass of rotrock.

"Brightness," said Jördis.

Vorosknecht jumped. I almost did too.

"Yes?" he asked.

She looked right at me. "It's unfair of you to expect her to meet you as a debater." I read nothing but mercy in this supposed insult.

"Yes. Yes, of course," said Vorosknecht. "I'm forgetting my purpose tonight." He glared at me, and I heard the heavy boots of Purples step closer behind me. "Ethicist Jagloben," he continued, "please leave us."

With my eyes, I implored Jördis not to, but of course she had no choice. She passed me, and I heard her footsteps echo until the door was closed.

"Kalyna Aljosanovna," he said. He didn't pace now, but stood still, looking me in the eye for the first time, unblinking. "Your Prince does not worry me. Your lame spymaster does not worry me. Your curse bothers me, personally, but it does not *worry* me."

He snapped his fingers. A Purple grabbed each of my arms. Here it came. My breath began to quicken as they lifted me. Perhaps I could fight my way out if—

"I don't like you. I don't like your kind. I don't like your curse if it is real, and I don't like frauds if it is not."

I took a very deep breath.

"It used to be," he sighed, "that the Purples existed to round up and punish mystics, heretics, and others with wrong ideas. That their ranks were filled only by the *faithful*; those forged deep in our darkness, full of strong ideas. But those beautiful days were before my time, and though my soldiers are quite loyal to *me*, and to the rule of logic and reason, I cannot simply wield them however I like. Having you killed would mean a day's worth of paperwork and hassle, because you are the Prince's new toy. Don't make yourself worth that hassle. I'm very busy." He smiled, then looked away from me, to someone behind me. "Instead, I recommend you tell your Prince that he can stop wondering what sort of powerful people are working with Selvosch, because it is the sort with a very loyal army."

He looked at me hard, as though I would miss the significance if he did not spell it out for me. I obliged him.

"Don't tell me that *you* are plotting against the King, Brightness!"

"Vulgar, stupid thing, aren't you? I am telling you because no one could ever mount a case against me on the word of a mongrel like you. Tell your little Prince, who has suddenly decided to pretend he has a backbone, and then keep entirely away from me and mine, until the Prince tires of you and you are kicked out or killed. I have wasted enough of my time with you."

The Purples' grip on my shoulders tightened.

"She clashes with my color scheme," said Vorosknecht, waving me away languidly.

I was lifted bodily and carried out through the door by my arms. Another bag over the head, another long walk.

A BALL MUST HAVE DANCING

As I was marched along with a sack over my head, the surrounding noise went from empty hallways, to crowds, to deafening music. I was being jostled from all directions, and it took me a moment to realize that the men who had been leading me along were gone. I removed the sack to find myself in a cavernous ballroom, filled with hundreds upon hundreds of dancers.

I *tried* to find a way out of there, honestly, I did. But a group of drunken dignitaries spun toward me with such violence that I wondered if, after surviving the Reds and the Purples, *these* were actually my assassins.

They spun in circles, and I was buffeted between a set of flushed, laughing faces. I burst out of the circle of faces toward what turned out to be the dead center of the dance floor.

No great lover has brushed so many crinolines as I did while caught in that ballroom and knowing no dances. A jumpy, brass-heavy music pounded from a great dais so far at the end of the room, it seemed miles away, even if the instruments sounded as though they were inside my ears. The guests' dances became more and more elaborate around me: each time I thought I had an idea of which step would come next, they did something else.

And so, I, certainly not dancing and clearly not a guest, was whirled through the crowd as I tried, in vain, to not bump into *everybody*.

I looked to the orchestra to orient myself, trying to keep its location in mind as I was battered about. Sweat streamed down my forehead, and I turned to see a second dais with a *second* orchestra. I soon lost track of which one I had been using to find my way, and I could see no doors. I felt more lost in this crowd than in a vast, barren steppe, as though I'd wander through these dancers forever. I'm not proud of it, but I *hated* their happiness so much.

I saw a glimpse of yellow through the crowd and stumbled toward it. A Prince's guard stood at the base of a set of stairs that went I knew not where. He was watching me, confused. I had never been so happy to see one of those uniforms.

I twisted between a pair of dancers who were trying very hard to look like they weren't groping each other. Past them, I recognized the Yellow from the Masovskan forest, and the top of our carriage where he had ridden. He said something to me, and I shook my head and pointed to my ears. He motioned me toward the staircase, and though it seemed a request, not an order, I followed.

"Enjoying the royal hospitality?" asked the Yellow, once we were far up enough that some of the din had softened. I felt strangely relieved in the presence of a man I'd seen daily during the last week. Even though he was one of my jailers, he was familiar to me by now.

"Better than I did yours," I said nonetheless.

"I hope you know I was only—"

"Following orders, yes. I know the feeling."

At the top of the stairs was a catwalk cut from the walls' rotrock, from which we could watch the guests conduct their elaborate dances.

The Yellow put out his hand to grasp mine in a greeting that super-seded chivalry and hand-kissing, because I wore a uniform the mirror image of his. After we shook, he saluted and I, a moment later, did a poor imitation.

"Sharpshooter Behrens," he said, smiling. "I shot the man bearing down upon you back in the Masovskan forest. The night we picked you up."

I took a deep, long breath, and then said, "Thank you. A moving man in the dead of night must have been a difficult shot."

The compliment clearly tickled him. "Only doing my duty. Shooting that man was easier than huddling behind a railing against Masovskan winds."

Behrens' given name, small, pointed beard, and accent all spoke to a lifetime in Rotfelsen, but his brown skin and tight curls suggested a family of mid-to-north Skydašian extraction. He may well not have even spoken Skydašiavos, but I suspected his insular Rotfelsenisch fellows still called him "the Skydašian," or worse. Perhaps behind his back.

"I've had quite the time tonight, so far," I said. "First almost killed by Reds, then roughed up by Purples."

"Ah, sorry to hear that. If I'd seen any of it . . ." He mimed shoot-ing his harquebus. "Sharpshooters don't generally duel, of course. So I'm free to assist Master Lenz while the others puncture duelists out-side." His actual harquebus was leaned haphazardly against a far wall, although he was also wearing a sword.

I considered telling him about the exact ruse I'd used to get away from the Reds, but decided I'd best keep my capacity for deceit to myself.

"Is it true that women can't be sharpshooters?" I asked instead. "I heard such a thing earlier tonight."

Behrens looked a little sheepish as he replied. "Well, yes. Back when our harquebusiers were first formed, guns of any sort were still in short supply here: sold only by shifty Loashti merchants to unsavory types on our side of the border. My forebears decided to pretend their scarcity was a strength, and so constructed rituals and mysteries: sharp-shooters in each of Rotfelsen's armies became rather silly, but intense, 'brotherhoods.'"

"You don't sound like you much agree with it."

He shrugged. "Maybe not, but I would lay my life down for my 'brothers' just the same. You know how it is."

I did not.

"Whether or not *I* agree with it," he continued, "the Yellows, Reds, and Purples only began accepting women into their ranks out of necessity. The Greens were snapping up most of the best fighting men. Some think they still are." He grinned and winked. "But we'll show them."

"Will we?" I asked. "I'm rather new to all this soldierly infighting. Are there . . . rules to it?"

"Sure!" he laughed. "Duels must be fought in certain places, violence must not touch the nobles—"

"But they watch it intently."

"Well, yes! But it's self-policing. If a noble is threatened, the guards involved are fair game."

"Or if the Reds *pretend* one is threatened?"

"Sure, of course. And a duel cannot be backed away from—"

"Unless you're a sharpshooter. Or don't care much for honor, like Lenz. Or a woman."

"Naturally, naturally." He screwed his lips to the side in thought. "Violence is, of course, forbidden between two soldiers of the same army."

"And when the King's Reds and the Queen's Reds are angry at each other?"

"Well, they do fight, yes."

"Does every rule have exceptions?"

"There are always extenuating circumstances, and sometimes one army changes its rules, and the others don't know immediately . . ."

"So no one knows the rules of engagement."

He smiled and shrugged.

This whole kingdom slept while its soldiers drove it into the ground.

"And what's a sharpshooter doing up here?" I asked. "Picking off Reds mid-dance?"

"Just keeping an eye open." He made a show of tapping underneath his right eye.

"So you must know who all these nobles are."

He laughed and scratched the back of his head, pushing his hat forward. "Here and there, one or two. I've spent the season closer to them than if I'd been on a Masovskan hill, but only just."

Even on the catwalk, which seemed reserved for guards and amo-
rous couples, an attendant with a trough of food passed us. He carried
little towers of crushed green ice, each on its own individual plate and
encrusted with pieces of peach, embedded like cannonballs that had
crashed into a fortress and remained lodged in its walls. Now this quieter luxury, away from the crowds but still attended to, appealed to me.
I may have looked too eager when I grabbed up a little tower for myself.

"What?" I asked Behrens, through a full mouth, as the attendant
padded away.

"Has Lenz been starving you?" He frowned.

"I wanted to try the Master of Fruit's work," I replied. "He's my
neighbor."

I admit it all only tasted like sugar and water, to me.

As I chewed through the ice, I enjoyed watching the drunk, dancing
fools below. I pointed to one, a woman who was tall and stately, and
seemed as popular as Selvosch. The current dance involved switching
partners regularly, almost constantly, but the partners never touched,
nor did anything suggestive. This woman was in high demand, with
dancers sometimes tripping over one another to be her next partner.
They did not even seem to speak to her when dancing—too busy con-
centrating on the strange steps.

"Who?" asked Behrens. The whole group kept twirling and shifting
away from where I pointed. At that moment, they were all doing some
sort of crab walk.

I managed to swallow my ice. "The tall, popular one," I said. "With
the burgundy dress, and the, er . . . prow."

"Ah? Ah! Edeltraud von Edeltraud, Mistress of the Rotfelsen Coin."

Now this name I remembered from reading Lenz's books on my
ride to Rotfelsen. I recalled that she had a lot of suitors, but had seen no
information on what the "Mistress of the Coin" actually did.

"That sounds cushy," I replied. "Why is she so nervous?"

Behrens crinkled his nose. "Is she?"

She most certainly was. Even from the catwalk I could see that her
many dance partners did nothing to make her happy—as clear as if she
screamed, "Leave me alone!" with each pass, each kick, each extend of
the tongue. Edeltraud von Edeltraud's stress was clear from her clipped
movements, her darting eyes, and the red marks she left on the bare
arms of female partners with whom she spun.

"And here I thought you were supposed to have good eyes," I needled.

"Well, now . . ." Behrens laughed.

"Is mastering the coin particularly stressful?"

Behrens thought this over. "I suppose it's a lot like being on guard duty, which is to say, long periods of inaction, during which one must be alert. In case it's ended by emergency."

"What sort of emergency?"

"Would you like to know Rotfelsen's most wasteful law?" Behrens smiled and leaned close, as though with a great secret.

I slipped into a playful smile. "Oh, yes."

"You see, whenever Rotfelsen's ruling monarch dies"—he paused and put out his left hand in a sign of warding off evil—"be it the will of the gods that such not happen in my lifetime—the Mistress, or Master, of the Coin must travel throughout Rotfelsen, with workers, to re-stamp *every single gold, silver, or copper mark in the kingdom* with the new monarch's face."

"Terrifying."

"They are given a year: a single mourning period. Bad luck to use money with a dead king on it, which, of course, does not stop many paranoid citizens from assuming the government is coming for their savings, and refusing to turn over even copper marks. Not unfairly: it's common to receive the wrong number of re-stamped coins. Hers is a job that many clamor for when the king is young and healthy, but if the position is left vacant in the reign of an old, wizened king . . ."

"They must catch officials with a net."

"Just so. Used to be that Masters of the Coin would lose their heads if the turnover didn't finish in time, because the wrong coinage could anger the gods. Nowadays, they would simply become an outcast and never again have an appointment."

So it was not everyday stresses of the job weighing on Madam Edeltraud, what with a young king. Perhaps Edeltraud, along with the distasteful Court Philosopher, was one of Selvosch's conspirators, and therefore expected the King to be replaced soon. Imagining the effort and resources involved to do this for an entirely new government, and the anger it could stoke from the people, put new possibilities in my head for what exactly would *happen* in just two and a half months at the Council of Barbarians.

I felt a numb fear at the violent end of the Tetrarchia, and a wave of excitement as convincing half-truths began to form in my head. This would merit a prophecy.

Edeltraud von Edeltraud finished dancing and started toward a side door.

"I wonder why she's so nervous," I said. "I'm going to follow her."

Behrens nodded approval.

I did not know how much he was in Lenz and the Prince's confidence, but as I started down the stairs, I hissed, "Tell Lenz that Vorosknecht is working with Selvosch!"

I did not see Behrens' reaction. I got down into the thick of the dancing once more, and began to push my way toward where Edeltraud had gone.

EDELTRAUD VON EDELTRAUD

I followed Edeltraud von Edeltraud into a small room with padded walls. She stopped and leaned against a wall, catching her breath after all that dancing, while I wandered the room picking up snatches of conversation and trying to look normal. Thankfully, it was the time of night that saw everyone too drunk to modulate their voices.

"—when the Council of Barbarians—"

"—I'll march right up to that arrogant goose and—"

"—is it true one of those southern armies got *inside the stone*, before High General Dreher repelled them?"

I stopped for a moment, to listen to that last one. If this unnamed drunkard at a party was telling the truth (and who could ever doubt *that*), if the Bandit States had amassed a force that punctured the rock even a bit, and if the High General was indeed covering it up, then something was *very* wrong. Unsubstantiated though it was, this was one more possibility for the Tetrarchia's demise. And, if the Bandit States united and invaded, running south with my family was right out.

"The High General insists it's untrue, of course," the drunk continued, "but surely *you . . .*"

"I'm sure I wouldn't know," someone replied.

I peeked around the corner and saw a drunk noble talking to a squat, pale, muscular woman who wore wool trousers and what looked to be the sort of frilled shirt some noblemen would wear, but cut for her figure from a scratchy peasant's linen. She held a long wool coat over her back and the shirt's sleeves were rolled up. I realized I had seen her on the stairs earlier in the evening.

"Well, but you're from Rituo, our only friends to the south," said the noble, dipping his head.

So she was a guest from our sometimes, sort of, kind of ally in the Bandit States.

"I'm sure"—she yawned, lifting her hand to her mouth and purposefully flexing her arms as she did so—"I wouldn't know." I wanted to introduce her to young Martin-Frederick Reinhold-Bosch, who so loved "martial" women.

"They say," the drunk noble stage-whispered, "there's a great Warrior Queen uniting your neighbors! And that she has sword arm thick as a tree and a—"

"I haven't the faintest," said the southern guest. She winked.

Was she here gathering information for a united invasion? Or working with Rotfelsen to stop it? Or was she simply a merchant, using her foreign status to toy with paranoid locals?

Whoever this woman was, Edeltraud von Edeltraud seemed to have her strength back, and I watched her leave the room. I counted to twenty before following her, and found myself in an annex with crystal walls and eight different doors. The Mistress of the Coin was no longer visible—in fact, there was no one else there, somehow.

A bit mystified by this place, I made a circuit around the empty crystal room, opening each door and looking down each hallway. These halls were all dimly lit, with vague silhouettes I could not make out, each looking nothing like the woman I was following. Thankfully, down the seventh hallway, I once more saw the recognizable shape of Edeltraud von Edeltraud.

I strode as naturally as possible into this hallway. Edeltraud von Edeltraud seemed to be looking for someone, but in the way of a drunk who wishes to seem sober and act as though they certainly are not lost. She didn't ask anyone anything, only looked anxious and purposeful.

Could this confused woman be part of a plot to destroy Rotfelsen from within? Or would the army rivalries spill into war? Or would the Bandit States invade? Why did I assume Papa's prophecy had anything to do with Rotfelsen in the first place? Possibly just because that's where I was. Certainly, most people in the Tetrarchia expected our end to come by way of Loasht, sooner or later.

I followed her into a room filled with flowers, organized in terraced troughs along the interior wall. There was also a vine in the center that writhed as though it were trying to escape the palace: at least this vine understood me. The far wall was one huge window, and the two walls that angled away from it were half bay windows in themselves. In the daytime, this room must have protruded right out into the sunlight. Besides the lamps, an eerie blue glow lit the flowers for guests to see—had I not spent so long reading *Bohdan's Botanicals*, I would not have known that this was because the top row was iridescent Quru moonblossoms. Edeltraud von Edeltraud glanced about this room, bit her lower lip, and left through another door a minute later. She paused only to take a dessert from the table by the door. It was sugar melted into flower shapes. I did not see any fruit in it, so I didn't take one.

After this, Edeltraud von Edeltraud disappeared down a long hallway. I started after her, but realized I was so close I could hear the shifting of her skirts. I stopped to wait, and prayed there wouldn't be too many doors for her to disappear through, this time.

Once a minute had passed, I continued toward where I *hoped* Edeltraud had gone. The hallway was dark and constantly twisting. I walked a long time before there were any doors. I still don't understand where in the palace it all fit: it must have writhed its way around many rooms, gradually traversing floors, and curving while seeming to go straight. After my audience with Vorosknecht, I felt that there were Purples around every corner. The hall did, at some of its turns, have alcoves: sometimes from these came giggles, running water, or low, seemingly inhuman, growls.

Then I came to a row of open doorways, and through them it appeared the party continued, even though the hallway had been nearly desolate. I glanced through each door I passed, as I hoped a guard on duty would do. I saw many soldiers in them, but not a single Yellow.

Some rooms that I passed: a maroon-lit room in which an ochre substance was being crushed into brandy and drunk by laughing guests; a chamber planted with short trees in which a round merchant stood on a table to regale bored nobles who thought him less than dirt; a nearly dark room in which a very intimate private dance was taking place between a number of couples, but none of them had my (self-appointed) charge's silhouette; a cave, essentially, in which a woman scantily clad as a boar chased a man dressed as a bird wearing a sorcerer's cap; and a series of rooms in which various games of cards, tiles, sticks, balls, and terrains were being played by screaming and laughing guests, between walls that matched the color of each game's primary component.

This was the top of Rotfelsenisch society, nobles and rich merchants who held the purse-, shoe-, and bodice-strings of the rock-bound kingdom. These were the people giggling like children as disaster loomed, whether from within or without. They were enjoying luxuries I'd never have imagined, while I was living in a *house* for the first time in my life, and while poorer Rots down in the depths drank brown cave water. I did not see Edeltraud von Edeltraud, nor did I see King Gerhold VIII. I felt sick.

The hallway ended abruptly at a chamber of natural rotrock, with a fountain in the middle whose water came from . . . somewhere.

In the corner, a crowd gathered around two noblemen who were being fanned. One had a bloody nose, the other blood trickling into his eyes. They were grumpy, but the cause of the fight seemed forgotten. Those surrounding them were attempting to talk them either into or out of an ensuing duel. I looked about the room: low mutters twisted amongst towers of fruit and meat that blocked out half the room, a liveried boy of about twelve stood in the center singing softly, and a magician was performing sleight-of-hand silently with minimal flourish. I did not see the Mistress of the Coin.

I stepped around a spire of pork (with a giant, wild boar's head on top, its fan-shaped ears brushing the ceiling) and slunk over to the window for air. Far below, in the courtyard, I saw small groups of soldiers posturing and fighting each other: tiny drunken figures lunging awkwardly, blades glinting. Greens against Purples, Yellows against Purples, Reds against Reds.

I felt a pang of protectiveness toward the Yellows, whom I did not know and probably would not like. Curse the power of a uniform.

I was about to turn back from boyish duels and the fresh night air, in order to look once more for Edeltraud von Edeltraud, when I heard Masovskani mutterings.

Masovskani is, I think, a beautiful language, which is easy to pick out even if you cannot catch the meaning, as it seems that every word has at least one "sh" or "tz" sound in it. So I heard the noises but not the words, creeping around the great tower of pork. I moved toward the sound, and the words became clearer.

"But if the King . . ." muttered a voice in halting Masovskani.

"What do I care for the King?" asked a second voice.

Something unintelligible.

"But if we are not careful—"

"The hammer will fall on him whether or not—"

"'The hammer'?" laughed a third voice, which sounded familiar. "So dramatic."

"Dramatic or not," was the reply, "we must be ready—"

"Never marry a man with a distinctive face!" a woman near me piped up *very* loudly. It was all I could do to not cough pointedly.

"Whyever not?" asked her companion. "I like the look of a face with some *character!*"

"If you marry a man with a distinctive *face*," the first replied with the unerring tone of one who gives advice because they have two years of experience on the other, "he will know immediately that the baby is not his. And even if he is too in love to see it, everyone else will, I assure you."

"But—!"

"And don't you take a distinctive lover either!" she added.

These two women had finished walking past me, but the damage was done. I finished circling the great spire of pork, and hoped the Masovskani speakers would have more to say.

Behind the meat was one last cluster of nobles, taking food from a small kitchen alcove with a serving window. There was also a lute-player relaxing on a divan, many rich men making verbal contracts that surely were *completely binding*, and a small curtain in the corner behind which some kind of rutting was likely taking place. Edeltraud von Edeltraud was there, speaking to two Masovskans, a man and a woman. They were dressed in almost-Rotfelsenisch clothing, but with puffy fur accents, and the woman, whose elegantly pinched face I could see, had the sallow skin and deep-set eyes of Masovska.

Two men entered the room, with a large group of Reds, and a smaller contingent of Yellows, but they were mostly blocked from my view by the pork. Everyone else in the room made a show of not reacting to them. Regrettably, one of these Yellows saw me and limped over.

"Well, hello!" laughed Lenz. "So nice to see you again, Kalyna Aljosanovna." He nodded at the lute-player, who began to play, masking our words. The music also masked the Masovskans' conversation, unfortunately.

"Hello," I said, looking at Edeltraud von Edeltraud. "Why aren't those Reds and Yellows fighting?"

"This is a Red room," he replied. "The *King's* Reds, mostly. A Purple would be barred outright, a Green would be 'allowed' in, but the guests would quickly disperse. Yellows are permitted, if they behave, because they serve the Prince."

Lenz said this in Masovskani; I quickly switched to Cölluknit.

"It's good Purples can't come in here," I said, "seeing as how Vorosknecht kidnapped me not long ago."

"Is that so?" Lenz took the hint and also dropped into Cölluknit. "What for?"

"Wait, is the Prince here?" I asked.

Lenz nodded toward the two men who had recently entered, surrounded by Reds and Yellows: they had moved more fully into my view, and I saw that one of them was our own Prince Friedhelm. The other one was unremarkable—Lenz told me that he was the King.

If inbreeding had rendered Prince Friedhelm's face particularly strange, it must have been because all those features had waited for him in the Queen Mother's womb, after sliding completely off of King Gerhold's smooth personage. The King was bland and characterless, a face that could be forgotten moments after being seen. If the Prince radiated power and a kind of sick charm, only the rounded gold lumps on a large necklace told anyone of the King's import. And thus, I beheld King Gerhold VIII.

"That's it?" I muttered.

"Why, he's positively beaming today," replied Lenz. "What did Vorosknecht want?"

"He wanted me to know he doesn't like me. And that he's working with Selvosch."

"Wait, he—"

"But right now," I interrupted, "I am *trying* to hear what the Mistress of the Coin is saying to those Masovskans. To make sense of a vision."

"Ah." Lenz snapped again at the lute-player, whose tune slowed and softened. "Then let us walk the room," he whispered, "and make conversation."

We began to walk toward Edeltraud von Edeltraud. For a moment, her companions were blocked from my view by a pair of rangy men in gold buttons making plans for a marriage of children.

"I suppose you know your Yellows are fighting outside?" I said to Lenz.

"They aren't *my* Yellows, and of course they are."

We curved around the rangy nobles, and I got a good look at the Masovskan man. It was Klemens Gustavus, the tyrant of Gniezto whose mercenaries I had fought Down Valley Way, when he tried to dispossess his eight-toed cousin. He looked awfully smug.

YOUR LOVELY ROCK

The other woman with Klemens Gustavus, I realized, shared many of his features. She must have been Bozena, the only daughter of old Gustaw Close-Hand.

"What?" whispered Lenz. "What is it? Do you see something?"

"I have seen them, in my visions, and I . . ." I blinked many times, for effect. "I see more now . . ." My eyes were closed.

I already suspected Lenz hadn't sent anyone into the court-room that day in Gniezto, and so I gambled that he didn't know the Gustavuses.

"Those are changing bank magnates from Masovska," I said. "Their names are Klemens and Bozena . . . something. They have a third sibling as well. Brother or sister I cannot yet see."

"And what of them?" he asked.

It occurred to me that the Mistress of the Coin would have a great deal to discuss with the owners of the Tetrarchia's largest changing banks, and that Edeltraud von Edeltraud's nervousness may have been due to simple economics. Perhaps there was nothing sinister here. Then I saw the uncaring smirk on Klemens' face and remembered the mercenaries in the forest on their way to Eight-Toed Gustaw from Down Valley Way. I remembered being nearly killed.

"They plan to kill the King," I said.

Lenz straightened suddenly, started to reach for his sword, then stopped himself. "Here? Now?"

I put two fingers to my forehead and "thought" very hard.

"Tonight. I see it. Very soon."

"I must tell the Prince," hissed Lenz. His belief in me was intoxicating.

My hope, at this point, was that when Edeltraud von Edeltraud and the Gustavus brats were put away, and there was no attempt on the

King, I could claim that I had stopped it with my prophecy. Of course, Selvosch had intimated to the Prince that *something* would happen to-night, but if it did, I could just claim that arresting these three hadn't been enough. If I was lucky, Edeltraud and the Gustavuses would act very close-lipped and suspicious because they were actually up to some good old economic chicanery together. If I was *very* lucky, they would actually be part of a plot. Whatever the case, I could probably keep sus-picions going until I was able to escape.

Unfortunately, Edeltraud von Edeltraud and the Gustavus brats seemed to have finished their deliberations. Lenz and I spoke nonsense to appear as if we were not listening.

"I'm afraid I must retire back to Turmenbach," Klemens yawned.

"We look forward," Bozena began, loudly, in Rotfelsenisch for all to hear, "to the rest of our visit to your lovely rock."

Klemens looked bored.

"Don't we, *brother*?" she growled.

"Oh yes," he said in stubborn Masovskani. He began to look idly around the room. "After all, it is so very . . . you know . . . here it is just so . . . so . . . stone."

Bozena shrugged and smiled at Edeltraud von Edeltraud. "The boys," she said in Rotfelsenisch, "will always be the boys."

Klemens was not listening. He had made a show of looking around the room, until he saw me. His eyes narrowed.

Lenz's back was to the conspirators, and I fought to keep from doing anything so damning (and pathetic) as hiding behind him. Kle-mens had seen me, and either he recognized me, could not remember where he had seen me before, or found me strange looking. I told my-self I appeared very different in my uniform, which was true, and that Klemens had been too disdainful in court to notice his audience, which was likely.

But he had certainly noticed Ramunas.

I forced myself to look back at Lenz. "Edeltraud is preparing to leave," I said in Cölluknit. "I will—"

"You stay with the twins. Warn the Prince."

"They aren't twins."

"Stay with them." Even in Cölluknit, he made sure to avoid any word for Masovskans. "You have followed her enough; she may notice. I'll go."

I didn't tell him I was worried Klemens had recognized me. It would mean admitting the Gift was not how I had learned of the brats, and I would negate a beautiful chance to extend my myth. A chance that had fallen into my lap.

I nodded. Lenz turned as though getting ready to leave, and rubbed his bad leg. Klemens whispered to his sister. Edeltraud von Edeltraud began to bustle toward the door. Was it my imagination, or was she glancing toward the King and the Prince? But then, who wouldn't?

Lenz disappeared through the doorway, and I backed toward a wall, hoping I would be out of Klemens' view. Then everything fell apart.

SMOKE

I am still not entirely sure what happened next. There are a few possibilities, although I suppose specifics hardly matter. After a few minutes of watching the Gustavus brats make some other goodbyes around the room, brown smoke streaked with blue began to billow out of the little kitchen.

Guests wondered at a parlor trick, laughed at what must have been the accident of a clumsy cook, and then became uneasy when the smoke continued to move toward them.

A strapping young man, finding the thousandth way to prove his manhood that day, was theatrically not bothered by the smoke, and let it surround him while others backed away. Then he spun and dropped to the floor in a fit of coughing. He stopped moving. Someone screamed. The Reds and Yellows all began to yell at once.

Everyone flattened against the wall, glasses broke, the lute stopped. One woman threw herself against the window so hard I thought she was going for the short way out. She hovered there instead, sucking in fresh air.

Soon the smoke overtook us all. I could not see whether the brave young man was dead or unconscious. I heard coughing, moaning, and pleading all around me. At the far end from the kitchen, near the window, the smoke was not quite so thick, and I could see outlines of the people around me. I didn't see Bozena and Klemens.

I think I vomited? I am not sure. I know I suddenly tasted Tural's peaches, but the flavor was corrupted, bitter, and twisted into something wicked. My insides burnt and I retched, and my joints seized up.

"You used too much!" someone said in Rotfelsenisch.

"Just hurry!" hissed another.

If there was more, I didn't hear it over my own coughing.

I turned to the window, and the woman who had been hogging it was gone, although I may have tripped over her. I threw myself against the sill and took a deep breath of night air. The dueling guards below did not seem to know anything was happening. They would learn soon enough, as I definitely vomited this time.

I heard a thump, footsteps, voices that were not hindered by coughing. I heard a sword leave its scabbard.

I looked back and saw nothing but smoke. Tasted it again as well.

A Noxious Mixture

The squirming Skydašian skrogdti plant, when cut, dried, and combined in an alchemical pot with burning jadestones and Lo-ashti fogwort, which only grows in the warmest of climes and takes its "fog" moniker ("ukungukuru" in Loasht) from the blue sediment that it discharges in every direction, converting the most brutal desert scene to something like a burning evening lost at the Cold Sea—creates a thick soup of smoke that is best characterized by its deep brown color, similar to the bark of a healthy pine tree, strung with streamers of sky blue. This issue, which secret societies of criminal eveningmen put to dastardly use and colloquially dub "pukevapor," creates the most unkind reaction in the humors, and any who breathe it in eventually cough, cry, and vomit until they have coughed themselves into a deeply painful unconsciousness. Many times, Adomas the Scoundrel has made use of it in order to steal the work of others.

In order to inhale this noxious mixture without such a reaction, one need only treat a wet rag with . . .

Safe or Missing

At the time, I did not stop to think where this quotation had come from, but of course it was a bit of *Bohdan's Botanicals* that had wound its way into my brain.

So, I knew that this smoke alone would not kill me, only cause extreme pain and unconsciousness, which is nowhere near as easy to turn and face as armchair swashbucklers would have you believe. Pain, vomiting, and unconsciousness are best avoided even when there isn't obscured violence going on in the midst of it, which there was. I heard, amongst the coughing, more struggle, the clang of swords, and the dull cutting of flesh.

The King was in this room, and the smoke must have been in aid of an assassination. I should have stayed by the window, but my mind kept screaming: *Assassination. King. Collapse. Gustavuses. I want to see Papa.*

In that moment, it made complete sense to me that I would have to do my—or Lenz's—job if I ever wanted to see Papa again.

The result of all this frantic thinking was that I leapt into the smoke, waving my arms. I was trying to stop someone from doing something.

I remember brown and blue, then darkness as I closed my tearing eyes. I couldn't breathe, someone hit me, a blade grazed my side, my knuckles creaked as the blade's owner got punched in the head. The assassins, whom I fancied to be the Gustavuses' hirelings, could breathe where I could not, but we were all just as blind.

More flailing, more hitting, more sounds of stabbing, something was sideways, all was dark, and then I sat up in a carriage. The smoke was back in the palace, many floors above me, and there was a clicking in my ears.

"The Prince is shaken up, but safe," said Lenz, pushing a blanket under my chin. My uniform was torn, and I was cut in more places than I remembered, but lightly. He looked worried.

"The King?" I coughed.

"Safe. Or missing."

I sat up, pushing the blanket off me. "What does that mean?"

Lenz sighed. "There was some sort of attack in a room containing the King, the Prince, some Reds, and some Yellows. All of the Yellows who were in the room are dead: run through." He raised an eyebrow. "Except us. The few surviving Reds insist the King was taken to safety, but that could be a lie. Either as part of a plot of the Queen's, some other plot that has Reds in on it, or a flailing attempt to cover their own incompetence."

"And there were the Masovskan merchants, too," I grunted.

Lenz nodded. "The official story: a fire in the kitchen, the King fell ill, and was whisked away to his rooms, while the Yellows died of smoke. We don't know the real story yet."

I slumped back down against the seat, numb. The carriage rolled between noble estates toward the servant houses. The night seemed quiet, peaceful. I groaned and twisted to look out the window. The Sunset Palace was as dark as it got (not very dark), and there was a wreath of smoke still twisting out one window and over the moon.

"Next time," I said, eyes watering, "you send me in *armed*."

Lenz nodded as if to say he would consider it.

"You're cut," he said.

"Because I tried to stop them." I coughed. "A fool idea. I hope this doesn't make me too *involved* in what's going on," I added. "You know that if I'm too close to what's happening, I will not see it anymore."

Always hedging my bets; always preparing for future lies.

Lenz didn't reply. I sat in the carriage, wondering if the King had indeed been abducted, or killed. Wondering if I'd just witnessed the start of the end of the Tetrarchia.

THE AFTER PARTY

In the carriage, through the palace grounds, and entering the servant house, I blinked in and out of consciousness. I felt as though I simply appeared at a dinner table on the third floor, like a fruit conjured into Tural's head. In fact, Tural was sitting across from me when I realized where I was. He looked worried.

"Have you wakened to the world?" he asked in Cöllüknit.

Lenz, who was standing and leaning over me, putting his weight on the back of my chair, did a very good job of looking as though he did not understand Tural's words. The knowledge that he certainly did reminded me not to confide in *anybody*.

Tural held out a cup of something. I took it and lifted the cup to my lips, only to smell acrid alcohol, and put it back down. I was shivering. I noticed I had been rudimentarily bandaged.

"Too good for Skydašian pear brandy, are you?" said Tural, in Rotfelsenisch. I think he was being playful, but it was hard to tell.

"I told you, she doesn't drink," said Lenz. His voice thudded somewhere too deep in my head. I wished for him to back away. I felt as though I were chained to him.

"Yes, yes, right," said Tural.

Skydašian pear brandy sounded, to my inexperience, like a quality liquor, rather than what would be hauled out for medical reasons. I blinked until the world around Tural bled back into place. That was when I saw that the table was full.

The room was dark, lit only by the warm glow of candelabras at each end and a large window coaxing in moonlight. Jördis the Chief Ethicist was there, her cheeks deeply rosy, and nothing in her face showing that she had been present during Vorosknecht's confrontation. They had all been drinking, and the table was strewn with plates of half-eaten Winter Ball leftovers: mostly dried fruit.

"What? Why?" I muttered.

"I was helping you upstairs after the maids patched you up," said Lenz, a little surprised I didn't remember, "and when we passed the party, Tural offered a drink, hoping it might help you come to yourself. You said—"

"No, no, no. Why . . . party?" I gurgled. I was immediately embarrassed and wanted to hide my face.

"Well—" began a stout bald man next to Jördis.

"Because?" Tural stammered.

"Why not?" said a small woman at the other end of the table.

Jördis smiled and leaned over the table toward me. She jostled a pile of raisins on the way, but didn't notice. She was so chipper and, well, normal, that I wondered if my audience with Vorosknecht had been a dream.

"Because the Winter Ball is over," she said, "and we can relax. No couriers with sudden moral quandaries, no emergency plum shortage, no night soil *situation*."

"And what's more," cried Tural, "leftovers!" He flourished toward the tabletop.

"Yes, yes," said the stout bald man, whose back was perfectly straight even while sitting. "Does anyone mind introducing us?"

I did not have the energy, but I did not need it. Many chimed in, even though Tural and Jördis were the only two I had met before: I was a soldier, a spy, a consultant, a hero, a researcher—someone even suggested I was an assassin. Not in such words, of course. Jördis did not give me away for a soothsayer.

"Charmed, Kalyna Aljosanovna," said the bald man, who looked around thirty years. He stood and leaned forward, to lightly reach across the table and take my hand, which he lifted as though to kiss, but did not. He was Rotfelsenisch to the core, but his pronunciation of my

Masovskan name was flawless. "And since no one has introduced *me*"—
he cast a side eye at Jördis, who just laughed—"I am Vondel, Tenth
Butler to High General Dreher."

"I thought Dreher didn't do parties," I said.

Vondel nodded solemnly. "Correct. Neither does he keep much
exciting food in his household. So, thank you all, for sharing your leftovers. I'm sorry to have missed the ball."

"No, you aren't," said Jördis.

Vondel allowed himself the barest, most ethereal, whisp of a memory of a laugh.

I nodded and tried to smile, and he was very good at pretending as
though I was being gracious while he sat back down. Overwhelmed as
I was in that moment, I made sure to remember this man—a butler to
the High General could be a useful font of information, even if he was
only the tenth one. (How many butlers did the General have?)

After a moment's silence, I gulped. "Please, all, continue what you
were doing before I arrived. I need to let the world become real again."

Jördis laughed. "So you do not drink, but what *did* you do?"

I kept my weary, ingratiating smile, but stared directly into her eyes.
"Very little. But I had some uncomfortable audiences."

She smiled back. "I can only imagine."

"Kalyna," said Lenz, "was caught in the kitchen accident." He
squeezed my shoulder hard. "It vacated the King's upper floors."

"Oh yes," said Vondel. "It was something quite noxious, wasn't it?"

"Yes. Something," said Tural. He seemed quite unconvinced that it
had been a kitchen accident.

They all talked for some time after that. Maybe it was twenty minutes or two hours, I don't know. I learned that supposedly every piece
of the Winter Ball had almost not worked, that numerous last-minute
fixes, and amazing feats of strength and ingenuity, were responsible for
each nonpoisonous drink, each ice sculpture that did not impale, every
pair of rivals who somehow did not run into each other, each morsel of
food that tasted right, and every window that someone did not tumble
out of. These, at the table with me, were the people who had made the
night's festivities possible, to hear them tell it. Of course, to hear *them*
tell it, their own underlings were all bunglers and idiots. I suspect a different story was being told in buildings yet farther from the palace, or
by exhausted workers descending back into Turmenbach.

For what it's worth, Tural—whom I had decided was my favorite—was not so dismissive of his subordinates, and Jördis—who was becoming my least favorite—did not seem to have any. Apparently, her job at the Winter Ball had been to prepare the Court Philosopher himself for any ethical questions posed by high-ranking nobility in light conversation. I wondered what her ethics said of covering my head with a sack and throwing me into his study.

The night's conversation ambled on. Someone asked where I was from, of course, and everyone seemed interested in the answer. ("Everywhere.") Eventually, thankfully, they got off the subject and back to the ball. The Master of Pillowcases was surprised at how few couples had used beds without permission; the Mistress of Periodicals was frustrated by dog-eared copies that had clearly not been read, only held open by those who wished to look engaged; the Woodwind Leader was pleased with everything; and the Lavatory Captain had to put up with my giggling, apologizing, and giggling some more. He graciously told me he was used to the reaction, and I was just happy for anything that kept me from worrying about the King. These were my new neighbors, whose work touched royalty in important ways that went unnoticed—and they liked it that way. Vondel was not, it turned out, one of my neighbors: he lived in a different servant house, but was friends with Jördis.

The laughter came easily, the leftover brandies and vodkas and ales flowed contentedly, and the shutter was eventually pulled down, only to rattle with cold winds, of which we felt the fingertips. More than once, Lenz suggested I get some sleep, and each time I surprised both of us by deciding to stay a little longer, and eating more fruits and nuts and pretzels. My body ached, and I felt exhausted, but not at all sleepy, and I found myself fascinated by the insights of the Master of Fruit on toilets, or the Lavatory Captain on ethics, or the Chief Ethicist on pillowcases, or . . .

Many toasts were drunk, and only the most perfunctory were to the King, Prince, High General, or Court Philosopher. I winced slightly at the mention of the King, and put him from my mind. There was a loud stamping and "Hear! Hear!" when we toasted Biruté, the Skydašian-born queen of Rotfelsen to whom many of the Reds were loyal. She certainly seemed popular. Perhaps Rotfelsenisch suspicion of one's neighbors and political enemies can overcome even Rotfelsenisch insularity. Or, perhaps, she was pretty and had a personality. (Both true, I would learn.)

Quite a few toasts later, we were simply raising our cups to "a job well done." My companions became so friendly and their pride so strong, and I so beaten down, but also comfortable, that I joined in on the third "job well done" and downed my pear brandy.

It burned and I coughed, which I had done *quite enough of that night*. I readied myself to be laughed at for such a reaction, but nobody cared. I waited for my brain to turn stupid, and nothing happened, except that I felt *warm*. Not just physically, in my fingers and toes, but in my . . . well, my feelings. It was nice, and I liked the people around me so much.

Then I caught myself thinking pleasantly about Lenz, and there was a cold snap in my chest. My face fell into something neutral.

"I'm going to bed."

Lenz reached to help me up. I ignored him.

"Vondel," I said, "if you please."

Always ready to do the proper thing, Vondel hooked my arm in his and walked me up to my room. He said good night, and by the time the door was closed, I was in bed. I got halfway through thinking, *I hope Papa will be*—and fell asleep.

WAKING

I woke up the next morning into what seemed a beautiful reality, in which I believed everything previous was the dream. Not just the Winter Ball, not just Lenz and Friedhelm and Vorosknecht, but the entire world as an imperfect place for unhappy people, *that* was the dream. I had simply spent a night in fitful sleep, wherein I had imagined war, starvation, rape, hatred, my father's illness, my grandmother's evil, my failure, Lenz's kidnapping, the Winter Ball's smoke, the King's disappearance, everything, and I had woken to the correct world, where all were happy, and things were as they should be.

Of course, then I woke fully and knew which world was real. I knew this because my jaw ached from grinding my teeth.

PART THREE

THROAT CUTTING IN AN ALLEY

Five days later, I learned to be wary of Lenz in a new way, when I saw him run his sword through a woman's throat, causing her axe to swing wide.

I was a few feet away, blinding a man in one eye. I am no slouch.

I realized then that the limping veteran, the spy who avoided combat and preferred dishonor to duels, was not so immobile as he let on. But I suppose I should explain why we were killing goons in an alley dusted with Rotfelsen's first snow of the season.

THE PRINCE'S BATHS

The very day after the Winter Ball, the Prince was, as I'm sure you can imagine, in a bit of a snit. Lenz looked almost as exhausted as I when he came to get me, and we were whisked back to the Prince's apartments. Specifically, to a small, hot, windowless room of tile, where Lenz handed a report he had written to a servant. We waited next to each other at a sort of soldier's rest, hands clasped behind us, facing a little round porthole door. Lenz began to sweat.

"This is a strange office," I said.

"Yes," Lenz replied.

The porthole door opened. Steam lurched out, and the Prince's voice echoed into our chamber, telling us to come in. We had to duck through the door.

Even after the ball, Prince Friedhelm having a series of private baths in his suites was a level of luxury that surprised me. This was not a tub next to a shitting hole, but a large marble chamber pocked with pools of different alchemically-enforced temperatures, rising steam, statues of nude figures (gods in the Ancients' stone, perhaps?), and a small army of attendants. There were no Yellows visible, and their uniforms would have been unbearably hot, but there were stands and statues and modesty screens that must have obscured doors hidden in the stone. I'm sure I could have been shot dead at a moment's notice.

Scattered throughout were small stations, often a table and stools, each with its own amenities. There was a food station, a liqueur station, a shaving station, a skin station, and an especially coy, hidden "relaxation" station. At the far wall, there was a huge, glorious opening that was blocked not just with a glass window, but two sheets of glass enclosing water. Between them, schools of small fish swam back and forth among lake plants, doing their best to avoid the larger fish also in residence. All the light in the baths came from this massive window, filtered through quivering water and the life swimming in it.

I felt a strange sadness for those poor fish, suspended in glass, who would be so confused if this whole place toppled around them, their glass shattered, and they fell out into the air before slamming into stone. Why I felt worse for them, in that moment, than anything else living in the Tetrarchia, I couldn't say. But then, maybe our country's end would simply be a massacre of human beings, and these fish would happily swim for whoever took over the Prince's baths next.

The Prince was sitting naked by a pool, being toweled dry by an attendant while he rubbed at his own shoulders with a piece of volcanic rock. Rippling shadows of fish flitted over his pasty skin, and he was shivering, so I supposed this was a cold pool he had just come out of.

"I still feel that smoke on me," he growled, to himself or his attendant. "And in me. It stinks of death, and it won't come off."

Lenz cleared his throat loudly.

"Ah, Lenz Felsknecht. Kalyna Aljosanovna." The Prince smiled with a friendliness betrayed by the split second in which he slammed down the volcanic rock onto his marble table. He stood up from his oak stool, and his attendant continued to towel him.

The urge, of course, was to stare at his nakedness. But I suspect he liked showing that even at his most vulnerable he had power—over life and death, over an army, over his attendants, over how comfortable or not we were—and so I gave him a cursory once-over, as I would have were he dressed, and then fixed my eyes on his clavicle. His heart didn't seem in it anyway.

"First of all," Prince Friedhelm continued, "thanks are in order. Kalyna, I believe you saved my life."

This was news to me, but I decided not to act surprised.

"Ah, how's that, Your Highness?" asked Lenz.

"She was right there in the fighting," the Prince explained, "when all the other Yellows in the room were dead. Yet I'm still here."

I nodded. "Your Highness, I only wish I had seen a vision of those attackers sooner, in order to save more lives."

Lenz looked unconvinced.

"However," the Prince continued, his smile fading quickly, even as he raised his arms so the attendant could towel off his sides, "I have not seen or heard a thing of my brother. The *Reds* say he was taken back to his rooms, but that can't be trusted."

"Your Highness," said Lenz, "let's not be hasty. Your brother may simply be resting after an ordeal."

"Or," replied the Prince, "the Queen's Reds have taken him somewhere. It may be time for the Twelfth Recourse."

"Your Highness," Lenz began, "I really think it's early for—"

"Well, I don't like it," interrupted the Prince. "People are starting to talk, and if he doesn't show his face soon, the talk may well concern putting me on the throne." He shivered at the thought, or at the cold. "It seems I did not do whatever it was Selvosch wanted in order to show that I was on his side, because they came for me as well last night."

"We don't know whether that's true, Your Highness," said Lenz. "There was a great deal happening at once, so perhaps you can still salvage your . . . erm . . . *relationship* with Selvosch, Vorosknecht, and the rest."

"Ah!" replied the Prince. "So now you recognize that it was a good idea for me to lead them on. Let them think I could be their pliable figurehead."

"No, Your Highness. I most certainly do not. But this is where we are."

"Mayhap," continued the Prince, ignoring Lenz, "Queen Biruté and her Reds are in on this, with Selvosch and the Court Philosopher. *Mayhap*, their plan was to marry me to the queen, let her be the real power."

"I . . . doubt it, Your Highness," said Lenz.

"Well, she's pretty enough, at least," said the Prince.

I rolled my eyes, but no one was looking at me. I stood as still as possible, both to ignore further attention, and because I was beginning to sweat considerably in this steam-filled room.

"Your Highness, let's stick to what we know," said Lenz. "Selvosch and Vorosknecht may not have turned on you yet. Perhaps, Highness, in last night's confusion—"

"Hang the confusion!" grunted the Prince. He turned and lifted his foot, to kick the stool he had been sitting on, but stopped, I suspect, because he was barefoot and it would have hurt a great deal. "They want me dead. Selvosch, that purple idiot, and whoever else!" He put his foot back down, then simply nudged the stool over with his knee, into the nearby pool. It didn't look very satisfying.

"Well, Your Highness," I chimed in, "I think I know who else." I curtsied.

"Will another round of names even help at this point?" the Prince seethed.

"It will," I replied, holding my curtsy, "because they will be easier to get to than Selvosch and Vorosknecht." I stood up straight and smiled.

I told the Prince of Edeltraud von Edeltraud, Mistress of the Coin, and of Bozena and Klemens Gustavus. I fabricated visions of them plotting together, talking about what would happen once the King was gone. Edeltraud would be about as hard to get to as Selvosch, but the Gustavuses, as important as they were, could only be Masovskan bankers in a Rotfelsenisch noble court. Though rich and powerful in their little world, they had only been such for two generations. If I could keep suspicions trained upon them, I could remain useful and alive, until I was able to escape with my father. Or avenge him. I did not feel much guilt at the deception.

"Lenz," the Prince began when I was done, "some of the attackers' bodies were left behind as well. See if you can find anything damning on them, now that we know this. And do put someone on Edeltraud. Selvosch and Vorosknecht will be expecting it, but hopefully she will not."

Lenz nodded and looked thoughtful. My heart pounded in my chest at the possibility of *nothing* being found to implicate any of these people. What if the Prince and Lenz spent all their time and effort following people who were not involved at all, while the real plotters got to the King—if they did not already have him—and set into motion the bloody end of the Tetrarchia? For neither the first nor the last time, I began to wonder if I would *personally* somehow be responsible for the great disaster looming.

Well, all the more reason to escape. Both to save myself and my family, and to take myself out of such a sensitive position where I could affect so much. I admit that I did, in that moment, manage to convince myself that my escape would partly be for the *good* of the Tetrarchia. But no matter my reasons, Prince Friedhelm was convinced I had saved his life, so it was a good time to ask for a little more leeway.

"Your Highness," I said, bowing slightly, "I assume you're aware of my Gift's reliance on greater context? In order to make sense of my visions?" I dropped about halfway into the level of obsequiousness I had used when dealing with Court Philosopher Vorosknecht. It felt right, with the Prince, to pretend a little less.

"Yes, yes, of course," he replied.

"Well, I was hoping to be given a touch more freedom: to be able to roam the palace grounds at will." Lenz opened his mouth, and I quickly added, "Unarmed, of course. This will allow me to get closer to more people, and to better understand their places at court."

"Lenz?" asked the Prince.

"Can't she be accompanied by a guard?"

"I recognize that I stand out," I said. "But I will stand out even more if I always have Yellows with me."

"I don't like it," said Lenz.

I turned to Prince Friedhelm. I did not say to him that I had (supposedly) saved his life and named more members of the plot: I gave him a look that said I trusted him to know that on his own.

"I don't see a problem with this," said the Prince.

Lenz sighed. "No weapons, and you will check in with the Yellows at your servant house every . . . let's say two hours."

"Of course." I curtsied. "Besides, my family isn't here yet. Where would I go?"

Lenz grumbled.

"Good," said the Prince. "Whom are you going to look into? Did you get any other useful visions at the ball?"

"I'm afraid I don't know yet if they are useful."

The Prince, still naked, looked at me expectantly. Waiting for more information. I supposed what I'd already given him only went so far.

"Something about the Bandit States, Your Highness," I said. "Some people seem to think their little nips at our borders have actually pushed into the rock itself, and that the High General is covering it up."

"That would be quite large to cover up," murmured the Prince.

Lenz shrugged. "But not impossible. The Reds manage our borders, after all."

"I haven't seen yet whether it's true," I said. "I was going to look a bit into the High General's underlings, as well as whatever I can glean from that delegate from Rituo, the woman who . . ."

"Andelka," Lenz offered. "I believe she's staying at Royal Inn of Ottilie's Rock."

"That's the one." I had never heard the name before. "And thank you."

"Fine, fine," said the Prince. "If you can bring me more plotters like these Masovskans and the Mistress of the Coin, then all the better."

Prince Friedhelm dismissed us. I had certainly set something in motion, for good or ill. Now I needed to hope that either Edeltraud and the bankers *were* against the King, or that I could pass them off as such until I escaped. And if they died for my lies, what did it matter? Everyone around me would be gone in two and a half months.

THE ROYAL INN OF OTTILIE'S ROCK

That night, while Lenz put his Yellows to work looking into the Gustavus siblings and Edeltraud von Edeltraud, I used my slightly longer leash to do a bit of my own investigating. I left my servant house about an hour past sundown, casually saluting the Yellows on duty at the front door.

"If I'm not back in two hours," I said, "it will mean I'm dead or captured, not that I ran away. I promise."

They looked annoyed at my flippancy. I winked and strode off with much unearned confidence.

As soon as I was out of the Yellows' sight, I changed my bearing significantly. I did not feel particularly *safe* running around the palace grounds alone at night, unarmed, and so I affected the quick movements of a harried servant running some errand. At least, in the dark, it would be harder to see how un-Rotfelsenisch I looked. I made my way toward the Royal Inn of Ottilie's Rock. Out on my own, at night, I realized that even Rotfelsen was getting quite cold now, particularly up on top of the rock where the winds could absolutely howl by. In a day or two, it would even start snowing—I could feel it in the air, or so I fancied.

Even after the previous night's excesses, I had managed to be surprised when Lenz told me that the palace grounds had their own inns: three in all. I had assumed that guests stayed in Turmenbach, the city below. It seemed those in the palace would do anything to pretend those beneath them did not exist.

The Royal Inn of Ottilie's Rock was just to the southeast of the barracks that housed the Greens up here on the surface—although the largest Rotfelsenisch army had stations throughout the kingdom. (So, too, did the other three armies, but very small and only in particular places.) I had used the inn's location near the Greens as further proof to Lenz that I shouldn't bring any Yellows with me. I was there to learn about our good friend from the Bandit States, not to start duels.

The inn itself was easy to find, as Ottilie's Rock itself was a huge, jagged outcropping that pushed up out of the ground, about as high as a small building. The inn sat on top of that, four floors dotted with inviting lanterns that illuminated patches of its brown wood. It looked precarious, but in a cozy sort of way: like it was the last outpost of humanity in some inhospitable place. In truth, it was only a short walk from the barracks, a servant house, and what appeared to be a cobbler's shop.

It was at this inn that, apparently, Andelka, the squat, muscular woman from Rituo, whom I had seen egging on drunken nobles the previous night, was staying. So I made my way up the stairs that had been carved into the rotrock, and made dangerously smooth by years of use. A gust of cold wind picked up and almost knocked me clear off Ottilie's Rock, which would have been a painful fall indeed. I wondered how many people had died on their way to, or from, this inn. Despite the cold wind, I felt a strange heat radiating up through the soles of my boots.

The first thing I noticed upon entering the tavern on the first floor was the warmth: it was warm beyond the fire cracking in a corner, steaming even. It was not dissimilar from the steam in the Prince's baths, except that a sort of pungent mineral smell hung in the air. The wooden tables and chairs were all nicely lacquered, I assume to keep from falling apart in the steam, and currently held only a smattering of patrons. I did feel that there was something very comforting about the tenor of the lanterns in that place, and the windows clattering from the wind, but I may have been prejudiced by seeing no *soldiers* for the first time in a week.

I did not see Andelka either, and there were only a few patrons scattered about, so I chose to lean awkwardly at the bar and attempt to get the attention of the keeper behind it. The bar itself was the only thing in the place that betrayed our position on the top of Rotfelsen, for it was a part of Ottilie's Rock that jutted up through the wooden floor, which had been built around it. The bar was long and mostly straight, although it had a few odd moments of curvature. Like the stairs outside, it had been worn down to a smooth sheen. When I leaned against it, the bar also generated a very light and pleasant heat. The keeper was a surprisingly tall man—hunching and bald, with a beautiful smile—who loped over to me.

"Good evening!" he said. "I don't believe you're lodging with us. Here for the ambiance?" His voice was surprisingly soft.

"It certainly is something. Where is all this coming from?" I waved away some of the steam.

"You didn't know? Ottilie's Rock has a natural hot spring inside of it, so downstairs there's a nice little cave with a sauna." He stretched his arms almost alarmingly far backward as languid steam hung about. "Even up here, it limbers up the muscles!"

"Marvelous!" I replied, smiling quite charmingly, I'm sure. "My name is Kalyna, what's yours?"

"Gunther. What'll you have?"

I supposed it was too late for a "normal" person to order a black tea, and less aggressive teas weren't popular in Rotfelsen: they wanted the tea mania, more than the flavor or ritual, to which I could relate. Given that, only the night before, I had drunk alcohol for the first time since childhood, I certainly didn't know what one was supposed to order at a "royal" inn.

"Well, Gunther"—I leaned forward—"what would you suggest?"

He smiled broadly, and twisted his body to grab a bottle from behind him without looking at it. His movements were both graceful and awkward, like a young cormorant that has learned its footing, but not yet the length of its legs. He brought up a small mug carved from rotrock and poured a clear liquid into it.

"I'm sure you have too discerning a palate for our ale," said Gunther.

I laughed. "Quite sure!"

I took a careful sip, and tasted something lighter than the previous night's brandy, with a greater number of flavors. I did cough, but he seemed to view this as the correct reaction, and nodded sagely.

"Starka," he said.

"Starka?" I coughed through another sip.

"Liquor from a simple potato, or other good, Rotfelsenisch root, thrown into a barrel with apple and lime leaves, or whatever else is to hand. The process is started at someone's birth, and the barrel is then hidden away in a cave, or buried in dirt." Gunther mimed this with his hands as he described it. "When that little baby grows up, the result is served at their wedding—or coronation. But, nowadays, some people make a lot more than they'll need and sell it." He shook his head. "I don't know whom this bottle was originally for."

"It's delicious," I said, truthfully, despite another cough.

"That mug was free because I knew you'd like it." Gunther winked, in a purely friendly way. "A silver mark for the next."

So expensive, but I supposed that was normal up here, so near the palace. Earlier that day, Lenz had begun to pay me, so I dropped two silver marks onto the bar, where they clunked pleasingly against the rotrock.

Gunther opened his mouth to protest.

"This is for the *next two*," I assured him.

He smiled and refilled my cup. "Now I know you aren't a courtier: they don't have taste, they only want whatever's expensive. So that's what I give them. But this"—he tapped the bottle—"is better." He stood up straight, and his great height was still surprising. "So, what brings you here?"

"Court, I'm afraid," I replied with mock humility.

"Well, isn't that a shame," he joked. "For the Council of Barbarians, I assume." Because, *of course*, I couldn't be Rotfelsenisch.

"Naturally. You see, Gunther, I represent a patron who is looking for a place to stay during the Council."

The keeper maintained his friendly manner, but I saw something in him changing, as he tried to figure out who, or *what*, I was. His smile remained, but his eyes grew distant.

"I'm fully convinced this is a fine place," I added, holding up my mug before downing the rest of my second helping. "But I'm tasked with finding out whether anyone will be staying here who might be, ah, dangerous to my patron."

Gunther screwed his face to the side, obscuring his lovely smile as he poured my third drink of starka. "I don't know that I can help you here, my friend. We don't discuss our lodgers. Boss' orders, you know."

"Oh, I certainly do know." I rolled my eyes to show that I entirely understood. Lenz was really the only *boss* I had ever had—unless you counted Grandmother—but I could empathize with someone who felt downtrodden. Never mind that this man poured liquor for minor nobles, and must have been paid well for it. I'm sure a keeper down in Turmenbach would have considered his struggles laughable.

Gunther's smile returned, and he poured himself a cup of starka before offering me another. I finished what I had and plunked down another silver mark. This seemed dangerous for one so new to drinking, but what else was one meant to do in the face of inescapable collapse and calamity? Drink, and try to escape—I was working on the "escape" part. I just needed to know whether the Bandit States would be a very bad place to run to.

"Perhaps," I continued, "I can ask you a few questions, at least. They may be slightly leading."

"Lead away."

"I was wondering if anyone from the Bandit States has been staying here. I'm sure it won't surprise you to know that my patron, like so many others, feels uncomfortable about our *friends* from Rituo and the rest."

He brightened a touch and poured himself another. He could really put it away, and I needed to make sure I didn't start trying to match him if I wanted to get anything useful done tonight.

"Well, who doesn't?" he replied. "And I don't much mind telling you because, you see, this is common knowledge, but our tavern is often crawling with those people."

And there it was. My uncomfortable, ironic stress on "*friends* from Rituo" had encouraged him, shown him that even though I was clearly not Rotfelsenisch (even if I partly was), I was certainly not of those people to the south. Now we were in agreement, which I didn't much like. The worst part was, he still had a very nice smile.

"Well, Gunther, as I'm new here, why don't you just tell me what everyone knows."

He laughed. "If someone from the Bandit States needs to a place to stay up here on the palace grounds, they are always foisted upon us. Like this one." He nodded toward the upper floors. "She comes down once a week to make a big show of spending money, then spends the rest of her time in her room, living *cheaply*."

I leaned closer, creating a conspiratorial air between Gunther and myself. He was good enough to oblige me by bending down.

"But why do they all stay here?" I asked.

"So the Greens can keep an eye on them, of course." He then stood up straight, no longer telling secrets. "That's the prevailing theory, anyway. No one can fully trust them, after all. I suppose an individual can be as good or bad as anyone else, but the way their little countries are always shifting and changing, you never know who's, well, on *our* side and who isn't."

Unlike, I thought, the extremely stable Tetrarchia, which was on the verge of violent collapse from an unknown source. Not to mention Rotfelsen's four armies, which were in *total* harmony with one another, and seemed as likely to bring the whole place down around our heads as anything else.

But if it was true that High General Dreher and his soldiers needed to keep an eye on Andelka, the woman from Rituo, perhaps these were normal precautions; or perhaps it was true that Bandit State armies had penetrated Rotfelsen itself recently, and the Greens wanted to be sure their ally from Rituo wouldn't go telling anybody. Or perhaps even Rituo was no longer our ally, aiding in this invasion, and Andelka was a scout or a defector.

Was Andelka as much a prisoner as I? It sounded as though she seldom left her room. Perhaps, if I could get to her, not only could I discover the Bandit States' part in the Tetrarchia's looming demise, but also find an ally against our captors—one who could help my family and me escape.

I asked Gunther a few more questions that went nowhere, and stood up, with the intention of sneaking upstairs and finding Andelka. But when I stood, my head reeled at all the starka I'd drunk. I chose to stumble back to the servant house. I was less worried about walking around alone at night on the way back, although not for any good reason.

The Yellows on duty were angry when they first saw me, as they had just been rounding up a search party. But when they noticed how I was stumbling up to them, they laughed it off.

THE KING REPAIRS TO HIS HUNTING LODGE

I woke up the next afternoon with my first real hangover. I regret to tell you it would not be my last. Another flesh-alchemist patched up my small cuts from the smoke-filled excitement of the Winter Ball, and told me again and again that, no, he could do nothing for a hangover.

The following three days (before that scuffle in an alleyway that I have mentioned) were a bustle of activity, in which I took little part. I spent them reading more of Lenz's secret histories, trying to find underlings of High General Dreher I could influence, and making regular visits to the steam-filled Royal Inn of Ottilie's Rock, hoping to set my eyes upon Andelka. She did not make herself known, and only being able to leave the servant house in two-hour increments made it impossible for me to lay in wait very long. I did become quite familiar with the schedule of Gunther, the tall, gentle-voiced barkeep.

Besides that, I spoke to my neighbors in the servant house, but learned little of note, just yet. I managed friendly chats with Jördis, but was loath to ask much of her. Who knew what she would take back to her master, the Court Philosopher? I also began to just barely appreciate food and drink far better than what I was used to.

I fell into a rather agreeable routine. I started to feel that the luxuries I was enjoying—solid walls, food and drink, well-fitted clothes, trips to the tavern—were something I was tricking my captors out of. These rich nobles and sneaky soldiers thought they were keeping me around for their plots, but then I would escape them with whatever I could carry. This was at least how I rationalized enjoying myself a bit.

Outside of the tavern and my little house, the Gustavus brats were apparently staying in Edeltraud von Edeltraud's mansion, which was nestled right near the Sunset Palace itself. Edeltraud and Bozena didn't show themselves after the Winter Ball, which was helpful to me in making them seem suspicious. Also helpful was that one of the attackers from the ball, who had been killed in the scuffle, had been found with Masovskan lesser grivnas in his purse. Carrying money from another kingdom was not unheard of, but neither was it normal: most businesses wouldn't accept it. Perhaps my wild guess had been correct.

Klemens was regularly seen returning to the Edeltraud mansion, although never leaving. I told Lenz I had seen a vision of him down in an enclosed city, which I assumed to be Turmenbach, the capital city just beneath us. This was, of course, because at the ball I had heard Klemens mention retiring "to Turmenbach." One of Lenz's operatives (simply a Yellow out of uniform) plied one of Edeltraud's servants for information, and learned that Klemens had a mistress stashed down in the city.

Apparently, Bozena also had a lover nearby, but the servant had no information on their whereabouts. I could have told Lenz that for free: in a land like Rotfelsen, a woman must keep lovers very secret because her consequences will be more dire. Klemens could be a cad, could sire bastards, and so forth, but Bozena would be at best upbraided and forcibly married, even if she was the real power of the Gustavus family (which I began to suspect). Lenz was none too happy that he had spent money on any information, however. Wasn't that my job?

I hoped I made up for it by "seeing" other facts about Klemens, Bozena, and their brother, Bernard, who had stayed home: full names, that they had just come into more money due to their father's death, that Klemens had killed a vagabond for fun. Lenz dutifully wrote them all down in his little books. Safe for all time—all two months of it.

The official word, during this time, was that the King was doing much better, but had repaired to his hunting lodge in the caves to the south, where he was stalking the giant coypu rats, wide as two burly men side by side, that lived there. He was apparently quite fond of doing this with no notice, leaving his Queen and most retainers behind.

Besides, everyone would see him again at the upcoming King's Dinner, wouldn't they?

While the King enjoyed his constitutional, Lenz and I looked for Klemens down in Turmenbach, which was built into the rotrock itself, and was accessed by bridges and ramps that wound down from the surface.

Turmenbach was a series of caves, sprawling in all directions from a central cavern that was itself larger than some cities I have seen. The rich mostly lived in huge manor buildings carved right out of the cave floors, which were generally as close as possible to the few great cracks in the surface that let in shafts of natural light—although there were also a few gigantic side caves that were entirely the home of this or that noble.

The rest of the city lived their lives in crowded streets or small networks of pockmarks up and down the walls. They traveled by pulley and catwalk, striding streets cut into stone and sometimes hopping over small crevices. Commoners would be knifed in small, dark tunnels that crossed only feet above private ones owned by nobles. Everyone there lived their lives as though such a place was entirely normal.

THE POPPYHOUSE

Hidden off to the side of Turmenbach's great, central cavern was a dirty little neighborhood made up of a mishmash of stone and imported wood buildings. The kind of place, apparently, where visitors stashed their secret lovers. Those streets, I was told, had once been *nice*—before the nobles hollowed out bigger and grander spaces—and so the neighborhood still sat beneath a sliver of sky. When I visited, that sky was dropping the season's snow into Turmenbach.

So, on the fifth day since the Winter Ball, hours before I saw Lenz kill an axewoman twice his size, he and I came to that rundown neighborhood and sat in a Turmenbach poppyhouse. It was little more than a cave with windows and a sign, really, where customers lay about on cushions, drinking poppy milk and dreaming poppy dreams.

We did not partake; poppy milk would have made our business there far less productive (though far more entertaining). Drifting through a poppyhaze while everything around me fell apart had a certain appeal, and the last few days had seen me relax my rules against alcohol, at least. But alas, we sat sober in the Reconstitution Room, which was placed at the front of the poppyhouse to show the street a respectable face. This was where customers recovered from their poppyhaze by sitting upright, drinking lots of water, and eating small, salty things. The fact that my jailer and I had been seated at the Reconstitution Room's window for nearly six hours was worthy of no one's notice. Lenz assured me that so-called poppy geniuses sometimes spent that long or longer reconstituting, in preparation for their next go-round. A morning haze and a dinnertime haze were normal bookends to their day.

If, as I often worried, the very rock of Rotfelsen would somehow crumble in the cataclysm to come, I envied these poppy geniuses who would know, deep down, that the ceiling and floor caving in were only part of the haze.

Lenz and I sat and ate olives, pretzels, pickles, nuts, and dried beet slices as we looked out a small window onto a cavernous Turmenbach street—more an alley, really. Through the window, all sorts of illicit customers turned the light snow on the ground to acrid slush. Winter had finally come to Rotfelsen, sort of.

In the Reconstitution Room, a girl of perhaps eight played a xylophone. There was no tune, just a simple and soothing rhythm loud enough to drown out the mumblings of the next table. No poppy genius wanted to realize, when he started to come down, that he had been blathering and now his neighbors knew the flavor of his illusions. The girl had been there as long as we had, and looked very bored. Lenz explained to me that she was the granddaughter of the proprietor (whom Lenz knew), and that she was being punished. This explained the hastily scrawled sign in front of her that read, "NO TIPS, PLEASE."

Through the window, I could see loiterers at both ends of the street. I knew them to be incognito Yellows, Prince Friedhelm's soldiers ready to enact a quite illegal secret arrest on our behalf. Lenz and I were simply there to oversee, to point out the right man if he ever showed his worthless face. We were bored and on edge all at once.

Lenz had once said we would "sit comfortably far from the dangers we see," after all. Ha ha ha.

"Just four," I said. "We should have brought ten."

"The Prince would not allow it," replied Lenz. "A small force is less likely to be seen. Secretly arresting a Masovskan magnate, based on a prophecy, isn't something the Prince wants to be known for."

"Well, if he does not trust my prophecies, I can leave."

"And yet here we are. Although it would certainly help if you could see a little *more*."

"If only I had seen you coming in the first place," I muttered.

Lenz stared out the window. The girl's plinking slowed as she got tired of pounding the xylophone. The man at the counter, her uncle, began to clap loudly at her, exhorting her to pick up the pace.

"The Prince trusts, Kalyna, but does not want to be seen if things go sour."

"Unlike you and I, who are so excited to be in the middle of it."

Lenz shrugged and shoved a fistful of almonds dusted with pepper into his mouth. Then he grunted, rubbed his bad leg, and fussed about repositioning the rapier in his belt so it didn't scratch the floor. A tired man at the table next to us got up and walked shakily toward the back cave for another haze, his second since we had arrived. The Reconstitution Room was luxurious by the standards of the neighborhood, but my days in the servant house had already spoiled me such that I found it dirty. I hated myself for this: the end was coming—with fire and sword and shattering—while I allowed myself to soften.

"You know," I said, "if the Prince were as careful about ruling as he is about *not* ruling, he might make a half decent king. Why doesn't he just . . . let this plot happen?"

"That is treasonous," Lenz grumbled.

"Arrest me!" I chuckled, arms outstretched.

He grumbled some more. If Lenz were particularly on edge, it may have been because after I nearly died in the pukevapor, he had allowed me to arm myself for this little excursion. My beloved sickle was at my side that day. He knew that I knew better than to attack him here and now, but it was one more small thing outside of my kidnapper's comfort. Something I could cling to, until the Yellows who were almost always watching me confiscated it again.

"Honestly," I said, "our Dutiful Prince is so dedicated to avoiding work that he has given himself huge amounts of it—being king would only pile a little more on his shoulders, I think."

Lenz said nothing.

I turned my stool to face him directly, staring at his left ear and gray temple. "Lenz," I said, "if the Prince decided he *did* want to supplant King Gerhold, would you help him? Or is that where your loyalty ends?"

He looked at me and said in a very slow whisper, "This is the second time you've asked me this. Do you *see* something?"

"No," I answered. Deadpan, to make him wonder. "Just curious."

Lenz's gaze returned to the window. Someone in the back cave had a coughing fit bad enough to be heard in the Reconstitution Room, over the girl's xylophone.

"You are," he mumbled at the window, "insane if you think I can answer that."

"Lenz, Lenz, Lenz!" I laughed, slapping his bad knee to rattle him. "It's an intellectual exercise!"

"In case you haven't noticed," he said, "the very fact that the Prince *refuses* to take the job is why we're in this . . . mess."

"So then you would help him to do so? Make your job easier, wouldn't it?"

"That is extremely not what I said. But I do think our good Prince could do well to be less cagey. He *is* a libertine, but would it be so difficult to show that he cares, at least a little, about keeping our kingdom afloat? Even if it is for selfish reasons."

"What monarch has nonselfish reasons?" I asked.

Lenz did not answer, but he did not disagree either.

"And what," I continued, "do you think Vorosknecht, Selvosch, Edeltraud, and the Gustavuses care about?"

"Power for Vorosknecht. Money for the others. If I were to guess."

I blew out a long breath, flapping my lips irritatingly. "But if the King does so little, why do they need to even supplant him? Why can't he be their figurehead?" He glared at me, and I shrugged, adding, "Context, Lenz."

"I would guess that they want more than one army on their side. High General Dreher has never struck me as hungry for power; he seems to relish living well within his means, and he knows how exhausting it is to use what power he already has. He seems most invested in maintaining the status quo. So the Greens and the Reds won't bow to the Court Philosopher. And now they know that neither will the Yellows."

"Well," I said, "old Friedhelm *tried* to trick them. He thinks he is very clever, doesn't he?"

"Yes," Lenz sighed. "That's why he hired us, after all."

"Hired you."

"Sure."

"And I still wonder whether he might not try to grab that power for himself."

Lenz shook and sat up straight. "Do you really think the Prince would have hired a soothsayer—"

"*Kidnapped* a soothsayer."

"—if he had plans to do . . . that?"

"Maybe he has no plans. Maybe"—I emphasized each word by wagging my finger—"he does not yet know he'll do it!"

"So you *have* seen—?"

"No, no. Not yet," I said.

Then I looked out the window for a long time, acting oblivious to Lenz's study of me.

Outside, at the far right corner, were two incognito Yellows, a squat man and a tall woman. They looked bored, and the novelty of seeing each other in off-duty clothing had long since worn off. Besides, there was only so long they could believably "loiter" before having to move farther down the street, and then later circle back.

The woman was the same tall Yellow who had taken me to the Winter Ball, whose name I had misheard as "Dugmush" because her mouth was full. It now felt too late to ask for a correction. Through the window, I saw her fiddling with her dagger, likely still frustrated at not having a sword; a "normal" Rotfelsenisch woman in a dress was not supposed to be so well armed. When she had been in uniform, I had found her strangely compelling, and also hoped that I, in my uniform, looked a bit like her. In a dress, however, she seemed uncomfortable.

The two disguised Yellows at the other end of the street had wandered away again, to avoid suspicion. This "street" was an enclosed tunnel, and its "buildings" were outcroppings and caves in the rock wall. I was never quite sure how any snow got in there. Across from the poppyhouse were apartments, and we had it on good (well, passable) word that in one of them lived the Turmenbach mistress of Klemens Gustavus.

"He's got to show eventually," Lenz mumbled. "Libido springs eternal."

"Until it doesn't," I added.

"Until it doesn't," he agreed.

"Feh," I grunted and slapped the table. "If only we knew where one could kill vagrants for fun, we'd have him by now."

Lenz smiled. "And do *you* have a lover waiting for you somewhere?"

I laughed and laughed and laughed. A man sitting near us, resting his chin on his hand as he watched visions dance away, jostled and fell onto his table. He looked at me, angry and horrified. I ignored him.

"I'm relieved you were so obvious," I finally said.

"Yes, well, no one's written a treatise on your love life."

"But you will?"

He shrugged.

"In the days since the Winter Ball," I said, "you have been respectful and decent. You've let me roam, within reason, you haven't pried into my affairs or shown off all you already know of them—so genial and comradely that I began to worry I wouldn't notice it when you became yourself." It was good to have these reminders. To know that I was a prisoner, always watched, even while living comfortably.

"I am always myself."

"Of course," I said, patting his hand mockingly, the way Grandmother would have. "I was worried about a subtle campaign of wheedling out my secrets. Thank you for your bluntness."

He cocked his head to the side and put his face in his hand. "So . . . *do* you?"

"What?"

"Have a lover?"

"Why?" I sneered. "You want to *fuck*?"

Lenz scowled and sipped his water.

"Naturally, it's no business of yours," I said.

"Perhaps there's a moonstruck someone waiting for you, then. Raising your child, perhaps?"

I turned away and kept my mouth shut. If I had someone waiting for me, I would have told Lenz I did not. As it was, I decided to let him believe in such a fabulous person of whatever gender. I fancifully imagined Lenz sending lackeys to all corners of the Tetrarchia only to discover, after years of searching, that I hadn't had a real sweetheart since I was twenty.

After years of searching indeed. The Tetrarchia had two months until breaking, violence, and death. Was I escaping south from a Loashti invasion? North from the Bandit States? Into the depths of Rotfelsen to escape squabbling nobles? Or would a starving peasants' rebellion sweep through and see me as another royal tool? Perhaps the other three Tetrarchic kingdoms would decide they just didn't *like* their insular neighbor. Or perhaps these would all happen at once. I was spoiled for terrible options.

Lenz yawned. "What, ah . . . what language do you and your family speak with each other?" he asked.

"You know," I sighed, "you can just stop prying, rather than coming up with such questions."

Truth be told, we spoke a sort of jumble, and in my thoughts, I changed languages based on my moods. Cöllüknit when I was sad, Masovskani when angry, Skydašiavos when happy, Rotfelsenisch when pragmatic. Sometimes I sang to Papa in Loashti languages.

"Just curious!" laughed Lenz.

"Well then, bring my family to me and you can find out."

"That reminds me," Lenz began, "I received word this morning: your father and grandmother arrived sooner than I expected."

"What?" I slammed my hand down on the table. "Why haven't you told me until now?"

"Wait, look!" Lenz hissed. "Klemens! Finally!"

MONUMENTAL GOONS

The youngest Gustavus brat was indeed across the street, leaving the building of his mistress. This was surprising, as we had expected to catch him *entering* it. Lenz looked perturbed, but not worried: the street only went in two directions, after all, and Yellows were at each end. There would be no mistaking Klemens, either, even if he had not been alone, and wearing his Masovskan furs.

Lenz knotted his brow and further mussed his unruly hair. "I thought he would have a bodyguard."

Klemens, calm and smiling, turned toward his right and began to walk down the street very slowly. The two Yellows behind him, at the far corner, did their best to not look like they were watching. From where Lenz and I sat, the other two—whom Klemens was walking toward—were hidden from our view by the poppyhouse's rotrock window frame. Still, they couldn't have been more than a few yards away. Why didn't they pounce?

Lenz yawned theatrically. "I think . . ." He yawned again. "That I need to stretch my leg a bit before it seizes up, you know? Let us take a stroll, Kalyna Aljosanovna."

"Don't think this conversation is over," I grumbled.

"What more is there to say? Your family is here. You're welcome. We can go see them once Klemens is good and trussed."

As we moved toward the door, we got a better view down the block: Klemens was still walking alone, followed by two Yellows. The other two, who should have been in front of him, were nowhere in sight. Klemens was whistling.

"Where the devils *are* they?" hissed Lenz.

We did not try very hard to exit the poppyhouse inconspicuously: it was the owner's professional duty not to notice strange things, and the customers' hobby. As the girl's soothing plink-plunking faded away, the other two incognito Yellows, the man and woman, sloshed across the snow in front of us, in too much hurry to be careful.

Lenz calmly watched them pass, but his calm evaporated when he looked where they were going: Klemens had an empty stretch in front of him, and then disappeared to the left, down an alley. Or was it another street? In Turmenbach, the difference between an alley and a street felt academic. The disguised Yellows who had passed us followed him into it and vanished.

Lenz moved quickly toward them. I didn't care for intrigue, but I needed to gain Lenz's confidence to effectively escape the country's death. Running headlong into danger at the ball had gotten me my sickle back, after all. Off I went, past my boss-captor, slipping my sickle into my hand. At least this time I wasn't guaranteed to vomit, but anything could happen.

It's good that I did. Run, that is, not vomit. I skidded into the alley, slipping on mushy snow, to find where Klemens' bodyguards had been waiting for us. Three of our disguised Yellows were there too, in a bent and bloody heap, one with his entire face laid open. The fourth, the Yellow who had taken me to the Winter Ball, was alive, held by her wrists with a knee in her back, as Klemens delighted in kicking her. She was then dumped over to join her comrades. Klemens had his sabre out, ready to hack at her prone body, but I fumbled in, and he stopped to look up. Her death mattered as little to him as her life.

I was now, effectively, alone in a narrow alley with Klemens and his three bodyguards, while Lenz limped somewhere in the street behind me. For however much use (I thought) he would be when he got here. The Yellows had surely been ambushed, while I at least *saw* my enemies, so I had that going for me. Klemens looked as maddeningly comfortable as ever.

"And who are you, madam?" he asked. It sounded cordial, even as he nodded his bodyguards toward me: two women and a man, all huge, all with huge axes. Next to those axes, my sickle felt like a toy. I brandished it anyway, and tried not to feel too ineffectual.

And here I had hoped coming down to Turmenbach, out of the hands of Vorosknecht and his Purples, would keep me safe. Ah well.

"I don't suppose it would help to throw the Prince's name at you?" I replied.

"Unsurprising," said Klemens. He shrugged.

A monster of a woman with long black hair loomed up in front of me. Her double-headed axe blade, end-to-end, seemed as long as I was tall. This couldn't have been true, but in that moment, nothing made more sense. She lifted her axe, blocking Klemens from my view.

The gigantic axeblade slammed into the snow and stone with a crunch. I had avoided it ably enough, but was too scared to move in and attack. I backed toward the mouth of the alley instead.

She stepped forward and wrenched the axe up out of the ground. Almost cut me in half with the motion. Yes, *double-headed*, right.

The male bodyguard had a golden beard that made him easy to spot from the corner of my eye. He approached my left side, and the third, a woman with a thatching of scars on her arms, was right behind him, each wielding their own unsettlingly large axes. The open street was to my back, but getting out of their reach seemed impossible.

"Lenz!" I yelled. I did not really want to warn him, but it seemed the best option. I choked it back as the axeman swung across at me. The blade screeched against the walls, and I ducked beneath it.

"Yes, yes, ambush," said Lenz as he limped into sight, rapier in hand.

The man's axe skidded off the rotrock wall and swung wide to his left. The black-haired woman who had come at me first was nearly shoulder-to-shoulder with him in that space. She had to skip forward like a child to avoid his wild swing, which made her look less dangerous. A narrow alley was not the place for such monumental goons.

The black-haired woman turned her skip into a run, past me and toward Lenz, as though this had been her intention all along. The man and the scarred woman both eyed me, stepping forward and back, nearly bumping as they traded places, not sure who should try first.

A light snow began to fall in through a nearby opening in Turmenbach's rotrock ceiling, adding to the slippery layer of brown slush beneath us. The alley was small and awkward, the bodyguards big, so I took a chance. I dashed diagonally at the axeman, head down, praying to someone. He paused before his swing, expecting me to check my momentum, but I abandoned my fate to the slush and skidded past him in the snow while his axe was still raised.

I slid uncontrollably toward the scarred woman. The man fumbled and half turned toward me, getting tangled in his comrade. In a moment I would hit the wall behind her, giving her a chance to cut me down. On my way past her, I flailed my sickle wildly. The axeman was still trying not to hit his comrade when she collapsed in a heap, her stomach opened by my sickle. He was very confused.

I rushed behind him, but the axeman managed to turn with me. Behind him, at the mouth of the alley, Lenz was peppering the black-haired woman with his rapier. He was much more mobile than I had expected. She avoided his attacks, but had no chance to respond.

The man facing me kept swinging, his blade clanking against walls and ground. I hoped his reach was too wide for Klemens to feel safe coming up behind me. I felt wind from the axe as I jumped back to escape, falling painfully to the ground. Sliding backward on my shoulders, the top of my head crashed right into Klemens' shin.

Surprised, he shoved me back toward his lackey. I suppose everyone was surprised. I managed to straighten up, twist past the axe and, using Klemens' gift of momentum, bring my sickle down across the man's face and into his left eye. He fell screaming and grabbed my knees, it seemed, for comfort.

At the same time, I saw the black-haired woman stopped in mid-swing by Lenz's rapier through her throat. She then crumpled to the ground.

I looked back at Klemens.

"Well." Klemens shrugged. "I guess . . ."

He broke into a run, bursting down the alley, past me and toward the street, hoping to get by Lenz and escape. I lifted my sickle as if to throw it, which would have been useless.

Lenz looked tired, and was heavily favoring his bad leg. Klemens ran past, sword flailing ahead of him to clear the way. Lenz stepped aside and thunked the Gustavus brat on the base of his skull with his pommel. Klemens dropped, groaning.

I kicked the half-blind axeman in the face to dislodge myself. I felt no guilt over taking his eye, but this felt wrong to me.

"You may be a better thug than soothsayer," Lenz called from the other end of the alley.

Was this a joke? Or was I not good enough at my job?

"Help me with these Yellows, will you?" he added as he limped toward me.

THE PRISONER

Three of the Yellows were dead. Now, my sickle confiscated once more, we rode back up through the city with an angry cargo, fastidiously tied and gagged in a compartment below our feet.

The only remaining Yellow was my "Dugmush," who was bruised but insisting she was fine. I found myself feeling simultaneously sorry for and scared of her. Her comrades had been killed, as she nearly had, and yet she seemed almost entirely calm, with something terrifying lurking beneath the surface.

But no amount of prisoners, murders, or tall women mattered enough to keep me from needing to see my father—I had never before lived apart from him.

"Where is my family?" I asked Lenz as the carriage began to creak its precarious way up to the surface.

"Safe. On the palace grounds," he grunted.

"Take me to see my father."

He coughed. "We're a little busy at the moment, Kalyna. Just now, we have two prisoners"—he stomped on the floor with his good foot—"one soldier, one soothsayer, and myself. We'll need to get Klemens good and squared away, and interrogated, not to mention gather whatever prophecies about him you can muster. I cannot spare you, or the Yellows to escort you."

I began to wonder again if Papa was alive at all, or if the possibility of his existence was being dangled in front of me, waiting for the perfect opportunity to break me by letting me know he was dead in a Masovskan ditch.

In silence, we ascended to the open air, where the snow had stopped, and the sun was out again. Lenz spent the time scribbling onto a piece of paper pressed against his good knee. Once we had lurched onto the surface, we rolled toward the giant walls of the palace grounds, and through them to that vast complex.

We were taken to where Lenz lived, in the officers' quarters of one of the barracks that circled the edges of the palace grounds. It was a squat brick of granite: painted yellow, naturally. In front was a pleasant little filigreed table and chairs, so that officers could pretend they were at a café. The carriage deposited us at its door, where we met Behrens, the sharpshooter, and a group of Yellows. Lenz explained what had happened, and they were all made suitably angry.

"We have the brat, and another," sighed Lenz. "No matter your inclinations, don't hurt them. Just put them away, *separately*. And once that's done, Kalyna and I will speak to our honored guest."

"Of course," said Behrens.

Klemens Gustavus' surviving guard was taken away, and I never did see him again. As he was just some mercenary, I hope that he was simply held for a bit and let go. Klemens had a bag thrown over his head and was marched right up into the barracks, where all the Yellows who saw him simply glanced at him and then turned away. They did this very purposefully, as if clearly signaling that they knew he was never here, and would not be surprised to never see him again. I found this terrifying, and I certainly did not forget that Klemens was only here because of my lies.

Lenz and I followed him upstairs through the barracks, lagging behind as Lenz's leg was greatly bothering him. By the time we got to Lenz's horribly messy office, I had entirely lost track of where Klemens had been taken. My jailer sat at his desk and began scratching away with a pen. I shoved some papers off a couch, sat down, and looked around.

What I could see of his rooms were less a study and a bedroom than they were two identical rooms that each played both all at once. Books, clothes, tools, cots, couches, bundles, all of these could be found in each room, scattered haphazardly. I suspect that before we worked together, weapons had been scattered about in the same fashion. The next room over had a real bed, and therefore must have been the bedroom, despite both rooms showing signs of having been slept in. I kicked over a pile of books, but Lenz ignored me and kept writing.

After maybe fifteen minutes of this, the Yellow who had survived our encounter down in Turmenbach—Dugmush, as I was now officially calling her in my head—reappeared. She was back in uniform, and appeared a completely new person; the bruises on her face only made her seem more formidable. She crossed to Lenz's bedroom and closed the door after her. I opened my mouth to ask, but decided against it. After another half an hour or so, I got too bored and angry that I wasn't with my father.

"What are you doing?" I grunted.

"Finishing up about our little adventure."

"Isn't that, you know, secret?"

"No more so than my theories on the King's virility, and the rest." He gestured unthinkingly at the pile of papers I had displaced on the couch.

"And if you're going to just sit there and write, why can't I go see my father?"

"Don't worry. You come across valiantly."

I sneered. "I'd rather be left out."

"No such luck." He finished writing with a big, theatrical flourish, and then stood up. "Well, let's go talk to our prisoner."

"Where exactly is Klemens Gustavus locked up, anyway? In your rooms?"

"Sort of!" he laughed. "We can't keep him in a prison when the state doesn't admit he's a prisoner."

Lenz walked into the bedroom, and I was curious enough to follow him. He asked me to close the door and, rolling my eyes, I did so. I saw no sign of Dugmush here. Lenz put both hands against the base of his bed, pushed, grunted, and almost collapsed.

"This . . . stupid . . ." he grumbled. He pushed again and collapsed, again, rather than push too hard from both legs. "Could you help me, Kalyna Aljosanovna? The *Prince's* rooms have perfect hidden doors that glide like greased knives, but I am not the Prince."

"You have a secret passage?"

"I wanted to slide it open and surprise you, but it is tricky and my leg is bum."

I stood above him, considering possible bludgeons in the disordered room around me. Then I sighed, got on my knees, and pushed. The bed groaned and swiveled out: the head was bolted to the floor, and the foot moved to reveal a rotrock staircase.

"These stairs are the only way to where we're going," said Lenz.

"That you know of."

"You first, please. It's quite steep, and I'd rather you not push me."

"Foiled again."

The stairs twisted so often I quickly lost track of how far down we were. Could one hide from a war here? Not if Rotfelsen's great rock was going to shatter, of course. Our footsteps echoed loudly, and I had to raise my voice over them to continue insulting Lenz.

"You aren't married," I said.

"Oh?"

"You took such an interest in my love life, it seems fair to pry into yours. No one who loved you would let you keep your rooms like that."

"Well," he said, "I'm young yet."

I prepared some other crack, but was interrupted by the muffled, hoarse, agitated screaming of a man with filled with rage, and with too much confidence to be scared. Yet.

"—and you fat, ugly, smashed-tomato-faced Rots wouldn't hear the rumble of your doom if you could get your fathers' cocks out of your ears long enough to—!"

At the bottom of the room were two bored Yellows in wooden chairs trying not to stare at a barred cell in the corner. In that cell was Klemens Gustavus, and in the whole chamber was his voice. I wondered if the "rumble of your doom" part was a normal threat, or proprietary knowledge. But how could he know anything? He may not have even been involved in the plot: I had invented a role for him out of my own childish anger, hadn't I?

"—go bathe in your auntie's menstrual blood in the summer home you built in your brother's ass, you—!"

"Seems a little sore," said Lenz. He was calm, but he had to yell to be heard.

"—slice up your pisshole so it opens like a peony in—!"

"He ran out of good things to say in Rotfelsenisch a few minutes ago," said Dugmush, "so he has moved on to Masovskani." She smiled brightly, reclining against the wall, with her hat halfway over her face, entirely relaxed despite the day's excitement. "I don't know what any of it means!"

"—flung from the top of the Sunset Palace dangling from your intestines—!"

"He's run out of good things to say in Masovskani too," said Lenz.

There was one lone torch on the wall, near the cell, and we stood mostly in the dark. I hoped that Klemens had not recognized me in Turmenbach, and would not do so here either.

"—may your ancestors rise from the grave in a thousand years to violate your descendants and— Oh." Klemens looked at Lenz and dropped his voice to normal, saying in Rotfelsenisch, "You have a limp. The one who cracked my skull."

"If only," said Lenz.

"This will all go much easier," suggested Dugmush, "if you let us jostle him a little now and then." She smiled again. An easy smile: the implication was troubling, but I couldn't help smiling back.

"No," said Lenz.

"Not shatter," she clarified. "Jostle. I owe him after he killed the others, and kicked me a thousand times."

"Five times," said Klemens.

She shrugged. "Lucky for you I'm unaccustomed to fighting in a skirt, and only had a dagger."

"I'm sorry," Lenz told the Yellow, "but no jostling."

She shrugged again and made a "well, I did what I could" expression, which she trained on me, then her compatriot, who shrugged back, and then Klemens.

"You're all going to die," said Klemens, pacing. "Not—not how everyone will die," he clarified, stuttering his Rotfelsenisch in anger. "I mean . . . I mean everyone in this room who is not me will die soon and ignominiously. That is what I mean."

The Yellow who had said nothing so far grunted.

"You do not do this to *me*," continued Klemens, grabbing the bars. "You won't kill me, and you won't keep me."

"Oh?" asked Lenz.

"I'm too important. You Rots, unable to see outside of your

depressing kidney stone of a kingdom, may think that no one outside it matters, but I am not some provincial Masovskan merchant. I run the biggest changing banks in the Tetrarchia."

"Yet you've already disappeared," said Lenz. "It'll make no difference how lasting that absence is."

Klemens seemed to have not considered this until now. He fell onto his cot and put his head in his hands.

And there was my guilt. I should have felt nothing close to sympathy for Klemens, a terrible man who killed because he could. But it's hard for me to keep seeing through the eyes of the helpless—I am just so used to seeing through my own. Here was a ghastly young man who could easily end up assassinated and never found based on my need to cover my own failure. Even he did not deserve to be a casualty of my fraud. Did he?

"Klemens Gustavus," said Lenz. "We know who you are, and we know that you, your sister Bozena, and Edeltraud von Edeltraud are involved in a plot against the throne. You can tell us what happened the night of the Winter Ball now, or you can suffer the consequences."

Lenz and I stepped closer to the cell. The guards sat up straight. Klemens dug his fingers into his greasy hair and looked up at us. He started to laugh.

"Against the throne? *Against*?" He laughed again, edged with desperation, and he began to shake.

We stood unmoving, silent.

"A plot against the throne? Tell you? Oh . . . oh hell, you're going to kill me." His voice strained and tears began to roll down his face. His hands shook, and he didn't think to sit on them—just moved them up and down as though looking for somewhere to put them. His sallow complexion began to turn red, and he began sobbing, then gulping for air.

"Just tell us," said Lenz. "Then you live."

If Lenz felt guilty, it did not show in his body language. I hoped it did not show in mine either. I had been nearly killed by Klemens' lackeys Down Valley Way because he had preferred assassination to sharing any part of his wealth. I hated him. Why couldn't he have the decency to strut and gloat? I wanted him cowed by his loss of power, but not so thoroughly that it was unsatisfying. Instead of a sadistic plotter, here was a sobbing man-child who reminded me of every time in my life I'd been caught and threatened, every time I'd been accused of impossible things, told to explain the unexplainable.

"Tell you?" Klemens laughed again, hysterical. "You kill my guards, hide me here, demand secrets I don't have about a plot *I am trying to stop* and—!"

"Trying to stop?" grunted Lenz. He moved forward, leaning against the bars. "What do you mean?"

Klemens muttered the defining traits of several Masovskan gods into his hands.

"Klemens," said Lenz, saying each following word slowly and carefully, "tell me what you've been trying to stop."

"Your Prince," Klemens sobbed. "And the Quarrymaster, and I don't know who else. They want to kill the King." He looked down as he spoke. "We planned a counterattack, to kill your damned Prince. But we failed, and now the King is missing."

Lenz made a noise deep in his throat, but otherwise did not seem to react much to this. "What," he ventured, "convinced you of this plot's existence?"

Klemens simply began to blubber, then hiccup, then shake his head. He seemed either to not have an answer, or to be entirely unable to speak out of fear. He raised his hands, as though to motion toward an obvious answer, but still no words came.

"Think it over, Klemens," said Lenz. "You may be able to save yourself. Perhaps your sister, too."

He turned to leave. I followed, and hoped I had not completely bungled everything.

MORE LIES

I had always thought that one's joints aching with the weather was an invention of Grandmother's. Or that if it were real, it was only for the very old. But as Lenz and I sat in another of his rooms, I could see that the cold outside caused pain in his left leg, although he was no more than thirty. He rubbed it, groaned, kept moving it up here, then down there, then back up again. He didn't seem to be exaggerating, although I harbored no doubts that if he needed to spring up and kill someone again, he could.

"That," grunted Lenz as he shoved papers off a chair in his suite, "was not what I expected."

I stood and said nothing.

"What *exactly* did you see?" he continued. "What exactly of Edeltraud and the Gustavuses planning to kill the King?"

I was in deep now, and the only way I saw out was more lies. What was I supposed to do, tell him I was a fraud who had lucked into a role in the highest court? The assumption would be that I was a spy from somewhere else—Loasht perhaps. These Rotfelsenisch always assumed Loasht because they couldn't place my background, and had very little actual experience with the Loashti. I decided the best way out was anger. I got up and stood over him. Lenz stared at me, unblinking.

"I saw three rich and powerful people who had orchestrated an attack, and I saw the King!" I waved my hands above my head. "What do you want from me? I see things, but I must also *interpret*. You drag me away from my family, whose years of experience can help me understand my visions, throw me in front the most bizarre and circular court, and tell me that there's a plot against the King!"

Lenz said nothing. I steeled myself, put my hands on his shoulders, and looked straight into his eyes. "I was ready to see plots against the King everywhere, and I must have seen their attack on the Prince, *who was standing next to the King*. What, by all the gods, did you expect?"

There was silence for a few moments. Lenz looked thoughtful.

"Can you tell me anything else?" he asked.

"Their plan, whatever it is, was called 'the hammer.' Or, at least, Edeltraud called it that." I smiled a bit. "Klemens thought the name was overdramatic."

"Hmm," said Lenz. "I suppose I agree with him on that, if it's true. Anything else? Anything *solid*?"

I glared at him. "Solid? No. For all the reasons I have just given you. But I've been visiting the inn on Ottilie's Rock, and learning some uncomfortable things regarding the Bandit States."

"Can you, ever, be more specific?"

"It seems the Bandit States have indeed been invading the rock itself, and that the High General has covered it up." I wasn't sure I believed this, but it seemed possible, and I needed something.

"Really?" Lenz scoffed. "Surely someone would have noticed that."

"How often does anyone up here speak to those on the outposts of your kingdom? How much power does the High General have over the people who live there?"

He looked thoughtful.

"For that matter," I continued, "couldn't a High General order massacres of his own people to cover up previous massacres by his enemies?"

"Is this something you have seen evidence of?"

"No, Lenz, I am making guesses. Something that even *I* must do. Let me get closer to Andelka to be sure. Some time near the High General wouldn't hurt either."

"Very well," he grunted. "I'll see what I can get out of Klemens."

There were a lot of ways my many, many deceptions could all come crashing down, but I still felt the satisfaction of having bluffed my way to safety, for at least the next hour.

"At least he wants to protect the King," I offered.

"At the expense of Prince Friedhelm, unfortunately. I don't know how we can convince him we're on the same side, now that we've killed his bodyguards, trapped him here, and cannot find the King."

"Hmm, yes, what a bother," I said. "So, take me to my family."

"We must report this to the Prince right away."

"After I see my family," I said. But he didn't even seem to hear me.

THE TWELFTH RECOURSE

And so we were whisked back up to the Sunset Palace once more. Lenz seemed almost as unhappy about it as I was. Soon we were in the Prince's study, and Lenz told him all that had happened today: about capturing Klemens, and what he had said in his cell. Lenz did not tell him about the poppyhouse, which was my personal favorite part of the day, but some people simply don't understand what matters in life.

Once he was done, the Prince shot up and began pacing intensely enough to wear a hole in his polished floor. This was the first time I'd seen him since our interview in his baths, and he did not seem to have spent the last five days in a good state. His fine clothes were disheveled, his eyes were bleary, and he was furiously smoking a pipe full of something that was not calming him down. He went on pacing for some time, and I found I could not care much for how unhappy he may have been. I just wanted to see my father.

"You know, Lenz," said Prince Friedhelm, finally, "I was already thinking it's time. But with what you've told me about Klemens, it is certainly time."

"Time, Your Highness?" asked Lenz. He sounded very much like he knew what that meant, but was hoping he was wrong.

"Yes, time! They're trying to kill me, it's almost the King's Dinner, and my brother is off *hunting*, supposedly. Such was my thinking over the last few days, but this Klemens character has decided me fully. If he's truly trying to *stop* these plotters against the throne, we need him on our side. And I only see one way to do that."

"But, Your Highness," began Lenz, "if your brother truly is off hunting, and he comes back—"

"He isn't, I'm sure of it. But if he *is*, we shall have an awkward reunion. Which is fine. We've never much liked each other." The Prince moved over to his bookshelf, and yanked one of the books so hard that it came off in his hand, revealing the hidden lever that controlled the hidden door.

I almost laughed. The Prince pulled the lever angrily and the door swung open, revealing a long staircase. These Rotfelsenisch loved their hidden passageways, I suppose.

"Hurry up!" Friedhelm yelled down the stairs. Then he grinned mirthlessly; Lenz put his head in his hands.

Soon enough, footsteps could be heard coming up toward us, and then an extremely bland-looking man appeared at the top of the stairs, huffing and puffing.

"Well . . . phew, quite the climb," he grunted. "I say, well, I made it, finally." He braced himself against the false bookshelf and smiled a clever little smile.

"What . . . ?" I asked, looking to Lenz.

"Meet the Twelfth Recourse," he sighed.

I looked back at the man. His smile disappeared, and his face became smooth, forgettable, vacant. I blinked four or five times as I felt the pang of recognition. He looked exactly like someone I had seen speaking to the Prince at the Ball: he looked exactly like the King.

He stepped toward me, his face that same vacant mask, then he broke back into a smile and bowed to me.

"I don't believe I've had the pleasure," he said. "Name's Olaf"—he winked—"but you can call me Gerhold VIII."

Lenz flopped back onto Prince Friedhelm's couch. Probably because of his leg, but it also carried with it the whiff of a great lady fainting in surprise.

"I cannot believe you're actually doing it," he grunted. He then quickly added, "Your Highness."

The Prince grinned. "And why not, eh?" He seemed very pleased with himself.

"And that you have now told Kalyna, as well," Lenz added.

"Well, if my brother has been kidnapped, how is she supposed to find him in her visions if she thinks that Olaf here is him, eh?"

"Just so," I said.

"I suppose," murmured Lenz.

I moved closer to Olaf, squinting at him. "How . . . ?"

"Flesh-alchemy, of course," sighed Lenz.

"But . . . like this?" I reached out, and almost grabbed Olaf's cheek to see if it would come off.

"Oh, far more than your garden variety alchemy," laughed Prince Friedhelm. He leaned back on his desk, seeming relaxed for the first time since the Winter Ball.

Olaf nodded at me. "Go on."

I pinched his cheek like he was a child. It felt real enough.

"We spent quite some time," said Lenz, "finding someone bodily similar enough to the King who also had . . . well . . ."

"No real ties," laughed Olaf. "No one will much care that I'm gone, you see."

"A drifter," added the Prince, "found living from ditch-to-ditch in the deepest caves. But a lucky drifter, in the scheme of things. He'll get to live like the King for a week or two."

"Until I'm poisoned or stabbed, or found out and *then* poisoned or stabbed," added Olaf. He hardly seemed sad about it.

Lenz grunted and threw his leg up onto the side of the couch, putting himself on his back. "After we found Olaf, we had the best flesh-alchemists spend weeks studying the King from afar, studying paintings and sketches of the King, studying even the gold marks that bore his face. Each focused on one part of his face, supposedly to reconstruct in case he ever had an accident, and then taught *those features* to other flesh-alchemists, without telling them whose face they belonged to. Everyone was sworn to secrecy, of course."

"Of course," echoed Friedhelm, absentmindedly.

"I've never heard of such a thing," I muttered, finally taking my hand away from Olaf, who smiled and became some semblance of himself again.

"Of course not!" laughed the Prince. "It's never been attempted before."

"The sad part," said Olaf, "is that if I survive this, they'll change me to not-the-King, but they won't be able to turn my face back to how it was." He shrugged. "No one ever spent weeks and weeks studying *my* face. No sketches, no paintings. A pity: I was quite handsome!"

Lenz dipped his head slightly in agreement.

"And you've lived down in a hidden room . . . ?" I began.

"For some time," laughed Olaf. "I can't very well go walking around like this. But the room has a window, so I could get used to the sun. It was torture at first, but now I rather like it. What's more, I had time to learn the King's manner. It mostly involves thinking of something else and looking far away." His eyes went vacant.

I absorbed that, and his seeming nonchalance about the whole situation. It was impossible for me to imagine this plan *working*.

"You must have spent that time learning how to be a king, yes?" I finally asked. "Polishing up on duties and such?"

Olaf snorted. "What duties? All I have to do is show up where I'm told, smile, nod, and not say anything *too* idiotic."

I opened my mouth and closed it again. Then I looked at Prince Friedhelm. He still seemed quite pleased with himself, so I decided now was as good a time as any to broach something that had been on my mind.

"Your Highness," I began.

"Mm?"

"If there are no real duties involved in being King of Rotfelsen—no complex decisions that must be made, no crushing responsibilities—why are you *so* insistent on avoiding the crown?"

"Kalyna . . ." Lenz warned.

I quickly added a curtsy and an, "If you please," so as not to seem too presumptuous.

Friedhelm was surprised at my forwardness, but then the corner of his mouth curled up, as though this was also something he *wanted* to tell. As though he thought he was about to be very charming.

"Why, Kalyna Aljosanovna," he said, "because it is *boring*. Crushingly, terribly boring."

Lenz looked up at this.

"For a man like Olaf, with no other prospects, it's the good life. But for me?" Friedhelm began to pace. "State dinner after state dinner, after state *luncheon*; presiding over fencing tournaments; staid little"—he yawned—"drinks with staid little functionaries; the opera, but always with some morose outer noble singing his own little aria about the taxes into my ear; siring absolutely, positively, *no bastards*." He made a face and shook his head. "Absolutely not. I shall have the privileges of royalty without *those* responsibilities. Let Olaf here"—he patted the man's shoulder—"handle the boring parts until we find my brother."

"And if your brother hasn't been kidnapped?" asked Lenz.

"Lenz, I tell you again that he *has*," said the Prince, leaning on his desk again. "And now his kidnappers will be trapped and confused. They'll want to prove that I've put a double on the throne, but won't be able to accuse me without exposing themselves." He grinned and clapped his hands together. "Meanwhile, you two will figure out where the real King has disappeared to. This will teach that ridiculous little Selvosch and that pompous Vorosknecht to turn against me."

"But," Lenz tried again, "Your Highness, if your brother is simply hunting—"

"Then mayhap this will teach him not to disappear like that. And when he comes home, I'll make a big show of re-changing Olaf's *pretty face*. After brother Gerhold is back on the throne, perhaps I'll lend him one of my bastards, since his *Queen* is unable to give him one."

"Are you sure," began Lenz, carefully, "you're not doing this *just* to see the look on her face?"

The Prince pushed off his desk and stood very straight, looking down at Lenz. "I have given you a very free hand, Lenz Felsknecht," he said quietly. "Don't you go and force me to rein you in."

Lenz spun to sit up straight, wincing as his bad leg was jarred in the motion. "Yes, Your Highness."

"And get off my couch," said the Prince. "You are dismissed."

So we were hurtling toward having two identical kings. If we couldn't have the fool, we would have the drifter with a death wish. Without either of them, we'd have the *Prince*. Gods, it was like I was seeing how everything would fall apart right in front of me, but with no way to change it. Unless I made it worse.

Lenz and I began to leave. I opened my mouth to remind him that *now* I needed to see my father, before the Prince spoke up again.

"Oh, and Lenz, please take Kalyna with you to the watchtower right away. I've hired someone else who should be able to help you find the King: You remember Chasiku, yes?"

"Oh. Yes, Your Highness," said Lenz.

We began to leave. Olaf waved cheerily, with seemingly no idea of the violent doom he would probably cause.

"I look forward to working with you!" he sang out.

THE WATCHTOWER

Soon I was back in a carriage with Lenz once again. He looked very irritated.

"This plan," I ventured, "seems ill-advised."

"I wouldn't go so far as to call it a plan," Lenz grumbled. "His Highness has a bad habit of throwing new ideas at a problem and just . . . seeing what lands."

"Like hiring a soothsayer," I said.

Lenz looked up at me. "You could say that." Then he broke into a laugh.

"What's so funny?"

"Chasiku," he laughed. "He's hired two of them, now."

"Two what?"

"Soothsayers," he replied, smiling.

I was quiet for the rest of the ride, until we reached the watchtower, which was made of rotrock bricks. Lenz talked to me, but I acted as though I wasn't listening.

This watchtower, Lenz explained, was one of the oldest structures on the palace grounds, and hardly in use anymore. It had been built in pre-, pre-, pre-Tetrarchic days, when Rotfelsen was a collection of small states, many of which planted capitals here on the surface: a confusing time, when who ruled which outcropping, or which tunnel, was never clear. The watchtower had originally been built to keep a lookout for armies on the surface, and was not high enough to look into the forests beneath Rotfelsen's bulging sides. In our modern, civilized age, it was for punishment: a good place to send a loud soldier for a day or two, where they could watch for absolutely nothing. It had apparently been easy for the Prince to requisition the watchtower for the use of his newest human bauble.

"A second soothsayer," I said as I stepped out of the carriage.

Lenz nodded.

"So the Twelfth Recourse wasn't enough?"

"I suppose this is Eleventh Recourse, Stroke Two," he sighed as he led me and a Yellow into the small circular tower. "Her name was brought up in our original search, and I even visited her in North Shore Skydašiai, but she said no. I suppose she changed her mind, and the Prince accepted."

"She got to say *no*?"

"Well, it was earlier in our search."

"In that case, will you be—"

"Letting you go? No," he said quickly. Then he grinned. "That isn't how Friedhelm operates. And besides, he seems to think you saved his life." He chuckled at the thought.

"Lucky me," I grunted.

"A second King, a second soothsayer," sighed Lenz. "We had better find Gerhold before the Prince replaces me, as well."

I snorted a bit at the thought. "Or before he brings in a juggler, and a dramaturge, and a bard, and—"

"Don't even speak that into existence!" said Lenz. "I doubt it is beyond him."

Well, this was a terrifying new wrinkle. Lenz likely thought little of my supposed Gift after that Klemens debacle, and this new fortuneteller was probably a fraud, like all who claimed to see the future outside of my small family. A more skilled fraud than me, likely enough. She would, I expected, do everything she could to discredit me. Or, at best, her lies would run counter to mine. And when I became even more useless than I already was, I would become only a prisoner who knew about a false king. Not a long life expectancy there, I suspected. How long had the Prince allowed those flesh-alchemists who cobbled together Olaf to live? Not long, I'm sure. My heart began to positively pound.

"As far as I know," I said, "only my family has the Gift." Best to start discrediting her *now*, rather than later. I hoped I would escape soon, but it's always good to plan for every possibility.

"Families grow and separate," said Lenz as he walked toward the center of the watchtower. "You might be surprised at your relatives."

"I have two relatives."

The watchtower was only as wide around as a big room. It was dark, with one guttering torch visible from the ground floor, and around the walls, there was a small, twisty staircase with a lot of bricks missing. A small pallet on a rope hung in the center.

"More stairs? You're not making your job easy, Lenz."

He smiled grimly and sat on the pallet. There was a wrenching sound above, and the pallet shook and began to rise.

"It's meant for supplies," said Lenz. "You'd better jump on now or take the stairs." When he finished talking, he had already risen past my waist.

I took the stairs. The Yellow followed me, to make sure I didn't try to cut the rope somehow.

At the top, the staircase curled around a system of pulleys and weights. The pallet was just surfacing, and a rope reached all the way down to the bottom, with some sort of counterweight hanging from it.

Lenz grunted as he flopped over onto the floor next to me, quite un-dignified. He pulled himself up. The top of the watchtower was a small open platform that led right out on all sides to a railing from which the surface of Rotfelsen could be viewed. We were up much higher than the nearby barracks or my servant house, yet the watchtower was hardly noticeable when it shared a stage with the Sunset Palace. There was one walled-off room up here, and the rest was open to the air. The room had a small wooden door, which was the only new-looking thing here, besides the pallet and its ropes.

That door was open. The small room had bedding on the floor, a few bags of what I took to be clothes, and no other openings except for a matching open door that led out onto the walkway that circled the watchtower. There was a figure in the room, sitting on the bedding, star-ing out that open door, with her back was to us. As I have mentioned, her name was Chasiku, and she was from North Shore Skydašiai.

A VERY SHORT HISTORY OF THE PRE-TETRARCHIA

Have I explained to you, whoever may be reading this, Skydašiai and its two shores? It would have been the strangest kingdom of the Tetrar-chia, were it not for the other three.

Long ago (but long after the Ancients and all that), a wandering tribe of sallow, pale people came to what would eventually be the Tetrarchia, and for some reason, settled in a frozen forest (Masovska). Soon after, they were supposedly followed by a sort of sibling tribe of stocky people both related to, and distinct from, that first group. This second tribe, smartly, settled in a pleasant seaside land next door (roughly half of Skydašiai).

These two tribes squabbled and split off for some time, until a host of entirely different peoples arrived, darker than any descended from those two tribes, and speaking languages like nothing that had been heard in the region before. They trickled into the nearby mountains, and these became the Quru.

Rots liked to think that they arrived fully formed, but this is of course untrue. The pink cheeked and often blonde people who came next gravitated toward the great rock nearby, for some ungodly reason, and fought amongst themselves within it for centuries.

These four groups were soon hundreds of small nations and city-states. Over time, they congealed down into roughly four, fighting and trading amongst themselves. But one more element was required for them to become the four groups that existed in my time.

The Skydaš Sea (or whatever it was called back then) cut off the north of our continent, except where the Quru mountains curled around its eastern end. The northern shore of the sea was visible from the southern, hanging golden in the distance. The not-yet-Skydašians on the southern shore sometimes sailed across to hunt and forage, but they never stayed. Monolithic Loasht loomed to the northeast, already ancient and sitting upon its guns; trading across the water, with no desire for new neighbors.

Then perhaps a thousand years ago, the *other* Skydašiai came. They wandered into the region from somewhere in the lands northwest of the Skydaš Sea, and settled right at its shore. The word "Skydašiai" did not exist yet, and these new settlers, with their deep brown skin and tightly curled hair, did not look like their new neighbors. This people happened to arrive during the lowest point in Loasht's most recent Era of Waning (which some whisper will soon end), and so were able to avoid being expelled or absorbed. They traded, fought, set down roots, and built cities.

There was no singular moment when the North and South Shore folk merged into one kingdom: their union was more gradual than the carefully negotiated formation of the Tetrarchia, centuries later. The two became symbiotic, with the North Shore providing a military bulwark against Loasht, while the South Shore grew abundant produce and became a trading hub. People began to intermarry, and rudimentary trade languages expanded into greater complexity. By the time a royal marriage was made between the two shores, their unification was a foregone conclusion.

Later, when the Tetrarchia was formed, Skydašiai (a word combined from two old languages that have long since merged and rendered the term gibberish) was a single country with a single language and set of laws. The North Shore and South Shore remained somewhat distinct groups through the centuries—with different physical characteristics on the outer ends, blending toward an almost homogeneous center around the sea, and with different customs throughout, depending on local specialties—but Skydašiai is Skydašiai. It is as much a land of wandering peoples settling down next to each other as is the Tetrarchia itself.

CHASIKU

She did not turn to face us. Skydašians of both shores tended to be a friendly, physical people—they liked to *hug*, but not Chasiku. She was sitting straight as the watchtower itself, with her legs pointing out in front of her. Cold morning light peeked in around her head from the door through which she looked. Her hair was cut extremely short, and I could see where the nape of black hair faded into the dark brown skin of her neck. She kept her back to me when she spoke.

"Good to see you again, Chasiku," said Lenz.

"Pleased to meet you," I offered.

"The limping spy I've met," she said. "But you're new. Average height. Some sort of mutt. Long, loose, curly hair, big nose. Scar on the upper lip."

"Uh-huh," I said.

Her back was still to me, naturally. A basic trick: she had either stolen a glimpse before I saw her, or pieced together clues from what Lenz, or Yellows, had told her.

"Pleased to meet you, too," I repeated, loudly and slowly.

She nodded her head slightly, toward the open door. "Kalyna Aljosanovna Tsaoxelek," she said.

"Kalyna Aljosanovna," I replied. "You must be confused."

"Oh!" She curved forward, away from us, like a tree that grows in heavy wind, then shook her head. "I apologize. That is not your name yet. It may never be."

I turned to Lenz and trained a *very* incredulous sort of look on him. Did he really believe her?

But then, he believed me. Didn't he?

"Maybe you will come around to her," he said.

"It's true," said Chasiku. "Maybe."

"That," I growled, "is just about enough of that." I stomped around the room to look into her face. "You may not need to look at me, but I prefer to see the person I'm talking to!" In order to better form fake prophecies about them.

I had expected that there would be a theatrical reason why Chasiku didn't show us her face: blindness (real or pretended) or great scarring. But no, when I came around, and stuck my head between hers and the door, she looked up at me uncaringly. Her face was smooth and unblemished, with high cheekbones; her eyes were large. She seemed willowy and hardy at the same time, if that is possible. As though you could easily snap her body in half, but she, head against her own rear, would only shrug and ask if you could do no better. She was attractive, I suppose.

"Yes. All right," she said, looking me in the eyes. "This is better?"

"Where do you come from?"

"Skydašiai."

"Yes, but . . . I mean, where did Lenz find you?"

"Skydašiai. Months ago. I turned down his offer, but have since decided I could use a change of scenery."

I looked up, past her, at Lenz. He looked back at me, but said nothing.

"You are giving me a headache," said Chasiku. "I feel the pounding of your death between my temples."

"Oh, really?" It was a stupid thing to say, but all that came to me.

"The Prince has told me about your family," said Chasiku, "and what you call 'the Gift.' You are all extremely lucky."

"*Lucky?*"

"My family," she said, "live on the outskirts of Kalvadoti, a great city. Even from so far away, where we see no one but those who come for our services, we are assaulted by the trembling delicacy of the people crammed into those buildings and streets. So many people, so many possibilities, every choice they may or may not make: it is all amplified, a constant thrumming behind everything. We have never called this a 'Gift.' It is a burden."

"That is all very sad, if true," I said. "My father is beaten by nonsensical imagery from across the world, so you will forgive my not crying for you. It also seems that your family has homes."

"I don't care to play at whose life is harder," she sighed. "The closer anyone is, the more of their futures dance before me. This whole place quivers of death more than most, as though none of you exist at all. It must be all these soldiers killing each other."

"And you feel my death, too?" I asked, trying to sound as unconvinced as possible.

Chasiku nodded.

"I thought," I said, grinning a little, I admit, "that I was going to marry this Tsaoxelek person, whose name I don't recognize. Now you say I'm to die soon."

Chasiku wrinkled her brow and cocked her head to the side to look at me, as though I had tried to get the better of her by pointing out that the sky was not blue, but *sky blue*.

"Sometimes," she said very slowly, as though to a child, "there may be *different things that can happen*. Is that so complex?"

I narrowed my eyes and stood up, back to the cold sunlight, arms crossed. "Yes, thank you. My family sees whatever is most likely."

"'Most likely'? What is 'most likely'?"

I shrugged. "Whatever we see."

She actually looked thoughtful for a moment; her eyes wandered over to the single decoration on her wall: a hanging tapestry that, to my view at least, was entirely abstract. I glanced at Lenz again, but he was watching her.

"Death, then," said Chasiku. "Death soon is what I see the most. Kalyna the wife of a man named Tsaoxelek is far less likely."

I wondered, was this woman a fraud trying to scare me, or planning to kill me? Or was she the real thing, and seeing, in her own roundabout way, the same ending of the Tetrarchia that my father had picked out of the future. Was all that death she saw because we had two kings? Or because Loasht would invade? Or because an earthquake would break Rotfelsen like an egg?

I looked at Lenz again, trying to intimate that if he believed her, he was a fool. He betrayed nothing of what he thought, unfortunately.

Chasiku melted back into the position she had held before. Her legs were still stuck straight out, across the bedding and the floor, pointing toward me and the door to the watchtower's platform. She stuck her arms out behind her and leaned on them, but remained almost entirely straight. She blinked again, closed her eyes longer, opened them, and sighed.

"And has she told you anything helpful yet?" I asked Lenz, over Chasiku's head.

"She only just got here," he replied.

"I am truly not interested in arguing with you," said Chasiku. "Your very presence here hurts me."

"Convenient," I grunted. "Privacy means fewer chances to say the wrong thing, more time to think out your 'visions.'"

Chasiku fixed her gaze upon me with a look that seemed angry and pleading all at once. I expected the anger, but the absolute desperation unbalanced me. There was something in her eyes that seemed to beg for my understanding.

"I need you to leave now, and take him with you. I am not so lucky as to have my mind pick and choose what it sees, as yours does. Even your father, it sounds to me, sees one thing at a time. To have you here, with all of your possible courses of action, and the things that could be done to you, oozing out of your every pore, it's as though I'm trying to read a book in Loashti while you yell Skydašiavos curses in my ear. Do you understand?"

I glared at her and repeated, "Very convenient."

The set of her jaw was tight, her eyes stared into me, seeming to beg for understanding while being disgusted at my very existence. After a lifetime of trusting what I observed in people—because how else could I have done my job?—it seemed almost believable that her power was real. Her pain certainly appeared so.

Chasiku would be fun to work with. Oh yes, a regular joy. All the more reason I needed to get out of this place. I reckoned my life had become cheaper than ever to Lenz, now that he had a newer, better soothsayer. Perhaps it was *her* false prophecies that would bring about the violent end of the Tetrarchia. There was a comforting thought, in a way.

"Let's go," said Lenz, turning toward the door we had come through. I stepped back around her and followed him toward the door. Apparently, on our way up, Chasiku had been the one to release the counterweight and thereby propel Lenz's pallet up to the top of the watchtower. Because she had known when we would be there, *of course*. From the top, Lenz could get the contraption working himself. I watched him go and wished he would crash.

Supposedly our presences, not our words, bothered Chasiku, but nonetheless we didn't speak anymore until we were out of the watchtower and in our carriage.

I Concoct a Desperate Plan

I was bone-tired as the carriage rumbled beneath me. Today I had killed, captured, interrogated, met a false king, and found that I was in danger of being replaced. I knew where Klemens was kept, and who Olaf really was, so there was no way being replaced would mean I could go on my merry way. I desperately needed escape.

"So," I began carefully, "my family . . ."

Lenz watched me silently for a moment, then yelled something to the carriage driver, and we turned.

We said nothing as the carriage pulled up in front of a five-story building on the palace grounds, wider and taller than my servant house, but similar in design. On my way out of the carriage, I looked at Lenz once more, trying to read him. Was I truly, finally going to see my father? It almost felt impossible by now. I hadn't seen him in almost two weeks—a lifetime. My hands shook as I went inside. I ran up a flight of stairs, and it occurred to me again that this could have all been a con on Lenz's part to string me along. Would I round the staircase to see more guards? Was it all a trick to root out any vestiges of hope? I shook and slowed my walk, not wanting to reach the top.

At the third-floor landing, a large man in a burlap apron leaned against a railing and scribbled furtively on a piece of paper. When I looked at him, he seemed not just annoyed and distracted, but angry that I was there. Who was this? What was going on?

"Oh, you must be the daughter," he grunted. "In there."

I felt a deep, and sudden, need to distract myself from uncertainty with violence. I wanted to hit him. At least then *something* would be clear.

But then I heard, "Is that you, freak?" and "Kalynishka!" and I stormed through Grandmother's room to my father's, giving him a hug.

I did my best to hide how tired I was, how ragged after nearly dying twice in the last five days. I acted as though I had picked my family's uncomfortably large rooms out myself, after a thorough inspection of the building. Grandmother insisted on knowing what I was *actually* doing, and why there were nosy doctor's assistants everywhere. That was who the man in the apron had been, and there were more of them, always scratching away with their pens, constantly underfoot. To get some privacy, I had to yank one such assistant out of my father's room and deposit her into the hallway. She yelped along the way.

Grandmother asked what my scheme was because there was no way, of course, that anyone would hire me to do anything. I was not fit to wipe the asses of elderly merchants. I ground my teeth further and didn't argue. Papa was proud, beaming even, though he knew no more than she.

"When are you planning to explain what's *really* going on here?" Grandmother yelled from her room, where she sat in a chair that she must have purposefully torn up in order to feel at home. "You ungrateful little—"

I slammed the door to shut her up. The noise scared Papa, and he began shaking like a baby mouse. I ran to him and patted his hand to calm him down.

"They have put our things in that closet, Kalynishka," said Papa.

"Yes. They'll be safe there."

"Oh, we have nothing worth taking, Kalynishka," he sighed, patting my hand. "The fish in Fántutazh Lake have changed, Kalynishka."

"Oh?"

"The stew tasted different this time than when I was younger; the lobsters must be dying off."

"I see."

"I'm so glad we're up here, not down in the depths again."

I nodded.

He let go of my hand before looking up at me and smiling. "You look well, Kalynishka."

"You always think that."

"Do I? Well, it is always true."

I smiled. We were both quiet for a few minutes, and I could not tell if this was the sort of comfortable silence shared by those who are at ease, or if there was something I *should* have been saying. Papa stared off into space, then suddenly snapped his fingers and looked at me, as though he had remembered where he left something.

"Kalynishka, the Tetrarchia will fall, do you remember?"

"I . . . Yes, Papa, I remember."

"It will crumble and topple."

"Literally?"

"I . . . don't know, Kalynishka. It's all so mixed up. But something will happen."

"Well, Papa, I do remember."

"Oh! Good, good." He patted my hand. "Soon, you know."

"I know. In about two months."

"So soon?" he mused as though he had an appointment.

"Yes, Papa."

"Oh, my. Well, do not forget."

"I won't."

"Also . . ."

"Yes?"

". . . our things are stored in that closet, remember."

"Yes, Papa."

We were silent again. I tried to calm myself down, to stop thinking about death and destruction, about unavoidable doom.

Looking at my tired father, I suddenly knew how fanciful any thoughts of a quick escape had been. He and Grandmother weren't going to just disappear in the night with me. I needed to work with Lenz until I had a real plan for escape.

And then, just such a plot began to roil in my head. We sat quietly in each other's presence a little longer, as I thought it through. It was a terrible idea, but worth a try.

"Papa," I hissed under my breath, grabbing his right hand in both of mine, which were so much more calloused than his. I could not afford to let Grandmother hear this.

"Yes, Kalynishka?" His loving gaze turned to one of sudden fear—fear that had not surfaced while he discussed death and destruction.

"Papa, I need your help with something."

His eyes widened. He looked excited that I needed his help, but also seemed terrified of failing me. I felt deeply guilty. He nodded firmly.

"A man is going to come up here in a few minutes and meet you. My master, I suppose. I need you to tell me if you *see* anything about his future."

"What kind of—?"

"Anything at all!" He started, and I immediately felt like a monster for interrupting him. "Even the most mundane thing may be useful." I just needed leverage.

He bit his bottom lip and nodded his head once.

"But Papa, it's *very* important you tell no one about this. Not the man, Lenz, not Grandmother, not *anyone*."

He nodded again, and I thought my heart would break. He always wanted to be useful, but the stress of pinpointing real things in his miasma of visions was so taxing. If only I were not so broken; if only escaping this country were not so vital; if only Grandmother did not adhere so firmly to her own cruel principles.

"If . . ." I stammered, patting his hand. "If you see nothing . . ." I was going to say that he shouldn't worry, but I needed to use whatever I could to escape. Or perhaps I just wanted to get the best of Lenz so badly.

"If you see nothing," I repeated, "*try harder.*"

He nodded again and seemed to understand, bless him. I would ruin him for our escape, and yet I still didn't know where we would *go*.

FATHER AND JAILER

I asked Papa to wait a moment and left his room, passing Grandmother and slamming the door on her. On my way downstairs, another assistant asked me what we had discussed. I ignored her.

I found Lenz on the ground floor, talking to a Yellow. I smiled at him and suggested he come up and meet my father.

"Why?" He seemed leery.

"I told them I work for the Prince, and though I didn't exactly lie, a corroboration might help keep Grandmother quiet."

"Kalyna . . . that's a lot of stairs." He looked down at his bad leg. "It's been a day."

"You've kidnapped me, forced me to work, put me in front of assassins and thugs, and involved me in . . ." There were Yellows and doctor's assistants around, so even though I was saying this in Masovskani, the next word was simply ". . . Olaf. The very least you could do is look my father in the eye."

Lenz sagged to one side and rubbed his chin. "Your father has the Gift, yes?"

"The Gift has him," I replied.

"Hm."

"Don't."

"Mm?"

"Don't try to make my father 'see' things for you."

"Whyever would I? I have you and Chasiku."

Was he sarcastic? Did he suspect I was a fraud?

"He sees nothing useful," I said, "and it would . . . it would cause him great pain to try." I choked, thinking of all the times I'd pushed Papa to see visions so that I could better cheat our customers. Thinking of what I had planned for today.

"What about your grandmother?" he asked.

"*Please do* ask for her assistance."

"I'll go," he sighed, and followed me up the stairs.

Lenz looked truly harried by the time we got to the third floor, as Grandmother loudly described his "lame, syphilitic leg." His limp was more pronounced than usual as we both perched by Papa's bed. Grandmother continued spewing invective from the other room.

"Pleased to see you again, Aljosa Vüsalavich," he said.

I tried very hard not to look surprised. Papa blinked up at Lenz with no recognition in his face.

"Lenz Felsknecht. We spoke in Masovska."

Of course they had. I imagined him asking my poor father a hundred questions and felt my face burn.

"Lanso, was it?" murmured Papa.

"Lenz. And I"—he raised his voice, half yelling through the door into Grandmother's room—"*serve our Highness Prince Friedhelm*!"

"Our highness of balls!" replied Grandmother.

Papa beamed at me, looked back at Lenz with fear and concentration, muttered a response, and nestled into his pillow.

Lenz ignored Grandmother and attempted small talk with my father: "Your daughter has been extremely helpful in the Prince's service," he lied.

"Yes," said Papa. He was deeply focused upon his lack of focus, and did not seem to know what he was agreeing with. "Yes, yes," he continued, "and the green crests of the Skydaš Sea scoop up skeletons of antennaed sharks that lived before humanity."

Lenz coughed and made his goodbyes.

"I'm heading back to my office, to try and straighten out the Prince's . . ." Lenz stopped himself and eyed my father, then said, ". . . business. You may stay for a bit. The Yellows will take you back to your house when you're ready."

When he passed through Grandmother's room this time, she sat silently with her lips pulled together, following him with her eyes until he was going down the stairs.

I looked at Papa, who seemed to be attempting to stare hard at something behind his own eyes. He noticed me, seemed frightened that I was there, nodded seriously to let me know he remembered what I'd asked, and then smiled, as though only just realizing the person in front of him was his daughter.

"Do you see anything?" I asked under my breath.

"Lots," replied Papa. "Lots and lots and lots."

"About Lenz?"

His smile faltered. "I don't know yet, Kalynishka. It's all so . . . so . . . so *much*." He pressed his hand to his forehead. "I will try to sort through what I've seen today, but it may take time. You know how my mind is."

"Not really, no."

He smiled again at that. "I won't forget."

"I know."

"And don't you forget either." He wagged his finger playfully.

"About the—?"

"Encroaching doom, yes," he whispered, as though gossiping about a neighbor. "Remember."

We embraced. He shivered less than usual, and I still felt guilty. I left the room.

BROKEN SHITWORM

"*What* won't your poor, beleaguered father forget?" asked Grandmother as I passed her.

I had considered the window, rather than going through her room yet again, but it was a long drop to rotrock. I kept walking and said nothing.

"Tell me what is happening, you wretched girl," she snarled. "What are you doing to my poor son, now? Haven't you ruined him enough?"

I stayed quiet as I approached the door to the stairs. Grandmother stuck out her foot as if to trip me, but pulled it back when she saw I would not stop.

"Tell me, you broken shitworm. What's going on?" She began to sound . . . concerned?

"If you must know," I said at the door, staring out, "why not use your *own* Gift to see?"

"My time with the Gift is done. That's your job, half-a-brain."

"Yet you still have the Gift."

"Of course I do. I am no sliver of a human being like you. I chose to carry on our legacy, and then when your father took over, I rightly chose—"

"But why can't you—?"

"*Because I should not have to*! Don't you understand that, you miserable thing?"

I turned to leave.

"You would not *dare* leave while I'm speaking to you!"

I was at the door. I *was* actually leaving, and it felt marvelous. I was a prisoner, but my jailers were more powerful than Grandmother. How could she stop me?

"If you don't come back," she yelled, "I will *tell them*!"

I stopped. I wanted to cry. I padded slowly back into her room.

She was in her chair, looking smug with her eyebrows raised, crinkling the tattoo above her left eye. I slammed the door, then passed her to shut the door to Papa's room. Grandmother slowly replaced her unlit pipe, clacking it between her teeth. She was so, so small.

"Why don't you sit, girl?" She pointed to the floor in front of her. "Not right to look down on your grandmother like that."

I did not sit on the floor, clean though it was.

"Tell me," she said calmly, "what's going on here."

I looked at her a long time, then said, "If it could save our lives, would you use the Gift?"

"It should not be *my* job to save our lives."

"If it could save our lives."

"Pray tell me, child, from whom we need saving."

"If I tell you what's going on, will you at least consider using your Gift to help?"

"Are we in mortal danger?"

"Will you *consider* it?"

Grandmother sat back and blew out a long gust of smoke-less breath through her pipe. She coughed and looked thoughtful.

I bit my lip and then stopped. I didn't want to look desperate. Something flapped by the window.

"No," said Grandmother, sighing. "No, I don't think I will consider it. What is mortal danger, anyway? Our line is done."

"You were deciding whether or not to lie to me."

"And aren't you *glad* I chose truth and honor, little fool? As I always do?"

Had I been on the floor, in her reach, she would have pinched my cheek.

"Always," she repeated. "I always tell the truth, regardless of what is 'safe' or 'considerate.' If that is uncomfortable, it is your fault for being so weak. You could get us out of any silly scrape if you were half the soothsayer your father was in his prime." She pointed at the closed door with her pipe.

I gripped my forehead to keep my skull from falling out. "Of course I'm not *half* the soothsayer he was." This next part came out very slowly, giving each whispered word its space: "I do not have the Gift." And then I started yelling. "Have you *forgotten* somehow? How can you hold me to the same standard?"

"Your father and I—"

"Have a Gift from the gods," I hissed, flailing at her, "which . . ." I wanted to yell it, let the Yellows and the doctor's assistants know, but of course I whispered again, "which I don't! I have done everything I can to keep us alive—"

"And a fine job of it you're doing," she said.

"You *are* alive, aren't you? Eating better than you ever have!"

"Eating too well. This decadence will poison us, like some . . ." She actually spat on the floor. ". . . *aesthetes.*"

"It is a magnitude more than *you* have done! I must—!" I cut myself off to lower my voice and begin again. "I must lie, cheat, and fight to keep us going in the way you and your blessed ancestors saw fit, while you squander your Gift and insult me."

"I have to insult you," she said. "No one else knows how defective you are."

"But why in the world won't you *help* me?"

"It is not *my* fault *you* are broken."

"Your blood's in my veins, demon. Perhaps it *is* your fault."

Grandmother looked hurt. I had actually hurt her in a way beyond simply existing. I had cut through her armor and injured her. Her eyes filled with sorrow and her pipe fell.

I wanted to cheer and dance, to caper about the room, laughing and pointing at her like a five-year-old. Then I felt guilty for thinking this about my own grandmother. *Then* I got angry at myself for growing so soft toward the old demon, who had never given me reason to be kind to her. I looked into her angry little face and knew I wanted to hurt her more.

Or perhaps it wasn't you, I considered adding, *perhaps my mother was the broken one. The one to blame for me.* I had never met my mother, what would trampling her memory matter?

I did not say this. It was too blasphemous toward a woman who may not have been the goddess my family described, but did not deserve to be used as a cudgel.

Now Grandmother and I both felt terrible. She told me to lift her and put her on the bed, repeating herself three times until I finally did as she asked.

"I might drop you, you know," I said as I felt her angry, gnarled little body curled into my arms.

"Won't be enough to kill me, *you know*," she said.

I put her on the bed.

"Why are you inflicted upon me?" she asked. "I always told your father that he should have had another child. Maybe that one would not be shattered inside."

"Anyone raised by you would be shattered inside," I mumbled.

"Eh?"

"I said he never wanted another child." I pulled her chair up to the side of the bed, just out of her reach, and sat.

"Never forget," she replied, waving a finger at me, "that continuing *our line* was always more important than whom you love or what you like or who you are or what you have. But much to my shame, you chose to ruin that."

"I did not *choose*—"

"My great-grandmother Aytaç's wife could not give her a child, so Aytaç found a man for a night and bore my grandfather Huso," she began, as though I did not know the family history by heart. "Married in the eyes of our family, but by no priest, they raised Huso together. When he was grown, Huso met my grandmother, who bore my father, Mildo."

I nodded and waited for her to finish.

"Mildo bore me, I bore your father, and your father found your wonderful mother, who bore you."

"I know."

"You then killed her—"

"I *know.*"

"—and as punishment, the gods made you our end. Instead of seeing the future, you *cause* it. Now I get to watch my son die slowly, and know that it is all over. You know, for a time, I thought you might still have some sliver of the Gift, useless but *there*. But it is clear you do not, or that you have chosen not to access it. You're too old to fix anything now."

"I am only twenty-seven," I growled, as I wondered why I was arguing on her terms.

She ignored me anyway. "Why couldn't you be more like your great-grandfather Mildo?"

I wondered the same thing.

"He never complained. He may have had complicated feelings around bearing a child, but he never complained." She sighed. "I am too good and kind a person. Sometimes it still hurts me to think that I caused my father so much pain."

She shook her head, and the next cough may have doubled for a sob. She stared at the ceiling.

"So much," she moaned. "I hurt my father so much." Another broken sob. Then she turned her head to me and grinned through it all. "But," she said, "at least I did not *kill* him."

I left. Her chair slammed to the floor behind me.

REGARDING CHILDREN AND SUCCESSION IN MY FAMILY

As far back as is known, the rule in my family has been that there is one child in a generation. A second is purposefully conceived only if the first has died. So, yes, when Grandmother said Papa should have had a second child, she was essentially calling me a corpse. Dead inside, at best.

This rule of only children existed, we were told, to keep the Gift from being split between multiple children, diluted. The logic of this escapes me, but then so does the logic of my physically resembling Grandmother more than my mother, as she has been described to me. It could be our ancestors simply didn't want the family to split into competitive branches with different customs, or were worried about what some great Soothsayer Conglomeration could get up to. I wondered if Chasiku was part of some long-forgotten offshoot, perhaps even the catalyst for our rule.

This rule did not mandate monkhood. There are root concoctions and gall bladder sheaths and the like that can stop conception, and still allow for a man and a woman to rut if they have tired of alternative activities, but they are not foolproof. Neither did the rule require relationships to be one man and one woman. My ancestors would bear a child with whomever they could have a child with, and raise that child alongside whomever they could stand to travel with—these did not need to be the same person.

In my teen years, I learned that I had neither time nor freedom for loving or sexual attachments. A boy is too likely to decide I am his, to insist I settle down, to expect Papa to survive on his own or happily move in with the new "us." They were often good enough people, I suppose, but they had no idea their happy future would completely alter the girl they found so alluring. Women were often easier to get along with, but I found it was a lot of work keeping track of which parts of the Tetrarchia fully frowned upon such relations, and which saw them as just two (or three) girls being "good friends."

I desired as much as anyone, but soon realized I couldn't afford to be with anyone while so much depended on me. So I kept my own company, with my own fingers.

This may have been ill-advised because, as a descendant of an old family of soothsayers, it had been my *duty* to have a child to carry on tradition. I put it off because no man would be willing to travel with us (Grandmother insisted this had been no obstacle for her), and caring for a child would mean so much time when I'd be incapable of caring for my family or doing my job. Then, around age twenty-five, I was lucky enough to have Grandmother decide that my childbearing days were over before they'd started. She chose to give up hope and revel in the misery of our line being over.

To my mind, at the time, these were the only reasons not to do my duty. Now, in hindsight, I recognize that deep down, I was terrified of having a child as broken as myself. A child without the Gift. How would Grandmother treat such a child? How would I?

A GALIAG ZIGGURAT

Behrens, the sharpshooter, saw me back to the servant house. We chose walking over yet another carriage ride. The thin layer of snow on the ground was already melting, and the flowers and hedges were still bright. A far cry from how frozen the Great Field in Masovska must have been, just then. This made me feel thankful for Lenz's interference in my life, and I had to drive that feeling right out.

"Been in a share of scrapes since you joined us," said Behrens.

"You could say that, yes."

"I begin to wonder," he went on, appraising me, "what would have happened had I missed that man in the forest. The night we followed you down toward the valley in Masovska, I mean."

"I would be dead."

"Is that . . ." He touched his temple. "Your professional opinion?"

"Common sense. Past possibilities are rather beyond my senses."

"Hmm. I don't know. I wonder what else our master saw in you that night."

"I was just starting to like you, Behrens," I said.

He threw up his hands. "Sorry! Just a curious sort."

"Most are."

He nodded.

"It seems I'm not quite enough for the Prince," I added.

"Oh, you mean Chasiku? Odd sort, isn't she? But, you know, the more the better, yes? I'm not the only sharpshooter in the army, either."

I thought on that for a moment, but decided I didn't much like the idea of being part of some coterie of soothsayers very much at all.

"Behrens, what do you think of all of the Prince's . . . *plans* and *experts*? Do you think the man knows what he's doing?" I kept it purposefully vague because I didn't know whether Behrens was aware of Olaf.

He laughed and made a show of looking around, to ensure no one was listening. We were out on a footpath, with no one close by. I could see the Royal Inn of Ottilie's Rock in the distance, and wondered whether Andelka was having a friendly conversation with a Green whose job it was to ensure she didn't escape.

"I try not to think about it too much, if I'm being honest. I'm in Lenz's good graces because I am very observant, but care for little but my sharpshooter brethren. This means I'm privy to a lot of strange information, and I think that if I showed too much of an interest in it, things might go bad for me."

"As in, you would be gotten rid of?"

"Or given a more important job."

"Do you care deeply for keeping the King in power? For keeping Rotfelsen and the Tetrarchia together?"

He shrugged. "Only insofar as it seems better than not doing so. If I wanted to be a soldier who *cared* about something, I'd be a Purple. And we see how that's working out for them."

"It may work out quite well," I replied, "if they succeed in taking power. Do the Reds or Greens feel anything for their charges?"

"I think that the Greens care about protecting our borders, and the Reds care about keeping either the King or Queen safe. But you'd have to ask them. As for the Yellows, our duty is to guard the Prince, but I don't believe many of us *care* for him."

"How scandalous," I replied in a clearly sarcastic monotone.

"Quite. I suppose most of us want, generally, to keep the palace grounds, and therefore the kingdom, quiet and safe. Relatively."

I wondered whether "quiet and safe" for the palace grounds really did mean the same for the people who lived beneath it. I decided not to voice this.

As we walked up to the servant house, Behrens concisely changed the subject: "A lady Yellow will accompany you to your room to make sure you didn't bring back any souvenirs."

I nodded. "Behrens, what would you do if the Court Philosopher ordered you, directly, to bring me to him?"

Behrens thought this over. "Well, I can't *directly* disobey Vorosknecht, but—"

"A good question, that!" chirped Jördis, who was ambling about just inside the house.

We both stopped dead in the doorway.

"Oh, don't worry about *me*," she laughed. "I'm off-duty! And my master's all hot air, you'll be fine!"

I faked a smile and said goodbye to Behrens, who did not fake it as well as I did.

"A nice seat on that one," said Jördis, under her breath, as he walked away.

I told her I supposed it was true. But ogling a body lost some of its thrill when I imagined that body as meat, cut up by a sword or crunched beneath rotrock.

Two months. Two months and a week, maybe. How specific was Papa's understanding of time, anyway? I sighed and went inside.

"Maybe you could make him into a Purple," I offered. "Get to look at him more often."

"I don't think he'd like it much in the Purples," she replied. "Any more than I would, if I had to be a *Soldier for Ideas*, as Vorosknecht calls it." She grimaced. "Besides, I suspect some of them would, ah, feel a way about his Skydašian ancestry."

I decided it wouldn't quite be prudent to ask her about what the Purples' "ideas" were. We began to make our way up the stairs, followed by a Yellow I did not recognize.

"I shouldn't even be cordial with you, you know," said Jördis.

"Because Vorosknecht—"

"I honestly don't know if he wants you beaten, killed, kicked out, or subordinate to him. He tells me very little." She grinned and shrugged. "So *I* don't bother hating his enemies. I'm sorry he ambushed you at the ball, for what it's worth. He only told me, minutes before you were dragged in, that we would see 'the Prince's mind-witch.'"

"And I, of course, never told you I'm a—"

"Why would it be my business? Who cares? We're all frauds here."

I coughed. "Well, I . . . I mean, I wouldn't say *that*."

"Oh, *of course* we're all entirely the experts we are paid to be." She winked. "And you and I love and respect the men we work for."

We stopped on the landing by our respective rooms. I leaned an arm against it and looked at her. "You take so little pride in your calling?"

"'Calling'?" she laughed. "Tural has a calling. I only follow in my father's footsteps. Never much cared for it, but I don't know what else I could do."

"I'm familiar with that feeling."

"Is your father a spy, too?"

I sighed. "No. And I didn't realize one could be a philosopher who doesn't care, unless one's philosophy is one of not caring."

"I regurgitate old books for Vorosknecht. No philosophizing necessary. Which"—she shook her head—"is fine by me."

"Well then, do those books say it is *ethical*," I asked, "to kidnap someone and threaten them with violence, whether or not that person is me?" Was Jördis aware of Vorosknecht's part in a plot against the King? The Court Philosopher had sent her out before discussing that part, but that could have been for show. If the King had been kidnapped, did she know where he was being kept?

"I told you," she said, "I'm off-duty. I'm not asking you *the future*, am I?" She said it as though the very idea of telling the future was laughable.

"I think you and Behrens, the Yellow you were admiring, would have a lot in common," I replied, "in your lack of caring."

"Is that meant as an insult?" She looked up at me in a way that was, at worst, mischievous.

"Not at all. I think some people up here care far too much about their work."

"I wholeheartedly agree."

We said our goodbyes, and I went into my room, where the Yellow searched me in a gentle and businesslike fashion, and found that I had stolen no weapons during this outing. She left, and I lay face down on my bed, nose in my pillow, staring blankly into an empty future.

My bedroom had become much more homey than I would have liked in the last few days. It was a prison, but it was mine more than any place I'd ever lived. I didn't share a space with Papa, Grandmother, transients, bandits, one-legged pimps, bulletfrogs, muskrats, or anything else. Sitting by the window, I had an endless expanse of fifteen unoccupied feet to the door: an embarrassment of empty space. Here I would sit, with the windows to my right and left, my back to the wall, and take very deep breaths. I had never been so alone in the place I slept.

There had been a few times before this when my family resided between real walls and doors. On the border of Skydašiai and the Tetrarchia's northeastern neighbor Loasht, there was a city called Galiag, and every few years it would be conquered by whichever country did not own it. Who owned it now? Would it be included in the Tetrarchia's collapse?

Galiag was contentious because if the Grand Suzerain of Loasht chose to invade the Tetrarchia, that city would be the gate by which their army entered our unwieldy country. Galiag was not contentious because anybody in their right mind wanted to live there. A land of burning winds, just as enjoyable as they sound, which rip up through the valleys to be channeled right into the city. Somewhere along the way, those winds must pass over deserts or lava flows or dragons or whatever it is that makes them burn so hot.

When I was a child, my family spent a summer—*a summer!*—in this place, which was Loasht-controlled at the time. The winds were so hot that at midday, one had to cower inside to keep from losing skin, and they were so strong that our tents were bowled right over. We spent one terrible night thinking our camp would hold in an alcove below a dune outside of town, and soon everything was shaking and moving. Papa had disappeared, Grandmother was screaming, and I was being pelted with stones so hot I suspect one could cook meat on them. I still have two scars from that: a round burn the size of a child's palm on my right ribs, and a rectangular pebble mark puckering a piece of my upper lip.

So we rented a tiny apartment in a disgusting little ziggurat. For reasons that are probably clear, rooms with windows were cheaper than those without in Galiag, and rooms facing east, where the wind originates, were cheaper still. We were on the ground floor, with a window facing the eastern valley and the farts of the gods. We could only afford such a place because Papa still told fortunes.

When the winds were at their worst, the room was almost fine. Down went the heavy shutters, and they would rattle from wind and fingernails, showing human silhouettes while we huddled the farthest from the shutters we could—not huddle *together* of course, since it was very, very hot. There was something thrilling about knowing death and pain were outside, and we were in there, separated by more than a tent made of animal skin. No, the winds were not so bad, but when they abated, the room was terrifying.

When the winds ebbed, we heard everything in any room near ours through those thin inner walls. Plots, cursing, rutting, robberies, abuse—every word of it leaked into our room. All complemented by the cries of hyraxes that scuttled in the walls. Outside the ziggurat was even worse, as the destitute, torn up by the winds that had just relaxed, scratched at our walls and moaned at our window. A window we could not keep closed all day, lest we die in that thick and overheated air. From both the neighboring rooms and the street outside, some of the people we heard wanted to get inside to us—to steal, to sleep, to rage, to talk. I didn't have my sickle yet, but that summer I gouged a man's eye out with my bare, little ten-year-old hands.

There *were* people who chose to live in Galiag. They were far from us, in the windowless centers of the ziggurats, rich and well-guarded. Perhaps they saw the sky at times, but certainly not often. Where we stayed was too rundown to attract anyone with money or power, but I did explore the ziggurat's innards a few times, when I was sick of being scared by the same people and decided to replace them with strangers. Those innards were all straight pathways that lead toward the center. The center was bronze, not brick, and the guards did not like me. That was my previous experience living between walls.

That crumbling ziggurat in Galiag came to me again as I sat by the window in my Rotfelsenisch room, looking out at a pleasant evening with pleasant snow. I noticed that I had, at some point, gotten myself a mug of brandy and a bowl of cheese curds.

I had spent five days living without Papa to care for, with servants making my food and cleaning my clothes, with space to call my own. Five measly days, and I had taken to drinking liquor and eating useless foods. I was a prisoner and I had become spoiled. Having so much space to myself had eroded what little decency I ever possessed: my clothes and books lay everywhere, curled around half-empty mugs that I had forgotten about days previous. I always suspected I only had self-control because I needed to care for Papa and not get yelled at by Grandmother, and it appeared I had been right. What a defective mess I was.

I sighed and stood up to pour another mug of brandy, and left my domain and prison to go talk to Tural.

PERSIMMON COUSINS

Tural opened up a thoroughly disgusting liqueur that he kept by his bed because I could not stand to go back for more brandy and have him see what a mess my room was. I described how exhausting my day had been, without telling anything of substance besides that Lenz and I did not see eye to eye. Tural, bless him, asked for nothing more.

"You and your boss seem to argue a great deal," he said in Rotfelsenisch.

"What else has a boss ever done?" I replied in Cöllüknit.

He brightened and said, "Nothing," in the same language.

"Have I interrupted your conjuring?"

"Oh my, no," Tural replied. "No conjuring is needed, not today." He laughed.

"That must be why you're smiling."

He nodded and held out the plate. "The day after next, and so soon after the ball, the King's Dinner looms, and all scatter like flightless parrots, but not the Master of Fruit. Never."

"And why is that?"

"Because I may now test my fruits with impunity, because they are in season and have arrived!" He gestured to a plate on his desk. "I know exactly what is ripe and how ripe, and I can taste them whenever I require. Everyone else has procrastinated until today, fighting off their decisions as humans do, but I could not *make* complete decisions until now, and so narrowed down every possibility months ago. In short, I am prepared. And the fruits are delicious."

"That sounds like a good place to be." And the opposite of where I was.

I felt helpless, able to do nothing but wait: wait for my family to arrive, wait for my father's prophecies to fall into my lap, wait for the Tetrarchia to crumble. In the meantime, I supposed I would eat good food, drink alcohol, laze about on the fourth floor of my prison, and prove Grandmother right. I decided to try learning more from Tural, in order to convince myself I was *doing* something.

"What exactly is this King's Dinner about?" I asked, wondering just how much of society Olaf would need to muddle through. "Didn't we *just* do this?"

Tural laughed, but not at me—a laugh of agreement that the royals' social calendar was all a bit much. He had a satisfying laugh, and a light salt and pepper at his temples. Quru doctors use tattoos to mark any injuries that they treat, such as the childhood injury above Grandmother's eye, and as he leaned back against his desk, I wondered idly if Tural had any such tattoos, and where.

"We did, I'm afraid," he said. "But this is a much smaller thing. Our good King hosts and attends an endless number of small state events. These monthly dinners were started by Queen Biruté as a way for her and the King to learn more about how their kingdom is run, but it has become just the same group of people who surround him at any other time, saying the same old things." He grinned. "But the meal must always be magnificent."

"Of course." I supposed this would be Olaf's coming-out party, as Gerhold VIII. What a terrifying thought.

"But," said Tural, picking up the plate from his desk, "I have put off one decision for the dinner, so lend me your taste buds."

"They're quite useless, I assure you."

"That can't be true." Tural pointed out the two sliced up pieces of fruit on his plate. At first glance, they were almost identical, except one was a bit waxier. "Upper red persimmon, tart." He pointed to the less waxy variety. "Lower red persimmon, sweet." He pointed to the other. Both were orange in color, to my eye, if leaning toward red. "Two cousins in the same family, one grows in the open, up here on the surface, where the Rotfelsenisch live like human beings, and the other grows beneath, where sunlight slithers into the rock. I cannot decide which to serve as the dessert starter tomorrow night. It will be the first thing eaten after dinner, but before the full dessert, a Quru cake."

"Is the Master of Cakes also Quru?"

He raised an ironic eyebrow and shook his head. "Rotfelsenisch."

"Ah. Disappointing cake, then?"

He opened his mouth to speak, paused for a moment, and raised his free hand, as though acquiescing to something. "Much as I would love to demean our Master of Cakes, and pretend that my Quru nature gives me some greater insight into our food, the fact is he makes extremely good Quru cakes. Even my mother would admit so, if she ever had a bite."

"I see."

"The cake will include many syrups, which were made from fruits I provided. However, the Mistress of Syrups is badly organized, and has not yet determined which ones she will use, so the dessert appetizer must be a fruit she does not have in syrup form. Hence"—a flourish—"red persimmon."

I nodded.

"Now," he continued, "I would love to know which you prefer."

"I truly don't think I can help."

Tural did not seem to understand.

"I don't really . . . *enjoy* food," I explained.

He knitted his brows together. "How do you mean? Was your mouth injured? Burned out? Or do you not enjoy the textures?"

"No, no. Nothing like that, I simply . . ." I thought for a moment. I had never really put these feelings into words before. "I have not, in my life, had the time or the money to learn to appreciate the intricacies of flavor. I have always needed what was fast, cheap, and filling."

Tural looked at me for some time. I was worried I would see deep pity in his eyes, but he only seemed thoughtful.

"Well, now you have the time and the money, don't you?" he said. "In a way I envy you, getting to experience the joy of new tastes."

Time, indeed.

"Besides," he continued, "fast, cheap, and filling can still be quite delicious."

I did not know how to respond to this. It truly hadn't ever occurred to me. I began to wonder how much of my unformed taste was due to my circumstances in general, and how much was simply thanks to Grandmother.

"Well," I said, "be that as it may, I'm certainly no expert."

"I did not ask for an expert's opinion," said Tural. "I asked for *yours*." He then produced a small knife and reduced each slice of persimmon into half-inch pieces. "Try a small piece. Please?"

His knife was sharp by the look of it, and it had a gold handle, so he must have taken it from the more distinguished palace kitchen where he did his work. A kitchen that was not checked by guards on the lookout for missing knives taken by an imprisoned soothsayer.

But before I could take it, I had to sample this fruit. I took a piece of each persimmon and admitted that they tasted the same to me. I asked him to describe their differences, and he happily obliged as I gave the fruit another try. Tural, without condescension, suggested I chew slowly, to savor, to look for certain aspects of the flavor. I had never eaten slowly before, except when my jaw had been broken, and at first it was maddeningly boring and frustrating.

But a strange thing happened: by my third piece of each fruit, I could swear I was tasting the difference between the two. Tural's own joy at the whole enterprise bolstered me further, and I realized I really did *like* what I was eating. And not just because there was sugar in it: I actually noticed each little fiber in the fruit's body, tasted the components that Tural swore were there.

Or fancied that I did. I may have simply learned that tartness could be good, and no more. But by my last piece of each, I had made a decision.

"Upper," I said.

Tural agreed, and celebrated by eating the rest himself. He bent back his head dramatically and closed his eyes to do so. He was a little drunk, and swayed slightly.

That was when I put a hand on his arm, to playfully hold him steady as I snatched his knife from the plate, hoping he had forgotten about it in his excitement. Same as soothsaying: take advantage of distractions. I palmed it and slipped it into my sleeve.

I felt guilty when he was finished and looked back at me, but not guilty enough to admit anything. Tural either did not notice the knife's absence, or felt that it was rude to acknowledge, which in Quru custom meant essentially the same thing.

We had a few more drinks and talked about nothing, as the knife threatened to fall out of my sleeve, and soon enough I took my leave.

I felt happy when I stumbled back the few feet to my room and shut the door. I secreted the knife inside an especially large book and flopped onto my bed. My chemically-induced happiness did not give me the space to stare into what the future might hold.

UP OTTILIE'S ROCK

The next day, I attempted to visit my father, to see if I could wring any visions from him, but was told by the Yellows outside that I was not allowed in without express permission from Lenz. Why, it was almost as though I'd escape with Papa in the night if given half a chance! (And leave Grandmother if I could.)

Instead, I chose that night to attempt a different sort of approach to the Royal Inn of Ottilie's Rock and Andelka, our delegate from Rituo, that most friendly of the Bandit States. I still had not seen her in the week since the Winter Ball, despite my many trips to the inn.

What I had gained, I suppose, was a better knowledge of Gunther, the keeper, as well as a few people staying at the tavern: lesser dignitaries staying on the second floor of the inn, in the "cheap rooms." These included a Rotfelsenisch bureaucrat representing a noble with quarries *deep* down in the rock, and a Skydašian merchant hoping to sell local politicians on a law regarding property taxes before the Council of Barbarians started. The most I had learned from them was that in addition to the second floor's "cheap rooms," the third floor housed the "good rooms," and the fourth contained the "Suzerain's Suite." This last one referred to how supposedly luxurious the suite was, such that if the Grand Suzerain of Loasht were to ever visit Rotfelsen (a thing that has never happened), they would stay in that very suite. Never mind that there were entire *mansions* on the palace grounds that could be rented out by visitors—this was beside the point. It was rather hyperbolic, but that is what the suite was called and, according to Gunther, the "Suzerain's Suite" was where Andelka was staying.

"In the grand suite, and only eating the cheapest food when she's up there," Gunther had groused.

So, this night, just a day after the Turmenbach mess, Olaf, Chasiku, and an attempt to drag new visions out of my father, I went back to the Royal Inn of Ottilie's Rock toward the later end of dinner time: when Gunther would be there and, I hoped, quite busy. Those staying in the "cheap rooms" would be drinking away their failures or toasting their successes, secure in the knowledge that they had only a short trip upstairs to their beds.

This time, I walked around to the back of Ottilie's Rock, which was shrouded in almost total darkness, save for the light from a few of the inn's rooms. Back here, there were none of the inviting lanterns, beckoning guests inside for respite from the growing chill in the air. No lights seemed to be on at the back of the "Suzerain's Suite" either.

I groped around in the dark for the servants' entrance that had to be there somewhere, and eventually found a small, rough, precarious set of . . . well, less *stairs* than *conveniently placed bumps and ledges.* The pathway here was narrower than my shoulders, and I marveled at how Gunther must have traversed it every night while full of starka.

I moved slowly up the jagged stairs, until the back wall of the building was almost close enough to touch, and then I (daftly) sped up just a hair, and slipped on the top step. I fell forward and flailed wildly at the wall, my hands hitting wood and my fingernails scraping until they stopped against a molding. I became utterly convinced that someone had heard my awkwardness, and so stayed perfectly still, legs sprawled out behind me, hands gripping the molding, midsection hovering in the air diagonally.

When I counted out a minute (and couldn't hold that position any longer besides), I pulled myself up to my feet.

I felt around the molding and found the back door, which was, surprisingly, unlocked. I crept inside to what felt like a maze of corridors that, from the smells and the noise, must've emptied out somewhere to the kitchens and the tavern, where I heard the Skydašian merchant laughing. I found my way to the servant's stairs with surprising ease, and didn't run into any maids, cooks, or other staff. Looking back now, I realize I should have thought this too easy; at the time, I was so shaken by my fall that I simply assumed the gods were balancing out my luck a bit. As though this was anything they had ever done for me before.

The stairs were dark and creaking, but I didn't seem to attract any attention, even when I alighted on the fourth floor. And when I tried the knob to what I assumed to be a servant's entrance to the "Suzerain's Suite," it turned and the latch clicked. Just as I finally began to doubt my good luck, the door refused to budge.

I held still for a moment in the pitch black at the top of the stairs, and heard nothing. I pushed at the door, and it gave slightly, but wouldn't open. It felt as though something was wedged against it.

For what felt an interminable moment, I pressed my forehead to the cool wood and tried to decide what I should do. Pushing harder and forcing my way in could make a lot of noise, but I had come so far already. What was I to do otherwise? Just turn around? I "worked" for the Prince, after all; our Bandit States visitors couldn't just kill me without causing an incident. Could they? Maybe even if I got caught, I could learn something.

I threw all my weight into the next push. There was a moment's resistance before the door opened entirely, and I found myself sprawling into more darkness, bound up with another body. We tussled, tangled up in one another, each trying to extricate ourselves. I kicked something metal that made a low clank, and I felt the person below me take a breath, as though about to yell something.

I panicked and reached out for where I hoped this person's face was. My hand brushed long hair as it clamped over their mouth—at the exact same time that I felt an impossibly strong hand cover my own mouth. Then a light shone into the room.

ANDELKA

"What," someone bellowed, "is going on here, by L——?!"

Even in that situation—caught and bundled up with a stranger, covering their mouth while they covered mine—I felt myself wince at the very sound of someone saying a *god's* name out loud. (I have, of course, not reproduced it here.)

I looked up and there, standing in a doorway leading to more of the suite, was Andelka: broad, squat, and pale. She wore a sort of armless and open dressing gown of silk brocade, and held a lantern that spilled light into the room, glistening off so many gold and silver surfaces that I couldn't quite make out anything. That light was also reflected on her powerful and veined arms, and the long, curved blade held in her free hand.

I looked down and, pinned beneath me, with his hand on my mouth and my hand on his, was Martin-Frederick Reinhold-Bosch, the young, blonde royal scion I had met at the Winter Ball. Even as I held his mouth closed, I saw his eyes widen with recognition, and then he winked.

I smiled back stupidly, before realizing my mouth was still covered. I rolled off him and we each let go of the other.

"Well," continued Andelka, "now you can talk, can't you?"

I was in a half crouch, Martin-Frederick was turning onto his knees and didn't much look like he was about to say anything.

"It was a love game," I said, almost without thinking about my lie before spitting it out.

Martin-Frederick laughed.

"You know," I continued, standing up, "*forbidden* and all that."

Andelka did not much look like she believed it. Martin-Frederick also stood, and I saw that he was armed, although his rapier was still sheathed. He began to reach down toward his belt, and Andelka waved her dagger, or machete, or whatever it was.

"Don't touch that sword!" she yelled. "Now why are you *actually* here?"

"Look," sighed Martin-Frederick, holding up his hands. "I work for High General Dreher. Yes, I was spying, but you're his guest, aren't you?" He nodded down to a piece of paper wedged into his belt, not far from his sword. "The orders are there. May I?"

Andelka stepped closer, holding up the lantern and waving her blade inches from his face. "Go on," she said.

Martin-Frederick smiled and nodded his head in thanks and began to slowly reach for the paper. Andelka nodded back. Then the young man darted backward, out of her reach, and seemed to go for his sword. Andelka yelled and swung at nothing.

Martin-Frederick laughed and brought up the piece of paper after all. He was uncomfortably at ease in this situation.

"Joking, joking!" he said, holding out the paper. "Read it for yourself. I'll wait."

Andelka snarled at him, set the lantern down on a marble and gold side table, and snatched the paper.

"You *can* read Rotfelsenisch, can't you?" Martin-Frederick couldn't help adding.

"Of course," replied Andelka. "Can *you*, little boy?"

I looked to Martin-Frederick, and nodded toward the lantern, attempting to ask, with my expression, if I should go for it: throw it down, start a fire. He gave a small shake of his head and smiled.

Andelka cleared her throat loudly and began to read in the flickering lantern light. "'Search the Rituo woman's papers for information about you-know-who. As she is our guest, try to be discreet and refrain from embarrassing her. But if she becomes a problem, you may bring in some Greens.' Signed, High General Dreher." She looked up, angry.

"And that's his seal," Martin-Frederick added. "But you know it already."

"That I do," sighed Andelka.

"My Greens are downstairs, keeping the servants quiet and out of my way in the kitchen. But now that you know"—he shrugged—"I'll call them up and they'll have a look." He bowed. "So sorry for the inconvenience."

"And what is she doing here?" Andelka waved her blade at me. She seemed to purposefully flex while she was doing it.

Martin-Frederick shrugged. "Love game. Thought it would be fun to sneak her in while I was at it."

"I shudder to think what else you people are doing in my room when I'm not here," said Andelka, not seeming to believe him.

"We'd have much less trouble if you ever left," replied Martin-Frederick.

Martin-Frederick Reinhold-Bosch

Martin-Frederick and I went down by the guest's stairs, to go have a drink in the tavern. Gunther was mostly hidden by steam, but greeted me as though entirely unsurprised I was there, which I took to be his professionalism. The tall keeper poured us cups of something he already knew to be Martin-Frederick's favorite—a liquor made from beets that I did *not* particularly enjoy—and we sat at a table in the corner of the tavern. The guests of the "cheap rooms" were being quite loud that night, and it was easy enough to talk. In the soft light, that young royal, who had once declared his interest in a "martial" woman to me, was still slim, beardless, blonde, and, I dare say, pretty.

"Well," I said, once we'd sat down across a small wooden table, "if it isn't . . . Marvin-Friedhelm?" I knew his name perfectly well, but I wanted him to *try* to stick in my mind.

"Martin-Frederick," he corrected quickly. "And I still don't know your name, or what sort of soldier you are. Or why you were up there." He leaned a little closer across the table.

"I was looking into rumors about the Bandit States," I said, answering only his third question. "But if you do work for the High General, you must already know the answers I was looking for."

He shrugged and sat back, trying to look like he didn't much care about what I wanted to know. It was the most awkward I had yet seen him.

"Perhaps," he replied.

I laughed charmingly and covered my face partially with my hand to pretend at masking it. This false laugh, intended to endear people to me, is much more musical than the snorting that happens when I laugh genuinely.

"Fine, fine," I said, through more fake laughter. "I am too tired to play around any longer." A lie, of course. (Well, I did feel too tired—but such is life.) "My name is Kalyna Aljosanovna, and the Prince *recruited* me as one of his soothsayers. The first and best one, naturally."

The young blonde marveled at this for a moment, as I had hoped he would. "I knew the Prince enjoyed surrounding himself with . . . experts"—he had clearly been about to say something less kind—"but I did not expect that. You know I'll have to tell High General Dreher about you."

I nodded. In fact, I hoped that he would. I was being forced to work by the Prince, I was very much at odds with the Court Philosopher, and the King was missing, so perhaps I could get something useful from Rotfelsen's strongest military power. Or at least learn where the High General stood.

"My turn," I said, as though Martin-Frederick wasn't the one with an official order and a band of soldiers upstairs. "What I was looking into was whether there is any truth to the rumors about the Bandit States invading Rotfelsen. That is to say, their armies actually getting inside of your lovely rock. I've heard quite a bit about it, but have seen nothing of the sort in my visions." I smiled and bowed my head. "Sometimes even my Gift needs a little help."

"Oh, *that*? Is that all?" He waved a bejeweled hand. "Not a chance. Not a chance! This whole idea hinges on the possibility that High General Dreher would rather lie to preserve his honor than do what must be done to keep us safe."

"And you don't think he would?"

"Not a chance!" he repeated. "If Rotfelsen were at stake, Dreher would publicly, clearly, ask the Prince and the King for help—perhaps even the Court Philosopher! What Dreher cares about is preserving the order and safety of Rotfelsen, not honor. Or perhaps, in *that* lies his soldier's honor. That's why he's been High General so long. And"—he grinned—"that's why he doesn't listen too much to men like me. You know"—he affected a deep voice—"'duelist adventurers' and 'royal thrill-seekers.'"

"If that's an imitation of our good High General and his favorite names for you, I'm afraid it's lost on me. I haven't had the pleasure."

"It's a gruff sort of pleasure, but I like that he treats me like any other soldier."

I sincerely doubted the High General did so.

I took another sip of beet liquor and made a face that Martin-Frederick apparently found cute. The guileless boy certainly didn't sound like he was lying about the Bandit States, and I could only take his word for it unless I could speak to the High General himself. I could always be wrong, but if Martin-Frederick was telling the truth, then I had my escape route nicely planned. Perhaps Papa's "fire and sword" would not come from the south.

From where then? But I shook that away and had another sip. It didn't matter. I just needed to get out. I was but one broken shell, in constant danger of losing my life even without Papa's doom prophecy bearing down upon us. I owed it to him to find our way south.

"Well, either way," I said to Martin-Frederick, "I would be very gladdened to meet with High General Dreher. Do you think you could arrange that? Surely, he listens to you a bit."

"Well, a *bit*, surely," he echoed, talking through a broad smile. He certainly did want to impress me. "I'll see what I can do, Kalyna Aljosanovna."

He raised his mug, and I clacked mine against his. We finished our drinks.

"Thank you, Melvin-Franklin," I said.

THE KING'S DINNER

Unfortunately, Prince Friedhelm "requested" my presence, as well as Lenz's, the next evening at the King's Dinner. It was held in a part of the Royal Party Apartments I, somehow, hadn't yet seen. It was a long, but low-ceilinged, dining room, with around forty people milling about a table that could probably seat fifty. It was soon made clear to me, however, that only fifteen would be *sitting* at that table. The rest—like Lenz and myself—would stand behind our masters and look serious and dutiful. I hoped we would at least get to pick at the leftovers.

There was a palpable tension animating those people who milled about and tried to act casual, waiting for a king they had not seen since the Winter Ball. It was suggested, in hushed tones, that soon an excuse would be made, and everyone would be asked to leave. Neither Selvosch the Quarrymaster nor Edeltraud von Edeltraud the Mistress of Coin were there, and I did not see Andelka of Rituo in attendance either, but Vorosknecht the Court Philosopher was, and I kept my eye on him. Perhaps *some* people had seen the King more recently than they let on, after all.

I reflected on the fact that I had recently seen the King's face, at least, and smiled. I decided to go talk to the Court Philosopher.

"Oh," he said when I approached him. "You're still here?" A Purple stood just behind him, a man that I think I recognized from our interview at the ball.

"So far," I replied. "Why? Have you a good reason for me to leave?" I grinned up at him.

Vorosknecht looked more annoyed than anything else. "I thought I had provided a compelling reason, but you must be dimmer than I realized."

"Perhaps I'm not willing to give up your charming company so easily, Brightness."

He grunted and flourished toward Prince Friedhelm, across the room, who was standing with Lenz and another Yellow I had met a few times.

"Tell me, fool," Vorosknecht began, "why the Prince needs three Yellows with him tonight when I am brave enough to be here with just one of my men." He nodded to the Purple behind him.

"I apologize, Brightness," I said, with a deep curtsy. "I did not realize you would be intimidated by the lame researcher and the unarmed prophet."

"Prophet indeed," he snorted. "I only worry what new problems you will blunder into. Your master was given a chance, after all."

"That is not how I remember the ball," I replied.

He yawned theatrically, stretching his arms high above his head. "I'm tired of this, and of you. I shall take my leave: the King isn't coming."

"Are you certain of that, Brightness?"

"Positive," he laughed. Vorosknecht nodded again at his Purple and turned his back to me.

"You should avoid telling the future to a prophet, Brightness," I called after him.

Without turning, he waved a dismissive hand at me as he walked toward the door.

Others began to notice that the Court Philosopher was leaving, and the murmurs and uncertainty grew. Various dignitaries began to make their excuses to each other, and to round up their attendants. I shot a look at Lenz, who seemed mortified. Prince Friedhelm was smiling calmly and fabricating his own excuses for leaving to a ruddy, stocky man in a green doublet.

Vorosknecht coughed loudly as he approached the door of the chamber, to ensure that everyone saw him leaving the room, insulted at the King's tardiness. He looked back over his shoulder, smiling imperiously at the guests, and so walked fully into a pair of Reds, who growled and shoved him backward. Behind those Reds, stood the King.

Vorosknecht stumbled and his smile dropped. He stood, tall and unmoving, watching the King's entrance with an intense, confused stare. His Purple stepped toward the Reds, but the Court Philosopher was smart enough to put out an arm and hold him back.

"I apologize for my lateness," drawled the King, as he scanned the room with his vague, uncomprehending face. When his gaze alighted on me, there was a brief twinkle in his eye, and I knew this was Olaf.

I saw relief in the faces of the dinner guests, as well as lingering confusion about what had taken so long, and about the King's week-long absence. I glanced in the Prince's direction, and saw that Lenz and the man in the green doublet certainly look relieved. Prince Friedhelm was perhaps acting too surprised: his jaw hung open in supposed disbelief.

There was then much bustling and noise as the important people found their seats, and everyone like me tried to find somewhere to stand. The floor of the dining room was rotrock, but smoothed and buffed until it shone like red marble, and caused each heavy oak chair to squeak and groan across its surface. In the middle of all that cacophony and chaos, I watched Olaf as he sat languidly at the head of the table. For the most part, he was doing a very good job of making the serene, vacant expression that was the real King Gerhold VIII's normal manner, but every now and then he would wince as a chair tore at the floor, or look suddenly to his side when someone flopped loudly into their seat. I hoped no one but me was seeing any of this.

Olaf was also studiously ignoring Queen Biruté, who sat next to him with a hand draped over Olaf's armrest. This was my first time seeing the Queen, and I must say she seemed too beautiful to be as inbred as her husband. She was also the only person in the room, besides me, who was not a pink Rotfelsenisch type, which immediately made me like her a bit. She was of Skydašian stock—probably a most careful mix of North and South Shores, to keep the balance of power in that kingdom going. She and Olaf were each leaning away from one another, and while he did not spare her so much as a glance, she constantly shot her eyes toward him, and then away, and then toward him, and then away. I hoped that the real king was as neglectful of her as his reputation suggested, and that she was just annoyed, rather than suspicious. But of course, this was the woman our Prince most suspected, and she commanded at least half of the Reds. I also began to wonder how long Olaf would be able to ignore so handsome a woman.

Vorosknecht, at least, did not seem to pay any attention to our false monarch. The Court Philosopher had gotten into a chair quickly, and was saying something quietly into his Purple's ear. The soldier nodded, and nodded, and nodded again, asked a question, and then nodded once more before quickly leaving the room. I assumed he was off to tell Selvosch and . . . whoever else was in on their plot, about the King's appearance. I wondered where exactly Vorosknecht had expected the King to be. Scared into staying in his rooms? Locked in a dungeon, perhaps? Sick from poison? The Reds who flanked Olaf betrayed nothing of their expectations or knowledge regarding him and his missing doppelgänger.

Prince Friedhelm was sitting in front of me, chatting with the ruddy older man in green, who I soon learned was High General Dreher. The same who had recently sent Martin-Frederick to search Andelka's rooms. I mostly saw his back.

"I admit, I wasn't sure my brother would show either," laughed Friedhelm, leaning in to be conspiratorial. "I thought he had been scared off by the . . . incident at the ball, you know?"

The High General chuckled, but did not agree with the playful, almost-traitorous comments the Prince was so fond of making. "I think our King is made of sterner stuff than you give him credit for, Highness. But then, I only saw him from a distance when he was a child—growing up together may have given you a different perspective."

"That may well be, High General. I think I am too familiar with him as a brother to see him as a King." The Prince shot his eyes at Olaf for a moment, then back to Dreher, and smiled.

The High General just smiled back and shrugged. Standing behind him, I saw, even in that small movement of his, what seemed to be a great deal of pain and effort.

"Welcome all," drawled Olaf at the end of the table, about four or five seats down from the Prince. "I hope you will enjoy your . . . our . . . ah . . . dinner. Together. And please do let me know if you have any . . . oh, you know, concerns."

Queen Biruté rolled her eyes for a moment. Was that a normal part of their relationship?

I had seen the real King, but never heard him speak, so I had no clue as to how accurate Olaf's Gerhold voice was, and I wondered if he was laying on the uncaring absentmindedness a bit thick. But no one stood up and screamed, "Fraud!" so I supposed we were doing all right so far.

The first course came out, but everyone had to wait for the King to start before touching their food. In front of each person was a little cup of brown broth with a perfect dollop of something yellow in the center, emitting a pleasing steam. Olaf took a small, noisy sip and proclaimed, unenthusiastically, that he was sure it was delicious. Then everyone began to eat.

Curious about his pained shrug earlier, I decided to watch High General Dreher for a bit. He held his body in his chair as though any extra movement would be excruciating, and when he ate, he bent his arm at the elbow and leaned down to sort of catch his food. Dreher must have been around sixty, but this went beyond the normal aches of age. His pain at simple movement seemed quite acute, especially in regard to his right arm, and I guessed he had some injury, or great sickness.

My feet were already starting to hurt as I stood behind the Prince and the High General. I glanced at Lenz, who was already heavily favoring his bad leg, slumping to one side. I stood straighter and grinned at him. He pretended not to see.

Olaf was looking with glazed eyes at an official I did not recognize, nodding almost imperceptibly as she spoke to him. He seemed to be doing a well enough job, but very little had been asked of him yet. The

Queen spoke to another courtier and continued to glance back at her "husband." She even waved her hand toward him, as though discussing him. I wondered if they had spoken before joining us for dinner and, if so, what was going through her mind right now. If Olaf pulled this off, would it be because he was a great actor, or because King Gerhold VIII was so much nothing?

Then I thought about how the King could very well be bleeding and broken in a dungeon somewhere, and felt bad for insulting him like this. Even a royal is just a scared person in such a situation, aren't they? (I'm not sure.) I decided to perk myself up by seeing how angry and flustered Vorosknecht was.

I looked across the table to where the Court Philosopher was sitting, but he was not staring at Olaf with a combination of confusion and anger, as I'd hoped. No, he was lifting a fork to his mouth and shoving a piece of meat into it while looking directly at me. I admit I was surprised to see his eyes trained on me, and my surprise probably showed. He continued to glare as he chewed slowly. What was he guessing at now? How much had he figured out? His Purple returned, and he mumbled something up to the soldier, while still looking at me.

I raised my eyebrows and smiled at Vorosknecht. After all, I knew *two* things that he did not: how we'd gotten a king here, and that all of his machinations would mean nothing when the Tetrarchia plunged into chaos and death. My smugness ebbed away, and I looked back at Olaf. I wondered, again, if his very existence, somehow more fraudulent than mine, would cause our end. The false King was looking slightly more engaged, leaning forward to listen to High General Dreher across five or so other people. The High General also leaned forward, with a pained grunt.

"Your Majesty," Dreher was saying, "I promise you that the rumors of the Bandit States' incursions into our fair country are spurious."

Olaf cocked his head to the side, a little puzzled. But it was Queen Biruté who spoke.

"Our *kingdom*, you mean, High General?" she said quickly, snapping out each word. "Our *country* is the Tetrarchia."

High General Dreher was silent a moment, and most of the table went quiet as well.

". . . told him that's not how you use a—" continued someone absorbed in their own conversation, before cutting themselves off when they realized no one else was talking.

Olaf turned slowly to Biruté and smiled halfheartedly. She smiled back, angrily. Olaf took an age to turn his head back all the way to face High General Dreher.

"The Queen," he said, "is quite correct, Dreher."

I frowned at Olaf. I worried that the King was too passive, and that even this slight bit of disagreement was out of character. I wondered whether Olaf was succumbing to a pretty face.

"Our blessed kingdom," Olaf continued, "is but one of four that make up our . . . ah, what did they tell me to say . . . our quadruple-blessed country."

High General Dreher was quiet for a moment, and I could not see his face as he looked at Olaf.

"True," laughed Dreher, finally. "But of course, if the Bandit States *did* invade Rotfelsen, they would also be invading our country, the Tetrarchia, would they not?"

Olaf smiled and nodded, and everyone seemed to relax slightly. I chanced a look at Vorosknecht, but he was eyeing his plate in that moment. I believe they were on the fourth course?

"Moot either way," the High General continued. "The point is, they have done no such thing. They gnash their teeth at our borders, but between our Greens and our alliance with Rituo, the Bandit States are kept well in check, I promise you."

"Well," said Olaf, "that *is* a relief, isn't it?" He slumped back in his chair.

"Indeed, brother," said Prince Friedhelm. "We need all the soldiers we can spare for when we host the Council of Barbarians, don't we?"

Olaf waved a lazy hand at Friedhelm. "Yes, yes, but we're hardly in danger there. Our allies are as invested in the Tetrarchia as we are. Oh, there may be rumblings in some of their backwaters about separatism, but it will amount to nothing." He coughed out a laugh. "After all, we've always had the most separatists right here, and we keep them under control just fine. Always worrying, aren't you, brother?"

There was some uncomfortable laughter around the table at that. Prince Friedhelm smiled without seeming very happy, and I did not know if this was all part of the play-acting, or if Olaf was taking his role too much to heart.

I thought about what Olaf had said regarding the Council of Barbarians not being particularly dangerous and remembered my father's prophecy. What was I doing, standing around, watching courtiers eat and trading barbs with a puffed-up philosopher, when I needed to get out of this place as soon as possible?

The next course came, and a nervous little server pushed past me to put small plates in front of Friedhelm and Dreher. Bored, I looked down over the Prince's shoulder to see cut up pieces of persimmon. So this was the beginning of the desserts, and soon this interminable night would be over. I smiled to myself and thought of Tural.

Someone was expounding more upon their worries about trade during the Council of Barbarians, and Olaf was pretending to listen. Or perhaps Olaf was *pretending* to pretend to listen. Whatever the case, he had not bothered to touch his persimmon slices yet, and therefore no one else did. Prince Friedhelm, always playing the sensualist, was drumming his fingers on the table with impatience about starting his dessert. I looked at the High General's vague annoyance, at the Prince's bejeweled fingers pattering on the table, and then again at the persimmon on his plate. And that was when I began to wonder if something was wrong.

The pieces of persimmon laid out on the Prince's plate weren't cut very evenly, or displayed very carefully, which was unlike all food I had seen served in the palace at this point. I leaned closer, almost touching the Prince, and saw the waxy sheen of the persimmon's innards. Hadn't Tural chosen, based on my input, to use the upper red persimmon variety? I closed my eyes and tried very hard to remember the fruits he had shown me, what they had looked like, and which one had been the waxier of the two. I tried, in a way, to *conjure*.

I remembered Tural's smile and high cheekbones; his pleasant smell and the flecks of gray in his hair. This was not what I needed to conjure. I remembered him happily pointing to the upper red persimmon, the tart one, which I had enjoyed. I definitely remembered it being less waxy in its appearance than what was currently on the Prince's plate. Perhaps Tural had changed his mind?

I saw Olaf's hand lazily move onto his plate, pushing around the thick and uneven piece of persimmon he had been served. I looked at Vorosknecht, and he was staring at Olaf, but that hardly meant much. Did it?

I leaned forward further and tapped Prince Friedhelm on the shoulder. I hoped very much that I would not look very stupid very soon.

"Those aren't the right persimmons," I whispered in his ear.

"What?" he hissed back.

"They look like the wrong kind," I said. I shut my eyes tight, as though to not see the deep amount of trouble I was getting myself into. "I just had a vision of someone dying at this table."

"Do you *know* it's the persimmons?" replied the Prince.

"I can't guarantee that. But look at how badly they're cut."

"I rather thought the cooks were getting tired," he replied.

"What's going on?" whispered Lenz.

Dreher glanced over at us. Olaf pressed two fingers around a piece of persimmon.

"Do we want to lose a second King?" I growled, my lips touching the Prince's ear, so no one else could hear.

"No," said the Prince, still whispering. "Kalyna, I suggest you let everyone know."

My eyes widened, and I felt my heart had stopped. I thought I could just feed the Prince the information and he'd do what he willed with it. I stood up straight. Olaf had picked up a piece of persimmon. Would I let him die to avoid everyone thinking me a fool? I considered it.

I took a deep breath, and brought up all the false confidence that I could.

"Your Majesty!" I positively boomed across the table. "Don't eat that!"

Olaf looked up at me, confused. But he dropped the persimmon slice. I wondered if the real King would have trusted me so quickly.

Everyone began to yell at once, some shoving their plates away as hard as they could. One of the Reds slipped up right behind Olaf, reaching for something on the table. I felt my body seize up in fear. I looked down at the Prince's knife, and wondered if I could grab it and vault over the table in time.

I had one foot on the Prince's armrest when the Red grabbed a bottle of clear liquor, poured it on a napkin, and began vigorously rubbing Olaf's fingers clean of persimmon residue. I deflated and stepped back down to the floor. The Prince turned and stared up at me confused.

"Well, what's the matter with the persimmons?" asked Dreher.

Vorosknecht said nothing, and did not seem to react much at all.

"Poison," I said, loud enough for all to hear. I found myself very much hoping that I was right and they were poisoned, and not that Tural had had a sudden change of heart regarding which kind to serve. I began formulating lies for what I would say if it was not, actually, poison: perhaps that I actually saw someone choking on their dessert?

"Bring the Master of Fruit in here at once!" roared the Prince.

"No, wait," I began, but I was drowned out.

THE MASTER OF FRUIT

There was a whirlwind of activity then, but the result was a very confused Tural sitting in a chair, surrounded by Reds. Some of the more squeamish dinner guests had left, but plenty remained, crowded up behind the Prince, the Queen, and Olaf, who were facing Tural. These remaining guests included Vorosknecht, who stood just behind the Prince, and Dreher, who was still seated at the table. Lenz and I were over by the wall, where we were supposed to look unobtrusive. A Red's large hands were on Tural's shoulders, holding him down in the chair. He looked searchingly at me, but did not say anything.

"Master of Fruit," began Prince Friedhelm, "are you aware that—?"

"Oh, let's just feed him his own fruit and be done with it," said Vorosknecht. "A quick test, and we'll save a lot of time."

Vorosknecht's one Purple soldier in attendance grabbed a plate of the offending persimmon and pushed it right into Tural's face. The Reds neither stopped nor helped. Prince Friedhelm glared at Vorosknecht. Olaf looked passive.

"It's just the best way," agreed Queen Biruté.

Was the Queen in on the plot? Seeing her agree with Vorosknecht, especially on the unimportance of Tural's life, made me begin to agree with the Prince on that. It would certainly explain all of her searching looks at her supposed husband.

"I hate to say it," said High General Dreher, who twisted his body toward us from his seat at the table, "but it may be our best option." He shrugged and winced.

The Prince turned farther, to look back at the High General. The Prince knew, of course, what I knew: namely that Vorosknecht was definitely in on a plot to kill the King. But of course, he had no proof, and neither knew nor cared about Tural. I saw him mulling over the High General's words, clearly considering it.

"Then how would we know who hired him?" asked Lenz.

"Hired? Hired?" cried Tural. "You hired me, Your Majesty!" He flailed his arms at Olaf, almost tipping over the plate in front of him. The Purple growled.

"What is this all about?" continued Tural.

"He's foreign," Vorosknecht pointed out. "Easy enough to guess: a Skydašian plot."

"How *dare* you?" cried the Queen, reeling toward Vorosknecht and shoving a finger in his face, even though he was much taller than her. "And this man is clearly Quru!"

"Well, that's less exciting." Vorosknecht smiled at the crowd behind him. "But Quruscan isn't far from Loasht, either."

There was a hushed whimpering among the remaining dinner guests and attendants at the thought that *they* were somehow adjacent to a Loashti plot. Prince Friedhelm looked pointedly at High General Dreher again.

"He's indelicate," the High General said, "but, again, not necessarily wrong."

"It's simply the best and quickest way to find out," agreed Queen Biruté.

"These . . ." Tural grunted, looking at the plate in front of him. "These aren't my persimmons!"

"Oh yes, very good," laughed Vorosknecht. "A bit late, aren't you?"

Tural suddenly shot to his feet, getting out of the grip of the Reds for a moment. They put their hands back on him, but didn't push him down.

"Sir!" he cried, clearly at Vorosknecht.

The Court Philosopher, for his part, seemed truly surprised at this outburst.

"I have never impugned your work," Tural continued, "and here you impugn mine!"

"What's that to do with anything?" laughed Vorosknecht. "I'm the Court Philosopher, and you're just—"

"*The Master of Fruit!*" Tural yelled. "I would *never* serve something of such an ugly cut and arrangement! You can believe that if I was to poison someone, they would *never* know until they were dead!"

I put my face in my hands. This had started well, at least.

"And," Tural continued, stepping on whatever Vorosknecht was going to say next, "there is one thing I'll say for you Rots: you insist on keeping records of everything!"

Prince Friedhelm tilted his head to the side and furrowed his brow at Tural.

"Most of the time," Tural continued, "it is a great nuisance, I must say." His chest was out, as though this was his great declaration. "But *these*"—he pointed disdainfully at the plate of persimmon slices held by the Purple—"are clearly lower red persimmon. And if you look at my acquisition and disposal paperworks, you will see that I signed the order to feed the King and his guests *upper* red persimmon!"

He went on to explain this paperwork in great detail, alongside all the bureaucracy that would come to bear once the dinner was over, in order to get these lower red persimmons, which he had *not* used, into the servant houses in the shadow of the Sunset Palace. He also explained how difficult it would have been to poison the already sliced (and, he pointed out, very evenly and thinly sliced) upper red persimmon, while poisoning whole fruits and *then* cutting them would be much easier. He was deeply thorough about everything, and I will spare you the bulk of it.

"Hmm," said Prince Friedhelm, finally. "So, how do we test it?"

"Your Highness," sighed Lenz, "it's much less dramatic than making someone eat fruit that may be poisoned, but we do have alchemists for that sort of thing. They check everything before it comes into the palace, of course."

"Just as I say," said Tural. "These were poisoned in the palace, behind my back!"

Lenz sighed. He had meant to leave that part pointedly unsaid.

"Yes, yes, good idea," said the Prince. He opened his mouth to issue more orders, then stopped himself, and turned to Olaf. "That is, brother, if you agree."

Olaf seemed to be falling asleep halfway through his nod of agreement. Queen Biruté's lips were pressed tightly together, but she nodded too.

"Well then," said High General Dreher, "I will leave you to your tests. It's all a bit technical for me, and I'm absolutely exhausted." He groaned and heaved himself up out of his chair.

"And how am I to know," began Vorosknecht, "that you won't lie and say these were poisoned just to protect the reputation of your newest acquisition?" He waved a hand at me. "This psychic of yours?"

All eyes went to me for a moment, and it was all I could do to stand tall. Prince Friedhelm said nothing because he knew there was nothing to say. If these were indeed poisoned, it was almost certainly Vorosknecht's doing, but he had just thrown doubt on the very idea. The techniques of alchemy were purposefully secret and obtuse, so it wasn't as though the King, Queen, Prince, and Court Philosopher (or their agents) could watch the alchemists and verify their findings. The only way to prove to all present that the fruits were poisoned was to force someone to eat them right there, while everyone was still gathered.

I believe that the Prince chose to let the Court Philosopher have that small victory, not because he didn't want to kill some poor servant, but because he did not want to contradict himself.

Everyone began to file out. Some seemed quite disappointed that there had been no deaths; this way, it was hardly a story to dine out on in the future.

The Reds kept a close cordon around Olaf as he made his way toward me. He took my hand limply, but let a smile twitch at his lips.

"Thank you," he said. "I do believe you saved my life."

"Think nothing of it, Your Majesty." I bowed.

Queen Biruté, standing next to Olaf, looked at me for a long time, with narrowed eyes. I did my best to stand still and accept her gaze. I did not know if she was suspicious of me because she did not trust the Prince, or because I had ruined her own plot for her husband, or if she thought all soothsayers to be evil witches, or if she thought I was cute. I thought about her willingness to let Tural die as I looked back at her.

"Yes," she finally said. "Thank you."

I bowed again.

Another Conspirator Legitimately Unmasked

The next morning, as the sun crept over increasingly leafless trees, I saw a carriage rolling to a halt from my window. It stopped in the sad, sludgy old snow that dotted the top of Rotfelsen and a Yellow ran out breathlessly. I had just enough time to throw on some clothes before he banged on my door, and I was whisked outside and into the waiting carriage.

I was surprised to see not just Lenz, but also Prince Friedhelm, sitting in the backseat. I was pushed in with them and the door was closed, but the carriage didn't start moving. Two Yellows standing outside the carriage began to have a very loud and conspicuous conversation about how the weather affected their old dueling wounds.

"Good morning, Kalyna," said the Prince. "We're on our way to a Red barracks to see how Olaf is coming along. Thought we'd stop by on the way."

"Of course, Your Highness." I managed to find some well of composure, despite being barely awake.

The Yellows outside continued to drone on—I suppose they were meant to drown us out, in case the Prince got loud.

Apparently, word had come back from the Prince's alchemists that the hastily prepared lower red persimmons had in fact been poisoned. And that the perfectly sliced upper red persimmons, which had been thrown unceremoniously into a garbage heap, had been perfectly safe. Regarding the poison's appearance, the Prince, Lenz, and I all felt quite confident that the Court Philosopher was to blame, but there didn't seem to be any good way of proving it.

"So," said Lenz, "now we will try to help Olaf manage the Reds' side of the investigation. I suppose we command two armies now."

"One and a half," corrected the Prince. "At best. The Queen's Reds must have been in on my brother's disappearance. Olaf will need to be careful—this particular rift between armies isn't helpfully color-coded." He shook his head. "That blasted woman. This is why I never married."

"Yes. Certainly. This is why," replied Lenz, deadpan.

"So," the Prince continued, "I wanted you to know all this right away, Kalyna, so that you can stop wasting your visions on the dessert man."

"You mean Tural, the Master of Fruit?"

"Yes, sure."

"Tural," I repeated. "Who almost died."

"I suppose. Now tell us who else is part of the plot!"

Just then, I could have killed the Prince myself. As though Tural were not worth a hundred times any royal on this damned rock. The Prince was already a little tyrant, and Vorosknecht was Vorosknecht, so their callousness had not surprised me, but it nurtured my distaste for them. High General Dreher, for better or worse, had seemed purely pragmatic—after all what is another death to a general? But I found myself particularly fixating upon Queen Birutė's part of last night's excitement—perhaps because I knew that Prince Friedhelm already suspected her. Or perhaps because I, for some reason, chose to hold her to a higher standard than all the breathless pink men.

"There must be someone else!" continued the Prince. "I let you run all over the palace grounds, wherever you please, to *read* whomever you like. Surely you've made something of your new freedom."

"Such as saving your life twice now?"

"But who else is working with them?"

"Oh?" I cocked my head to the side. "Is that all?"

They both looked at me intently. I had, of course, spent most of my time and energy looking into Andelka and the Bandit States, only to be led to the High General. And I was thinking of the High General, with his man Martin-Frederick, more and more as something to be used *against* the Prince. So none of those investigations had rendered anything I much wanted to tell Friedhelm and Lenz. Nor, for that matter, had I learned anything useful about how the Tetrarchia would crumble in on itself, or who would cause it. But I remembered Tural sitting in that chair, being threatened with death, and I remembered a number of sidelong glances toward our imposter King. The answer to the Prince's demand seemed clear.

"Well," I said, "Queen Birutė, of course."

Friedhelm laughed and clapped his hands in excitement. "I knew it! I *knew* it!"

"Your Highness," said Lenz, shooting a doubting glance at me, "this is hardly something to celebrate. If the Queen is—"

"Oh, we'll get her now, won't we? We'll pry those Reds away somehow."

Lenz stared at me while the Prince prattled. Finally, Lenz reminded his master that they had more to do that day, and ushered me out of the carriage.

Just outside the carriage, the two of us stood for a moment in the now days-old snow, which had so far received no reinforcements. It was mixed with dirt and dead leaves, as though autumn was still preserved beneath our feet. I shivered a touch.

"Are you quite sure you saw the Queen?" Lenz hissed in Cöllüknit. I nodded.

"Doing *what?*" he added.

I looked directly into his eyes. "Telling her Reds to kill the King," I said. "I saw it after finally being near her at the King's Dinner, so it is in our future." I shrugged. "Or it was later last night."

"The real King or . . ." He mouthed "Olaf."

"That I don't know," I said. "But either is bad, isn't it?"

"The latter," he sighed, "could mean she is on our side, but doesn't realize it. That she wants to rescue the King."

Instead of responding, I simply nodded to show the most vague, and possibly ironic, assent. I'm sure it was maddening. The lie had come so easily. But now, with a moment of quiet, the enormity began to appear in my head, even if I did not exactly feel *guilty*. I didn't need real powers of prophecy to feel that I had just put the whole Tetrarchia, immutably, on the path to destruction. That, by implicating the Queen to the Prince, I had all but assured that this rock would be torn apart beneath me.

Lenz sighed theatrically, placed his hands on his hips, and tapped his good foot against the ground. It sluiced through the old snow and did not make a satisfying sound.

"Well," he said, still quiet, but switching back to Rotfelsenisch, "I hope we'll have this all sorted before the Sun's Death."

My mind had been so stuck on Papa's prophecies that I first thought this meant the sun would actually die soon. Could the sun die? I must have looked confused.

"That's Rotfelsen's solstice, Kalyna. In just a few short weeks."

"Ah. Not another ball, is it?"

"Thankfully, no," he said. "But you've wintered here before, you must know of it."

"If you can call it winter." I kicked the watery snow.

"Yes, yes, but it gets cold and dark enough that in the middle of winter we gather, and—"

"Who's 'we'?"

"Families and friends come together in their homes, with food and ale and . . ." He trailed off. "Ah," he said, when he realized why I had not heard of the Sun's Death.

"This sounds very insular," I said. "Will you visit your family?"

"No," said Lenz. "Have a good day, Kalyna Aljosanovna." He lifted himself back up into the carriage.

I went back into the servant house, and spoke to Tural, giving him the news about the persimmons, which he took with such a calm, "I told you so" manner that he reminded me of Grandmother. But, you know, an appealing version of Grandmother.

He then grew a touch angry, but only because two good batches of persimmons had been ruined. He didn't even think to ask anything so vulgar as *who* had done the poisoning, or *why*. I found that I did not feel particularly guilty about implicating a royal on his behalf, even if he would have abhorred the idea. He never had to know.

PART FOUR

LOCK IT AWAY

The Reds spent the next few days rifling through the kitchens, and scaring the poor workers, and the Yellows spent them sniffing around Vorosknecht's and Queen Birutė's apartments, but nothing useful was found either way. I do not know how much influence the Prince and Lenz had over even the King's Reds, through Olaf, at this point, but those soldiers certainly didn't seem to be doing anything particularly useful.

But then, neither was I, at least not insofar as it would help find or stop whoever had tried to poison Olaf. My focus was still entirely upon escape. With every new wrinkle in the catastrophes unspooling around me, I imagined only the ever-growing probability of what my father had foreseen. If Martin-Frederick could be believed, the Bandit States were not, in fact, invading, and that was all well and good. But *something* must have been going on there, for High General Dreher to be keeping such a close eye on Andelka and "you-know-who." Vorosknecht was, it seemed, attempting to kill our false King, while the real King was hidden from us, and I had implicated the Queen in a (justified) fit of pique.

I did my best to ignore the continuing feeling that I was *causing* the Tetrarchia's impending collapse. After all, these powerful idiots had been undermining each other for years, so how was one imprisoned faker supposed to waltz in and ruin the whole place? (Dare I admit, even now, that a part of me felt satisfaction at the thought? That the narrative of me being plucked against my will, dragged into their court intrigues, and tearing everything down had a thrill to it? If only I could have destroyed only the monarchy, the nobility, and the armies, leaving everyone else alive and well. That, I think I would have been happy to do.)

Whatever the case, I tried to focus on my escape. I wanted to see if my father had picked through his visions to see anything useful about Lenz, but avoided visiting for the next two days. I told myself this was because it would strain him to have me asking, every day, whether he'd found something helpful, which may have been partly true. But I was also getting comfortable, and Papa and Grandmother were reminders that we were not *meant* to be comfortable. Besides, for once in my life, I did not have to take care of him myself. He was in good hands.

I had somewhat free rein over the palace grounds now (in two-hour increments) because Lenz guessed, correctly, that I would not leave without Papa, whose building was guarded. In the absence of useful information on my captor, or any word from Martin-Frederick Reinhold-Bosch, I devised schemes.

I was set on the Bandit States as our destination, as it was the closest way out of the Tetrarchia and had not, I hoped, been raiding Rotfelsen anymore than before. What's more, I knew which obscure villages and tunnels in lower Rotfelsen to take there, but how to escape the palace grounds? Even if we could give the Yellows the slip, we needed a mode of transportation for Papa and Grandmother. I considered hitching a ride with the Skydašian merchant at Ottilie's Rock, perhaps convincing him we were traveling performers, but didn't know when he would leave. I wondered if I could fake my own death and tell Grandmother where to meet me, but couldn't trust her (and couldn't trust Lenz to let them go after my death). I even prayed to my two favorite gods to deliver me, even though they were my favorites in part because they were not known for seeing devotion as transactional.

I spent a day in my room, hatching and abandoning these plans as I ate leftover Quru cake, sipped whatever brandy was to hand, and sewed some of the gold marks I'd been paid into my clothing. But soon, the chances to procrastinate became too tempting: I could read one of Lenz's books, apologize more to Tural about his near death, or try to wheedle information out of others in the house. These were all ways to convince myself I was doing something helpful, but of course, the usefulness was all in my head. I had nothing new to glean from these sources that would help me *escape*. So I did what any self-respecting plotter and charlatan would do—I repaired to a tavern.

My hope was that a change of scenery, combined with regular walks back to the servant house, through ever brisker and windier air, to let the Yellows know I had not escaped, would knock the cobwebs out of my head. What's more, I was still hoping to hear from Martin-Frederick Reinhold-Bosch, and through him from High General Dreher, one of the only people whose power rivaled the Prince. But I did not think I could just traipse right up to the Green barracks and risk being seen doing so.

I spent two days moving back and forth between my prison and the Royal Inn of Ottilie's Rock, chatting with Gunther, and plotting in that steamy room over tea, alcohol, and meals. It felt like a new low (or high?) in my decadence. I wanted to see Papa, but I was glad I could avoid seeing Grandmother, not just because she was awful, but because she would tell me I was drinking too much and lazing about. And she would be right. On the second such day, a greater snow finally fell upon Rotfelsen, and I got to experience my first time trudging home drunk through snow up to my knees. I found it strangely pleasant.

On the third day, I finally decided to see my family again. I crunched out through more snow toward the building where my father and grandmother were housed. I had felt so inactive lately that walking was far preferable to another carriage ride, no matter how cold the wind.

In the building's entryway, I met the Yellow I was still calling "Dugmush" in my head, for lack of something better. She cheerily followed me upstairs. I ignored my nagging embarrassment at not knowing her name—what would it matter in the long run?—but could not ignore her. I was beginning to find her easy confidence alluring, although whether it was a yearning *for* her, a need to be *like* her, or a morbid *fear* of her, I wasn't sure. Likely all three.

I also ignored the doctor's assistants in their burlap aprons, scurrying about underfoot as I went up the stairs. I crossed through Grandmother's room, and also ignored whatever terrible things she had to say.

At the door to my father's room, another doctor's assistant stood in front of me and said, yelling to speak over Grandmother's invective, "Your father needs rest, you know . . ."

I growled at the assistant, and she scampered away. My grandmother kept yelling, and the Yellow decided she could guard me well enough out on the landing. I went into Papa's room and slammed the door. He looked at me with surprise, excitement, and unease, but he repeated his old joke:

"Welcome, stranger, to the tent of Aljosa the Prophet! In this humble place I will untangle the strands of fate that— Oh! It's you, Kalynishka!"

I smiled and took his hand tightly. It was not as clammy as normal. He really *was* being cared for here. I looked down into his sweet face, and wondered whether it would be best to stay here, in comfort, until the end came for the Tetrarchia. Was it worth trying to escape so badly, and tearing him away from his care? Would it be so bad to haunt the crumbled remains of Rotfelsen until I was allowed into a hell?

I sat down next to Papa and touched his face. He positively beamed up at me, and I felt warm inside. He had so much trouble seeing clear visions, what was I doing trying to get him to help me? Trying to wheedle ammunition against my jailer from him?

"How are you doing, Papa?"

His eyes twinkled. "I saw a thing," he mouthed to me in a mixture of three different Loashti languages.

I stiffened. "About the . . . limping man?" I replied in Cölluknit.

Papa nodded excitedly. "Kalynishka, I . . ."

I gripped his wrist so tightly in anticipation that, after a few seconds, he twisted slowly and moaned. I was hurting him. I loosened my grip.

"Yes, Papa?" I croaked.

"Never, Kalynishka," he whispered. I did not know what he meant. "Not even around Mother. Not around the doctor, nor her scratchy assistants who never leave me be. I didn't . . ." He looked frustrated, he wanted so badly to explain to me. "I . . . I locked it away."

"You didn't speak of it. Even during your . . ." I did not want to say "rants."

"My screaming nights, yes!" he cried, relieved at my understanding. "And I will keep it from everyone but you, Kalynishka."

I patted Papa's hand. "I know you will," I lied. "I have always been able to count on you when I need to, Papa," I lied.

He then told me what he had seen. He promised again that he would tell no one. Papa was going to hurt himself so much holding onto this secret for his ungrateful daughter.

PAPERWORK

"What are you making my poor son do for you *now?*" cried Grandmother as I passed through her room again, onto the landing.

I answered her by slamming her door. The Yellow, Dugmush, who had been waiting for me, smiled and shrugged.

"Ready to go?" she asked.

The doctor's assistant I had scared off earlier began to slip past me back toward Grandmother's room and, I assume, Papa's.

"Of course," I replied to the Yellow. "But a minute, if you please."

"You're the boss," she said, even though I was not. I found her easy trust in me a touch thrilling.

She shrugged and leaned back onto the banister, one long leg sprawled out to the side, and yawned. The assistant had her papers clutched tightly to her burlap apron, and was trying to get around me. I leaned down to look at her.

"Excuse me," I said, making a concerned face.

She looked perplexed and uttered awkward half-words. She slowed, but did not stop. The assistant was smaller than me, and only doing her job. I would feel guilty about this. Later.

She passed me, and I said, "I just wanted to talk to you about—"

This was when I kicked her in the back of the knee. She folded backward and waved her arms, looking terrified. I snatched the papers out of the air and winced when she hit the floor. The Yellow at the banister seemed to wake up and start toward me. I stepped around the assistant and, even as I heard the soldier's footsteps, glanced down at the papers in my hand.

As I thought: she had been copying down what Papa said, during his fits and otherwise.

"Just one moment," I said to Dugmush. "I'm not trying to escape."

The Yellow followed but seemed only curious. I dashed toward the other end of the landing, where a bigger doctor's assistant was poring over something. He was a thick man, heavily muscled, his voice deep and bewildered.

"What's—?"

I hit him in the nose and he reeled, then I grabbed his throat and jumped toward him, using my weight to knock him over. He was big, but not particularly fast; the muscles were to hold down injured, squirming soldiers while they had limbs cut off them. He crashed to the floor beneath me, and I let go of his throat. Leaning in the doorway, Dugmush barked out half a laugh before thinking better of it.

"Are you going somewhere with this, ma'am?" she asked. "I was only told to keep you from running off with your family, but I suspect Master Felsknecht would not appreciate all this."

I stomped past the prone assistant toward a desk, which I ransacked for more papers, yanking out the drawers. I wasn't allowing myself to feel worry, just anger. Rage at Papa's most secret moments, his pain, being put on display. The fear would come later—I could not afford it yet.

"Just a few minutes," I said. I turned to face her. "Please."

"Did they *do* something to the old man?"

"Somewhat."

I threw an empty drawer behind me with a clatter. The thick male assistant groaned. The small female one was at the doorway now.

"What are you doing?" she screamed. "Those are medical documents!" She looked at my guard. "Aren't you supposed to stop her?"

"Only from escaping," was the reply.

No one saw me smile bitterly as I continued my search. There were papers documenting the edges and silhouettes of the futures Papa saw every day. Here was a good reminder of where I stood in Lenz's clutches. No matter how many secrets I was told, I was still a prisoner.

My father had the best medical care possible, but it was not free. It was not unconditional.

How much could be learned from these papers? Had my father truly kept what he saw of Lenz's love life secret? Worse still, had my fraud been exposed? My heart positively pounded against my chest. My neck and fingertips went cold.

In a fit of childish anger, I kicked one of the wooden drawers that lay at my feet. It broke against the wall, and the small assistant yelped. I stormed back toward the stairs, and she tried to bar my way, but faltered when I got too close.

"Follow me," I told Dugmush.

"Of course," she laughed.

"What is happening out there?" screamed Grandmother.

DOCTOR AUE

Doctor Aue was a thin woman with a snub nose who barely looked at me when I burst into her ground floor office. She was standing at the side of her desk—in stockings and breeches, dressed "like a man" because she was a *doctor*—bent over a collection of medical drawings. The Yellow, whom I was still ridiculously thinking of as Dugmush, leaned in the doorway, and I felt both bolstered and threatened by her presence. Behind her was the rattled female doctor's assistant, looking anxious. The larger male assistant was, I think, I still lying on the floor above us.

"Yes?" said the doctor.

"What is *this*?" I asked as I shoved a paper into her hand. "And where are the rest of them?"

She smoothed it out over the meticulous drawing she had been inspecting of a man having a tumor drained. She sighed, rolled her eyes at me, looked down at the paper, picked it up, blinked and moved it far away for a better view, then brought it back to where it had been, and finally read.

"'There are flowers,'" she said. "'Orange hydrangeas, and a boy is running through them. His mother is on a horse. The ocean is capsizing Loashti fisherwomen. They are crying out for their gods, but they are drowning. Purple. Blue. It blinks. The walls of a fortress house a family of rats. Lights everywhere, she cannot see her father anymore.'"

Doctor Aue squinted up at me. "I don't know. What is it?"

"I suppose," I muttered, "that out of context . . ."

"Shall I go on?" she asked. "There's much, much, much more. 'The tiger is coming for him, but he is too aroused to run.' That's a good one."

I snatched it out of her hand. "My father, your patient Aljosa Vüsalavich, is very sick, and sometimes he raves. These are records of what he has ranted about under your care. Is that a standard treatment?"

Doctor Aue blinked many times. "Huh." She looked at me, looked at her assistant, and then slowly circled back to sit behind her desk. Her office was small and very cold, with every inch of wall covered in drawings, instructions, and sometimes dried innards I could not place. None of this looked like decoration; it seemed every object on the wall had been put there in a moment when Doctor Aue needed to see it immediately.

"Is that what this is, Louisa?" Doctor Aue's gaze shot right past me and my guard to the assistant out in the hallway. There was a very long silence.

"Yes, Doctor."

"Huh."

"Do you," I said, "honestly suggest this went on without your knowing?"

"A nice thing," she replied, "about being a *very good doctor*, is that I can afford to have scruples. Sometimes. My job is to help my patients, most of whom are nobility and would never allow their utterings to be recorded. What's more, since it has nothing to do with how your father *feels*, it's a waste of my staff's time and effort, and could jeopardize his trust in us, which can be dangerous."

"But . . . ?"

"But, if Lenz Felsknecht had told me, with the Prince's voice, to copy down your father's ramblings, I would have been required to do so. Lenz, I'm sure, knows that I would carry out this task while also complaining and petitioning bitterly against it, which is why he instead went straight to Louisa here." Her eyes darted back to the assistant, although I wondered how well the doctor could see any of us. "Didn't he?"

I looked over my shoulder. Louisa nodded.

"And you did the right thing by listening to him," said Doctor Aue.

I shook the papers noisily in my hand. "I thought this was a waste of time and effort?"

"And it's the duty of any Rotfelsenisch citizen to waste their time and effort on royal aims, if asked. That includes myself and my busy little bluebirds here. If he told them to do something, and told them to not tell me, that would be their duty even if he hadn't offered money. Which I am sure he did."

She looked past me for confirmation. Louisa must have nodded again because a moment later, the doctor looked at me, or my forehead, and continued, "Yes, quite. Well. Now that I know, I will begin petitioning. But hard to say much will come of it."

I stared down at Doctor Aue for a long time. She began to trace a finger over a graphic illustration of hemorrhoids.

"Please leave those papers," she added.

I slammed them onto her desk, to which she did not respond.

"Thank you for taking care of my father," I managed to say.

Doctor Aue said nothing more, but her finger stopped tracing hemorrhoids for a moment. I walked out of the room.

I began back toward the stairs, but Dugmush moved to block my way. She did the courtesy of not grabbing or pushing me.

"Sorry, ma'am," she said, "but given all that, I don't think I should let you go up there, just now. I'm only supposed to stop you from escaping, but I think that if you told your family about all this on my watch, I'd never hear the end of it." She shrugged.

"Of course," I growled. I couldn't bring myself to thank her for letting me go as far as I had. I felt a wild fear begin to rise in me, but tamped it down. "Tell the other Yellows, when they look for me, that I'm at the tavern."

DISAPPEAR

I went back to Ottilie's Rock and drank too much. I was trying to make my hands stop shaking. Trying to tell myself that if Papa had betrayed my secret, I would've been dead by now. But I didn't believe it. Lenz or the Prince could have been toying with me, or using me to wheedle visions out of my family. I drank until my breathing finally slowed. Until even Gunther began asking me to slow down. Until the Yellows that stopped by every two hours to check on me began to blur together.

I woke up with what is still one of the worst hangovers I have ever had. I was also on a small couch, covered by a blanket, in a small wooden room I did not recognize.

"Ah, ma'am!" cried a maid, as she passed through the room. "You're finally awake."

I sat up and felt that my head would spin off of my body up into the sky. I wanted to cry, but worried that doing so would make me vomit.

"Where am I?" I managed.

"Just a maid's quarters," she replied. She pointed to the beds in the room, which may as well not have existed until she revealed them. "That nearest one's mine. You slept like a rock all night. It's early afternoon by now, ma'am."

I mumbled some sort of thanks to her that was, I'm sure, not sufficient, and stumbled to my feet. I went to the nearest window and saw Yellows outside, standing about in the snow, looking bored. Or at least I think they were—my vision was blurry enough that they may have been gigantic talking flowers. Well then, I was in no hurry to leave and report in to my captors.

I decided to partake of the sauna beneath the inn. As Gunther had told me, it was simply a cave, where a few people wrapped in towels sat on rotrock outcroppings and ignored each other's presence in steam so thick they could pretend they were alone. My first inhalation down there was painful, and the very air seemed to assault me, but by the end, I found it agreeable, despite the ongoing invective of Grandmother's that ran through my head the entire time.

Loafer. Aesthete. Drunkard. Monster. If you like the steam so much, why aren't you cooking for your father?

Grandmother. Papa. Oh gods. I must have been exposed by Lenz's treachery. But was it even treachery? Or was it simply the cost of getting to sit in this sauna after drinking too much expensive starka the night before?

I managed to replace my stockings, skirt, blouse, and bodice over wet skin, lacing everything with fingers that hardly listened to me, and tromped back upstairs into the tavern proper, sweating profusely. And there, like a blonde, arrogant messenger of the gods, was Martin-Frederick Reinhold-Bosch, the young swordsman, sitting idly at the same table we had shared after our misadventure with Andelka of Rituo. His eyes brightened when he saw me, but the deeply steamed nature of my joints meant that I made my way over quite slowly.

I opened my mouth, but he interrupted me: "Martin-Frederick Reinhold-Bosch," he said quickly.

"Oh, I remember." I sat, and allowed him to kiss my hand. I tried to smile. But my eyes weren't fully open.

"I was hoping I would find you," said Martin-Frederick. "The funniest thing happened. Here I had been, trying and trying to get our good High General interested in speaking to you, and being ignored!" He seemed genuinely frustrated.

"Aren't you glad he treats you like any other soldier?"

"Well, when it's *appropriate*, yes. But then, a few days ago, he calls me to his office first thing in the morning and says, 'I want to speak to that Aljosanovna woman.' Just like that!"

"Was this just after the most recent King's Dinner?"

"Why, I believe it was."

It was good to know my performance had impressed the High General. Martin-Frederick poured me some tea. It was over-brewed, but I was hungover and still breathing heavily from the sauna, so I felt as though its bitterness would somehow chase the poison out of me.

"So then," said Martin-Frederick, "would you like to meet him?"

"I would be delighted."

"Now?"

"Of course!" I said this before I even thought it through. Perhaps I should have waited until my hangover wore off, but if Lenz was reading about my fraudulence right now, I was out of time. Besides, I felt relaxed just then.

So we walked, side-by-side, out into that clear morning at the top of snow-covered Rotfelsen. Martin-Frederick was a small man, but, even while relaxed, the feel of his arm told me that he was all muscle. No matter how I felt about him, it was, again, rather nice to touch another human body—one that wasn't trying to divorce my soul from mine. The paths were mostly full of servants dashing from building to building, or heading up toward the palace on their way to a full day of carrying, tiptoeing, and being spat on.

The Yellows guarding the tavern noticed us, of course. As we walked out onto the snowy surface, the four of them bore down upon us.

"Ma'am?" said one of the Yellows.

"I get two hours, don't I?" I replied.

I vaguely recognized the Yellow who had spoken, but did not know him by name. He narrowed his eyes at us. "And where are you going?" he asked.

"It's a secret," replied Martin-Frederick.

"Master Lenz—" the Yellow began.

"What's the matter?" interrupted Martin-Frederick, looking back over his shoulder. "Don't trust her?"

My head was beginning to pound again at hearing my kidnapper's name. Surely, I had been found out. Or would be soon.

"Not about trust, sir," said the Yellow. He and his comrades came up quickly behind. "Just orders, you know?"

"Of course," said Martin-Frederick.

A troop of ten Greens appeared from seemingly nowhere. The Yellows stopped dead.

"What do you think their orders are?" asked Martin-Frederick.

The Greens glared at the smaller group of Yellows. One Green spat on the ground. I felt a thrill at power being exercised *for* me, for once in my life. It was replaced by a pang of fear for the Yellows, whether or not they deserved my sympathy. Those Yellows, caught between duty and being outnumbered, stood their ground.

"Go on," said Martin-Frederick, waving a hand at the Yellows. "Disappear."

As though this gave them permission to act on their fears, the Yellows turned away and walked very quickly, but did not run.

"We had better go before they come back with friends," said Martin-Frederick, exhilarated by the whole thing.

One of the Greens looked like he wanted to disagree, so eager were they for a fight, but Martin-Frederick shook his head, and the soldier went silent. The Greens had never hassled me personally, and, according to Lenz and his books, they were Rotfelsen's biggest, and best trained, army. The one that came the closest to actually protecting its people.

Four armies in this one kingdom, itself one of four kingdoms in a larger country, all desperate to tear each other apart. The place was trembling with potential violence—with all that death Chasiku had supposedly felt. Imagine, for example, if a fight did break out, and a stray bullet killed Martin-Frederick, or someone even more important than him. Rotfelsen was easily one duel away from exploding. I hoped this thought was simply the product of an overemotional hangover.

"I wish this was my own social call," laughed Martin-Frederick, as we half-ran eastward, toward a series of hedges and away from the Sunset Palace. I admit a part of me agreed with him. I was not terribly interested in Martin-Frederick, but who wouldn't enjoy running from a bit of trouble with a pretty boy?

Behind a hedge of orange flowers, we came to what looked like an outhouse, but it wasn't near a building. It was padlocked and guarded, built from green-painted rotrock as though lazily pretending at camouflage against the hedges and grass nearby. No one had painted orange flowers on it, regrettably.

"High General Dreher," I asked, "wishes to take breakfast with me in there?"

"Sort of," said Martin-Frederick.

"'Sort of' in a way that means 'not at all'? I try to avoid following soldiers into strange rooms."

Through most of my life, I would have done anything to avoid groups of soldiers, and yet here I was. Being yanked to and fro by soldiers was simply what one did on the palace grounds, and I'd gotten used to it already. Disgusting.

"Even if it's the first step toward getting out from under the Prince's thumb?" asked Martin-Frederick.

The Greens guarding the outhouse undid the padlock and opened the door. Inside was a platform ringed by a cage, hanging on pulleys that squeaked beneath the green stone roof. It was the sort of thing used to transport goods from the surface into the depths of Turmenbach. Martin-Frederick got in first, to show that it was safe.

"Well," I said, "that's unexpected."

Martin-Frederick flourished toward the cage around him. Perhaps the High General really would help me. The end was coming soon anyway, and I decided I'd do what I could to live a bit longer. In I went.

GLAIZATZ LAKE

I was packed in very close with Martin-Frederick and one other Green. The young swordsman was a little too theatrical about his gentlemanliness, but at least it meant he didn't jam himself against me. He would not tell me where we were going besides "down."

The cramped cage holding us plunged down through a narrow tunnel for some time, wobbling and clacking and sometimes banging the walls. This was particularly fun for my pounding, starka-soaked head. Our descent was slowed by the pulleys—else we would have died—but it *felt* like a free fall. There was a lamp clattering above us that miraculously never spilled its oil. At least it was all too loud for conversation.

We were going to Glaizatz Lake. I didn't know this yet, but I'll save you that little suspense, since the revelation likely means nothing to you. But I'd been to Glaizatz Lake before.

There is no Glaizatz Town or Glaizatz Hill or Glaizatz Region or Glaizatz Oblast, just the lake. A big, circular lake murmuring in a great cavern somewhere in the center of the red boulder that is Rotfelsen. The lake is too important to Rotfelsen as a water supply for unpredictable towns to be allowed to form near its surface, so the only people there are pulleymen, guards, fishermen with permits, Turmenbach teenagers sneaking in to look brave, and guides who lead young children and their bitter grandmothers up thin, rocky paths to see the surface of the lake itself.

When I was six, we were in Rotfelsen for a time, and Papa allowed me to visit the lake because I begged and begged and pleaded and begged. But Papa couldn't make it up those paths, not by then, and so it was Grandmother who took me. I would say she never forgave me, but I was unforgivable long before that. We saw the surface of the lake, its mossy walls streaked with thick, pointed gashes, with its pulleys and buckets, its guards, its railings for outsiders to gawp behind, the lights that flash and throb beneath its surface. Our guide was a sprightly woman, perhaps a decade older than Grandmother was, who ran up and down the rocks like a lizard.

Glaizatz Lake, I learned from the sprightly guide, does not emit patches and bursts of light from nowhere; it is filled with barely visible creatures that shine when threatened by larger fish.

"The wiggly little shrimp," she said to me in a chirp that should have felt condescending, even at six, but didn't, "bounce about in the lake together, looking for safe patches of water in which they can float, still as rocks, and contemplate the love of the gods. But when the heathenish fish that wish to eat them during their contemplations thrash up to them, the wiggly little shrimp exude a light derived from their own divine understanding. This blinds the heathenish fish and, more importantly, attracts even larger fish, with larger *teeth*"—she lunged at me, squeezing her hands like little shark mouths; I think I laughed and cringed—"who, drawn by the light and the true understanding, gobble up the heathenish scavengers and save the wiggly little shrimp. Understand?"

I nodded enthusiastically. On the way back to Papa, I had devoured half a grilled "heathenish" fish, which the guide had given me for free when Grandmother refused to pay because it was too "fancy" for me. Unfortunately, I proved Grandmother right by becoming too full, and when I complained of stomach pain, she slapped the rest of the fish from my hand.

"Now it's no one's," she hissed.

I don't know why I remember this so clearly.

Whether or not the shrimp understand the gods (and who am I to assume that they don't?), their light shows frequently succeeded at protecting them, by signaling the fishermen to kill their predators.

After all this, Grandmother dragged me back down. We spent our time in one of those towns with no sunlight that are stuck into tunnels far lower than the surface of Glaizatz Lake. The town had a spigot stuck into its eastern wall, which was one of the edges of the bowl that held the lake, with all its glowing shrimp and heathenish predators. This single spigot oozed grimy, sometimes bloody, water that needed to be sifted before drinking, and was guarded by Greens.

High General Dreher

Eventually, our cage popped out of the ceiling of the cavern. After perhaps half an hour in a tunnel confined to the width of three sets of adult shoulders, a split second saw us hovering at the top of a monumental cave. Glaizatz Lake itself was maybe seven miles across, and the cavern was wider than that. Our cage felt unmoored, floating in the air above the circular lake, which was alive with the blinking lights of wiggly little shrimp, strewn with boats, obscured by buckets on pulleys, ringed with ledges on which workers slept in shacks. The whole place was eerily quiet and muffled, just as I remembered it, thanks to the soft, thick, absorbent moss that grew on every wall.

Would Glaizatz Lake crumble too? Would those in the towns at its base be crushed, drowned, or shot to pieces? Where would all its water go, then? Flooding those towns perhaps, filling up the rock. Or draining down into some hollow in the center of the world.

Martin-Frederick, next to me, laughed good-naturedly at my gasp. "Surprised? It's—"

"Glaizatz Lake," I muttered to myself, not meaning to interrupt.

"Yes. Oh. You knew?"

I nodded, holding onto the bars and looking out over it all. "I have never seen it from above before. Incredible."

Martin-Frederick looked pleased.

"What I don't know," I said, "is what this *thing* we're in is called."

"A lift," said Martin-Frederick.

"Simple enough."

Our tunnel must have been a hollow pillar right through Turmenbach. We sped down, and only when the lake reared up to slap us did · we slow. Our cage clicked lightly onto a small island of rotrock no larger than my bedroom, on which High General Dreher was seated at a wooden table. Behind him was a Green.

The cage clanked open, and I stepped onto (somewhat) solid land once again, shaking from the trip.

"You'll excuse me if I don't get up," said Dreher. "Good to see you again, although I don't believe we've been introduced. I'm High General Dreher. Please sit."

I gave my name and sat across the square table from the High General, while Martin-Frederick sat around the corner to my left. The space at my right, where a fourth person would have sat, was taken up by a huge roast. The Green who had taken the trip with us stood by the open cage. There was a tall lantern on a pole stuck into the ground behind the High General, so I could only see his face when wiggly little shrimp flashed nearby.

"I know that was excessive," said High General Dreher, "but I do love to take my breakfasts down here."

I leaned forward on my elbows and forced a smile. My head was throbbing. "Right out in the open, yet this might be the most private place in the Tetrarchia, hm?"

"Exactly," said Dreher. "It's the only island on the lake, you know. Barely visible from the shore."

"There are theories that it doesn't reach the lake's floor!" chimed in Martin-Frederick. "And that there are larger creatures further below!"

"There are theories about everything in this place," sighed the High General.

Martin-Frederick and I were left to serve ourselves, and so the young man enthusiastically cut the roast for me before I could stop him. The knives on the table were quite sharp, which perhaps showed the General's trust in his guests. Or, perhaps, showed that there was nowhere to run.

The roast was tough, and there was nothing to go with it—I was now so spoiled as to be disappointed with the perfectly edible. I remembered the papers documenting Papa's ravings: all that good food I'd eaten recently had not been *free*. I should have been happy with tasteless nourishment.

Martin-Frederick took a bite of the roast before gleefully throwing a chunk into the lake to watch the water light up around it.

"So," said High General Dreher, "what did you and the old bejeweled purple chatterbox discuss during the ball?"

"Nothing interesting." I shrugged. "He just wanted me to know that he's very important, and that I should leave as soon as possible."

The High General laugh-coughed, and was then silent for a few moments. "Yes," he finally replied. "That sounds like him. But you're still here."

"And not bruised, that I can see," said Martin-Frederick.

"Impressive though his suites are," I said, "*he* didn't drop me into the center of Glaizatz Lake."

The High General looked up, concerned. "I'm not trying to impress. I just—"

"Of course," I said. "That's why you succeed."

He leaned back and groaned, looking uncomfortable at the idea of being too ostentatious: the type of officer invested in looking like a common soldier. A common soldier who ate breakfast on a private island and commanded Rotfelsen's largest army. A common soldier who commanded a young prince. A common soldier who seemed to never be called by his given name. (It was Franz, but I learned that later.)

I felt that I immediately understood the High General. He was respected and feared throughout Rotfelsen as a straightforward, no-nonsense man, and he was as much a fraud as I. The only difference was that he did not seem to realize it. No one with that much power is *common*, no matter how plainly they speak.

Another flash of wiggly little shrimp gave me a closer look at Dreher's face than I had gotten at the King's Dinner, where I was mostly behind him, or far away. It was a square and ruddy face, like it had been carved from the rotrock itself. More important than his face was the care with which he made every movement, as though always trying to minimize pain, just as he had at the dinner. That morning, I felt I sympathized, even though my movements were only painful due to a hangover.

"I suspect Vorosknecht," laughed the High General, after a few careful bites, "wants to scare you away for the same reason that I'd like to bring you closer."

I set down my knife and fork. "Oh?"

"Because you're a mind-witch!" said Martin-Frederick. He smiled at me as though the act of smiling rendered this accusation meaningless.

"Martin-Frederick," said Dreher, "please."

The young man opened his mouth to respond, and then seemed to change his mind. He smiled at me and shrugged apologetically.

The High General looked at me silently. No flashes from the lake came to tell me his expression.

"I am a soothsayer," I said.

"That seems like something the purple windbag wouldn't like," said the High General. "For reasons he would term as 'moral.'" He laughed at this, although it quickly became another cough.

Martin-Frederick moved to pat the High General's back, but was waved away.

"And what are your morals, High General?" I asked, once his cough had subsided.

"Whatever protects Rotfelsen," he replied immediately. "If I got caught up on whether things were 'right' on some higher, moral plane, I would not have an army at all."

"Vorosknecht has an army," said Martin-Frederick. I could've thanked him for pointing out the obvious so I didn't have to.

"Vorosknecht," grunted Dreher, "can afford to be highly selective about his ideals. He can have all his statues and parties and jewelry and cordials—he can be decadent because he does not need to protect our people."

"Except from bad ideas," I added.

The High General laughed at that, which was good. I was genuinely enjoying seeing the man whose soldiers had brought me to his island in a restricted cave, miles beneath the capital, call someone else "decadent." It was honestly great fun for me—I enjoyed playing along. My audience with Vorosknecht had been difficult because I could not tell where his beliefs ended and his fraud began. Dreher seemed to truly believe his own nonsense, which endeared him to me, in a sense.

"Personally," he said, "I'd much rather your abilities—be they curses or gifts, I hardly care—be used for the good of Rotfelsen. I'm glad Vorosknecht doesn't recognize their utility, but you are wasted on princely intrigues."

"Perhaps," I allowed.

"Whose fortunes do they have you telling?"

"Whoever's the Prince requires."

"Mine?"

"If you like."

"No, thank you," Dreher said quickly. "I mean, did the Prince ask for my fortune?"

"Not yet, no. Or I could look at the future of your battles against the Bandit States."

"No. No, thank you. Unnecessary. Our relationship with Rituo has only been improving."

I cleared my throat, glanced to Martin-Frederick, and then back to Dreher. "Even when taking into account, ah, '*you-know-who*'?"

Dreher let out a long, irritated breath and looked at Martin-Frederick, who gave another apologetic shrug. The High General made a dismissive gesture with his hand.

"I am a straightforward man," he said. The kind of thing straightforward men *always* say. "The rumors of some Warrior Queen in the Bandit States are true, in that a few little states, farther south, have been knitted together by someone. But she's no real threat—not now, anyway. We're simply keeping an eye on her, and ensuring that Rituo continues to help us destabilize her."

"I see."

"Do you *like* telling fortunes for the Prince?"

I could imagine most any answer to this going wrong, but given the fights I had seen between Yellows and Greens, I made my choice. "Of course not."

"Do you need *help*, Kalyna Aljosanovna?"

"I don't follow."

"Look," said the High General, "it's clear enough that Friedhelm and his lackey are holding you against your will. At the dinner you were in uniform, but unarmed. I don't know what they have on you, but when he tires of and discards you—if you live that long—who will protect you from Vorosknecht, I wonder?"

I grinned. "A High General, maybe?"

He laughed. "Maybe. I feel for your position, truly, but sympathy alone isn't enough for me to risk helping you. I'm sure you understand."

"I do." I appreciated Dreher's upfront nature, no matter how many layers of artifice it required.

"I think," he said, "that I could use your help to maintain order here in Rotfelsen. And that, if you helped me, I could do far more than protect you from the Prince."

I pondered this for a moment, which he graciously allowed me to do. There were clearly things he was not telling me. But then, who could blame him? We had a false King under his nose—I wondered how his desire for order, for maintaining the peace, would conflict with that.

I considered what I could gain from the High General, in this moment, if I told him about Olaf. Perhaps he would rescue me right now, but perhaps, with no reason to think I was loyal, he would have me killed and then start a war with the Yellows. I decided to hold onto that piece of information, for now.

I leaned forward with both hands on the table. "Can you help me escape Prince Friedhelm?"

"I'd like to try."

I sat back. If the High General treated me like a normal underling, and not a prisoner, it would be much easier to disappear in his service. Although I wondered if I'd feel guilty about running out on someone I found a bit pleasant, despite everything.

"I like the sound of this very much," I said, letting real excitement and relief bleed into my voice. "But how do you know I don't actually love the Prince's service? How can you trust me?"

"What's the most you can do if you're lying? Tell the Prince I don't like him? Hardly a revelation."

"Well then, what can I do now, to prove that I can be helpful to you."

"Do you know why the lights of Glaizatz Lake are so mysterious?" asked Dreher.

I kept silent, expectant. No one spoke for a long time. Everything we ate and drank was cold, and somehow there was a draft in that cave, yet I sweated out liquor and steam.

"No, no," said the High General, laughing, "that wasn't rhetorical, I'm really asking. You're a prophet; I thought you might know."

I laughed with him. "Sir, I only see images, and they are often useless without context. Please go on."

"Meaning that if you know the mystery, you may be able to learn its answer."

"You see, General?" said Martin-Frederick. "I told you she'd be useful! Before you even saw her at the dinner, I told you!" He flourished at me.

"You did," Dreher conceded. "I'm glad to know you have an eye for talent."

Martin-Frederick seemed pleased by this.

"Kalyna," said Dreher, "I've been told that there are mountain pools and steppe bogs in farthest Quruscan with creatures similar to these, who carry in them tiny flames to light up their predators or prey."

I nodded. This was true, I had seen them, but they were nowhere near as bright or numerous as the wiggly little shrimp in Glaizatz.

"Have you been there?" he asked. "Is that where you're from?"

"Yes, I have. And only partly."

"Well, do you know the difference between those in the steppe bogs and these?" The General pointed down at the water. Shrimp flashed accommodatingly nearby.

"No," I said.

"The sun." He did not point up. "The ones that flit around in Quru pools have the sun above them half the day, like most decent creatures."

I nodded. It seemed inopportune to point out that most of his fellow Rots seldom saw the sun. That even his soldiers were mostly drawn from such people. That we were currently in a cave.

"The, ah, explanation that most who pay attention to these things give—for the Quru shrimp, I mean—is that half the day they pull the sun's light into themselves. Just enough, or their tiny translucent bodies

would burst. They hold this inside in order to release when necessary."
He laughed quietly. "Of course, who's to say this theory is trustworthy?
It's also said that when they release the light, it actually burns their en-
emies, which seems unlikely."

"Wouldn't water douse their flame?" asked Martin-Frederick.

"So, the answer that I wonder if you know," continued High General
Dreher, "is this: If their Quru cousins receive light from the sun, what
illuminates the little ones down here?"

"The divine love of the gods?" I offered.

Dreher coughed appreciation at that, which was satisfying.

"In a way," said Martin-Frederick, trying to be cryptic.

The High General shot him a look. "No one knows," he said, "but
there are *theories*. Does that jog the slivered future in your brain?"

"Not yet."

"Hmm," he said. "Hmmmm."

"No one knows what's at the bottom, you know," said
Martin-Frederick. He was leaning far forward. "Some say there isn't
one. The lake just keeps doing, down through the middle of the rock,
and into the ground below it."

"Well," I said, "I will grasp for new visions and find your answer."

"That would be lovely," said High General Dreher. "When you do,
tell Martin-Frederick here. Then we'll plan your extraction."

"I'll do you one better," I replied as I cut another piece from the
roast. "Come get me and my family from my servant house on the night
of the Sun's Death. Everyone will be tired, and full, and I will certainly
have something for you by then. If you aren't satisfied with what I tell
you"—I shrugged and gestured upward with the skewered piece of
meat—"you can drop me right back with the Prince, or wherever else
you like."

I had no idea what I would say when this time came, or how long I
would work for the High General, but I was giving myself an ultima-
tum: have a plan by the Sun's Death or die with the Tetrarchia.

Dreher looked at me, silently, for a good long time. Then he smiled.
"Wonderful."

I smiled back and nodded and ate the chunk of roast I had been
waving about. It was still underwhelming, but my alcohol-wrung body
cried out for nourishment. "Thank you," I said when I'd swallowed most
of it, "for the liberation, and for the breakfast."

High General Dreher nodded and looked off across Glaizatz Lake, rubbing his right side with his left hand.

Martin-Frederick chattered at us as we continued to eat. I don't remember what he said, as I was too busy trying to think of what answer to this strange question would most please Dreher.

He was certainly my best chance for escape, and I was now even more confident that fleeing south into the Bandit States was the way to go. What's more, with Lenz poring over Papa's ramblings and clearly on the brink of learning my secret, the sooner the better.

Dreher was the most likable source of power I'd yet met in this rock, but that was because I felt I immediately understood his flaws and desires. He was personally likeable, but still a general, and no general can be a good person. The Tetrarchia saw no large-scale wars these days, but border towns carried bad memories of what men like Dreher were capable of.

Still, it was difficult to connect the man in front of me to that. I did not understand enough of armies and politics to know whether High General Dreher oversaw carnage or only stuck pins into maps in his office. Which of these is worse is its own question.

No matter. It couldn't hurt for me to make up something about the bottom of Glaizatz Lake and see what I could get out of it. I would use anyone as a means to escape the Tetrarchia before spring.

MOLDERED LUNG

Breakfast was finished quietly, goodbyes were grunted, and soon Martin-Frederick, the Green who had come with us, and I were back in our small cage, or "lift." The Green yanked a cord, and we were hauled up toward the surface. It was slower going (and quieter) in this direction, but whatever pulleys and counterweights and buckets of water were doing the pulling made decent time. I wondered about what poor villages we were passing through—what people might be just on the other side of the shaft's stone walls.

Martin-Frederick made little conversation on the way up, mostly compliments on my ability to charm Dreher and my prophetic powers. When the sun became visible above us, and I knew we were nearing the surface, I said, "I do hope the High General will be healthy."

"What do you mean?" asked the young swordsman.

"Well, a fighting man suffering from moldered lung, it must be frustrating for him. His days of charging embankments are long past."

The sound of the old general's cough, and the movements he could and could not make, had been as clear as day to me, and guessing at a man of action's frustration was just as easy. The biggest gamble had been deciding to not try impressing Dreher directly with my insight. Best to let the lackey do the talking: the High General did not seem the type to appreciate a show-off.

"How . . . ?" For a moment, Martin-Frederick was stunned at my insight, before muttering, "Oh, yes. Of course. The future."

I grinned. "On the subject of the future . . ." I began.

"I feel we've hardly discussed anything else," Martin-Frederick interrupted. "But I suppose that's true of most people. Until they're old, then they discuss the past."

I nodded as though what he was saying was wonderfully profound. The lift clanked closer and closer to the surface.

"But yes, what about it?" he asked.

"Well, as I mentioned to your High General, my Gift requires context, and I'm afraid I won't be getting down to Glaizatz Lake very often."

"Oh, you mean because of my uncle, the evil prince who's keeping you captive?" he laughed, as though this very true statement were something from a play.

"Yes," I replied. "So if I had a better idea of *what exactly* High General Dreher wants me to see, then I would know when I have seen it."

"Or not seen it."

"Just so."

The cage clanked to a stop in the green outhouse and I stepped out, less wobbly this time. Martin-Frederick followed, and I stopped just outside, breathing in the fresh air for a moment.

"Then context you shall have," he said, smiling at me in the morning light. He was at least nice to look at, if not to talk to. "But don't tell him I told you . . ."

"Why would I?"

"Well, if what I'm about to explain comes up in conversation, maybe you could tell him that you saw it . . . You know, in one of your prophecies?"

I knotted my brows. "I don't lie about my abilities. It is like a duelist's honor."

"I see. Shall I not, then?"

"Tell me."

He laughed. "Finally, I have something that *you* wish to know. Well, High General Dreher is convinced that the very Soul of the Rotfelsenisch Nation lives in that lake."

I was quiet for a moment, and leaned back against the outside of the little hut that enclosed the lift.

"The *what?*" I finally asked.

"The Soul of the Nation. Some silly idea the High General picked up that every nation—"

"Rotfelsen is not a 'nation.' It's one-quarter of a nation."

Martin-Frederick waved this away. "You may not understand. But you've been to all corners of our Tetrarchia, and so you know it isn't so simple. Each of the Tetrarchic states still sees itself as its own nation with its own people."

He was stating what was, to him, fact, and I suspected my disagreement would invite more explaining, so I nodded. Of course, citizens of the Tetrarchia didn't go around thinking of themselves as "Tetrarchic" every moment. But neither did most people think of themselves as Rotfelsenisch or Quru or Skydašian or Masovskan most days. If my travels had taught me anything, it was that people were far more likely to identify themselves by their geography, their town, their neighborhood, their politics. Only those in the corridors of power (or, like Martin-Frederick, aspiring for them) thought the world was defined by the broad lines the Tetrarchia had painted across the grasses all those years ago.

I nodded.

"And each of those nations," he continued, "are supposed to have their own individual 'Soul.'" He snickered at the thought. "Loasht, too, and everywhere else. Maybe a multiheaded monstrosity for the Bandit States? I don't know. The ideals and archetypes of a nation bound up in some spirit that guides its fate, you know."

"How abstract," I replied. "I always heard of spirits as being rather straightforward and small: a dead person's memory, a wind-sprite in a mountain, a source of courage, that sort of thing. A small part of everyday life."

"Exactly!" he laughed. "Whereas this Soul of the Nation is the sort of theory fanciful scholars come up with on long boring nights, while taking many different substances and trying to make sense of their people's history." He shrugged and shook his head. "But history doesn't make sense—it's just things that happen!"

"Well, those drug-addled 'fanciful scholars' you describe don't sound like the High General."

"No. He's a pragmatic type whose highest calling has always been protecting our kingdom. But theoreticians can hook a man like him if their fantasies are told the right way. Particularly if he's led to believe he can *guide* this Soul."

I cocked my head to the side. "But it sounds to me like the Soul of the Nation is a rhetorical exercise more than a—"

"Mostly, yes. But, you see, there's a . . . sect."

"Naturally."

"A small group of deranged—if you ask me, but don't tell Dreher I said so—thinkers who believe this Soul of the Nation is a real thing that actually lives in the stone. Or beneath it."

"Perhaps they're just too literal minded."

"Now *that* sounds like our beloved High General," he sighed. "So many hours spent staring at Glaizatz Lake and its mysteries—strange shrimp, singular moss, ancient lacerations up the walls—has led our good Dreher to the inevitable conclusion that the Soul of the Nation is a real thing, which lives at the bottom of that lake, deep in the rock, or below it, feeding the shrimp their light."

"The love of the gods after all," I said. "He should talk to the tour guides."

"Oh, he has! Although he doesn't think of it as a god, exactly. Whatever it is, he thinks that *pleasing* it, if it exists, will benefit Rotfelsen. So he hopes you'll prove its tangibility without his pushing, in order to prove him right."

"And yet you tell me . . ."

"I hope you'll be able to give him proof to the contrary. I think that his fancies are beginning to get in the way of his aims. Chasing phantoms does not protect our borders, you know." He made a face. "And he thinks that this 'Soul' is disgusted by all of the 'decadence' going on above it. Personally, I rather fancy nice things."

"If he's so obsessed, he may not believe me."

"I maintain hope that our High General can be reasonable in this, as he is in most things."

I thought for a moment, tapping my chin. "And, of course, there are plenty of strange creatures in the world: What if he's right?"

Martin-Frederick laughed and threw up his hands. "I'm not against the idea of the thing existing. If you prove it, I will happily prostrate myself before it, offer sacrifices, or whatever one does. But his hope is that you'll find it, while mine is much more mundane: I hope to take you to the opera."

"That"—I grinned—"would be much easier if I were liberated."

"I agree," he said. "First, your rescue from the evil Prince. And then, down in Turmenbach, there will be a production of *The Leper's Five Tits*, a wonderfully popular comic opera! Performances will begin near the end of winter, when dignitaries are beginning to stream in for the Council of Barbarians. The Grand Opera House will be filled up to its brim."

I bowed slightly and tried not to think about the Council, and how it had to be related to Papa's apocalyptic vision. I intended to leave the Tetrarchia behind me before this opera would begin its run, anyway.

"I would be delighted," I said. "Have a fine day, Martin-Frederick Reinhold-Bosch."

"And yourself, Kalyna Aljosanovna. I look forward to seeing you again soon."

Two Greens were ordered to escort me back to my servant house, but when I asked to go somewhere else instead, they happily complied. At least I was not *their* prisoner as well. Once the Yellow barracks were in sight, the Greens let me walk the rest of the way by myself, rather than start a fight.

SURVIVE TO TELL THE TALE

I marched right up the stairs to Lenz's rooms. I played in my head, again and again, how I would yell at him when I got there. I tried not to think about my need to escape, about what he might know; I just wanted to be angry at him for what he'd done to my father.

I also tried not to think about whether this even was something done *to my father*, so much as something that terrified me because it could lead to my entire fraud being laid bare. Because it reminded me that I had not given Papa a doctor, a room, and good food; they had been granted to help me forget that I was a prisoner.

On top of everything else, my head was still pounding with that hangover.

But one foot in front of the other, I stomped up the stairs and into Lenz's messy rooms. There were papers everywhere, as usual, and I wondered which ones might contain what my father muttered in his most private and vulnerable moments. Through a door, I saw him sitting on the bed in the next room, speaking to someone I could not see. My face was twitching with how badly I wanted to throttle him.

"Lenz!" I bellowed as I moved toward him.

He turned and looked puzzled. I opened my mouth to say more, just as Olaf's stolen face appeared in the doorway and he smiled at me.

"What?" I gurgled.

"Well, hello!" laughed Olaf.

I entered the room, and saw that Prince Friedhelm was there as well. So-called Dugmush, the Yellow who had guarded me when I discovered Lenz's surveillance of my father, shut the door and waited outside. All the thoughts of what I would yell at Lenz drained away. For now.

"Yes, Kalyna?" asked Lenz, still seated.

"What . . . ?" I began, but was unsure how to continue.

"What am I doing here?" laughed Olaf.

I nodded. I wondered the same about Prince Friedhelm, but thought better of questioning him. The "King" was here, but the Prince was everyone in the room's boss. Seeing the Prince and the "King" in Lenz's messy bedroom seemed *wrong* somehow, like a city guard out of uniform, or a calm god painted hovering above an ancient scene of destruction.

"Well," said Olaf, "the King and the Prince are beginning to spend a bit more time together. Mending our relationship! It gives me an excuse to get away from the Reds for a bit, since we don't *quite* trust them." He shrugged. "And who knows if they trust me?"

"The more Yellows we can have around Olaf, the better," added Lenz.

"So far so good!" laughed Olaf. "I've never had a more comfortable bed, finer clothes, or better food."

"Except for the persimmons," added Prince Friedhelm.

"I never expected to survive this adventure, but it's nice to get a taste of the good life beforehand. I must say I hope we find Gerhold, or that I die, sooner rather than later—I was not prepared to keep up this charade for more than a few weeks."

I looked at Olaf, studying his stolen face. What life had he left behind to be so cavalier? He certainly seemed to be enjoying himself. As someone with the extremely gauche and commonplace need to *survive*, I truly could not understand his thinking.

"Running out of things to tell the Reds?" asked Prince Friedhelm.

"Oh no," replied Olaf. "They're used to silence from me. It's the Queen."

"Speak to her as little as possible," said the Prince. "I foolishly used to think she only disliked my brother as much as I do, but it is clear now she is part of this. She is trying to expose you."

"That's not the impression I've gotten," said Olaf.

"Oh really?" Lenz replied. He glared at me.

"Well, perhaps I am too simple to understand," Olaf conceded. "But so far, she has simply been reminding me that she and I—that is, that she and the King—have been trying to have children."

"Olaf," snapped Lenz, "you haven't . . ."

Olaf threw up his hands. "By all the gods, no!" He shook his head. "And not just because we could sire all kinds of bastards. That would be an awful thing to do to anyone, wouldn't it?"

Lenz nodded. The Prince smirked.

"She is just trying to fluster you," said Friedhelm. "Goad you into admitting the truth, probably where you can be overheard. Having your baby wouldn't help her cause any more than if she bore some other bastard."

"Well," I cut in, "we had better find the King so you can survive to tell the tale."

Friedhelm glared at Olaf. "You had better never tell the tale."

Lenz stood up and grimaced slightly. "Why don't we go find out what our friend Klemens Gustavus knows, yes? That *was* the original reason you brought Olaf here."

Prince Friedhelm nodded absentmindedly, and we got started on moving Lenz's bed to once more to reveal the secret stairway. It was good that Dugmush helped because the royalty—even the false royalty—were not about to lend a hand.

Counter-Conspirators

So, the five of us—Lenz, the Prince, the false King, the Yellow I called Dugmush, and myself—all went down that same winding staircase to the secret cell where the spoiled little Masovskan murderer Klemens Gustavus was held. I damned the vertical, rock-bound kingdom, and its many sets of stairs, under my breath. I also damned Lenz, again and again, as I waited for my moment to have him alone.

Lenz and I entered the little room first, where another Yellow waited outside the cell. As before, the light was mostly on Klemens, and we were in shadow. Prince Friedhelm stepped out behind us.

"Back to kill me?" sighed Klemens. He was standing, leaning forward, with his aggravating little bully's face squeezed against the bars.

A thought occurred to me, and I glanced back to where I knew Olaf must be, at the bottom of the staircase, hidden from view. I am at least decent at theatricality, and so motioned to him to stay out of sight, hoping he saw it. Lenz and Friedhelm either did not notice, or played along.

A moment later, Dugmush emerged, meaning she must have passed Olaf. I smiled, which Klemens took as confirmation that we would kill him now. Then the Prince stepped forward enough to be in the light. Klemens reeled backward and made a strangled sound somewhere in his throat.

"Well?" screeched Klemens. "What do you want? Do you want me to *apologize* for trying to kill you before you kill me?" His Rotfelsenisch seemed to crumble around the words he wanted to say, but he puffed out his chest with, I suppose, a kind of bravery. "You like to see your enemies die, Prince? I swear I will haunt you until the end of your days!"

The Prince chuckled quietly, not arguing with anything the brat was saying. Klemens' nerve seemed to already be flagging.

"Tell me again," Friedhelm finally said, "why you and your conspirators wanted me dead."

"*Counter*-conspirators!" Klemens growled.

"Rather a mouthful," I said.

"*We*," Klemens continued, "were trying to stop *you*, Selvosch, and the rest from killing your brother."

Prince Friedhelm said nothing. He just stood there and smiled.

"Did . . ." Klemens gulped. "Did . . . I . . . did we succeed?"

Prince Friedhelm now laughed louder. Louder than I had ever heard him laugh, or speak, and it echoed through the room. It was deeply sinister, I must say. As he laughed, the Prince turned toward the staircase and nodded at it. Olaf emerged into the dim light, his face as vacant as the real King's. Klemens blinked many times.

"You . . ." he stammered. "You are the King?"

"So far," said Olaf, with a nod.

"Huh," said Klemens.

"Despite the rumors," Friedhelm began, "my brother and I get along well enough. For siblings."

"There was an attack on me that night," said Olaf, "though it did not come from my brother." He stepped closer to Klemens. "Thank you for saving my life."

Friedhelm cleared his throat loudly, and I suspected he didn't much care for that improvisation. Klemens laughed triumphantly, and I immediately hated the rich monster all over again.

"But *unfortunately*," Friedhelm continued, "your attempt on *my* life threw us somewhat. So we would very much like to know who you are working with, and what you know about our enemies. Who are also *your* enemies."

Klemens nodded enthusiastically.

"Kalyna," said the Prince, "will he behave himself?"

I had rather forgotten that I was there for a reason, and jumped at my name. I nodded to the Prince and stepped forward into the light, right up to the bars, staring into Klemens' face. He looked very pleased with himself.

"He will," I said. "Today, at least."

A Yellow unlocked Klemens Gustavus' cell and, with that, he was free. Freer than I, in fact.

It occurred to me then that Prince Friedhelm had created a false King who obeyed his orders, and was presently using that tool to extract the names of Klemens' fellow counter-conspirators. What a terrifying man I worked for—did he *really* want his brother to return to his throne? Was this purely momentum?

Whatever the case, Klemens fell for it fully, and I did enjoy how stupid it made him look to me.

So we all went back up to Lenz's apartments, where Dugmush got a flame going in the fireplace. I hadn't noticed just how cold the winter had become until I felt that warmth.

Klemens sniffed at the state of the place, and made a big show of finding it disgusting and common. That he was only seeing it at the royals' mercy did not seem to cross his mind. Then, in those messy rooms, Klemens Gustavus laughed about the whole "misunderstanding," and happily told the "King" about his counterplot. Now that he was free, he also treated Friedhelm and Olaf as, at *best*, equals. The Masovskan banker also enjoyed pointing out what good terms he was on with King Lubomir XIII of Masovska. Friedhelm seemed to find this amusing, and Olaf did not react.

I will spare you Klemens' self-aggrandizing and long-winded explanation, and simply tell you that Klemens and his sister, Bozena, were working with Edeltraud von Edeltraud, the Mistress of the Coin, whom I had followed at the Winter Ball. Edeltraud, it seemed, had been approached by Selvosch, much as Prince Friedhelm had been. It seemed also that, like the Prince, her desire for immediate comfort had outpaced her hunger for power. Edeltraud had been promised a high place in the new government—although who would *rule* that government had been left vague—if she could ensure that, after the King was overthrown, Rotfelsen's money would keep flowing as it always had. The offer that had been meant to sway her was that, once King Gerhold was out of the way, the Rotfelsenisch coinage would only need to be collected and reminted *once*, replacing the royal face with a yet-to-be-chosen symbol, and then never altered again. Edeltraud von Edeltraud had been too short-sighted to see past this first overhaul, which would still have to take place within a year. If she failed, she would have to explain herself to an overzealous and unstable new government.

Selvosch had also told her that "someone with an army" would be on their side. This had probably meant Vorosknecht, but for *some strange reason*, Edeltraud had suspected the King's scheming, degenerate brother, *simply* because he was the kind of man to hire spies, prophets, and doubles. So, Edeltraud had reached out to some business acquaintances, and she and the Gustavus siblings had bought some assassins of their own for a counterattack. These would-be assassins had been paid in Masovskan money from the

Gustavus coffers, hence the lesser grivnas found on one of their bodies.

"We were in such a rush to arrive in time for the Winter Ball," Klemens sniffed, "that we did not have time to stop at one of our *own* banks. Cleaning up some legal nonsense back home, you see."

Klemens was questioned on who else his "counterconspiracy" knew to be part of the plot against the King, but he knew less than we did. He was not told that Court Philosopher Vorosknecht was part of the plot, nor that Queen Biruté supposedly was.

I kept quiet through most of this talk, partly because I worried that Klemens would recognize me from Masovska, and mostly because I was waiting for a chance to get Lenz alone. Klemens, sitting languidly across one of Lenz's chairs, warming his feet by the fire, had barely glanced at me.

"But," I finally said, "why do you and your sister care what happens in Rotfelsen? The new marks would spend the same."

"We run the largest changing banks in the Tetrarchia, Loashti," he said.

"I'm not—" I began.

"So our trade depends on the four kingdoms . . . oh, you know, playing nice."

"What does one King or another matter to that?" I asked.

Klemens furrowed his brow and cocked his head to the side. "Loashti," he said, "these people want to *leave* the Tetrarchia."

A LOT OF YELLING

So that was it. The end of our country. It had to be. There was no doubt in my mind, but I still didn't know *how* it would all happen.

We stayed in Lenz's chambers for some time, discussing the fact that Vorosknecht and Selvosch wanted Rotfelsen to back out of the Tetrarchia entirely. The Prince was shocked and affronted at the very idea.

"Separatism?" he cried. "*Separatism*?! That's supposed to be for sad bumpkins in forgotten corners who speak outmoded doggerel languages! Not for nobles in the very seat of power! What could they be *thinking*?"

Lenz, despite his own surprise, kept trying to describe the long historical view on such things to Friedhelm, who truly could not care less. Olaf kept his face blank.

Eventually, it was clear that the discussion was going nowhere, and that Klemens was eager to be on his way. So off he went.

A few minutes later, Friedhelm and Olaf were donning their "royal disguises" in order to get back to the palace, where they belonged. These disguises were just a pair of ratty wigs, clearly meant to signal that it would be shameful to admit to whatever they were up to, but also shameful for royalty to try *too hard* to fool anybody. The hope was that people would begin to notice that the Prince and the King were closer than everyone had thought.

Soon, Lenz and I were alone in his rooms. Dugmush was out in the hall, and we didn't even have a prisoner below us. Lenz deflated into a large wooden chair shaped like a raging hawk. I began to pace.

"This sort of nationalism seems to have been born in our own depths, but has since been popping up in all corners of the Tetrarchia," he sighed. "The idea is that backing out of the Tetrarchia will make a people stronger. More *themselves*."

I kicked over a particularly tall pile of folders, made up my mind, and stomped toward him, grabbing one of his books on the way.

"I shudder to think what would happen if our country's ties were simply broken in such a way," he said.

I had no strong personal feeling that the Tetrarchia needed to remain unified, but such a violent withdrawal, during the Council of Barbarians, simply had to cause the destruction I'd been dreading. These people were rushing right toward my father's prophecy. But I had Papa's other prophecies on my mind.

"I've heard of similar things in—"

I threw a book at him; it clipped his shoulder.

"Kalyna, what is this?"

"Have you heard from Doctor Aue yet today?" I asked. Picking up whatever was to hand: a pile of papers.

"No," he replied as he stood up. "Should I?

I threw the papers at him, but they sputtered out into the air and floated to the floor.

"Of course!" I growled. "Why pay for his care if you can't also use him?"

"Ah, I see." He grabbed a folder and waved it in my face. "I'm ending that little project anyway, because this"—he threw it into the crackling fireplace—"is nonsense."

"I told you it would be."

"And now I know for myself." Lenz began to pace, slowly and unevenly.

"My father is sick, and you—"

"Gave him the best care he has ever had."

"You betrayed him. Kept him prisoner, held his life over my head."

Lenz put himself right in my face, then. "Because you are a prisoner," he hissed. "Of course your father is held against your good behavior. And your behavior has been as underwhelming as your prophetic powers."

Did he know? Had Papa betrayed me? Or was Lenz truly angry that nothing useful was in those records? Nothing of my fraud, nothing of what Papa had learned about him, nothing of the end of the Tetrarchia.

Whatever the case, I would keep bluffing until I knew for sure. It was all I could do.

"Is this about those damn Gustavuses again?" I growled. "I told you that—"

"Vague," Lenz spat. "Everything you see is so vague. I'm still not sure the Queen is against us, but now the Prince—"

"I would see more *clearly*," I said, "if you hadn't dragged me so far into all this palace intrigue in the first place!"

"Oh yes, that's right," he laughed, "if you're too involved in a future, you cannot see it."

"Yes, and—"

"*And*," he continued, "you have to be near a person to see their future. Very convenient way to explain never seeing anything."

I said nothing. Those were the actual rules of the Gift, for those who really had it, but there was no way to argue *that*.

"Talking to Chasiku, and seeing how her powers work, has been enlightening," he said. "Your father's Gift is unfocused, but I begin to doubt whether *yours* even exists."

I felt cold. I could not feel my fingers. "I did not ask to be your personal psychic!" I sputtered. "You don't drag Chasiku all over this damned rock. Use her and let us go!"

"Chasiku," he replied, "doesn't *need* to be taken everywhere to be useful. And you know too much to be let go."

"That's just it!" I cried. "You knew from the start I can't see things that involve me, yet you have dragged me into this . . . this nest of ridiculous intrigue! Of course I don't see enough for you."

"Pathetic."

"If there ever can be an 'enough,'" I continued.

"Pathetic," he repeated.

"You"—I lowered my voice, working very hard to push confidence back into my words—"are not the only one who can pry into another's relationships." I remembered what Papa had seen about Lenz.

Lenz laughed bitterly and reeled away from me. "How hollow. Now I know you have nothing."

I shrugged. I wanted to blurt out what I knew, but I still planned to abscond with the help of the High General during the Sun's Death, so I said, "I am fickle and capricious."

"You," he said, "are more trouble than you're worth."

"Then have me dragged out and killed!" I shouted, loud enough for Yellows in the hallway to hear. I ran up and waved my hands in his face. "Do it, if I'm too much trouble! Have my family slaughtered and stop worrying!"

I had caught him off guard, which was, of course, the point. Lenz blinked many times and leaned away from me.

"Kalyna Aljosanovna," he said. "I, too, am a prisoner here. The Prince—"

"You have resources! Money, carriages, secrets. You could run!"

"I cannot leave the King to . . . wherever he is."

"I don't think much of you, Lenz, but even you should be smart enough to not care about something so silly as royalty."

"I—" he began.

I clapped my hands loudly in his face, interrupting him. I only had one thing left, so I used it.

"What does *one worthless king* matter?" I hissed. "This will all be rubble in two months!"

There was a long silence. An orange-and-sky-blue butterfly landed on a nearby windowsill.

Lenz opened and closed his mouth a few times, then took a deep breath. He composed himself, sat down, crossed his bad leg over his good, and set his back straight.

"I'm sorry, Kalyna Aljosanovna, what was that?"

So I told him.

THE FALL OF THE TETRARCHIA

I told Lenz that *I* had seen the fall of the Tetrarchia in terrible violence, and that *I* could see nothing of the cause. That was the only fabrication.

No weak skirmishes and redrawing of borders, war will pour in like a deluge, change will come to all with fire and sword. To the whole Tetrarchia. The survivors will not live the same lives beneath different flags, they will be ruined and enslaved, or strung out beneath the sun with their entrails stretched across the landscape and their children thrown into the Quruscan steppes or among Rotfelsen's shattered remains. It will crumble and topple.

I quoted Papa almost exactly, and hoped that the specificity, the belief in my face and voice, would be clear. I sat slumped on a bench piled with books, my elbows on my knees. As I spoke, I stared at a book on the floor and memorized every squiggle in the marbling along the edges of its pages.

When I finished, Lenz sat still for a few moments, his eyes wide. Then he leaned toward the door and yelled for Chasiku to be brought to us.

"Why didn't you mention this earlier?" He spoke softly, not even angry.

"What reason have I had to be forthright with you?"

"But this . . . this is no simple kidnapping or palace coup, this . . ."

"Exactly. What would it matter to tell you? It will happen."

"How fatalistic."

I laughed. A different false laugh—the mean one. "My family rather tends toward fatalism. This is coming, and"—even now, I couldn't ignore an opportunity—"this has loomed so large in my visions that it's made seeing anything else difficult."

"Well, if you can't see past two months!" Lenz stood up and paced awkwardly again. "But . . . why is changing this any different from changing other prophecies? You and your family make a living giving people fortunes that *can* be changed."

"This is bigger."

It seemed that Lenz was taking me seriously now. Perhaps it was the conviction in my voice, combined with having just heard what Vorosknecht and his conspirators were up to, but Lenz was talking as though the end was real.

Papa had not betrayed my secret. Not once. He had screamed and twisted in the night, tormented, without me there to hold him, but he had said nothing about my fraud or what I'd asked him to do. I wanted to cry.

"But can't we stop it?" Lenz wasn't really asking, so I didn't answer. He was just talking as his mind twisted around. "If this were immutable, you and your family would have seen it years ago, your father would have seen it before you were born. It's possible *now*, and it can be made . . . impossible, but we need to know more. This plot against the King must be a catalyst . . ."

He was right that here, in the seat of power, there was a chance that we could change the thing. I began to think that I should simply come clean to him, sell myself as the translator of my father's ramblings. It would make my life easier (if I wasn't killed for it), and make it much less likely that the Tetrarchia would fall based on some false future I made up to get out of a situation, like the Bandit States invasion that I no longer expected, or the Queen's part in the plot (which still felt quite possible to me).

I am a fraud, my father saw the doom of the Tetrarchia, please don't kill me, came to the front of my mind. I moistened my lips to speak.

At that moment, a Yellow announced Chasiku. Her arrival immediately curdled any desire to unburden myself. Maybe it was to keep her from being smug, or maybe the moment had simply passed. Either way, current discomfort won out over abstract future dangers. I hoped my cowardice had not doomed us all.

Chasiku looked even more uncomfortable than me, however. The newer soothsayer, my replacement, was shivering when she came in, and had a scarf almost entirely around her head. Lenz moved to help her to a chair, and she slapped his hand away before stumbling over to fall into the farthest possible seat from us. Most of her face and body was covered, but that bending, long-limbed physicality was still visible, hidden beneath.

"It's not *that* cold, is it?" I asked her.

"This is not cold," she growled from beneath her scarf. "Why have I been dragged in front of all these dying soldiers? It pounds at me, destroys me from within. It's been like this for *days*, and bringing me here makes it so much worse."

Lenz opened his mouth to explain, but I stood up and spoke first. "You did say that everyone here stinks of death, didn't you?"

"Yes, yes, including you," she spat.

"Hmm, interesting," I replied. "Could that be, oh I don't know, the imminent destruction of the Tetrarchia?"

Chasiku clawed the scarf off her head to look up in my general direction, although not directly into my face. Seeing her face again, I was still surprised at how put together, and unblemished, she was. I suppose I assumed that all soothsayers ran from mobs, had scars from Galiag windstorms, and learned to cut men down when it was needed.

She blinked many times in quick succession. "Could it?" she murmured.

"Of course, you *see* so much," I said, "and yet—"

"When I got to this sad little kingdom," she interrupted, "I was accosted by so much, *including* images of shattering rotrock. I thought that was a normal occurrence here, but I begin to wonder if it was"— she waved her arms about—"the whole place."

Lenz stepped forward. Chasiku, eyes closed, became tense all over. She no longer shook.

"Was that Rotfelsen itself . . . ?" she muttered.

"It will be," I said. "*That* I have seen."

I felt myself fill with confidence at my ability to pass for prophetic. This confidence was wrung from the doom that faced us all, but I felt no worse because of it. I am that terrible of a person, I suppose.

Chasiku glared up at Lenz. "Why did you bring me here and not tell me of this?"

"I just learned it a few moments ago," he replied. "Why didn't *you* tell me? When you agreed to come here, you didn't see that this was looming?"

"No," she replied. "But it explains a great deal. Part of why I chose to leave Kalvadoti, was that most of what I saw was getting confusing, brutal, and short. My family just accepted it, but I thought a change of scenery would show me other possibilities . . ." She trailed off.

I made an obnoxious flourish with both hands. "Surpriiiiiiiiise."

She did not seem to notice or care, so I said, "Well, you wouldn't have escaped it in Skydašiai anyway. Rotfelsen may crumble. But the rest of the Tetrarchia has its doom just as assured. Armies, chaos, and the like."

"Then why didn't I see this before?" she sighed. "My family and I *have* had difficulty seeing clearly lately. I need more time to consider this."

"I'm so glad we have lots of time," I said, turning to look idly at some books on a shelf.

"Thankfully," said Lenz, grinning in a sickly sort of way, "we have two soothsayers to figure this thing out. You two can work together."

"Only two?" said Chasiku. "I thought you had a whole family."

"Aljosa is not well enough to help," said Lenz. "And Vüsala turned me down."

I stood up straight so suddenly I hit my head on a shelf. "What?"

"I offered your grandmother a position when we first moved them into their new home. She . . . rejected it."

It was good to laugh. I wiped away a tear of joy when I was finally able to speak. "I would give so, *so* much, just to have seen that rejection."

Lenz smiled weakly.

Chasiku looked uncomprehendingly from me, to Lenz, to me, to Lenz, and said, "Can I *leave?*"

"Yes, of course," said Lenz. "But I *expect* you two to look into this together. And soon. Perhaps each one's visions can help illuminate the other's, if you can put your egos aside. Maybe Kalyna's . . ." He waved his hands, looking for the word. ". . . proximity will help? Either way, I can't have you two at each other's throats at a time like this."

Chasiku ignored him and growled, "Why can't anyone make decent *coffee* in this forsaken rock," as she all but ran away. She slammed the door.

I glanced at where she had been, and wondered why she got more freedom than I. Possibly because she wasn't actively trying to escape, which reminded me . . .

"You should come to my servant house for the Sun's Death," I blurted out.

This surprised him, and Lenz turned to look at me. "The Sun's Death? Why?"

"It might be nice. And you can convince the others in my house that we're friendly. That I'm not a prisoner."

He looked skeptical.

I grunted. "Fine. I would like to see my family, and if they come to my home, you'll want to keep an eye on us, won't you?"

"I'll think it over," he grunted.

"And that's all I ask," I said with a very large grin. Then I paid him an ironic salute. "Until then, I will see what I can see," I sighed.

"This isn't just about where King Gerhold is being held," said Lenz. "I know you don't much care for Rotfelsenisch royalty, but everyone—"

"Don't play moralist against me *now*," I growled. "If," I continued, "I could save Olaf and Tural and every farmer and cook and prostitute and merchant and barkeep in our drawn and quartered country, I would. They are *all* my people, remember? Even the Rotfelsenisch. But I cannot save everyone."

Because I am broken, I thought.

TEA IN THE ALCOVE

It felt like weeks since I'd last been in my servant house, even though I had only left it the previous day. Since then, I had terrorized some poor doctor's assistants, plunged down to Glaizatz Lake to eat with High General Dreher, learned a secret about Lenz, visited a hidden prisoner with the Prince and the "King," and told Lenz that our terrible end was nigh. It was starting to get dark, but it wasn't really evening yet: the Sun's Death indeed.

The servant house had a little alcove on the first floor: a windowed bulge popping out of the building's side. As I walked up toward the house, I saw Tural sitting there with a teapot, looking out at the snow, which sat in patches, mere inches from the alcove, so close it looked as though Tural was sitting outside. He seemed far too content to be conjuring his fruit flavors.

I waved to him, and he nodded very slightly. I went inside, took off my coat, and turned directly to the left of the door toward the alcove.

"I know this time is yours," I said in Cölluknit, "but would it disturb you to have company?"

Until I spoke, Tural had looked like an artist's rendering of a man in deep thought: lean legs crossed, elbow on his knee, chin on his fist. Only the slow steam rising from his teacup had told me this was not a painting. When I spoke, he turned to me and smiled broadly.

"It would please me to share."

Tural reached into a shelf in the tea stand and pulled out another cup, which he then flipped right side up with his thumb. He poured me tea, and I did the slow, steady, open-palmed hand gesture that the Quru sometimes preferred over saying "thank you."

"No!" he said, in guttural Rotfelsenisch. "No, no, no, no, no. None of that, now. We aren't in the steppes, and you needn't flourish for every word. I certainly don't."

I smiled and sat. The tea was radiant snow-cave leaf, a dark green drink that was nowhere near as blunt in its power as the black Masovskan tea I was used to. Its very smell warmed me.

"Delicious," I said.

Tural thanked me with a hand gesture, and I chastised him for it.

"No fruit?" I asked.

"My great joy in fruit was drained years ago," he said, back in his native Cöllüknit. "A *tragedy!*" He clasped his hand to his chest.

I had noticed that his white chef's jacket was unstained and there were no seeds in his cravat. I also noticed (for the first time?) that he was handsome.

"But," he went on, "right now is almost the best part of the Rotfelsenisch year: when it becomes beautiful to live in this half-burst pimple filled with blood."

I made a face at the image. "Winter? Why is winter so great here?"

"I left my home," he began, raising his voice, "because there is hardly any fruit alive there, half the year. Too cold, everything freezes. What appears in spring gave me my love, but every year I dreaded when the mountains would heave with snow, and the bushes would lose their leaves. So I traveled to escape that time, and to learn more. Nothing to me is so sweet, varied, and wondrous as fruit, you see. Nothing else shows the fingers of the gods through the world in its every little line, strand, and membrane."

"Vegetables?"

"Well, yes. But I also have a sweet tooth. So! I traveled, landed here where winter is mild, and stayed."

"Winter is even less oppressive in Skydašiai," I offered. "And nonexistent in some parts of Loasht."

"Too little winter for me," he said. "Skydašiai produces most of our fruit, of course, but I like a little cold, in the air *and* in the people. They are too friendly."

"And this is the dark story of how you left your home. But you haven't told me why winter is the best part of the year, here in the bloody pimple."

He grinned. "I used to dread winter, now winter is wonderful. I still must work, I must sit and conjure, but the Sun's Death is the one meal I needn't prepare for. No one wants *berries* at the Sun's Death, they want lamb and ale and hard brown bread to soak in stew." He smiled wistfully and looked back out at the snow. "It's marvelous."

"That's sad. You came out here for the love of something, and now you hope for its absence."

Tural shrugged. "I still love fruit. I love it as one loves the family member whose presence is longed for, and then whose absence is a relief."

"I know just the one. And what family do you share the Feast of the Sun's Death with, then? Or do you take the opportunity to go home to Quruscan?"

"I don't, you know," he laughed softly, "visit my family very often anymore. They feel I have been 'Rotfelsenized.' Or even"—he lowered his voice—"what some call being 'Tetrarchized.' You know, taking this great, silly experiment we live in as an identity." He laughed at the thought. "No, a few of us in the servant house with nowhere else to go have a little meal here. At this point, I would not miss it."

I must have looked very pathetic because he quickly added, "You will be joining us, of course?"

I nodded and thanked him, my mind turning over possibilities for escape to the south. Could I somehow bring Tural with us? I did not want him to die when the great pimple fully burst and collapsed. (This way of seeing Rotfelsen was now seared into my mind, it seemed.)

I leaned forward with a playfully conspiratorial air, and began, quietly, to speak in a Cöllüknit dialect specific to the far Qoyul Mountain, at the very edge of the Tetrarchia. Many who knew the language of Quruscan, but were not native speakers, would not understand me. To Tural, I must have sounded like a bumpkin.

"Lenz also needs somewhere to go that evening," I said.

Tural nodded sagely.

"I would like to organize for him a surprise, as he has been working too hard. But because of my duties, I can't leave the palace grounds."

"Oh?" He raised an eyebrow and leaned closer, quizzical. Winter or no, he still smelled of berries; they must have soaked into his skin.

"Could you do me a favor down in Turmenbach?" I asked.

Tural sat back, and unfortunately, I couldn't smell him anymore. He looked out the window and scratched the nape of his neck under the cravat. He looked at me again, hand still on his neck, and his sleeve fell slightly. I saw a Quru medical tattoo, jagged like broken bone, on his wrist.

"I suppose I could, now that I am in my slow period," he said. "But considering the last time I found myself in a room with Lenz and yourself I was nearly fed poison in front of the King, I worry that this is more of your . . . intrigue."

"I promise you that it is not more palace intrigue." I very purposefully added the world "palace."

"Well, that's good. Sometime soon, I hope you will explain to me what you and your boss are really up to."

This was the most prying he had ever done, bless him.

I nodded and said, "Thank you." I put a hand on his shoulder in a most Rotfelsenisch way. "You are remarkably calm, in your off-time."

He laughed. "I will be fed up with it soon enough, and I will yell and scream for more to do."

Then I explained my *surprise* for Lenz. Well, part of it.

SOMETHING WRONG IN YOU

My next step, if I was to escape with my family during the night of the Sun's Death, was to learn more about this "Soul of the Nation" theory that, according to Martin-Frederick Reinhold-Bosch, had so captured High General Dreher's imagination. In this, I did not seek *truth*, partly because I took the idea itself as fanciful garbage, but mostly because truth did not serve my purposes. Whatever "truths" I offered about the Soul of the Nation could then also be enhanced by the quite damning truths about Prince Friedhelm's little masquerade with Olaf.

All I needed was to tell the good High General enough, one way or another, for him to take me into his services—at least for a day or two. Once I knew the lay of the land in his service, where I would hopefully not be a prisoner, the rest would come to me. (I hoped.)

I considered asking Jördis, the ethicist in my servant house, if she'd heard of this "Soul," but I did not trust her. Dreher and Vorosknecht did not seem to get along, and letting the purple windbag know that I was courting the High General's favor—and through philosophical theories, no less—seemed like a clear road to failure. Besides, Jördis was as mercenary as I.

I spent a day in my room, combing through book after book to see if I could find anything on this Soul of the Nation concept, but came up empty. Neither Lenz's own secret histories, nor the other volumes he had placed in my room for me, so much as mentioned the thing.

The next day, I considered taking a trip to the Royal Inn of Ottilie's Rock, but quickly admonished myself for this: Did I *really* think Gunther and his regulars would be able to help me with such an esoteric concept? Of course I didn't, I merely wanted an excuse to do something nice, for a change. I shook the thought out of my head, sighed, and decided to go talk to Chasiku, the Prince's second soothsayer. Lenz had insisted we "work together" after all. I let the Yellows in front of my servant house know where I'd be.

"If I'm not back in two hours, come find me there."

I did indeed hope that Chasiku could help me make sense of what was going on, but also her very presence was nagging at me. A second soothsayer was a constant threat of my fraud being discovered. Not the biggest threat I faced, but one that I could actually confront, unlike the Prince and the Court Philosopher and the onrushing doom of the Tetrarchia itself. She was a danger to me, but I did not have nightmares about her. So while part of me hoped to get real information from her, another part wanted to get one over on Chasiku, before she did the same to me. It was petty, but it felt like the only way to have some measure of control over my life.

So I went up the stairs of Chasiku's tower, to see her out on the walkway, leaning against the railing in the cold, with a mug in her hand. It was a cold, sunny day, the trees were all bare, and the only bright colors I saw were my own powder blue and persimmon orange dress, and Chasiku's patterned shawl of two-tone gold, green, and black. She did not turn toward me.

"Someone may think unkindly of seeing you in green," I said.

"I prefer for no one to see me at all." She sighed and motioned forward with her mug, toward the view, as though she were looking at me. "Well, you're in trouble. What *are* you planning?"

If one can grin without smiling, that is what I did. "Don't you know?" I replied.

Chasiku seemed only weary in her reply. "I see the *future*, Kalyna, not the past or present—beyond what I am seeing right now." She gestured again toward where she was looking, off the very edge of Rotfelsen itself.

I moved closer and glanced down. It was bright up here, but below, where Masovskan forests must have been sitting in the shadow of this great piece of rock, I saw only the top of a heavy fog. Rotfelsen may as well have been a pebble floating in a cloudy sky. Off in the distance, I saw the curved backs of creatures that never showed themselves on a clear day, only ever half visible, slithering through the fog. I felt a bit dizzy and stepped back. Chasiku turned to look at me.

"And now, all I see is an insecure fool," she said, motioning toward me with her mug, and then taking a sip. She made a face. "The coffee here is execrable. I've started making it myself, but the beans are so stale by the time they get here." She drank some more anyway.

"It's like that everywhere in the Tetrarchia besides Skydašiai," I said. "If they have it at all."

"Awful," she said, then took another sip. "I am getting bits of your future that are ever more ridiculous. Still death, but stranger, and at whose hands, I cannot tell. You have truly stepped in something. What's wrong with you?"

"What's wrong is that this place is falling apart and I'm trying to—"

"No, no. I don't mean what's wrong with you right now," she interrupted. Chasiku trained her eyes on mine, perhaps because she remembered I preferred it. "I mean, what's wrong with you, in general."

I narrowed my eyes.

She seemed confused. "There's something wrong *in* you. Something broken."

"Why do you say that?" I asked as evenly as I possibly could.

"Because I see bits of your future, and when it isn't death, it's all staring into space or apologizing to your father. Whatever is corroding you is so distracting."

I took a deep breath, and told myself that she was making this up to undermine me. "And so it is only me that you see? Nothing about the Prince, or the King, or our High General, or Vorosknecht?"

She looked down. "I am trying, but you cause so much . . . so much noise. And the King has been difficult to get a grip on. I met him, for a moment, but things seemed off. Like he existed, but also did not."

So she had been introduced to Olaf as the King. That she saw something wrong did not prove her powers to be real, however, as she could easily have noticed something off about him—to be a false prophet, one must be very observant. I wondered, too, whether Friedhelm and Lenz were revealing secrets to *her* that I was not made privy to.

"The destruction of this place is knocking around my mind," she continued, as though each word were a painful grasp at making me understand, "sweating death from every pore. I agreed to come here because I wanted to get away from Kalvadoti, that terrifying and bustling city. Now I've learned that I'm not just doing new work, I am, *apparently*, all that stands between the entire Tetrarchia and destruction."

Was she, I wondered? Was that the position I would leave Chasiku in, if I managed my escape? (Or, for that matter, if I botched it and was killed.) Well, it was too late to start worrying about her now, so instead I reacted to the insult.

"'*All* that stands between'? Now wait, I'm here, too—"

"You are worthless," she said. "Lenz will listen to you more than you realize, and he will assassinate, will throw armies at this plot, while the end only becomes more likely. Your power is empty, your whining threatens to overcome even me, and whatever you do, the end *only becomes more likely*. And your . . ." Her jaw clenched, her body shook. Chasiku seemed to be in pain: not the sharp pain of a cut, but the quivering ache of trying to thread a needle with a sprained wrist. "And your family of diluted psychics will continue to pick away at my concentration with your hatred of each other and yourselves, unless you, Kalyna, *tell me what is wrong*."

"I am sorry to inconvenience you," I said.

She stopped. "Wait," she muttered. "How did that all sound to you?"

"How do you think?"

She looked at me again. "I don't know? I was trying to help."

I stared at her for a long time. Was that true? I could not make sense of her.

"Look," I finally said, "I came here to ask you about something specific. Think you can manage that?"

Chasiku drained her terrible coffee, made a face, and then bowed sarcastically. "Come into my chamber then."

The Soul of the Nation

Chasiku's room now had a desk, a real bed, and a stack of books of its own. The only ornamentation was still the tapestry on the wall, which seemed to just be a mass of colors.

"Have you heard of something called the 'Soul of the Nation?'" I asked her.

"I believe the phrase may be used in some old poems," she replied, leaning forward over her desk, with her back to me. Its top was mostly empty, save for a few stacks of paper and a quill. "But it rings a bell," she added, shuffling through the papers. "Have I heard it in the jumble running through my mind recently? Or perhaps it's simply in those somewhere." She waved the other hand backward, toward the stack of books.

She continued her shuffling, and I looked through her volumes. These were different than what was in my room: secret histories of Lenz's with titles like *Supplemental* and *On Separatist Movements*, alongside books by others such as *Quarry Economics Vols. I–VII*, *The Foolishness of Utopian Thinking*, and *The Tracts of Rotfelsen's God-counters*. Some of these volumes seemed as slapdash in their binding as Lenz's histories, and others did not even have titles written on their covers. They looked like the sorts of dissident literature that I had seen in Hidden Markets, such as the one where I'd bought my sickle treatise.

"Heady stuff he's left you," I said.

Chasiku nodded. She was still riffling through her own scribblings at her desk.

"Yes," she said. "I think he hopes it will further clarify what I see in my visions." She snorted. "I have been reading them when I need a break."

I squinted at a book with a very long title whose pages seemed to have been adhered with spit. It seemed Lenz thought much more of Chasiku's intelligence than mine, as I had no lofty works of political or theological theory in my room. I did not let on to her that I was insulted, and besides, Lenz wasn't exactly *wrong* in this—I found even the titles mystifying.

But I sat down on Chasiku's bed and began to page through them anyway, hoping I could find something. Chasiku eventually sat at her desk, and began alternating between looking through papers and star-ing off into space. It was almost companionate. At one point, a Yellow came to check on us, and I waved him away.

After a few hours, I was flipping through *On Separatist Movements*, trying to make sense of it, when a pamphlet fell out: *The Secret of the Soul of the Masovskan Nation: DO NOT COPY! DO NOT QUOTE! BURN THIS IF YOU SEE A SOLDIER!*

Well, who could resist that? I gave it a read and, other than this pamphlet clearly having been written by Masovskan dissidents, about the supposed "soul" of Masovska, I did not learn much beyond what Martin-Frederick had already told me. Until the very end:

Once more, please be exhorted to NOT ever for ANY reason share these great truths with the authorities. Even if you think those authorities MAY be sympathetic.

A popular trap they will lay for you: "If a nation can have a collective 'soul,' then ours must be for the whole Tetrarchia, as that is our nation."

DO NOT FALL FOR THIS! If you agree, you will anger the SOUL OF MASOVSKA. If you disagree, they will lock you up as a TRAITOR. Avoid the issue entirely by NEVER SHARING THIS DOCUMENT WIDELY. Our time will come.

Martin-Frederick had told me about this Soul of the Nation idea so casually, but then he didn't believe in it. It made sense that the the-ory, whether taken literally or metaphorically, would be criminalized: I had read no poems passionately composed to the Tetrarchia, seen no singular identity applied to its people. It, collectively, was no one's motherland.

"Do you mind if I keep this?" I asked Chasiku, holding it up.

"Yes, yes, fine," she replied, as though we had not just been silent for hours. "Have you received any new details about it?"

"About the Soul of the Nation?"

"The what? Are you still on that? No, no. The violent end of our Tetrarchic Experiment."

I tucked the pamphlet into my blouse. "Afraid not," I replied. "A pity about all that awful death on the way: I'd let the whole structure burn down, if we could save the people." It was an imprudent thing to say, but I wanted to better understand where Chasiku stood.

She looked at me and nodded very slightly. "I shall have to try re-summoning the vision of shattering rotrock that I saw," she said. "Perhaps I can figure out what causes it. It's all well and good to worry about plots, but it may be a simple natural disaster, right when the Council of Barbarians is taking place. We have earthquakes up in the North Shore, do you have those here?"

"*I* didn't grow up in Rotfelsen. But I can't imagine they do, or else . . ." Well, or else it would all crumble, wouldn't it? Neither of us bothered to voice it. Instead, I stood up and said, "I shall leave you to conjure."

When I moved away from her bed, Chasiku all but pounced from her desk onto it, as though I had been hoarding it from her. She lay back, head propped up, hands behind her head, staring at her tapestry.

"If your family," she began, "only sees what's 'most likely,' then seeing everyone's futures changing like this must have been confusing."

This had not actually occurred to me until she said it. I wondered what hells Papa must have been going through the last few months. I even started to think on how this may have affected Grandmother, but thought better of it.

I opened my mouth to thank Chasiku for the surprisingly sympathetic words, but she continued before I could:

"No wonder you are all such fools," she said.

I sighed and turned to go. But then I had a thought.

"Chasiku, if you want to help out a poor fool—"

"Helping fools is the only thing I have ever done consistently."

"—perhaps I can ask you one more time about this 'Soul of the Nation' thing. I promise I will be specific."

She rolled her eyes.

"Have you seen anything beneath us? Down where the caves and the lake—"

"Oh, is *that* the underground lake I've been seeing in your futures?"

"In *mine*?" I gulped. "What did you see there?"

"I saw you in the waters, and something beneath you. Glowing."

"Beneath me?" The glowing little wiggly shrimp stayed near the surface, as far as I knew. "What was it?"

KALYNA THE SOOTHSAYER | 277

She shrugged. "Some very large glow. It isn't what kills you down there, if that's what you're wondering."

"I wasn't."

"Or is it? It's so hard to tell these days. But I think it will be the drowning or the bullets, or the many large fish."

"Thank you," I muttered.

"Any time." She actually smiled. Was this her way with customers, a genuine desire to connect with me, or glee at my death?

LEINGARDE'S COMPREHENSIVE GUIDE TO BANNED COMIC OPERAS

The next day, I sent Martin-Frederick Reinhold-Bosch a copy of *Leingarde's Comprehensive Guide to Banned Comic Operas* that I found on one of the shelves in my room. (Chasiku got complex theory, I got warbling "crafty servant" archetypes.) With the book was a very kind note, saying that it had made me think of him. Inside the book, at the first page about *The Leper's Five Tits*, was crammed a second note, saying, "I look forward to seeing your carriage at the Sun's Death. I have found what you need."

I hoped this was not too blatant, lest a Yellow find it. I also hoped it was not too subtle, lest Martin-Frederick miss it.

I heard almost nothing from anyone for days. No Martin-Frederick to confirm or deny getting my message. No Prince Friedhelm discussing his plans to ensnare the Queen, or take over the Reds. Nothing from Lenz about the end of the Tetrarchia, the King, whether my erstwhile jailer would even come to the Sun's Death, or whether my family would be allowed to attend. He did send a little extra payment for the "visions" of Papa's that had been written down during his screaming nights, along with a note saying how pleased he was that Chasiku and I were "working together." It was decent of him, in a way, but I needed him to come to the Sun's Death if I was ever to escape.

I was questioned by a couple of Yellows about my jaunt with Martin-Frederick and the Greens. I told a lot of truth: that after the King's Dinner, High General Dreher had wanted to meet me, and that he wanted my prophetic opinion on a boring personal matter. If they thought it was something more sinister than that, it was their own fault for always getting into fights with the Greens, wasn't it?

My escape plan was set, so I spent much of that time waiting for Yellows to be free enough to escort me to my family, since I was still not allowed to visit them on my own. Once there, I tried my best to pack their things in a way that did not *look* like I was packing their things, and assess my father's ability to travel. He desperately wanted to leave, but he was also "so comfortable, Kalynishka. Just so comfortable here." At least I was finally able to keep him company when the Gift came for him again, a duty that I had been neglecting for weeks (as Grandmother continued to remind me). He saw nothing new that I could use, but the important thing was that I was there for him.

"Is Dagmar with you this time, Kalynishka?" asked Papa, one night. I cocked my head to the side. "Who?"

"That would be me, ma'am," said the Yellow in the next room, who had graciously been allowing Grandmother to scream at her for a bit, instead of me.

Yes, this was the tall, striking blonde woman I'd thought of as "Dugmush," and had decided it was too late, and too embarrassing, to ask her name. I felt that I would die, just then, and spare everything congregating around me the trouble.

"Ah!" I finally said, turning to look at her. "Well, good to meet you, Dagmar."

"Likewise." She winked at me.

But I didn't want to start learning the Yellows' names *now*, particularly not one I found rather attractive. I was on the cusp of escaping and leaving them to their deaths, if I was very lucky.

The two weeks until the Sun's Death stretched into those voids of seemingly infinite darkness that happen near the solstice. I spent them in my head, reading histories that had not been written by Lenz. I read of ancient, pre-Tetrarchic societies because, while those times were no more savage, modern historians were much more eager to describe their savagery. All the better to cry, "See how humanity improves!" Dark, old things seemed right for those days. Besides, if Masovska could survive the Year of Massacres, Rotfelsen the Jackal Disaster, and Quruscan the Decade of Avalanches, perhaps we could survive the coming catastrophe.

Or *they* could. I would be in the Bandit States. I wished very much that the pale, pink, hidden Rots hadn't decided to name their solstice "the Sun's Death."

THE SUN'S DEATH

The day of the Sun's Death had *some* light: the morning burst into terrible brightness for what felt like a few moments. In that time, the servant house bustled with activity as a feast was prepared, and the big, third floor dining room was decorated.

Everyone I encountered as I ducked beneath dead branches, and stepped around carefully composed piles of earth, assured me this would be an embarrassing shadow of what a Feast of the Sun's Death should be. They were all quite disappointed it would be my first.

"Only five main dishes!" a cook exclaimed, taking a break because five main dishes afforded him infinite time to chat.

"No new coats of paint on the walls," mumbled a maid as she decorated the dining room. "Closer to the palace, there would be a new coat over the walls, just so someone with *talent* could adorn them." She shrugged. "Down here, there are no great tableaus or grand old trees dragged up thirty stories, just some branches and my scribblings."

She insisted I not call her an artist. As she spoke, she was engaged in painting, on the space between two windows, a golden sun body with the orb of the sun for his head. He (that is, the personified sun) ran terrified through a wood lit only by himself, as star-headed wolves bayed and chased him, each wolf an individual, each one facing the sun from a slightly different angle. All this while the moon looked gleefully on from above, using his hands to block his own light from confusing the wolves, although moonbeams peeked out between his fingers.

But she was not an artist, she said, and this was nothing compared to the murals that would cover whole walls at a "real" Feast of the Sun's Death. Her lifetime ambition, it seemed, was to someday work in one of the nearby noble houses, dabbing in the smallest details at the House Artist's direction. The Sunset Palace, which loomed just out the window, right next to her painting, was further than she could ever imagine going.

And all this work, which the first- and second-floor servants insisted was the lowest of the low, was being done for *us*. I had met the Prince, the Court Philosopher, the High General, and the King (sort of), and seen the rich at play at the Winter Ball, and so had come to see

Jördis, Tural, and the rest as plain, normal, working folk. But they were
not. Breaking their backs to give us a nice feast were the menials who
lived below us, and who, here on the palace grounds, lived lives that I,
through most of my own life, would have seen as luxurious.

Whether it was guilt about my new station, or revulsion for the nobility, I felt a deep need to show the servants that I, too, knew how to
do real work. They laughed in a friendly way and sternly forbade me
from helping.

"It is nothing. Nothing!" cried the servant house's head butler. "This
is hardly even a dinner to us, I promise you. Certainly nothing close to
the *Feast*."

I was idling in the dining room as he inspected every surface. It was
now just about time for the sun's, well, death, which is to say it was early
afternoon and the sky was red.

"Well, what did your family do for the Feast of the Sun's Death, Johann?" I asked. "Paintings a mile high, whole trees, runners of red fabric
as far as the eye can see?"

Johann coughed to cover a laugh and turned to face me. He was
prim and perfect as a head butler should be, but for the scar down his
face, which meant he was not presentable enough to be head butler in
a more prestigious place. He could, I had been told by a cook, make a
hefty sum as a third or fourth butler in a noble's house, but felt it was
beneath his experience.

"Of course not," he said. "Of *course* not. But that is different. We
are on the *palace grounds*, and what's more this is your *first* Feast of the
Sun's Death. I wish it could be more satisfactory."

I shrugged. "But I won't know it's meager if no one tells me."

This line of reasoning did not please him.

The smell of old wood around us was only slightly noticeable mixed
in with that of food from below. I had been down there recently, before
being shooed away, and it seemed there was only paprika and butter
and sweat to breathe, with no air left at all. Up on the third floor, it was
pleasant, and light reflecting off the red silk that was hung everywhere
made it seem that the paprika had actually floated up here physically,
in one big cloud. Some of the old branches had been picked for their
perfect gnarls and twists, while others had been broken into shape, but
every branch, while quite dead, seemed to yearn for the sky, for the sun
that was not there. Circling everything were the maid's paintings of

the personified sun figure's life, death, and rebirth. These were small, none wider than my shoulders, but I appreciated the intimacy of them. I don't claim to know art, but I do know that the sun felt warm when I gazed at him, and his absence was chilling. I was told these would be painted over tomorrow.

The long table where I had eaten so many times was draped in red. This was the sun's . . . I don't know, blood, I suppose. Eight places were set, all around one end of the table for ease of conversation, while the other was covered in variously sized decorative plates, which were empty.

Eight seats. I didn't know how many people were originally meant to be at dinner, so I couldn't tell if my *surprise* had been planned for, or if Lenz or my family would join. We would see.

Candles, hundreds of them, were stuck onto any part of a branch that would hold them. A boy of maybe fourteen, who looked both bored and terrified, stood in the far doorway holding a metal bar taller than he was, with a douser on the end. He was our bulwark against burning the whole place down. The candles were mostly red or blue, with a good number that were a swirl of those two colors. Scattered about were also a few with a dark brown and tan check pattern right in the tallow, and a smattering of your average yellow-white candles.

I remember the candles so well because I idled about, staring at them, for some time. They had been lit hours ago and were already leaking multicolored globs.

"So sorry, ma'am!" chirped the douser boy in a cracking voice.

"For what?"

"The white candles, ma'am." He looked at the floor. "We were out of the other colors, you know. And we usually have a smattering of purples, yellows, and greens, you know, just in case someone—"

"Oh, I hadn't even noticed!"

"Nice of you to say, ma'am," he said to the floor. Then he seemed to remember that he was meant to the watch the flames and looked up, terrified.

I wanted to sit at the table until dinner began, but suspected this would alarm the staff. I leaned back against an open window and felt a cold winter wind on my back, which was nice in that building of paprika and steam. I smiled at the douser boy, and he gulped.

I didn't want to sit in the quiet of my room, so I stood there awhile longer. I thought about the season and the comfortable servant house,

I listened to the bustling around me and watched the douser boy glare about the room, from one candle to the next, endlessly. If I went to my room I would only think more about my plan, and it was much too late for *that*. I had considered and reconsidered and re-reconsidered my impulsive, devious, and cruel plan. The conclusion I had come to was that it was our best chance, even though it was terrible and would likely get us all killed.

Besides, what was there to do in my room? I had already packed what I could.

The Feast of the Sun's Death, Almost

At first, four people milled about the dining room, feeling that, with eight seats, we needed at least one more diner to be seated. These were myself, Tural, Jördis, and, again, her friend Vondel, the stout, bald Tenth Butler to High General Dreher, whom I had met after the Winter Ball. Most of our neighbors were off with their families, and the dining room was all so quaint and friendly, so free of the divisions that were always felt at court. So very nice and, if everything went as planned, I was going to ruin it.

Seeing Vondel again allowed me to compare him to our servant house's own head butler, Johann: Vondel was younger and less experienced, but worked in the Sunset Palace, and therefore was prestigious enough to sit with us while Johann bustled. Vondel seemed to have endless poise, which Jördis found amusing.

After a few more minutes, Lenz arrived. He looked uncomfortable, but I was happy he was there at all. I must have smiled when I greeted him because after that, he looked *much more* uncomfortable.

He was followed by two fully armed Yellows whom I knew by face but not name. I found myself wishing that one had been Dagmar. They planted themselves at far sides of the room.

"Kalyna Aljosanovna," said Lenz. "When you have a moment, I have some news for you regarding our"—he glanced sideways at the others—"business."

"Subtle!" laughed Jördis. "Careful, Lenz; you've got a High General's man and a Court Philosopher's woman standing right by you." She jabbed a thumb behind her. "And also Tural."

"My work is too lofty for one master," sniffed Tural.

"Yes, well," said Lenz, "deep down we are all King Gerhold's, aren't we?"

"That," said Jördis, "is a toast. Down, everyone, find your seats!"

We did, all five of us bunched around one end of the table. I sat with two empty chairs to my left and Tural to my right, next to him was Jördis, then Vondel, an empty spot, and Lenz, who was across the table from me. Lenz was almost a rival for Vondel at sitting bolt upright, as though about to run off at any moment, but it was nowhere near as graceful in him. His discomfort did not please me as much as I had hoped.

Jördis leaned over Vondel and patted Lenz on the hand. "We need to get some ale into you, I think."

"Yes," said Lenz, smiling.

Jördis smiled back sweetly, turned to the main doorway, and took a deep breath to scream for ale.

"What? No!" Vondel interrupted. "Not yet, Jördis; you are a monster."

Tural chuckled, Jördis rolled her eyes. I am sure I looked confused.

"This is the only reason you bring me, isn't it?" sighed Vondel. "To keep you in order."

"And here I thought we were friends," said Jördis.

"Everyone join hands," said Vondel, raising his own. "Unless we're waiting for . . ." He pointed to the empty places.

"No, no," I said. "They won't mind."

"Excellent." Vondel inclined his head toward me at just the right angle to communicate, *If you say so, but I do not believe you.* I was amazed at what he could convey with such subtlety. Like Klemens Gustavus in a Gniezto courthouse, if he were pleasant and friendly.

We all joined hands with our neighbors. Tural's was surprisingly soft.

"O sweet sunlight," Vondel began, "bleed through the night and cut down through our rock where even daytime finds you scarce, deliver us from . . ."

Thus began the Feast of the Sun's Death. Vondel hardly seemed interested in what he was saying, but he took great satisfaction in saying it. He went on for some time.

After what felt like ten minutes: ". . . you grow up the cave-barley that makes our ale, and now we drink deep of that ale so we may pass the time of your death all the quicker, and wake into your new life and warmth very soon.

"Now," he continued, to Jördis, "you may call for—"

Casks of ale slammed onto the table, and the plates and mugs jumped. Butlers began pouring the thick, black liquid into our goblets. This was an entirely new sort of alcoholic beast to me, and I admit that to my untrained tongue, the first taste was of bitter mud. But, as usual, I saw others enjoying it and soon grew accustomed. Surely they knew better than me.

At some point, while Vondel spoke, the plates covering the other side of the table had been piled high with roasted root vegetables, strings of anemic greens, hunks of lamb, egg noodles, and much more. After coughing down a few draughts of the ale, I reached toward a plate of carrots.

"I suppose we can supplement this ale with—"

Vondel stopped me with a glare. "The guest," he said, "must be taught the Order. We do not eat anything yet, and not the carrots."

"Oh."

"*Certainly* not the carrots."

I hadn't even been particularly hungry. I put my hands in my lap and waited.

There was much more after that. Vondel had a long speech about the sad vegetables and springtime—complete with a rote comparison between the green of the vegetables being served to eat and the Greens that he served. This was followed by a bracing tradition that had us all up and walking circles around the table to see who was the drunkest. I honestly thought this had to be made up, until I saw how easily even Lenz, with his bad leg, went along with it. Why, he almost seemed to enjoy himself.

All the ceremonial food that had been laid out ahead of time was meant to be eaten as part of the Order; we were nowhere near the meal. When we finally got to those sage-buttered carrots ("These that feel your great light even when they are in the dark and beneath the world, like so many of your people"), a third Yellow tromped into the room and stood at attention.

"Two more to dine," he said. "Aljosa Vüsalavich and None of Your Damn Business."

I smiled.

"Show them in," said Lenz.

Slowly, up the stairs, came the sound of a woman peppering

someone with curses, interspersed with low mutterings of "yes, ma'am" and "of course, ma'am" and "uh-huh, ma'am." Then a large Yellow came through the door, carrying Papa in his arms, crushed to his chest. Papa was in his best silk brocade caftan from the days when he still ran the business, and his arms were wrapped around the soldier's neck. Grandmother was right behind them in a stunning array of Quru scarves over a many-layered dress. She was yelling.

"Be sure you don't bump his head against— Oh, it's you."

In all my years of fraudulence, I don't know that I have ever faked so good a smile.

"Grandmother! Papa! So glad you could make it!" I ran to them, embracing both. Grandmother, for all her bile, was too suspicious of the surroundings, and my affection, to fight me off. I don't think I had hugged her in more than twenty years.

With a strained smile, I introduced everyone to Aljosa Viisalavich and Vüsala Mildoqiz. "I don't believe either of them has taken part in this feast before," I added, "but I hope you will be charitable."

Papa's face broke into a huge smile as he looked around the room.

"This! These branches and cloth and candles, and the *carrots*! Oh, the carrots!" he cried. "I have *seen* this. Again and again, caught between sharks and robberies and ladies walking to town! I have *seen* this in so many homes of pink-cheeked people, like some of you, but only in flashes, in silhouettes: I never knew what it was!"

He reached out, and the Yellow took him over to the nearest decorations. Papa ran his hand over a silk stream of red, and touched the dead branch. The douser boy looked very uncomfortable.

"All along it was the Feast of the Sun's Death I saw," Papa continued. "I never knew because we have not passed a winter in Rotfelsen in some time. Some time indeed."

There was a very long silence then. Eventually, I had to answer the expectant stares.

"Yes, well, uh . . . Lenz and Jördis already know this, but, ah, I am a soothsayer. So there's that. My father and grandmother are, too. Yes." I think that I rubbed my hands nervously as I said this.

Vondel, professional that he was, seemed to note the information same as he would my middle name, had I one. Jördis remained confused by Papa's gibberish. Tural almost fell out of his chair.

"What!" he cried. "And you did not tell me!"

"Vorosknecht called me a 'psychic' at the King's Dinner," I replied.

"I was not paying great attention," said Tural.

"No wonder they've kept you around," growled Grandmother. "No one knew what you are."

"Well," Tural went on. "Well. I am sure you have had reasons."

"Thank you, Tural," I said.

"Have you," stammered Papa, "have you already walked around the table?"

"We have," said Vondel, standing. "But there is much more to come, Aljosa Vüsalavich. I am so glad to share this time with you." He moved to Grandmother, took her hand, and before she had a chance to say anything, he was off to Papa, bowing. The Yellow did a nice job of dipping Papa in a mock bow right back.

"But you must be cold," continued Vondel. "Please sit. The carrots are warm, and the ale is warm enough."

"Oh!" laughed Papa. "Oh yes, thank you!"

I saw now that his cheeks were red, his hands shaking. I had been too preoccupied to notice. Too busy looking to see if Lenz had any inkling what was coming. Too busy trying to look calm before my moment came.

Eventually, we did get them seated, with Papa between Grandmother and me, thankfully. Three of the on-duty Yellows stood against the wall, one behind each member of my family. It was clear who the prisoners were here, and Tural furrowed his brow at me. None of the Yellows present were Dagmar, possibly because she had allowed me to assault the doctor's assistants, and was now on first-name basis with my father. None of them were Behrens, my sharpshooter friend, either. I felt sure this was on purpose.

So, on went the Feast, in which so far there had only been light nibbling. Vondel began the first song, "Blood-Green Pastures of the Rotfels," which seemed less like a prayer than a drinking song. Grandmother shocked me by joining in. She even knew all the words to the verses, which were complex and easy to mumble through until the rousing chorus.

"What?" she snarled at me afterward. I had said nothing.

Everyone at the table had gotten very good at pretending Grandmother was whispering inaudibly when she insulted me.

"I didn't realize you knew this song."

"Monster, monster," she sighed, shaking her head. "I know the Order inside out. I did have a life before you two were born."

"Pity you still do," I mumbled into my ale. Papa smiled at me.

"Now," said Vondel, "who can tell me, and our guests, wherefrom came the red cloth that adorns the dead trees of—"

"Hello?" came a voice from the stairwell. "Hello? Third floor, is it? The third floor?"

Lenz stiffened. I grinned.

"Yes! Yes!" called Tural. "Right up here!"

A slight, chestnut-haired man burst into the room, red-cheeked and breathing heavily, but not hard. He had the easy movement of a martial bearing that had relaxed over the years: coordinated, but not stiff. Clutched to his doublet of unaffiliated gray was a large bag, at his hip a rapier.

"I am so sorry to be late," he laughed. His voice was musical. "Hellishly difficult to find paste-breads today; I should have put in orders a week ago, but what's done is done." The man smiled at everyone, looking at Lenz last.

Tural smiled with recognition at the newcomer, then turned his smile toward Lenz. Lenz's eyes were wide, his lips pulled together, his face the mottled gray of the sky before a torrential rain. He looked like he was going to burst. The Master of Fruit then glared at me hard, with a disapproval I felt in my stomach.

So this was Lenz's lover, whom my father had strained himself to find in his visions.

SURPRISE!

Gabor was a handsome man, if boyish for my taste. He appeared to be around twenty, in the moments before one saw the crinkling at his eyes betray him for closer to thirty. Lenz had done well for himself. Gabor could have done better.

I knew, from what Papa told me, that Lenz visited Gabor in Turmenbach regularly, at the home they used to share. I suspect no one in Rotfelsen—possibly including Gabor and Lenz themselves—would have considered them to be spouses, but "husband" was the word Papa had used. What part, I wondered, had this relationship played in putting Lenz so closely under the Prince's thumb?

"Kalyna . . ." said Lenz from across the table.

"What? I learned that your friend here would be all alone on the Sun's Death, and I thought that sounded very sad."

He narrowed his eyes as though trying to see my very brain. "You *learned*."

I smiled sweetly.

"Didn't you hear I was coming?" asked Gabor, cocking his head to the side to look at Lenz.

"No," said Lenz.

"You've been so busy lately," I said. "It's been hard to get hold of you."

Gabor crossed over behind my back, toward Lenz's side of the table, dropping his bag into the hands of a waiting servant as he did. On the way, he clapped a hand on Tural's shoulder and begged Vondel not to get up. He approached Lenz, and I saw no awkward almost-kiss, no longing embrace. Gabor grabbed Lenz's shoulder much as he had Tural's, and gave it a good, hearty pat. He then plopped down next to Lenz, smiling, and Lenz nodded brusquely back, keeping his eyes trained on me. I did everything I could to not look out the window—to not check if Martin-Frederick was out there yet.

Gabor introduced himself to the rest of us informally from across the table. Vondel was uncomfortable about this, but Jördis ribbed him into relaxing.

"Please, please," Gabor said, arguing the point playfully, "in the shadow of the Sun's Death, we're all family! Otherwise we freeze!"

This was, I gathered from Vondel's smile, a reference to a prayer in the Order. Probably a bit we had already done.

Gabor claimed to know me through Tural, and acted almost as though the two of them were old friends. They had only just met, after I had asked Tural to find and invite him.

"Now," said Vondel, once introductions were done, "as I was saying: Wherefrom comes the red cloth that—"

"Ooh!" cried Gabor, pouring himself ale. "We're almost at the meal then."

Everyone gave this a laugh, the sort that showed it was a joke made every year, with the only surprise being who would make it. Yes, everyone had a good laugh except for me, who still did not know what was going on. Even Papa and Grandmother, the people with whom I could always share my alienation, knew these stupid words Vondel was saying, and understood the meaning of the red cloth or dead branches or why the carrots were so different from the . . .

Good. This was good. I didn't want to get too comfortable. My hands twitched and I thought about violence. About the use of small violence to escape great violence. This was my neighbors' last chance for a decent Feast of the Sun's Death—next year's would happen in refugee camps or Loashti prisons, if it happened at all—and here I was to desecrate it.

Vondel had apparently been giving his speech about the significance of everything around us, with others joining in. I hoped I looked like I was listening, but I didn't absorb a word of it. As Vondel spoke—sonorously, I must add—Jördis smiled the smile of warm nostalgia. Papa showed inklings of understanding, Grandmother glared at her plate but chimed in, and Gabor took a moment to smile at me.

Lenz continued to stare at me hard. His mustache twitched. He was trying, I think, to figure out how and why I had done what I had done. He wanted to know what my plan actually was.

WHAT MY PLAN ACTUALLY WAS

Well, it wasn't to expose Lenz's secret relationship to the world, although I'm sure he suspected otherwise. I do not *think* I am that cruel, but why would anyone believe me?

No, my plan was to get my family into a coach provided by Martin-Frederick Reinhold-Bosch, which would take me to the High General, whom I would then regale with visions of Glaizatz Lake and the truth about Olaf, Prince Friedhelm's pet pretender. This may well start its own war, but this place was on the verge of destruction already, and *that* could not be blamed on me. Could it? I felt bad about what this meant for Olaf, but he seemed to welcome death.

When everyone was nice and relaxed near the end of the night, I meant to retrieve Tural's knife from my room and hold it to Gabor's throat. I would keep him hostage in the carriage to ensure Lenz's good behavior. Then, once I was safe with the High General, I would make plans for my family and me to escape him as well. He would be busy, and I would earn his trust with lies about the Soul of the Nation, and the truth of the imposter on the throne.

It was a plan likely to end in my death, I grant you, but it seemed my best option. Most guards got the Sun's Death off, and Martin-Frederick would vouch for me. Besides, Gabor was smaller than me, and if I could get my hands on him, we would see just how strong Lenz's sense of loyalty to his master was. Would he let someone who knew about Olaf go, to save his beloved's life?

This was my terrible plan. It had a lot of possible failings, and I had just found a new one: I *liked* Gabor.

THE FEAST OF THE SUN'S DEATH

The meal was finally underway. The steam that rose from heaping plates of meat and grains, the twinkling light of hundreds of candles, and the alcohol in my body, gave the whole room a gauzy feeling. It seemed Jördis' laughter was taking physical shape in the air, like a warm fog.

And I wasn't even drunk. I had sipped when the Order told me to drink deep, and I had nursed a mug of ale in between so as to not seem suspicious. I wanted to be sober when it was my turn to play kidnapper. I couldn't afford clumsiness or warm feelings.

"So!" Gabor yelled a little too loud. He had a low tolerance, which was good. "What goes on in the Sunset Palace these days? You all must know who's been skewered, and which mouthy viscount's been thrown from a window, yes?"

"Our Kalyna here fought off an *assassination* attempt," said Jördis, pointing across the table's corner at me and smiling.

"It was a *kitchen accident*," I murmured.

"Oh?" said Gabor, sitting up straight and looking over at me. "Who was the victim?"

"A roast," I said.

I made a show of being very full and needing to move, so I stood up and began to pace. Papa looked at Gabor and blinked a lot.

"We," said Vondel, almost puffing up his chest, "do not *know* at whom the assassination-that-was-not was aimed. Perhaps we could be enlightened?" He raised an eyebrow at me and smiled with exactly one-eighth of his mouth.

"Kitchen accident," I repeated, moving idly toward the window, which wasn't far from Lenz and Gabor.

"Do I . . . ?" muttered Papa.

"It was a kitchen accident," echoed Lenz. He had finally stopped staring at me every second.

"Oh, please!" laughed Gabor, patting Lenz on the back.

Lenz closed his eyes when he was touched.

"The stories trickling down to Turmenbach were good enough for you before, Lenz," Gabor continued, "but now you know the inner circle!"

Lenz sighed. "But there are so *many* inner circles." He almost smiled. "Piled on each other like pangolin scales."

"When you lived together?" asked Papa out of nowhere.

"I'm sorry?" asked Gabor.

What little relaxation Lenz had found disappeared. I did not risk looking out the window for Martin-Frederick and his coach.

"You two," said Papa. "You lived together."

"Oh! Yes," answered Gabor. "We fought together in the army, and afterward pooled our meager pensions to buy a property neither of us could have afforded on our own. Why do you ask?"

I waited for Papa to answer, and my eyes may have been as wide and horrified as Lenz's. Gabor's calm was amazing to me, and without him there, I suspect Lenz would've been bleeding from the nose and eyes.

Papa cocked his head to the side and blinked a few more times at Gabor. Then he sat up straight and said, "Just curious. You seem to be great friends."

I fancied that the exhalation of pent-up breath from Lenz and myself could have put out every candle in Turmenbach.

"We are!" said Gabor, seemingly unfazed. "You are very observant, Aljosa Vüsalavich, you know that?"

Papa turned on the charming little "you can trust me" smile that I had not seen on him in at least a decade. It was an expression I practiced in the mirror almost daily. "I suppose it's a gift," he said.

Lenz actually smiled and looked up at me quizzically. I tried to look reassuring. Perhaps I succeeded, perhaps he was simply exhausted. Papa began to babble across the table at Gabor, who listened intently and asked many questions.

Ale flowed, food was shoveled, the night wore on. I made it over to the window and glanced out. There was a small coach there that did not belong to the Yellows. I couldn't see who was in it.

If Lenz was no longer tense, neither was he personable. He spent the rest of the night slumped in his chair, trying to extinguish something in his chest with alcohol. Jördis, Gabor, and Papa did most of the talking, and no one seemed bothered by Papa's nonsense. He even managed to sneak a few sips of ale without Grandmother yanking it away from him. I moved back to my seat.

I never forgot my plan, but it had fallen so far back into my head as to be a vague buzzing when Lenz lurched unsteadily to his feet.

"Kalyna Aljosanovna," he said, "I know it is . . ." He choked and gurgled, cleared his throat, and continued. "I know it is the Sun's Death, but may we, you and I, speak business privately?"

"Yes. Of course." I stood. "My room is yours."

I gouged my palms with my fingernails as I waited to see if he'd go for it.

He trod slowly and loudly across the room, staring downward. Everyone was silent, even though they didn't know what was happening. Gabor looked very concerned, and I felt a pang of guilt.

The Yellows guarding the room (and fastidiously removing all knives from the table the moment we finished with them) began to follow and were waved away. Lenz pointed at Grandmother and Papa and mumbled something. The Yellows stayed. My heart began trying to jump out of my chest. It was my chance. A better chance than kidnapping Gabor, perhaps.

I followed him up the stairs to my chamber.

YOU CAN'T PLAY THE HERO NOW

"It wasn't fair of them, you know," said Lenz.

He was sitting in my chair. The one against the wall and between the windows, where I felt the most safe and could view my whole room. On his way to it, he had not lit any candles, but had grabbed one of my half-empty mugs of day-old (at best) brandy, sniffed it, and taken it with him. I stood over him, but my eyes wandered toward my bed. Tural's knife was under the pillow.

"What wasn't fair?" I asked. "Not fair of me to bring Gabor—?"

"Did I say 'you'?" he spat. "I am not that drunk." He sipped. "It wasn't fair of *them*."

"Whom?"

"The army. Rotfelsen's army."

I said nothing. He wanted to tell me whatever it was; there was no need to ask.

Lenz's face was barely visible, but starlight quivered in the windows behind him. Most of the servant houses were dark, but the noble manors and Sunset Palace beyond them were lit up in nearly every window as the Feast of the Sun's Death played out. I became very aware of the fact that Lenz could probably see my face in that light, so I crossed over and sat on my bed to his left, in shadow. The hilt of the rapier on his belt glinted a foot away from my knees.

"They encourage it, you know," he said.

"What?"

"Men."

"Oh?"

"For morale," he said.

It seemed that this was meant to illuminate for me the entire tale that was in his head. When I didn't respond, he finally clarified.

"For morale," he repeated, "many armies encourage their soldiers to rut in the night, hoping that, being lustful, sentimental youths, they will be quicker to trust and protect one another when battle comes with the morning. The Greens are entirely male: they think women will fail on campaign, and no one wants pregnant soldiers."

I nodded.

"Can you imagine?" he laughed, pushing back his hair, which managed to fall over his face and stick straight up at the same time. "Can you imagine how the minds of comfortable old commanders can justify eagerly throwing fit young men at one another when in the army, while soundly condemning the same activity so much as a second after discharge?"

"Of course I can."

"It's chivalrous when our boys are youthful and the army is out in the world," Lenz continued, "but past twenty-two years of age, it's disgusting and childish. Because 'old' men—and I am not so much older than you—are disgusting, no longer lithe and beautiful. Two grown men together are considered either so arrested as to be fools, or entirely amoral. So"—he pointed at nothing—"the *army* gives men like Gabor, like myself, a taste of what we will miss for the rest of our lives. It's all so . . ."

"Arbitrary. Yes."

"A policy for dilettantes!" he seethed. "For men who wish to try new things and throw them away. Or men like Friedhelm, who simply wish to scandalize by *pretending* they try such things."

"I can see how that would make you angry."

"Of course you can. That's why you brought *him* here."

I sighed loudly—perhaps a touch theatrically—and said, "*That* is not why I brought him here." It was considerate of him to phrase it this way, so I didn't have to lie. Not that I mind lying.

"Oh, really?" said Lenz, halfway between sardonic disbelief and a desperate need to believe.

"Really," I said.

"*Saw* him, did you? Saw me visiting him."

I nodded. "Many times. At the house in Dunkel Cave, with the lattices and the orchids. It's nice."

He coughed loudly. "It was my house, too, before the Prince yanked me up here to work for him."

"So you have often said to Gabor when you look around the place." I shrugged. "Or will."

"How melancholy," he grunted.

I leaned over across my bed, propped up on my right arm. And if the fingers of my right hand happened to slip underneath the pillow, what did it matter?

"It certainly doesn't bother me if you flout Rotfelsenisch convention," I said. "I only wanted to show you that I, too, could put my enemy's loved ones under my power."

"Are we still enemies then?" he sighed.

I took a deep breath and let it out in a long sigh. I supposed I *had* taken advantage of Lenz's need for secrecy, even if that made me queasy. If others could know about Gabor, Lenz would surely have brought a Yellow or two into my room.

Lenz tried to see the palace grounds through the window over his right shoulder, but seemed uninterested in turning far enough around. I wondered if Martin-Frederick was out there in that coach, if Lenz might see him. Then Lenz looked at me again, waiting for some sort of explanation.

I gave him one.

I shoved myself up with my right hand, the knife glinting out in the open as I moved off the bed. Every part of me pushed toward him at once. I pivoted on my left foot, lifted my right, and stepped on the hilt of his sword. The small, gold-handled knife stopped against his throat.

Lenz didn't look scared or angry, yet. He showed only a dull surprise as the mug slipped from his fingers. I caught it in my left hand.

"Let's not make any noise," I said.

The knife blade was quite sharp, and when he nodded it shortened the stubble on his neck. I put the cup, carefully, on the desk. I loomed over him, left hand on his shoulder, right hand holding the knife to his throat, right leg pushing down his rapier.

"So," he rasped, "you brought Gabor for him to be here when you finally kill me?"

"Killing you is the contingency plan. I just want to leave."

"You'd leave the Tetrarchia behind to rot when you could save—?"

"I can do nothing. Nothing but escape. You seemed well convinced of my uselessness recently."

"Look, I'm sorry I said—"

"I don't *care* what you said." I leaned in closer, his sword pivoting under my foot, my weight pushing against the blade. "Just let me go. You have my replacement."

He shrugged as much as he could without being killed. "I can't. I need you."

"Let Chasiku do my job."

"Chasiku," he gurgled, "hasn't saved Olaf's life. Besides, if one was enough, I wouldn't have brought her here in the first place."

I pushed the knife harder against his skin. It was sharp enough that a small red line began to show beneath it.

"I've already been compromised by my soft heart tonight," I said. "Let me go or I kill you."

"I can't stop you now," said Lenz. "You may kill me and try to leave. The Yellows are too trusting of you as it is; you might make it. Before Gabor hunts you down."

"Then why not save your life in the process?"

"Because I need you to stay. I cannot force you, so I will ask." He swallowed carefully, and I moved the knife a fraction of an inch away to avoid cutting him further. "If it were only about finding King Gerhold"—he gulped—"I would let you escape and face the consequences. I swear I would."

I could not tell if this was true, but I could feel the possibility digging into my resolve.

296 | ELIJAH KINCH SPECTOR

"Please," he said. "Please stay. I'm begging you. I need all the help I can get to save everyone from what you've seen."

"Maybe I was lying."

"If you were not in a hurry, you would plan a better escape. Please, help me save the Tetrarchia."

"It is not your job to save the Tetrarchia."

"What you foretold will happen right when the Council of Barbarians meets in *that* tower!" He pointed behind himself with his thumb, at the Sunset Palace, without moving his shoulder. "That is not coincidence."

I felt myself begin to buckle as I imagined *something* happening at the Council, and then the whole rock crumbling. Then I got angry. I put my weight on my right foot, pushing his sword further down and pulling his belt into his stomach—because I couldn't press the knife farther without killing him.

I had to fight to keep from yelling. "You abducted me, put me in danger, and held my father to keep me in line. You can't play the hero now!"

"Fine," he said. "Both of us have—"

"No! Not 'both of us.' This hasn't been some equal arrangement where I gave as good as I got. Whether or not you *enjoyed* having power over me, you had it."

"Then let's make it one."

A long pause. "One what?"

"Equal arrangement."

"You're joking."

"I am too terrified to joke."

I was about to call this into question, when I realized he was quivering beneath me.

"Go on," I said.

"You agree to stay until we have either unmade the disaster, or been crushed in it—you agree to do all you can to help the Tetrarchia's *people* survive. You get full freedom of movement: no checking in, no limits, armed to the teeth if you like."

"And my complete freedom from this rock once it is all over?"

"That is up to the Prince, but if we survive, I will try."

"How can I trust that you won't throw the Yellows at me the moment I let go of you?"

"Tell me what I can do to convince you."

I didn't know, but I was tempted. The comfortable living, the care for my father, the fact that it was probably too late to get out in time: if I were given my freedom, these would be good reasons to live up to the bargain.

And perhaps it was only repetition, but Lenz was beginning to chip away at me, to make me believe that *I*—monster, broken shitworm, failure—could save the people of the Tetrarchia. I did not want those who had been beaten down as much as I, worse than I, to suffer all the more. My family had been chased out of every part of that quartered country, but I loved its peoples even so. They were motley and divided, but they were, all of them, *my* people.

The four monarchs would be in one place, so near, when everything fell apart, when this rock broke and the rest of the country was subsumed by war and chaos. He was right, damn him, that wasn't a coincidence, and I was close enough to do . . . what?

I had already risked my life just to get Eight-Toed Gustaw from Down Valley Way his inheritance, and my family would have died without me to support them. The end of the Tetrarchia was so much larger, and yet I was risking no more. Perhaps dignity, but what is dignity to a fraud? I had risked my life for less so many times, and now I was going to run when I could save *everyone* in all four kingdoms? Or rather, when there was even the slimmest chance that I could save them?

I pulled the knife away, but not too far, and maintained my position of power over Lenz.

"I hate this," I admitted. "It feels like you're *granting* me freedom."

"I came here to grant it," said Lenz, slowly rubbing his throat. "But last I checked, you took it at knifepoint instead."

"You would have already been dead by now," I said, "if I hadn't come to like Gabor in the last few hours. I'd hate to see him a widower, even if he has made a terrible choice with his life."

Lenz smiled. "I like him, too."

Some part of me wanted to smile back, but I fought it. "Again, how can I trust you?"

He sighed and looked thoughtful. My knee was getting sore, so I moved my foot from his rapier handle. But I held the knife near his left arm, ready to cut him if he reached for it.

"Neither of us," he said, "want a scene while Gabor is here. I don't want him to know I'm your *jailer*, and you don't want him trying to help me."

"Really?"

"I met him in the *army*, Kalyna."

I sighed.

"I will leave, with my Yellows," he said, "and your family will stay here tonight. It will be monumentally easy for you to fly before dawn. If you don't, then meet me at my barracks, first thing tomorrow. We will have a civilized conversation about where we stand, and Chasiku's role, and this whole blasted mess."

"I meant: How can I trust you the moment I let go of you?"

"Ah," he replied. "I am still quite drunk."

"Will you even remember granting this to me in the morning?"

"I will." He burped. "You have scared my mind into some kind of lucidity, even if my body is still sluggish."

I stepped away from him. I didn't know what else to do. I still disliked him—possibly hated him—but I felt damned inconvenient sympathy for him. Not for his position in this moment, but for how the Prince's service had wrenched him from the one he loved.

Lenz stood, swayed, fell across my desk, and stood again. His hair went in all directions.

"Maybe," I said, "we should not meet first thing in the morning. You'll be hungover."

"I'll manage," he said. I could see him in the light from the windows now, and his left eye seemed trapped in a permanent squint, even though he was not looking at anything. There were glittering bubbles of spit in his mustache. "I will see you in the morning."

"If I don't run away."

"Will you?"

"I think I will."

Lenz smiled weakly and inched his way toward the door, hands against desk, shelf, wall, whatever would hold him up. When he got to the door, he yelled downstairs: "Get my coach ready! And bring Kalyna Aljosanovna's"—another gulp—"bring her sickle up! It's in the backseat compartment!" Then he turned and shrugged at me. As he stumbled down the steps, I also heard him mutter, "And stop hiding the silverware from her. It's embarrassing."

The night wrapped up quickly after that. Lenz and Gabor left together almost immediately, and Papa seemed very tired, so Jördis, Tural, and Vondel all took the hint and retired. The servants had already made up guest rooms for my family in the servant house.

I could hardly believe I was doing it, but once the Yellows were gone, I ran outside to where I had seen the small coach through the window. It sat just outside the walls, in shadow, seemingly empty, but when I approached, a blonde head popped up and Martin-Frederick Reinhold-Bosch opened the door, leaning out into the moonlight. Behind him was a Green. I squeezed my fists until they hurt: escape was right in front of me.

"Things have changed," I hissed. "I can't leave now."

"What have they done to you?" The young blonde leaned farther down, his face inches from mine.

"Nothing! Just a change of plans." And then I added, as though it was a favor to him, "But you are correct: the High General's 'Soul' does not exist."

Martin-Frederick stared at me for a moment, eyes wide.

"Don't tell him yet," I added. "We'll meet again soon, and you and I can decide how best to break it to him. But, for now, you need to leave before you're seen!"

He screwed his mouth to the side. "A pity. I want to know more, and Dreher had a task for you and me to do next. Together. Ah well." He grinned. "Until our next meeting, Kalyna Aljosanovna."

He leaned forward, as though expecting a kiss. When he did not receive one, he bowed theatrically and nodded to the Green.

A whip cracked and the coach rode off, with Martin-Frederick gripping something inside and hanging out of the open door, continuing to bow. I could see his white teeth in the moonlight.

I laughed at myself as I went back to my room. I was not going to escape tonight, with Martin-Frederick or otherwise. I had decided it. I wanted to stay and, well, *save* the Tetrarchia. Ludicrous as it was, I began to think that, while I would likely fail, I had as good a chance of success as anyone else. This made me feel powerful.

Unfortunately, I was not going to have a nice, civilized meeting at Lenz's barracks the next morning—in fact, I would feel quite powerless right away. Of course, I did not know that yet.

PART FIVE

I DID NOT RUN

I slept with my sickle clutched against me, like the good luck charm Grandmother threw away when I was nine. ("Garbage. Nothing can fix *your* luck!") I felt safe, even though I was doomed. I had an ally—I didn't like or trust him much, but I believed what Lenz had said to me that night.

Until I was awoken, violently, by a couple of Yellows I had never seen before. They shook me, yelling something I could not make out, and I knew I had been betrayed. I continued to know this all the way to the Sunset Palace, in hastily thrown-on woolen stockings and a nightgown, beneath a large coat and scarf, shivering in the cold as I still clutched my sickle. They had not taken it away from me, but what would one sickle matter against an army? It was still dark, and the

Yellows kept yelling, but I was barely awake and could not retain any of it other than "Prince," "Lenz," and "now."

And, soon enough, I was in the Prince's study. Prince Friedhelm was lying on his back on the couch, flanked by nude statues and covering his face with his hands. Lenz was leaning awkwardly against the Prince's desk, even more disheveled than usual, one hand playing idly with the letter opener, next to a large, round-ish bundle in purple fabric.

When I stepped in, the Prince quickly twisted to look at me, then groaned and resumed his position. Lenz hardly looked at me at all, and I began moving toward him, in order to kill him.

"Oh," Lenz finally mumbled. "You're still here. That's one small bit of good news this morning." He sounded very unenthusiastic.

"Well, if I'd known you were lying," I growled, inches from him now, fingers tight on the handle of my sickle, "I'd have—"

"No, no," he sighed. "You misunderstand. We have a . . ." He could not find the word, and weakly indicated the bundle next to him on the desk.

The bundle was sloppily wrapped, the purple cloth distributed uneasily around it. I became curious enough to give him a reprieve, and warily moved my sickle under my armpit, pressed to my body, and moved toward the bundle.

"Go on," moaned Prince Friedhelm.

I had to pick it up to begin unwrapping it. It was heavier than I expected. I pulled part of the cloth away and saw a blank human eye staring up at nothing. I admit I gasped.

"Keep going," grunted the Prince.

I didn't really want to, but I continued. I saw flesh that was pale and waxy even for Rotfelsen, and then I began to see familiar features. I saw Olaf's face.

"Olaf!" I gulped out as I dropped the dead, heavy thing. A door creaked. "Yes?"

I turned and, standing in the hidden doorway in the Prince's bookshelf, was the King's face, smiling and winking.

I looked back down at the head, which was rolling along the floor, then back up at the man standing in the doorway. The head thunked sickeningly against a foot of the couch, and the man in the doorway looked down at it. Uncomprehending, at first.

"King's dead," I said.

Olaf finally realized what he was looking at, and began to retch.

A FIGUREHEAD

Once Olaf's breakfast had been cleaned up, he sat on the Prince's couch, staring at the floor. But definitely *not* staring at the head that shared his face, which had *not* yet been cleaned up. Prince Friedhelm sat next to him, and did look down at the head, pushing it lightly back and forth with his foot. They almost looked like brothers, that way.

"No, no, no, no, no, no, no," muttered Olaf.

"There was a note," said Lenz. "Not signed, but the cloth is purple, and . . . well, who else would it be?"

He handed me the note, which, like the head it had been bundled with, was oddly bloodless. The note read:

"WE DON'T KNOW WHAT YOU'RE PLAYING AT WITH YOUR FAKE, SO WE STARTED ON ONE GERHOLD, AND SOON WE'LL GET THE OTHER. WE CAN'T PROCLAIM HIM TO BE A FAKE, BUT NEITHER CAN YOU TELL ANYONE ABOUT WHAT WE'VE DONE. WE NEVER NEEDED HIM, OR YOU, AS A FIGUREHEAD."

Head was indeed underlined. Vorosknecht thought he was very clever, I'm sure.

"Maybe it's a fake," I said.

Lenz and the Prince looked up at me. Olaf didn't move.

"You made one, after all." I waved a hand at Olaf. "Maybe they found some flesh-alchemists to do the same."

Lenz shook his head. "One thing we could not change in our good Olaf, was the teeth. A very trusted doctor took a look, and *that*"—he pointed to the head, which lolled between Friedhelm's feet, staring at the ceiling—"certainly has Gerhold's teeth. It seems Gerhold has also been dead quite some time, and the head was, ah, preserved."

"Oh gods," moaned Olaf.

"He may well have died the night of the Winter Ball," added Lenz.

"Why did you rewrap it?" I asked.

"Because we didn't want to *look* at it," sighed Lenz. "It's King Gerhold VIII."

"No," said the Prince. He clapped a heavy hand on Olaf's back, and the false King seemed about to vomit again, but held back. "*This* is King Gerhold VIII."

"Your Highness!" cried Lenz, standing up straight. "This is really too much!" He limped over toward where all the royalty in the room, alive, dead, and false, was concentrated. "This is ridiculous, you simply can't! Retire Olaf and become King. We can change his face today, get a little loose with the timeline of your brother's death, and then still pin it on Vorosknecht. Somehow."

Olaf nodded quietly.

"It's time to end this farce," Lenz concluded.

"The farce," said the Prince, "would be me throwing the rest of my life away rotting on that throne! I know it's hard for you people to understand, but royalty are *divinely appointed*, each for their own uses. Women like my mother to continue the line, men like my brother to bear the burden of rule, and men like *me* to enjoy its fruits."

"With no consequences," said Lenz.

"Yes!" replied Friedhelm. "When have consequences ever come into it? And you have the gall to tell me to 'end' the 'farce.' I hired you to save my brother's life, didn't I? A fine job you've done!"

"Hired? *Hired*?!" Lenz yelled, putting his hands on the Prince's shoulders and shaking him. "Coerced, blackmailed, kidnapped. Not hired!"

I couldn't help smiling a bit at that. It was like hearing myself speaking to Lenz.

Prince Friedhelm, however, had had enough of Lenz's insolence. He pushed aside Lenz's hands, stood up, and backhanded the spymaster across the face. Quite hard, it seemed. I lost my smile.

"Last I checked," said the Prince, "you were in the army, and I'm a gods-damned prince."

"And princes eventually have to be kings, don't they?" growled Lenz.

There was silence for a moment, as the two men glared at each other. I coughed loudly, and could hardly believe what I was about to say.

"Lenz might just have a point, Your Highness," I suggested. "What's more, your duty aside, our jobs would be much easier without so many layers of fakery folded atop one another."

The Prince reeled to face me, and he seemed an entirely different man than the one I'd first met. *This* gnarled, twisted, angry, petulant face—this was the face of a man about to have someone killed. Someone most people wouldn't miss, even if they knew about her. I calmed myself by remembering that the moment I decided to help Lenz rather than escape the Tetrarchia, I had essentially signed my life away.

So, I continued: "Whatever the morality of blackmailing him, and kidnapping me, think of how much time and effort would have been saved if Lenz had not spent the last month and a half trying to keep me from escaping, and . . ." Deep breath. Why not? ". . . I had not spent it trying to escape. Why, I even told him I thought the Bandit States were invading." I laughed. "A lie to cover my escape. Your brother would still be alive, had you gathered underlings who *cared* to be in your service."

"It sounds to me," said the Prince, "like you two are traitors."

Lenz opened his mouth to speak. But the Prince interrupted him: "And don't say anything about *earning* your allegiance, Felsknecht. I am royalty, remember?"

"You are royalty when it suits you," said Lenz.

I fancied that, by bringing Gabor to the palace grounds, I was responsible for this surge of courage and impudence in Lenz. I liked that.

Prince Friedhelm stared at him for a long time. Olaf moaned to remind us all that he was there.

"Well," said the Prince, turning away from Lenz, "true enough. And it still suits me little. So much time wasted doing a King's piddling chores." He shrugged. "Olaf, you are now royalty, too. King for life, my man." He patted Olaf's back hard. The false king burped.

"Olaf as your figurehead sounds like an awful lot of work," I said. "Why not just take the throne?"

Friedhelm laughed and shook his head as he turned to face us. "He won't be a figurehead. We'll get rid of the Queen and replace most of the Reds, so Olaf can hold dinners, kiss babies, and find a new Queen. Then he and that Queen can secretly have a bastard child of mine, to keep the line going. Lenz will teach Olaf more about politics, and it will be out of my hands." He clapped them together to show this.

I shook my head in disbelief. The Prince hardly seemed to mind. The urge to have us killed seemed past.

"Now," he said, "you two have saved *this* King from a plot before, so please do try to continue doing so. And find out who Vorosknecht's allies are so we can kill the whole lot of them, eh?"

Lenz nodded numbly, I shrugged, and our interview was over. I hardly knew where to start.

A TASTE OF FREEDOM

Olaf, unsteady on his feet, went back through the secret entrance to the King's—well, to his chambers. Lenz and I left as well, through a normal door. When we left, Lenz spent the whole way down the Sunset Palace's many, many stairs cursing under his breath. Once we got outside, he took a deep lungful of crisp, winter air, and looked at me.

"Despite my leg," he said, "I think a walk will do me good. Will you accompany me?"

I was still in my nightgown, but I had a big coat on over it, and a walk sounded nice, so I agreed.

For the first ten minutes or so, we spoke very little. Now and then, Lenz would say something like, "I can't believe him," or "this is a nightmare," and then I would laugh quietly to myself and shake my head. As far as I knew, we weren't going anywhere in particular, and this suited me fine. I was walking with Lenz, but there were no soldiers with us, and I could simply *leave* if I wanted to, and walk somewhere else. What a heady feeling it was. Why, I could have kicked him in the shin (the good one; I'm not that monstrous) and run away, had I desired to do so just a bit more than I already did.

And I must say the surface of Rotfelsen looked beautiful that day, or perhaps choosing to stay put me in a better frame of mind to enjoy it. It was finally, truly winter up here, but not a bitterly cold one, if one was properly bundled. It was snowing again, lightly, but green grass and rotrock still burst out here and there, seemingly reflected back and forth between sun and snow forever, until the colors were dazzling. Winter flowers in light blues and purples could also be seen, beneath barren bushes and surrounded by broken lines of variously sized paw prints. It was all so delicate. Which, of course, then made me think of how *delicate* Rotfelsen itself would turn out to be, along with the whole Tetrarchia. I took a deep breath of sweet air and tried not to think about it too much.

"You don't seem to have told the Prince about my doom prophecy," I said, after we had been walking for some time.

"Sometimes," Lenz replied, "our bosses do not need to know everything."

I suppressed a laugh, but could not help snorting quietly.

"It's true!" he added, looking at me and smiling slightly. "I suspect that if Prince Friedhelm knew, he would try to run, with an entire retinue of servants and soldiers and lovers, causing a panic. I fully believe that the plot we're up against is tied in with the end of the Tetrarchia, so if we have him focusing on the conspiracy, he can remain blissfully ignorant on the rest."

"Or," I began, "escape can still be on the table. You and I, Papa, Gabor." Maybe Tural.

"Your grandmother?"

"Why ruin a perfectly pleasant and harrowing escape?"

"Well," said Lenz, "honored as I am to be included in your escape plans now—"

"Only because I suspect Gabor wouldn't leave you."

"—I still meant everything I said last night, about working together to save this . . ." He looked around at the snow and the rotrock crags and all that. ". . . beautiful, stupid place."

"Now you're getting into the spirit," I said.

"So, I suppose if we must protect the, ah, King, then . . ." The words were souring in his mouth.

I shrugged. "You know how I feel about royalty. But I like Olaf, so if anything, I am now *more* inclined to—"

"Please don't finish that thought, Kalyna," he begged. "I'm sure I know, and I'm sure I do not want to hear it. I'm shaken enough as it is."

I shrugged. I *did* like Olaf, and yet the thought of him remaining as King seemed easily like another path to destruction. But what other options were there? The Evil Prince?

Martin-Frederick also came to mind. He was, after all, in line for the throne. Perhaps a silly young man, who still had room to grow in his life, would be a better choice.

"Now," said Lenz, "let's talk about something nice, like how you certainly meant to kill me a few minutes ago."

I grinned at him. "I thought you had betrayed me."

"An auspicious start to our partnership."

"Don't be silly!" I clapped him hard on the back, and he coughed. "The *start* of our partnership was when you kidnapped me in the middle of the night! Let me handle the auguring—it's my job, after all—and you focus on whatever it is you're good at. Then we save the Tetrarchia."

Lenz sighed. "Have you seen that?"

"Oh, gods no," I laughed. "We will have to bring it about ourselves. So, now what?"

Lenz, still walking slowly beside me, stared down at me. "I was going to ask *you*. As you say, that's your job. Partner."

I wondered for a moment if we were on good enough terms for me to be honest about the Gift, and my original fraud. I quickly decided that this partnership was much too shaky for that.

"Well," I said, "we could always try assassination?"

"Of Selvosch, maybe. But Vorosknecht and the Queen may be too difficult to get to."

In all that had happened, I had almost forgotten how I had implicated Queen Biruté. I considered telling Lenz that had been something I made up on the spot, but then reconsidered. After all, who was I to say that I hadn't accused her based on my own intuition? She ran half the Reds, and had been quick to agree with Vorosknecht at the King's Dinner, after all.

"What about the Greens?" I asked. "They're the largest army by far. High General Dreher wouldn't much care for the Court Philosopher and the Queen banding together to depose the King, would he?"

"Unless Vorosknecht can expose Olaf, or at least cast doubt upon him. Last I checked, our good High General Dreher is no great fan of Prince Friedhelm. He groups him together with Vorosknecht, as a decadent, soft aesthete."

I looked up, and noticed that we were nearing the Yellow barracks where Lenz lived.

"I may be able to help with the Greens," I ventured.

Lenz narrowed his eyes and looked down at me. "How?"

"Dreher," I began, "and his underling, a little royal named Martin-Frederick Reinhold-Bosch, may have been interested in . . . liberating me from your grip."

Lenz laughed sadly. He lifted a hand, as though to press it to his forehead but, having done that a great deal this morning, scratched his cheek instead.

"And why was he interested in that?" he asked.

"Firstly"—I held out a finger—"because he hopes to learn from my Gift, and I *was* trying to escape. You remember that. Secondly"—another finger—"because, as you've mentioned, he hates the Prince."

Lenz groaned.

"*But*," I continued, louder, "that is because he, like everyone, thinks Friedhelm wants to replace his brother."

"Which he has," sighed Lenz. He sounded very tired.

"Well, we won't tell the High General *that*." I waved it away. "Perhaps, rather than a spy, two prophets, and a doppelganger, our good Prince should have hired a propagandist."

"Oh, he did," muttered Lenz. "Quite dead, now."

"But," I continued, "if I can convince Dreher of the truth—"

"*Part* of the truth."

"Of course, of course." I did not explain to him just how comfortable I was with untruths. "Have you spoken to Chasiku about . . . all of this, yet?"

Lenz shook his head. "The Prince doesn't want her to know about Gerhold. *You* were already in too deep to not tell you."

"See if she figures it out herself," I said. It was a terrifying thing to imagine them doing *to me*, but I suggested it nonetheless. This is why it's awful to begin feeling comfortable: you'll do anything to keep that sliver of comfort.

Lenz grunted noncommittally.

"Why are we at your barracks?" I asked, as we were now quite close. Perhaps a handful of yards.

"Are we?" Lenz looked up. "Oh! I was just wandering, must have been drawn here. Gabor, ah, stayed over last night." Lenz smiled, slightly, in spite of everything. "I hope he hasn't left yet."

"He's too good for you," I said.

"I know."

And that was when someone began shooting at us.

ON GUNS

I admit I hadn't yet interacted with guns much in my life—the people who wanted to kill me generally couldn't afford them. Guns had only been available to the Tetrarchia, in any noticeable numbers, for perhaps a hundred years, and only by the grace of Loasht. Their design schematics, the best ways of making them, and gunpowder itself, all came from that country looming in our north, who sold them to us for a nice profit. Unfortunately, up on top of Rotfelsen, the people who wanted me dead were of a quite better class than I was accustomed to.

Many theorized that Loasht sold us guns in order to push the Tetrarchic kingdoms toward killing each other; others suspected that we were only sold terribly out-of-date models, leaving us defenseless against shiny new firearms; and some believed that the guns had spells woven upon them, so that they could be made to jam, or even explode, from miles away by Loashti "sorcerers." Personally, I think that Loashti merchants only wanted to make money off the strange and combative country to their south, and hardly cared about whatever plots their Grand Suzerain may have been concocting. But this, of course, went against the popular idea of a monolithic, decadent, and inherently sorcerous Loasht bent on our destruction. (Loasht had its own uneasy relationship with so-called "sorcery," but that is another conversation.)

The point is, I wasn't very used to guns. In my time in Rotfelsen, I had *seen* them quite a lot, carried by soldiers, but had hardly ever heard the report of such a weapon since Behrens and his comrades shot up goons in the Masovskan forest. So, when the first shot rang out at Lenz and I, as we were walking idly back from the discovery of a regicide, I simply froze. Startled and confused, I stood completely straight, and stayed completely still.

Lenz's body flopped to the ground, and I looked down at him from where I remained standing, puzzled by his odd behavior. Then I looked behind me and saw puffs of smoke blooming from a small copse of trees, one of many that dotted the surface, pretending that Rotfelsen was a normal kingdom with normal ground. I heard more of those terribly loud noises, and what I now know is the sound of a bullet whirring quite near one's head. I flinched, but did not think to duck.

"Lenz!" called a voice from somewhere in front of me that sounded miles away, with all the noise around my head. I turned back to gawp at the barracks, where Gabor was in the process of dropping from a second story window, twisting, grabbing a windowsill, and then landing on the little filigreed officers' table in front of the building. He broke some crockery and fell into a run along the rotrock ground, drawing his sword.

As Gabor ran in a sort of zigzag toward the trees, a group of eight or so Yellows appeared in and around the barracks door, tripping over each other, tangled up as they tried to draw swords or load harquebuses. Gabor was far ahead of them, untouched by gunfire (as was I, but I didn't realize why just yet), when one of those Yellows took a bullet beneath the eye and fell back against the yellow wall.

Finally, I thought to drop to the ground. It was Gabor's unthinking anger at the thought that Lenz had been shot, and the dead Yellow staining the wall, that made me realize what was going on around me. In my defense, it had only been scant seconds since the shooting began. I turned to Lenz, to see if he had dropped on purpose, or been hit.

"Gabor, be careful!" he cried.

Gabor reached the trees, seeming not to have heard Lenz. The hidden attackers became much less hidden then, bursting out into view and beginning to run from the copse. They wore no uniforms, nor colors of any particular allegiance, and were masked; but I had my suspicions. One of the masked men tried to reload his harquebus as he ran, so Gabor stabbed him, and he fell lifeless to the imported dirt. The rest, perhaps six of them, were out of Gabor's reach.

"Are they *all* running from him?" I asked. "I know he was a soldier, but—"

"Are they what?" Lenz grunted. He craned his head around, then looked back at me. "They're running *toward* us."

I hopped back up and saw that a group of Yellows was still bungling forward to intercept our assailants, but would not reach them before the masked men reached us.

"Kalyna . . ." muttered Lenz. He was still on the ground, trying and failing to pull himself up. This was something much more than his normal limp, but I did not have the time to ask.

I growled at him, which I know I should not have done, before reaching for his hand. He grabbed mine tightly, and I began to pull. Just then, someone grabbed my other *hand*, and yanked at me. I turned and saw a slender man with his face hidden behind a white silk mask, covering all but his eyes. I gurgled something out as I tried to release myself from his grip, still pulling up at Lenz with the other hand.

I was stuck in a very silly looking position, I am sure: bent toward Lenz, my arms out in both directions, feeling dragged between these two figures. I decided to remedy it by kicking the masked man very hard in the gut. I made sure to throw myself into it enough to yank Lenz upward. Both men groaned in pain at the same time, but neither let go. The masked man did double over, however, which put his head near my waist. So—my arms still held between both, like in some circular peasant dance—I decided to knee him in the face.

He pulled himself back up just in time for me to look like a fool, kneeing at the air and going off balance toward him. The masked man had also gotten his breath back, and began to speak.

"No, no, no, no, Kalyna!" he cried. He lifted his other hand, which held a bejeweled rapier, and used the tips of his fingers to pull off his mask. "I'm here to save you!"

It was Martin-Frederick Reinhold-Bosch, and he was grinning at me, his face flushed with the excitement. From his expression, it immediately became clear to me what this whole fiasco was in his mind: the righteous rescue of a downtrodden woman from an evil prince and his lame underling.

"Oh. Balls," I said.

This was about when the Yellows crashed into the masked men, and it all became a great mess of yelling and fighting. The only person with any sense of clarity seemed to be Martin-Frederick himself, whose attention was entirely trained upon me.

"I don't need saving!" I tried to yell over the battle.

Martin-Frederick was about to respond, when Gabor twisted his way into the skirmish and swung his sword at the back of the Martin-Frederick's head. How the young man knew to duck is a mystery to me, but he did. He let go of me and turned to parry Gabor's next few strokes, hopping sideways, the grin never leaving his face.

Lenz's hand was still in mine, and I tried to pull him farther from the fighting. Gabor, still looking furious, attacked Martin-Frederick a few more times. The young man laughed and leapt entirely out of his reach.

"Away!" yelled Martin-Frederick. "There are more coming!"

And with that, the masked men (who I now realized were Greens) began extricating themselves, although none did so as gracefully as their leader. The Yellows cursed them for cowards, while Gabor spared Martin-Frederick only a fleeting glance before he ran over to Lenz. More Yellows were indeed running to join us from the barracks, too late to do anything besides shake their fists.

Once it was all over, there were only two dead: the Yellow shot as she exited the barracks, and the masked man Gabor had killed. There were quite a few light cuts and scratches amongst the Yellows, and Lenz had been shot. I don't know if it was particularly lucky or unlucky that he had taken the bullet in his bad leg.

HONOR

There was a great deal of fussing after the attack, and we helped Lenz over to the officers' table outside the Yellow barracks. It was perhaps a touch too cold to sit outside, but we all had our blood up from the excitement, so it seemed comfortable enough, for the moment. Beneath Gabor's skeptical eye, a Yellow was conducting rudimentary field medicine on Lenz's leg, to staunch the bleeding while we waited for the flesh-alchemist.

Once Lenz's patching was finished, he sat very still, breathing in and out slowly, while Gabor sat near him and tried very hard not to hold his hand. I stood over both of them, and decided to speak in Skydašiavos, just in case. The Yellows near us kept watch, but gave us space to talk.

"They were trying to rescue me," I said to Lenz. "That was why their shots never hit me."

"From whom?" asked Lenz, in the same language. It sounded like he knew the answer.

"From the *Prince*," I said, letting that word stand in for, *the evil, scheming Prince who has coerced us into his service and supplanted his brother.*

"Hm," said Lenz.

Gabor hardly seemed to mind that we were speaking over his head. He was thinking his own thoughts.

"What a mess," I grunted. "Remember how we wanted to make them our allies?"

"Who?" said Lenz.

"That was Martin-Frederick Reinhold-Bosch," I replied. "I suppose that he, or High General Dreher, decided to speed things up. To 'help' me."

"Dreher?" Gabor said suddenly, looking at me. "What about Dreher? In Rotfelsenisch, if you please."

Lenz leaned over and said quietly to him, "I suppose those were Greens."

"I killed a Green?"

"Most like," said Lenz. He looked sad.

"Well," sighed Gabor, "isn't that a pity? As a retired Green myself, I don't much relish the thought of fighting more of them." He shrugged. "But there's nothing for it, yes?"

"Nothing for . . . What do you mean?" I asked.

"Their leader, the young one"—Gabor smiled warmly—"I'll need to fight him again."

"What? No!" I gasped, running around the little table to Gabor's side. "He was trying to help me, he thinks that our boss is attempting a . . ." I silently mouthed the word "regicide." Then I continued: "We're on the same side, so we should—"

Gabor shook his head. "First he shot Lenz, then neither he nor I had a conclusive victory."

"Gabor, I'm fine," said Lenz. "Just a wayward bullet lodged in flesh that's already thickened and scarred. It isn't as though he was after me, and even if he was, it was a misunderstanding. And he certainly wouldn't know that you and I are . . . what we are."

"Not the point," laughed Gabor. "Lenz, it's not even about you, really. We crossed swords and all that."

"I'm sorry, is this about *honor*?" I hissed. "What a ridiculous thing. We are trying to—"

Gabor turned to me and grinned. "Yes, but don't worry about it. Why, when I was younger, some of my closest friends were those whom I'd fought first. I may well bind your alliance!"

"And if one of you dies?" I asked.

"Then one of us dies." He shrugged and smiled. "That's a swordsman's life, you know?"

Gabor seemed entirely at ease. I looked at Lenz imploringly, but he was too busy staring at Gabor with a mix of affection and irritation.

TSAOXELEK

Lenz insisted that I be escorted by Yellows at least for the rest of the day. So far, my new freedom had involved one trip with Yellows to the palace, where the King was dead, and one trip back, with Lenz, during which he had been shot. Now I did not feel particularly free. One of the Yellows that escorted me was Dagmar, and she seemed eager for more trouble.

"I heard about *this* whole fracas too late," she bemoaned, pointing a thumb backward at Lenz, whom Gabor was helping up. "You need to stop having so much fun without me."

Dagmar's presence was welcome to me now. That lean body would enact violence to protect me. She felt like safety.

I hoped very much that Lenz and Gabor were going to go have it out, and that Lenz would talk Gabor out of trying to fight the annoying young Martin-Frederick Reinhold-Bosch. I still wanted to make High General Dreher our ally, and I also did not want either Martin-Frederick or Gabor to get killed.

I felt strange when I returned to my servant house, like the world around me was vibrating, but no one else noticed. There were no longer Yellows stationed outside the house, and Dagmar and the other left entirely once I'd entered. I supposed this was freedom.

Everything inside was quiet, as it was the day after the Sun's Death, and it seemed all the residents were milling about or sleeping off their food and drink. Unfairly, I found it distasteful that people could go on about their normal lives when the King was dead, an impostor was on the throne, and everything seemed to point, unerringly, toward the most awful collapse.

Jördis must have been up at some point because she was napping in the first-floor alcove. I looked down at her, and wondered what she knew about what her master was up to.

I lay down in my bed and tried to think of what in the world I should do next, but it all just seemed too big, and my onrushing end seemed assured. There was a knock, and I sat up to see Tural standing in the doorway. I had not even closed the door to my room.

"So," he said in his brusque Rotfelsenisch, "what was I a part of last night? Eh?" He was a sinewy thing, leaning a shoulder on the doorframe. Was he always so handsome, or only when he was quiet?

I laughed weakly and sat up. Last night seemed so long ago.

"First there was the King's Dinner," he continued, "and I asked no questions. Then you asked that I bring your boss' friend, and still no questions."

I nodded wearily. He was right to be fed up with me.

"But, I bring him and then . . . something strange in your boss, yes?"

"Yes," I agreed. "Lenz has . . . kept me a prisoner here, until now," I said. "And I brought Gabor in as a way to threaten and control him in return." I smiled awkwardly until my cheeks hurt. "And that is that."

Tural looked unhappy, concerned, disapproving.

"But," I added, "we've sorted it all out, and I'm no longer a prisoner. Everything is fine, and Gabor is safe!"

"Really?" he asked.

"Yes. I promise."

"If you're a prisoner, I'll—"

"I'm not."

"All right," he said. "Good. Because I am not sure how I would have ended that sentence. All right. Yes. All right. The next time you need something from me, even if it is just to talk, Kalyna . . ." he grinned. "Just *tell* me."

"I will. And Tural?"

"Yes?"

"I stole your knife."

"Yes."

"Sorry. You can have it back."

I somehow pulled myself to my feet and picked the knife up from where I had dropped it the night before, after deciding I wouldn't open Lenz's throat. I walked up to Tural and tried to hand it to him. He did not smell like fruit today.

"Keep it," he said. "But next time you need something that's . . . not right, you tell me, yes?"

"I will."

"Good nap." He turned to leave.

"Tural?"

"Mm?"

"What's your surname?"

He stopped. In Quruscan, surnames were often secret from any who were not close to one's family. Descriptors and nicknames were used to tell people apart, not unlike certain Masovskans, such as Eight-Toed Gustaw from Down Valley Way.

"Why?" he asked. "You've spent time in Quruscan, you know better than these Rotfelsens."

"Are we friends?" I spoke Rotfelsenisch, but used a Cöllüknit word for friend.

He sighed. "We are."

"And I am also Quru, and you know mine."

He laughed. "Aljosanovna is different, and you know it. But I'm Tural Tsaoxelek."

I had suspected.

"Thank you, Tural Tsaoxelek."

"Tural will do," he said. "Good nap." He left.

Tsaoxelek. The Quru name Chasiku had claimed to see appended to mine in one possible future. Were she a fraud, like me, she would have needed to find out that Tural and I had been very lightly flirting, and then somehow discovered his secretly held surname. I was more and more inclined to think she was the real thing, which led me in some troubling directions. First, that there *was* some sort of great light beneath Glaizatz Lake, playing into whatever High General Dreher believed, and contradicting what I had told Martin-Frederick. Second, that I was probably going to die down there. And third, that there was indeed a whole other family (or even collective of families) of people with some other version of the Gift, while I was still bereft of it.

None of this convinced me to jump on Tural the next chance I got. In fact, it made me more wary. The weight of possibilities. But if Chasiku's Gift was real, and did in fact see futures in a different fashion than Papa's did, there was at least a small chance of a future stable enough for Tural and I to both be alive and married. If so, how could I make such a world possible, whether or not Tural and I became joined within it?

Romantic entanglements, and something beneath the lake, together led me toward one place: Martin-Frederick Reinhold-Bosch. If I could convince him (and through him, Dreher) that we were on the same side, then we would have a civil war of Yellows and Greens against Purples, probably with the Reds split. I didn't much like the idea of a war at all, but if this could happen before the Council of Barbarians, perhaps the end of the Tetrarchia itself could be avoided.

This was when my mind fully seized upon the idea of putting Martin-Frederick on the throne. After all, between the false king and the evil prince, why not someone who at least had potential? He was young yet, but that meant he had time to become someone better, and he certainly knew more about the workings of the court than Olaf. Not only was he likely the best choice, but how better to get the Greens onto our side? Surely Lenz could put together some family trees that would nicely paper over the succession, if Friedhelm allowed it.

With the possibilities buzzing in my head, I wrote to Martin-Frederick.

I hope you will give me a chance to explain.

—Warm feelings, K

I summoned a courier, but those who served my house had grown accustomed to not being called on by me, and he gave me a blank look for a long time before finally dashing off. Then I fell into a dreamless night's sleep.

GABOR

"Just how good are you?" I asked Gabor.

"Great!" he laughed. "At what?"

"With a sword. How good with a sword?"

"I get by," he said, with a smile that suggested he did more than get by.

In Papa's original vision of a meeting between Lenz and Gabor, he had seen every detail of the house deep in its cave, with its lattices and orchids. Specifically, he had seen a sign that said "DUNKEL CAVE." This is how, after some time with a map of Turmenbach, I had been able to tell Tural where to find our guest for the Sun's Death.

Now I was in the home Gabor had, until recently, shared with Lenz in the (I thought) whimsically named Dunkel Cave, well underground on the south side of Turmenbach. Gabor and I were sitting out on his veranda, which was lit with blazing torches and looked out over a garden of cave plants: huge mushrooms, multicolored mosses, wrinkled liverworts, and broad green leaves that somehow caught trickles of sunshine, or something like it. Snow was piled up in the corners, though I was unsure how it had gotten there.

Gabor was in a very large housecoat that had almost certainly been made from a rug and, despite giving off a sort of languid noble air, had served me tea himself. I saw no one else in the relatively clean house. Lenz must have decided not to tell Gabor that I had planned to bargain with his life at the Sun's Death, because Gabor seemed happy to see me.

"You get by?" I asked him.

He nodded. "I got through the 'Skirmishes,' fought off Bandit State raids many times, and these days I do little but garden and practice swordplay." He looked out at his mushrooms and smiled, then opened his mouth to continue and hesitated, looking a little embarrassed. "I . . .

come from an aristocratic background. Strictly minor, but nonetheless I grew up expecting to spend a few years under High General Dreher and then, you know, live on family money forever." He shrugged, and stretched out the next word far too long. "Buuut being disinherited for . . . well, you know"—he winked—"doesn't suddenly change one's habits. Working every day comes naturally to Lenz; I tend to live off our pensions and what he makes, and when things run scarce, I hire out my sword, here and there."

"You're that good?"

"I hope so. In all honesty, most jobs only require a basic competence."

It occurred to me that if Klemens Gustavus had not been so insistent on hiring giant protectors, Lenz and I might have met Gabor in the alley by the poppyhouse. That would have been interesting.

"How much do you charge for a little light stabbing?" I asked.

"Oh, I'd never charge a friend."

I felt a pang of guilt, took a deep breath. "You *do* know Lenz and I aren't friends, yes? We work together and don't get along."

Gabor raised an eyebrow. "Did I say anything about Lenz?"

I wasn't used to someone being so quick to call themselves my friend; it made me uncomfortable. What did he want from me? Where was the catch? Was this how life went for people who were able to live in nice, clean, safe buildings? I expected to wake up covered in pig shit again, still drunk, still fifteen.

"We *are* friends, aren't we?" Gabor added.

"I . . . suppose so."

"Good, good!" he laughed, patting me on the shoulder. My tea spilled. "Now, Lenz has told me you're no slouch yourself. Why do you need me for your skewering?"

"I don't. I was hoping to talk you *out* of stabbing someone."

"Why, who?"

"The young Green. Martin-Frederick Reinhold-Bosch."

He deflated slightly, but kept up his smile. "Oh! That one. I don't plan to stab him. Just a few nicks."

"Must you fight him at all?"

"I'm sorry, Kalyna, but we have already had this conversation. And I'm sure the young man would understand as well."

"Perhaps. But he hasn't been in real war, you see."

"This isn't about *war*, Kalyna." Gabor sat back, thoughtful. "Technically, I've never seen war either. Just the Skirmishes with Skydašiai because the Tetrarchic kingdoms can never go to 'war' or the whole thing would fall over. Just, you know . . . slap-fights between brothers." He laughed at the phrase, and then his smile dropped away. "But slap-fights in which I *slaughtered* my Skydašian countrymen, sometimes while they begged for mercy. Because I was told to do so. And we were all so young: children, as I would measure it now. Younger even than this Martin-Frederick."

He became quiet, staring past me and pulling at the brown hairs of his eyebrow.

"I'm sorry, Kalyna, where was I?"

"Your fight with Martin-Frederick isn't about war."

"Oh! Yes, quite right. *War* would be hunting him down and slaughtering him. Like I slaughtered the man who first shot my poor Lenz in the leg." He clicked his tongue distastefully. "This is honor, a duel, a challenge. You may find it silly, but men like Martin-Frederick and I, who get by on our swords, just like to know whether or not we're better than each other."

"But, Gabor, you must understand, not only are the Greens an important ally for us to have, but Martin-Frederick is also my friend." Was he? I wasn't sure.

"And, as I told you, after this he may well be mine. It really does often work that way. There's something *intimate* about a duel. And they hardly ever really end in death. Usually a cut, some scars."

"Did you and Lenz ever duel?"

Gabor let out a laugh from deep in his gut, quite unlike the pleasant one he usually had. "Gods, no! He never would have stood a chance. That's not the kind of intimacy I mean." He screwed his mouth to the side. "Well, *sometimes* it was. Before I met Lenz." Gabor leaned forward and patted my hand. "But I promise you, Martin-Frederick is too young for me."

"He is not that kind of friend." But I was thinking more and more that he might be a halfway decent king, compared to the other options.

"Yes, of course," said Gabor. "But you'd prefer I not kill him."

"Very much."

"Well, I don't intend to."

"But can't you—"

"We will fight, Kalyna. And it will work out for you. You'll see."

I sighed and looked away for a moment, admiring his garden. Then I looked back, brow furrowed.

"How did you mean '*see*'? Lenz has told you what I am?"

"Of course! A soothsayer."

I smiled as I felt myself slip into lies, confidence games, and false charm—as surely as if I'd been back in our tent. Gabor had been so quick to tell me about himself and his past, he seemed almost desperate to know what I thought. Somehow (I can't imagine how) he must have gotten the idea that my opinions *mattered*. What's more, as Lenz still believed my great fraud, so too did Gabor. Doubly so, perhaps, as he hadn't spent weeks failing to get useful visions out of me. I wondered if Lenz had told him about Chasiku.

"Gabor," I continued, "the better I know someone, the weaker my Gift becomes concerning them. If we *are* to be friends, this may well be the first and last time I can tell you anything of your future."

He nodded and leaned forward. I put out my hand and took his; it was calloused and lined.

"You want to know whether you win."

He nodded. I could tell from the set of his jaw that a disastrous future vision would not stop him from what he felt he needed to do. The duelist, sellsword, and soldier in him did not particularly fear death, or killing.

"Well, I admit that I have been trying to see it, and it's been hazy. Part of why I came down here, Gabor, was to see if I could 'part the mists,' so to speak."

He was hanging on my every word.

"It could be," I continued, "that your own indecision has been causing the future to be cloudy. Perhaps, even as you told me it would be a harmless duel, you also saw young Martin-Frederick as a man who'd tried to kill Lenz." I did not tell him how close *I* had come to killing Lenz.

"Well . . ." he muttered. "Well, of course. And Lenz has been kept up there, away from me, all this time."

"But I do believe you have firmed up your resolve, Gabor. After all, I'm seeing much better now."

"And?"

I smiled broadly. "Gabor, I will not tell you who wins. That would take the fun out of it. But I will say that, if you go easy on the boy, you two will indeed come out of it with just a few scratches, and as lifelong friends."

Gabor slapped his own knee and sat back, full of wonder. It had been almost too easy. When was the last time someone had gone into a reading trusting me so much?

"Well, that's lovely, Kalyna! So good to know neither of us will die."

I hoped very much that I had made the right choice.

A BRIEF GLIMPSE OF LOVE

I spent the way back to the surface imagining Gabor and Martin-Frederick as fast friends after a few sword exchanges, followed by a future in which Martin-Frederick was king, and Gabor his right-hand. I tried very hard *not* to think about what would happen if Gabor, puffed up by my "prophecy," decided not to take the duel seriously.

I went back to the servant house, where my family were being moved into new lodgings: Lenz had used the Prince's name to empty out two rooms on my floor; the Lavatory Captain was unhappy about leaving, and I missed him.

I needed to speak to Papa, and the sun was already setting in the early afternoon when I went into his new room, which was on the other side of Tural's from mine. Grandmother's was far at the other end of the floor because Lenz was merciful.

I didn't knock before entering. Papa was propped up in his bed, wearing his coat and three layers of blankets.

"Welcome, stranger," he cried out in Masovskani, "to the tent of Aljosa the Prophet! In this humble place I will untangle the strands of fate that— Oh! It's you, Kalynishka!"

I felt the warmth of a real smile in my cheeks and took his hand. "You are peppy today, Papa!"

"Of course!" he chirped. "We stay in these new rooms tonight, and then we leave Rotfelsen tomorrow!"

I felt my face tighten in an attempt to not frown, as showing my feelings would only make him feel worse.

"No, Papa, we will not be leaving tomorrow."

His face fell. I was a monster. He slumped down and lay on his side, and I leaned down to look into his face.

"When will we leave?" he asked.

"When I have saved the Tetrarchia." *If Prince Friedhelm allows it.*

He looked thoughtful, and this overrode his sadness. "That sounds like a big job."

"Not everything about the Tetrarchia; just from the great doom that you saw."

"Oh. Oh! That, yes." He smiled now, from his sideways head. "I still see it, you know. Now and then. Is it soon?"

"Very."

"Oh, good!"

I knotted my brows at him, and Papa actually noticed my reaction.

"Good because that means we will leave soon!"

"If I can stop it."

"Oh, you will, Kalynishka." He struggled and wrenched his right hand out from under the covers to pat mine with it. It was warm and sweaty. "I know you will."

"Have you seen that?"

"Oh, no!" he chirped. "Just death and destruction. Entrails, shattering, so on, so forth, so good. But I know you will because you are my Kalynishka!"

I felt warmth and happiness and quickly doused them both. I had no right.

"Perhaps, Papa, but I need more of your help, if you can give it," I said. "It should be much easier than last time!" I added quickly.

Papa nodded. He still smiled.

"The man you saw before, whom you met at the Sun's Death? Gabor?"

It took him a moment, but then he nodded. "Gabor. Yes. Yes. I do hope I did a good enough job before with finding what you needed, and keeping the secret."

"You did wonderfully, Papa." I embraced him. "You were as focused and wily as you have ever been. It was a joy to see." I meant it, too.

"Why . . . why thank you, Kalynishka."

I moved back, hands still on Papa's shoulders.

"Gabor will be fighting a duel soon," I said. "Can you see it?"

Papa bit his lip and rolled his eyes up into his head. Unfortunately, this was when Grandmother opened the door and shrieked.

"You! You little . . . little . . . *shirker!*" she cried. "Get away from him. *Get away from my son!*"

She walked up slowly, but I sat unmoving and stared at her, like a fish blinded by the light of a wiggly little shrimp. I didn't move or react until she slapped my face with her leathery hand. I blinked and continued to stare at her. Then Grandmother removed her pipe and hit me on the top of my head with it.

That was when I stood up. My cheek stung more from affront than physical pain, but the top of my skull ached, and I couldn't help rubbing it like a chastised child.

"Do your job yourself, you broken thing, and trouble my son no more!"

She then let loose a stream of Cölluknit curses that I will spare you. Cölluknit curses, you see, are too long in their original forms to be used effectively, and so are shortened when screamed. This means that a literal translation, without the context that comes with knowing the language *and* the people, is inoffensive and nonsensical. She screamed things like, "Green shoe blue rock dead fish old king," in rapid succession, a total of maybe one hundred words. I, of course, knew that just two of them (you may guess which two!) were enough to mean I was made of feces scraped from the backside of Quruscan's greatest pervert. The economy of it all is stunning.

She stopped when someone else who understood what she was saying interrupted.

"What *is* happening in here?" yelled Tural, also in Cölluknit, from my father's doorway. "By all that is just, I've been trying to conjure for the past hour!"

"And who are you?" screamed Grandmother.

"Grandmother, you've met him—"

"Kalyna, is your family going to be this loud—"

"I will be as loud as I—"

I actually put my hand over Grandmother's mouth. I held it firm. She tried to bite me and yank down on my arm, but failed at both.

"Tural. Sorry we disturbed you, but *out.*" I pointed to the door with my free hand.

Tural left. He looked angry, but he always looked angry when he conjured, and this was my family, so I didn't much care just then.

Speaking of my family: having given up on biting, Grandmother licked my palm to make me let go. I did so, recoiling and wiping my hand on her scarf.

"You will rely on my poor son for nothing else, monster," she muttered.

"Even if it kills us?"

"Even if it kills everybody."

I looked down at her for a moment. Had she seen the end? If so, she would never act on it. I strangely admired her restraint.

"Fine," I said. "I'll find this future another way."

She raised a thin, white eyebrow, and the tattoo above it crinkled. "What other way?"

I couldn't help grinning. "You and Papa aren't the only ones up here with the Gift."

Wonder came into her face. So neither of them had seen Chasiku, it seemed. No great surprise; they had never been near her, and they already knew me too well to see my future.

"Not the only . . ." she mumbled. "You don't mean that you . . . Kalyna, have you . . . Kalyna my child, have you awakened . . . ?"

Then I saw it in her eyes. She thought I had the Gift at last, and with that thought there was hope, as well as something else. Something I had seen moisten Papa's eyes many times, but never Grandmother's . . . except, when she was looking not at me, but at her son. I almost gasped.

Love. She was filled with it; seemed to stand up straighter.

"No," I said. "There's *another* soothsayer here."

Grandmother slumped into the chair I had left. The love left her eyes and she stared at the wall.

I must admit that I *savored* this moment. It's foul, but I did.

"No," she said. "No no no, that's impossible."

"But true," I replied, leaving. I began to laugh at her in an ugly way. A real laugh.

"Impossible. Throughout history there has only been our family, one at a time, through the generations."

"Now *that*," I said from the doorway, "is impossible. A line like that could be wiped out so easily. There must have been someone else." I continued laughing at her, from my gut.

Grandmother looked up, her face twisted with anger and crumbling, poisoned love. "Take me to this fraud."

"No."

"Freak! Monster! Take me to this faker now!"

"No, Grandmother."

I slammed the door on her because Grandmother always brought out the best in me. When I walked by Tural's room, his door was closed.

I did go ask Chasiku about Gabor and Martin-Frederick.

"Why?" she snapped. "Don't you worry about *your* death, about what will kill everyone around us? Why these two?" She was sprawled across her bed, on her stomach, talking into a pillow.

"Because a lot depends on it. Can't you just try?"

"Yes. Yes. Fine." She was silent for a moment, then, "No, afraid not. I can't pick two ridiculous Rot men dying out of the hundreds that I see all the time."

"Great. I am glad you tried so hard. What uniforms are those hundreds that are dying wearing then?"

"All colors. I say, don't you see *anything*?"

"My Gift is being stubborn."

"Sounds like a good problem to have."

And she would say nothing more to me that day. I hoped this counted as "working together" enough for Lenz.

When I returned home, I had a note from Martin-Frederick. He apologized for having been so busy lately, and asked that I join him in a bit over a week in Turmenbach, at the Grand Opera House. If I could just get him, and through him, High General Dreher, on our side, then we would have Rotfelsen's largest army. We could save the Tetrarchia. Then we could accuse Vorosknecht of (genuine) regicide, and the Prince could abdicate in favor of Martin-Frederick, saving Olaf from continuing his charade. We could save my father.

I wrote him back to say I'd be delighted.

A Battle Written in Stone

Rotfelsen had finally, truly found its winter. Snow was now piling up and the winds chilled the bone, although it was nothing like what must have been happening in Masovska's Great Field just then. Down in Turmenbach's stage district, only slivers of sky were visible, and yet the streets were piled with snow. I gazed idly out the window of a carriage that I had hired myself, passing lanterns and snowdrifts. For the first time, I realized Turmenbach was beautiful, in its way. Pity.

The thin crack of sky became a rough circle above as the carriage splashed into a great rotrock cavern. The door opened, the driver said, "Ma'am," and flourished, and I stepped out into the cavern that served as Turmenbach's Grand Opera House. It was somehow far colder than the surface, and the walls were covered with great divots in no clear order or pattern. At the far end was one great craggy outcropping, which I would soon learn was the stage. All throughout was the clanking of the shovelfolk doing their thankless duty.

Shovelfolk were teams of men and women dedicated to keeping everyone from getting buried. They hauled away snow, melted it with torches, carved out walkways, hacked at ice, and were ignored by the people around them. To the citizens of Rotfelsen, they may as well have been alley bats snatching up mice. If Rotfelsen ever saw *real* winters, the shovelfolk would have been heroes of the realm. Instead, it was a seasonal vocation forced upon the destitute, excepting a handful of nobles who "selflessly" joined this group to feel like they were in charge of *something*, the way a noble was supposed to be.

Groups of shovelfolk were guiding the snow into a great pit on the right-hand side of the stage, where another group had torches to melt it. Up on the stage, holding a shovel that was only used to point while giving orders, was Martin-Frederick Reinhold-Bosch. He wore a doublet of red, green, purple, and yellow, all very shiny and gaudy and spreading over his torso in various patterns. The four colors of Rotfelsen's government gamboled up and slashed through his doublet in perfectly equal amounts, except for pinpricks of green that littered everything. It was all quite impressive. He also had a cadre of four Greens keeping an eye on him.

"Ah!" he said when he saw me. "You came!" Martin-Frederick vaulted down from the stage, and I admit I was impressed to see him not slip on the sludge. He threw aside his shovel, and the rest of the shovelfolk continued to work just as well without his supervision. His was a vanity position to show how much one of Rotfelsen's royal sons cared about the people.

I put out my hand for him, as I forced a smile. "Yes, well, I am free to come and go as I please."

He kissed my hand. Then the young man stood up straight, still holding my hand, and looked me over for a moment. "I think I like you better in a uniform."

"And I like you better when you aren't shooting at me."

"They were *never* shooting at you," he replied, still smiling. "And I would never touch a harquebus myself. Beastly Loashti things."

He then led me in a stroll, arm-in-arm, around the outer edges of the opera house, under the fiction that he was showing me the place. Huge piles of snow were wedged up against the walls, sagging toward us and waiting to be melted.

"Do you mind," I began, once we were farther from other ears, "telling me what exactly it is you think you're doing?"

"Naturally," replied Martin-Frederick, with a grin. "I am supervising the shovelfolk!"

I sighed. "I mean your *attack*, Martin-Frederick. What were you thinking? What was that all about?"

"But I told you, Kalyna Aljosanovna, it was a rescue!"

"And I told *you* at the Sun's Death that I did not—"

"Well, you know, I thought old Uncle Friedhelm had you under some sort of greater duress than before: that he had forced you to say what you did the night of the Sun's Death. So I talked Dreher into giving me some men to liberate you and put a bullet in the spymaster."

I ground my teeth, closed my eyes, and tried again. "But if I had been under greater duress, why would that have *changed* by the very next day?"

Martin-Frederick raised his free hand and mimicked a gun. "That's why a 'pop' in the skull for the spy, yes? Pity he was only wounded. It all went rather Skydaš after that."

I must have looked confused.

"Old Green talk," he clarified. "Gone Skydaš—gone bad, like that fermented bread they eat. You understand."

Now that I had begun to appreciate food, I had another reason to hope the Tetrarchia would remain: I needed to try this bread.

"Fine," I said. "*Thankfully*, Lenz is still alive."

He stopped walking, almost yanking me backward just by standing still. "Now, Kalyna, I say! I almost begin to wonder if I shouldn't have tried to rescue you at all!"

I let go of his arm and turned to face him. "You *absolutely* should not have. That—!" I realized that my voice was echoing, and the Greens were looking my way quite intently. I continued, quietly: "That is what I have been telling you, over and again. What I don't know is why you would not listen to me until now."

Martin-Frederick Reinhold-Bosch put his hands on his slim hips and looked at me, incredulous. "So you'd prefer I left you in Friedhelm's clutches?"

I sighed. "I would prefer that you listened to what I told you, and showed some trust in me."

"And if you were under some sort of, I don't know, spell?"

"What do you know of spells, Martin-Frederick?"

"That some strange person, wreathed in bones, can, from miles away of course, mutter and imitate your downfall. He will burn herbs and chant, and tear at his greasy hair, until you follow the exact routine he is demonstrating for you."

"That is not how spells work," I said, even though I had no idea at time. (In truth, I can say now, he wasn't far off.) "*I'm* the 'mind-witch' here, remember?"

"Well now, I don't think of you as a . . ." He trailed off and, for the first time, his smile seemed to falter a little. Martin-Frederick knitted his brow and looked at the slush beneath. "Kalyna Aljosanovna, I'm sure I'm sorry. Please do understand that I only wanted to help."

I smiled very nicely and told him I forgave him. Then we chatted a bit about nothing much, and I felt very strange walking casually, arm-in-arm with some kind of prince, inspecting the strange shapes in the walls, while destitute men and women shoveled and carried and cursed all around us.

"You should see this place when it's full of people," sighed Martin-Frederick.

I looked at him, and then at the shovelfolk who were, currently, all around us. I echoed his sigh, but for my own reasons. I supposed it was too much to ask that Martin-Frederick be a better king to his people than any *other* monarch was, but I still hoped he could be improved—molded.

"Your average drama or mummery only half fills the place," he continued, "which leaves space for milling about, and some benches are often brought in. But *The Leper's Five Tits* will fill the place!"

Just in time for its walls to crash down, perhaps. Although physical collapse wouldn't even be necessary if soldiers hemmed in the audience. I suddenly imagined tens of thousands of Loashti soldiers, all with guns more powerful than what they sold us. They could shoot or burn or let trampling do most of the work. In an attempt to stop thinking about *that*, I leaned over to inspect a dip in the wall as Martin-Frederick kept talking.

These dips and gouges and outcroppings slashed throughout the walls played the parts of benches, catwalks, and even elevated private boxes for the rich, complete with velvet pillows. I looked at a shallow dent in the wall near the ground: it looked just like the impressions of spinal ridges that graced the roofs of so many of Rotfelsen's tunnels.

Across one section of this dent was a vertical shape taller than me, driven deeper into the stone, and I tell you there is no way it was anything besides a claw mark. I looked up at the other shapes in the wall, some deep enough to use, some only decorative, and began to see the truth etched out across them: a dip where a head or tail had sunk into rotrock like it was butter, a line where a long body had been whipped across the side, a series of gouges where a grasp had come up with only stone. Everything that could be reached and used by humans had been worn down over the centuries, but the shapes still told a story.

The Grand Opera House had been carved out by a fight between two or more of those thousand-legged burrowers, and . . . something else. Now, thousands of years later, it was like seeing huge, unknowable creatures fight in the darkness through brief flashes of far-off lightning.

Did any of these things still exist? Was worrying about conspiracies a waste of time?

"It is marvelous and powerful to be surrounded by so many people, all enjoying something together," said Martin-Frederick.

"Ah?"

"I have a box reserved for us."

"Yes, of course," I muttered, glancing at an oblong nobles' box far above his head. Its bottom half was smooth from use, but its top half still showed lines like sections of a giant caterpillar. Those sections were interrupted by deeper lines that could only have been teeth; the mouth that held them, when it whipped its prey about and slammed it into the rotrock, must have been circular.

"Martin-Frederick," I began, "did you ask me to meet you all the way down here just to show me where we'll be seeing the opera?"

"Yes! And thank you for accepting," he said. "But I also wanted to show you the Grand Opera House itself." He leaned in eagerly. "Do you wish to know its origins?"

This time, unlike on the way to Glaizatz Lake, I didn't step on Martin-Frederick's chance to tell me about where I was. He expounded upon the major theory of the Grand Opera House's forming, which I had just guessed, and felt extremely smart telling me about it. I nodded and smiled because I was trying to make the Prince and the High General into allies, and possibly Martin-Frederick into a king. He could be a bore, but that certainly seemed our best option.

"And *that* is the only reason you brought me here?" I asked when he was finished.

"Not only," he sighed. "I also rather fancy you, if you hadn't guessed."

"I did not need my Gift to see that," I said. "I'm quite glad you didn't burn our bridge entirely and kill Lenz."

"As am I, now, I must say. But what to do about Uncle Friedhelm?"

"And why can't Prince Friedhelm be your ally?"

"Well . . . I was told that he . . . hmm . . ."

"Besides," I continued, "I never did get to tell you *why* I canceled our first escape."

"It would be quite decent of you to do so," he laughed.

I had a lie prepared for this. A lie to convince the pretty blonde and his boss that I had been feeling out the Prince's true allegiances, and that now I had them, and they were to the crown. Then we would present the High General with Prince Friedhelm and Olaf together, much as we had for Klemens Gustavus. What's more, Olaf would then say that, as he was unable to have children, he was now adopting Martin-Frederick Reinhold-Bosch as his heir. I opened my mouth to begin it, but no one heard me.

"You there, boy!" cried a voice from the entrance, echoing through the Grand Opera House. "Are you ready to give me satisfaction?"

It was Gabor.

A DUEL

"Satisfaction?" Martin-Frederick yelled across the Grand Opera House. "For *what*, pray tell?"

Gabor hopped over a stream of melted snow running out of the cavern, his every movement and every moment of stillness showing great control. It was amazing to watch. This friendly, small man communicated so much that was threatening in a twitch or a blink, and when he steadied the rapier on his hip, it somehow said he wanted nothing more than a fight. The Greens went for their swords. The shovelfolk ignored him, and continued melting piles of snow.

"We didn't finish our last engagement," replied Gabor.

Martin-Frederick, for his part, was equally skilled at showing disinterest. A stifled yawn, loose movements, a wandering eye. I took this to be all part of the game these sorts of genteel duelists played. (I was more familiar with back-alley brawls and the like.)

The Greens who were there to guard Martin-Frederick started toward Gabor, ready to draw their swords. He smiled at them as they stood between him and us.

"Ah, hiding behind Greens again?" sighed Gabor, beginning to remove his left glove, finger by finger.

"Of course not," replied Martin-Frederick. "Do we have some quarrel, sir?"

The Greens did not move out of Gabor's way, but neither did they draw their swords. Gabor removed his left glove entirely, smiling past the guards at Martin-Frederick.

"A disagreement. We crossed swords. I'm sure you remember—after all, *I* was not masked."

Martin-Frederick laughed with what seemed to be genuine humor. "And so you wish to kill me?"

I managed to bite back a protest. This was not supposed to turn deadly: I hoped it was all posturing.

"I wish," said Gabor, "to see who is better."

With his left, ungloved hand, Gabor made a rude gesture. Then he threw the empty glove to the stone ground. Quite a way behind him, on the far wall, the gouges from a great set of ancient claws seemed a wreath about him.

"Then you shall have satisfaction," said Martin-Frederick.

"This doesn't need to be deadly," I hissed at the blonde.

Martin-Frederick Reinhold-Bosch looked at me and laughed. "Of course it doesn't need to be!" He looked at his guards and waved a languid hand. "Out, all of you. Shovelfolk, too. I won't have it said that my loyal underlings helped me to kill this fool."

The Greens grumbled, but looked like they understood, and began to leave the Grand Opera House. The shovelfolk left with much rolling of their eyes, which Martin-Frederick did not seem to notice. Within a few short minutes, the whole of the great cavern had only three people within it: Gabor, Martin-Frederick, and me. Suddenly I found myself very cold in there, with the snow in huge piles, melting all around our feet, and so few bodies about.

Gabor had done nothing to agree with, or refute, Martin-Frederick's talk of killing. Was this a normal part of the back-and-forth of these things? Was it about cowardice?

"Gentlemen," I implored, moving between the two men. "You are both my friends, and this is all a misunderstanding."

"Then he should apologize for his comment about my being masked," said Martin-Frederick. "I was, after all, trying to save his *friend.*"

I bit my lip to stop myself from calling Martin-Frederick a child. That never discouraged a young man from being childish.

"Masked or not, what does it matter?" said Gabor. "I don't care what you get up to, young man, but we never finished our fight. My fingers ache at such a lack of resolution. It is, well . . . unsatisfying."

"But you're on the same side!" I pleaded. "Try not to kill each other."

Martin-Frederick turned to me and shrugged, as though he could do nothing to change the situation.

"I'm sure," said the young blonde, "you won't mind if we dispense with seconds. I am at your service this instant, and Kalyna Aljosanovna will bear witness."

"Naturally." Gabor's voice rose musically.

I haven't seen many duels in my time. I suspect that, had there been a greater audience, these slight, deadly men would have shaken hands, crossed swords, gone back six steps, twirled, or what have you. As it is, they stripped to their shirts, unceremoniously drew their rapiers and, within a second, Gabor had circled to the left and lunged at Martin-Frederick.

The boy pivoted his blade only slightly to deflect this. I learned just how slim my understanding of swordplay was when I assumed, in that moment, that Gabor was off-balance and had lost. He recovered instantly, and neither seemed surprised. He had not expected to hit his mark so early, I realized: he had been giving Martin-Frederick a jump.

And they were off, faster than I could follow. The two men circled each other, swords rebounding. I could not tell the difference between an attempted cut and slapping someone's sword aside. Their eyes never left each other's blades, and yet both stepped effortlessly over and around piles of sludge, or cracks in the rotrock floor.

Within a minute, they had quickened. Each of Martin-Frederick's movements became faster, harder, more controlled, matching Gabor well enough. I had expected the boy to be easily riled and overwhelmed by a professional, but I suppose there was a reason Dreher kept him around.

Martin-Frederick advanced, and Gabor gave ground with each riposte, finding less time for his own thrusts. Gabor began to slip in the melted snow. Martin-Frederick's back was to me, and he seemed a faceless machine. I could see every line of worry on Gabor's face, or at least fancied I could.

I began to have the sinking feeling that this bore greater similarity to a knife fight in an alleyway than I originally thought.

The younger man feinted to the right and then slipped back to the left, bashing against Gabor's defense. He pivoted, striking from one side and then the other, left, right, left, left again. Gabor's back was now against the wall.

My lips were dry, my throat cracked. I had told Gabor that neither would die; *I* had told him to "go easy on the boy."

Again and again, Martin-Frederick's blade was deflected from Gabor's body by only a hairsbreadth. Gabor ducked a stab at his chest, but it cut across the side of his neck. I gasped. He rolled backward to avoid the next, into a low gouge in the wall that held a loveseat. Martin-Frederick seemed annoyed as he jabbed at the rolling figure.

Gabor got to his feet and shoved over the loveseat, which set Martin-Frederick back for perhaps a half second. The younger man jumped forward again, blocking my view. I saw only Gabor's shoulder as he leaned forward, and both men stopped moving.

I rushed up, and saw Gabor's blade sliding away from Martin-Frederick. The young blonde slipped backward, falling into a sitting position on the wet stone. I felt a rush of relief as I saw him there, legs out and back straight, elbows on his knees. He looked like he was catching his breath.

I rushed to Martin-Frederick to see how badly he had been injured. I sat beside him, bracing his back with my hand, as he sat there.

"Martin-Frederick, where did he get you? Are you alright?" The hand on his back came back covered in blood.

"Oops," said Gabor, winding his right shoulder. "Maybe next time."

Martin-Frederick was dead.

BEFORE HIS BLOOD DRIES

Gabor rocked back on his heels. "Sorry about that, Kalyna. I tried!"

I shook Martin-Frederick's body with numb hands. I felt all our chances to ally with High General Dreher, to save the Tetrarchia, going up in smoke. I felt the absence of a young man who had been vital and alive moments before. An arrogant one, surely, but he could have become a better person someday (unlike me), and even a good king. His body was limp. I *missed* him.

Gabor stepped forward to wipe his blade on the front of Martin-Frederick's shirt. I must have looked affronted because when he saw my face, he seemed shocked and said, "I tried to go easy, like you said, but he got me in a difficult position, Kalyna. I couldn't help it. Did you care much for him?"

"Not really," I said to the back of Martin-Frederick's head.

"Well, at least there's that, eh?"

"Gabor?"

"Yes?"

"Run."

"Excuse me, Kalyna?"

"Run. There must be a service entrance in this place. Get out of here and go to Lenz's barracks. He has a secret chamber. I'm going to call for help."

"Now?"

"Before his blood dries. They're right outside, and I need to—"

"I really am sorry that—"

"Later. Go now."

And Gabor was gone, silently into the darkness at an alarming speed.

I took a series of deep breaths, counted to twenty, put both hands right in his blood, smeared some up my arms for good measure, and screamed my lungs out. Screamed like I couldn't gather the faculties for the word "help." Screamed like I was the one dying. I hoped I sounded terrified, as though a man I cared for had been killed by a violence I didn't understand. I hoped I did not sound like I was screaming with frustration at the end of my plans. I hoped that I could twist this into something useful.

I screamed until the Greens were peeling my bloody fingertips from the corpse's clothing.

A CLEAR CASE OF ASSASSINATION

High General Dreher's office—the one *not* in the center of a subterranean lake—was at the top of a Green barracks, and only two rooms larger than Lenz's. I wondered how many secret chambers it had, but perhaps he didn't need them: he had Glaizatz Lake. In all, it was the sort of suite I expected: consciously pared down and near the soldiers. Did the Greens love him half as much as he wanted them to?

The small ruddy man was at a desk covered in papers and knives, and whenever he opened or closed a drawer in his desk, I heard a clink of heavy glass: I'm sure there were many medical ointments and potions in there. The remains of a roast sat at one end of the desk, looking as dull as the one I had eaten on the lake with him and Martin-Frederick. How many of these sad roasts had the young swordsman eaten with the High General? To think that they had been among his last meals was deeply depressing.

Dreher looked at me sternly, but not harshly. He was trying not to scare me, and I was trying very hard to look scared, because it helped me to seem raw from Martin-Frederick's death. I was depending quite a bit on the camaraderie that can be found amidst loss and high emotion.

"So," said Dreher, "his name is Gabor. I know that much because apparently you called him such before . . . Martin-Frederick sent the Greens away." He said the dead man's name as though he was irritated at himself for being irritated by Martin-Frederick's stupidity. "Do you know his family name? Anything else about him?"

"No," I said, shaking my head. I realized I did not actually know Gabor's full name, so that, at least, was not a lie. The rest would be.

"Do you know why he attacked Martin-Frederick?"

I noticed his use of the word "attacked" rather than "challenged," or "dueled."

"I believe," I said, carefully, "he was involved in the, ah, fracas the other day, when Martin-Frederick tried to rescue me."

Dreher sighed and sat back, grunting in pain. "Damn young fool, I never should have let him do it. So this Gabor is a Yellow?"

"I don't believe so, High General." I was unsure, as yet, how far I could go in incriminating Gabor to get Dreher on my side, if I needed to do so. But I knew for damn sure I would not reveal his relationship with Lenz.

"And why didn't you want to be rescued, Kalyna? I could still use your Gift over here, with the Greens."

I leaned in closer, both hands on Dreher's desk. I let my very real desperation at how everything was spiraling out of control, at how it felt that everything I did led toward Rotfelsen literally crumbling around us, bleed into my voice and he looked truly surprised.

"Because I have gotten in good with the Prince!" I growled. "Because I know his plans, and I think you will be surprised. And I have seen something *glowing in Glaizatz Lake* besides! Something strong." I added that last part onto Chasiku's vision: if he thought it was Rotfelsen's Soul, then of course he would want it to be strong. Whatever that meant, for a glowing something or other.

Dreher opened his mouth, then closed it and looked thoughtful. He leaned forward as well, until his face was inches from mine, his fingers steepled and his elbows on his desk.

"Kalyna Aljosanovna, I think you are shaken up by what's happened today."

"I suspect so, High General, but—"

"Please call me Franz. And let me ask you: Did you much like Martin-Frederick, Kalyna? I know that he was fond of you."

I nodded. "He was brave, and kind to me, and pretty. I—" I stopped myself, seeming unable to get out the words, before starting again. "I allowed myself to hope he might keep me as a mistress."

"I think he would have," said Dreher, patting my hand. "Do you think he was assassinated?"

"Gabor is not a Yellow."

"That's not what I asked you. Was it a fair duel?" It was clear from his tone that High General Dreher already had an opinion on this question: he thought it was his enemies coming after him. What he wanted, what he *needed* for me to gain any modicum of his trust, was a confirmation of what he already "knew." And I happily threw Gabor to him.

"Well, Franz," I said, "the fight was *technically* legal and honorable, but he was an older, more experienced duelist who goaded Martin-Frederick to anger." I gulped. "He gave the young man no choice, pretended at little skill, and then cut him down. I believe he was a professional swordsman." This last part was, of course, true. I felt the words curdling in my mouth as I said them, but my old need to say what a mark wants to hear was too strong. I am proud and sickened to say that none of my distaste showed.

High General Dreher sighed for a long time, and it seemed to pain him. "Martin-Frederick," he finally said, "was young and impetuous, but he had so much potential."

I nodded.

"What's more," he continued, "no one assassinates my officers with impunity. We will capture this man, with your help, I hope."

I nodded again.

"Please go home and get some rest. We shall talk more tomorrow."

The High General poured us two mugs of a Masovskan pine liqueur. Very foreign, I thought, for a man obsessed with the Soul of Rotfelsen. Almost "decadent."

As though he'd read my thoughts, he sheepishly said, "It's my one vice."

He lifted his mug, and I did the same.

"To Martin-Frederick," he said.

"Martin-Frederick Reinhold-Bosch," I sighed.

We drank. It warmed me down to my stomach. Or maybe I was warmed by knowing that I had hooked High General Dreher. And all it had cost me was the betrayal of a friend and a pretty young man's death.

CHANCES DWINDLE

"You did what?" sighed Lenz, the next morning.

"Gained High General Dreher's confidence."

"There is a manhunt on for Gabor, who is trapped beneath my room."

"Well, he *did* kill Martin-Frederick. After we both asked him not to fight the duel. Does he mind it?"

"Not as much as he should," grumbled Lenz. "He's mostly worried about his plants."

"Something needed to be done to get the High General on our side," I said. "We're all dead if we can't stop this. So I made the most of a bad situation. And now you can have him near you."

"How did you end up using my lover twice? While I have found none of yours?"

"He was convenient, and I'm too unlikeable to have lovers."

"Untrue," said Chasiku. "Surprisingly."

We had been traveling up to the top of her tower on the pallet as we argued. I had told Lenz about Gabor and Martin-Frederick's duel, of course, but also about Dreher's belief in the Soul of the Nation, and Chasiku's vision of something glowing, which, whatever it was, could be used to manipulate the High General. Chasiku, now, was sitting in the open air, with her back to the view and her head against the metal railing, her arms hanging over her knees.

"Well," I said, stepping off the pallet. "No lovers recently."

"Yes," said Chasiku. "But that can change soon, if you lie."

"I don't care enough to lie," I lied. "And how does your family pro-create, Chasiku? If you can't stand to be around people?"

"What do you two want?" she asked.

"To know how your family—"

"What is she up to?" Lenz interrupted me, pointing in my face as the two of us walked out to the railing.

"Why not ask me?" I offered.

"I have." Lenz turned to Chasiku and specified, "Where is she going with this?"

"Hard to say," said Chasiku. "Cause and effect are chasing each other around in my head. There are thousands of actions that she, or you, may take, but our chances of surviving the next month only dwindle. The short version: I don't think she knows where she's going."

"Sounds right," I said.

Then Chasiku looked thoughtful, and added, "Well, *our* chances are dwindling, Lenz. Yours and mine. Kalyna's odds of survival seem to be improving."

"That's . . . interesting," he said, turning to me. "Planning to run out on us?"

I wasn't, but I shrugged. Was I?

"Anything else?" he asked Chasiku.

She shook her head.

"Your Gifts," said Lenz, "have a great number of limitations."

"If soothsayers could pick out the future perfectly," I began, "the first one would have been kidnapped by a king millennia ago, and that king's family would still rule the whole world. Why do you think we suffer in obscurity?"

"Kalyna," said Lenz, "do you really think you can gain Dreher's confidence? Convince him that we're on his side?"

"I do. He likes me, and thinks I could be useful. More fool him. I'll probably tell him some secrets and prophecies to get his full trust."

"What kind of secrets? About Gabor and me?"

"About the Prince, Lenz. Dreher doesn't care about you."

"Fine. Tell him all about Friedhelm for all I care, just don't tell him anything about the King. Do either of you have anything else that can be helpful?"

We didn't, so I went back to my servant house to ponder. Instead, I spoke to Tural for a bit. He was deeply anxious about the Council of Barbarians, which was now only a month away. He had been the Master of Fruit four years ago, the last time the Council was in Rotfelsen, but he only remembered a blur of frantic activity.

He and I then played a strange game where I gave him the names of fruits, and he muttered long sentences about them in return. He imagined different ones together, and wove long histories of each, how they interacted with the culture and times of their land of origin. To hear Tural tell it, none of human history would have happened without fruit. Did you know that the beginning of trade between the North and South Shores of Skydašiai was for apples? This may be entirely untrue.

We talked into the night, and near the end, I found myself wanting to kiss him. I remembered what Chasiku said, and did not do so. As I fell asleep, my thoughts were instead on High General Dreher.

DINING WITH THE HIGH GENERAL

I began to regularly visit High General Dreher for dinner, and we always consumed the same sad, bland roast. It reminded me of myself before palace living spoiled me, but Dreher had access to *so much* good food, which he happily ignored.

On the first day, after some pleasantries about the hunt for Gabor, Dreher began to speak about his vision for Rotfelsen itself, in vague terms. So, I gave him a little push by telling more of what I had supposedly seen beneath his lake. I took what Chasiku had seen, something glowing at the bottom, and embellished.

"Something is down there: something alive and glowing bright that will soon stir. It waits in repose for . . . I'm not sure what."

There was a very long pause. When Dreher rasped, "When?" he was barely speaking.

"Soon. I don't know more, yet." I brought out the old prophetic classic of looking off into the middle distance, as if seeing something there.

"But you said yesterday that it was 'strong.'"

"I did. It cannot be fully viewed, but it looms large behind all I see." Arms crossed, I flicked my eyes back to Dreher's. "The Soul of Rotfelsen," I said.

High General Dreher pounded on the table and jumped out of his seat in excitement, and then moaned in pain, but hardly seemed to care. "I knew it!"

He huffed his way around the desk to me, putting a large hand on my shoulder, and said some nonsense about how even my foreign Gift saw the greatness of the Rotfelsenisch people. I did not disabuse him of the notion as I should have. When I considered a corrective, I pictured the Greens and Yellows killing each other, each thinking the other were regicides, and then the Purples swooping in (probably with mercenaries, as well) to take out the Reds and topple the Tetrarchia. It seemed a likely cause of our country's doom, so I smiled and flattered Dreher regarding the special place of the Rotfelsenisch people in this world. Insensible love of one's kingdom never made much sense to me, but it must have included love of the King, and that was what I needed from Dreher.

Over the next few days, I fed him more about the Soul of the Nation, and about the importance of Rotfelsen as a kingdom. It was easy enough to get Dreher to spend his meals with me, easy enough to show I agreed with his view of the world. I may not know the ways of courtly intrigue and politics, but I have always been a manipulator. Every time I saw him smile at a comment, every time he asked me to come dine with him again soon, I felt a warmth like that of love and friendship. It feels so good to play a role, to feel smarter than the other person, to appear to them as someone who is not *me*.

The strangest part of it all to me was that, even as I listened to Dreher's assertions of the Rotfelsenisch peoples' pride of place in the world, of how the Soul would cure them of foreign corruption and vices, I never stopped finding Dreher personally pleasing. He came across as humble, attentive, and interesting, even when I *knew* he was, at best, our begrudging ally, whom I was deceiving. But then, what did I know? Maybe that *was* the Soul of the Nation down there. The gods have created so many strange and wondrous things in the world.

One evening, I broached the topic of Prince Friedhelm.

"You may," I said, "be surprised at where his priorities actually lie."

Dreher took another bite of his sad roast and laughed. "Are you trying to tell me that our Prince is not an evil schemer?"

"I . . . well, that isn't entirely inaccurate. But a schemer can be useful, and he thinks that the King—"

"Is a fake," Dreher interrupted. "A fake that the Prince has put there. Did you know that?"

I did not have to fake my stunned silence. I knew about Olaf, of course, but was not sure how Dreher had found out, or why he was telling me. One particularly terrifying possibility began to nag at me.

"I . . . did not, High General."

"Franz."

"Franz, I must say, it's hard to believe. Why are you telling me this?"

"Because I want you to understand what your master is capable of, and I want you to use your Gift to help my cause, instead."

"And what is your cause, Franz? I thought I knew, but I begin to wonder." I felt a sinking feeling in my gut.

"Rotfelsen, of course. I have never pretended it is anything else. You have seen its Soul, and so you understand its greatness."

I nodded. I was not sure what else to do. High General Dreher stood up and moved to the door of the office.

"Kalyna Aljosanovna," he said, "I would like you to join myself and some others in an after-dinner drink. The Greens will show you the way while I collect our friends. Please do not call me 'Franz' in front of them."

Our friends. Oh, this was bad. Whatever was going on here, it was troubling.

"Oh, and Kalyna," he said, "Martin-Frederick once told me that your Gift showed you my . . . condition. If tonight you are asked for a demonstration of your powers, use something *else*."

"Of course."

He gulped and looked away, out the door, embarrassed. "Do you know . . . ? That is, how long do I have?" His voice quavered not, I expect, from fear of death, so much as from fear of seeming weak.

"Your condition won't end you any time soon," I said, sagely and with great confidence.

He sighed and nodded, though he didn't turn to look back at me, and left. I was led out of the High General's suite by two very deferential Greens, and had no way of letting anyone else know where I was going.

PLOTS AND PLANS, POTS AND PANS

That night I was wearing a sky blue dress with a dark green (*total coincidence*) bodice, and my sickle, which the Greens let me keep, was slung at my side like a sword. I was taken out of the High General's barracks, and to one of the large mansions near the palace. The Greens were still deferential, but answered no questions.

I was then left alone in a chandeliered parlor full of plush chairs with landscape murals on the walls, but no windows. I listened to the pleasant clink-clank of kitchenware from the next room. Pots were being stirred, and something was being fried. Who was I about to see, and what was Dreher's goal? I had a strong suspicion, but tried to talk myself out of it because, if I was right, the odds stacked against me were overwhelming.

When Dreher arrived, the first thing I saw behind him were great swaths of green and purple. My fears were correct, and I managed to act unsurprised when Court Philosopher Vorosknecht ducked his ridiculous hat through the doorway.

Filling out the room was a group of very rich nobles. One was Selvosch, others I vaguely remembered from the Winter Ball: a woman who had been just a little too drunk, a man who had gotten too excited when someone sat on his lap, and those sorts. So these were the regicides: thirty or so powerful people and their bodyguards. I was introduced to royal advisors, magnates, and priests of a few disparate

344 | ELIJAH KINCH SPECTOR

gods. Vorosknecht did not look happy to see me. Even less happy to see me, almost hiding behind him, was Jördis.

"What is *she* doing here?" the Court Philosopher asked the High General.

"Lending us her power," replied Dreher. "I hope."

Vorosknecht scoffed as though he could not get full words out. I grinned at him.

"Kalyna," said Dreher, turning to me and looking very serious, "you must understand that, though I like you, your life depends on these next few minutes and these fine people."

Vorosknecht almost said something, but bit it down.

"I," continued Dreher, "am going to give you privileged information now. You see Kalyna, we all—you are giving me a look."

Now or never. "You are the regicides. You kidnapped and killed King Gerhold, and now are looking to get rid of his false replacement, along with the Prince, and take over Rotfelsen, removing it from the Tetrarchia entirely."

"This is your prophet, isn't she?" someone squeaked.

"She's a devil," said Vorosknecht.

"Do we succeed?" someone else asked me.

I smiled in that general direction, although I didn't see the speaker. "Looks that way. But things can change."

Jördis was very intently studying the floor.

"I cannot believe you have done this, Dreher," said Vorosknecht. "What does she have to gain through loyalty to us? Put her *below* and forget her!"

At the word "below," many people cringed.

"Wait, wait, wait!" cried Selvosch, pushing his way forward. "Do you . . . truly have the *Sight*?"

I almost laughed at his wide-eyed intensity, but I nodded. "I do. And besides my problems with the royal family—for example, a prince who kidnapped me—I submit to His Brightness Vorosknecht that seeing the future makes me predisposed to side with the winners."

Vorosknecht scoffed, but no fortuneteller or swindler has ever starved by telling someone they're a winner. I smiled and did a very good job of looking at ease.

"So what now?" exclaimed Vorosknecht. "Tell her our secrets—"

"She already knows our secrets," someone said.

"—and induct her into our mysteries—"

"Vorosknecht," said Dreher softly. "She's seen it."

"What?" spat the Court Philosopher.

Selvosch, who was still leaning over me, knew exactly what this meant. His eyes widened.

"*It*," repeated Dreher. He pointed down. "The Soul."

"You can't possibly think—!" As suddenly as he had yelled, Vorosknecht stopped. He pursed his lips very tightly before grunting, "Go on."

I smiled graciously. All my power went into not appearing scared; everything else needed to convince them would flow from that. I told them there was something glowing beneath the lake, in the deepest parts of Rotfelsen. Reactions were mixed; clearly this Soul of the Nation cult was not the only reason for regicide. Some looked bored, some shrugged it off, but Dreher, Selvosch, and some others looked as I must have as a child spending my first winter night in the Ruinous Temple: hearing the low murmur of wintering merchants, looking up at lanterns and animal skins heavy with snow far above me, feeling that it was all quite magical. Vorosknecht looked intently at Dreher.

"Are you sure?" blurted Selvosch. This man who had wielded so much social power at the Winter Ball now seemed so fragile, as though his every belief in the world hung upon what I—whom he'd just met— would say.

"I can't guarantee it's what you're hoping for, but I saw what I saw and would not tell you if it were otherwise."

High General Dreher turned to Court Philosopher Vorosknecht and hunched in his direction, arms out, inviting a response. The Court Philosopher glared, but did not refute me.

"I suppose," he said, very slowly, "the gods would not allow a cursed and deluded devil to see such divine truths. If she has seen it, and seen it *correctly*, which it seems she has, we must believe her." The words were moldy vegetables in his mouth.

I smiled sweetly. A few others let out sighs of relief. No one in the back grumbled, because if anyone disagreed . . . well, they could take *that* up with the Greens and the Purples.

Dreher nodded at a nearby Green to offer me his arm in order to help me up. The High General shrugged apologetically at being too weak to do so himself.

"Now that we are all done standing around and determining that you will not be sent below, let me explain."

BRANDY SLINGS

We all moved into the room where I had heard the melodic preparation, and the conspirators spread out to chat, served drinks by men in green livery. Given the company and the atmosphere, it was no different from a small chamber during the Winter Ball: powerful, well-dressed people talking, laughing, and drinking, surrounded by stunning art none of them looked at.

"Lovely to see you here!" I said to Jördis, a bit too loudly.

It appeared that even her well-honed smile could not match my own false friendliness because she faltered and laughed awkwardly. "Yes, yes, you too, Kalyna."

"It's good that I have finally found something that you truly care about, Jördis." I winked at her. "Or did you just find yourself here, following in your father's footsteps? Perhaps you're hoping it can all pass you by."

She coughed loudly and looked around her. "Well, I . . . I don't know . . . I mean that is . . . Excuse me please, Kalyna."

She showed me that perfect bow again, and scuttled off. I continued schmoozing, and learned more of these peoples' plan.

The plan was that all Tetrarchic monarchs (including Olaf), as well as their advisors, would be killed at once at the Council of Barbarians. The Reds, split between the Queen and false King, and exhausted from preparation for the Council, would be easily overtaken, along with the Prince's degenerate Yellows. The coup would be sprung, and a new age of independent Rotfelsenisch glory rung in to the sounds of clanging swords and harquebus blasts. The deaths of every leader at the Council would break the Tetrarchia entirely and make Rotfelsen a sovereign nation.

But, beyond this clear plan, was a garbled sense of the *why* of it all: there seemed to be little shared by the group beyond "overthrow the government." Everyone had their own reasons: Martin-Frederick (I was told) had in fact *wanted* to be king, Selvosch wanted complete control over all mining with no oversight, Dreher wanted a militarized Rotfelsen free of "corruption," and Vorosknecht wanted "a country based in reason." It was hard to imagine a military dictatorship with an unprepared king and a long list of philosophical rules standing up on its own, all while making less off its mines. Everyone wanted power, but after the breaking up of the Tetrarchia, all their ideas diverged. Did every single one plan to betray the rest? Who would replace Martin-Frederick now? What's more, half of them were mesmerized by tales of a magic being in the lake that would somehow represent all of the cave-bound pink people. Perhaps the only common cause was nationalism at the expense of all else.

But the viability of these peoples' ideal government had little to do with how dangerous they were. I simply didn't want the great, big pimple to pop while I was on it, and for the rest of my home to eat itself.

Given the Rotfelsen-centered nature of their cause, it didn't terribly surprise me that Queen Birutė was, in fact, entirely uninvolved. A Skydašian import was not in high esteem here, so she was meant to die with the other kings and queens. I hoped it was not too late to untangle the mess I'd made by accusing her.

It was cold that night, and I drank what was called a hot brandy sling (which tops brandy with hot water, sugar, and spices), and ate fried slices of reindeer cheese as Dreher explained that he would sweep out decadence and rot. Vorosknecht was visible behind him, gleaming in purple and jewels as he communed with a Purple: a man of about my size with a too-easy and mirthless grin. Jördis tended to hang about behind them. After some time, Vorosknecht approached me.

"And you aren't loyal to this Prince? Or his limping spy?" he asked, loudly.

"You mean the men who kidnapped me?" I laughed.

"Yes, them. How *did* they replace the King?"

I shrugged. "They did that right under my nose, and now I trust them even less, if that is possible."

"Amazing powers you have."

"The fake looks the same in the future as he does in the present," I sneered. "I'm afraid this is all new to me. But at least I can look forward to seeing Prince Friedhelm and Lenz being—ah, what was it High General Dreher said?—sent below, yes?"

Someone behind me choked, just a little, on their drink. Vorosk-necht glared in the direction of the choking, and it stopped. Dreher smiled uncomfortably.

"Ah, Kalyna, there are many here with delicate sensibilities," said Dreher.

I lowered my voice and smiled at him. "But what exactly does it mean?"

A bit of silence, and then Vorosknecht said, "Oh please, High General, you've told her everything *else*."

Dreher shrugged. "There's a building down by Glaizatz Lake. It used to be a prison, nothing too strange about that. Belonged to the Court Philosophers, who could put the wrong-thinking down there."

"What a glorious time," sighed Vorosknecht.

"When control of Glaizatz Lake came to me," continued the High General, "it became mine, but I had little use for it, and it fell into disrepair." He made a short motion toward the Court Philosopher. "But then Vorosknecht told me about the Soul, and we began working together, and put it back into use. Secretly, of course."

"And who goes in there?" I asked, although I felt I knew the answer.

"Our enemies," said Dreher. "It's where Gerhold went, when he was alive. We have others down there who have gotten in our way—Greens and Purples who would not fall in line, that sort of thing—and it's where Martin-Frederick's assassin will go as well. It's always good to have more—we'll use them."

"Now, I feel like this is a stupid question," I asked, lowering my voice, only speaking to Dreher, "but use them for what?"

"Come down to the Lake with us, and we'll show you."

"I would love to. When?"

"You'll know when it's time," he said

"Well, that's all very spooky and ominous," I laughed, letting others hear me. I was happy to play the uncouth commoner: I wasn't going to fool anybody by acting noble or Rotfelsenisch, and it allowed me to ask probing questions.

Dreher seemed pleased with me, and Vorosknecht insulted me a few more times. I didn't learn anything else useful.

"Kalyna Aljosanovna," said Dreher as we were leaving. "Welcome to the New Rotfelsen."

I smiled magnanimously.

SHUDDERINGS

When I got back to my bedroom, daylight wasn't far away. I had smiled and laughed all night, been free of visible fear or discomfort; I had understood the people I was with implicitly, and they had been lucky to have me and all my great power.

I slowly lay down in bed, and proceeded to hold myself and shudder uncontrollably until midmorning. I had to let out every feeling I'd missed. Two extremely powerful men who I'd thought at cross purposes were, in fact, allies. The leader of Rotfelsen's largest army was aligned against me in ways that were entirely irreconcilable. He not only wanted to take over the kingdom, he wanted to destabilize the entire Tetrarchia, no matter how much death and misery it caused.

I could not imagine what chance we had to prevent utter destruction, and once more, I considered running. But I had made my choice. Knowing Dreher and Vorosknecht's ridiculous reasoning only made me want to stop them more.

Apparently, as I lay shaking, Grandmother yelled at me from down the hall, and Papa had one of his spells, in which he cried out and writhed and saw hundreds of unconnected images. That night, once again, I wasn't there for my father.

When I was up, I almost avoided him again: I had gotten so accustomed to not seeing him every morning. But now he was mere steps away, and I made myself go say good morning.

"Oh! Oh, Kalynishka," he sighed from his bed. "Did I miss you last night? I don't remember if you were there."

I almost lied. "Sorry, Papa."

"I know, I know, but you're very busy these days. Running around, seeing people. Today I think you'll hear something important from . . ." He lowered his voice and looked around for Grandmother. ". . . the *other* one."

I raised my eyebrows. "You mean the other sooth—"

"Shhh! Shhhh shh shhh!"

"You aren't bothered by her presence?"

"I'm overjoyed, Kalynishka. She will do your job, and we will leave here."

"Soon, Papa."

"Except for the disaster that will end everything," he said, as though realizing he had forgotten a hat. "That is soon."

"Yes. Papa, do you remember Glaizatz Lake?" I smoothed his forehead; it was dry and warm.

"Of course! I didn't get to visit myself, but you and Mother did."

"Do you . . . know if there is anything beneath it?"

"Like what? I don't believe there's much. The water keeps going down, I've seen that. Down into an ever broadening emptiness. Does that help?"

"Perhaps. Are there spirits there?"

My father was quiet for a long time, leaning against the headboard. He looked out the window, at the wall, leaned over to look at the closed door. We had been speaking a mélange of all the languages we knew.

"Quiet this morning," he said. "Where is Mother, I wonder."

"Father. A spirit? Do you see it?"

"I don't like to look for spirits, Kalynishka. It ends badly."

"How so?"

"Badly."

He would tell me nothing more, and eventually I left. It was eerily quiet as I did so: Grandmother's door was closed, and I heard nothing from her room. I hoped she was sick or dead.

I knocked on Jördis' door, and heard nothing. I knocked again, louder. Still nothing. I thought to myself, *How would Dagmar knock on a door?* And pounded relentlessly, throwing my strength into each impact. Still nothing.

"Jördis? I just want to talk!"

Not a thing. So I went out and walked to Lenz's barracks, flanked by Yellows, for my protection.

Tea Cookies in a Dungeon

When I got down the winding stairs from Lenz's bedroom, into the hidden dungeon where we had once kept Klemens Gustavus, the door of the cage was open wide, and Gabor was performing pull-ups from the bar atop the doorway. At a small folding table, looking over a plate of mottled yellow and brown tea cookies, sat Lenz and Dagmar, the latter of whom was watching the stairs and looking intent.

"Kind of you to join us," said Lenz.

"Well, I've been busy," I replied. "But I couldn't think of anywhere else to go for cookies."

"A gift from Tural," said Lenz.

"We're old friends now!" laughed Gabor, his voice heavy with exertion.

"No tea?" I asked.

"Couldn't get it down without spilling," garbled Dagmar.

She had been so still when I came in, had looked so focused: this had been because of a mouth full of cookies. I began to suspect that she never had serious thoughts, but only wished to do violence, relax, and eat. I envied her that, and realized in that silly moment that I *wanted* her. In some capacity, anyway.

"I hope you've been productive," Lenz sighed. "Did you get the High General on our side?"

I laughed and laughed. "Oh, my sweet Lenz," I said, slumping into a chair. "High General Dreher will never be on our side."

"Hates Prince Friedhelm that much?"

"Well, yes, but that's not why. He's been in with Vorosknecht the whole time: one of the other 'powerful people' Selvosch mentioned to Friedhelm." I let my head fall back against the chair, staring up at the dark ceiling. "It feels like a lifetime ago. Our Dutiful Prince probably should have just joined them."

"Oh," said Lenz. Then: "Oh! Oh gods. Oh no."

I nodded.

He slumped back in his chair and looked at the ceiling. "I never thought he had that sort of lust for power."

"He doesn't," I replied. "He thinks he is doing it for the good of Rotfelsen."

Lenz groaned.

"At least," I added, "there is good news." This was the best way I could think of to frame another one of my great mistakes. "Queen Biruté is *not* part of their plot. You were right, Lenz: what I saw must have been her suspecting us of being *against* the King."

Lenz turned to glare at me. "I knew it," he said.

"Friedhelm said the same thing when I told him the opposite."

"Friedhelm is a fool," Lenz replied.

"Hey!" Dagmar bellowed through more cookies. "Watch what you say about our Prince!"

Lenz froze.

Dagmar swallowed, stared at him intently, and then broke into a laugh. "You should see your face! Of *course* Friedhelm is terrible."

I wondered if she was just having fun, or deflecting his ire from me.

"So then," huffed Gabor, still doing pull-ups, "at best, we are looking at a civil war with the Greens and Purples on one side, and the Reds and Yellows on the other?"

Lenz seemed to sag at the thought. "If we can convince the Queen to join us. And even then, I don't much like the odds. The Greens are so large . . ."

"No," I said. "We will end this before it becomes a war." I grabbed a few small cookies, each about the size of a child's thumb. "I want to avoid as much death as possible." I punctuated this by popping a cookie in my mouth.

"Whoops!" laughed Gabor, dropping down to the floor. "I suppose I shouldn't have killed the young man."

"It's fine," I said through crumbs. "It has ended up making my life easier, and apparently he meant all along to supplant the King in favor of Dreher and Vorosknecht and their ilk." I sighed and closed my eyes. I felt I was already forgetting Martin-Frederick's face. "I know he didn't believe in everything Dreher does, but what a disappointment that he was happy to let them destroy everything." I opened my eyes and looked at Gabor. "How is my assassin?"

"Bored!" Gabor replied. "I think I'd rather be up there where everyone is looking for me than safe down here. At least it would be interesting. I think that he"—Gabor pointed at Lenz—"keeps me in this prison because if I came upstairs, I'd clean his rooms. I'm not the most tidy, but without me, this one lives like an animal."

"That's enough," said Lenz.

I ate another cookie. "Martin-Frederick's death has been useful, but I'd still rather avoid more."

"Well," said Lenz, "we must nonetheless prepare for war and death. Do they trust you?"

"I think the High General does, and Selvosch. I have encouraged their . . . religious feelings."

"Their what?" asked Lenz.

"Gabor, Dagmar, do either of you speak Masovskani at all?" I asked.

They both shook their heads. I smiled apologetically. "Sorry, spy things. You know."

I gave Lenz a brief report of all that had transpired the night before, in Masovskani, to keep Olaf a secret. I did not see any glimmers of recognition in the others' eyes.

"This is an entire mess," Lenz sighed afterward.

Gabor, full of energy, began to run back and forth across the small room, jumping up against each wall and vaulting off it to run toward the other. It was tiring to watch. I laughed at myself for ever thinking I could have held him hostage. Dagmar's eyes followed him disinterestedly.

"When will you learn more?" asked Lenz, switching back to Rotfelsenisch.

I ate another cookie; they were lemon-hazelnut. "Can't say. They seem more interested in grabbing me when they want than in giving me a clearly drawn schedule. They want to show me something with the prisoners, down at the lake."

"So secretive!" laughed Gabor.

"We *are* in a hidden dungeon," offered Lenz.

"But with cookies," replied Dagmar.

"And they have a secret dungeon, too," said Lenz. "At Glaizatz Lake."

"Why can't we just assassinate the lords high and get it over with?" mumbled Dagmar.

"I'd love to," I sighed. "But they're always squirreled away with a host of guards. Perhaps when they next grab me, I can kill Dreher, and possibly Vorosknecht too, before I'm murdered, but there are more of them than those two. Did I mention Jördis was there, too?"

Lenz grunted.

"What if," Gabor puffed, walking over to the table, "you had help?"

"What? No," groaned Lenz. "We're going to prepare for a quick, decisive war. Maybe I'll ask Edeltraud von Edeltraud and the Gustavuses for help. If they can use their considerable fortunes to hire mercenaries, we'll have three armies, and we might even win."

"Let them capture me," said Gabor.

"What." Lenz glared back at him.

"Let me out," said Gabor. "Kalyna can turn me in to gain more trust, and then when she's taken down to Glaizatz Lake for one of their secret meetings, she releases me, and we kill all of them."

"Releases you," said Lenz, as he stood up, "from the secret underground prison? And then *you* kill *all* of them? Will you listen to yourself?"

"Dreher did say that many of the prisoners already down there are Greens or Purples who didn't want to betray the Tetrarchia," I said.

"Why, that's perfect!" laughed Gabor. "I can spend a few days in there, getting them riled up, you release us all, and there you have it!" He clapped his hands. "Dreher: dead. Vorosknecht: dead. The rest of their fools: dead."

"Absolutely not!" cried Lenz. "This is ludicrous."

Gabor narrowed his eyes, and I decided it would be good to end this argument. I changed the subject: "We should go speak to Chasiku."

"I agree," said Lenz. "*You* stay here, Gabor. Someone will bring you books."

"Not the ones you wrote, I hope," said Gabor.

"I knew I liked you," I said.

Tell Them Everything

I appreciated that Lenz was coming more and more to Chasiku with his questions about the future because it might mean he was thinking of me less for that sort of thing. I wondered if I should make everything easier and come clean, but that went against my very nature. I was a terrible, broken, failure of a soothsayer, but what would I be without even that?

When asked what she saw now, Chasiku said, "They will come for you soon, Kalyna."

"Who?" I asked.

"The big men: the sick one and the liar, you know."

"Who's sick?" asked Lenz.

"Dreher," I said. "Quite sick, in fact. How will they come for me?"

"To take you down . . . down there again, where it's dark and bright. To induct you into their mysteries. Or to kill you. Depending."

"When?" Lenz asked her.

"Soon. In the coming weeks. Maybe."

"I can use this to dismantle the regicides," I said. "With Gabor's—"

"No," grunted Lenz.

"Maybe," added Chasiku. "But your actions so far have only made destruction more likely." She said it as if it were obvious.

I was about to respond when there came a shrieking from the bottom of Chasiku's watchtower.

Lenz was surprised, and even Chasiku seemed baffled. I felt myself sag, my neck droop, my insides go numb. It was Grandmother.

"You let me up there right now, you worthless nothing!" Down at the bottom of the watchtower, Grandmother was a dot: a scarf with its hands on its hips. "You are a waste of your mother's life and my son's juices, and if you don't lower that thing right now I will—!"

"What?" I cried, leaning over the precipice, the pallet floating by my head. "You will *what*? Come up all those stairs by yourself, maybe?"

"I will tell them things about you!"

"Things?" murmured Lenz.

I wondered again if I should tell Lenz the truth about my Gift, get the game over with so I could focus on my new persona of reluctant spy.

I lowered that pallet. Grandmother glowered the whole way up, but I stared right back.

Once she was up there, Lenz began, "Nice to see you—"

"Quiet. This is all your fault," she snapped.

Lenz sighed.

"I," proclaimed Grandmother, a finger in the air, "have known my share of frauds—"

I winced.

"—and *you*"—she pointed at Chasiku—"are the most brazen I have ever seen!"

"Oh?" said Chasiku. "Please explain."

"Where do you come from, faker?"

"Kalvadoti on the North Shore of Skydašiai. My family is large and has been there for generations."

"You're a liar," said Grandmother. "No soothsayer stays in one place, none has so many children."

"You must have split off from us centuries ago," said Chasiku.

"*We*! From *you*!" Grandmother sputtered and gave her a look she had never given even me. "We trace our line back thousands of years."

"Humanity is old and so are you, but . . ." Chasiku looked puzzled.

"What?" I asked.

Chasiku's finger sort of spasmed as it pointed to Grandmother again and again. "Does she know about the end? She must."

"*She*," I said, "has foresworn her Gift."

"But does she know?" repeated Chasiku.

"Oh!" cried Grandmother. "The great-great-grandfather of all tricks! 'I know a thing but will not tell you.' Of course. Who are your bastard father and whore mother, fraud?"

"My family hate being around people too much to make rutting our profession," said Chasiku. "My parents cannot stand each other, and this"—she waved her hands around the room—"is already more people than I would ever like to be around at once. Someone must leave. I think it is you."

"That's not how the Gift works!" screamed Grandmother.

"Then I don't possess it. Leave."

"Kalyna," said Grandmother, "you are not to associate with any of these people again." She shook a fist at everyone; the joints in her arm popped. "This playing at intrigue and politics, or whatever you're trying to cram into the emptiness inside you, will make your father cry. Come, now!"

I looked at Lenz, annoyed, and Chasiku, bemused.

"No," I said. "I'm busy."

Grandmother was already halfway to the pallet when she realized what I said. She turned, spat, and glared at me with a look that still, in my adulthood, terrified me.

"If you don't stop this nonsense," she said, "I will *tell them*."

I stood very still. "Tell them what?"

"You know what, you freak, you waste of the gods' breath."

I stared at her and hoped I was not shaking. "Go on."

She put a gnarled hand to her forehead; a puff of air whistled out the end of her unlit pipe. "You stupid, *selfish* girl, I am trying to *help* you. Why do you never see that?"

I sat in silence. Everyone else was purposefully looking at the walls.

"I am trying," she continued, "to help keep you away from these . . . these *charlatans*! I did not think you could tarnish our family's legacy any further, but I was clearly wrong."

"Then go on," I said. "Help me. Tell them. Tell them everything about me. Go on."

"My own granddaughter . . ."

"Now. Tell them."

Grandmother narrowed her eyes, turned around to look at everyone else, one by one, then back at me. Her mouth tightened.

"You threatened to tell them," I said. "Do it. Do it or I'll never take you seriously again."

Her whole face puckered. She was at war with herself in a way I had never seen.

She said nothing, turned, and stormed out to the pallet. I heard her release the rope to descend. I hoped she'd fall too fast, and break everything.

Part of me was disappointed she hadn't told them.

"Well," said Lenz, "what was she going to tell us, hmm?"

"How should I know what a 'dark secret' is to a woman like that? Could have been anything: the first person I slept with, that time I stole a bauble when I was five, anything."

"Hm," he grunted. "You shouldn't let her treat you like that."

"It's fine," I said. "She'll die soon."

Chasiku coughed.

"Do you see her death on the edges of your vision too?" I asked her.

"Everyone I have seen in Rotfelsen has the stink of near death on them," said Chasiku. "Except her."

There was silence.

"When everything falls apart," Chasiku continued, very slowly, "when we fail, in every way we fail, *that one* will somehow survive."

I looked at where the pallet had been.

"The old demon will outlive us all," I sighed.

"And in one possibility," Chasiku continued, "she escapes on your shoulders, after you abandon us."

"I think I would rather die," I said.

DISPASSIONATE

After this, I was exhausted, and I slept for what felt like a day or so. I was awoken by Dagmar in the late morning of the next day.

"Up with you," she said. "Lenz has been talking to the Prince, and wants you to join them." She gallantly turned away while I got dressed.

As we left, I glanced at Jördis' closed door. In a carriage on our way to the palace, Dagmar, with one leg up across an empty seat, threw a sheaf of paper at me.

"Lenz wants you to read this on the way."

It was a new draft for Lenz's ongoing life's work, his secret histories, dated to the previous day. The ink was still wet at the end, and it was full of misspellings, from which I will spare you. The final draft would also probably involve Lenz himself much less. It read:

Today I told the Prince about Aljosanovna's discoveries regarding the identities of our regicides: he easily believes Dreher's part, but has not, of yet, managed to stop suspecting Queen Biruté. After that, he and I, with Olaf, who is now King Gerhold VIII, had a sad little meeting with Bozena and Klemens Gustavus, the Masovskan bankers. They were very obsequious, spoke a great deal about how honored they were to be "favored" by the King, and told us they were on our side without promising anything. It was a waste of time.

After that, Olaf took me to his apartments and asked for my help. Seeing him as the King, I said yes before knowing what he needed.

"Lenz," he said, "I have told Queen Biruté who I am."

I made quite a few exclamations. After Olaf convinced me to sit back down, I asked him why.

"Well, she and the King were hardly close, so she didn't mind how little we spoke to one another, but they were trying to have children, remember. When she first got suspicious, I said just what you told me: that I was worried I couldn't have children at all. But she's quite invested, after all and, with the real Gerhold dead, I couldn't just say 'I don't feel like it' forever, could I? She had begun replying with things like, 'Well, neither do I. But it's what we must do!'"

He spoke as though he was my underling, begging me to forgive him.

"Now Lenz, you see what a position I was in? It isn't often that a person is so straightforward about these relations, but when they are, how is one to respond? Keep turning her down and make her more suspicious, do her a great injustice by sleeping with her falsely, or tell the truth? What would you have done?"

I said something about ignoring her entirely.

"But we must attend so many functions together!" Olaf continued. "And besides, I thought that if I could get her to understand, perhaps we could unite the Reds. So I told her. I had to. I told her that I was meant to just be a quick replacement for a few weeks, and how out of my depth I felt now that I was King, and I admit I broke down a little bit."

He was quiet for a bit, and I asked him what she had said in return.

"She said, 'I have never had someone come up with such a lie to avoid sleeping with me.'"

"I'm sorry, Olaf. What?"

"And then she said that she knew it was a bad time for jokes, but couldn't help it."

Note: I must be sure to include this in my file on the Queen.

"Then," Olaf continued, "she got very serious and asked me what I looked like before. I didn't take her meaning, so she explained that if we're to have children together, and they look off, she'll be the one accused of adultery. Flesh-alchemy is too new for us to know whether it would make my . . . issue look like Gerhold or me. I told her I didn't think I had any great, hereditary disfigurements."

I was pulling out my hair at this point, but managed to tell him that she was not, in fact, one of the regicides.

"Oh good! That's very good. Because after that we had dispassionate relations."

"Fools," I said once I'd finished. "They're all fools. And so am I."

"I haven't read it," said Dagmar, "but I agree."

THE KING AND QUEEN REPAIR TO THEIR HUNTING LODGE

When I entered the Prince's study, I was greeted by the sound of someone screaming, "No, no, *no*! I will not allow it!"

It appeared that Prince Friedhelm was yelling at Olaf, who was sitting calmly on the couch. Lenz was at the Prince's desk, watching.

"I'm sorry, brother," replied Olaf, who looked entirely calm as the Prince stood over him, fuming, "but there's nothing to allow. It's decided. Unless you outrank both myself *and* the Queen."

"The fraud and the traitor, you mean!" cried Prince Friedhelm. "Lenz, talk some sense into him!"

Lenz shrugged.

"Don't you want a niece or nephew, brother?" sang out Olaf. "I'll be back soon! Or at least in three weeks, for the Eve of the Council."

"Olaf," asked Lenz, "what exactly are you and the Queen planning?"

"A vacation!" laughed Olaf. He looked right past Friedhelm, at us. "Do you know of Lady Starost, by any chance?"

"I believe I've written about her," said Lenz. "There were rumors about her and the Queen."

"All true," laughed Olaf. "They're quite in love and have been for years, but always with the understanding that Biruté would also be, ah, intimate with the King. For the sake of heirs."

Lenz clapped a hand over his eyes, as though trying to not see what was happening before him. "Did you tell this Starost about . . . ?"

"About me? Oh no, of course not!" Olaf laughed. "Biruté is keeping our secret. But she told Starost that she and the King—which is me—are beginning to . . . get along much better. Lady Starost was overjoyed because she had been worried about the lack of an heir, and suggested we all take a trip together, to get away from palace life and be a bit freer. Lady Starost also invited along a man she knows whom I've found quite handsome, and—"

"This is a travesty," muttered Prince Friedhelm. He began to pull at his hair. "The bastard child of a fake, a traitor, and possibly two degenerate, childish nobles will doom the Tetrarchia."

"I thought you wanted the King to have children," I said.

Friedhelm rounded on me, glaring wildly. "*Royal* children. *Rotfelsenisch* royal children. Our family is divinely appointed."

"Biruté doesn't wish to adopt your bastards, brother," said Olaf.

"Of course not," spat Friedhelm. "Because she wants to usurp you and control the kingdom."

"Not at all!" laughed Olaf. "And we can worry about that later. This will just be a nice time: like one of those Skydašian farces, with all the running around and slamming of doors, except that we'll all know why we're there, and no one will be jealous! I hope."

"That sounds," I began, "like so much more fun than what I will be doing."

"Oh? And what's that?" asked Olaf.

"Does no one else care about what is happening here?" cried the Prince.

"Infiltrating a cult," I replied to Olaf. "But not a fun one. They just think Rotfelsenisch people are better than everyone else."

"Ew," said Olaf.

Friedhelm walked over to his desk and sat down, glaring over it.

"You," he said to Olaf, attempting to be calm, "are the King of Rotfelsen. The King simply cannot have this sort of scandal." He pressed his hand to his face, massaging his eyelids and letting out a long grunt. "If he could, then, well . . . I would be King."

There was silence at that. The implications were lost on none of us. Olaf, finally, stopped smiling and looked seriously at Friedhelm.

"There will be no scandal," he said, "Your Highness. The King and Queen will be on holiday together to reconcile themselves to one another, and therefore better represent Rotfelsen at the Council of Barbarians. The only whispers will concern the ways in which the royal union was weak before, but is now strengthened." Olaf sounded positively responsible.

"Honestly, Your Highness," Lenz added, "with everything we now know about the regicides, having Olaf and Biruté away from the palace is a good idea. Safer for them."

Friedhelm was quiet. Thoughtful. I wondered if he was thinking of having us killed. I thought again of the flesh-alchemists who had "made" Olaf, of the doctor who had looked at the teeth in poor Gerhold's disembodied head, of all of the Prince's earlier "Recourses" who were no longer alive.

"This once," Friedhelm grunted.

Olaf stood, and nodded.

Just then, Queen Biruté came in and sang out, "Dearest, we're ready to go!"

"*Sister*," said Prince Friedhelm, "please keep the royal reputation in mind."

Biruté looked him in the eye. "That, coming out of your mouth, is truly the strangest thing I have ever heard." She took the hand of her husband's doppelgänger. "But I always do."

"See you at the Council," said Olaf, as they moved toward the door. "We've told the Reds, jointly, to listen to you in all things related to security, Your Highness. Tell everyone we'll be at the hunting lodge, shooting giant rats."

"And where will you actually be?" asked Lenz.

Biruté put a finger to her lips, and the two left, chattering. At least someone was happy, in all this.

If we could get this all sorted out, and save the Tetrarchia, I rather envied the new life Olaf would have in front of him. But of course, living outside of what was normally acceptable was much easier for a king: Lenz and Gabor only wanted to live quietly together, and that had been interrupted by the Prince. And yet Lenz and Gabor still had the protection of their ranks, and could live their lives much easier than many others. All I had to do was think back on women I had known to begin feeling resentful of Olaf and his luck.

The Prince immediately turned toward me, as a new outlet for his anger. "Well?"

"Well what, Your Highness?"

"What Lenz told me: that you're in good with Dreher and the regicides, and that *she* is not one of them. Is this true? I begin to believe I can trust no one."

"It is," I said.

"Tell me everything that happened."

So I did, including Chasiku's visions of my soon being down in Glaizatz Lake with Dreher, Vorosknecht, and the rest. I only left out the great, terrifying, encroaching doom that was beating down the doors of the Tetrarchia.

"Well," said Friedhelm, "find a way to get someone else down there!" He was sweating, his hair flopping everywhere. "And *kill them*! Do I have to decide everything for you?!"

Lenz nodded curtly, and we left. On the way out, Lenz managed a smile.

"I convinced Olaf that the vacation was his idea," he said. "If he told the Queen, who knows who else he might tell."

"I was worried about that," I replied. "What if he tells his traveling companions after all?"

"Either," said Lenz, "the Tetrarchia will be crushed and it won't matter, or we'll be in a better place of power to protect our secrets."

"*Your* secrets. If we succeed, you're letting me go."

"If it is at all possible."

It felt silly, meaningless even, to discuss what we would do after we won. I certainly felt the crushing weight of our inevitable failure bearing down on us, and I had to believe that Lenz did as well. Now, I would just try to enjoy the ride.

KNOW YOUR PLACE

That evening, I was attacked.

Now that I could traverse the palace grounds armed, I admit I had gotten too comfortable. Certainly, violence sometimes broke out in the vast flat gardens and uneven crags of the surface, but it was always of the dueling or partisan brawl variety, and it wasn't as though Martin-Frederick would have a group of Greens start shooting now. The same comfort that had led me to get used to a bed and walls, to alcohol and good food, told me that this was a place where I was relatively safe, up until the rock would shatter beneath us all. Besides, there were Reds everywhere, trying to clear out the troublemakers for the Council of Barbarians.

The point is, I was not being as careful as I would have been, for example, on my way to Gniezto from the Great Field. When I heard running, I assumed it was just a group of Reds on their way to do something important, to the extent that I thought about it at all. So I passed, unthinkingly, behind a great, high wall of shrubbery and was punched in the left side of my face, wobbled, and was shoved to the rotrock below.

"Not the face, horse-fucker!" someone hissed. The voice jumped at "fucker," suggesting it belonged to the person delivering the kick to my ribs.

I twisted and caught the next kick in my hip. It wasn't dark, but I could barely see my attackers: five or six, pink skin, brown clothing, a flutter of purple here and there. They kept kicking at me as I tried to pull away.

One of them leaned down to grab me, and I kicked their chin with both feet. I turned this into a painful roll backward, pressing my spine hard into the rock below, but managed to move up into a weak crouch and draw my sickle. I held it above my head, looking up at them through the curve of its blade.

The five attackers were dressed normally but their purses, pommels, and various other trimmings and accessories tended toward purple. One near the back was holding his chin, which made me smile.

The man in front was familiar, but I didn't place him immediately. His hand was on the purple tassel that hung from his rapier's guard.

"Listen," he said in the voice that had grunted *horse-fucker*, "we don't like you much, and we are here to knock you around. But you come at us armed, and we will have to do the same, and then you might just die. We don't mean to kill you."

"Just 'knock me around,'" I spat.

He nodded, and laughed at nothing.

My breathing came with difficulty, my body already ached, and I felt as though my lips were swollen, whether or not they were. Then I remembered where I'd seen him.

"You're one of Vorosknecht's," I croaked. "I saw you at the lake. You were never more than two feet from him."

"Sure, sure, but I am off-duty."

"Of course you are."

"Well?" He drew his sword an inch from its sheathe.

What a terrible decision he had given me. Vorosknecht wanted me to know he had sent these soldiers to humble me, and to know he had *officially* done no such thing. I ground my teeth and gripped my sickle tightly. The urge to crash amongst them and cut up their faces was strong. They had attacked me. Why not take every possible retaliation? Maybe I could even win.

But these were not bulky henchmen in a too-small alley. These were trained soldiers who had been chosen for this, and I was already hurt.

My hand shook as I lowered my sickle. I sneered. Even then I considered stepping forward and raising it back up into their leader's gut. At least he would be done with.

I dropped the sickle.

Need I tell you what happened next? I acquitted myself as well as can be expected from one who's been beaten and chased all her life, in every corner of our land: I punched and kicked and bit and threw myself upon them with great tenacity. They followed their directive to avoid my face as best they could. At one point, the man whose chin I'd kicked got frustrated enough that he pulled a dagger, and the leader punched him in that same chin for it.

But don't let me sound appreciative. They beat me savagely, and though in the end some had bruises, bloody faces, and (I hope) cracked ribs, I was the one on the ground, holding my stomach, coughing and moaning. I couldn't speak, I felt as though I'd never again move or breathe. My knees were pulled up, my arms were around my midsection. I stared at the soles of their boots.

"There we are," said the leader. "Now you understand, we simply do not like a mind-witch. You see?"

I gurgled.

"Our master, of course, knows nothing about this and would not condone it if he did."

I coughed. In my mind, it was an insulting laugh.

"But," he continued, "if somehow he *did* know, and somehow he *did* condone it, and wanted me to give you a message—and let me remind you that he does not—that message would most certainly be:" He leaned down, his mouth by my ear, and I prayed for the strength to turn and bite him. "'Know your place.'"

I coughed many more times. I wanted to say that the message was clear enough without words. I also wanted to threaten this man's mother with murder. I couldn't speak. They left.

DAGMAR

"Well, they certainly knew their business," said Doctor Aue.

It was the day after my beating, and I was sitting up in bed against a wall of pillows while Doctor Aue dabbed at my ribs and stomach. Lenz had insisted on bringing his favorite doctor, and he now stood a few feet behind her, his mustache matching the frowning line of his mouth. At the door stood two Yellows: Behrens, the sharpshooter who had saved me back in Masovska, and Dagmar, the tall one. They assured me that Jördis was not home next door.

"What do you mean?" Lenz asked the doctor, before I could.

"You said," she answered, to me, "they were meant to send a message, and not to damage you irreparably. They wanted you to be presentable, yes?"

I nodded, and somehow even *that* hurt.

"Well, I think they have at most broken one rib. I think! Hard to say without opening you up!" She laughed at this. "I'll bind it, and you should be reasonably well in a few days, if very sore. As I say, they knew their business." She smiled at my stomach, not my face.

"Well, good for them," I croaked.

"Quite! You will heal entirely. Eventually. I expect."

To this day, the middle finger on my right hand is regularly sore and easily hurt. I think I tried to block a boot with that hand and failed. Aue was a good doctor, as far as I could tell, but a doctor is no more a prophet than I.

"Gentlemen must turn their heads," Doctor Aue called out in a singsong. Lenz and Behrens did so as she lifted my nightshirt farther to inspect my chest. She made a pained inhalation and said, "This will hurt for some time."

I nodded.

"But only bruises. Deep bruises," she added. Doctor Aue dropped my nightshirt back down and tucked it into the covers around my thick wool stockings before singing, "All done, gentlemen!"

Lenz and Behrens looked at me again, and both seemed worried. I thought they were being silly: I wasn't dead, after all, and I had taken worse beatings in my time.

"Rest," said Doctor Aue, "rub this on it." She set down a jar of dark green gunk strung with lines of pink. "You will know to put on more when your midsection stops smelling terrible. Also, avoid spirits, which thin the blood, rich foods, which thicken the blood, and dark tea, which quickens the blood. These indulgences tell the gods you don't care about your health."

I nodded blankly. Doctor Aue leaned forward to pat my shoulder affectionately and, though I was dressed, her hand touched the one spot that wasn't bruised. She was a good doctor.

"Really," she said, "you'll be fine. They wanted you to know that they *could* break you, but they didn't want to, yet."

"Is it surprising that this doesn't make me feel better?"

Doctor Aue looked reassuringly in my eyes, and then away. "I suppose not, but you'll be alright this time."

"Thank you."

"And you *might just* have had this coming, after what you did to my poor assistants."

I said nothing, but she smiled in a friendly fashion.

As Doctor Aue got up to leave, there was a knock on my door. It was Tural, pushing Papa in a chair that glided (and spun, and teetered, and got stuck) on little wheels. When I saw Tural, I began, casually I hope, to lace up the open front of my nightshirt. I didn't want him to see me blotched with bruises.

"Nice to see you again, Aljosa Vüsalavich," said the doctor as she passed my father on the way out.

"Yes, yes, you too," he replied, with no idea who she was.

"Kalyna," said Lenz, "your subterfuge isn't working."

Papa was rolled up to my bed to hug me. I saw Grandmother glaring in through the door from the hallway. She stood there, silent and unmoving, like an angel of death.

"What do you mean?" I replied to Lenz, "The doctor said I'll be fine!" Papa nestled into me as I spoke, gripping me intently.

"And next time?" said Lenz.

"There won't be a next time. I have everything planned." This was a lie. "Tural, do you mind giving us the room?"

"I am sure I don't want to know," he said.

As Tural left, he tried to talk Grandmother into leaving with him, but she remained in the door, still as a statue, and glared. Finally, she slowly lifted her arm and pointed at me, before silently mouthing the words, "Got what you deserved."

Dagmar, at the door, looked at me inquisitively, as if to ask whether Grandmother should be shut out of the room. I almost shook my head, before realizing that I did not have to say no.

Is this warmth in my gut what power *feels like? Or am I bleeding internally?*

"What you deserved," Grandmother repeated, this time making just the rattling beginnings of sound in her throat, and dragging out the last syllable. She trained that evil look on me, sucking air in through her nose. Papa still held me tightly.

I nodded slightly at Dagmar, who looked down at Grandmother, shrugged, and moved into the doorway, blocking the old demon from view entirely. Then she closed the door, slowly, in Grandmother's face.

Gods and hells and Ancients and monsters, did that ever feel *glorious*.

"Unsettling," said Lenz.

"I can do nothing about her, but I have everything else planned," I said. "All of this"—I indicated my midsection with both hands—"is proof I've shaken up Vorosknecht." Papa hugged me tighter and my body ached, but I wasn't about to stop him.

"Shaken him up?" asked Lenz. "Wasn't he supposed to trust you?"

"He did this because he's intimidated by my influence over Dreher, not because he suspects. He's scared of me, so I can force him into a compromise."

"Influence," said Lenz, bracing a hand on my bed and leaning over it, to get the weight off his bad leg, "that you can use to unobtrusively learn their plans in order for us to counteract them. When we have our war."

"Well yes, *if* I fail at stopping all this first." I grinned. "Trust me. We're partners!"

Papa finally looked up from hugging me and declared that he needed to sleep. When the door was opened, so that Tural could come and get him, Grandmother was gone. The door closed, and I was now alone in the room with the military types.

"Well, *partner*," said Lenz, "will you please stay home and recover?"

"I need to do something first. Then I'll rest."

"Fine," said Lenz. "I would like you in relative working order on the Eve of the Council."

The Eve of the Council was the night before the first official meeting of the Council of Barbarians. It was marked by a feast, and its full name was The First Hallowed Evening Proclaiming the Future Thaw Upon Which the Divine Monarchic Council of Pure Blessed Blood for the Furtherance of the Greater Eastern Tetrarchia as a Bulwark to Its Devious Neighbors and a Net Spread to Catch the Dropped Blessings of Its Gods, Will Meet and Present Themselves, Weaponless and Free, for Inspection Before Falling Upon Food and Drink with Great Strength. It was when we supposed the regicides would strike, and it was about three weeks away.

It was also when the very Tetrarchia would crumble, and everyone I knew would die. And we still did not know exactly *how* it would happen.

"I intend to stop them before that," I said.

"Well, good for you," he said. "Did you know two of the other three Tetrarchic monarchs are already in Rotfelsen?"

I did not.

"We've received word," Lenz continued. "Their unwieldy entourages are already dragging their way through our tunnels, stopping at cities, shopping for the fête, bickering with one another."

"Great," I said.

"Kalyna, stopping this on your own, beforehand, is *stupid*. Our armies are the solution."

"That's not what Prince Friedhelm told us to do."

"He's a fool."

"I know."

"Whatever you do, Kalyna, I'm not letting you run around without protection anymore, and *that* is final. You need a bodyguard."

I think he expected me to protest, but I was very sore. "That sounds lovely," I said.

Lenz smiled very genuinely. "Dagmar," he said, "please keep an eye on Kalyna."

"Why not?" said the lean, broad-shouldered Yellow leaning against the door. She winked at me again, and I prayed she would never know I had gone weeks knowing her only as "Dugmush."

"Dagmar is very good," said Lenz, "and isn't known to be *mine* more than any other Yellow."

It was easy to see why: Dagmar always seemed too relaxed for power games. Yet here she was.

"And you, Dagmar," I said, "you're already all caught up on the . . . ah . . ."

"Destruction of the Tetrarchia because we don't know why, ma'am?" she said, smiling. "Yes, ma'am."

"Good," I said, tripping over possibilities in my mind. "Good, good. If you, Dagmar, can act as my loyal guard, who would happily go Green with me, then they might let you come down to Glaizatz when the regicides meet. If I have someone who can fight—"

"Kalyna," said Lenz, "I'm giving you a bodyguard, not an assassin."

"Are you sure?" I asked.

"Whichever," yawned Dagmar.

PURPLE HALLWAY

Later that same day, not long after rubbing Doctor Aue's pungent goop all over my bruises a second time, Dagmar and I stood in the purple hallway outside Court Philosopher Vorosknecht's study in the Sunset

Palace. I hadn't seen the place since I was dragged there during the Winter Ball.

"Is it true," asked an on-duty Purple, leaning toward Dagmar, his voice dripping with his intentions, "that Prince Friedhelm is trying to quit his addiction to young boys? Or is he as ravenous as ever?" He grinned widely.

"Why should I know or care?" asked Dagmar.

The Purple was confused by her answer for all of a half second. Then she broke his nose with her fist. I liked Dagmar more and more.

The Purple slid down the wall and sat on the floor, moaning and holding his nose. It had twisted in a new direction before he grabbed it, trying to keep it on his face. The other Purples surrounded Dagmar, who threw her hands in the air and laughed. It wasn't a mean or cruel laugh: very genuine.

"What?" she asked. "Isn't this how it works? I'd ask for all your dueling cards in a line, one after the other, if I could, but your master must change the laws first. Women can't duel, so I broke his nose." She shrugged. "Seemed fair."

The Purples grumbled to one another but did nothing else. I, in my blue dress, and with no yellow accents, pushed right past them and pounded on the door to Vorosknecht's study, since we hadn't yet been announced to him.

The door was opened by the man who had led my beating the night before. His gasp was suitably satisfying. We pushed past him, to where Vorosknecht stood behind his desk, next to poor old Meregfog's skeleton. The man who'd opened the door ran back to stand at the Court Philosopher's other side.

"Kalyna Aljosanovna, what a pleasant surprise," sighed Vorosknecht.

"You're a fool," I said, walking right up to his desk. Dagmar stood behind me.

"Whatever do you mean?" asked Vorosknecht.

I put my hands on his desk and leaned over it, getting my face much too close to his. "That you're a fool, Your Brightness."

His face twisted as he smelled the awful goop smeared on my bruises.

"Kalyna Aljosanovna, I don't—"

"I am one of Dreher's advisors now. You don't want me as your enemy."

"What are you talking about?"

I looked at the Purple behind him. I could remember him kicking me, could remember seeing that face obscured by his fists. I grinned, which I'm sure looked ghastly. "What's your name, soldier?"

Silence.

"Oh, come now, I'll learn it anyway, the next time we regicides are all together!"

"Keep your voice down!" hissed Vorosknecht.

"You're his personal guard, I'll know you soon enough. Your name."

Vorosknecht nodded.

"Alban," murmured Alban.

"I'm sorry?" I said, leaning toward him.

"Alban!" he said louder.

"I *am* sorry, I don't hear you. Vorosknecht, your man doesn't know how to speak to one of High General Dreher's adv—"

"Alban, *ma'am!*" yelled Alban.

I stood up straight and smiled. I'm sure Dagmar also smiled.

"You should have Alban here killed for assaulting me," I said. I lifted my right hand in a supposed sign to Dagmar, although we had worked out nothing of the kind. "My woman will do it for you, if you like." I heard her step forward. Alban flinched.

So *this* was how having a henchman felt! No wonder everyone up here liked it so much.

"What is this all about, Kalyna Aljosanovna?" asked Vorosknecht.

"Well, either your man and his friends assaulted me for no reason, in which case we have them executed, or you sent them to do so. We both know the answer, of course, and it was an idiotic thing to do."

"Why?"

I breathed out in exaggerated annoyance. It was a good way to cover wincing from the pain of my beating. "Because *I* am the only person capable of wresting Dreher from your control over that Soul of the Nation garbage."

Vorosknecht stood still and straight as Chasiku's watchtower. "Go on."

"What's to go on with? You told him about it, I have *seen* it. Maybe he'll listen to you over me, but we all know the fanciful theorist and the no-nonsense leader will be at odds once the King is deposed. I'm the safer option. Especially because I haven't got an army."

Vorosknecht grinned. "Saw it, did you?"

"You don't believe me?"

"You weren't the first to visit me today," he said.

He wasn't still anymore. In fact, the Court Philosopher began to walk idly along the side of his desk, toward the purple bust of himself and the glass liquor cabinet. He was comfortable now. What had I missed?

"Well," I said, "that stands to reason."

"As a matter of fact"—he drew out his words interminably—"you weren't the first *of your family* to visit me today."

"Oh?" I managed to squeak.

"Your grandmother had a very interesting story to tell me about you."

She wouldn't, I thought.

"I admit," sighed Vorosknecht as he wheeled toward me, "even *I* never thought you were so bad as a"—he cleared his throat—"'broken shitworm who killed her own mother.' Did I get that right?"

She had told him. The old demon had really told him.

LIE TO EVERYONE

One day when I was seven years old, we were camped somewhere that may have been Masovska, and may have been Quruscan. We were traveling from one to the other, and had stopped for the night, setting up camp a good distance from the road, using the same tents that would be packed up in Papa's room at the servant house twenty years later.

Back then, I had no idea my father was holding the pieces of himself together just enough to care for me. In my memory, he was as strong and smart as anyone I have ever known; stronger and smarter, really. I remember helping him pitch camp as he walked around on his hands, hands with which he drove each stake into the ground with one blow (or so I recall it).

I remember that after the work of setting camp was done, I jumped onto Papa's back and loudly insisted he gambol about with me. He plucked me off. His beard was still brown then.

"Oh, Kalynishka, Kalynishka, no. Papa must rest!"

"Did you always not have legs, Papa?"

"Now, Kalynishka," he laughed. "You know you should not ask people questions like that."

"I know!" I cried. "I did not ask 'people,' I asked *you!*"

He patted my head. "Kalynishka, I did once have legs, but I don't remember them."

"And you don't miss them?"

"How could I miss what I never knew? And I can still beat you in a race, Kalynishka!"

I suspect my father would still have been faster than me when I was twenty-seven, if his mind had not fallen apart in the intervening decades.

At seven, I jumped up and down. "Let's race!"

"Not now, my love, not now."

He walked on his hands over to a rock beneath a tree and lay down to rest. This exchange, innocuous though it was, has always stayed with me, and became a particularly potent memory after Papa stopped pretending he was fine. As I look back now, it seems he probably *was* just tired that day, but to myself at, say, thirteen, it was a horrifying presentiment of what was to come, heavy with meaning that may not have been there.

On that day when I was seven, it had been only two weeks since Grandmother first told me I killed my mother. Of course, at that age, two weeks is a very long time, so I felt I had been wrestling with this my whole life, and also that Grandmother *must* have forgotten the conversation.

This was why, later that night, I took a walk out in the nearby grasses, thought for a long time, and then came running back, shouting excitedly.

"Papa! Grandmother! Papa! Grandmother! I'm fixed! I'm fixed!"

Papa, sated, was taking a second nap by the fire. Grandmother sat nearby and grabbed my shoulder when I was close enough. Her fingers gouged and hurt me.

"Quiet! Don't wake my son with your nonsense games!" she hissed.

"But, Grandmother," I said, trying to lower my voice, but each word ending higher than it had began, "I have the Gift! I was out in the field and there was a buzzing in my head like a bee was in there, but it was not a bee, and then I fell down and saw a vision and I have *the Gift!*"

374 | ELIJAH KINCH SPECTOR

Papa slept through my excitement. Grandmother looked down at me, puffing smoke through her pipe.

"Really," she said.

I nodded.

"What did you see?"

"I saw that . . . next year, Gniezto will have great rains!"

"Really?" She smiled, relaxing her grip. "That's good!"

I grinned and nodded. I felt a wave of relief: she believed me, and now I would be normal.

"For how long?" she asked, still smiling. "Will it come in from the north or the south?"

"Uh . . ."

"Go on, girl, will it be just enough to help the crops, or so much that it washes them out? Will there be thunder and lightning? Wind? Hail? Will it be early or late spring?" Her smile was hard.

"Well . . . that is . . ."

"When you felt this," she continued, shaking me, "did the 'bee' in your head seem angry or placid? Did it hurt? Did it feel nice? Did you lose your balance or decide to lie down to better concentrate?"

"I . . . I don't know, Grandmother, I—"

Her smile finally dropped, and she slapped me hard. I almost fell into the fire.

"Don't ever waste our time and our hopes with this nonsense again, useless child," she said through her teeth. She hit me again. "To survive, you must lie to everyone. But not to us."

OTTO

Twenty years later, in the Court Philosopher's study, it seemed Grandmother had actually told someone else the truth.

"What do you have to say about that, Kalyna Aljosanovna?" asked Vorosknecht. "Going to deny it, defame your ailing old grandmother?"

Ailing, indeed.

Vorosknecht walked right up to me, exploiting his height to make me look up. Which I did, right into his eyes.

"No," I said. "I never had the Gift. It's a sham. My father and grandmother do, but not I."

I had considered continuing my lie, no matter the evidence, as I always did. But the Court Philosopher had made up his mind, and I didn't need us to spend the next ten minutes arguing. Better to turn this new wrinkle toward my original aim.

Besides, even to someone I hated, it felt *good* to say that out loud.

Dagmar, unflappable as always, did not seem to react to this.

"Ah-ha," said Vorosknecht slowly. "Ah-ha." He drummed his fingers on his desk. "How did you know about the persimmons?"

"I guessed. You're not very subtle."

"Subtle or not, I've outed you."

I shrugged. "And? It changes nothing."

"Unless I tell Dreher."

I grinned. "And deprive him of his greatest proof that the Soul of the Nation, which will guide Rotfelsen into his hands, exists? You know he's clinging to that mightily now—you made him too great a fanatic, *fool*. Now you just might lose him."

Vorosknecht looked irritated, but he no longer looked smug.

"Listen, Otto," I sighed, putting a hand on the Court Philosopher's shoulder, and shaking him. Alban stepped forward, as though I were attacking his master. "Otto, Otto. We're a pair of frauds, you and I, and we're also the pillars bolstering our great High General's faith in *a magical lake spirit that will lead the pink men to glory*. A ridiculous notion, but at this point, if either pillar is shattered, well, his belief may never return."

Vorosknecht pulled his shoulder from my hand and backed away.

"Oh, Otto! Don't be like that!" I laughed.

"If you didn't leave this room alive," he said, "the High General could still believe you had seen it."

Dagmar stepped in front of me. I rested a hand on my sickle, which was on my right hip, and the other on a rapier, which was on my left. I didn't know how to use the sword, but it looked good.

"In that case," I said, "Dagmar here could just kill you. She can do it before Alban gets over the desk."

Dagmar's hand was on her sword, two inches of steel showing. Alban didn't move.

"You would both be executed for it," said Vorosknecht.

"But Your Brightness," said Dagmar, "once I'm caught, I'll tell the tribunal, honestly and truthfully, that I lost control of myself when you questioned my mistress' honor." She smiled. "I will swear up and down that she called on me to stop, even as I butchered you like a hog. Oh, I'll be executed, but Kalyna will face no consequences, and you'll have traded your life only for *mine*."

I could have kissed Dagmar. Vorosknecht looked angry, and genuinely shaken.

"Stand down, Dagmar," I said. "I want His Brightness to be my friend. We have the same purpose: we want to keep Dreher in the dark."

Vorosknecht chewed his lip.

"Well," I said, "not my *friend*, but you know."

"What do you *want*?" asked Vorosknecht.

"When last I saw you, you said something, mockingly, about inducting me into the mysteries of your Soul of the Nation cult."

"Yes . . ."

"Induct me!"

"Dreher is already planning on it," he spat. "Even though our mysteries are *currently* limited to Rotfelsen's best, brightest, and richest. You are not they."

"Lucky me. I expect it will come in the middle of the night?"

"As it did for him, yes," said Vorosknecht. He was wary, but he was answering me.

"Then don't fight him on it. Warn me ahead of time when it will be, prevail on Dreher to let me bring my woman here"—a thumb back toward Dagmar—"for protection, and prepare me for the mysteries, so that mine will be *particularly* auspicious. Then I will *see* the Soul of the Nation, way down in Glaizatz Lake, ordering its servants to . . . well, whatever you like." I grinned.

Vorosknecht rubbed his beard.

"*And*"—I sweetened the pot—"I can give you Lenz and the heretical works about the Soul in his library, which may undermine your own . . . interpretation."

This was probably a cruel offer. I made it nonetheless.

"Alban here told me to know my place," I said. "Well, I do. It is beside Dreher."

"So the mysteries, your thug here, my trust, Dreher's trust, secrets, the schedule," grunted Vorosknecht. "And then the Soul of the Rotfelsen Nation will certainly want our victory over the Tetrarchia, and a return to true Rotfelsenisch philosophy."

I nodded. "Yes, sure, whatever that means."

"Anything *else* you need from me, fraud? Or will all of that be enough?"

"Just your understanding that if Alban ever comes close to me again, Dagmar will kill him."

"Happily and easily," said Dagmar.

Court Philosopher Otto Vorosknecht, His Very Brightness, looked at me for a long time.

"I may do some of this," he said, "if it suits me."

Dagmar and I

As we walked in the shadow of the Sunset Palace, I cleared my throat loudly, and Dagmar said nothing. The rush was leaving me, and I was in a lot of pain.

"Dagmar," I finally began, "the truth of what I admitted in there, about myself . . ."

"I don't much care, ma'am," said Dagmar.

"Don't call me 'ma'am' when we aren't putting on a show. You work for Lenz, not me. And you can be honest."

She turned to me as she walked and grinned. "In that case, I don't much care. I *was* being honest. I became a soldier for gold and excitement, and had little of the second until you showed up. I don't care what you are or aren't." She winked at me.

"You have got to stop doing that."

"Is that an order, ma'am?" She did it again.

"No."

"Good."

We walked back in silence.

Perfectly Safe

"Dagmar!" snapped Lenz. "I thought you were supposed to keep her safe!"

"She's fine!" laughed Dagmar, presenting me with two open hands as though I were a pie she had baked. "Perfectly safe!"

"Well, what's done is done. Now you can be inducted into their mysteries and learn more about their plot."

"I can do more with Gabor."

"You mean his silly notion about getting arrested on purpose?"

Normally, I would have gotten uncomfortably close to Lenz, to make him uncomfortable. But I knew I smelled bad, and we were now on the same side.

"Yes," I replied. "He's already in danger; let's make use of his danger."

"Seems to me," said Lenz, "you already have. Martin-Frederick's death has benefited you very much."

"It's benefited *us* very much, Lenz! And with more of Gabor's help, we can stop this before it starts. We can save *everyone*."

"We get Gabor arrested, and he goes into that secret prison."

"As opposed to the one you have him in now? And we'll wait for Vorosknecht to tell me when I'm being inducted, so Gabor will only be imprisoned for a few days! He's a strong man, and it was his idea. The Tetrarchia's doom concerns him as much as it does us, and you are not his father or his master."

"I should never have told you how formidable he is," said Lenz.

"You two have a secret love; you don't get much chance to brag about him."

He smiled at that. "Kalyna, I want what you're proposing to be possible, I do. But Gabor isn't enough." He sighed and shook his head. "This would be a much easier decision if it were our only choice, but if you fail at this, and then we *win* a battle on the Eve of the Council, I must face a life alone."

Lenz wasn't used to discussing these feelings. He didn't tear up, and his voice didn't quaver, he just stared forward and spoke softly. I felt guilty.

"Then let's even the odds," I said. "We'll have him arrested with, say, ten Yellows. Dreher said they can always make use of more."

"'Make use'? Gods, what will they do with them? Why can't you just risk your own life? Mine would be harder without you, but I wouldn't miss you."

"Well, you should not have—"

"Kidnapped you, yes. And you'll never let it go."

I nodded.

"But," said Dagmar, "if he hadn't kidnapped you, none of us would know what was happening, and I'd be guarding a bathroom right up until the Tetrarchia crumbled."

I couldn't very well argue with that. I still wished that I had been in the Bandit States this whole time.

KALYNA THE SOOTHSAYER | 379

MY RECOVERY

Since Vorosknecht and I were now allies in fooling Dreher, I didn't want the High General to see that I'd been beaten up, so I finally went home. The hope was that I had done enough to be allowed a few days' recovery before diving back into my stupid plan. I could wait for other people to respond to *me*, for once.

I eased myself carefully into bed and began to rub Doctor Aue's terrible goop onto my torso. Then what I most feared came to pass: Grandmother barged into the room.

I readied myself for a long string of invective, followed by a story, followed by what exactly she had told Vorosknecht and why, along with how she had thought to go to him in the first place, and how she had gained an audience.

Instead, Grandmother simply glared and said, "We are leaving now."

"No," I said.

"You deserved that."

"What?" I asked with feigned innocence.

"Having your flawed nature exposed to the purple man."

"No." I shook my head.

And she barged right back out.

I felt my whole body relax at her absence. Let her continue betraying me. I didn't care anymore. (Of course I cared, but less.)

Doom, war, destruction, and who knew what else was coming, but for three glorious days I padded about the servant house, slept a great deal, spent time with Papa, hardly saw Grandmother, flirted with Tural (or at least thought I was), and did not go outside. I communicated with anyone who didn't live in that house by messenger. Even without brandy, dark tea, or heavy foods, it was delightful.

Jördis was barely at home during this time, but I did manage to catch her, and she smiled as though nothing had happened, even after I closed the door to her room, and we were alone.

"Your boss doesn't much like me," I told her.

"Well, we already knew that, didn't we?"

I opened my blouse, which was an incredibly uncouth thing to do, and showed her how bruised I was.

"*Ouch,*" she said. "I am sorry, Kalyna, but you know how he is. He doesn't much like being challenged and, well, your involvement in his affairs may be more challenging to him than when you were officially his enemy."

"Don't you mean *our* affairs?"

Her smile finally dropped, but she still seemed quite calm. "I only go where my master tells me," she said. "I have never lied about how much I care for his ideals."

But she also, apparently, had not cared enough to expose his treason months ago.

"I am sorry he had you beaten, as I was genuinely sorry when he ambushed you at the Winter Ball. But I'm not sure what you expect to get from me, beyond an apology."

I let it go after that, and Lenz began putting incognito Yellows on Jördis. She was spending most of her time in the palace.

On the second day, I received a visit from an extremely uncomfortable man whose clothing showed no affiliation. But I recognized his face as one of those Purples who had beaten me alongside Alban. I had been bundled up in the chair in my room, but when I saw him, I immediately found the energy to be up and about, bustling and folding papers, and pouring myself radiant snow-cave tea and generally showing that I was *just fine*. He sweated a great deal, and handed me a small piece of paper that only said: "TEN DAYS FROM NOW. EARLY MORNING. YOU WILL BE DUNKED. YOU CAN BRING YOUR YELLOW." Vorosknecht gave no more details, but I had drawn *something* out of him, and he was not currently having me beaten or killed.

On the third day, a Yellow brought a note from Lenz, that said, "Fine." It went on to tell me that ten of the hardiest Yellows had volunteered—the types who dared each other to do dangerous things, or hit each other for fun—to be arrested with Gabor. They would be caught carousing in the Royal Inn of Ottilie's Rock, which was conveniently very near the Green barracks. I would make sure that they were particularly irritating to Gunther, the keeper there, which would make them quite easy to find, as he would tell anyone who asked about them. I felt a little bad about it.

I burned Lenz's letter.

GABOR'S ARREST

"I have found Martin-Frederick's murderer," I hissed under my breath to High General Dreher. I was sitting in his study in the Green barracks, nervously tearing at a small piece of paper. The bruising on my face was almost entirely gone now—at worst I looked a little puffy, like I had been crying and not been beaten.

He sat forward so quickly it must have set something in his torso out of sorts because he began to cough, and finally wheezed, "Truly, Kalyna Aljosanovna?"

I nodded, and then looked about as though I was deeply disturbed. "Yes. I . . . I saw glimpses, in my head, of this man laughing with his cronies, celebrating his success. They're hiding the assassin in the closet of their rooms on the third floor of the Royal Inn of Ottilie's Rock."

"Are they armed?"

"Yes. Ex-soldiers, I think."

"Hmm." He sat back and rang a little bell on his desk.

"But," I said quickly, "do try to take them alive. So we can learn more."

"Of course, Kalyna. We always want more able bodies in our prison."

"You still haven't told me why."

"Soon, Kalyna. I promise."

I smiled. A smile of haggard relief at justice being done. High General Dreher grunted as he got to his feet, and came around to the desk to take my (artfully quivering) hand.

"Thank you, Kalyna. I have never . . ." He shook his head and smiled. "I have never had reason to trust someone not of Rotfelsen before."

It was two days before my initiation. A week after that, everything around us was due to end. But we still did not know exactly how.

A HOLLOW PROMISE

"Are you ready for this, Kalyna?" asked Lenz.

I was in my bedroom, stinking of Doctor Aue's ointment, with everything cleared out of the room's center so I could clomp up and down the floor with my sickle, now and then glancing at the desk. Lying open upon it was my sickle fighting treatise, showing page after page of old drawings of dismemberment. I sliced at the air.

"Of course not," I said.

"Well, it doesn't matter. Gabor is down there, and I'm sitting up here and imagining it."

"As am I," I said. "But I promise you, Lenz"—another slice, up through the air—"that if I survive tomorrow, I will make sure Gabor does, too." It was a very nice promise that I had no way to keep.

"And you're sure High General Dreher said he was arrested without incident?"

"Oh yes. He and his 'friends from the war' all gave up right away; there was no fighting."

"Good." Lenz looked like he wanted to pace, but my practicing kept him still, lest he walk into the blade. "We should have taken Jördis prisoner," he added.

"*That*"—I raised the sickle and spun—"is your answer to everything."

"And look how it turned out. You're telling me what to do now." Lenz actually smiled. I don't know what Gabor told him before running off to be arrested, but it must have been reassuring.

"Besides," I added, "we would make the Court Philosopher suspicious if we did that. Where will you be tomorrow?"

"Up with Chasiku." Lenz pointed up, above his head. "Hoping she can give me an idea how our chances change with your . . . actions."

I nodded. "I hope Olaf is staying hidden."

"I'm sure he's fine," said Lenz. "Between what he, Biruté, and whomever else are enjoying, it feels awfully unfair that Gabor's down there."

"At least you have someone." I was breathing hard now, and I set down the sickle to start stretching.

"Are you still hurt?" he asked. "Can you even do this?"

"As you said, it doesn't matter if I'm ready." I spoke to my ankle as I tried, and failed, to touch my toes.

There was silence as I stretched more.

"Tomorrow, huh?" he said.

"Tomorrow."

"And you really think you can—"

"Yes," I lied. "I wouldn't do this otherwise."

"If it works, what will we do?"

"Move on."

THE NIGHT BEFORE MY INITIATION

"Kalynishka," said Papa, "you are going to do something."

"Yes." I leaned over his bed.

"I'm not seeing your future," he clarified. "I am not *that* far gone. But I see things happening around you. Large things."

"I hope so. Do you know what?"

He shrugged. "Fighting, death, anger, eyes."

"Thank you, Papa."

"You are going to do something."

"Yes."

"Do it well, Kalynishka."

I nodded. "I'll try." I sighed and took his hand. "But you never like it when I hurt people."

Papa nodded as many times as I just had, his head moving as far up and down as mine. "Of course not, Kalynishka, but sometimes it is what you do. Sometimes you do it for me and your grandmother. Necessary?"

"I'm not sure tomorrow is necessary."

"I *am* sure that if you think it might be, it is," he said, patting my hand. "I will see you tomorrow."

I didn't have the heart to tell him how likely it was I would die tomorrow.

Grandmother never came out of her room, and I did not go to see her.

I tried to go to sleep. It was still relatively early, although the sun had, of course, been down for hours. I lay awake, staring at the ceiling, heart racing. There was nothing for me to do until tomorrow.

After what must have been an hour, I got up, padded down the servant house's hallway, and knocked on Tural's door.

He was wearing belted silk pajamas in a deep blue, with buttons running up the side. He looked annoyed and then smiled when he saw me. His whole body moved as one to invite me in, but I stayed in the doorway. After the King's Dinner, and having him bring Gabor to the Sun's Death, I had kept Tural out of all of my plots. He had almost died at Vorosknecht's hands once, and he deserved the chance to just focus on his fruit. But I had to say *something*.

"I may not survive tomorrow," I said.

He blinked quite a few times at that, and then looked at the floor. "You told me to just *tell* you, next time."

"That I did. Do I want to know why?"

"If you'd like," I replied. "But it's complicated."

He nodded and looked at me again. "Best not get into it, then. You probably need your sleep."

"I suppose." I smiled. Warmly, I hope.

He smiled back and nodded. I hung in the doorway, my body sort of swaying in and out of the room. It was all very awkward and teenaged.

Finally, I took a breath, closed my eyes, and I said in Cöllüknit, "Tural, will you come to my bed tonight?" Even though I was still sore, still had fading bruises, still could not get the smell of Doctor Aue's goop off of me.

When I dared to open my eyes, he was still there, and so was his smile. This was a good sign.

"Kalyna," said Tural, "I would like to very much."

I think I smiled too widely then. I felt pleasant jitters rise in me.

"*But*," he continued, "I cannot. I don't care for propriety, but I know I've never slept unattached with someone and not awoken with a stinging need to be, well, *attached*. Whether or not it was a good idea."

I felt the flutter in my chest die down.

Tural continued, "I don't say that if we do this, we must be married. That would be silly—we're too old for such illusions. But I know that, for my sake alone, if we do this, and if you survive whatever is going to happen, I would need to know we would make a try at *finding out* whether or not we could be married."

Kalyna Aljosanovna Tsaoxelek, I thought.

"Does that make sense, Kalyna?"

I nodded numbly.

"Can you, Kalyna, promise me we would try to find this out together?" he asked.

I liked Tural very much, and I knew, from my own feelings and Chasiku's vision, that our marrying was something that could, *conceivably*, work. But I knew, instantly, that I did not want it to. Whether what I felt could become love was not the point: my duty was to my father, and he could not survive staying in one place. Not any more than I could imagine Tural leaving Rotfelsen to travel the world with us.

For that matter, even without my father, could *I* survive staying in one place? Could I, broken as I was, put so many of my hopes for security and happiness into one person? Tural was handsome and kind, but also persnickety and set in his ways—and how those flaws would *grate* upon me if I changed my whole way of life for him.

But what could it hurt to tell him "yes," I wondered. I would surely die tomorrow. If I did not, there was the good chance that we all would soon enough. And if somehow my plan worked and everyone, myself included, was saved? What then?

I could still leave with my family once it was all over. I could avoid Tural, or tell him I changed my mind, or even admit I'd lied. What did it matter? I would soon be gone. I could lie tonight, and then do my duty to family and Gift by attempting to become pregnant by him—perhaps I would even succeed, to Grandmother's shock. Or I could lie to Tural, and limit myself to the great world of things a man and a woman can do together that will not conceive. Whatever the choice, with so little chance of a future, why not lie for an exciting tonight? It would be far from the worst thing I had done on Rotfelsen's surface. Far from the worst lie I had told.

"No," I said. "I can't make you that promise."

He nodded and smiled sadly. "I assumed as much, but I would have kicked myself had I not made sure."

"Thank you for your honesty."

"And yours, too."

"Good night, Tural. I'm going to . . . Good night."

"Sleep well, Kalyna."

When I turned to go, Tural almost said something: I heard the sound of his mouth opening, a slight inhalation. But there was nothing, so I went to my room.

I considered finding an attractive Yellow (such as Dagmar, or a stranger), but decided against it because they might see me as a superior to be pleased no matter their will. So I lay on my bed and used my hands. Looking back now, I wonder if Tural did the same that night. At the time, I didn't think about Tural at all.

Once I was done, I still couldn't sleep. With lust somewhat sated, all I had left was fear, and it would not let go. I grumbled to myself, and tossed and turned in my bed.

Then I wondered idly if Prince Friedhelm would sleep with me if I prostrated myself before him. I imagined this and laughed myself to sleep at last.

PART SIX

My Initiation into the Mysteries of the Soul of the Rotfelsenisch Nation

They came for me early the next morning, a group of three Greens who inquired respectfully after me at the door of the servant house. Dagmar brought me downstairs, and we met the Greens at the front door. I made sure my nightshirt was laced up so they couldn't see my bruises.

"Why wasn't I told about this visit?" I demanded.

The Green in front sighed and said, in the voice of rote memorization: "The Mysteries of the Nation do not warn, and they do not wait. You will come with us now." He then inclined his head and added his own "Ma'am."

They waited outside the servant house as I got dressed. I did it quickly; no need to keep anyone waiting. I had laid everything out the day before. A simple wool skirt in bright blue, the same sort I had spent my life wandering, fighting, and prophesying in. Beneath that were warm wool stockings tucked into the knee-high boots I'd been given for my short stint as a Yellow. I wore a yellow blouse covered by a thick leather vest that would not stop a blade, but might at least make it rethink its direction, and atop that a heavy green wool coat and orange scarf. From a belt on my waist dangled my sickle, which was expected, strapped to my left thigh was a long dagger, and in my right boot was Tural's knife with the gold handle. My hair was up as much as it could be, although curls fell everywhere.

I had spent a half hour the night before practicing at throwing knives, but only ever managed to hit my desk with the handle. The gold handle was dented when I gave up.

I took a deep breath and left. On the way out, I didn't see Papa, Grandmother, Jördis, or Tural. Only maids and butlers going about their morning duties. Dagmar followed me silently.

Outside the servant house, there was a large carriage with black curtains over its windows. I almost laughed at how melodramatic it was. The Greens helped me in and seemed unsurprised by my sickle, or by Dagmar, which was a good sign. We were blindfolded, even though the curtains were opaque, and off we went. The morning was quiet and chilly.

The carriage rumbled awhile, and I suspect we went in circles. Every time it bounced, my ribs hurt. When we stepped out, I found it rather cute how intently the Greens pretended they weren't putting me into a lift down to Glaizatz Lake, even as we descended. When we landed, I was still blindfolded, but I knew we were at the edge of the lake. The quiet lapping of the water, and any other noise, was muffled by the moss that ran up the walls

As we walked by the lakeside, I heard splashing and saw, through my blindfold, the light of the wiggly little shrimp. I suspect they were being purposefully riled up for my benefit: soldiers tromping in the shallows, kicking at the water.

Then there was a rustling of cloth and the lights disappeared, although I still heard muffled splashing. I was led upon the stone in a great series of twists and turns, spirals and circles. Back, I suspect, to exactly where I'd started.

"Kalyna Aljosanovna!" boomed a voice. "Soothsayer and prophet of far-off lands, you are in the presence of the hidden chosen!"

The voice was almost certainly Vorosknecht's, and the urge to say, "Is that you, Otto?" was strong, but I fought it. I waited quietly for them to continue their farce.

"Do you know why you're here?" he said. He was forcing his voice into a lower register, but it was definitely the Court Philosopher.

"To submit myself to the mysteries of the deepness beneath Glaizatz!" No one had told me exactly what would need to be said, so I guessed.

I heard some muttering, and then my blindfold was removed with a flourish.

I stood in a black silk tent, the top higher than I could make out, and the sides wide enough that one draped wall fluttered over a corner of the lake itself, bringing water inside. In that water could still be seen the odd blinking light of shrimp, but they were no longer being provoked. All that tiny bit of light served to show me was the soldiers standing in a circle around the silk walls, in purple and green uniforms. I could see nothing else; all was darkness.

Were they truly going to induct me, or was this a secret execution? All I knew was that Dagmar and I were surrounded by enemies in the dark.

"Kalyna Aljosanovna," said a different voice. Quarrymaster Selvosch's, I think. "Is it true that you, *even as a foreigner*"—a good thing about darkness is no one can see you roll your eyes—"believe in the purity of the Rotfelsenisch nation and the truth of the spirit of light, built from our goodwill and strength, that resides beneath our very feet, guiding the fate of our great stone?"

"Not only do I believe it," I said, taking a long pause for effect, "*I have seen it.*"

More murmurs, from in front of me. I heard a strange rasping somewhere behind me.

"A being beyond god or demon," I continued, "beyond physical form. Swirling warmth and light, made from, and maker of, the goodness of your people."

The lie was easy, but I almost choked on the word "your."

"Seeing," said Vorosknecht, "is not enough."

Some sort of sign must have been made because torches were lit in the hands of four soldiers, and the rest of the enclosure flickered into view. I still couldn't see the top: it must have been hanging from Glaizatz Lake's massive ropes and pulleys far, far above.

There were probably twenty soldiers visible here, equally split between Purples and Greens. Among them were some faces I recognized, including an angry-looking Alban.

In front of me was a great dais of what looked like heavy onyx. I didn't know how they had gotten it down here. Behind it were ten figures: one had a tall hat, another was hunched. I assumed those to be Vorosknecht and Dreher. It was not as many as I'd met before, but these were only the people involved in the regicides' religious aspect. I must say, a part of me felt relieved that I certainly did not see Jördis' outline amongst them, although I wasn't sure what difference that actually made.

At least no one had made a move to kill me yet.

To my right was the water, and to my left I could see, through the tent, the outline of a lit up building, which must have been the prison. I looked behind me and saw what the rasping noise was: perhaps twenty-five people, all kneeling in rows, with ropes binding their wrists and connecting them to one another. Their clothes were tattered, and their mouths were gagged. I fancied that one of them looked like Gabor, but in the darkness, it was hard to tell.

As the torches grew brighter, I looked back in front of me, and saw more faces: many I didn't have names for, along with Dreher, Vorosknecht, and Selvosch.

Someone to Dreher's left growled, "There's a Yellow here. And they're both armed."

Dagmar grunted with exertion. I turned to face her, just as she was theatrically tearing off her yellow jacket and throwing it on the rotrock beneath her. In a show of extra zeal, she stomped on the jacket. Then she looked up, grinning, in her shirtsleeves and darker yellow trousers.

"I could take the rest off too, but I don't think it would be decent," she said.

I smiled at the audience. Some of them laughed, which I took as a good sign. I looked back at her, and used it as an excuse to look past her, at the prisoners. Their heads were bowed, and the soldiers surrounded them.

KALYNA THE SOOTHSAYER | 391

"Commendable," said a begrudging Vorosknecht. "But we still need to disarm you."

"Of course." I bowed.

Soldiers came and took my sickle and Dagmar's sword. Naturally, we both had hidden weapons, but we were their allies, and it would have been an affront to search us. I casually scratched my left leg with my right boot heel, to remind myself that a dagger was there.

A soldier with a torch walked closer to the dais. Dreher had the smile of a proud sponsor or teacher, or perhaps pet owner. I winked at him, and he smiled wider.

"Kalyna Aljosanovna," he said, resting his elbows on the dais, which, despite its appearance as heavy stone, wobbled, "I have recommended you for this honor not only because of your exotic Northern Gift, but because of the dedication you have shown to us, our cause, our Soul, and a great people to whom you don't belong."

I curtsied.

"Kalyna Aljosanovna," he continued, "of Masovska and Loasht and places foreign"—I gritted my teeth—"are you prepared to submerge yourself in Glaizatz Lake and bring yourself closer to the Soul of the Rotfelsenisch Nation? To endear yourself to its goodwill as a righteous subordinate? To cleanse yourself of foreign corruption in its pure waters, before they are muddied with our enemies?"

I curtsied again and nodded.

"Advance," said Vorosknecht.

I began to step forward, and stopped when I realized he was speaking to his partners, not me. They circled out from behind the dais (which shook some more as they bumped into it) and proceeded with the ceremony.

I won't bore you with the whole thing. There was a lot of walking in circles and call-and-response chants amongst those Ten Noble Regicides (who were supposed to be called The Ten August Nobles of the Soul). Quite often, one would turn too slowly, or forget to turn and bump into another, or a few lines of response chanting would be mumbled nonwords except for "Soul of the Nation" and "Ten August Nobles of the Soul," or someone would hiss "no, no, skip that part." *These* were the people in grasping distance of toppling our nation, of somehow killing untold thousands. Vorosknecht, of course, was perfect in his movement and enunciation, and never stopped letting me know, with his eyes, that he wished I were dead.

The worst part of this ceremony was when a soldier was sent to scoop up water from the lake, and I had to drink it, blinking shrimp and all. They were too small for me to taste, and I barely felt them, but I somehow felt guilty, even though I ate meat regularly. Why do we feel any of the silly things that we feel?

"Are you ready," Vorosknecht asked me, *eventually*, "to drop your body into the waters of Glaizatz Lake, Kalyna Aljosanovna? And to emerge reborn, or *drown?*" His preference was clear.

I nodded.

"And do you," the Court Philosopher continued, "with the power of your sight, see that the Soul of the Nation, which dwells beneath, wishes to begin being sated on the blood of its enemies?" He waved a hand at the tied-up prisoners behind me.

I was both aghast and unsurprised that these ridiculous nobles, with their made-up cult, had gotten all the way to human sacrifice. Vorosknecht stared at me hard, willing me to remember that I had agreed to say that the Soul saw whatever he wanted it to see. I'm sure he had a plan to expose me, or at least murder me, if I did not.

I nodded again, and prayed that I had not just, personally, condemned Gabor and the others to death.

Dreher came right up to me and whispered. "You must swim out a bit and let yourself drop deep. Remain underneath for as long as you can before you swim to the surface. If you think you can do better, go up for air and try again. Don't be afraid to stay so long that you pass out. We'll haul you back. If you feel a pull on the rope and you aren't done, give a pull back. If they feel nothing in return, out you come."

I felt myself begin to overheat under all my layers of wool. "'Swim'? You mean I don't just, I don't know, dunk my head?"

"Oh no," he said in my ear, "we try to get as close to the Soul as we can. Without dying, of course." He laughed.

"Did you do this, General? Even with your . . ."

"Condition?" he whispered. "I had Greens swimming alongside to help, but you're a healthy girl from a wild place."

I nodded. "Thank you. I'll do my best."

"And when you're back, we'll start on the prisoners!" he said. He seemed cheery about the whole thing.

Suddenly I very, very, very much wished I hadn't dressed in wool and leather for combat, and was not burdened with hidden weapons.

I removed my wool jacket and leather vest, laying them by the shore of the lake. I took off my boots carefully, desperately willing Tural's knife to stay inside the right boot as I lay it down. I still had a great deal of heavy wool on, but there was no way to remove my stockings or skirt without everyone seeing the dagger strapped to my thigh. I would simply have to do my best.

A rope was tied around my waist and fastened to a metal spike that had been driven into the rotrock ground. All of the Ten Noble Regicides crowded around the piece of lake that sat underneath the silk tent, and seemed rather at a loss for how to act, now that they did not have a chant or an order in which to stand. I wondered if anyone planned to mention this to Vorosknecht in the future: "Wouldn't the Submersion be grander if . . . ?"

These ten were mostly men, and I hoped none of them were getting in close just because I was (barely) undressing. They did seem eager; maybe they wanted to see how foreigners floated.

Many of the soldiers also crowded in behind them, and the rest watched from where they stood guard over the prisoners. What else did they have to do? I looked back, planning to give Dagmar a meaningful look, but she was already creeping away from the crowd.

I stepped into the water slightly, and saw that at this part of the lake, there was an immediate drop-off to great, murky depths: there would be no wading in. Standing with just my toes in the water—well, my toes in thick wool stockings, which were soaking in the water—I looked down into that great expanse, lit only by guttering torches behind the Ten Noble Regicides and wiggly little shrimp below. I turned back to look at everyone watching me.

"Do I . . . say anything first?" I asked quietly.

There were chuckles. These dangerous fools felt quite smart in the presence of someone even more ignorant of the Mysteries than they.

"No, no," said Dreher, in a benevolent fashion, with a hand on my shoulder. "To this group, your words will mean very little until you've done it."

I nodded and looked back into the water. I wondered if Vorosknecht had ever done this or if, as the founder of this little cult, he had been exempt. I stared into the dark waters.

"Well," I sighed, "off I go."

It was a stupid thing to say. I took many deep breaths to saturate my lungs and dove into the water.

I am lucky enough to be a good swimmer, ever since that boy at Fántutazh Lake showed me how to perch in the water-bound trees and catch the fish that eat the moss there. Following his tanned legs through the water was a great motivation to learn. But I've never taken much pleasure in swimming for its own sake. What's the point if you aren't doing it in order to kiss a boy in a tree?

I decided to give them a show. The longer I was in there, the closer they would think I was getting to the Soul of the Nation, and the longer Dagmar might have without being noticed.

Swimming beneath the surface of Glaizatz Lake was quite the experience. It was so dark, above and below the water, that it was easy to become disoriented. The shrimp blinked all about, and a part of me always wished to move toward them. Sometimes much larger creatures brushed my legs, unseen outside of a scale or an eye appearing in the light of a shrimp's fear. Swimming in a wool skirt isn't easy, but at least it gave me a barrier against those things I couldn't see.

The rope meant I had a decent idea of where I was in relation to everything else, although it also meant I couldn't go too far. Staying near the surface, I was able to move out from under the edges of the black silk tent, and see dots of light quivering through the water. I also saw torches near and far that went up the walls of the great cavern, illuminating them better than I had seen before, showing the moss that lived there, and the great, pointed gashes in it that I remembered from my childhood.

It all seemed blissfully removed from, well, *me*. I was in the quiet and dark, decorated with little shrimp who blinked in and out of my field of vision. Anything could have been happening above, really.

When my lungs began to hurt, I straightened myself perpendicular with the surface and allowed my body to slowly, carefully float toward the top of the water. My nose and mouth eased above the surface, and I took a series of breaths, hoping no one would see or hear the water breaking. I caught a strange smell, but assumed it was just another of the lake's oddities. After this, I slipped back down and swam around a bit longer. There was a tug on the rope, I tugged back to let them know

I was alive. I went up once more, only nose and mouth, and took more breaths. Again that smell, like burning hair, but I slipped back down and swam longer.

There was another pull on the rope. Before I could respond, I was being yanked back toward the tent. As I looked out through the water, I saw the torches flickering in and out of view.

I pushed my head into the air, smelled burning hair, saw smoke everywhere, and heard yelling and the clashing of metal. The tent was burning and, in the way silk does, emitting huge amounts of smoke. My heart quickened.

My rope was still being pulled, so I curved about under the water and slipped out my dagger, struggling with the waterlogged rope, sawing at it. Whatever was going on up there, the shrimp had noticed, and they began to pulse and shine faster and brighter than before. Fish and eels thrashed about me on all sides. I don't think Glaizatz Lake had ever seen a battle by its shores.

I felt myself dragged toward the shore, faster, then slower, then faster: whoever was reeling me in had other things to do. Once I sawed through the rope, I was so close I would have been inside the tent had it still been standing. Silk burns terribly fast.

I didn't want to go above, to put myself in danger or see my plan failing, but my lungs were sore, and I tasted metallic streams of blood snaking through the cold water. I pushed up, and popped my head and chest out, immediately feeling how heavy I was.

Here is what I saw: a battle in smoke between those in uniforms and other, harder-to-see figures. A lot of flashing steel, quite a few prone bodies, and Dagmar in the thick of it, in her shirtsleeves and more than happy to attract our enemies' attention.

I also saw Gabor, haggard, but spry as ever. In the moment I was watching, he jumped over one blade in order to stab the owner of another; it was quite impressive, and I wonder if anyone else who survived that day saw it. I must be blessed. What I could make out of the fighting seemed furious, and many bodies were already floating halfway into the lake, turning the waters murkier.

There was a group huddling by the dais that I took for the Ten Noble Regicides, but it was hard to say. A soldier was thrown back into the dais, and it broke, gushing tan splinters and revealing the black-painted spruce frame it had always been.

I saw this whole tableau in perhaps two seconds, but it looked, by the gods, as though this plan was *working*.

Then a Purple saw me and yelled something, and there were harquebuses leveled. I dove, leaving Dagmar and Gabor to their fates.

I didn't hear the reports of the harquebuses, but the bullets that punched down into the water spiraled past me. I panicked and swam away from them, which meant not only across the lake, but further down, into the depths.

Everywhere a shrimp brightened, I now saw other creatures, some dredged up from depths and caverns humans never saw, twisting and swimming in all directions. Confused as their fish minds could be, torn by bullets from above, clouding the waters with their innards. I saw stray fins, tentacles, and eyes float past me.

None of this mattered to me at the time. My mind had, for some reason, decided to prioritize safety from bullets over air, and down I went.

The agitation of the lake creatures grew, and I tasted blood again and again, which I doubt was human. My lungs began to ache, and I was buffeted on all sides. I didn't see bullets anymore, so the need for air took hold, and I began to swim frantically in the direction I thought was up.

I will tell you now that it was not.

LIGHT

So I swam toward what my stupid body took to be the surface. Maybe if I had the Gift I would have known better.

Soon the fish and eels and whatever-else of Glaizatz Lake were so thick around me I could hardly move. Battering me, getting caught in my hair and my dress. My lungs burned, and I knew I would die. I had expected to die today, but not like this, not without even *knowing* if we had saved the Tetrarchia.

Would I go to one of the hells that tortures you by letting you see how the world goes on without your presence? Or one of the hells that tortures you by refusing to show it?

Then I saw light peek out from between the fins and arms and tails and tongues. It was to my left: I had been swimming sideways, not up, toward the far walls of the lake. I turned and swam toward the light as my body felt like bursting. That light had to be the surface.

As I went, the creatures of the lake began to clear out, which I assumed was because I was nearing the air. The light grew brighter, larger, until it was impossible that this could be the cavern's torches. I don't know why I kept swimming toward it; perhaps I was so far gone I thought it was the sun.

The light was white, yawning bigger and bigger, and I finally realized that in swimming toward it, I was swimming straight down, away from air. The light seemed to fill the entire bottom of the lake.

The lake, need I remind you, was seven miles across.

Was this the Soul of the Nation?

A sort of blot appeared at one of its edges, and slid down over the light. A dark circle moving toward the center; a miniscule dot that was far larger than I. I was fascinated. I floated in the water, entranced, staring down. My head, deprived of air, began to think this dot was the beginning of a cancer on that Soul, caused by me and my actions.

Then I realized it was the pupil of an eye.

Some deep foreboding gripped me (finally), and I began to swim up, away from it. But even as I did, I looked down, watching this great eyeball that was the very size of Glaizatz Lake itself, if not larger. In that eye, I searched for intelligence, for benevolence, for, I suppose, a soul. The pupil centered itself and then began to move again. It flitted here and there, tracking each thing in its domain, up, across, down, with no reason or purpose beyond an animal's alertness when it smells blood.

I saw reflected in that eye an empty and singular mind. As you see in the face of a fish that has been drawn from the water and does not yet know it's dying, glassy and emotionless, but feeling pain.

Glaizatz Lake had no floor: it only tapered down to this, something living in a cavern below Rotfelsen, or in the very depths of the world. A great, blank, cold-blooded animal peering into our little rock, so much larger than anything that had dug tunnels through Rotfelsen, or fought in what was now the Grand Opera House. A creature of a size that could destroy this entire rock and all its people with a swish of its tail, if it had a tail.

I swam faster for the surface. Every part of my body pained and waterlogged. I am sure that, though I was but one speck in Glaizatz Lake, this great eye locked onto me and me alone for half a second, and I have never been so scared before or since.

As I neared the surface, the lake's creatures seemed to have calmed, and the pupil rolled away again, back to the edge and out of my sight. Soon after, the great eye closed, the lake darkened again, and I burst out of the bloody and body-clogged surface of the water. I was coughing, sputtering, and, I think, crying, although with so much water and blood everywhere, it was hard to tell. I swam for the nearest shore, heaved myself onto it, and passed out. If someone came and killed me, what did I even care? At least it would not be that thing.

MOVEMENT

I was shaken violently, but my eyes wouldn't open. I heard clashing and yelling, and a great thrumming beneath it all, but there was a clicking in my ears that obscured everything. I wasn't touching the floor; mostly dry hair brushed my face.

"What . . . ?" I burbled.

"Not now!" grunted a voice by my head, vibrating my cheek. My face was buried in someone's neck. I smelled sweat.

I got my eyes open. There was a Green, his face straining with exertion, his sword falling toward me. I screamed, but it came out a croak. His sword was stopped by another blade. I was gripping something tightly; was it a sword? Was I waking up in the middle of fighting? The clicking in my ears began to fade.

"I said not now!" yelled Dagmar.

The Green's sword was stopped again, and I felt myself lurched toward him. A hand that wasn't mine pushed his face away, and then he was run through by the sword that I thought I'd been holding. I wasn't. Something dashed across my vision, and I thought it was Gabor.

The Green fell to the floor, and my world finally expanded, but not by much. I was in a small, enclosed lift cage; the rumbling I heard was its ascent. The rushing walls of the rotrock tunnel came into focus, as did the wildly shaking lanterns above us. Purples and Greens crowded in on us, the lift swaying and tipping, but I bounced even more. My feet were dangling, whipping about; my arms were over a strong pair of shoulders, gripping a vest for dear life. To my left, Gabor was fighting.

Dagmar was also fighting, and I was on her back, whipping around with each of her movements.

"What's happening?" I said into her ear.

"We're fighting," answered Dagmar, spinning as she exchanged sword strokes with two men who were each hardly a foot away.

Gabor slammed into the wall to our left, grunting as his sword flicked out and opened a Purple's cheek. Then Dagmar killed the soldier, and I felt her shoulder slow for a moment, as her blade hit resistance in his body, and then quicken as it slid the rest of the way, and back out.

"Yes!" cried Gabor, pushing himself off the bars. "We're fighting!"

"So we didn't win?" I asked.

"Not as such," said Dagmar. "Now shut up."

I complied. My legs felt like wet yarn, dangling as Dagmar carried me, leaping through the small space, stepping over bodies to create more of them.

Moments later, it was over. Gabor breathed hard, smiling and wiping off his sword, and Dagmar lowered me, gently, to the floor in a corner of the lift. I counted six dead soldiers on the floor—I could hardly imagine how they, and the three of us, had even fit in this space, let alone fought here.

Not that *I* had done any fighting.

Dagmar crouched down in front of me, like she was speaking to a child. She even wiped my wet hair out of my face. I think I sort of chirped.

"How're you doing?" she asked, arms resting on her knees.

Gabor came up behind her and dropped my boots, jacket, and leather vest to the floor near me. His clothes were ragged, his face bruised.

"Fine?" I gulped. "You did all the work." I shook the water out of my head. "I saw you fighting and dove right back into the water."

"So?" said Dagmar. "We were fine, and there were at least four harquebuses pointed your way: to come out would have been suicide."

I couldn't meet their gazes anymore, so I looked at the floor, where the empty, dead eyes of a man stared up at me. He must have been younger than twenty-five. I kept looking at him as I fumblingly fit my wet stockings into my dry boots.

Going back in the water may have been the smart thing, but I knew that wasn't why I'd done it.

"What happened?" I gulped.

"Dagmar set the tent alight, and then cut us loose," said Gabor.

"I had to knife a few of their soldiers on the way," added Dagmar.

"Oh," I said. "Good." I had one boot on when I finally looked up at them again. "Is . . . is that good?"

"Yes!" cried Gabor.

"Eh," added Dagmar.

"Did our plan work?" I coughed.

"Well," said Dagmar, "Gabor, his friends, and some other imprisoned workers all put up a good show, for how little they must have been fed."

"Very little," Gabor agreed.

"We fought, and we killed many, but seven of the ten regicides got away. Including Dreher and Vorosknecht."

"Oh."

"They're ahead of us in another lift, on their way to the surface," said Gabor. He shrugged.

It would be some time before our enemies reached the surface, but we could do nothing, warn no one. This had been as terrible as all my plans. What I would have done for Ramunas' messenger lammergeier now.

I put my head in my hands. We sat in our lift full of corpses, with no idea where on the surface we would emerge. Somewhere below us, the freed prisoners were finishing up with the enemy soldiers. I hoped they wouldn't kill them all—it wasn't their fault, really. Was it? My only booted foot slid out, and I mistakenly kicked the dead soldier near me in his dead face.

My heart pounded, my head throbbed. It was all over, and I had failed. The whole point had been to kill the ringleaders, and instead I had revealed my allegiance, and they'd gotten away. I suppose we'd saved the prisoners, but this was still the end. With nothing else to do, I tried to wring the water out of my clothes. My hands quivered. In my mind, I saw the great, white eye. Now I knew from where the wiggly little shrimp drew their light. The lift screeched against the tunnel.

"Did you see the light?" I murmured. "Did it reach you from the water?"

"What? Like their Soul?" laughed Dagmar. "I think I saw some of the shrimp sync with one another for a moment . . ."

"No. Not like the Soul or the shrimp. Something else."

"A near-death illusion," said Gabor. "I've had them myself."

I shook my head. "Can't we go any faster?" I moaned.

"No rush!" laughed Dagmar.

"Indeed," added Gabor. "They must be waiting for us at the top."

"What if we get up there," I sighed, "and it's already war?"

"Then we'll fight," said Dagmar.

I shook my head. I never was cut out to be a soldier.

They began to regale me with how the fight I'd missed had happened. Dagmar and Gabor seemed awfully calm, and I half-listened as I tried to not pass out from fear. One of the regicides had been killed, two more taken prisoner. The lift dragged us ever upward. I nodded aimlessly.

Gabor laughed. "You see! I told you she'd want to take prisoners."

I nodded again.

Dagmar rolled her eyes and put a copper mark in his hand. "I wanted to kill them all; Gabor said you'd be angry if we did."

I nodded again.

Then they had found me and fought their way to a lift. They told the story as if we weren't all doomed.

How could they be so calm? I felt sick, I was sore, my lungs hurt, and I was shivering with cold, soaked through as I was in late winter. People have faced war in better shape. The lift kept screeching and dragging us upward.

"How many of ours died?" I asked.

"No time to count," said Dagmar. "Plenty."

Another thing to feel guilty about. How many had I led to death?

There was a loud burst above us, and a corpse in the back of the lift shook. Someone was shooting at us.

SHARPSHOOTERS

Dagmar extinguished our lantern to make them shoot into the dark.

Leaning over the mouth of our tunnel, with the sun blazing above them, were two silhouettes, and whenever one started to reload, the other fired. We did our best to flatten against the sides of the small lift, which shook and hit the walls of the tunnel.

"Do you have that little knife?" asked Dagmar.

I popped Tural's gold-handled knife out of my boot and gave it to her. Dagmar flung the knife upward, her body snapping up, leg kicking out. One of the figures above made a choked noise and disappeared. Moments later, a harquebus fell amongst our feet.

"Show-off," I grunted.

The other outline disappeared. They must not have realized none of us knew how to reload the gun.

Gabor, sword in his right hand, hefted the harquebus in his left for show. We all crouched as we hit the open air, which I had been sure I would never see again. It was midmorning. Blindingly so.

This lift didn't have a little building around it, unfortunately, but popped up into the air beneath a gazebo. There were high hedges around us, and off to our left I saw Chasiku's watchtower, reaching far above, which at least gave me my bearings for the few moments I expected to live.

The man Dagmar had killed with the knife was a Purple, as was the other shooter who was, inexplicably, also dead. There was a Green's corpse as well, and otherwise, no one we could see. It didn't *sound* like the surface had exploded into war, but how else to explain the dead bodies?

"Well," said Gabor. "I'm glad they weren't waiting for us, but this is all a bit eerie, isn't it?"

I nodded as we stepped out of the gazebo. We were all so exhausted; it was certainly preferable that we get into no more fights. Then, of course, there was a yell, and ten more Greens came running around the hedges toward us. I heard a moan and realized it came from me.

This whole day had all been my stupid idea, so I took the lead in front of the two trained soldiers, sickle raised, and ran forward, expecting to die.

At least I wouldn't be killed by the creature below the lake.

A tall man with a scar and a sabre in his hand was in front of his men. We met, his sabre dropped toward me, and then he jerked to the side and was dead before I had done anything.

"Ha!" Dagmar cried.

The rest of the Greens looked confused. Another dropped.

I stood still, confused, until Dagmar and Gabor leapt past me. I shook my head to clear it and joined in.

Grunts and impacts sounded around me, and I was quite lost in it all. If there's a good thing about being outnumbered, it's that you can flail and trust you won't hit a friend.

But then, we hardly got a chance to *hit* anyone. Gabor and Dagmar did a bit of cutting, but the Greens kept dropping of their own accord. I fancied I heard distant shots.

One particularly large Green had been absolutely within inches of killing me, executing a perfect lunge entirely outside of my weak defense, when he had suddenly spun like a dancer and died.

I looked up to see puffs of smoke coming from Chasiku's watchtower every few moments.

When there was one Green left, he pressed himself against the hedge to our left, to hide himself from the watchtower. He looked so confused and terrified that I felt for him. Then he was shot *through* the hedge, and died.

"Not complaining," said Dagmar, "but what's going on?"

"This way," I said between heavy breaths, pointing toward an opening in the hedge.

But first I went and retrieved Tural's knife.

BANG

"Did you see that?" yelled Behrens as he bounced down the last few steps of Chasiku's watchtower. "Did you *see that?*"

"Yes, yes!" I laughed as he hugged me. "What was I seeing?"

"Something amazing!" he said.

At the top of the watchtower, a group of Yellow harquebusiers leaned against the railing and looked down at us. They were clean, their yellow uniforms smooth and sharp. Dagmar, Gabor, and I were rumpled, dirty, and stained with blood, my hair a scraggly mess. I smelled of lake creatures, and I was shivering. We must have been a sight.

"Miss Chasiku," said Behrens, "she comes to my barracks and asks for me, you see."

I had an idea of how difficult it must have been for her to leave her watchtower and go deliberately to a place full of soldiers. I nodded at Behrens to continue.

"And she tells me that soon you'll be killed, unless I bring, ah, 'a gaggle of your shooting friends.' Once we're all lined up on her balcony, she—well, ma'am, I knew that she was a soothsayer, like yourself, but I didn't expect anything like this. Half of us, we didn't even see whom we hit. She just stands there, you see, with her eyes closed, and she points.

"'No, no,' she says to me. 'Why are you aiming, idiot? Point. Bang. Point . . .' and I say, 'Bang, miss?' and she nods, you see?"

I saw very well now. Behrens and his sharpshooters had gone one after the other: Chasiku, eyes closed, would point, and the sharpshooter would aim right along her arm and fingertip to shoot. This was how they hit targets they couldn't see, or that were in the middle of a mad dash.

Targets. I mean people, human beings.

I thanked Behrens, who loudly insisted he didn't deserve it. I tried to enjoy his excitement in victory, but I couldn't stop thinking of what else might be happening, where else the Purples and Greens were going. Yet even *that* was a welcome reprieve from that great eye, which was still throbbing in my mind, like when you stare at the sun and then close your eyes. It was lurking somewhere beneath the lake, in Rotfelsen's depths.

"Did she see anything else?" I asked, failing to keep my voice down. I nearly screamed it.

"Yes," he said. "Miss Chasiku saw that the regicides were going to do something, so she sent Lenz off to your servant house."

My scalp prickled. I began to shake worse than when I'd been on Dagmar's back.

HOSTAGES

As many Yellows as chose to follow me hopped into a carriage, and when we got to the servant house, I leapt out and ran inside screaming for Papa. Johann, the head butler, got in my way, demanding to know what was going on. I ignored him and went up the stairs three at a time, with the soldiers all trailing behind me.

I threw myself into my bedroom, and saw two dead Yellows and one living person. Sitting in my chair, feigning calm, with one leg crossed over the other, was Selvosch the Lord High Quarrymaster.

I was inches from stabbing him when Behrens grabbed me and held me back. The Quarrymaster's supposed calm drained away. The Yellows filled the doorway and the hall outside, keeping anyone else out.

"Kill me," shrieked Selvosch, clearly hoping that I would not, "if you want the hostages to die!" He said these bold words even as he shivered.

"Where?!" I managed to scream in his face. I must have looked like actual death to him, crusted over with blood, eyes wild, trying to twist out of Behrens' hands.

Selvosch managed to grin. "With us. And if I don't join the others within the hour, they die."

I finally stopped straining against Behrens' hands. He did not quite let me go, just yet.

"It will take us longer than an hour to bring up the regicides we captured down in Glaizatz Lake," I said. "You need to give us more—"

"Keep them," said Selvosch. "Or kill them. They believe in the Soul of the Nation, and they'll die before they talk."

"Then what do you want from us?" asked Dagmar, stepping forward.

"Bring us your false King," said Selvosch, "and you can have them back."

"We don't know where he is," I replied.

"I doubt that."

"We don't," I pleaded. As far as I knew, no one left on the palace grounds had any clue as to where Olaf, Biruté, and their paramours had absconded to. "And he likely won't be back for a week. Not until the Eve of the Council."

Selvosch shook his head and stood up. "Bring him to us, and you get them back. Try to intrude upon the palace, without that supposed King in tow, and they die."

He began to walk toward me, and the rest of the Yellows, expecting us to part for him. When we didn't, he went around, and squeezed out into the hallway. I stared straight ahead, at where he had been. Then I slumped into the chair, hearing Selvosch's boots on the stairs. I began to cry, and they were big, ugly tears.

"Did they get Lenz, too?" hissed Gabor. He looked down at the dead Yellows, who must have accompanied Lenz there.

I just shook my head and shrugged because I couldn't speak.

"Why do you think Selvosch called the king 'false'?" asked Dagmar.

"Who knows?" said Behrens. "Soul of the Nation garbage to delegitimize him, I'm sure."

There was a thump in my closet, and Dagmar ran over to open it, sword drawn. Her sword's point, and the barrels of two Yellows' harquebuses, met the figure that tumbled out onto the floor.

It was Papa. He lay limply on his back.

I knocked them aside as I ran to him, still crying, grabbing him, blubbering incoherently as I held his rigid body. Then he blinked.

"Can I move now, Kalynishka?" he muttered in my ear.

"Yes, of course!" I cried, hugging him. He relaxed into a heap in my arms, and we sat in a pile on the floor, surrounded by Yellows. I told him how much I loved him in perhaps three different languages.

"Your friend with the mustache, Lanzo?" said Papa. "He came here with his men and told us to keep quiet, said we were in danger. Well, you know, Mother began screaming and screaming at him, and at his soldiers, daring them to kill her. So he put me in there and said to stay very still. Until it was safe to move."

"But, Papa, if you're here . . ."

"Yes!" he cried, grabbing my clothes, hands turning white, as though he had just remembered. "They took Mother, and your friend!"

I blinked the tears away many times, and then I laughed. Genuinely, but evilly, I think.

"Lenz and Grandmother," I choked out. "They only took Lenz and Grandmother!"

I pulled myself up, giggling, and started toward the door. Gabor grabbed my arm.

"Kalyna, where are you going?"

"To kill Selvosch, of course!" I said, grinning like a mischievous child. "They only took Lenz and Grandmother! I'm going to go kill them."

Gabor yanked me back violently.

"You may not care for your grandmother," he hissed, "but we will have a plan before we go and get Lenz killed. Is that clear?"

His handsome, youthful face, which had been so full of joy even during all the carnage earlier that day, was suddenly hard in a way I had not seen before.

"He doesn't deserve someone caring about him so much," I grunted.

"Neither do I," he replied. "But he also saved your father. What do *you* deserve, Kalyna?"

I shrugged and went back to Papa. Behrens and Dagmar helped me sit him up in my chair, and I sat on the floor next to him, stroking his hand. I reflected upon the fact that Lenz had saved my father from being taken, and knew that I had to rescue my kidnapper. If nothing else, I refused to owe him.

THE DELEGATIONS BEGIN TO ARRIVE

Selvosch had been right about the two regicide plotters we had captured: they wouldn't say a thing. Dagmar asked if she could *convince* them, but I did not let her. I suspected no one was offering Lenz the same kindness. The captured regicide soldiers didn't seem to know very much, and it would be very easy for their masters to deny any accusations that came from them. So, we shoved them, seven in all, into that one cell beneath Lenz's barracks, and convinced some Yellows to feed them regularly. We did not know what to do with them, but at least they were very uncomfortable.

As far as we could tell, Vorosknecht and Dreher were curled up in the Sunset Palace, with a coterie of regicide plotters and loyal soldiers, holding their hostages—who may or may not have included Prince Friedhelm—and making sure that we came nowhere near them without Olaf. "We" in this case was myself, Chasiku, Gabor, and any Yellows not already in the palace. So, without Prince Friedhelm, whom we had not heard from since Glaizatz Lake, and so must have been trapped in the palace; without Lenz, who was at best a prisoner; and without even King Olaf or Queen Biruté, we were all that was left. No available royalty also meant no one could get the Reds on our side, and they were busy keeping the peace for the Council of Barbarians. Jördis, for her part, had entirely disappeared: her clothes and furniture were still in her room, but her papers and books were all gone.

The day after our battle at Glaizatz Lake, Gabor, Dagmar, and I found ourselves in Chasiku's tower, trying to formulate some sort of plan. Everyone kept looking to the two prophets in the room, for obvious reasons, but Chasiku kept seeing Rotfelsen falling apart, and all I could think of was what I had seen in Glaizatz Lake. Or *beneath* the lake. Papa had seen an "ever broadening emptiness" down there. How big could the thing be? What sort of shape took up that space? Every time I considered it, my mind reeled, and I felt almost drunk.

So we sat around with no real leaders, reminding me of a play I saw in my youth, in which a town lost all of its adults, and the children had to lead themselves. I believe it ended with the children being slaughtered by an invading army: it was a morality tale.

After we had said a great deal with no actual progress, I was leaning against the railing of Chasiku's tower, idly watching streams of dignitaries make their way up from Turmenbach, and into the Sunset Palace. I believe I was seeing a Quru delegation of some sort, based on the enthusiastically waving flags of almost prismatic colors and patterns, and the deep red robes. It certainly wasn't large enough, or elaborate enough, to be Queen Sevda of Quruscan, but was likely some group of mountain officials. They were chanting, "Barbarous! Barbarous!" in Cölluknit, and many were laughing.

"Remind me why we can't just sneak in with them and murder our enemies?" I asked.

"Everyone's being checked at the door," muttered Dagmar, "by Greens and Reds. Someone would tell our friends hiding out in there."

"There must be someone who can get us in," said Gabor. "Tural's been going in and out, right? Couldn't he, I don't know, pack us in barrels of peaches or some such?"

"He doesn't have access to those until they're already in the Palace," I sighed. "Besides, I doubt he would even have time to listen to us right now." And I wanted to keep him out of danger, to the extent such a thing was possible.

"This is interminable!" cried Gabor, tearing at his hair. "We're just sitting here, and Lenz may be *dead* by now."

I laughed. "No, no, he's the spymaster, they'll keep him alive to help them catch the King and the Prince. But Grandmother has probably made them angry enough that they've killed her already."

"You're probably right," Gabor mumbled. Then he realized what I'd said and looked up at me. "Gods, I hope not!"

"Then you're the only one," said Chasiku.

I nodded.

"But I've still never seen her death," Chasiku added.

"Well, great," I growled, turning my back to the railing and staring at the three of them.

Chasiku was sitting straight on her bedroll, drinking her homemade coffee with a grimace, Gabor was against a wall, and Dagmar was actually lying on her back on the hard floor, her hands behind her head. This was who I had: the woman I had called a fake, the man I had planned to kidnap, and the guard whose name it took me weeks to learn. By the gods, I actually missed Lenz.

And now it was about a week until the Council of Barbarians would begin, and everything would crumble. But how?

I thought again of the eye beneath Glaizatz Lake. It had intruded around the edges of my thoughts all day, and it was easy enough to imagine its connection to the shattering of Rotfelsen. But how would these deluded nationalists cause it to destroy us? I opened my mouth to speak, but couldn't bring myself to. The others would either find me mad, or be faced with something they could affect even less than the regicides.

"Have you seen anything useful, Chasiku?" I asked. "Or are you only not seeing my Grandmother's death?" And then, I very quickly added: "And obviously *I* haven't seen anything useful."

Chasiku just smiled and shrugged.

We all stood around for awhile, as more pieces of Cöllüknit wafted up from below.

"The Masovskans are supposed to start showing up tomorrow," said Dagmar, stifling a yawn. "At least that's what they tell me."

"Oh no," I said.

"Oh no, what?" asked Gabor.

"Dagmar, with me," I sighed. "I know who can get us into the Palace."

THE EDELTRAUD MANSION

Dagmar and I found ourselves approaching a sprawling and decadent mansion, one of many that were in a nice little line just in front of the Sunset Palace. Poor, departed King Gerhold VIII's grandfather, Gebbrandt II, had convinced (or forced) his major officials and lesser relatives to come live in this part of the palace grounds, where he could hold them beneath an imperious eye. All these estates were of Masovskan wood, not rotrock, so that they would not become fortresses.

The particular one we were about to enter had a metal gate that looked impressive but would stop very little, surrounding a couple acres of gardens with a mansion in the center. As we came closer, the building seemed to consistently reveal itself to be larger than I expected.

This was the home of Edeltraud von Edeltraud, Mistress of the Coin, and friend—or at least begrudging host—to the Gustavus siblings. A butler with the nose of a boxer welcomed us and led us into a drawing room filled with paintings, sculptures, and couches of stone housing voluminous cushions. On one of those couches was Klemens Gustavus, the spoiled scion of the changing bank, who had tried to have his own cousin killed in Masovska a lifetime (or a few months) ago. And who, of course, Lenz and I had kept locked up for a bit. Everyone makes mistakes.

Dagmar spent most of the way there telling me not to trust Klemens, and that I should let her kill him.

"Let's not forget that he killed my comrades," she hissed. "And kicked me many times."

"We *had* ambushed him," I replied.

She only harrumphed.

Klemens was having tea with Edeltraud von Edeltraud herself, whom I had not seen in person since I followed her around during the Winter Ball. Upon seeing me, she stood up, welcomed me, and then began to leave.

"I want no part of whatever you will discuss," she said. "I don't want to be involved!" And she disappeared, as though she had never been there.

"Please sit," said the young banker in halting Rotfelsenisch, motioning to a small stool that was, pointedly, lower than the couch he was on. Klemens seemed delighted to see me, which I took as a bad sign.

If I was positioned lower than Klemens, Dagmar, standing behind me with her hands on her hips, cast a shadow over both of us.

"Kalyna Aljosanovna!" he continued, once I had sat. "My old jailer! Looking beautiful as always."

I could not help laughing at that, but I think he took it as modesty, which it was not.

"I'm sorry again about our misunderstanding," I said. Being forced to look up at him made this apology feel particularly infantilizing.

"Oh, don't even begin to speak to it!" he laughed. I had only ever seen him be dismissive or frightened, and so this friendliness was disarming, no matter how false. "It worked out, we are on the same side, and we have kept the King alive so far."

There were a few things wrong with that last phrase, but I said, "Yes. He is alive and happy at his hunting lodge."

"Truly?"

I nodded.

"Then all is right with the world! Why, I'm so happy with how things have turned out that I do not even blame you for that mess back in Masovska."

"I couldn't possibly know what you mean."

"Of course." Klemens sat back, and crossed one leg over the other, and *there* was the hateful, dismissive child from the Masovskan courtroom.

Dagmar coughed. "I don't know what this is about, but do I need to hit him?"

I shook my head.

Klemens laughed. "You needn't worry. I'm not so dull as to start killing advocates in Gniezto. My cousin can have his little windfall, and *you* can give me direct access to the King!"

"What are you doing?" snapped Bozena Gustavus, in Masovskani, as she stormed into the room.

I heard Dagmar's sword clank against her hand, but she did not draw it. Bozena stomped up and looked ready to hit her brother, but she did not do so.

"Why don't you just tell her everything, you fool!" she cried, still in Masovskani. She glowered at him for another moment before turning to me, and switching to Rotfelsenisch. "What do you want from us, witch?"

"Watch your tone," said Dagmar.

"Oh, come now, sister!" laughed Klemens. "She is our august ally, and she sees the future!"

I opened my mouth to answer Bozena's question to me.

"She is not our ally!" She sneered at him. Despite the rest of us, she had gone back to Masovskani. "She is a royal tool with no power."

"Keep it to Rotfelsenisch, please," grunted Dagmar. "So I know whether you're threatening to murder us."

"If I may!" I all but yelled. "All I am looking for is passage into the Sunset Palace."

"Into?" grunted Bozena.

"*Our* enemies," I said, "have hostages, have taken control of the palace, and are keeping us out. The King is blessedly away, but he will be back soon. Just because you have no longer been involved in trying to stop the regicides, does not mean they are done. If you do not want the King, as well as the King of Masovska, and the other monarchs besides, to be *assassinated*, we must get into the palace."

"Things got away from your spymaster, did they?" laughed Klemens.

"Yes," I snapped. "Clearly."

"You should have left it to us," replied Klemens.

I smiled and nodded.

"And what do we get in return?" asked Bozena, back in Rotfelsenisch.

"An unbroken Tetrarchia, for one," I answered, "in which you can continue to do business. And your lives, besides."

"But you understand we would be putting ourselves in danger for you," she said.

"We are all in danger."

"Not good enough," said Bozena. "We have only your word on that. You will kill these regicides, if you get in?"

"Or throw them in a dungeon forever."

"In that case"—she flourished a hand at her brother—"we will need a new Court Philosopher, won't we?"

"You're not suggesting a Gustavus?" I replied, coughing out the name.

"And why not?" asked Klemens. "I've always had a philosophical nature."

I laughed at them. I had been a conniving fraud long enough to recognize the simplest games when I saw them.

"And maybe Bozena as the High General?" I asked.

"Oh? Will they need one of those, too?" asked Klemens.

"I would love," said Dagmar, "to see you try to get siblings, and Masovskans at that, into those titles."

"Maybe we should get rid of both positions altogether," I said.

"Well then," sighed Klemens, "what about Selvosch's quarries? Who will take those?"

There it was. He had started out high and outlandish to make this seem plausible. Bozena nodded her agreement.

I found imagining the government of Rotfelsen overrun with Gustavuses to be at least a little entertaining, and smiled.

"I am not the King, of course," I began, "but with him away, and the Prince and spymaster trapped in the palace, I can only say that I'll do what I can." I grinned. "Which is a lot. I've grown quite close to the King, you see." I leaned forward, elbow on my thigh and chin in my hand, staring straight into Klemens' eyes. "So, if you can get, say, twenty of our people into the palace, then the King will be very grateful, and I will do all I can to encourage him." I sat back. "If not, then I doubt any of us will survive the Council of Barbarians."

Klemens looked up at his sister, who was standing beside him, gripping his shoulder. She sighed and nodded almost imperceptibly.

"Capital!" said Klemens. "You and your Yellows can come in with us."

"Thank you." I bowed my head.

"Then I shall see you again on the Eve of the Council!" he said.

I started. "The Eve? That's a week away! What about tomorrow? I thought the Masovskan delegation—"

"The *royal* Masovskan delegation," Bozena corrected. "Merchants who can afford to take part in the Council and petition the clerks and politicians, we all show up right before it starts."

A whole week. How much damage could they do in a week? And a week knowing that the eye was . . . down there. But then, had it *always* been down there? Was Rotfelsen that precarious? Was the world?

"Can Edeltraud get us in earlier?"

"Oh my, no!" laughed Klemens. "She's terrified of being seen in there again, ever since she first turned down Selvosch and the regicides. Why, she's hardly left the house!"

I sighed and took my leave. I did not see Edeltraud von Edeltraud anywhere along the way—she had disappeared.

"See you in a week, Kalyna Aljosanovna!" called Klemens.

"Don't trust them," Dagmar muttered. "We should kill them and be done with it."

I shrugged and shook my head.

WAITING FOR THE COUNCIL

The following week was awful, and largely uneventful besides. It was almost spring, but Rotfelsen was actually hit with its biggest snow yet, on top of everything else.

Every day of that week, Tural would come back from long hours in the Sunset Palace, with nothing to tell us beyond kitchen gossip, most of which was only kitchen-related. We did learn from him that no one in the palace had seen the Prince, which was worrying. He also told us that whenever Yellows had tried to enter the palace, as they normally did, the Greens would not officially bar their way, but always provoke them until particularly egregious brawls broke out. Purples would then jump in, outnumbering the Yellows, until the Reds would disperse the fight, sending the Yellows back to their barracks.

The full force of the Yellows was in flux, running drills and patrolling the palace grounds at the behest of their extant commanders. Those who had been part of Lenz's espionage, at least, would listen to Dagmar, Chasiku, and I.

"It is almost as though," I said, "having four separate armies in one place is a bad idea."

"I suppose I never thought of it that way," said Gabor.

I then thought about how much better *no* army would be, but I did not say this out loud.

That was the extent of what we got out of Tural. Gabor hired someone to go take care of his plants, and then spent most of the time pacing in what had been Grandmother's room, and sometimes coming to chat with Papa. Dagmar never left my side.

I spent a good deal of that week with Papa, both because I was quite sure we would all die in a few days, and because I hoped against hope that he would see something new and useful. He did not.

However, Chasiku did.

On the night before we were set to infiltrate the Sunset Palace (if the Gustavuses hadn't forgotten), a Yellow I didn't recognize woke me up and told me Chasiku wanted me to come over to her right away. I roused Dagmar from where she was sleeping outside my door, threw on a big scarf, and off we went. As soon as we were up in Chasiku's tower, Dagmar sat down against the wall and closed her eyes.

"Wake me if someone's killing us," she said. Then she began to snore, lightly.

Chasiku was out at the railing, looking off into the darkness. She was shivering, but hardly seemed to care. I joined her, and began to lift my scarf onto her shoulders. Chasiku whipped her face around to glare at me.

I froze for a moment, then continued to put the scarf over her. She grunted.

"Well?" I asked.

"You saw something down in Glaizatz, didn't you?" she said. "I knew it when I was seeing your future before, and you have been very reticent to talk about it."

The eye in the bottom of the lake had continued to haunt me. I nodded.

"I didn't want to scare anyone," I whispered, slipping into Sky-dašiavos.

"Well," she said, "if you don't tell me, I shall be driven mad by seeing pieces of it with no context."

I sighed, and I told her. I told her about eye that had glowed, that had looked at me, that was definitely not some Soul of Rotfelsen, just a large, dumb creature in the depths of the rock. Or below even that.

"That . . . likely explains why the whole rock will fall apart," she said.

"I have tried not to think about it, but yes. It's the only thing I can imagine causing that."

She nodded.

"But," I ventured, "if Rotfelsen has stood all these years, what would cause that thing to . . . thrash about beneath us now? Has it always been there? Does it travel around through the depths of the world? Are there . . . *more* of them?"

"One thing at a time," said Chasiku. "I saw something new tonight, Kalyna. I saw soldiers in purple uniforms marching what seemed an unending number of prisoners down to Glaizatz Lake and, down there, slaughtering them. Over and over, for what may have been days." She blinked her eyes, not looking at me, and I fancied I saw tears there. "Thousands dead, and I saw every single one. Each silent or pleading person, every single face in its last moments. I saw them all in a *moment*, Kalyna."

I had nothing to offer. I simply nodded.

"Then," she continued, "I saw the crumbling again, the rock coming apart. I saw soldiers in purple startled by it, and then crushed in the midst of their endless murder."

A thought appeared somewhere in the back of my head, a glimmer of an idea. Then it grew and grew, and I had a sickening feeling.

"Were they throwing the bodies into the lake's waters?" I asked.

She nodded.

"That was their plan with Gabor and the rest, some kind of human sacrifice for what they *think* lives down there," I continued. "But we stopped it. When I saw the eye, our battle had already filled the water with some small amount of bodies and blood."

"You think that clouding the waters with blood and bodies, with pieces of humans, will . . . irritate it?"

"Chasiku, I saw no thought behind that eye. It was blankly panicked. If the water is clogged with dead, the fish will begin to thrash and die, they will not be able to see or hunt, it will simply change their lake, and their little fish minds will be confused."

"And so perhaps that great, big fish mind will also be confused, and alarmed," she said. "Or at least inconvenienced or irritated, like someone spat in its eye. Or it may feed on those fish, somehow, either when they come down into its depths, or when it reaches up into our lake."

The thought of it *reaching up* made my skin crawl. And I remembered those great gashes in the walls of the cavern. Which I had seen as a child, and again when I went down there to be "initiated."

"And if it's irritated, or can no longer hunt here," I muttered, "it may just decide to leave for somewhere else and . . . turn around."

I bent over until my forehead touched the railing with a muffled clang. I stared at my feet and began to breathe very fast. Neither of us said anything for a few minutes.

"Sneak me in with you tomorrow," said Chasiku. "It would be torture for me to be in the palace at its normal capacity, let alone during the Council, but I can't just sit here and trust . . . *you* to fix this without me."

I snorted. "What could you possibly do?"

"Tell the stupid boys where to shoot."

I stood back up. "Fine. Give me back my scarf."

She did so.

THE EVE OF THE COUNCIL

I woke up on the Eve of the Council expecting something to happen, but, at first, nothing did. The Council of Barbarians proper would begin the next day, but there would be the Opening Invocation tonight. I still felt quite certain that those invocations would be when our regicides would make their move, as it would be the first time all four monarchs would be in the same place. Unfortunately, by that morning, I had heard nothing from Olaf and Biruté, and nothing from Bozena and Klemens Gustavus.

At midday, I was sitting in my chair, with my feet pulled up and my knees against my chest, grinding my teeth and staring into space, when a messenger came from the Gustavuses. Half an hour later, myself, Dagmar, Gabor, Behrens, a beleaguered Chasiku, and fifteen loyal Yellows were outside the Edeltraud mansion, all hidden in a large carriage. We were well armed, and I had decided to wear trousers that day. For violence, whether or not it made sense.

Outside the mansion, in the surprisingly bitter cold of late winter, was a huge crowd of people, maybe a hundred. Klemens Gustavus was standing on top of a pile of crates, yelling and pointing, but no one seemed to be listening to him. Dagmar, Gabor, and I left the carriage and made our way to him.

"There you are! Finally!" snapped Klemens. "What are you waiting for? Get in!"

"Get in where?" He did not hear me over the crowd, so I repeated it, yelling.

Klemens jumped down in front of me and pointed behind him. "Into the crates! You and your flunkies!"

Dagmar barked out a laugh. I looked at the crates, blinked, and looked back at Klemens.

"What a miserable man," said Gabor.

"You have a hundred people here," I said, "can't we just blend in? Throw cloaks over the uniforms until we're in the palace?"

Klemens' eyes looked like they would pop out of his skull, and his sallow face went red. "A hundred people, Kalyna, with *a hundred* Council passes stamped what feel like *a hundred times* by the correct dignitaries, Kalyna! They do not make a habit of letting just anyone in, do you understand that? These aren't just our retinue, some of these are from our sister changing banks in other parts of the Tetrarchia. And everyone had to be verified by someone in their place of origin *and* here." He flung an arm off to the right. "We are even *trying* to expand to the Bandit States, so we have a group from Rituo. *Rituo*! Do you know what a nightmare it was to get papers from the Bandit States! If I knew what was right for my *business*, I would have skipped that, thrown them into these crates, and *you* out on your asses!"

I let Klemens regain his breath before I smiled and patted his shoulder. "Thank you so much for your help, Klemens Gustavus. Your ability to pull this whole retinue together just shows what a fantastic quarrymaster you will be."

"Thank you, Kalyna Aljosanovna. Now get in the crates."

Dagmar stared hard at Klemens for a long time. Gabor shrugged and began to climb into a crate.

"I don't think we should do this," whispered Dagmar, so close I could feel her breath.

"We have to get in there," I sighed. "We have to find the Prince, ally with the Yellows trapped in there, and stop the regicides before they ruin everything. And I am out of ideas on how to do so."

Dagmar shrugged. "Well, you're the one who makes tricksy plans. So."

In we went. My crate was full of musty, but pleasant, Masovskan furs. It wasn't as though I thought Dagmar was *wrong* exactly, but I had not found another way in. Dagmar's shin was pressed against my face, and Gabor's head was against my stomach. What would happen would happen.

"Just in case," muttered Dagmar, as she pulled out a dagger and almost cut Gabor.

Our crate was nailed shut, sealing us in and almost gouging my shoulder. I could hear the rest of our people climbing into the others, as Klemens was screaming, "And don't any of you tell anyone that there are people in the crates, if you value your jobs or your lives! It's for a *surprise!*"

That it was. I hoped.

After what felt like forever, we were lifted up by angry men who kept grunting Masovskani curses into our ears, and loaded onto something. For the most part, all I could see was Dagmar's leg, but it was sometimes dappled by the midday sun peeking through the boards of our crate. I could feel puffs of cold air from outside, now and then, but crammed in with other people and heavy furs, I was sweating awfully. I hoped I did not smell too bad, first because it would make the others in my crate miserable, and second because I began to fancy it would somehow give us away.

We were close to the palace, but the ride felt interminable. I wondered what Dreher and Vorosknecht were up to, if Grandmother had gotten herself and Lenz killed yet, and whether the King and Queen had arrived, or were still off in their love nest.

The same cursing men lifted us back off the carts, and began to carry us into, I hoped, the palace. Something was blocking out the sunlight, now.

"Who're you?" came a disdainful voice.

"The Gustaw Gustavus Changing Bank," said Klemens, "and affiliates, with gifts for—"

"What kind of gifts?"

"Furs and fish, mostly."

I was thankful that I had not been put in a crate of fish.

"Let me take a look."

"My good man, the crates are nailed shut."

"Well, I still think we should—"

"Hey!" another voice cried. "Who are they?"

I felt Dagmar tense. Her dagger had been out and ready the whole way, and she began to reach for her sword with the other hand. I suppose she wanted to pull it out the moment the crate opened, but mostly she just kicked me in the face a little.

"Just more affiliates, my *good man*," growled Klemens.

"Did you bring hangers-on from the damned Bandit States?!"

"Well, yes! We're trying to open a bank in Rituo."

"Andelka and the Rituo delegation have already—"

"But this isn't—"

"You can't just—"

"You there, Rots!" cried Bozena, from somewhere behind me. "You come and take a look at their papers, and tell me whether or not they're in order, yes? Rituo is our *ally*."

"Watch your tone, Masovskan."

"Come look at their papers, first."

Inspection of their papers took a long time, and there was much complaining about some parts being in the language of Rituo, which the soldiers certainly did not know. The inspection of everyone else's papers went on even longer, and Dagmar remained tense throughout. Sometimes she muttered, "I'll kill him. If nothing else, I will kill him."

Finally, I heard a soldier murmur to another: "What about the crates?"

"We'll probably have to read a series of gods-damned *books* in five languages detailing everything in there. We've wasted enough time, and have plenty more to check in. Let them through."

"Yes, sir. Besides, the way those fish are smelling, I'd rather not let any more stench out."

And in we went. The noise of soldiers yelling, birds chirping, people screaming that they had papers, all melted away and became the bustle of the Sunset Palace in utter disarray before a big event. A cheery butler told the Gustavuses where to put us, as a much less cheery one screamed at a group of people who were, I think, mopping the floors.

I kept listening for Tural's voice, even though I knew we couldn't be near the kitchens. I did not hear him.

We were carried a bit longer before we were set down. Dagmar began to writhe in anticipation. I heard low voices that I could not make out, and we were lifted again. This time, there was no cursing, just grunts and jostling as we were carried. We went like this for some time, and the bumping became worse.

"Something's wrong," grunted Dagmar.

"Just keep quiet," hissed Gabor.

Dagmar arced her foot upward, almost kicking me again, and began to slam on the top of the crate.

"Stop it!" I whispered.

Voices finally came from outside the crate, grumbling something in Rotfelsenisch. Dagmar kicked again, and the wood began to give. The crate was dropped to the floor, and my teeth cracked together from the impact. Dagmar kicked again, and the top of the crate broke outward.

In a moment, her sword was out, slicing through the furs, and she was on her feet. Then she didn't move.

When I managed to pull myself out of the crate, at first all I saw was Dagmar's yellow uniform against a vast ocean of purple. I blinked a few times.

The three of us were surrounded by Purples, with their swords and harquebuses pointed at us. The walls behind them, and everything else in view, was also purple. There were no other crates or allies or bankers in sight. It seemed the Gustavuses had indeed betrayed us.

"I knew it," growled Dagmar.

THE GRAND SUZERAIN

Dagmar, Gabor, and I were led down another purple hallway to a small door that opened into a room that was now familiar to me: Court Philosopher Vorosknecht's study. There was the purple couch, the great desk, the gaudy paintings, the glass liquor cabinet, the bust of the Court Philosopher himself in purple-stained marble, and the skeleton of poor old Meregfog. The door closed behind us and became one of the paintings.

Ranging about the large room, and out into the adjoining halls, were about twenty Greens and twenty Purples, including the ones who had brought us there. Some sat, some stood, two Greens in a hallway were even throwing a small Loashti rubber ball back and forth. Vorosknecht stood, looking smug, but harried, behind his desk, with Alban at his side. Slumped into the great purple couch was High General Dreher, surrounded by Greens who looked quite out of place against the room's predominant color. Selvosch sat near Dreher, on a little stool, shaking with . . . some sort of feeling, I'm sure.

In the center of the room, were three figures, bound and gagged. Lenz and Prince Friedhelm were covered in bruises, from what I could see. Lenz seemed to have had the worst of it, with old blood crusting in his mustache, and one of his eyes so swollen I was not sure he could see out of it. Grandmother was there as well, but she did not seem to have been beaten. She seemed to be trying to bite off and swallow her gag, in order to be free or to choke to death in spite.

"Well, hello everyone!" I chirped, because I could think of nothing better to say. Grandmother glared at me, and I grinned at her.

We were divested of our weapons and shoved to our knees near Vorosknecht's desk, with our hands hastily tied behind our backs. In those few moments, I saw so much of what the last week must have been like for the leaders of the regicides. Dreher was breathing hard, as though even that movement was painful, with his hands braced against his knees. It seemed that he would have bent over entirely, with his face between his knees, if he was not keeping his red, unblinking eyes fixed on Vorosknecht. For his part, Vorosknecht's beard was unkempt, and he could not stop drumming his fingers on his desk. He also glared across the room at his partner. The High General and the Court Philosopher didn't seem too fond of each other at all.

"Perhaps now we can get some answers," sighed Vorosknecht. "And if not . . . oh well."

"Answers would be ideal," snapped Dreher. "After your Chief Ethicist disappeared right when she could have been useful."

Vorosknecht shrugged. "Alban, I believe the High General had words for our witch."

Alban grabbed me by the rope around my wrists and dragged me across the floor until I was in front of the purple couch, where Dreher leaned forward and slapped me. It was surprising, but it didn't hurt much.

"How *could* you, Kalyna?" he said. His red face was full of anger; his bottom lip quivered.

I looked up at him. "So, they haven't killed you for bringing me into the fold yet?"

"We were all taken in by you," said Selvosch. He seemed on the verge of tears. Such love for the Soul of the Nation, I suppose.

Vorosknecht cleared his throat behind me, as though he very much wanted to dispute that "all" of them had been taken in. But he said nothing.

I had gotten to them. I was captured, I would probably have my throat slit any minute, but I had gotten to them and that warmed my heart. The anger in that room was so thick and palpable. What had they screamed at each other during the past week? How many attempts, or perceived attempts, at undermining each other had there been? How miserable and sleep-deprived were they and their men? I felt a tingle just imagining.

"Well, now you have me," I said. "I suppose you win."

"We won when we had the Prince," sighed Vorosknecht. "He led us on a merry chase for days through all his hidden tunnels and whatnot, but we got him in the end. And in here, no one else in the palace can hear him or the spymaster scream."

"Now, we just need one of you to tell us where your false King is," sighed Dreher. "I'm honestly surprised at how well the Prince has held up."

"That's because none of us know," I laughed. "He and the Queen have disappeared. Beat us all you want, we still couldn't begin to tell you."

I remembered that Olaf had promised to be back for the Eve of the Council. If he kept his word, he would be delivered right into their hands.

"And if we began on your grandmother?" asked Alban, from behind me.

I craned my neck around painfully to look at him, and grinned. "Please do."

"Disgusting," grunted Selvosch. "To care so little for your own family. No Rot would ever—"

"Oh, stop it, Selvosch," moaned Vorosknecht. "I'm sure even the pretender will be back for the Council, so let's just kill them and wait it out. The worst-case scenario is we kill *three* monarchs and take over the palace."

I heard Alban, still standing behind me, draw a knife.

"Not yet!" cried Dreher. He leaned forward closer, his red face inches from mine.

"First, Kalyna, why did you do it?"

"Do what, *Franz*? Exploit your beliefs?"

"Have this . . ."—he waved a stubby hand at Gabor—"*animal* kill Martin-Frederick. Tell me you saw the Soul of the Nation. Make me look like a fool. All of it!"

Alban snorted. "'Look like'?"

"Quiet, Alban," laughed Vorosknecht.

Dreher glared over my head. "Quiet!" he screamed. Then he looked back at me. "Kalyna," said Dreher, "A little spying is one thing, but to play with our beliefs like that. Why did you do it?"

"Because it was fun, Franz," I replied. My own grin became infectious, and very genuine: I couldn't stop it. And I was not entirely lying.

Dreher raised his hand to hit me again.

"Let me, High General," said Alban. He stepped across and backhanded me hard enough to knock me onto my side. I tasted blood. From there I saw only boots, and the purple-stained wood of the floor.

"Oh, that's cute," I said, my cheek pressed into the floor. "Hit me for the High General: that will convince everyone that the Purples and the Greens are one big group of friends."

Dreher wanted some sort of absolution from me, and that could buy me a few minutes, but for what? Would Chasiku and the others come save us? Most likely, they were in a dungeon or dead. I could try to prolong my death, but either way, these men would win and the whole Tetrarchia would fall. Crushed by the whim of some great . . . *fish*. I felt like the condemned man who chews his last meal slowly: taking up time for the sake of one more breath. My mind raced for other ways to stall.

At least they hadn't gotten Papa. He would be safe and comfortable until the end.

"What do you mean?" groaned Selvosch. "What do you mean about a big group of friends?"

"Exactly what I said. You're all waiting to betray each other, and you act like friends. It's cute."

"An easy lie," said Vorosknecht. "Alban, bring her here."

"Come up here, Loashti," grunted Alban.

I was dragged up to my feet and over to Vorosknecht, so I could look him in the eye.

"Tell us where you hid your pretender," he said, looking down at me, pointing with his long fingers. "This is your last chance, before Alban slits your throat."

"I told you what a fool you were before, Otto," I laughed, making sure to get some spittle flecked with blood in his face, "back when you and I planned to string Dreher along with this Soul of the Nation garbage. But even *I* didn't realize just how blitheringly stupid you are."

"What?" roared Dreher behind me. It was followed by the sound of him wheezing.

"Now wait, High General, wait," stammered the Court Philosopher. "This is clearly a trick. Alban, kill her."

"Don't you dare!" shouted Dreher. "If you want her dead so quickly, maybe there's truth in what she's saying." He had moved closer.

"Come now, High General," groaned Vorosknecht, pressing his hands to his eyes in consternation. "Haven't you believed enough of her lies?"

Dreher's voice was right behind me. "What are you saying, witch?" I fancied I could smell the bland, sad roast on his breath.

"You honestly believed," I began, "all of Vorosknecht's stories about a powerful Soul of the pink people's nation, one that would be pleased by human sacrifice? You really think we weren't stringing you along?"

Dreher shoved me aside to get in Vorosknecht's face. I slammed against the purple bust of the Court Philosopher. To my left were the purple-stained bones of Meregfog, his old pet.

"Is this true?" cried the High General.

"Of course not. She is just trying to get to you, High General. We've learned all she knows, and she's trying to stay alive."

I pressed harder back against the cool marble of the statue, feeling for any rough edges I could use for my ropes. It was quite smooth. Maybe Vorosknecht often rubbed it for good luck, or some such. I needed more time.

And then, all at once, the best way to keep us alive a little longer came to me. If I survived, I knew I would never stop feeling I had betrayed myself. I started to laugh again. It was a laugh calculated to sound threatening, cruel, evil, but the truth is, it started deep inside me, in a well of self-loathing.

Both men stopped yelling at each other and turned to me.

"What?" ventured Vorosknecht.

"What I know hardly matters," I said. "You *should* be wondering what the Grand Suzerain knows."

That shut them up for a moment. The Court Philosopher understood it first, and his eyes widened.

"The Grand Suzerain of Loasht?" he whispered.

I grinned. I think there was blood on my teeth from when Alban had hit me. "And he knows *everything*." I leaned forward, eyes wild. "Do you truly think that assassinating your four little monarchs will make you safe? That conquering this backward rock will *make you safe*? What do you honestly think will happen when this ailing, sectarian, four-part government crumbles?"

Dreher looked shaken. "The Rotfelsenisch nation," he began, "will rise and—"

"The armies of Loasht," I interrupted, "will swarm through this broken experiment and crush you while you're weak. More soldiers than you can imagine, with guns like you have never seen." I laughed some more. "Rotfelsen is not so strong a fort, and there are more of our soldiers amassed at the border than there are pink idiots within this rock."

"No," said Dreher.

I nodded. "Oh, yes. Whom do you honestly think I've been spying for in Rotfelsen all this time? Lenz? *The Prince?*" I turned and spat in the direction of the bound and gagged captives. Prince Friedhelm's eyes were so wide that I wondered if he believed me.

I could tell from the faces of Dreher and Vorosknecht that they certainly did. The second easiest thing to make a customer believe, after what they *want* to be true, is what they *suspect*. To them, this was the pieces falling into place: Loasht was always the great threat, looming and unknowable, and I was *foreign*. There is much more Rotfelsenisch in my blood than there is Loashti, but what does blood matter anyway? Mine doesn't even bother to carry the Gift.

"Quiet, witch!" yelled Alban.

He stormed up to me to hit me, even as I saw fear in his eyes. I acted as though I wanted to avoid being hit, and moved into a position where, I hoped, it would look normal for me to stagger off to my left. Then I let him strike me, and did so. I laughed some more, a laugh of pain at betraying myself, and of gleeful satisfaction at conning them all. I hated myself, but it was *thrilling*.

I turned to my left and right and continued to smile ruefully, now at Dagmar and Gabor. They looked appropriately horrified.

"Kalyna? You can't be serious!" cried Gabor. He overplayed it a touch, but no one else noticed.

I stumbled back until I felt Meregfog's pedestal behind me. "Pathetic." Now I tasted even more copper, so I smiled in Vorosknecht's direction with a bloody mouth. "Still think it's a good idea to work behind Dreher's back, Otto?"

"She's lying, of course!" yelled Vorosknecht.

"Why would I lie now? You're going to kill me, and I know it. But I will go to meet my reward with the ancient Lords of Loasht in their fortresses. I will die knowing I brought Loasht glory."

Alban drew a dagger. "Then I suppose it's time to—"

"Stop!" yelled Dreher, walking over and pushing the Purple away from me. "Every time you plan to kill her, you convince me that she's right about you."

"Come now, High General," groaned Vorosknecht, crossing the room to us. "You aren't really going to listen to this—"

"You traitor!" Dreher continued. "You agreed that she was seeing the Soul! You must have been in league with her, and with Loasht!"

I laughed and laughed, and pressed my ropes against old Meregfog's fangs. I hoped very much they were no longer poisonous. As the two men yelled at each other, the Greens and the Purples in the room began to amass, glaring and murmuring.

"Really now, this is too much!" Vorosknecht growled, throwing his hands up in the air. "You're going to believe the professed Loashti spy over me? You don't think she may have hoodwinked me as well?" He waved an arm at me.

I stopped trying to cut my bonds, as they were looking at me once more. I could not tell if I had made any progress.

"Why not? I'm a soothsayer," I laughed. "I did see your country's puny soul, but the Loashti one is so much *greater*."

"Do you honestly expect us to believe you are a Loashti spy *and* a soothsayer?" snapped Vorosknecht.

"If they have them," said Dreher, "then who better to use as a spy?"

This next lie played so heavily on vile beliefs that I almost couldn't bring myself to say it, but I did: "Loasht has deep and ancient magics borne in our very blood, you fools. Where do you think my Gift comes from?"

"She's a fake!" yelled Vorosknecht, looking back at Dreher.

"Oh?" I sneered. "Is there *some reason* you think I'm a fake, Otto? Some reason you knew, but never told Dreher? Perhaps my grandmother can enlighten us!"

Vorosknecht was silent.

"Believe me or not," I sighed. "But I know you're each planning to have the other killed once the assassinations are finished."

They were both quiet then. I don't know if either of them had specific plans for the other one's end, but there was no way they could both create the Rotfelsen they wanted while working together, and they knew it. They must have known it during this whole week spent at each other's throats, with nothing to unite them but getting to tonight's invocation. What's more, their most loyal soldiers and commanders— here with them—must have also known it.

As a matter of fact, it was not the leaders who broke first: it was a Green who drew his sword. The epaulets on his uniform suggested he was one of Dreher's commanders.

"You!" he cried, leveling his sword at Vorosknecht. "First you seduce our High General with your fairy tales—"

"No!" yelled Dreher. "It's not a fairy—"

"—and then you plan to assassinate—!"

Alban knocked the man's sword aside, and clubbed him over the head with the pommel of his dagger. A group of Greens drew their swords. Purples loyal to Alban drew theirs. It was all very quiet for a moment. As everyone else stood still, the Green who had been clubbed wheeled about awkwardly, trying to catch his balance.

Then, as he turned, he inadvertently sliced Selvosch's arm with the tip of his rapier. No one was on Selvosch's side, but someone had been cut, and they all exploded.

ALBAN

The room and its adjoining hallways became an unbalanced blur of green against a great canvas of purple, and soon there were splatters of red as well. Dreher and Vorosknecht were yelling at their soldiers, but no one could hear them. I backed up against Meregfog and began desperately trying to cut my bonds on his teeth, thinking how silly I would look if I poisoned myself and died.

A Green backed up toward me, and ducked beneath a Purple's wild sword swing. To avoid it, I threw myself backward, crashing to the floor with the stand and the skeleton beneath me. My back hit the stand hard, and I lost my breath. I heard the crunching of bones and hoped none of them were mine.

I had never noticed before that, on the ceiling of the study, there was a large painting of Vorosknecht bowing before the gods of wisdom. I laughed hysterically at the look of quiet dignity on this gigantic version of the Court Philosopher, even as I reached desperately for Meregfog's fangs. I could no longer see the fighting, I could only hear it.

I managed to wrap my hands around a long fang. One side was so sharp that it cut me, and I felt my hands become slick. The fighting got louder. Somehow, with my bloody hands beneath my own body weight, I managed to cut the rope apart. I rolled onto my side, and found myself with the use of my hands. I scrabbled around for a better look at what was going on.

I turned just in time to see High General Dreher punch the Court Philosopher in the face. The two began to fight, and I felt an inescapable glee. Throughout the room, the forty or so soldiers were hacking each other to bits, yelling about betrayal, and generally making a mess. Lenz and Friedhelm had scooted off, beneath a far table, trying to stay out of the way. Grandmother, it seemed, had already rolled to some other part of the room—I did not see her. Closer to me, Dagmar writhed against her bonds, while Gabor lay on his back across a prone Green, trying to grab a weapon with his bound hands.

I hopped up, shakily, with the long fang in my right hand, like a small knife. That's when Alban, through all the commotion, saw that I was free.

He roared something and ran toward me. I reached for the closest thing, and hurled Meregfog's skull at him. It burst into pieces against his forehead, and he staggered. Then he was attacked by a Green.

I turned to Dagmar, quickly cutting her free with poor Mcregfog's fang.

"Finally," she grunted as she shot up to her feet.

She turned to Gabor, but he had already freed himself with a dead Green's sword, while I took the corpse's dagger. Gabor avoided four or five blades that weren't exactly aimed for him, and skewered a Purple who had been distracted with someone else. He snatched her sword as she fell, and threw it behind him, to Dagmar.

"Get behind the desk," I hissed. "I would rather they kill each other and we just mop up whoever's left."

"Not without Lenz!" Gabor called over his shoulder. Then he plunged into the battle.

"I'm going to help him," grunted Dagmar. She became a daffodil blur in that purple room.

Well, *I* went behind the desk. I cowered there and felt very silly with a dagger in one hand and an old fang in the other, peeking over the surface to watch everyone else fight. The Greens and Purples were really going at it, and I felt confident that many of them had expected this confrontation to come. Just not for another day or two. They were cutting each other to pieces, knocking over all of Vorosknecht's fine furniture and art, pulling down tapestries, and spraying blood everywhere. Gabor was weaving his way through, toward where Lenz and Friedhelm were huddled under a table, not even aware that Dagmar was protecting his back, letting no one get close. That woman was like iron: it was inspiring, terrifying, and enticing.

At one point, in a far corner of the room, I caught a glimpse of Grandmother. She was hiding behind an armchair with a fiery look in her eyes. It was the worst thing I'd seen all day.

"Oh gods," I mumbled to myself. "What do I do?"

Suddenly, on the other side of the desk, Dreher and Vorosknecht popped back up into view. The High General had the Court Philosopher in a headlock, and was dragging him backward, yelling and cursing. Selvosch stared at them from behind a statue, shaking.

Two Greens started toward them, to help Dreher kill his rival, until one of the Greens was very surprised by a sword poking out through his chest, and the other took a dagger across the throat. Alban burst between the two of them, sword and dagger in hand, and began trying to pull Dreher off Vorosknecht.

I ducked down beneath the desk and hoped no one had seen me.

"Loashti charlatan!" was suddenly screamed inches above me.

Selvosch was sprawled atop the desk, his head over the side, in front of mine. He was gesticulating wildly toward me.

"She's here! The witch is here! It's all her fault, we need to stop—"

I jabbed Meregfog's fang into his shoulder, and he howled and slid away, tumbling off the desk into some other direction. Regrettably, he took the fang with him.

So much for hiding. I popped up and began to run for another corner of the room. I could no longer see where Gabor and Dagmar were through the wall of Greens and Purples. For a moment, above it all, I saw a Purple standing up on the couch, laughing and fighting someone off, until he was run through from behind by a Green. The table beneath which Lenz and Friedhelm had been hiding had long since collapsed, but I had no notion of whether or not they were still under it.

I ran behind the statue of Vorosknecht and waited a moment, looking for the next safe spot in this chaos. I saw the large glass liquor cabinet, and went for it. I was almost touching it when Alban tackled me.

I managed not to be knocked over, so instead we did a sort of dance together: me stumbling backward as he stumbled forward, our arms entangled, unable to get at each other with our weapons. My flailing leg kicked over the liquor cabinet as I went. I heard it crash, but never saw it, which is rather a shame.

Our strange little dance ended with me crammed into a far corner of the room, but too close up against Alban for him to bring his rapier to bear. I grabbed his sword arm with my free hand, and knocked it against the wall until the thin blade bent, and he dropped it. I tried to stab him with my dagger, but he jumped back and avoided it. Over his shoulder, I saw the battle raging on.

Then, I did a very stupid thing: I threw the dagger at him. In my defense, I knew I was not capable of hitting him with the blade. But I knew he'd see a metal *something* flashing toward him, and I followed just after it, hoping he'd flinch.

He did, holding up his arm to protect his face as the harmless handle of my dagger hit him. Moments later, I was upon him, both of my hands gripping his wrist, trying to shake his last weapon out of his hand.

Alban hauled back his free hand and punched me in the face. My mouth was already very bloody, and I grinned.

"I already know how hard you hit," I choked out.

A quick moment of surprise was enough to get his dagger out of his hands. Unfortunately, it practically flew away, behind him, and now there was just the two of us and our fists, alone in this room of violence.

I didn't want to back away, so I allowed him to hit me again. I hooked my left arm around his body, my face next to his, chin over his shoulder. Our cheeks touched. I punched him in the stomach three times with my right, hooked my leg behind his, and shoved him back. He fell, but grabbed the front of my blouse to pull me with him. Rather than trying to pull free, I put out a foot to stop myself, and stomped on his chest.

None of the other fighting mattered now. Not Dreher and Vorosknecht, not Gabor and Dagmar, not Lenz, and certainly not Friedhelm and Grandmother. I stomped on him again.

Alban swung a leg up and caught me in the chin. I staggered back, and he turned over, crawling toward where the dagger had fallen. But he still thought a simple kick to the jaw was enough to stop me. I am not the strongest or the fastest, but I've been hit a lot in my life. I didn't spend a childhood being walloped by brigands and townsfolk and competitors for nothing.

He had barely moved by the time I was sitting on his back. I slammed my hands as hard as I could against both sides of his head, smashing his ears and, hopefully, bursting his eardrums. He cried out, and I grabbed his ears tightly, and began to slam his face into the wood floor, again and again.

"How good are you without six of your men, Alban?" I shrieked. He couldn't hear me.

He struggled and reached backward for me, turning his head as far as he could. I saw half of his face, and his eye socket looked wrong, shifting beneath the skin. I punched him, and he went limp. I held his hair in one hand and kept punching him anyway. I was beyond thought or care. I didn't even hate Alban: he was just a cruel man doing his cruel job, but he was here to be hit.

I wasn't even listening to what was going on around me. If a Purple had decided to come up behind me and slit my throat, I could not have stopped them. All I heard was noise, and all I did was continue to beat this man with my bloody hands. Until, finally, I was too tired, and I just stopped. I sat on top of him, panting and shaking.

My hands quivered until Dagmar grabbed them, and yelled something to me that I didn't hear. I shook my head. There was nothing in the world but Alban and my bleeding hands. Dagmar yelled it again, and pointed.

I turned, and saw a great wave of Yellows streaming into the room. Behind the first row of them was a group that carried a sort of palanquin made from the top of a crate. Perched upon it was Chasiku, pointing feebly with a hand shaking as much as mine.

AN AUDIENCE WITH THE KING

I mumbled, or yelled, I don't know, as Dagmar held me tightly, pulling me away from Alban's limp body. The Yellows who had come into Vorosknecht's apartments were quickly followed by an even larger group of Reds, who yelled and pointed weapons until everyone was still.

I was standing up, leaning against a wall, covered in blood and surrounded by broken furniture, when Olaf entered the room. He looked pristine in his ermine and scarlet silk, a ceremonial sword gleaming at his side.

"I say!" he laughed. "What in the world is going on here?" He looked around, seemingly tickled more than anything else. Until he saw me and ran over. Olaf bent over to look into my face, putting a hand on my shoulder. "Kalyna, are you alright?"

"Did we win?" I whispered.

"Well, I hope so!" he laughed. "But what happened, are you—?"

Queen Biruté appeared at his side. She was in immaculate dark blue robes, and placed a delicate hand on his shoulder.

"*Your Majesty*," she whispered. "The Reds are watching."

Olaf smiled at her and stood up straight. In a moment, I saw his face change to that blank Gerhold expression.

"Well," he said. "My, my, you've all made quite a mess." The King and Queen then wandered off to inspect the Court Philosopher's apartments.

I saw Chasiku being laid out on the purple couch, which was now stained with blood, and I staggered toward her. Dagmar followed, ready to catch me if I fell.

"Chasiku. Chasiku!" I didn't mean to yell, but I still had panic sitting somewhere deep within me.

Chasiku did not move.

"Did we win?" I cried. "Do you see the . . ." I looked about at everyone in the room: scores of Yellows and Reds, as well as captured Greens and Purples. I switched to Skydašiavos. "Do you see the shattering? Did we stop it?" I grabbed her shoulder and began to shake her.

"Kalyna," she moaned, her head swiveling toward me. "I can't see Rotfelsen shattering anymore, in any future. At least not this year. We won. I am in so much pain. Leave me be!"

I let go of her and slumped to the floor. I did not even care that I was wedged between Green and Purple corpses.

THE INVOCATION

Eventually, I was pulled up off the floor and cleaned up. When all was said and done, about seven Greens and Purples had survived the fight in the Court Philosopher's apartments. There was not a single dead Yellow, as they had burst in just at the end, when the others had done most of the work on one another. It turned out that Chasiku, Behrens, and the rest of our secret invasion force had been taken to a storage room. There they were let out of their crates by smiling Gustavuses, who, of course, had *no idea* how one crate had been misplaced. It seemed the bankers had hoped *I* would die, but that Chasiku and the rest would save the Tetrarchia.

Chasiku had indeed led those Yellows, from her palanquin, to where the battle would take place. There were Purple guards out front, but with Chasiku's guidance, their legs were shot out from under them before they saw anyone. This commotion in front of the Court Philosopher's apartments was what brought more Yellows, the Reds, and eventually the King and Queen.

Gabor and Dagmar had indeed saved Lenz and Prince Friedhelm, although Dagmar took a few small injuries protecting Gabor as he untied them. Neither Lenz nor the Prince was able to be particularly helpful after that, as they had spent days being beaten.

While the room was being cleaned up and inspected, a visibly shaken Gabor took me aside and told me that he had seen Grandmother slit an unconscious Green's throat. No one else had seen it happen, and Gabor hadn't the slightest idea what had driven her to it. Grandmother, of course, refused to say anything beyond insults: at me, at Lenz, at the Prince, at her captors, and so forth.

The surviving Green and Purple soldiers from the battle were arrested, as were a blubbering Quarrymaster Selvosch and a stoic High General Dreher. Court Philosopher Vorosknecht—the one I would most liked to have gloated over—was dead. The High General had expressed his martial courage through a table leg, and stove in his onetime ally's skull. When I heard this, I looked up at the purple bust of Vorosknecht, still standing and untouched, and thought of what a shame it was that his end hadn't come by being crushed beneath it.

Alban also survived, by the way. He was thrown in prison as well, of course. I heard later that I had permanently deafened him in one ear. I felt neither guilt nor joy: really, we had both been doing our jobs. His just carried the requirement of being a bad person, while for mine, being a bad person was a nice extra.

Chasiku was carted back out to her tower, and I was thrown into a yellow uniform and dragged to the evening's invocation, which would preface the Council of Barbarians. Lenz was excused from duty that evening, in order to convalesce.

The Feast of the Eve of the Council took place in a great hall that had, somehow, not been used for any part of the Winter Ball, nor anything else I had attended. Months spent as a royal pawn, and

KALYNA THE SOOTHSAYER | 435

I could still get lost in that damn palace. The room had a ceiling, hung with wreaths, that was higher even than that of the Grand Opera House.

I stood with a group of Yellows up in the rafters, watching a priest of the goddess of springtime drone on in front of a great crowd of courtiers, dignitaries, advisors, minor royalty, their spouses, and whoever else was able to get in. The front row of this audience was conspicuously empty, with no Dreher, no Vorosknecht, no Selvosch, no Edeltraud, and a very heavily bruised Prince Friedhelm, still resplendent in yellow. Behind the man giving the invocation sat Queen Sevda and Consort Kagiso of Quruscan, King Lubomir XIII and Queen Thora of Masovska, King Alinafe of Skydašiai, and King Gerhold VIII, lately Olaf, and Queen Biruté of Rotfelsen. Besides the empty seats, and the overwhelming presence of Reds, in the near-total absence of Greens or Purples, it seemed that nothing had changed.

I kept waiting for shots to ring out, for battle cries to sound, but the old man just droned on. I imagined the creature with the eye in the depths of the world ripping through us all with its tentacles, or fins, or hands, right through the great hall and the rotrock itself. But nothing of the kind happened, and the old man just kept blathering. We had avoided the end of the Tetrarchia, had avoided civil war, and had even kept the battle to a small group of rooms and fewer than a hundred dead. So why did I feel like a failure? I'd nearly died, and killed, for the broken and unwieldy Tetrarchia, and the similarly ruptured Rotfelsen, to continue on just as before. I had fought for sameness and stagnance, and that was what we got.

I sighed and looked over the monarchs again. Some looked intense, some bored, and I think it was Lubomir who was asleep. Olaf maintained the blank expression of his forebear, with empty eyes looking at nothing. But every now and then, a small smile would appear at his lips, as though he was fighting a laugh at what a strange place he was now in. He wasn't looking at me, but I could not help smiling back. That was something.

A GREAT DEAL OF CLEANUP

The Council of Barbarians continued along its way, and I had very little do with it. Those of us who worked for Prince Friedhelm were rather busy.

I had this beautiful idea of winning a moral victory by going to Dreher and convincing him that his plot had been wrong all along. In my mind, he would realize I was right and tell me everything, letting us hunt down the rest of his compatriots. But the ex–High General had nothing to hold onto but pride, and refused to say a word. Three days into the Council, he killed himself. We never did find out where he got the poison, and it seemed that his last words were whatever he yelled while crushing the Court Philosopher's skull. Perhaps it is silly, but I was glad he lived long enough to learn that I was *not* in fact a Loashti spy.

Jördis, it turned out, had been in hiding at the servant house of her friend Vondel, Tenth Butler to High General Dreher, who had not been important enough to be involved in anything. Jördis, true to her nature, had wanted to see who "won." She had apparently remembered my little bluff about a soothsayer siding with the winners, and so once she realized I was not, in fact, on Dreher and Vorosknecht's side, she had decided the best option was to disappear for a bit. When it was all over, she allowed herself to be arrested, along with many promises to help however she could.

It seemed that old Meregfog's skeleton really was all out of poison, as Selvosch grew quite talkative. Not to me, of course; he hated me. It was Lenz's idea to send Jördis in to speak with the Quarrymaster, as she seemed so keen on proving her trustworthiness. So, Selvosch saw Jördis, a high-ranking subordinate of Vorosknecht's, as clear proof that the movement was gone, and we didn't tell him otherwise. He didn't need to know how little she cared for ideology. Selvosch told her who else was in on the plot, as well as that the other Greens and Purples had, largely, been expected to fall in line once the coup began, without being given time to think much about it. Jördis did not demand a full pardon based on this, but heavily suggested she would do whatever *else* was necessary to obtain one.

Selvosch also babbled about when Vorosknecht had first brought up the Soul of the Nation, and I couldn't help feeling that this moment, and whatever was in the Court Philosopher's own head, and whatever chance encounters he had, must have been what redirected Papa's futures from stretching for decades toward, instead, an imminent doom. I think we would need to read Vorosknecht's mind to know for certain what he had done and what he believed, but that mind had been splattered across his carpet.

Most of the regicides were tried in royal tribunals that I was not privy to. I don't even know if I wanted them to be treated well or harshly, only that royal tribunals make me nervous by their very nature. Give me a muddy Masovskan courtroom, full of gawkers.

Doctor Aue had quite a few sounds to make over Lenz and Prince Friedhelm's injuries, but they were nursed back to health. Lenz felt that he had been particularly ill-used in the past few weeks, and I supposed I could not disagree.

It seemed that we had saved the Tetrarchia. In the long term, of course, something terrible lived beneath us. In Rotfelsen, or beneath Rotfelsen, or beneath the entire Tetrarchia.

Oh yes. I also went alone to see *The Leper's Five Tits*. Not as some honor to fallen Martin-Frederick, the would-be nationalist king, but his tickets were given to me, and it seemed like a good thing to do. It was funny!

KING GERHOLD VIII

"I hate this," said Jördis. She was draped from head to toe in purple, but of a more reasonable style than Vorosknecht had worn. And no hat for Jördis. It was the fourth day of the Council of Barbarians.

Two Purples were straightening her caftan, until she waved them away. We were in a small room in the Sunset Palace, along with Lenz, who still looked viciously bruised, and Dagmar, who hung behind me.

"You asked what you could do for a pardon," said Lenz, "and we need a Court Philosopher immediately. The role will be stripped of its real power, and you'll hate the duties, so I think it works out."

"Rotfelsen will be well-served by a Court Philosopher who doesn't want the position," I added.

"Well, you've got that," grumbled Jördis. "My father would be *so proud*." She glanced at the mirror and sighed. "I look like a grape."

"But not a prisoner," I said. "And you have soldiers now."

"Not a full army, of course," she replied. "Which is fine. Maybe this will keep the soldiers from all fighting each other all the time." She did not sound hopeful.

A great shift had taken place, and a forced exodus. Along with Jördis, there was a new High General: an oblivious young man named Engel, who had simply been the most likable officer to have no part in Dreher's treason. Now he and Jördis both commanded Greens and

Purples who were mere shadows of themselves: the first a small honor guard, and the second about half its original size. I suspected that, in five to ten years, the Yellows would be the next great threat to the Tetrarchia. I would have to ask Papa.

"Jördis," I began, "do you . . ."

"Have anything to say to you, Kalyna? No, not that I can think of. Other than that I could have been a better neighbor. But I saw the light, didn't I?" She grinned.

"I suppose."

Prince Friedhelm appeared in the doorway. The bruises were starting to fade on his face, and his yellow robe was so long that a pageboy carried the end of it.

"Lenz, Kalyna, come with me right away."

We all moved to follow him, and he pointed at Dagmar.

"Not you, Yellow, stay here," grunted the Prince.

Dagmar clicked her tongue and leaned against the wall.

Lenz and I went with the Prince to his study, where Olaf was waiting. He was sitting on Friedhelm's desk, grinning from ear to ear.

"It's all such nonsense, isn't it?" he laughed. Olaf threw up his hands, waving them around. "Everything! All of it! Why, just today I swore, by the gods and my royal blood, that I would protect the, ah . . . Oh, what was it, brother?"

Friedhelm slammed the door behind us. "The Freitabranden Moss Caverns in the southeast district of—"

"Yes, yes, I'll learn it all," laughed Olaf. "Eventually. I'm King now, aren't I? Time to push me out of the nest, I suppose. I've gotten very good at thinking about fun things during long speeches."

"I would like nothing better. Now why did you request *my* remaining Recourses?" He sneered. "Other than you, that is."

"Oh, because they're going to be mine now, brother. You don't need them anymore."

"Yours?" I groaned.

"With the option to leave entirely, if you wish," Olaf added quickly. "After all, you saved my life and my kingdom!" He giggled at this last word. "And, Friedhelm, I believe you only needed them, and me, because Gerhold wouldn't listen to you about all the threats to his reign." He hopped off the desk and walked toward Friedhelm, his hands clasped behind his back. "Well, I promise you that Gerhold is now *very* aware of them, and would like the tools to fight further threats. What could you possibly need them for?"

"Well, I—"

"You want me to stay alive on the throne, yes? To take over all these boring functions, so you don't have to? Well, lay the responsibility at my feet." He winked. "Brother."

Prince Friedhelm stood still for some time, then he exhaled very slowly. "You will pay me for them."

"Of course, of course! I have a whole list of your people I want, and what I think they're worth." He clapped Friedhelm on the back. "You won't be disappointed! I'll be the best King you ever installed."

Olaf then pushed past Friedhelm, to put a hand on my shoulder, and another on Lenz's. "Well, you're both free to stay in my service, or leave!"

"I will . . . stay," said Lenz, weighing each word, "if I can live down in Turmenbach again."

"Granted!" Olaf clapped his shoulder.

"I'm already gone," I said.

"Of course! But I hope you'll let me send you along with some payment, and a few useful gifts to remember me by."

"I . . . sure, why not."

"Splendid, splendid!" Olaf spun about and walked back to the desk. "Now, brother, I've brought the paperwork, so we can just take a look right now." He pointed to a sheaf of papers with the King's seal still dripping upon it. "You two may go. But Kalyna, I'll definitely want to talk again before you disappear!"

Prince Friedhelm continued to stare at his new "brother" for some time. Perhaps he was planning to supplant Olaf after all, someday, but it wouldn't be *my* problem. Lenz could deal with that. Although I did also wonder if the Prince wanted me dead, now, to keep his secrets.

In the doorway, I looked back at Olaf. He bugged out his eyes at me and mouthed, "Isn't it *mad*?" before turning to business.

BLOOD COMRADES

"You put some little fat woman into the Court Philosopher's chair!" cried Klemens Gustavus. "If we had known women could hold that position, we could have tried Bozena after all!"

It was the fifth day of the Council of Barbarians, and I was in the mansion of Edeltraud von Edeltraud, Mistress of the Coin, with a good ten Yellows besides Dagmar. I had not fully left the Prince or the King just yet.

"What's done is done!" said Edeltraud von Edeltraud, who was sitting in a large chair. "I'm just glad it's all over and done with, without real bloodshed."

"And that the King is young and will live a long time," sneered Klemens. "So you won't have to mint all-new marks."

"That does not hurt," said Edeltraud.

"Neither will those quarries," added Bozena.

"I do not have Selvosch's quarries yet," said Edeltraud.

But she would, as I had already heard. Better than the Gustavuses, perhaps.

"This is all academic," I growled. "Klemens Gustavus, do you want to tell us how I ended up in the Court Philosopher's hands?" I knew the answer, of course.

"Oh?" He cocked his head to the side. "You mean when we smuggled you into the palace, specifically so that you could kill him, and then you found him and did exactly that?" He shrugged. "Who can say? The world is full of mysteries, you know."

"Quite mysterious indeed," I said.

Klemens smiled and moved toward me. Dagmar thrust her body at him in a feint that made him jump. Then she laughed. Klemens took a deep breath and extended his hand to me.

"No hard feelings, yes? It was a whole mess in Masovska, of which you only saw the end. Then here in this awful place, we thought we were on different sides, and you killed my men and kidnapped me, but still we came together." He clasped his fingers to show this, and then extended his hand again. "I know we were only doing our small part for the Tetrarchia, but you could not have saved thousands of lives without our help. We are blood comrades now." He said the last sentence in Masovskani, in which the term "blood comrades" had a particularly strong meaning.

I stared at him for a few moments. I was a killer, it's true, but Klemens was a *murderer*, and I, at least, saw a difference. We had needed his help and that disgusted me, but I suppose these are the sort of allies one must make when playing with the fate of a country. I hardly even cared whether he had betrayed us: that at least was understandable, with how we had treated him. But I could not look at him without seeing the men who had been sent to kill Eight-Toed Gustaw from Down Valley Way, and imagining those who had been sent to other inheritors—the men I hadn't stopped.

I looked Klemens right in the eyes, smiled, and shook his hand firmly.

"Blood comrades," I said in Masovskani. Then in Rotfelsenisch, "Allies, now and forever. All is forgiven."

Klemens smiled genuinely, and Bozena seemed relieved.

Perhaps it was hypocritical of me to give my forgiveness, and what amounted to a serious Masovskan oath of alliance. Perhaps I should have spat in his face, told him what I thought of him, stormed out. But it's always best to avoid making enemies, until you come for them in the night. I am a liar, after all.

GOLDEN KNIFE

That same day, I stood in Tural's doorway once again, as I had so many times. We'd hardly had a chance to speak since my "initiation." He was conjuring a flavor, but when he saw me, he snapped right out of it.

"You're leaving soon," he said in Rotfelsenisch.

"I plan to," I replied in Cöllüknit.

"Are you sure?" he asked in the same.

"No. But I will anyway."

He nodded and looked down, then walked up to me, smiling. There were slight creases at the corners of his narrow eyes. His mustache looked like it would have felt nice.

"I had hoped we would get along well," he said.

"We do. And could have gotten along even better, were I more selfish."

He sighed. His breath smelled like earthy tea.

"Did I tell you," I began, my hands shaking as I avoided his eyes, "that in one of the futures Lenz's other soothsayer saw, I had your surname?"

He smiled and shook his head, as though I had told him something endearing. "No, you did not. Ha."

I tried to take a deep breath. I felt the very real possibility of future love hanging there in the air between us like dust, and disappearing. It was the closest I think I've ever come to seeing the world the way

Chasiku did. But I simply could not allow it to happen, not with the way that I needed to live my life. Spending all this time up here with Tural, and even Martin-Frederick, had made me realize how lonely I was, but it was not right to subordinate my entire life to escape loneliness. Better to find someone who could assuage my loneliness on the road—who would expect very little from me.

"I still have your knife," I said, holding it up. "Would you like it back?"

"Someone was killed with that knife, weren't they?"

"Not by me."

"Please keep it."

Stupidly, I had already started trying to hand it to him. He put his hand on mine and gently pushed it back toward me.

"Please keep it," he repeated.

I am sorry to sound maudlin, but his hand on my hand was the longest amount of time that Tural ever touched me. Out in the hall, Dagmar was whistling very loudly, in order to not hear what we were saying.

THE EYE

I never told anyone but Chasiku about the great eye I had seen at the bottom of Glaizatz Lake. What was the point in telling Lenz, or the Prince, or Olaf? What would they do, shoot at it? Who was to say there weren't things like this under every mountain and lake in the world? People live in all sorts of dangerous lands, and a great rock was always going to be strange and precarious.

I hoped that its presence in my thoughts would lessen, but to this day, I often think of the moment it glanced at me. And when I do, I want to cry.

On the sixth, and penultimate, day of the Council of Barbarians, I went to speak to Chasiku about it. She shrugged it off.

"I'm always seeing terrible things," she said.

"And are you going to stay here?" I asked in Skydašiavos.

"I will," she said. "When I saw the Purples slaughtering all those people, down in Glaizatz, it was honestly one of the worst futures I have ever beheld. It's stained my mind."

"Then why—?"

"Because, Kalyna, sometimes, in new visions, or even in person, I see those people. The same faces that were begging for mercy, cruelly cut down and discarded, I see them living now: smiling, grumbling, cursing, *alive*."

"That's wonderful."

"Often it still hurts," she continued. "Seeing them reminds me of that vision, reminds me of their deaths. But I will stay. I'm working directly for the King now, apparently."

"I never thought you'd stay anywhere in order to be around people."

"Kalyna," she said. She still didn't look at me as she spoke. She was leaning against the railing of her balcony, staring off the edge of Rotfelsen into a clear early-spring sky. "Where I come from, my family is . . . well . . . Imagine your grandmother and her expectations, if she were thirty people."

I shuddered. Though Chasiku was not looking at me, she laughed.

"Have you worked in North Shore Skydašiai before, Kalyna?"

"Many times."

"In the big cities?"

"We often avoid big cities."

"Well, my family are a perfect example of why you do. We're a business: a great, stifling, powerful business, that forces out competition."

"Ah," I said.

Chasiku turned, ostensibly to face me, and leaned her back against the railing. But she looked above me. "Detachment is forced upon us from a very young age. Your grandmother may be terrible, but at least she yells at you, and that is emotion. Believe it or not, Kalyna"—she grinned—"I chose to get away from my family because I am *friendly*, comparatively. I wanted to be near people." She spread her arms and continued to smile the most I had ever seen. She had a lovely smile, really. "This is me being friendly."

"Chasiku, you're a much better soothsayer than I am."

"Or will ever be," she added. Not being mean, just frank. I couldn't tell whether she had learned the truth about me. "But it's because of you that this place no longer beats me with the deaths of thousands—at least, no more than any other place. I could not have done my part without yours."

"You're welcome for that, I suppose."

"Oh, and Kalyna?" She trained her face on mine, but still her eyes wandered.

"Yes?"

"Someday you will not be a soothsayer. I promise you that."

This might be the greatest thing anyone has ever told me.

SPRINGTIME

I was in Papa's room on the final day of the Council of Barbarians, packing up the tent rolls. It was one of those sunny days that comes in the early spring, still cold, but promising more. I even heard chirping again. My hope was that if we left right away, we would not be caught in the great surge of traffic that would leave the palace grounds tomorrow morning. Papa was buoyant.

"Are we leaving, Kalynishka?" he asked from his bed, for the fifth time.

"Yes, Papa. Soon. Didn't you like it here?"

"Oh, I did. I did! But, you know, a prophet must wander."

I nodded and folded his clothes. I was smiling.

"But Kalynishka," he asked after a few moments, "did *you* like it here?"

I sighed. "I suppose I did, Papa. Parts of it, anyway."

"Would you want to . . . to stay?" He sounded terrified of the idea, but thought he was putting on a brave face for me.

"Well—"

"Don't you spoil your daughter, Aljosa!" cried Grandmother, bursting into the room.

"Well now, Mother," said Papa. "Don't say it like that. If you are too angry about it, she *will* want to stay."

"She *does* want to stay," growled Grandmother. "She wants to stay and rut with the fruit-man. She wants your grandchildren to smell of durian, my boy."

"She does *not!*" cried Papa.

"Grandmother," I asked, "are you packed?"

"You want an old woman to pack her own bags? You've been off the road too long. You'll do it."

"In a moment," I sighed. "Maybe."

The door to Papa's room was open, but Gabor knocked on it anyway.

"Kalyna!" he cried. "Lenz is on his way up, but I ran here first to say goodbye! I think he wants to talk to you about, you know, spy things."

Gabor gave me a hug, which was odd. He had killed a number of people because of me, starting with Martin-Frederick, but now he was only a slight man wrapping his arms around me.

"You will let me know if you come by Rotfelsen again, won't you?" he asked. "Even if"—he lowered his voice—"you don't let *him* know." He motioned his head back toward the door and winked.

I nodded and patted his shoulder. "And I'll let you know if I need more stabbing done."

"And I you, if I need someone beaten to a pulp!"

"Not so loud, please."

Lenz appeared at the doorway, leaning on a cane, which Doctor Aue had promised him, by the grace of many gods, he wouldn't need after a month. He and Gabor glanced into each other's eyes for one short moment, and it was perhaps the most demonstrative I ever saw them. Then Gabor laughed and rushed through a beam of sunlight to go say goodbye to my father.

"How are you there, Aljosa?" he asked, and they began to talk.

"Hello, Kalyna," said Lenz.

"Good morning," I said.

"Kalyna, I really am sorry that I—"

"If I ever see you again, I will still bother you about the kidnapping, but in the end, I suppose . . ." I sighed. "Well, you were also the Prince's prisoner, and we both did distasteful things in his employ. And I *suppose* it was all for the best, what with saving the Tetrarchia."

"Saving the *what?*" screamed Grandmother. "What did you people *do?*"

"Now, now, Granny," said Gabor from where he sat on Papa's bed. "Come over here and talk to your son and me. You'll be leaving soon, and I want to know *everything* about your strange family's history before you do."

Grandmother looked angry and doubtful, but couldn't resist the chance to give a younger person a lecture about the perfect lineage that I had besmirched.

I walked over to Lenz. "I still haven't packed my things," I said as I left the room.

In the hallway, we passed a chair where Dagmar dozed lightly.

My bedroom was brighter than my father's. Even though it was very cold out, I had left the window open overnight because I needed to remind myself how it felt to shiver in my sleep. I began gathering up a few volumes: ancient histories, *Bohdan's Botanicals*, and the like.

"You can keep those," said Lenz, as he hung in the doorway. "Just don't take any of the ones I wrote."

"Oh, come in already," I said.

Lenz did so.

"Kalyna, is Olaf sending you off with enough gold marks?"

"Too much would make us a target," I said. "I only asked for what could get Papa put up somewhere with walls and a doctor, now and then. More importantly, he's giving us a good carriage and some horses. But not a carriage that *looks* too nice, I made sure of that: something the army got sick of. We're negotiating what else I can bring with me, to keep us safe."

"Good, good." He looked about and poured himself a drink from a bottle on my desk. "You threatened my life in this room," he said.

"I threatened your life a lot; I got the closest here." My back was to him as I tried to make as many books as possible fit in a case.

"Are you *sure* about leaving?" he asked.

"I always have been."

"Yes, but . . . now you could stay of your own accord. You could have walls, a ceiling, mild weather. Olaf would be delighted. Doctor Aue is here, and Dagmar and Tural."

And the eye.

"I know what's here," I said.

"Kalyna," he said, "you hate being a soothsayer."

I wondered if I should just tell him the truth.

"And?" I asked.

"If you stayed here, you could work for me."

"I've had enough fighting."

"Not fighting. You figure people out, and understand how to . . . how to . . ."

"Take advantage of them."

"Well, yes! And that makes my job much easier, and much less violent."

I began to laugh.

"Don't laugh at me, Kalyna," he said through his own chuckles. "Yes, we killed some people, but you did an amazing thing. I know you don't much like royalty or our government, I know you don't much like me—"

"Well, in that company, you're not so bad."

"—but you like Olaf, don't you? And think how much better your life, and your father's life, could be if you stayed here."

"You finally learned to leave Grandmother out."

"We were locked up together for a week."

"Well, she'll be gone soon."

He came closer, crossing the small room. "Does no part of you want to stay and do something different?"

I finally turned to face him. "It doesn't matter what I want. It doesn't even matter what's best for my father's health because Doctor Aue can make him comfortable, but she cannot cure his mind. He *needs* to travel, he needs to continue in the world the way he has, watching me practice our family's calling because he does not know how to handle anything else. Every time he sees me, Lenz, he asks me when we're leaving." I ran my hands through my hair and then gripped it at the nape. "I think I *want* to stay," I admitted as I stared at my boots. "I want to sleep with Tural and talk to Gabor and keep an eye on Jördis in her new position and have Dagmar as my body-guard so that *I don't have to fight ever again.* I even want to work with you, Lenz, because I've gotten used to it. But until my father . . . until later, what I want doesn't matter. There will come a day when I will be devastated, but also freed."

"And now you'll go out and . . . sell your Gift."

I wanted to be angry, but in Lenz's eyes I saw only sadness and pity. He still thought I had a Gift to squander. I took a deep breath. All this time I had kept the secret, except from Vorosknecht, who was dead; Alban, whom no one would listen to; and Dagmar, who didn't care. But here was Lenz, with whom I had been through so much, still under the influence of my fraud. And saying it out loud to those others had been so satisfying.

"Lenz," I said. "I need to tell you something."

He leaned on his cane and looked down at me with an open, mysti-fied expression, that wiry hair stuck out in all directions. This was a man whose presence and knowledge I'd feared, and now he hung upon my next word. And I wanted so badly to unburden myself.

"Lenz," I said again, "I honestly will miss you. Even though I don't like you."

He smiled and shook my hand.

Of course I didn't tell him that I was a fraud. Of course. What in the world would that have accomplished?

EPILOGUE

We wandered throughout the spring and did many things. I still sat at Grandmother's feet, still brought her food, and she still cursed me, but it bothered me less and I didn't let her hit me. It was easier to see the regard in Papa's eyes, to remember it in Tural's, Olaf's, Gabor's, Lenz's. I don't tell you I was, or am now, a happy person, but I will say that now, as I write these words, I am more content than I ever thought possible. That year was when I started inching toward who I am today.

The following summer, we returned to the Great Field, north of the town of Gniezto, in the kingdom of Masovska.

"What are you doing, freak?" cried Grandmother one balmy summer night. "If you go and get cut open, you will kill your father."

I wore leather trousers, my hair was up, I had the sickle on my right hip. A warm breeze shifted the field's grasses as we sat just inside the open tent.

"Don't you do this, shitworm," Grandmother continued.

I stood up, my hair brushing the tent, and kissed her on top of her ancient head. "Shut up."

I stepped out of the tent as she yelled through a mouthful of sage-buttered carrots. To my left, Papa waved from the fire pit, where he sat in his wheeled chair, laying out batter into a sizzling pan. He preferred cooking this way to the alchemically warmed pot. A lantern burned far above him, hanging from one of the turrets of our carriage.

"See you in the morning, Kalynishka!" he said.

I buckled on a sword and walked past the other tent to the edge of this year's hill.

Olaf had been happy to send someone along with us, for our protection, so now we were four. Six, if you counted the horses.

"So"—a laugh—"who is this man again?"

"Some petty extortionist working for the Gustavuses," I replied. "We're starting small."

"Well, that's better than nothing." Dagmar cracked her knuckles. "Traveling with you three has been better than guard duty, but just barely."

I looked up at her and feigned insult, mouth agape.

"Oh, settle down." She patted my cheek.

"Do you think our little assault lies within the King's orders?"

She shrugged. "My orders are to keep you safe."

I nodded.

"And *then* Skydašiai?" she asked. "I've never dueled before."

"Sure. Skydašiai."

"Finally. Shall we?"

Dagmar leaned down and kissed me intensely. She never expected more from me than this: a kiss, some time alone, light words, a bit of excitement. Once we managed to disengage, I nodded, and we walked down the hill into the warm night.

FURTHER READING
(AND VIEWING)

Secondary-world fantasy settings don't spring fully formed out of an author's imagination. Unfortunately, I wrote the first draft of this book around a decade ago, so I hardly remember most of its influences. (For example, I can't for the life of me find where I learned that sickle-fighting treatises were a real thing in medieval Europe. But they were, I promise.)

Nonetheless, here are some references of note I do remember:

Vanished Kingdoms: The History of Half-Forgotten Europe (sometimes under the much less romantic, and greatly inferior, subtitle *The Rise and Fall of States and Nations*), Norman Davies (2011)

Nothing influenced the world and larger plot of Soothsayer more than this book. It explores European nations that completely disappeared from the world and, through them, how nebulous our modern ideas around national identities and borders really are. It's also a history book in which the author is clearly subjective, and sometimes grumpy, which I love.

With Fire and Sword (Polish: *Ogniem i mieczem*), Henryk Sienkiewicz (1884; I read the 1991 W. S. Kuniczak translation)

"Alexandre Dumas–style historical adventure novel set in Eastern Europe" is a concept that narrowcasts to me so intently as to be almost parodic. This book is also how I first learned about the Polish-Lithuanian Commonwealth, without which the Tetrarchia absolutely does not exist. (But beware: it's from the nineteenth century and, unsurprisingly, offensive at times.)

The Thirty Years War, C. V. Wedgwood (1938, revised 1957)
Another great bit of history on how shaky the seemingly set foundations of modern Europe are. This book taught me a lot about the strange way the Holy Roman Empire was run, which was also a major influence on Soothsayer. Wedgwood has a real gift for quickly sketching each individual in a long procession of historical figures.

F for Fake, directed by Orson Welles, cowritten by Orson Welles and Oja Kodar (1973)
A dizzying, rambunctious, and insightful treatise on fakery and expertise, edited together in a way that feels thirty years ahead of its time. I would often watch scenes while writing this book, just so I could soak in the rhythm of Welles' speech and editing.

Acknowledgments

It is wild to me that so many incredible publishing professionals have thrown their weight behind some silly ideas I came up with ten years ago, and I can't thank them enough.

My agent, Hannah Bowman, has been a tireless advocate for my work and an invaluable guide to publishing for my *extremely* neophyte ass. She was also a huge help in improving the book: please guess which major character, and entire related subplot, came from conversations with her.

Erewhon felt like the perfect home for *Soothsayer* even before I knew that their editor, Sarah Guan, was interested. Sarah has done amazing work to make this book the best that it can be, and I was overjoyed when her first comments were along the lines of, "But could we have *more* of the politics?" (Yes. Yes we could.) As I write this, promotion has just started, so I've only seen the beginning of what Martin Cahill is capable of on the marketing side, but it's already staggering.

Sasha Vinogradova's cover is stunning, and elegantly captures so many aspects of the book's vibe and iconography. Cassandra Farrin's interior design expertly conveys both the gravitas and lightness that I was going for in *Soothsayer*. Copyeditor Lakshna Mehta has done an exemplary job of fine-tuning the language while maintaining Kalyna's voice.

That voice of Kalyna's, and her very thought process, would never have existed without Ed Park's course on writing in the first person. (Or, for that matter, without Charles Portis's *True Grit*, which was assigned reading.)

As to friends and family: My spouse, Brittany Marie Spector, has been the first reader of my work as long as we've been together, and has never been content to just tell me it's good and pat me on the back. Simon Leaver-Appelman, Martine Neider, and Anna Bristow were all extremely helpful early readers for *Soothsayer*. Long before this book, Simon was also indispensable in helping me develop my writing style.

I'm also a fourth-generation writer. My father, Lincoln Spector, has been a freelance humorist and tech journalist for much of my life, with side projects in film criticism, poetry, and Purim spiels. My mother, Marilyn Kinch, has been a fanfiction author for decades. My grandmother, Rebecca Newman (her memory is a blessing), traditionally published one novel, self-published another, taught writing for years, and even hosted a public-access TV show on writing.

I never got to meet my great-grandmother, Sarah Spector, but I identify strongly with her. When she wasn't distributing leftist literature in her old folks' home, she was writing an (unpublished) novel based on her experiences growing up in the shtetl and immigrating to New York. The half-remembered, and mostly obliterated, Yiddish world passed down from her part of the family is deeply important to the themes and milieu of *Soothsayer*.

I also have to thank the friends and partners who make up the strange, bicoastal Venn diagram of found families in my life. My fellow artists, queers, leftists, and diasporic Jews, as well as the fine folks who are none of those things but tolerate us.

And you. Thank you for reading my book. I love you.

Thank you for reading this title from Erewhon Books, publishing books that embrace the liminal and unclassifiable and championing the unusual, the uncanny, and the hard-to-define.

We are proud of the team behind *Kalyna the Soothsayer*:

Sarah Guan, Publisher
Diana Pho, Executive Editor
Viengsamai Fetters, Assistant Editor

Martin Cahill, Campaign Manager
Kasie Griffitts, Sales Associate

Cassandra Farrin, Director
Leah Marsh, Production Editor
Kelsy Thompson, Production Editor
Lakshna Mehta, Copyeditor
Rayne Stone, Proofreader

Samira Iravani, Art Director
Alice Moye-Honeyman, Junior Designer
Dana Li, Cover Designer
Sasha Vinograd, Cover Artist

. . . and the entire Kensington Books team!

Learn more about Erewhon Books and our authors at erewhonbooks.com.

Twitter: @erewhonbooks
Instagram: @erewhonbooks
Facebook: @ErewhonBooks

Reading Guide

EREWHON

✳ About the Author ✳

ELIJAH KINCH SPECTOR is a writer, a dandy, and a rootless cosmopolitan from the Bay Area who now lives in Brooklyn. His first novel, *Kalyna the Sooth-sayer*, received acclaim from NPR, Nerds of a Feather, Tor.com, *Foreword*, and *Paste Magazine*, among others. His next novel, *Kalyna the Cutthroat*, is expected in 2024. You can find him at elijahkinchspector.com.

✳ Book Discussion Questions ✳

These suggested questions are to spark conversation and enhance your reading of *Kalyna the Soothsayer*.

1. Discuss the theme of storytelling in the book. How does Kalyna tell stories to advance her goals? What stories do you think Kalyna believes about herself? What are some of the stories the Tetrarchia tells its citizens?

2. Another major theme of *Kalyna the Soothsayer* is ethnic identity. What are Kalyna's identities? How do you think these identities inform the choices she makes throughout the book? How did your own identities (ethnic and otherwise) influence the way you experienced the story?

3. Which parts of Kalyna's personality—self-critical, calculating, paranoid, cunning—are a result of her family upbringing, and which are from the reality of her life in the Tetrarchia? How do you think Kalyna's personality and worldview help and hinder her throughout the story?

4. At the end of Part Four, Kalyna decides not to escape and instead to stay in Rotfelsen and attempt to save the Tetrarchia. What do you think *really* keeps Kalyna in Rotfelsen? Do you believe Kalyna's stated reasoning for her actions, or is she under the influence of other motivations?

5. Kalyna describes herself as a liar, but which characters are truthful in *Kalyna the Soothsayer*? Which are trustworthy? What is the nature of "truth" as a concept in Rotfelsen?

6. When Kalyna and Chasiku first meet, in Part Three, Chasiku describes her family's experience of soothsaying. How do you think Chasiku's family would perceive Kalyna's family? If they were to meet, how do you think the two groups would interact? Why?

7. The cover of the book depicts multiple possible futures for the Tetrarchia. What do you think will become of the Tetrarchia after the events of the book? How would the prophesized fall of the Tetrarchia play into your theories, if at all?

8. Do the Bandit States and Loasht remind you of any real-world countries? Nations can have many different types of relationships with each other; what are some variations you've seen in our world? Do those between the Tetrarchia and its neighbors remind you of any other examples of international relations?

9. Why does Prince Friedhelm work so hard to keep a king on the throne of Rotfelsen? Does Rotfelsen need a monarchic government? What would happen to the Tetrarchia if it didn't have kings and queens?

10. If you were the author, what would you like to see happen in the sequel? Are there any places you want to see more of? Which characters would you want to read more about?

✳ Excerpt from ✳

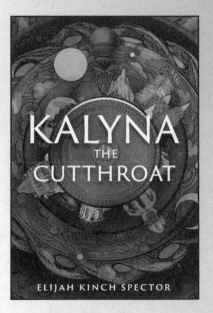

Keep reading for an excerpt from
the next book in the Failures of Four
Kingdoms series, *Kalyna the Cutthroat*.

How I Left Abathçodu, with the Help of Farbex the Good Donkey

"Get moving where?" I asked breathlessly as Dagmar began to push me down the street, away from my pursuers. My pursuers who had been my neighbors for nearly a year.

"I don't know," she said. "Away. You're the smart boy." Her Cölluknit was halting, but did the job.

"Why—?" I took a deep breath and tried again. "Why are you here? I'm glad to see you, of course, but it's been three seasons."

She moved into the next intersection, looked down every street, and then seemed to pick a left turn at random.

"Thought you could use some help," she said. Then, suddenly, she stopped so abruptly that I bumped into her. She rounded on me. "You *can* pay?"

I blinked. "I . . . What will you do if I can't? *Un*-save me? Throw me back to them?"

"No. No. But we will go our separate ways."

My mouth went dry. I must have looked very strange, standing in the middle of the street, slowly licking my lips as I stared fervently at nothing.

"I can pay," I said. "If we can get my things."

Dagmar looked thoughtful for a moment, tapping a long finger against the side of her nose.

"Do you . . . erm," she began. "Do you speak Rotfelsenisch?"

I shook my head, and then offered, "I can *read* it decently."

Dagmar groaned and stared off into space, as though she would read the words she needed there. She said something that was certainly a Rotfelsenisch oath or insult. There was still shouting in the distance, and it sounded as though the chorus was growing.

"Do you have," she began again, "anywhere safe you can wait? A friend or, ah, ally?"

I thought about this, as the voices clamoring for me got louder. Dagmar did not seem particularly worried, which I took as proof that we were, for now, safe. I felt like a child relieved that an adult was now here to fix everything, though she was younger than me.

My one-time friend, Manti Dumpling Akram, was of course right out. He may have truly thought that bringing me to the local authorities would have helped me, but his thoughts and intentions did not matter to me anymore. Certainly, I could hope that my terrified flight had shaken his resolve—perhaps even shaken his trust in the fairness of authority—but I was not about to turn right around and ask for his kind of "help."

I wondered whether Crybaby Vüqar, a fellow scholar, would protect me out of professional courtesy, but of course he'd been Akram's friend long before he'd been mine. Besides, the Tetrarchic citizens I'd met, even when they were being friendly, were quicker to see the differences between themselves and outsiders than any similarities.

"Think faster, smart boy," said Dagmar, as she grabbed me by the collar of my jacket and dragged me around a few corners, into an empty yurt. We were at the base of a hill covered in yurts like friendly little mushrooms, right where the wooden buildings ended in this part of town. Dagmar deposited me onto a stranger's bedroll.

"What would you have done if someone were home?" I asked, feeling surprisingly mild about everything.

"No one is," she replied, standing by the entrance. "Lucky them."

Would the librarians help me? I had become familiar with a number of them, and perhaps those who spent all day buried in old texts would better understand the historical context of my current situation. *Or*, as the guardians of the Library of Abathçodu's system, integrity, and order, they would prefer that things go back to the way they had always been. Either way, I had never discussed much with any of them outside of searching for books. That was the way of the Library.

"Find the Loashti!" came from outside. It sounded like the person yelling was running right past us and up the hill.

Dagmar grumbled something at me in Rotfelsenisch, which I assumed meant "hurry up" or similar. At some point she had silently drawn her sword.

I remembered the temporary, and clandestinely placed, statue I had seen some months ago, "Alımjun the Feckless Grocer Ejecting Me from Her Store, as Rendered in Twigs and Curtains," and wished I'd known the name of its sculptor. Perhaps that person would have hidden me, purely out of spite for that grocer, my landlady.

"Maybe Doctor Eldor?" I finally asked.

"Sure," Dagmar hissed.

"Do doctors in the Tetrarchia have any . . . *code* about how they help people? Perhaps that supersedes the government's wishes?"

Dagmar's passable Cöllüknit broke down at that question, so she stared at me as though I had babbled curses and mysterious Words of the Gods. Backwards.

"Let's try Eldor," I sighed.

"Sure," she repeated. Then she peered out of the yurt and beckoned to me.

The bottom of the hill was quiet now, and I did not even hear yelling in the distance. Had they given up? Had the whole city been roused against me, or just a small, angry aberration? Perhaps there were even competing groups, and Akram and Vüqar were leading the faction who wanted to keep me "safe" in official custody.

Whatever the case, I felt safest with Dagmar and her sword. She was not bothered by my being Loashti, because she hardly ever seemed bothered at all.

I managed to get my bearings and lead us to Doctor Eldor's without incident. The streets were mostly quiet now, which, given the bustling school and its merry students, was worrying. It was dark, but not that late yet.

When we arrived at the same small wooden building where Akram and my "friends" had, the previous summer, attempted to trick the learned doctor into "reading" my many tattoos, Dagmar flattened against the wall next to the door. I knocked.

Eldor opened the door slowly, cautiously. She was a stout, gray woman who always looked inquisitive, and warm candlelight radiated from behind her. When she saw me, she stopped opening the door, and left it halfway.

"Is it an emergency?" she asked. "Did they hurt you?"

This moment of seemingly genuine worry, even if it was purely professional, made tears come to my for the second time that night. I very pathetically wiped them away on my sleeve.

"Not yet," I whimpered. "Will you let me hide here?" My voice cracked. "Just—just for a little while?"

Eldor only hesitated a moment, but in that time I fancied I saw a thousand calculations and emotions cross her eyes. Then she opened the door.

"Come in. It isn't illegal to harbor you, yet. Just frowned upon."

I rushed in, and Dagmar appeared behind me, like a looming Death Spirit with her sword a pale glint angling out of her cloak. She followed me in before Eldor could fully react.

"Who is that?" she asked, as Dagmar kicked the door closed.

"My protector," I said.

Eldor nodded at the bare blade. "And that is for . . . ?"

"You, had you turned him down," said Dagmar, as she sheathed her sword. It did not sound like a threat, just a fact of life.

Eldor, in most classic Quru fashion, asked no further probing questions. She led us through the small front room of her home, which was where she treated patients, complete with a small couch and a number of strange instruments. I had been here, not long ago, when my throat had swollen up at the advent of spring. Eldor had given me some concoctions for drainage that had me feeling human again in a few days, which was lovely, but a bit slow compared to many Loashti medicines.

Off to the side of Eldor's office, there was an open door into her husband, Big Rüstem's, workshop, where we could see piles of hay and cane, plaster heads for temporary statues that had not yet been constructed, and small models no more than a foot high. Dagmar craned her neck for a closer look at the artist's domain.

Meanwhile, Doctor Eldor took us into a different, smaller back room, which contained a low table, with sitting pillows on the floor, a multicolored lamp hanging from the ceiling, and wall shelving stacked high with jars. She closed the door and sat on a pillow; I joined her nearby. Dagmar put her left boot on the face of the table, leaning forward, resting her left elbow on her knee and dangling her hand idly. That this was extremely uncouth could be read in the slight curl of Eldor's lip.

I could now see Dagmar's face fully in the light from above, refracted through red, green, blue, and yellow glass. The sellsword looked just as I remembered from the previous summer: a lean, pale face, with brown eyes searching suspiciously even while she seemed unbelievably calm. She was less sun-burnt than she had been, and I think she had a new scar: a nick below her jaw.

"Only one exit," she said.

"Either you trust me, or you do not," said Eldor, looking up at her. "In here, if anyone comes to the door, they will not see you. If Rüstem's workshop door was closed, it would make them suspicious."

"Just saying," replied Dagmar, shrugging. She leaned down further and shoved at my shoulder in what was meant to be a friendly fashion.

I nearly screamed in fear and imagined pain. Shaking, I gripped my own knees tightly and attempted to will myself into stillness. Dagmar gingerly removed her hand.

"So, smart boy," she said, "where is your . . . um . . ."

"Things?" I offered.

". . . money," she finished, at the same time.

I stared down at my knees, took a deep breath, and tried again to be still.

"No . . ." I gulped, then tried again, closing my eyes. "No money if you don't get my books." It was not courage—only the thought that going through all of this *and* losing my Commonplace volumes would be too great a calamity.

"Yes, yes, I'll get your *things*. I just forgot the—" another Rotfelsenisch curse, "—Quru word for 'things.' Why must such a simple word have six syllables?'

Eldor opened her mouth to answer, but I shook my head at her and she decided against it.

I, with Eldor's assistance, spent some time trying to give Dagmar directions to my rented yurt behind Alimjun's shop. Eventually, we laid it out on the table in a makeshift map fashioned from piles of some powdered root from a nearby jar. Once it was clearly visible to Dagmar, she understood the way immediately.

"And when you smell fermented peppers," added Eldor, "head toward the scent."

"Why didn't you *start* with that?" sighed Dagmar.

She finally removed her foot from the table, and then shook herself out of her cloak. Underneath, Dagmar was wearing thick leather trousers and a blue blouse, billowy with a number of small red feathers sown into it. The specks of red rippled as she rolled up her sleeves. Dagmar's arms were long, wiry, muscular, and absolutely etched with scars: they were nearly as covered as mine were with tattoos. Some of those scars were still red, and Eldor widened her eyes at them.

"It gets cold up here at night," I said. It was a stupid thing to say.

"Cute," replied Dagmar. Then she was gone.

After a few minutes, I got up to inspect Eldor's jars. She watched me quietly, and seemingly dispassionately, from her seat on the floor.

"Are you a doctor of some kind?" she finally asked, as I gazed at a jar of dried mushrooms. "Or a scholar of healing? I would be very disappointed if *now* I learned that you had been a fellow doctor, or whatever the Loashti version is, and we had not discussed it."

"No, no. I'm not. May I smell these mushrooms?"

"Yes, but don't take in too much vapor."

"I am a scholar," I continued, "of folklore and—Ooh, what a smell!— ritual, and the like." Now was certainly not the time to say that I studied curses. "Many of these are used in ceremonies I have studied."

I could positively hear Doctor Eldor raise an eyebrow at this.

"Loashti sorcery?" she asked.

"Why would I study that in the Tetrarchia, Doctor?"

She made a vague noise of labored assent, which turned into a noisy throat clearing.

"I only mean," she said, "that is why people here fear you. Loashti sorcery."

"And what, pray tell, *is* Loashti sorcery?"

"Well, if they knew, they might not fear you!"

"Loasht," I said slowly, "is much more virulent about stamping out what it considers to be 'sorcery' than the Tetrarchia has ever been."

She made a thoughtful, but not at all assenting, grunt. I went back to fawning over her collection.

I got the feeling that, regardless of my area of study, or my origin, mine was simply a *personality* that Eldor would never have liked: chatty, fanciful, and argumentative. And yet, she was protecting me while Akram, who did like me, had not. He may have thought he was, but that was beside the point.

I next browsed Eldor's collection of preserved cacti, and we had a nice, long silence, until she said, "They are not bad people you know?"

"Who?" I asked. I still faced the jars, but no longer saw them.

"The people here," she said. "In Abathçodu."

"I am sure some of them are bad and some of them are not bad," I replied. I did not turn to face her, but scrupulously inspected labels. "Just like anywhere."

"You know what I mean."

"You mean, the people who were chasing me through your streets—"

"Yes."

"—because of some faraway change in policy—"

"Yes."

"—that no one here can fully articulate—"

"Yes!"

I had never heard her yell before, so I quenched whatever I had meant to say next. I took a deep breath instead.

"They're scared," she said.

I wanted to tell her that *I* was scared. That I was alone in a foreign place, hunted by those with the luxury to be "scared" in packs. To chase down and overpower the unimportant, isolated, powerless scholar who "scared" them so. But said none of that. Instead, I walked back over to the table, sat down on a pillow, and looked at her.

473

"All right," I said, "they're good people. They are just scared. What do you wish me to *do* with that knowledge?"

"Just—don't judge them too harshly."

"I hardly see how my judgements of them will matter."

"I respect you," said Eldor. "You are clearly learned, and it must have taken great courage to come study here in the first place."

I sucked my teeth audibly.

"And so," she continued, "I wish you to have a little mercy in your consideration of my neighbors, given their context."

At least ten possible responses came to my mind, but I imagined each one would have made Doctor Eldor angry, sad, or more argumentative. I wanted her to keep sheltering me, but I could not bring myself to concede that I was in any place to give "mercy." How did my opinion of the people chasing me through the streets matter?

Thankfully, after a short silence between the two of us, Dagmar returned.

My mercenary savior now *sat* on the face of the small table, with her dirty boots on the floor. (She almost stepped on a sitting pillow, but I saved it.) Her sword was sheathed, her elbows rested on her thighs, and she was sweating and breathing hard. In front of her, on the floor, sat one of my packs.

"I grabbed all I could." She winked. "I hope it was the right yurt."

It was. Inside were some Quru clothes, most of my money and valuables, every volume of my Commonplace Book not back in Loasht, and a few of the other books I had brought with me. Not all, but I wasn't going to be picky: my own volumes contained all I'd recorded of my research thus far, alongside anything else that caught my eye. Dagmar had not brought, however, any of my glass bottles or dried gourds, which contained not only the sorts of ingredients that Doctor Eldor had so much of, but also what I used to keep my skin and hair as soft and beautiful as was possible in this dry climate.

Also in the pack were a few library books, as of course Dagmar had not taken the time to pore over what was mine and what was borrowed before throwing things in the bag. These I left with Eldor to return.

"And please do," I added. "I won't have it said that I stole your books, besides."

Doctor Eldor nodded sagely.

As I handed her the last one, *The Miraculous Adventure of Aigerim*, Eldor stopped just short of taking it. I looked down and saw a splatter of fresh blood on the cover. Eldor looked up at Dagmar.

"What?" asked the sellsword.

"They are just *scared*," Eldor repeated, as though Dagmar had been present for our conversation. Or as though I directly controlled her.

Dagmar grinned. "They are now."

Eldor trained a withering look on me.

I readied myself to leave, and Eldor insisted that I keep the stained copy of *The Miraculous Adventure of Aigerim*. I didn't want to waste space on a light, romantic adventure—which was, crucially, not light *to carry*—but I was beginning to wonder what might set the doctor off and cause her to throw us to her neighbors.

"So," said Dagmar, "how do we get you out of town?"

"I . . ." I gaped. "I thought you had a plan?"

"I don't know the city," she said. "And I'm not much of a planner."

"It's still dark," said Eldor. "Maybe you can sneak out?"

"Someone will be watching the borders," said Dagmar.

"Abathçodu doesn't really have set borders," I added.

"Well," the sellsword replied, "*someone* will be *somewhere*. And I can't cut through everyone."

Eldor's eyes widened, and her jaw clenched. Dagmar did not seem to notice.

"There must be a way we can sneak out," muttered Dagmar. "What are those . . . uh, silly statues all over the place?"

"You mean, the statues my husband makes?" said Eldor.

"Yes, exactly! Those daft things of sticks or mud or hay that break, or go tumbling down the mountain, if you so much as look at them."

Eldor pressed her lips together, choosing not to justify the artistic life of her home. I must admit that I that moment I felt more of a kindred spirit with the doctor, and with the city that was persecuting me, than I did with my brutish, indelicate savior. There is a lot to consider there, another day.

"Maybe we can do something with them," said Dagmar. She mumbled for a bit in Rotfelsenisch, and then added in Cölluknit: "What would that one do?"

At the time I did not know who "that one" was, nor even their gender, thanks to Cölluknit's single, universal pronoun.

475

"Doc," said Dagmar, "which cliffs offer the softest landing?"

"Well . . ." began Eldor.

"Wait . . ." I tried.

"You know," Dagmar continued, "with a lot of, um . . ." she mimed something unintelligible. "With a lot of little bumps rather than a long drop. Preferably with some nice thickets as a cushion."

"A cushion?" I asked.

"But not too soft!" added Dagmar. "Some sharp bits would be good. Bits that catch and cut down on the . . . the ah . . ." She mimed some more.

"Momentum?" offered Eldor.

Dagmar nodded and looked relieved.

According to Dagmar, what "that one," whoever they were, would have done was mad, senseless, and dangerous. But it was also the only idea that anyone offered.

And so it was that Doctor Eldor, Big Rüstem, and their "large assistant" (Dagmar in a cloak and hood) trudged through Abathçodu carrying a new work of the artist's. This statue was of hay, held in by some of the hoops and planks of an old barrel: it depicted Farbex the Good Donkey, a popular character beloved for his jolly rotundity. Big Rüstem spent the whole way grumbling that anyone who got a good look would be disgusted at how bad a job he had done—but of course this was because he had thrown Farbex together at the last minute, with myself bundled inside the friendly animal's straw guts.

What a terrifying ordeal this was. I was encased in a prison weak and pliable enough that I fancied I could be seen and heard, but stiff enough that I could not move. The beloved Farbex had been chosen to give me lots of padding, but the reason I needed such was particularly ghastly.

From what I could hear, many residents of Abathçodu did see Big Rüstem's statue of Farbex, but none saw it very well. They were all quite busy looking for a Loashti sorcerer.

After some particularly harsh and violent words from a passerby, I heard Dagmar whisper, so quietly that I'm sure no one else could hear her: "Don't cry now."

It must have looked like she was speaking into merry Farbex's much celebrated rump, and that image did stifle my tears.

Once the statue of the Good Donkey was planted in its spot, Doctor Eldor's large, clumsy assistant bumped it.

"Oops," said the large, clumsy assistant.

All was spinning and falling, bouncing and cutting, terror and pain. Finally, I lay curled up in my hay prison, not even attempting to free myself. Hours later, I was wrenched out of whatever thicket I had ultimately landed in, and then Dagmar eviscerated poor Farbex, freeing me.

"No more lazing about," she said, throwing down my pack. "Is anything broken?"

"I don't know," I said as I tried to stand. It took three attempts, but I managed. I was bruised and shaken, with my clothes torn and my skin lacerated all over. Certainly, neither of my arms felt as though they were quite correctly fitting in their sockets, but they could move, at least.

"You seem whole." Dagmar clapped her hands loudly and grinned. "Looks like the burs and spines of the famed Quru stinkbrush did their work well!"

"At least," I sighed, "I was in there so long that I can't even smell it."

"How lucky!"

"Oh yes."

"Then let's go, smart boy!"

"Where?"

"Away. Then we figure out the rest."

I nodded numbly, for I was numb all over, and followed Dagmar down the steep rocks. It was morning now, and Quruscan's springtime sun was just peeking over the mountain in pink lines. I could smell the flowers around us, and even hear chirping and movement nearby. There was no path here, just gnarled beige trees, low gray brush, and blooms of every color I could possibly imagine. When I looked behind me, the cliff face above was such that I could not even see Abathçodu.

"So, how did you know to come save me?" I finally asked, after we'd walked for perhaps an hour.

Dagmar, in front and cleaving the brush with a long dagger, grunted back, "I saw that things are going bad for some Loashti. Remembered I dropped you there." She shrugged. "Thought you might need help."

477

"Going bad how? I still hardly know myself."

"What I heard," she explained, "was that Loashti with papers in . . ."—she seemed to be grasping for the words—"pink, robin's egg blue, orange marble, or lime are not Loashti. Ex-Loashti. Outcast aliens." Dagmar kicked over some sort of small dirt mound that must've been a creature's home. "I knew some people here would take this chance to . . . oh . . . you know . . ."

"Act upon their worst impulses regarding the Loashti?"

"Yes! I think. My Cöllüknit is still not . . . great. But it's easy to make Tetrarchics turn on Loashti." She looked back at me and grinned. "Not everyone is as reasonable and tolerant as I." She winked.

"What a pity," I murmured in Zobiski.

To her credit, Dagmar did not demand to know what I had just said in my native tongue. Whenever I would speak in that, or Loashti Bureaucratic, she acted as though I had said nothing. I did the same when she let Rotfelsenisch words hack their way through her throat.

Dagmar seemed to hold no great animus toward Loasht, or indeed anybody. She was even-handed and nonplussed with everyone—and also willing to kill everyone. (Or most everyone.)

"Do things in the Tetrarchia," I asked, "usually change so suddenly after every Council of . . . well . . ."

"'Barbarians'? Say it if you mean to say it." She cut her way through another thicket. "But no. I've guarded Prince Friedhelm at . . . five or six Councils? Usually nothing happened that would . . . " She lapsed into Rotfelsenisch.

"That would change day-to-day life?" I offered.

"Close enough." She shrugged, her back still to me. "That is, until the last one I attended. Sort of. Since then, things have been much more . . . ah . . ."

"Fluid?"

"Yes."

"When was your last Council? Were you there when the Blossoming started last year?"

"No, no. Year before."

The vines on a tree began to writhe on their own, seemingly in anticipation of Dagmar and her dagger. Instead of cutting at them, she went around, and motioned that I to do the same. I dutifully did so, and trudged after her in silence for a few minutes.

"Wait," I said. "How did you know my papers were pink?"

"Went through your . . ."—another Rotfelsenisch curse—". . . *things* while you slept."

"Of course."

"'Things,'" she muttered. "What a word to—"

"You do know I have less money than when you last went through my belongings, yes? Those were savings. I've been studying in Abathçodu, not doing paid work."

"Smart boy," she tsked, waggling a finger over her shoulder at me, "I *last* went through your things was when I retrieved them five hours ago." She destroyed a bush that puffed out dust as some sort of useless defense against her, causing her to cough. "Besides, work has been slow for me lately—not many blood debts or duels in Quruscan. I am not sure why I've stayed."

She finally cut our way to a path, and made a cry of joy, before spitting loudly on the ground. The path was small and winding, but it was something. We began walking side-by-side.

"No," she growled under her breath, "I know why I've stayed." She sounded disgusted with herself.

"Why?"

Dagmar's back straightened and her eyes widened.

"Did I use Cöllüknit?" she asked.

"You did."

"Huh."

We were quiet for some time as we moved downhill along the path. Dagmar kept looking around to see if we were followed, or anticipated, but we seemed to be alone. I mostly tried to not think about how hungry I was becoming.

"Do we know where we're going?" I asked eventually.

"Rather," she said. "We're looking for ziplines to the steppe. Down there we'll find a place that may contain a person I know."

"Dagmar, that could mean almost anything."

"Look," she said, stopping and turning toward me, "did you like falling down the cliff in a roll of hay?"

"Of course I did not."

"Well that was the best *I* could do. I told you I am not a planner. I am a stabber. But I cannot stab your way back to Loasht. You do want to get back to Loasht, don't you?"

I hadn't even considered it. I had been so caught up in escaping Abathçodu.

"I don't know," I said. "If I'm no longer Loashti, can I even go back?"

That last part only occurred to me as I said it, and suddenly I was overwhelmed with a feeling of impossibility, of the insurmountable.

"You can if we sneak you in," said Dagmar.

"Is the whole Tetrarchia is now hostile to me?"

"You'd have to ask the whole Tetrarchia."

I moaned, and realized how parched my throat was. I would die here in the Tetrarchia, hunted and despised I would never again see the lands of my forebearers, who had been forced to become part of Loasht, and were now, it seemed, being forced to sever themselves from its embrace.

"I suppose I have to go back," I said. "See if this is all some bureaucratic *mistake* the Academy can fix for me." It seemed unlikely, but the Loashti Academy had sheltered my kind before. "And if not, to find my family and . . . figure out what all we can do next."

"So, that's a yes to getting back into Loasht?"

"I suppose?" I croaked.

"Then you need someone wilier than I," said Dagmar. "I know what I am, smart boy: a blunt thing you point at what needs killing. You need a planner, like I said. Someone who is, you know, tricksy like. Erm . . ." She added something else in Rotfelsenisch, before adding, "Do you know what I mean?"

"Not really."

"A cutthroat!"

"Don't *you* cut throats?"

"Well, yes!" She threw up her hands, angry at our inability to communicate. (But not, thankfully, angry at *me*.) "But you need someone... someone 'cutthroat' in the way they do things. The way they use things. And use people."

"No scruples?"

"Yes."

"A scheming manipulator?"

"Exactly!" She gestured broadly toward me. "Thank you!"

I nodded to show her I understood, although I was confused. And worried.

"What you need," she said, "is reason I stayed in Quruscan so long. She'll figure this out!"

"Oh. Good."

"Yes, yes," Dagmar continued, beaming at me. "Not a scruple on that one. Not the ghost of the father of a scruple!"

I stared down at the path and felt as though I would faint.

Commonplace Book, excerpt from My Wondrous Travels, Vol. 2: Outside Loasht *by Dust in the Air is . . . whose full name is lost to history. Copied down, and later translated from Loashti Bureaucratic to Skydašiavos, by Radiant Basket of Rainbow Shells.*

There is simply no reason to visit the Tetrarchia for one who is not a merchant, or a dragoman escorting a merchant. Its wonders—such as the great rock of Rotfelsen and the congested forests of Masovska, home to a temple even older than Loasht—are so normal to the locals that they never think to treat them as attractions. They are such a simple group of peoples that they fail to understand how strange their lives and homes are.

What's more, for a merchant, such as myself, there is hardly ever a reason to go beyond Skydašiai. I had hoped that, in visiting the other three Tetrarchic kingdoms, I would find stranger textiles and produce, new dyes or spices; but perhaps their only great accomplishment is how seamless and easy trade within the Tetrarchia is. In this one way, perhaps, Loasht could even learn from them (Loasht is, of course, much larger). Anything interesting that can be bought in the Tetrarchia can be bought in Skydašiai: at a slight markup, yes, but you will save much by avoiding travel through inhospitable lands.

Honored Reader, you may take it from me, who was traveled to all of the farthest places: there is simply no reason to visit Rotfelsen, Masovska, or Quruscan.

481

More from Erewhon Books